DEAD MAN'S INK

Dear Rosa
so great to meet
you at HWIB2018!
so much love,
Phillip Hart K

REBEL • ROGUE • RANSOM

REBEL

CALLIE HART

REBEL
Copyright © 2015 Callie Hart

Formatting by Max Henry of Max Effect

LIVE FOR SOMETHING OR DIE FOR NOTHING

For *JESS*, for always having my back.

For *CJ*, for being sweet and adorable, but also being secretly evil like me.

For *LILLIANA*, for being hilarious and making me laugh when I should be crying.

For *ASTRID*, for drinking wine with me and putting up with my crap.

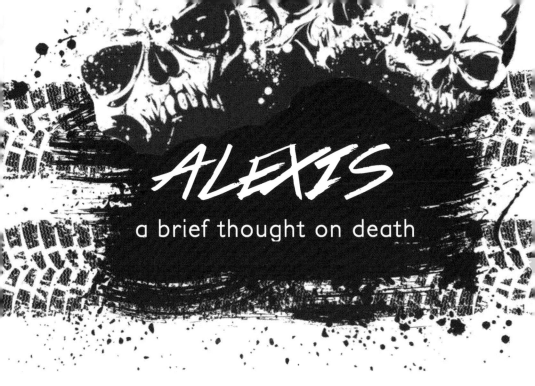

ALEXIS

a brief thought on death

I never thought I'd die on the streets of Seattle. I never thought I'd be the kind of person to wish for death, either. You ask people what frightens them most in this world and nine times out of ten, you'll get the same universal answer: death. The Great Unknown. That one last wild ride. I used to be one of those people, paralyzed by the mere thought of non-existence. Seems a lot has happened recently to adjust my outlook, though. Now, I've realized there are more frightening things than simply ceasing to be. Living, for example. Continuing to breathe, even though it feels like your heart is shattered into a million pieces and you can't possibly go on another moment. Continuing to feel, even when your nerve endings are so frayed and overloaded from pain inflicted by others. Continuing to hope, despite the odds of rescue growing smaller and smaller each day.

I never thought I'd die on the streets of Seattle. I never thought I'd want to die. Beg for it. Wish for it constantly. I suppose my ingratitude for the great gift this life poses might be hard to comprehend. Perhaps if I started from the beginning, you might understand.

Here.
Let me explain.

ALEXIS

2012

St. Peter's hospital looms over the city, the building a crouched, disapproving sentinel blaring light and sound into the night. Fog blossoms on my breath. Curled around my takeaway coffee, my hands are finally beginning to thaw out. I'm listening to Led Zeppelin on my busted iPod with the cracked screen, watching people stream in and out of the hospital, and imagining their stories. Filling in the blanks from the expressions on their faces.

Broken leg.

Chest pain.

Only one more shift before the weekend, thank god.

New baby.

Lost loved one.

It never ceases to amaze me how a person's face alone can convey so much of what they're feeling, especially when they don't know they're being watched. I've seen the whole world crumble and be reborn at least five times before the cell phone, in the pocket of my thick Parka, rumbles against my stomach. It's my dad.

"I'm so sorry, sweetheart. Are you still on the bus?"

I smile. I smile because the old man is clueless. "No, I'm outside. I've been waiting for you for half an hour."

He groans. In my mind I can see him pressing his fingertips into the creases of his brow, trying to figure out the problem he's presented with. Because there's a problem. There's always a problem. "Ah, okay. All right, I'll be out in a moment. A little girl just came in. She was in a car accident. Her whole leg's shattered. They asked if I could stay behind and monitor her while they operate, but I'll just tell them to—"

"Dad?"

"Yes, sweetheart?"

"It's fine. I can catch a bus back to your place. It's not a big deal." This is not the first time I've said these words, nor will it be the last. Since I decided to stay in Seattle and go to college here, it's been tradition to go back home every Sunday to hang out with my parents. They're big on church, big on Jesus. They like it when I spend Sunday nights with them. Most of the time, Dad's working, though, and Sloane, my older sister, is following in Dad's footsteps, training to be a doctor, so she's hardly around either. Usually it's just Mom and me, and I'm used to that. Used to the endless cups of tea and church gossip. Used to doing the dishes after dinner and sitting in comfortable silence while we watch whatever inane reality TV show Mom's hooked on at the time.

"You're sure you don't mind?" Dad asks. This is a script both of us have repeated countless times; we barely need to think before the words slip out of our mouths.

"I'm sure, Dad. It's okay. Go and anesthetize the crap out of that kid."

Dad tuts—is crap a curse word? Dr. Alan Romera sure thinks it is, but then again, the old man thinks *shoot* is a curse word. His disapproval is, as always, mild and affectionate, though. "Love you, sweetheart. I'll see you when I get home. Tell your mother not to put dinner in the oven for me, okay? I'll heat it up when I get back."

No dinner in the oven means he won't be back until well after midnight. I tell him I love him too and hang up the call. My role as voyeur is at an end. I drain the remnants of my coffee, shove my ear buds back into my ears, and begin the long walk across downtown Seattle to the bus depot. It's not often that snow sticks here since it's so wet. I feel like a little kid again as I trudge through the four-inch covering that carpets the sidewalk, tucking my face into my jacket, trying to keep warm as I listen to Robert Plant sing about letting the sun beat down upon his face. I pass a homeless guy hunkered over in a shop doorway, the only person out on the streets in this frigid weather.

I come from a family where giving is second nature. The ten-dollar bill I pass to the man vanishes quickly into the many folds of jackets and shirts he's wearing as protection against the cold, his quick, distanced eyes blinking thanks at me as I hurry down the street. I'm almost halfway to the depot when I can no longer hear Robert Plant singing anymore, and the ground feels like it's shaking apart beneath my feet. A convoy of motorcycles sweep down the street, engines snarling, drowning out all other sound. You don't get many packs of motorcycles traveling through the city. The sight is bizarre enough that I stop and watch them pass, until the very last of them disappear around a right-hand turn at the intersection behind me. They're gone from sight, but the sound of their rides echoes off the tall buildings for at least another twenty seconds.

Dad calls men who ride motorcycles *temporary citizens*. He's seen so many fatalities over the years, so many decapitated heads still inside crushed helmets. He swears blind if he ever catches me on the back of one of the things he'll ground me for life. The patients he's dealt with in the past are usually riders of sports bikes, though, aerodynamic things designed for going way too fast. The men who just passed me—at least twenty of them—were on machines constructed from polished chrome and exposed engines, handlebars way too high, exhausts way too fat. Society tells me they are criminals. Perhaps they are.

I carry on toward the bus depot, my iPod shuffling through

songs. The streets are clear by the time I find myself closing in on my destination. Everyone's playing it smart tonight, already inside, enjoying the warmth and a hot meal. That's exactly where I'll be soon, and I *cannot* wait. I'm getting ready to cross over the street when a tall man with silvered hair staggers out of the darkened side alley beside me.

I don't hear him—the music blocks out any sound he makes— and the sight of him suddenly emerging from nowhere has me jumping out of my skin. My heart slams against my ribcage, adrenalin fires through me. There's blood in the snow. He's bleeding. I tear the headphones out of my ears, and then he's lurching toward me, one hand outstretched.

"Help...please help...me," he gasps.

I skitter away from him, clutching my hands to my chest. It's a natural reaction most people would have, I think. A terrifying old man, dressed in a torn great coat, and covered head to toe in blood comes flying at you from out of nowhere, and your first instinct is to run. Not people like my father or my sister, of course; they would run straight toward someone like that. It takes a heartbeat to get myself together before I realize this guy needs me to be like my dad. Or like Sloane.

"What...what happened?" I hurry forward, unravelling the scarf from around my neck, preparing to use it to staunch the bleeding, wherever it's coming from.

The old man's eyes grow round. Suddenly he's not staggering toward me anymore; he's backing away. "No..." His voice comes out in a ragged, wet rasp. "*No!*" The look on his face is sheer terror. And he's staring at something behind me.

I've seen enough films to know what comes next. The hand that clamps over my mouth. The iron grip of the arm that wraps around me, pinning my arms to my sides. The weightless, stomach-churning sensation of being lifted off the floor by someone much bigger and much stronger than me.

I try to scream. Pain rips down my throat, but I barely make a sound. The hand covering my mouth captures my cry and shoves it back inside me, effectively putting me on mute. My heart's racing. I can't...I can't see properly. Black spots dance in my vision. I've never been good with small spaces, and being trapped inside this person's arms is a very small fucking space. I react. I'd like to say I remember the training I received from the on-campus security team, showing us how to protect ourselves when out walking alone late at night, but that's not what this is. This is the panicked flailing of a twenty-one-year-old girl gripped in the deepest throes of fear.

I bite down on the hand and taste blood. A loud hiss from the man behind me lets me know I've caused him some discomfort, but the bastard doesn't let go. My feet are still off the ground. I lash out, kicking backward. My heels hit shinbone and strong muscle, but the grip around me doesn't falter.

"What the fuck you doing with that bitch, *hijo*?" a voice demands. The accent is strong and thick. "Get her off the fucking street."

I've been too terrified to take in much, but now I see the bloody man, on his knees, staring off up the street. He looks devastated, like he knows this is the end. His abject hopelessness hits me like a wave; this man, whoever he is, knows he is alone right now and no one is coming to his rescue. Which means no one is coming to my rescue, either.

He looks up at me, his mouth hanging open, and shakes his head. "I'm sorry," he tells me. I try screaming again, with just as much luck. My captor tightens his hold on me and then we're moving, heading into the darkness of the side alley. Fuck. I know it instinctively: if I disappear into the darkness of this alleyway, I will never be seen again. And pinned to this stranger, struggling with every last ounce of strength I possess, there's absolutely nothing I can do about it. I see the face of another man, a Hispanic guy with a shaved head and a spider tattoo underneath his right eye, as he moves forward and grabs hold of the bloody old man under one arm. He spits on the old man, takes hold of him, and drags him behind us into the alleyway.

Dumpsters, trash, broken wooden crates; there's nothing back here to indicate someone is going to come along at any moment and save us. The sound of footfall—many pairs of boots—rings off the walls on either side. We reach the iron railings of a tall gate in the middle of the alleyway, dividing it into two, and this is where my captor stops. He spins us around, and for the first time I see exactly just how much trouble I'm in.

Seven men, all with guns drawn, stare back at me. The same cold, indifferent look marks most of their faces; only one man wears a different expression—the guy who dragged the old man behind us. His victim is laying face down on the concrete, shoulders shaking, and now he has turned his attention to me. And he looks...*excited.*

My stomach drops through the floor.

He's wearing a black Parka with grey fur trim, which strikes me as odd fashion sense for someone of his...*standing.* It's also strange that I should be thinking things like this when he's stalking toward me and sticking his face into mine. Regardless of his fashion sense, I know with certainty I'm looking into the eyes of a killer.

"You scream...and I'll cut your tongue out with *this.*" He draws a narrow, six-inch knife from the pocket of his jeans, sharp and cruel-looking, and I know he's being very, very serious. "You hear me?"

I can't tell him yes. I can't even nod. I'm far too scared to have any sort of control over my body. Instead, I manage to blink at him. The Hispanic guy accepts this and nods to his friend. "Uncover her mouth so she can speak, fuckhead."

The hand lets go of my face, though the arm around my chest doesn't loosen any. "You know this old guy, *puta*?" Spider asks.

I shake my head straight away. I don't want to give him any reason to get angry. His boys all look bored, but this guy...this guy looks like he could get riled up, and easily.

"Let the girl go. She doesn't know me," the old man on the ground groans. He shouldn't have opened his mouth; one of the other men boots him in the chest so hard I hear a snapping sound. Without looking over his shoulder, Spider guy says, "Don't worry, my friend.

We'll get to you in a moment. But in the meantime..." He strokes the back of his hand down my cheek, running his tongue over his top teeth. "You swear you don't know this guy?"

"Yes," I whisper. "I swear."

With little more than a blur of black material, Spider pulls his hand back and lashes out. Pain rockets through my head, surprising and sharp. I open my mouth, trying to gasp in a breath, but it won't come. He hit me. He *hit* me, and he looks like he enjoyed it. He smiles at me, nodding. "I think I believe you. But I have to be sure. What did he say to you, pretty? Did he tell you something, huh?"

I've never been struck before in my entire life. I can't even remember my parents striking me for misbehaving as a kid. A tiny part of me is roiling with anger at the treatment, but the rest of me is shocked, paralyzed with fear. "He didn't tell me anything. He asked for my help," I whisper. Spider laughs at this.

"He asked you for help, pretty? That's kind of ironic, no?" The question is rhetorical. He nods to the man holding me, and the hand comes descending over my mouth again. Spider presses the tip of his knife into his index finger, turning around so he's facing the old man on the ground. I catch the glint of a gold wedding band on the old guy's finger—somewhere out there this man has a wife who is probably worried about him. It's late, and it's dark. He could have been on his way home when these guys jumped him. He could already be late for his own family meal.

"So, what we gonna do with you, *ese?*" Spider asks. "That was some crazy shit you just pulled. You seriously thought running was a good plan? And I thought you guys were supposed to be smart. Educated and shit." He spits on the ground. I can't see the expression on his face, but I'm betting his eyes are glinting with that same poorly concealed depravity he fixed on me a moment ago. This man thrives on power. He thrives on blood, and from the way the old man on the floor is shrinking away from him, I think he knows it, too.

"I...I can't help you. You know there's nothing I can do," the old man says. His voice catches in his throat. "Just...just let the girl go. Please."

Spider looks over his shoulder at me, one eyebrow arched into a bemused black line. "Her? You're begging for *her* life?" With a shrug, Spider crouches down, still playing with the knife. "What about your life, Conahue? Not worth begging for?" he asks.

The old man—Conahue—swallows. The action looks painful, as though he's swallowing razor blades. He looks up at me and I see the last flicker of fight in his eyes fizzle out and die. "You're going to kill me anyway. Begging is probably a waste of what little breath I have left."

Spider barks out a sharp blast of laughter. "Your life's been in your hands for a long time, my friend. We gave you plenty of warning. When my employer asks for something, he gets it. There are consequences if he doesn't. Hence this little...*meeting*, my friend. You could always change your mind? Do as he asks?"

Conahue gives a brief shake of his head, breathing heavily. His face, underneath the congealed, drying blood, is mottled and ashen. "I've never lied. I've never taken bribes. I've never let a piece of shit gang lord get away with murder."

"Ah, so you're a man of morals?" Spider asks this, twisting the knife over in his hands.

"Yes," Conahue gasps. "Not that Hector would understand that. He hasn't suffered a guilty conscience a day in his life."

Most of the men snort at that. It appears as though the majority of them agree, and they're proud of the fact that this mystery man, apparently their boss, isn't inconvenienced by a functioning moral compass. Conahue struggles to push himself upright, but Spider tuts at him, wagging the knife back and forth in front of his face. The action is enough to stop the old man in his tracks.

"You do realize," he says, "that the whore Hector's accused of killing was a junkie, right? She was a drain on your country's precious resources. You'll die for some cracked out bitch you don't even know?"

Resolve flashes in Conahue's eyes. "I will."

"So be it." Spider acts slowly, extending his arm with deliberate purpose so Conahue can see what he's doing. From my vantage point, still a foot off the floor and unable to turn away, I witness the point of the weapon press down into Conahue's chest and travel slowly, slowly, slowly, into the man's body. Conahue's eyes widen, a look of mild disbelief coming over him as he starts to convulse.

A pool of thick, dark red blood begins to rise up out of the wound, around the blade of the knife, and then around the hilt when Spider has driven the weapon all the way into the other man's body.

I scream, but there's no sound—only a high-pitched out-rushing of air from my lungs. The vice-like grip around my chest tightens, and a sharp pain lances through me—my shoulder, burning, suddenly on fire. Spider draws the knife out of Conahue's body; the old man is still alive, but the muscles in his face fall slack. He's not got long left. He reaches up a shaking hand and clutches at the wound in his torso, his feet twitching. Spider watches him, back still turned to me, with such stillness that I get the feeling he's mentally recording this—the life slowly slipping out of his victim, absorbing every fine detail of the moment so he can replay it again later.

A violent crash of sound roars down the alleyway, and I'm suddenly hit with the sensation of it—a wall of noise slamming into me, rattling my bones. I don't know how I didn't hear it before. It can't have registered through the fear, the horror of watching that knife disappear into a man's body. The guy holding onto me turns along with everyone else to see what's going on; a motorcycle has pulled into the alleyway behind us.

The high wrought iron railing is all that stands between me, trapped with this group of killers, and the single biker on the other side. The bike's headlight spears through the darkness, lighting us all up and eliciting a chorus of Spanish curse words from Spider and his friends. "What the fuck is he doing?" one of them hisses.

Spider snarls, pacing to the railings, knife still in hand, though it's now dripping with blood. "You're too late, *ese!*" he hollers. "It's done.

Run back to your *cabron* and tell him he's fucked. And so are you!"

The growl of the engine cuts off abruptly, so that Spider's last words sound outrageously loud against the following silence. The guy holding onto me clucks his tongue derisively when the figure on the bike climbs off and lowers the hood on his sweatshirt—a handsome guy, late twenties, with dark hair and dark eyes. From the way he walks toward us, I can tell he's built like a tank. He's wearing gloves. He reaches to the back of his waistband and produces a gun.

"Are you fucking kidding me, *ese*?" Spider laughs. "There are eight of us and one of you. You gonna shoot us all through the railings before one of us gets you?"

The biker on the other side of the gate doesn't say anything. He has quick eyes. He takes in the scene before him—the old man on the floor behind us; me clasped tightly in someone's arms, my mouth covered; blood splattered on the top of my Converse shoes; the other men behind me. He sees all of this, and his face remains completely blank.

"You realize what you've done," he says. He doesn't look at anyone in particular, though it's clear he's talking to Spider. He looks down at his gun, snaps back the action and then frees the clip containing the ammunition.

Spider takes hold of one of the railings, the steel of the knife in his fist clanking against the steel of the gate. "I did what had to be done, *pendejo*. You're a man who gets things done, I've heard. You should know all about that."

The biker on the other side of the gate casts his eyes upward from under drawn brows, apparently not even remotely fazed by the situation. He presses the first bullet out of his clip into the palm of his hand, and then fits the clip back into the gun. The gun goes away, back where it came from. "Borrow your knife?" the biker asks.

Spider shrugs. An evil smile spreads across his face. "Sure, *hijo*. Why the hell not?" He reaches his hand through the gap and drops the weapon into the snow. The biker comes closer, bends and collects the knife. He's only three feet from me now. I can see the club patch stitched onto his hoody over the right hand side of his chest—Widow Makers—along with the small separate patch underneath that, which says *V.P.* The club's emblem—a fleshless skull flanked by two guns and surrounded by stitched roses—is so close I could reach out and touch it, if only my arms weren't being pinned to my sides.

The biker glances at me quickly—an assessing, curious look—and then he bends over the contents of his hand and begins scratching the tip of the knife against the bullet. A rustling whisper runs around the group behind me.

Is he really doing it?

He's marking that round?

No way.

The biker finishes whatever he's doing and then holds the bullet between his index finger and thumb for Spider to see. "You want this?" he asks. From the eager look in his eyes, Spider definitely does want the round. I just don't have a clue why. In fact, I have absolutely no clue what's going on. Everyone else seems to know what the biker's actions mean, and all I can do is wonder.

"I do believe it's customary to hand it over," Spider says, amusement thick in his voice. He reaches through the railings and holds out his hand. The biker slowly shakes his head. He looks at me.

"I'll give it to *her*," he says.

Spider's face twists into a scowl. "As you can see, my friend is a little tied up at the moment."

The Widow Maker tips his head to one side, casting dark eyes over me and lifting both eyebrows. "Something tells me this woman isn't your friend, Raphael." And then, to me, "Are you his friend?"

I don't know what the hell to do. My mouth is still covered, but I could probably shake my head. And then the guy holding onto me would probably snap my neck for pissing them off. My eyes widen, my tears blinding me. How the hell can this guy be so calm when it's clear I'm being held against my will? It's fucking obvious Spider, this Raphael person, whoever he is, isn't my friend.

"Huh. I don't think she's feeling very talkative," Raphael muses.

"Still. I'll give it to her, if it's all the same to you. This is worth it, right?" He curls his fingers around the bullet, making a fist. "You've been waiting for it for a long time. Pushing buttons, involving yourselves in shit you have no business involving yourself in. And now you've gone and done something entirely irreparable—" His eyes travel over my shoulder, back toward the man on the ground, whom I presume must be dead by now— "and you're finally getting what you want. A blood bath. All you have to do is let her take this from me."

Raphael seems to consider this for a minute. He then sucks in a sharp breath, gesturing an impatient flick of his wrist at the man holding me still. "Put her down, Martin."

The grip around me is instantly gone, and my feet are on solid ground. My legs don't feel like they're going to hold me, though. I feel like Bambi taking his first steps. Raphael produces a gun of his own and thrusts it into my face. "Go on. Go and take it," he snaps. A hard shove from behind pushes me forward, and Raphael moves to stand behind me. I then feel something I never imagined I would ever experience in my lifetime: the muzzle of a gun pressed against the back of my head. My limbs lock up; I can't fucking breathe.

"Walk, bitch, or I'll put a hole in your skull."

I lock eyes on the biker through the railings; he gives me an almost imperceptible nod, like he's willing me to come forward. I do as I'm told. My heart's kicking wildly against my ribs as I put my right arm between the railings and hold out my open hand. The biker steps forward, closing in on me and taking hold of my wrist. He places the shining, tarnished gold piece of metal into my palm and curls my fingers around it tight.

"Tell them you're a virgin," he murmurs. "Whatever happens, make sure Hector knows that."

"The fuck you saying to her, *ese*?" Raphael snaps. Before I can register what the guy has said to me I'm yanked backward, away from the stranger and away from the gate. I almost lose my footing. I hear the soft clicking of a gun being cocked behind me. "Open your hand. Tell me what you've got there," Raphael snarls in my ear.

My fingers barely work; it takes serious effort to stop shaking and open my hand. Inside, I can see the slightly scuffed bullet, see the scratched marks on its surface.

"What is it?" Raphael demands, jabbing the gun in my back.

"It's...it's a bullet."

"And what does it say on it?"

"It says..." I turn the metal over in my hands, trying to focus through my tears. "It says *WAR*."

Howls of raucous laughter explode behind me; Raphael reaches forward and snatches the bullet from me, holding it up for his friends to see. "War!" he shouts. "Fucking war!"

The bullet is clearly a declaration, and Raphael and his men are overjoyed by it. The biker gives me a firm, meaningful look; he holds my gaze for a long moment, and then he turns around and pulls up his hood. Somehow, through all the laughter and rough housing going on around me, I hear the creaking of the snow under his boots with every step this stranger takes away from me. The Widow Makers club emblem is emblazoned in white across his back; it's the last I see of him as he climbs back onto his bike, starts the engine and rides away.

Hands take hold of me again. Raphael's still grinning from ear to ear as he squeezes my arm. "We're done here," he says.

"What are you going to do with me?" Strangely, I almost feel like laughing. People ask that question in movies, when they're kidnapped and taken from their homes and their lives, stolen away from everything they know and hold dear. I never thought that it would one day be me asking that question.

Raphael smiles a cold, dead kind of smile. "Oh, *Chiquita*, we're not going to kill if you if that's what you're worried about. No, you're much too pretty for that." He strokes the back of his hand down my cheek again, the same hand he hit me with before, and a wicked light sparks in his eyes. "You're going to come with us. My name is Raphael...but from now on, you will call me *master.*"

ALEXIS

Three of Raphael's men disappear and return shortly after in a beaten-up panel van. The windows are so dirty I'm surprised the driver can even see the road. I may be powerless against so many of them, but that doesn't stop me from fighting like a hellcat when they try and make me get in the back. I'm reminded of a poem, a famous one by Dylan Thomas, '*Do Not Go Gently Into That Good Night.*' The title in itself is comment enough for the situation I find myself in. The poem demands the reader kick and scream against death, and that's exactly what I do. I kick and I scream, because getting in the back of that van is the same as dying, and I don't want to die. I want to go home and listen to my mom gossip about her church friends. I want to do the dishes, and I want to watch TV. I want my sister, always so strong and distanced from everything, to come and find me and save me. I thrash so hard that another of the men has to take hold of my legs in order to restrain me.

"*Let me go! Let. Me. G—*" I choke on the last word. My head spins as something hard and blunt impacts against the back of my skull.

"Get her in the fucking van," Raphael snaps, and then another heavy thud connects with my head. No spinning now. No fighting or screaming or clawing furiously for my life. Only a sinking sensation and blackness.

Only blackness.

The void envelops me, whisks me away from the events of the last half hour. I sleep, or lose consciousness, I don't know. It feels like I'm still awake; I can feel the side-to-side rocking motion of the van as it takes corners. My ears still hear talking, distant and muddled, but I can't make out the words.

We travel for a long time. I have no idea how long. It could be hours; it could be mere minutes. Everything is a blur. I'm in pain and I'm wet, chilled to the bone.

When I fully regain consciousness, there's no pretending I'm still out cold. I throw up onto the bare metal flooring of the van, my stomach fiercely rejecting everything inside it. My head is killing me. I want to cry, but I can't. I simply don't have the energy.

"Fucking stinks back here," a male voices complains. "Open the window, asshole."

There are more comments about the smell I've created by puking. I feel like informing them that they shouldn't hit people so hard over the back of the head if they don't want to deal with the side effects of concussion, but my tongue feels fat and swollen and I can't breathe properly.

Fuck.

What the fuck am I going to do?

This is the part where I think about who's going to be looking for me. Mom will have called Dad to see where we are, and he won't have answered because he's in the OR. She'll maybe have called Sloane, but my sister will be out with her friends, celebrating another day's survival as an intern. Mom can't have called Matt, my boyfriend, because she doesn't even know he exists. None of my family do. Too many questions. Does he go to church? What is he studying? Where is he from? What are his prospects? Is he being respectful?

The answers—doesn't go to church; not studying *anything*; from Mount Rainier; no real prospects; and hell no, most definitely *not* being respectful—would not go down well. So, long story short, my family will have no clue where I am, and neither will Matt.

I throw up again, and this time it's not from the concussion. It's from the overwhelming sense of dread cycling through me, feeding on itself, growing by the second. There's one question playing on repeat inside my head, and I'm too much of a coward to face it yet. It's there if I stop thinking even for a second, though:

Are they going to rape you?
Are they going to rape you?
Are they going to rape you?

I'm more afraid of this than I am of dying. I'm more afraid of something I have only thus far shared with two people in the whole world being forcefully taken from me than I am of losing my life. If I die, I'll just be dead. If they do unspeakable, horrific things to me, I will relive that experience every time I open my eyes each morning. Every time I close my eyes at night.

"Left up here, brother. Not far now," a gruff voice says.

The van's suspension is shot to hell. My head bangs painfully against the floor as the vehicle swerves and leaves the road, turning onto what must be a dirt track. Someone snickers, and I get the impression it's at my expense. I'm sure to evil bastards like these, a skinny girl, hands bound behind her back and lying in a pool of her own vomit, is a highly entertaining sight.

I try not to think about how vulnerable I am. I try not to think about what's going to happen when the van's engine stops spluttering and we reach wherever we're going. All I can concentrate on is my breathing, trying to keep it even. I'm dangerously close to hyperventilating, and I don't want to pass out again, which is what will happen if I let my panic take hold of me.

I breathe in. I breathe out. I breathe in. I breathe out.

"She's got some great tits," a different male voice says. I haven't heard this guy speak before, and I'm shocked—he has no accent. He sounds like he's from Seattle, though I know whoever he is, he must have some Mexican heritage. Each and every one of my captors appeared to be Hispanic. I barely register that they're talking about my chest until a hand suddenly grabs hold of one of my breasts. I try to open my eyes at this stage—being manhandled wins out over my splitting headache—but I can't see anything. They've blindfolded me. I kick out with my legs and manage to shove myself away, out of the reach of wandering hands. It still feels like the hand's there, though, squeezing and kneading my breast; my skin is crawling, prickling with the intensity of my disgust. Matt's never touched me like that before. Whenever he's touched me, it's been to bring me pleasure. Whoever just grabbed hold of me did so for their *own* pleasure, a fact painfully clear by the way they pinched and rolled my skin.

"What the fuck you two doing back there?" Raphael demands. I know *his* voice. He sounds suspicious, but then I've yet to hear Raphael sound anything but. "Don't touch that girl, motherfuckers. You heard me lay claim, right? I'll cut out your fucking tongues if you so much as look at her."

Two disappointed grunts follow after that.

Someone in the front cranks up the radio to obnoxious levels, and the sound of Taylor Swift's, *We Are Never Getting Back Together* blasts from the rear speakers. My head must be right next to one of those speakers, because it feels like it's on the brink of explosion. I used to like the song, but now? Not so much. The situation descends into outright weirdness when someone in the van, I can't tell who, begins to sing along. Enthusiastically.

My body is singing in *pain*. My shoulders are throbbing from the discomfort of having my wrists bound tightly behind my back. Thankfully my hands themselves have gone numb from lack of blood supply, so at least I'm now being spared that particular agony.

Less than fifteen minutes later, the van pulls to a jerky stop. Raphael is the first out; I can tell from the way his voice fades and then cuts off altogether when his door slams shut. The music is still blaring, though it's not pop music anymore. It's Mexican rap music. Angry. Hostile. Violent.

The rear doors open, and suddenly someone has hold of my ankles. I'm pulled from my cowering position in the back of the van, and I hit the ground hard. The drop from the vehicle to the ground must only be two feet, but my shoulder impacts first, sending a white hot flash of pain charging through my back and neck.

I cry out, but no one says a word. Hands find me, more than one pair, and they lift me roughly to my feet, pulling me forward. I hear nothing but Mexican rap music and the frantic staccato of my own heartbeat. I stumble after whoever is dragging me behind them, tripping on unseen obstacles and rolling my ankles. The music fades away, and my heartbeat grows even louder.

"Now, you'll keep your fucking mouth shut, you hear me?" a voice commands. Raphael. Of course, Raphael. "If you want to live, you don't breathe a fucking word." He yanks on my arm, unbalancing me, and I drop to one knee, only to have my arm almost wrenched out of its socket as I'm tugged to my feet again.

Without being able to see, my other senses have come alive. A saccharine sweet smell hits me—the smell of sugared almonds and cotton candy. There's a screeching sound—a screen door opening?—and then I'm jerked to a halt.

"And what is this?" a male voice asks. The timbre of that voice is low and rumbling, husky with a thick accent. Spanish, but not Mexican Spanish. It's softer, more muted than Raphael's hard intonation.

"This is *mine*," Raphael replies. "I picked her up along the way. The judge is dead, by the way. In case you were wondering."

"I wasn't wondering. I gave you a job to do, and I expected you to do it. What I didn't expect you to do is bring a stranger back to my home."

The way this person speaks makes something very clear; he is pissed. Seriously pissed. It's the quiet, careful way he parts with his words that gives me that impression. I've had a severe case of mouth sweats ever since I threw up back in the van, but now my throat is miraculously dry.

"She's been blindfolded the whole time. She doesn't know anything," Raphael says.

A cracking sound, and then the dull, slow thudding of feet against wood. One step. Two. Three. The voice is closer now.

"Has she seen your face?"

"Yes."

"Does she know your name?"

There's a brief pause. And then, "Yes."

"Does she know...*my* name?" The malice in this question makes my palms break out in a sweat. I'm beginning to get the feeling Raphael's fucked up in kidnapping me, and *I'm* going to be the one paying the price.

"Yes," Raphael answers. "She does. But she's never gonna be out of my sight, *Padre*. She won't be a problem."

"The girl isn't the problem here, Raphi. You are currently the problem. You do shit without thinking, and that is a really fucking big problem for me, you understand?"

So I know this guy's name? That must make him Hector, surely? He is Raphael's boss. Raphael doesn't say anything to him in return, though his hand tightens around my arm, fingernails digging into my skin. I squirm, trying to free myself, but it's a complete waste of energy.

"Take the blindfold off her," Hector commands.

A piercing light stabs into my head, making me gasp. Daylight? *Daylight?* It was eight thirty in the evening when I first came across the unfortunate Judge Conahue. I blink up at the sky, horrified when I see the sun's position directly overhead. That would make it almost midday, or around that time anyway. How the hell is that possible? I was dazed after being hit on the head, but I thought I'd been mostly conscious. Obviously I was wrong, otherwise I wouldn't be surprised by the fact that at least eighteen hours have passed since I was taken.

Eighteen hours. That means I could literally be anywhere. Definitely out of Washington State. Any hope of rescue I might have been harboring plummets.

"I see why you risked pissing me off, Raphi," Hector says. I lower my gaze and I see him—a tall, dark-haired man with startling green eyes. He's clearly of some Latin descent, though his skin is more golden than olive. Maybe in his mid forties, he reminds me of the pediatrician I used to see when I was a kid. Except there's an air of something *not-quite-right* about this man that Dr. Hereford didn't have. Something that makes the hairs on the back of my neck stand to attention.

He holds out a hand to me, his cool mint-green irises locked firmly on my face. I don't know what the hell he expects me to do. My hands are still firmly tied behind my back. Hector doesn't even turn his head; his eyes simply travel from me to Raphael, and then my captor is moving quickly, hands fumbling to pull a small knife from his belt so he can free me. I'm in instant pain. It's like my hands are on fire. Blood rushes back into my fingers so quickly and intensely, the piercing sensation takes my breath away. Hector reaches down and takes my right hand in his, and massages his fingers over mine, making a clucking sound at the back of his throat.

"You'll have to excuse my friend here. He can be very uncivilized when the mood takes him."

Raphael's getting antsy in my peripheral vision—he clearly doesn't like anyone else playing with a toy he considers his—but something primal within me is warning not to look away from Hector. He's beautiful in an odd way.

And terrifying in every other.

Despite his consideration for my screaming wrists and his apparently sincere apology over my treatment, I haven't forgotten what I heard back in that alleyway. This man is suspected of murder. The murder of a woman. And I am currently at his mercy.

"What's your name, sweet girl?" he asks, smiling, head tipped to one side, as though I'm a delightful mystery he's looking forward to unraveling.

I clench my jaw, torn for a moment. I shouldn't tell him my name. I shouldn't tell him who I am. I don't know why, but I know it with a certainty that makes my heart race in my chest. "If it's all the same to you, I'd rather not say," I inform him. Hector's smile fades. A flicker of disappointment flashes across his face—I have been a bad girl. Hector's focus flits to Raphael again, this time accompanied with a single arched eyebrow.

"Sophia Letitia Marne," Raphael reels off. "Twenty-one years old. Student at the Cornish College of the Arts in Seattle."

I can't avoid my reaction now; my head whips around so I can look Raphael full in the face. He's lying to his boss. Sophia isn't my name. I sure as hell don't study at Cornish. I recognize the information, though. Raphael's almost black eyes are glinting with a barely suppressed fury that confirms my suspicions: he hates having to answer to someone else. Hates it with a vengeance. Hector holds out a hand to Raphael; he seems to know what his employer is requesting from him. He reaches into his pocket and pulls out an intimately familiar object —my wallet.

He snaps the clasp open and fishes out a card, which he hands over to Hector. I'm hardly a party girl, but last year a group of my friends wanted to hit a club to see a DJ play, and I was the only one underage at the time. Luke, the boyfriend of one of the other girls, made up a fake driving license for me. I'd memorized the card's details before going in, chanting my borrowed name and date of birth over and over again in case any of the doormen asked me, only to be let in without even having to produce the damn thing. I then proceeded to forget my fake persona altogether.

My real driving license is sitting on my bedside table at home, snapped in two. I broke it at least a month ago, and since I'm living on campus and don't have a car at the moment, replacing it has been very low on my list of priorities. There are no credit cards in my wallet, either. Nothing else to give away my real identity. A cold sweat of relief breaks out across my face. Hector studies the license, studies me, studies the license again. He grunts, handing it back to Raphael.

"Well, Sophia," he says, giving me a small smile. "It would appear you've gotten yourself into a bit of a situation. Are you content with Raphael as your new master?"

Am I content with Raphael as my...? I'm at a loss for words. I'm pretty sure I'm covered in my own blood from where I was hit over the head. I reek of vomit, and my wrists are banded with a deep purple ribbon of bruising. I hardly look like the sort of person who came willingly to their newfound servitude. My mouth opens, but I struggle to find the right response to the question.

"Let me put it this way," Hector says. "Are you going to make trouble inside my home, Sophia? Because I have a zero tolerance policy when it comes to trouble within in my home."

I haven't given much thought to the building Hector is standing in front of, but now I take a closer look at the place. The two-story Colonial, white weatherboard with green shutters, looks like something out of Little House On The Prairie. It's quaint, with its wrap-around porch, swing bench, and multitude of potted flowers balancing on the windowsills. I'd expect this place to belong to some frail, little old Southern lady. I can picture her rocking slowly on the swing, drinking her endless glasses of sweet tea. There are no bars on the windows, and no security gates or armed guards. But...there is also *nothing* else out here. Not a single building for as far as the eye can see. Just desert. A burnt, alien landscape with no roadways, no stores, or any way of making contact with civilization.

"Well?" Hector asks.

"What if I say yes? What if I *am* going to make trouble?" I don't really need to ask this question, though. I know all too well what he's going to tell me before the words have a chance to leave his lips. Raphael snickers, a wickedly sharp, crackling laugh. Hector just shrugs his shoulders.

"One of the many bonuses of living out in the desert, so far from prying eyes, is that shallow graves are easy to come by, my dear.

Should you wish to incite chaos here, to disrupt my peaceful life, you can bank on finding some permanent real estate of your own out here."

Somehow, I've strangely been holding myself together since I was grabbed from the side of the street. I've cried, yes, but I haven't completely lost it. Until now. My legs buckle out from underneath me, ditching me in a heap at Hector's feet.

"I need to go home. I have to go back to Seattle. My family...my family will be worried about me. The police—"

My head is kicked to one side, pain slamming through my already delicate skull. I didn't see the hit coming, but I can certainly feel the echo of it relaying around my body. I can't breathe. I can't see through the tears welling in my eyes.

"You'd be wise not to mention the police in my presence again, Sophia. They aren't a group of people I like to discuss." Hector sinks down into a crouch. He reaches into his pocket and then holds his hand out to me, offering me something inside—almonds. I was right about the smell. Candied almonds. "Why don't we just say...no kind of law enforcement should be spoken of from this point forward? It will make a happier life for you, and a happier life for me. Don't you agree?"

I nod, cautiously touching my hand my face, trying to cup the stinging sensation. To make it go away. Hector's eyes narrow at me. "Why don't you take an almond? They're delicious. Don't you find them delicious? And then Raphael will take you inside so you can speak to Ramona. If you're polite to her, she may find you some fresh clothes."

This man is insane.

Certifiably insane.

He flipped so quickly, violence surging out of him like the unexpected eruption of a geyser. He's unstable, and I don't want to risk pissing him off again. I get the feeling he wouldn't flinch away from killing me if he thought I wasn't going to be compliant. I reach out and take a sugared almond between shaking fingers.

"Good girl. Eat it," Hector coaxes.

I force the small almond past my lips, and the explosion of sugar that follows makes my mouth ache.

"That's it. Perfect." Hector nods appreciatively. He stands, the action so quick and fluid that he makes me jump. He strokes one hand against the top of my head, *shhh*ing me, and then turns his attention to Raphael.

"Get her inside. Make sure she's given a room on the south side of the house." He turns and climbs back up the steps that lead up to the wrap-around porch, opens the screen door, and disappears back inside the house.

That leaves Raphael and me, with my stomachful of knife-wielding butterflies. "On your feet, girl," he snaps at me. The insanity is back in his eyes again. I want to turn and run. I want to blindly flee this malevolent, charming house and run until my legs can't carry me any further. I would do it too, if it weren't for the group of grim-looking men leaning up against the van I arrived here in. They all have weapons—a vast array of differently shaped guns and knives, small and large. But mostly, I don't do it because of the baiting edge in Raphael's words. It's almost as if he's willing me to disobey him, to run, to try and free myself...so he can have the pleasure of capturing me all over again and teaching me a lesson.

I get to my feet.

I go inside the house.

I think, perhaps, I will never see my family again.

REBEL

seven years ago

"**Get down, get down, get down! Watch your fucking head, Duke. You nearly caught that round to the face.**" Hands pull at me, bringing me to the ground. I've been trained, but boy am I fucking green. My lungs are burning with adrenalin and dust and the shitty realization that I nearly just died.

Cade is on his back beside me, choking on the dirt. Overhead, the powerful blades of the helo that just dropped us into the middle of this shitfight thump at the air, blasting us with even more dirt and dust as it gets the hell out of dodge.

"On your feet, boys. Keep low!" Richter hollers. So far, I've followed Richter from the academy, through basic training, all the way across to the other side of the world, and now it would seem I've followed him straight into hell.

They warned us how bad it would be. We believed them, too, but the reality of what we're facing is beyond anything we could possibly have comprehended. Richter's grabbing at my flak jacket, jerking me upright. He's signalling to me, tipping two fingers to my right. "Got company, Duke. You're on right flank. Shoot anything that moves. You okay, son?"

"Five by five." I nod frantically, my finger on the trigger of my M4 Carbine, but I'm screaming inside my own head.

"You're on point," Richter yells. "Take a deep breath and accept this." That's his thing—accept that you are where you are. Accept that only *you* are in control of whether you come out on the other side alive. I push myself up onto my feet, my boots scraping against a fallen street sign half buried in the dirt road. Then we're moving. Cade's at my rear, gun aimed over my shoulder, protecting me. That's our way. We always protect the man in front. In this instance, my heart is in my throat and my dick is hard, and I am in charge of protecting everybody. There are seven men at my back, counting on me to choose a safe passage for them through this madness.

We've navigated our way down three streets, choked with burned out cars and building rubble before we make contact. Gunfire rains down from overhead, immediately making my job almost impossible. "Down, down, down," I yell. I can't see a fucking thing. The narrow street we find ourselves in is being used to dry sheets—the stained white and yellow and salmon-pink cotton barely shifts on the slight breeze, blocking whatever may lie at the other end of the street from view.

Could be anything back there. We can't pull through this way. I hold up my closed fist: *freeze.* All eyes will be on me back there. I know they'll have already stopped moving and are crouched low behind me. More shots fire overhead, really fucking close. Like *right on top of us*, close. I hold my hand up in the air, my index finger raised, and I circle it over my head: *rally point.* Move back to the rally point. We need to find another way. I'm backing up, crouched low, scanning to find the shooters on the roofs over our heads when we hit smoke.

Smoke on the ground means another unit must be close; they're trying to conceal their whereabouts, too. Couldn't have come at a better time. I see Cade's pack in front of me, PRESTON in big black letters across the material. There's shouting up ahead, along with the rattle of more shots fired.

A cloud of smoke blows across our path, and then I'm stumbling, tripping, falling forward. I'm cursing myself out when I hear the metallic zip of a round firing no more than two feet over my head—exactly where I was standing a second ago.

"Fuck." *Get up, get, up, get up. You need to move. Get your ass up* now. I push myself back, onto my feet and I can just about make out the faint shapes of my unit ahead of me. They haven't realized I've fallen behind. I'm less than a second away from calling out to Cade when a darker, more solid shape is rushing toward me, materializing out of the smoke.

Non-American, military age male. He's holding something in his hands. Takes me the length of a heartbeat to recognize it as a weapon—an AK47. And he's pointing the fucking thing straight at me. My training kicks in, and I'm lifting, aiming, firing my own weapon before I can think straight. The guy who was rushing toward me falls back, not making a sound. I hear his weapon clatter to the ground, but aside from that the only noise comes from up ahead, from people shouting in English and Farsi. And from their guns.

My blood is raging through me as I hurry forward, my cheek pressed up against the sight on my M4. I keep low, and I stay on my toes. I don't know where I hit him. Could have been in the heart. Could have been in the shoulder, for all I know. The last thing I need is for him to sit up and start shooting as soon as I draw close enough.

The guy doesn't sit up, though. He's flat out on his back, eyes fixed upward, his chest hitching up and down as he chokes on his own blood. I got him in the neck. The motherfucking neck. *Jesus.* He's holding both hands up to the raw wound across his throat, trying to stem the blood that's pumping out of him, but it's a futile task. He might as well be trying to hold back an ocean's tide. I'd nicked his carotid, barely scratched it, but it's enough to be the reason why he dies. His eyes swivel in his head, staring at me, showing way too much white.

He says something to me in Farsi, his voice gurgling out of his mouth, and then he drops his right hand, patting loosely at his side for something. He's looking for his gun.

"Don't even fucking try it, asshole," I snap out. The guy on the floor—he's a young guy, maybe twenty-two, can't be any older than me—doesn't heed my warning, though. He hands scrabble in the dirt, groping, and then he's holding a handgun. Fear radiates off him as he aims the thing at me.

"Drop it," I tell him. "Put it down."

He has tears in his eyes now, blood pumping rhythmically through the gaps between his fingers. He knows he's about to die. He says something else in Farsi, something I don't understand, and I can see the moment he decides he's going to do it. He's going to shoot me. There's a split second in time between that moment and me firing my rifle.

Crack!

I shoot him in the head, almost right between the eyes. We're trained for hours as we become riflemen, laid out on our stomachs, to always go for the head. Always go for the heart. But seeing a real human being, eyes glassy and still filled with tears staring blankly back at you with a gaping hole in his forehead, is very different than being proud of the tiny tear in a paper target on some range in a US Army base. Seeing that hole in his head makes me feel like I'm gonna fucking throw up.

The worst part? The worst part is that my dick is still fucking hard inside my pants. They warned us about this, too. The cocktail of hormones and adrenalin pumping around your system in a situation like this has the most fucked up effects on the male body. I thought they were joking. I sure as hell didn't think it would happen to me.

I look down into the eyes of the man I've just shot and killed, and I know I'll never forget his face. I'll never be able to rid myself of the horror I'm feeling right now.

"Jay! Jamie! What the *fuck*, man?" I look up and Cade's standing

there, the butt of his gun pressed against his chest, a wild look in his eyes. He sees me, sees the guy lying on the ground. Shock transforms his features. "Holy fuck, man. Do you know who that is?"

I just look at Cade, unable to respond.

"Dude, that's fucking Aarash Zubair. He's Ahmad Zubair's son."

Of course, I know who Ahmad Zubair is. He's the head of all Taliban activities in this area. He's been on our watch since before we even arrived. Cade takes out a small point and shoot camera and takes photos. It struck me as some cold shit when we were given the cameras and told to do this, but it makes sense. We need to identify people. And in this case, prove it is who Cade thinks it is.

"Did he say anything to you before you shot him?" Cade asks.

I nod, feeling my body come back to me. My cheeks prickle, feeling odd and strange. "Yeah. Something like, *enen waheen.*"

"Enen waheen? What the hell does that mean?"

"I don't know. I don't know."

Back at base, Cade shows his picture to Richter and it's confirmed. The man I shot *was* Aarash Zubair, son of Ahmad Zubair. One of our translators also confirms what the guy was saying before I shot him:

Enen waheen.

I am alone.

REBEL

now

Three years ago, my best friend went missing. Three years ago, my whole life changed. It's amazing how dramatically the foundations of your very self, the very basis of what makes you *you* can tilt on its axis, and you can become something *other*. Something dark. Something disreputable. Something bloodthirsty and violent.

Suffice it to say, I am not the man I used to be.

I am no longer good.

As president of a motorcycle club, I find I'm presented with daily opportunities to prove just how *bad* I have, in actual fact, become. A beating here. An armed robbery there. That's the small stuff. The shootings, the gunrunning, the drug dealing—that's the stuff that scandalizes the ghost of the man I used to be. But guess what? Fuck. That. Guy.

He let his family walk all over him. He had his heart ripped out when the one bright element in his life was taken from him. He was the weak bastard that cowered in the dark when he should have fought. If I'd have been the man I am today back then, on the night Laura was kidnapped, I might have reacted more quickly. I might have found her. I might have saved her. *I might have saved me.*

But I didn't. So now I'm the guy who steals and breaks shit, and I'm the guy who enjoys it as I'm doing it.

"Put him on his ass, Carnie," I say, snapping open my Zippo. Carnie, our one and only Widow Makers prospect, does as I tell him. He shoves the man he's holding at gunpoint down onto the ground. Meet Mr. Peter Hartley, forty-three, severe gambling problem, and a penchant for beating small, defenseless Asian women.

Do I care that he gambles too much? Not particularly. I care an appropriate amount, since Mr. Hartley is really fucking *bad* at gambling, and it's my money he's been losing.

But, do I care that Mr. Peter Hartley likes laying his fists into the bodies of small Asian women? That would be a resounding *hell yes.* I probably would have let poor, blubbering, snot-nosed Mr. Peter Hartley off with a couple of black eyes and a week's extension on his loan repayment, had I not seen the black eyes on the girls who run his massage parlor. A real man does not hit a woman. A real man does not hurt a woman. Fuck, even sorry-ass, pathetic attempts at men do not raise their hands against women while I'm around. Not unless they want to lose their balls in the most painful manner possible.

"Pl—please, Rebel. *Please!* I swear, I'll have the money to you by the end of tomorrow. I can sell—I can sell—"

Mr. Hartley has nothing left to sell. He knows it, and so do I. "I don't care about tomorrow. I care about the phone call I just received. I care about my boy here having to bring me down to this shithole to see what you've done, Peter."

A look of confusion transforms the guy's face. "What—what do you mean?"

I grab hold of his arm, lifting it up so I can take a look at his hand. His right hand. The one that carries the full force of his blows when he swings. His knuckles are red raw and covered in half-healed scabs. "You're a fucking mess, Pete. What on earth have you been up to?"

He lifts his shoulders slowly, an uncertain shrug. "Oh, y'know. I like to box."

"Who you been boxing with, Pete?"

"Just—just the guys, y'know."

"No, I *don't* know. Which guys?" If there's one thing I hate on the face of this planet more than weak men, it's weak men who are also liars.

"Just some guys, some friends of mine. I train down at O'Rourke's every Thursday. What have my knuckles gotta do with the five grand I owe you, man?"

I glance up at Carnie, who is still thrusting the muzzle of his gun into the back of Peter's neck. "He train at O'Rourke's?" I ask. Carnie gives me a nod. A lot of my guys train at the permanently sweat-soaked fighting gym down on Fourth, though personally I choose to do my workouts in private. I let go of Peter's hand, shaking my head. "So you know how to punch, then, Pete, huh?"

He looks up at me as though this is a trick question. "Yeah? I guess I do."

"See, now that's bad. Very bad. That means when you hit those girls downstairs, you're not just some asshole loser who takes his insecurities out on women. You're an asshole loser who takes his insecurities out on women, *and* who knows how to make it hurt while doing it."

His eyes go wide—it's like a light bulb's just gone on somewhere inside that thick skull of his. "What? No, man, I don't hit my girls. I would never do—"

I smash my fist into the bastard's face. Peter isn't the only one who knows how to hit, after all. I pull back my right arm again, considerably more powerful that Peter's, and I power my fist straight into his jaw a second time, this time knocking him over. A welt of blood sprays from his mouth, raining down on the thread-bare carpet of his tiny office. It smelled of stale sweat and Cheetos in here, but now it mostly smells of blood—that metallic tang never fails to set my heart racing in my chest.

"What the fuck, man? I said I never hit them!" Peter spits on the ground, ejecting a small, white pearl of a tooth from his mouth. "Fuck, man, you knocked out one of my—"

I hit him again. And again. And again. I hit him until I break out into a sweat. The motherfucker is out cold and lying in a pool of his own blood, and I can barely raise my arm by the time I've decided he's had enough. Carnie laughs under his breath; he's lowered the gun and is leaning against the wall, arms folded across his chest with an amused look on his face. Makes his slightly crooked, many-times-broken nose appear even more off center.

"Well. Saved me a job there, boss. You know he's gonna be out of commission for weeks now, though, right? You aren't gonna see that money the end of the month at least."

I heave in a deep breath, wiping the back of my hand across my forehead. "If that motherfucker's even walking before the end of the month, you come back here and go round two on his ass, you hear me?"

Carnie gives me a mock salute. "Loud and clear."

I'd stick around and wait for Mr. Peter Hartley to wake up, just so he knows the deal here, but Carnie and I are suddenly accosted by four small, defenseless Asian women. Turns out they're not so defenseless. None of them are over five foot five, but that doesn't stop them from charging into Peter's office, screaming at the top of their lungs in Chinese. They split up, two of them hammering their fists into Carnie's back, the other two heading straight for me.

I duck around the overflowing desk, putting some space between the charging women and myself, but it's a wasted effort. They come straight over the damn thing, still hollering and shouting.

"What the fuck they saying?" I shout over the top of them.

"You're asking *me?*" Carnie yells back. One of the women bites his shoulder through the white T-shirt he's wearing; he howls in pain, and that's enough for my boy. He pivots around and grabs hold of the two angry masseuses by the hair, one in each hand. "I'm gonna start breaking some of your rules if we don't get the hell out of here,

36

dude," he yells.

I admit I'm losing patience, myself. So far my attackers have managed to scratch my face, and the most furious of the two is currently trying to go for my nuts. There's one quick way to resolve this. I reach into my waistband and pull out my own gun, an AWR Hawkins 4.

The screaming women fall instantly silent. They back up, shooting both Carnie and me hateful glares as we sidestep out of the room. Once we're out of the office and charging down the stairs, they start up with the screaming again, barreling at breakneck speeds after us.

"How fast can you start your bike?" Carnie calls over his shoulder.

"Faster than you, brother." We burst into the main room of Hartley's massage business—the legal, non-brothel part—and even more women start screaming. From there it's a short distance out onto the street. The door nearly rockets off its hinges as we slam through. True to my word, my engine's snarling before Carnie's. We leave the women in the dust.

We reach the clubhouse just after nine, our faces still aching from laughing so hard. Set back off the road, surrounded by high fences, the clubhouse is a squat, industrial-looking building from the outside. The front yard is crowded with bikes—rows of shining motorcycles, old and new, lined up like a pack of guard dogs. Every MC has a business front—a necessary evil when trying to explain to the law where your money's come from and what you get up to all day long. The Widow Makers are ink monkeys. We're the guys who mark you up with that pretty little butterfly you've always wanted, seductively placed just above your hip. We're the ones who tattoo the name of your boyfriend onto the curves of your cleavage one week, only to be the ones to cover it with someone else's name the next.

A neon sign—*Dead Man's Ink Bar*—sends electric blue reflections across meters of polished chrome as it blinks off and on in a steady pulse. Dead Man's never closes, so that light is never switched off. We pull up and park underneath it, kicking back our stands, and swinging off our bikes.

"Hey, lookit," Carnie says, pointing back over my shoulder. "V.P's back."

And so he is. Cade Preston, Vice President of the club, went on a recon mission for me three days ago with some of our boys. His bike, a dirty great big Star Bolt with an olive green tank, is propped up in its usual spot against the side of the building.

We had news that a club friend was being leaned on by Los Oscuros, a mixed breed cartel. And not just a club friend—my uncle. The fact that he's a federal judge is something I overlook on account of the fact he made his house my own whenever my father got sick of beating my ass as a kid.

"Sweet. He must have squared everything away quicker than expected." We rap my knuckles against the tank as I pass Cade's bike—still warm. Inside the clubhouse, there are no celebratory shots of Jack being passed around. The place is full, nearly every single member of the club seated at tables, some parked on the edge of the pool table. There are a lot of stern looks on faces. Arms folded across chests. I spot Cade immediately, leaning against the bar. The look on his face speaks volumes.

"What? What happened?"

Cade speaks three words:

Raphael Dela Vega.

Before he's finished saying them, before he's had a chance to personally bring my world crashing down around my ears, I already know it. I already know my uncle is dead.

REBEL

"**I** called it. I didn't have any other choice." Cade closes the door to my den behind him, shutting out the steely looks of the Widow Makers crew—there are twenty-three people gathered out in the bar, because they all knew before I did: we are at war with Los Oscuros. Cade saw my dead uncle's body lying in the snow, and he handed over that bullet, just like I would have done. Except I would have given it to Raphael straight between the fucking eyes. "You okay?" Cade asks, as I slump into the seat at my desk.

No other member of the club would ask me if I was okay right now. They're hard men, who deal with their issues the hard way: silently. Cade, on the other hand, has known me since I was eight years old. He knew me before all of the goodness got torn out of me. He knows I am *not* okay.

I just shake my head, staring down at the gun I've drawn from my belt without realizing and am now holding in my hands. "How did he die?"

"I don't know." Cade's ominously silent for a moment. "But there was a lot of blood."

I close my eyes, trying to fill my lungs with some air. It's not working. "Okay." I inhale. Exhale. Nod my head. "Okay." The second time I say it, I'm closing a door. Ryan Conahue is dead. There's nothing I can do to bring him back now, but there are a number of things I can do *about* his death. My first instinct is go take this fucking gun, climb onto my bike, ride all the way from New Mexico to Seattle, and torture that motherfucker until he begs to die. "Do you know where they're staying?" I ask. "Hector and the others?" It's not just Raphael that needs to die. His boss is the one who ordered Ryan's death. He is as guilty, if not more so.

"They've left Seattle," Cade says. He places his hands on the back of the chair he should be sitting in, leaning forward. "They're back in L.A."

Back in L.A. That means Raphael's hightailed it straight to his boss to tell him the good news. Hector's been pushing for bloodshed ever since he moved up into the States. He wants our business. Well, that's not strictly true. He wants our gun and drug business. He's done everything in his power to take that business from us, but our clientele is loyal. And paranoid. They don't trust new faces. Now we've drawn swords, as it were, Hector must think he's going to wipe us out. Give the gang lords we deal with no other choice but to deal with them instead. This whole clusterfuck of a situation is political, mixed in with the fact Ryan was in a position to send Hector down the line for a very long time.

"You know this isn't your fault," Cade says softly.

I somehow manage to tear my gaze away from the gun, so I can look up at him. "And how the hell have you come to that conclusion? I told him to stand his ground. I told him we'd fucking protect him!"

Thankfully Cade doesn't say another word on the subject. He knows the dangerous glint in my eye. He knows when I'm on the very brink of a total meltdown, and he knows better than to give me the final push. This *is* my fault. No two ways about it.

My friend drops his head between his braced arms for a second, sighing. "This might be nothing to concern ourselves with, but

Raphael had a girl with him."

"What do you mean, a girl?"

"Just some young thing off the street by the looks of things. Nice clothes. Had that moneyed look about her."

"She wasn't one of his crew?"

Cade shakes his head. "She was terrified. I told her to say she was a virgin."

That's potentially one of the only things that will save a girl once Hector's guys get their hooks in them. Hector may want my guns and coke, but his main area of interest lies in human trafficking. A beautiful virgin is worth more than a whole shipment worth of AKs if you sell to the right buyer. "I wanna see this girl. You got footage?"

"I got something. Not a very clear picture, though." Cade pulls a thumb drive out of his pocket and tosses it to me. I slot it into my computer, opening the file as soon as the device registers. Cade is right—the picture is for shit, but it's good enough to make out the shape of a woman, walking down a darkened street.

The woman stops, turns, watches something farther down the street.

"That was us," Cade tells me. "We knew Ryan was in the area. We were looking for him." His face creases into a look of remorse. A look that worsens as Ryan's figure appears on the screen, a meter from the girl. He frightens her. She staggers back, and he falls to his knees in the snow.

My heart rises up into my throat. I understand why Cade looks so fucking guilty now. They missed my uncle by mere seconds.

My eyes feel dry; I don't think I've blinked since the footage started playing. Ryan holds one hand up to the girl—a plea for help if ever I've seen one. The stance of the girl, the way she's holding her own hands to her chest, makes me think she's going to run from him. But she doesn't. She surprises me and takes a step forward. More dark shapes appear on the screen—Raphael and his friends. I watch the girl getting grabbed. I watch those fuckers dragging Ryan back into the alleyway. And then there's nothing.

"She was going to help him." I hear myself say the words, but they don't really register. Not until I find myself saying them again. "She was going to help him." I take a deep breath. "So now we need to help *her*."

ALEXIS

Ramona is a tall, slender woman with the traces of what might once have been a hair lip. If it was, her surgeon was very talented. Raphael hands me over to her with a clipped and considerably angry burst of Spanish, and then I'm whisked away. The woman has to be in her late twenties, though the tired look in her eyes gives her the appearance of someone much older.

"What you done to piss him off?" she asks, though she doesn't really sound like she's interested. A good job, really, since I have no intention of making small talk with her. The sugary sweet smell I caught outside is even thicker inside the house. We walk down a long, narrow corridor, and Ramona stops at the end, opening a door on the right. Inside, a confusion of pastel tulle awaits—dresses upon dresses, hanging on rack after rack. An entire room full of forgotten prom dreams.

"What size are you, girl?" Ramona asks. She smacks some gum. I don't answer. She rolls her eyes and storms into the room, yanking a yellow dress off the closest rack and thrusting it out at me. I can see the label—size six. My size. I take it from her, because I sense she'll only go get Raphael if I don't and I do *not* want that.

"How long have you been here?" I ask.

"Five years," she replies. "Five loooong, boring-ass years. Come with me."

She takes me upstairs and down another long, corridor, right to the end again. She opens the door to the room that must be directly over the prom room. Most worryingly, she opens it with a key. "Go on. Inside."

Inside, I go.

"Get washed up. I'll be back in an hour to do your hair and shit. Don't go trying to jump from the fuckin' window or nothin'. Had a girl do that one time and her damn legs exploded." With that very cheerful parting word of warning, Ramona closes the door, locking it behind her.

I am alone.

Despite what I was just told, the first thing I do is dump the hideous dress on the bed, and run to the window, checking to see if it's open. My jaw nearly hits the floor when I find that it is. Why the hell would they leave the windows open if they were planning on kidnapping people and holding them hostage?

Because you're in the middle of nowhere, a small voice in the back of my head reminds me. *And how would you get down, anyway? That's a big drop. A really big drop.* It could be my eyes playing tricks on me, but I think I can actually see a patch of rust-colored dirt directly under the window. Do people's legs actually explode when they hit the ground after a fall? I have no idea, but my stomach is balking at the prospect of giving it a shot. There's no handily placed downpipe to shimmy down like in the movies. Nothing to gain any purchase on at all. Fuck.

I give up the jumping from the window idea, and decide on searching for another means of escape. The room is markedly bare, though. There's a double bed, freshly made by the looks of things. A dresser against the far wall, though when I open the drawers, they're all empty. A sink complete with dripping tap stands in the corner—the kind the Victorians used to put in every bedroom back before the introduction of the en-suite bathroom. My heart leaps in my chest when I see the mirror mounted on the wall above it. I could smash it and use one of the shards as a weapon. But I'm not even halfway across the room when I realize the mirror isn't actually a mirror at all. Instead, it's a highly polished piece of metal, screwed tightly into the wall. I try to prize the screws out, but I only succeed in making my fingers bleed. The nails don't budge an inch.

A weak desperation sets in after that. I stalk the perimeter of the room, eyes scanning for something I may have missed. Something, anything, I can use to get the hell out of here. There isn't anything. Once that really hits home, I curl myself into a ball in the corner of the room and I cry. I cry so hard I make myself sick, my stomach muscles trembling from the second round of purging. I'm rinsing out my mouth, my legs trembling underneath me like two frail stalks of corn, when the door opens and Ramona walks in. She doesn't seem impressed that I'm not decked out in the yellow dress yet.

"Fuck's sake," she hisses. I move away from her so that my back's pressed up against the wall, but she doesn't seem to care. This whole thing feels a little rote on her part. With quick, rough hands, she takes hold of my soiled T-shirt and forcefully removes it from my body. I'm too stunned to struggle. She unbuttons my jeans next, and drags them down. My legs get a good hard slap when I refuse to lift my feet at first. I relent after the third strike, miserably raising them one at a time so she can bully my dirty, wadded-up jeans free from my body.

She leaves me in my underwear while she fills the sink with water. I'm made to remove those too when she's done, though—*if you don't do it, I will.* I cover my breasts with my hands, awkwardly trying to make myself smaller as Ramona uses a clean, white face cloth to scrub at my body. The water's warm, but it might as well be freezing cold. Every time she touches me, I nearly jump out of my skin. My humiliation is complete when she thrusts the cloth between my legs, forcing my hand out of the way.

"You want to make him unhappy?" she snaps. *Him* being Raphael, no doubt. I do not want to make him unhappy—the bastard is unhinged—but I don't particularly like the way my lady parts are being prepped for some unknown event, either. Ramona tuts as she plucks with her fingers at my pubic hair. I'm not a particularly hairy person, but she seems revolted by what I've got going on downstairs.

"This needs to go," she informs me. "You look like a fucking virgin with that fuzz going on."

I'm hit with a sudden memory—the mystery biker's words to me as he gripped hold of my wrist. *Tell them you're a virgin. Whatever happens, make sure Hector knows that.* Even the firm look he gave me as he walked away was reaffirming what he'd said to me. I haven't even considered what it might mean for my situation right now, but he seemed so insistent. And he hated Raphael; I could see that in his eyes, too. I open my mouth and tell Ramona what he told me to say, choking on the words. "I *am* a virgin."

Ramona rockets to her feet, taking a step back. "What?" She looks like I've just slapped her.

I contort my arms around my body again, trying and failing to cover too many parts of myself. "I'm a virgin. I've never been with anyone before," I say in a small voice. This is a flagrant lie. I lost my virginity when I was eighteen to the first guy I ever loved, Joshua. We'd been dating for two years through the final years of high school. We'd finally committed ourselves to each other the week before he left for college in Oklahoma. We'd known it was over but we still loved each other. It was a final, gentle moment, one last gift that was shared between us before we said goodbye. Since then I've only had one sexual partner, Matt, but we've hardly been shy about what we've wanted from each other.

Ramona casts a doubtful eye over me. She doesn't believe me. "How old are you?"

"Twenty-one."

"Ain't no white college girls virgins at twenty-one," she tells me, as though she's an authority on the matter.

"My family's religious. *I'm* religious. No sex before marriage." My cheeks burn like charred ember when I go to Church these days—there's never been a woman so wanton sitting in the pews of St. Augustus Catholic Church. When I'm feeling particular penitent, I'll go to confession and take my Hail Marys on the chin, along with the partially visible scandal that marks Father Richmond's face.

Ramona stares at me some more. I'm probably blushing—I've never been manhandled like a piece of meat before. Hopefully the woman's taking my rosy glow as embarrassment over my confession to *her*. "You never been touched by a boy? Ever?" she asks.

I shake my head.

Ramona tosses the face cloth back into the sink with a wet splash, tutting under her breath. "Put the dress on anyway. I'll be back in a moment." She leaves me, naked and shivering, wondering if I've done the right thing or if I've just made things infinitely worse for myself. I have no clean underwear, so I climb into the pale yellow dress without any. The thing is a frou-frou monstrosity, all ruffles and pleats. There's even a satin bow that ties just under the bust line. I tie it, all the while wondering if the strand of ribbon is long enough to hang myself with if it comes down to it. I wasn't joking back in the van; I would rather die than be violated by a bunch of strange men.

Twenty minutes pass. I sit on the edge of the bed, counting my heartbeats. It's strange that the treacherous organ in my ribcage insists on skipping along so steadily, when it seems as though the intensity of my fear should have stopped it dead by now. I hear voices after a while—loud ones—and then the thunder of boot steps out in the corridor. The door rattles as the key is fumbled, inserted, twisted, opened, and then Hector, Raphael and Ramona storm one by one into the room. Raphael's face is twisted into a rictus of rage. Hector simply looks like he's being inconvenienced.

"Lie back on the bed," he says.

I lock my ankles together, my arms clamped firmly around my body. "No."

Hector laughs, looking at Raphael. "You always bring the spirited ones back, huh?"

"She's not a fucking virgin, Hector. No way. She's lying."

"And why would she do that?" he asks softly. "I'm presuming you didn't tell her of our business here?"

The creases in Raphael's face deepen. "No," he admits.

"Then the girl is probably a virgin." He turns back to me, walks over to the bed, and places a hand on top of my head. I cower from his touch, which seems to displease him. He grabs hold of my chin in one hand, lifting my face so I'm looking up at him. "Lie back on the bed, sweet girl, or I'm going to make you. And I don't want to have to do that, because I don't want to hurt you, you see. Do as you're told and I'll be quick. I promise."

My tears return, blurring out the world. Maybe that's a good thing. I don't want to see their faces as I slowly lie back down onto the bed. Hector throws back the skirts of the yellow dress, and I bite back a cry of shame. His hands are cold. They push my legs apart, and then his strong, thick fingers are investigating, parting the folds of my flesh, demanding entry.

I start to sob. I should have thought of this. Centuries ago, they used to confirm a maiden's virtue before she could be sold off to a husband. And now Hector is going to find out I've lied to him, and I'm going to pay the price. I should have just kept my mouth shut. I cry out as Hector's finger probes deeper inside me. It hurts. The horror of my situation has my whole body clenched tight, locked up and rigid, which makes what Hector is doing to me pinch and burn even more.

I hold my breath, my fingernails cutting into the skin of my palms as I wait for it to be over. For him to call me liar. For more pain to arrive. I'm praying for Matt to come in here and save me, but he won't. He can't. No one can.

"She's telling the truth," Hector announces. *What?* I can't...it takes a moment to register what he's saying. He *believes* me? He withdraws his finger from inside me, and even that stings. Lifting his hand, he takes his index finger and slowly slides it into his mouth. "She's sweet, too. She has a sweet pussy."

My stomach roils, making dark threats. If I had absolutely anything left inside me, I would throw it up all over the bed.

Hector gives Raphael a conciliatory slap on the shoulder. "You know the rules, my friend. Virgins belong to me. Maybe next time you should fuck them before you bring them home, huh? That way there would be no doubt." Raphael's lips are pulled back into an ugly sneer.

"Hector, she is *mine*! I—" Hector snaps his right hand out, backhanding Raphael across the cheek. It probably didn't hurt all that much, but the action silences Raphael in an instant.

"I don't repeat myself for anybody, Raphi. You know that. Please, remember yourself." Raphael clenches his jaw. He nods once, staring the older man directly in the eye. Hector ignores him; he faces Ramona, maintaining a cool, effortless calm. "Get some pictures taken. Post them immediately. Make sure she gets sent to one of the cartels. I don't want her opening her mouth about the judge to any of our other clients. Highest bidder wins out. I want her gone within twenty-four hours." He storms out of the room, wafting a sickly sweet cloud behind him as he goes. I close my legs slowly, pushing down the layers of the dress, crying silently.

I'm to be sold. Like a piece of meat, an object, nameless and unimportant, I am going to be *sold.*

ALEXIS

Ramona disappears and comes back a while later with a small point-and-shoot digital camera. I'm less than compliant when she tells me she wants to take photos of me. I start kicking and screaming, and she counters my refusal with two heavy set women, who hurry into the room and pin me down on the bed while she forces something—a pill—down my throat.

The two women keep me pinned to the bed, grunting as I try and wrestle free of them, until Ramona's happy that whatever she's given me will be taking effect soon. They leave, then, and Ramona smirks as I try launching to my feet, only to find that my arms and legs are made out of rubber. I hit the ground hard, but it doesn't seem to matter. In actual fact, nothing really matters anymore.

She makes me pose in my yellow dress, dead eyes staring straight down the lens, and then she makes me strip. She tells me how I'm to stand or sit, how I'm to hold myself, and she snaps off picture after picture of me, the flash burning another flare of color into my retinas each time. When she tells me to sit on a wooden chair and open my legs for her, I come to my senses long enough to refuse, and she slaps me around the face.

"You'd better just do it, white girl. You don't want to make this hard on yourself," she says to me, her voice softening. It's as though Ramona is both the good cop and the bad in this scenario, which makes it hard to know how to react to her—I never know which side of her I'm dealing with at any one time. She gets her way in the end. I open my legs and close my eyes, and the flash doesn't bother me this time. I think maybe she'll tell me she wants to take the shot again, eyes open this time, but she doesn't. Maybe the people who will be viewing these pictures like when a girl's shame is evident, along with the most private parts of her body. Maybe that's what excites them.

"Don't worry," Ramona says, as she hovers in the doorway, half in, half out, her job done. "You'll be out of here really soon. The men who are gonna bid on you, they take good care of their possessions. If you're good to them, do as your told, you won't want for anything. It's a better fucking life than you would have had here with Raphael."

She says this as though she might know from personal experience what a life with Raphael might be like. I have no choice but to put the yellow dress back on. Ramona leaves me alone in the bare room, my clothes, the clothes I wore in another life still quietly stinking of vomit in the corner, and me curled up in the middle of the bed, too empty and too *nothing* to even cry anymore.

I eventually fall asleep. I don't dream, which is a small blessing. It's dark when I'm woken up—by a silhouette standing in the doorway. Raphael. "You fucking lying whore," he spits.

I sit bolt upright on the bed, my head spinning. The drugs from earlier have mercifully worn off, but now I feel sick. Adrenalin washes through me in a powerful tide that jumpstarts my heart, sending it into overdrive. Where is Hector? Ramona? Without them here, I don't feel safe. Not that I'm safe *with* them here, but at least they would protect their goods, as it were. "You've been touched before. I know it. I can fucking smell it on you," Raphael snarls.

He takes one step into the room, and I push back on the bed, my hands and feet scrambling for purchase against the sheets. "I'll scream," I whisper. My voice cracks—so much fear, so much adrenalin—and I think perhaps he might not have heard me. "I'll scream," I say again, this time louder, more confident. Raphael snorts.

"Scream all you like. It won't get you anywhere. You've been bought and paid for now, bitch. And from what I know of your new owner, you're gonna wish you'd never been born. Get ready. They're already coming for you."

Ramona's warning—*be good and your new owner will be good to you*—was apparently a waste of breath. If Raphael thinks whoever's bought me is a bad person, then I am totally fucked. "Come with me," he commands. I get to my feet, my head spinning from lack of food and panic, and follow after him as he leads me back down the stairs. In the corridor, he stops abruptly, turning on me. My head smashes against the wall as he pins me by the throat with one powerful hand. "You should know, Sophia Letitia Marne, that I have a very long memory. And I hate being fucked around, especially by whores. I don't like not getting what I want. You got a sister, huh? Any family? I am going to find your family, Sophia, and I'm gonna make them pay for your little lie. You hear me? And then, when I've fucked and killed your mother and all of your sisters, I'm going to send you pictures. And you'll know that their deaths were because of you." He spits in my face, then—a huge, wet ball of saliva and phlegm that hits me on the mouth and cheek. "Just wait and see if I don't," he whispers.

A door next to us opens, sending a rectangle of orange light spearing through the darkness, and Hector appears in the doorway, hands on his hips. "Thank you, Raphael. That will be all," he says. My legs almost collapse out from underneath me when it doesn't look like Raphael is going to let me go. But he does. He squeezes my neck one last time, fingers crushing my esophagus, and then pushes away from me, growling under his breath. He charges down the corridor and then out the front door, slamming it hard behind him.

"Why don't you come and wait with me, Sophia?" Hector asks. I'm too paralyzed by what just happened to even contemplate answering, let alone following after him. He takes hold of my elbow and guides me into the lit room he just appeared from, where he sits me down on an overstuffed wingback chair and hands me a tissue. I wipe my face mechanically, too numb to do anything but breathe.

"I should kill you."

My head snaps up to find that Hector has sat himself down opposite me. I see the room properly now—the rows and rows of shelves along the walls, jammed with books. The writing desk. The fireplace, in which a fire is crackling enthusiastically. This must be his study. Hector bridges his hands together and crossed his right leg over his left, studying me with those green eyes of his. They looked sharp and calculating in the sunshine earlier, but in the muted light they now look watery and inconstant. Like they aren't any one fixed color and could easily change with the man's mood. "I hate being lied to, sweet girl. Why did you tell me you were something you weren't?"

It suddenly feels like I'm choking on my tongue. He knows. He knows I'm not a virgin. "I don't know what you mean," I say. Hector tuts disapprovingly, shaking his head.

"I've slept with hundreds of women, my girl. I know what an intact hymen feels like. And yours is most definitely broken."

I don't answer. It's better to keep my mouth shut than to confirm or deny the fact. Hector shifts in his chair, apparently getting comfortable. "So really, I should kill you. I would never normally risk such a liability out there, walking and talking, mentioning my name in places it ought not to be breathed. But, you see, I'm currently under investigation for murder. You may know a little something about that, given Raphael's interaction with Judge Conahue, perhaps? No?"

He dips his head, mouth open, clearly waiting for me to say something. I don't. "You can imagine how awkward it would be if the authorities chose to visit my home while one of my men was burying a body out the back, of course. They have very unique ways of finding buried bodies these days. Freshly disturbed earth is a bit of a giveaway. A lucky thing for you, Sophia. A very lucky thing." A clock on the wall chimes, making me jump. Three a.m. Hector sucks on his teeth, tapping his fingertips together, as though he's thinking on something. "Selling you is the easiest option for me right now, so yes, I have played along with your little ruse. Raphi's a hot head. He can't be trusted to have nice things unfortunately. He breaks them, and then refuses to clean up after himself. You leaving this place is best for everyone all round. But let me tell you, Sophia. I heard what Raphi said to you just now. Raphi is a man of his word. He will look for your family, and he will kill them if he finds them. I am in a position to prevent that from happening. All I require from you is that you keep your mouth shut. You don't talk about me, ever, to anyone. You don't talk about my home or my employees. Does that sound like a fair trade to you, sweet girl?"

My throat is as dry as the Sahara, but I still manage to croak out an eager, "Yes."

Hector nods. "Then we have an agreement. I would advise against breaking it, Sophia. I have eyes and ears everywhere. I also have an uncanny knack of discovering if people have been opening their mouths, when they should be keeping them firmly closed."

"I won't say anything, I swear." I almost can't believe he's letting me go with another cartel. Seems to me that it would be easy enough to send me out with Raphael a couple of miles into the desert and have him put a bullet in the back of my head, but I am not stupid enough to question him. He stands up and takes me by the elbow again. "Time for us to wait outside. I don't particularly like the man who has purchased you. I'd prefer he didn't have to step foot inside my home. Come."

Hector is weirdly protective about his home, but then again he's weird all round. I let him take me outside onto the veranda, where he sits me down on the bench swing. "Please don't move from this spot." Hector paces with that deliberate, unhurried gait of his down the steps to where Raphael is standing, staring out into the desert. I'm left to do the same. Without any light pollution out here, the dark black velvet of the night sky glitters with an explosion of stars. I have no idea where the rusted van I was brought in here has gone, nor the men that traveled with us. No vehicles, no other people, nothing. Just us, the house, and the stars. Yet again, I'm tempted to slip silently off. The men's backs are turned. It would easy enough to do right now, but the fear of what they will do to me when they catch me—because there is no *if*—is enough to keep my bottom firmly planted on the bench.

I hear the rumble of engines before the lights come into view. It's hard to tell how far away the convoy of cars is in the darkness, but it seems as though there are many of them. I count one, two, three, five different sets of headlights. My whole body is begging me to get up and run, to flee, to see how far I can get at least, before I'm trapped with yet another group of insane, violent men, but it's too late for that. Too late for anything but to sit and watch the approaching armada of cars float toward us on the horizon. It's a full five minutes before they're close enough to make out the great plumes of dark dust and sand being kicked up behind the vehicles in their wake. There are seven cars, not five. Why so many? Hector said he didn't like the man who'd bought me. Maybe the feeling is mutual. Maybe the extra muscle is to ensure there's no trouble as the deal goes down.

I'm on the verge of hyperventilating by the time the cars, a mix of sedans and dirty four by fours arrive in front of the house. Hector walks out to the lead car. A window buzzes down, and he shakes hands with the dark figure inside. Men begin to pour out of the cars. Every single last one of them is Mexican. Covered in tattoos and sporting a variety of weapons, they don't look any friendlier than Hector's people. The last person to get out of the cars is grossly overweight, dressed in a cream suit, complete with panama hat. And he's wearing sunglasses. At three thirty in the morning.

Hector slaps the man on the shoulder, grinning and shaking his hand. They speak in rolling, loud Spanish together, and the men standing around them burst into laughter. The fat man signals one of his guys forward. He's carrying a brown paper bag—the kind Mom used to put my lunch in back when I was in elementary school. Hector doesn't touch the bag. It's Raphael that takes it from the other guy, perhaps his counterpart within this other cartel, and begins withdrawing bundles of money from inside. I can't see what denomination the money is in, but Raphael lines up ten stacks side by side next to each other on the hood of the fat guy's car.

Hector casts his eye over the stacks, nods once, shakes hands with the obese man one last time, and then climbs back up the stairs toward me. "You go with him now," he tells me. "And remember what I said. You open your mouth..." He doesn't need to finish his sentence. "I hope I never see you again, Sophia Letitia Marne." And with that, he vanishes back inside the house.

When I turn to face my fate, there are at least fifteen men staring up at me in the dark. The majority of them are leering, eyes already eating up my skin, devouring me whole, though the fat guy doesn't appear to be even half as interested in me. He steps forward, gesturing me forward with an impatient beckoning motion of his fingers. "Come on, child. I have guests arriving at my home shortly. We have to hurry."

Another thick Spanish accent. I think doing as he asks is probably the smartest thing I can do, and yet I just can't force myself. My body will not comply. I want to go home. More than anything in this world, I want to be back in Seattle. The idea of voluntarily leaving with these men makes me sick to my stomach. If I do that, my whole world is going to change. I know that without a shadow of a doubt.

"Juan, go and fucking get her," the fat guy says, talking to one of his men. I see the sneer spreading on Raphael's face as a tall, thin man with one hand firmly gripped around a gun stalks toward me. I don't have the courage to back away. I freeze to the spot, my mind racing. Juan climbs the steps, hooks one wiry arm around my waist and then half-drags, half-shoves me back down the steps after him.

"Put her in my car," the fat guy says.

And that's what Juan does. I am unceremoniously bundled into the back of the lead car—a dark sedan with blacked-out windows. Juan climbs in the front driver's seat, and then the rest of his crew helps the fat guy lower himself into the back with me.

The doors slam, the sound of a shotgun ringing out into the night, and that is it—I am sold. People have taken longer to buy a pack of cigarettes. Juan starts the engine, and we're moving within seconds. I swivel in my seat, turning to watch as the black, black outline of Raphael grows smaller and smaller behind us.

"So. You're the piece of pussy who's been causing all this fuss?" the fat guy asks. He lays a meaty hand against the bare skin of my thigh, grunting with approval. "You may call me *Mr.* Perez," he informs me, as though entertained by the use of the English address, instead of the Spanish. "And now, I have some friends who would very much like to meet you."

REBEL

Being the president of an MC is a lot like being the president of a small country. There are things to consider. Firstly, traffic laws. Convince your constituents to not ride around in their cuts. If they ride around wearing their cuts, people will be able to identify them. And where's the common sense in that? Secondly, diversity is king. If your entire club is made up of white guys with shaved heads, you start to look suspicious. And besides, no one Widow Maker is better than another, regardless of the color of his or her skin. The only hierarchy we subscribe to is this: Prez's word is final. If Prez isn't around, V.P.'s word is final. Thirdly, gender equality. Ain't a single man born on this planet without the good graces of a woman. Clubs that refuse women in their ranks are fucking retarded. After the cuts, what's going to attract more attention than a bunch of angry-looking dudes riding around on motorcycles? Nothing. Throw a couple of women in the mix and suddenly you're a hell of a lot less conspicuous.

The Widow Makers are black, white, Asian, Hispanic, male, female—you name it, we got it. Our bikes aren't the kind of things you'd see being built on *Orange County Choppers*. Yes, a good percent of the Widowers' rides are monstrous cruisers built out of chrome, exhaust pipes fatter than they have any sane reason to be, but we have street fighters too. Sports bikes built for speed and cornering quickly. Tourers built for comfort. Road-legal dirt bikes that can turn on a hairpin and jump a fucking mini van if they have to.

The Widow Makers aren't your average MC. We're a bit of everything. We blend into the background. We're covert. We fly under the radar. We're the only MC in the United States of America that operates like this. You may be asking yourself why we hide who we are from the prying eyes of the public. The answer to that question is simple:

We're not just a motorcycle club. We're criminals. And we're really fucking good at not getting caught.

JULIO'S COMPOUND

I hear the cars pulling up around four am. Carnie hears it, too. He was sleeping, silent, not one muscle twitching, but the low rumble of tires on hard-packed earth has jolted him awake. His Beretta—he calls her Margo. After his mother—is in his hand, ready to shoot. One of Julio Perez's employees lifts his semi-automatic, aiming it at Carnie's face.

"*Calmate*," the Mexican says. He has the look of a stone-cold killer about him. There's nothing going on behind those blank, dark eyes of his. Carnie winces up at the guy, shifting in his chair. Margo goes back into the waistband of his jeans.

"Do I not look calm to you, asshole?" he asks. Carnie hasn't been prospecting for us for long, but he's got fucking stones like bowling balls. He's never really looked the part—tall and gangly, glasses, side parting. He's basically a thirty-three-year-old hipster redneck. I found him half beaten to death just outside a bar in Midland City, Alabama. I wasn't going to waste my time scraping him off the ground, but Cade went through his pockets and found out he had his light aircraft license. Not surprising, given that Midland City's the location of Dothan's regional airport. He was a crop sprayer for a living before we picked him up. Spent his time dusting fields with enough weed killer to deform an entire county.

After we hauled his ass to the hospital and kept an eye on him for a while, he became our prospect. When we're outside the clubhouse, the guy is on my hip at all times, learning how the fuck to behave himself. Other times, he's also a runner. What he runs at any one time depended solely on how we are making our money that month. Pot. Guns. Stolen goods. If it's illegal, odds are Carnie's hauled it across state lines in the back of his Cessna 208. There's only one thing we don't touch, and that's girls.

Until now.

Andreas Medina, Julio's right-hand man, makes a low tutting sound, looking up from the bank of security cameras he's studying. "What you want with this bitch, anyway?" he asks.

I remain slouched in the leather armchair of Julio's security center, eyeing the two punks that have been left behind to keep watch over us. Just because Julio's doing us this favor doesn't mean he trusts us. Especially since I'm bribing him. "She's hot," I tell Andreas. "I saw Hector's post go live and thought to myself, 'Now that's the kind of pussy I need in my collection.'"

Andreas grunts. It's plainly clear that he doesn't believe me. News about what happened in that side street in Seattle is spreading fast. Los Oscuros and the Widow Makers are at war. Everyone with enough common sense is battening down the hatches, preparing for the storm to hit. Julio and all of his men must know that this girl we're paying them to fetch for us was involved in my uncle's death somehow. That's why I'm paying the fat old fuck a hundred grand to do this job for me.

The sound of approaching vehicles grows louder. Andreas doesn't ask me any more questions about the girl; he's too busy verifying that the cars slowly rolling into view on the security cameras are the same seven cars that left the compound four hours ago. A burst of static erupts from the radio sitting on the desk in front of Andreas. "*La tenemos. Abre la puerta,*" a voice advises. *We got her. Open the gates.* Doesn't sound like Julio, but Andreas does as he's told. On the grainy, pixelated screen, a set of huge, high gates swing outwards, letting the cars drive slowly, one at a time into the compound.

Carnie shoots me a stern look, and then stands. "Time for us to be going then."

We should probably stick around inside and observe etiquette. After a business dealing with Julio, it's customary to sit with the man and have a beer. We can't afford that luxury tonight, though. I'm bone tired, and we need to get this girl as far away from California as possible. If we loiter here too long, the likelihood of her being murdered by Los Oscuros grows by the minute. I get to my feet, stretching out my body.

"Been a blast as always. Boys."

Andreas jumps up too, holding out a hand. "Why don't you just slow your roll, *ese*? Julio might want to confirm the exchange." I pull out my cell phone and pull up the transaction confirmation. One hundred thousand dollars, cleared into the account details Julio gave me.

"Merry fucking Christmas," I say, pushing past him. The guy who threatened Carnie with his semi-automatic a moment ago steps in front of me, blocking my way. He lifts his chin, daring me to do something. "What do you think happens if I don't walk out of here?" I whisper. "What do you think happens if there's even a scratch on me when I leave?"

The guy blinks at me. He doesn't move.

"It's okay, Sam. You can let him by." Andreas places a hand on the guy's shoulder, which seems to descale the threat level somewhat. They both move out of the way so I can exit, swiftly followed by Carnie. "Hey, Rebel," Andreas calls after us. I glance over my shoulder. "There will be an end to this, y'know. You can't hold it over him forever. Julio ain't just some punk you can fuck with. We will get the files back."

I give him a lazy smile, flashing teeth. *I'm not afraid of you.* "As always, such a pleasure doing business with you, Andreas. I'm sure we'll see each other again soon."

As Carnie and I hurry out of Julio's villa, three half-naked women run down the corridor in front of us, screaming. They vanish through a side door, tits and ass flashing everywhere, and then they slam the door closed behind them. "Working girls?" Carnie murmurs.

"I doubt they're here for the free tacos."

Carnie spits on the ground, shaking his head at another guard as we exit though the front door. Outside, Julio Perez is heaving himself out of a dark sedan, groaning with the effort. He's wearing fucking shades at night. Carnie elbows me, jerking his head at the fat fucker, as though he can't believe what he's seeing.

I laugh under my breath. "Right?"

Julio catches sight of us—must see us snickering at him—and flips us off. He finally manages to pull himself out of the car. "Motherfuckers," he growls. "You should think twice before laughing at my expense. What you think this is, a fucking circus?"

"Something like that," I answer. "Where's the girl?"

"I slit her throat and left her ass out in the desert," Julio snaps. The driver of the dark sedan climbs out of the car and stands there, staring at us like he expects us to start shooting or something. I know it's a bluff, though. I have dirt on Julio. The kind of dirt even an Untouchable like him wouldn't want getting out. He'd never risk the files I stole from him being made public knowledge. The cops already wanna lock him up; it's not them he's afraid of, though. It's other gangs that would come after him if they caught wind of some of the stuff he's been up to. Double-dealing. Skimming. Flat out stealing from the skinheads. Bad shit.

"How 'bout you stop wasting my time and hand her over, Perez? That way we can get out of your hair and you can get your ass to bed."

Julio grunts, clearly unhappy. He pulls the door of the car open wider and moves aside, and there she is, sitting on the back seat. The blurry girl from Cade's security footage. The girl who witnessed my uncle being murdered. Her hair, thick and dark, has been pinned up into fancy twists and knots. Dark eyes peer out of the darkness, fixed on me, wide and round—she's afraid. I can see it on her the moment our gazes lock. She's wearing some sort of dress, looks like a fucking prom dress. All poofy and flouncy. That's the last thing I fucking need.

Julio jerks his thumb at her, gesturing for her to get out of the car. She slides forward, gathering up the dress so she can clamber out into the night. She's taller then I expected. Still a foot shorter than me, but taller than she appeared in that video as Hector Ramirez's men tossed her in the back of that van. She doesn't move. Looking from me to Carnie and then back to Julio, she doesn't seem to know who to be more afraid of. I take a step forward.

"What's your name?" She looks at me, throat bobbing, eyes shining brightly, and shakes her head. "What, you're not gonna tell me your name?" I ask.

She shakes her head again.

"All right. Suits me fine." I turn to Julio. "Andreas has proof of funds. We're done here."

Julio paces toward me, his wide body swinging as he walks. He speaks so only I can hear him. "You may have me by the balls, but you know me. You know the type of man I am, Rebel. Do you understand what I'm telling you?"

"You're telling me that you're working on a way to kill me, I'm betting." Julio just stares me in the eye, neither confirming nor denying. I slap him on his shoulder. "Good luck with that, man. You know where you can find me."

But Julio won't kill me. He won't even fuck with my club. He knows there are measures that have been taken. He knows the repercussions, what will happen to him and his *familia* if he does.

His men have gathered in front of the villa, glaring at us, as Carnie and I begin walking toward the gates. As we pass by the car, Carnie takes hold of the girl's wrist and tugs her along behind him. He's firm but not rough. She looks like she's about to have heart failure, though. She pulls back, trying to wrestle her arm free. Carnie doesn't let go. He doesn't give her any other option but to follow us. She stumbles, crying out, but Carnie simply pulls her to her feet and carries on walking.

If Julio's gonna shoot us in the back, now's when it'll happen. But as we reach the gate, the high wrought iron barricade slowly swings open.

"If you know what's good for you, you won't come back here," Julio calls after us. I don't look back. Neither does Carnie. We walk right out of the compound, the girl in tow behind us, to where we've left our rides.

Carnie starts the engine of his bike, revving it so we can't be heard. "What we gonna do about the dress?" he asks. He's having the same thoughts I did as soon as I saw what she was wearing. The girl can't get on the back of a motorcycle wearing something so big. It'll get caught in the wheels or something. I turn to the girl, scanning her from head to foot. She's started to cry low, exhausted, barely there sobs that shake her whole body.

"What are you wearing under there?" I ask her.

She looks up at me, and bam. It hits me at possibly the most inopportune of moments: she's fucking beautiful. Even when she's crying, face covered in running mascara, she's breathtaking. I can't afford to be standing around like an idiot in the desert, checking her out, though. "Did you hear me? What are you wearing under that ridiculous fucking dress?'

"Nothing," she whispers. Her lip trembles, making her look really young. In fact, how old *is* she? She looks like a kid. A kid in a bullshit dress, wearing nothing underneath.

"Carnie, give me your knife," I say.

Carnie hands it over, slapping the well-honed blade into my palm, handle first. It's a serrated, mean-looking thing—great for scaring the ever-loving shit out of people when they're not behaving themselves. The young woman standing in front of me turns a ghostly pale white when she sees it.

"Please. Please don't hurt me. I—"

I grab the hem of the long dress she's wearing and I begin to hack at it. The girl stops talking. I work quickly, cutting the skirt of the dress so that it rests about mid-thigh, throwing handfuls of tulle and other lacy shit onto the ground. When I'm done, I straighten up and the girl's arms are locked around her body, her eyes clenched tightly closed. Her legs are on show now, and they are mighty fucking fine.

"Which bike you wanna ride on?" I ask her, pointing to them. She looks at me like she doesn't understand what I'm asking her. "You pick which bike, which means you pick which one of us you're trusting to carry you."

"What if I don't trust either of you?" she asks carefully.

"Then I pick you up and put you on the back of my bike anyway," I tell her. She lets go of herself long enough to wipe the tears out of her eyes. "That one, then. The bigger one." She points to my bike. I grin so hard it feels like my face is gonna split apart.

"Good choice." I'm aware of the fact that Julio hasn't closed the gates after us; he's still watching us from the entrance of his villa, bulky form silhouetted against the light spilling out from inside. I start the engine of my Ducati Monster, snapping my wrist as I gun it, warming up the cylinders. I climb on, turning my attention back to the leggy girl at my side. "Get on," I yell over the roar of the Ducati.

She just stands there, shivering.

"I mean it. Get on this bike, or I'll have to come get you."

The girl shrinks in on herself, her shoulders rounding, pulling up to her ears. For a moment, I think I'm actually gonna have to do it. I think I'm gonna have to get off my bike and forcefully put her on it. I'm seconds from doing exactly that when she cautiously steps forward and throws her leg over my ride. I can feel her looking for something to hold onto, a handrail at the back like the street fighters have. She's not going to find anything, though. I reach back until I find one of her arms, and then I pull it around me. "Now's not the time to be shy, sweetheart. Hold onto me and you'll be fine."

I'm not stupid; I know the last thing she wants to do is wrap her arms around me and get all up close and personal, but we don't have time for me to explain why holding on is a good idea. We really need to get the fuck out of here.

"You been on a motorcycle before?" I ask over my shoulder.

"No." She answers very quietly, but I can still hear her over the roar of the engines.

"Then the smartest thing you can do right now is hold onto me and not let go until I tell you. Unless you want to die, of course?" Slowly, very carefully, her other arm snakes around my waist. "There's a good girl." I gun the engine again, jerking my head to Carnie. "Let's get the fuck out of here before they change their minds and kill us after all."

"Copy that." Carnie takes the lead. He burns off into the desert, and the only thing I can see as I charge after him, an unknown woman clinging onto me for dear life, arms growing tighter and tighter as we go faster, is the red flicker of his taillight.

SOPHIA

I'm going to die.

The cool desert air whips through my hair as we burn the night, ruining the intricate style Ramona created so that I'd be pretty when my new owner came to collect me. My heart is in my throat. I press my cheek into the back of this stranger's back, and I stare out into the abyssal darkness, not seeing anything. Not caring. Practicing at stilling the screaming panic in my head.

This can't be happening.

This can't be happening.

This can't be happening.

This is happening.

This is happening, but it will be okay.

Everything will be okay.

Eventually, we come to a highway—god knows how these guys knew which direction to head in—though everything is still pitch black. No streetlights. No other cars. Nothing. I loosen my grip around the guy's waist, not that I don't feel like I might be tossed out of my seat any second. The seams in the blacktop make regular thrum, thrum, thrum noises as the motorcycle's wheels travel over them. I think about jumping.

What are the chances of me seriously damaging myself if I throw myself off this bike? What are the chances of me dying? It's almost as if the guy in front of me guesses what I'm thinking. The motorcycle speeds up, tearing up the open road, the engine roaring in my ears. No chance I can do it now. I'd be road-kill the second my body hits the ground.

I allow myself the luxury of a few tears as we travel on, on, on into the night. There seems to be no end to this journey. It feels like I'm going to be trapped here on the back of this motorcycle forever, forced to hold onto a man who paid a huge amount of money so he can do god knows what to me. So he can *own* me. That thought makes me feel sick. My head's still spinning from where Raphael's men hit me, which doesn't help.

I can feel the last reserves of my energy draining from me, my body falling limp, as the sun begins to peek over the horizon. We pass a Winnebago at first light, the driver honking his horn at us in greeting. He obviously hasn't seen another person on the road for a long time, either. As we pass the souped-up vehicle, I catch a glimpse of the guy behind the wheel—he's grinning, wearing a bucket hat, the kind people only ever wear on vacation, and there's a small kid in the front seat beside him. They both look so damned happy, flashing their middleclass smiles at us. I wonder if they can see the terror in my eyes as I whip by them in a blur.

Probably not.

The guy with the glasses on the other motorcycle revs his engine, and suddenly the front wheel is off the ground. He's pulling a wheelie. I can hear him hollering as my guy pulls forward to catch up with him. Underneath my now very lax grip, I can feel his stomach muscles contracting as he...as he *laughs*. I hate him. It's wrong that he should be laughing at the stupid, reckless behavior of his friend after he's basically just kidnapped me. Tertiary kidnapping—that's what it was. Raphael first, then that Julio guy, and now this one. I've been passed from pillar to post like lost property. The worst part of now being bought and paid for by this new guy is that he's really good looking. There's no way he would have a problem getting any girl he wanted, which makes me think scary things. Maybe normal women won't let him do the things that he wants to do. Maybe his sexual proclivities run so dark that he can only act out his fantasies on people who have no choice in the matter. That could be part of it, too—the sense of power he'd feel as he took something precious from someone who didn't want to give it.

An hour after we hit the highway, the guys pull into a diner at the side of the road—Harry's Place. My body is aching from sitting on the back of the motorcycle for so long; my back, my butt, my shoulders, my legs—all of me is throbbing or complaining in one way or another. It hurts even more when the guy kills the engine and makes me get off, my limbs protesting at being straightened out after remaining in one position for so long. The guy swings off the motorcycle and kicks out the stand, letting the heavy machine rest.

I quickly look around, wondering if I should run. Now that it's light and I can see where we are, that doesn't seem like a good plan. Arid desert stretches on endlessly in every direction, the landscape without life or vegetation. Orange rocks and dirt forever.

"I wouldn't if I were you." I snap my head around. The guy I rode with is standing in front of me, hands in his pockets, mouth pulling up at one side. It's almost a smile, but not a friendly one. He looks amused. "People die out there without trying very hard. That's why our good friend Julio built his compound out there. No chance anyone's gonna stumble across him, if you catch my drift."

I glare at him, wrapping my arms around my body. This dress is not the kind of thing I want to be wearing on the side of the road in the middle of nowhere, with the sun really starting to heat up. I have far too much skin on display, especially since half the skirt was hacked away by a really sharp knife.

The guy standing in front of me tips his head to one side. "We'll find you something a little more appropriate to wear soon."

He's wearing a black T-shirt with the sleeves cut off, and worn-out jeans, white sneakers on his feet. Tattoos cover every available inch of his skin from the shoulders down—colorful sleeves that I only allow my eyes to skim over before quickly looking away. I have no idea what a person like *him* would consider more appropriate attire for *me,* but I'm not looking forward to finding out. "Where are you taking me?" I demand.

The other guy, joining us, laughs. "Pissy, ain't she?" He spits on the floor.

"Seems so."

I want to get smart with them. I want to ask them if being witness to a murder, kidnapped, assaulted, violated, and sold would make them pissy, but I don't know much about these people yet. They've yet to show me who they are. Whether they're violent people. They look like violent people.

The one I rode with smirks at me. "I'm Rebel. This is Carnie. We're taking you back to our clubhouse. If you have any further questions, you can direct them straight to Cade."

"Who's Cade?"

Rebel—obviously not the name his parents gave him when he was born—points a thumb over his shoulder. "Cade's the guy sitting in that Humvee behind me. I believe you've already met."

Sure enough, there is a black Humvee parked in the lot, twenty feet away from where we're standing. I can't see much through the dark tint on the windows. The car's massive—looks like something that belongs in an army convoy, not sitting in a diner's parking lot. The door opens and a broad guy in a black hoody jumps down from the driver's side. I don't recognize him at first, but as he gets closer I see more and more of his face. It's the guy from the side alley, the one who gave Raphael the bullet. The one who told me to say I was a virgin.

His face is expressionless as he arrives next to Rebel. "Went off without a hitch?" he asks.

"Surprisingly. You got everything prepped?"

Cade nods. "The guys have been warned. We should arrive back early evening or so."

Rebel nods. "Okay. Don't let her out of your fucking sight, you hear?"

"You know it." Cade steps closer to me, and that's it; I've been transferred over to yet another person. Rebel climbs back on his motorcycle and he doesn't look back. He and Carnie burn off into the early morning without even acknowledging me again. I stare after them, wondering what the hell is going to happen next.

Cade takes hold of me by the arm, pulling me in the direction of the Humvee. Eyes fixed straight ahead, he doesn't look at me as he opens the passenger door of the monstrous vehicle and waits for me to climb inside. I shuffle backward instead.

"Who are you?" I ask.

"I'm Cade," he replies.

"I'm not asking what your name is. I'm asking *who are you*? Are you guys some sort of sex ring or something? Do you trade in people that are stolen off the streets? Are you going to use me up and then kill me?" I feel a little braver around this guy, so the questions flow one after the other. I probably shouldn't feel brave around him, but he did tell me to lie to Raphael and Hector. Part of me wants to believe that's because he was trying to save me from whatever horrors Raphael had planned for me. Equally, it could mean that he simply wanted his boss to have me instead of his enemy.

"We're not gonna kill you," Cade tells me, glancing at me out of the corner of his eyes. "And we don't deal in girls, either."

"Then why won't you just let me go? You could just send me back to my family. I swear I won't breathe a word about what I saw."

Cade places his hand on my back and pushes me toward the car. "'Fraid we can't do that. Rebel needs you."

"He *needs* me? What for?" I have no choice but to climb up into the Humvee as Cade moves to my left and urges me forward.

"Not my place to tell you, kiddo. Just keep your head straight. Don't freak out on me and everything will be fine. Rebel will get what he needs, you can go back to Seattle and everyone's happy." He slams the door closed and walks around the car, but he doesn't get in. He locks the doors and heads inside the diner, instead.

As soon as he's vanished inside the building, I get to work. There has to be something in here I can use as a weapon. Something I can use to get free. A cell phone to call my dad. I check the glove compartment, on the backseat, underneath the front seats as best as I can, contorting my body into awkward positions in order to get my head down into the foot wells, but there's nothing. Not one scrap of paper. Not one piece of trash. Not even an owner's manual. The interior of the car is spotless.

I don't realize Cade has returned until I hear the driver's side door opening. I'm on my front, looking under his seat at the time, which is where he finds me. He has a brown paper bag in his hand and a bemused expression on his face. "This isn't our first time at the rodeo, kid," he tells me. "Where are you planning on going, anyway? We're in the middle of nowhere."

I push myself upright, slumping back into my seat. "I don't suppose it'd matter where I go, *asshole*. All I'd need to do is find a payphone. I'd call the police and have them come arrest all of you, starting with that psycho Raphael and his weird boss."

Cade nods, passing me the brown paper bag. He gets in, starting the engine. "Raphael is definitely a psycho. Hector, too, when you get to know him."

The smell of melted cheese hits me, and I realize what I'm holding. Food. Actual, real food. I haven't eaten anything since back at Hector's ranch. I glance over at Cade, trying to suss him out.

"Is...this for me?"

"Before you start complaining, they didn't have any salads. If you don't want it, I'll gladly take it off your hands."

I close my hands around the paper bag, holding onto it tightly. "I *do* want it." It's annoying that he thinks just because I'm a woman, I'm allergic to carbs and a little grease. I manage to hold my tongue, though. If he wants to pretend like he knows who I am, based on the fact that I have tits and a vagina, then let him. That's his loss. Cade pulls out onto the highway, and I tear into the paper bag, finding a simple grilled cheese and a chocolate muffin inside. Neither of us speaks. He drives. I eat.

I've never enjoyed a grilled cheese sandwich as much in my entire life. The heaviness of it sits in the pit of my stomach, solid and weighty, which is reassuring. If I have to go without food again for a little while, I'll manage. I don't know when but I've decided that I'm going to make a break for it as soon as I can. At some point on our journey from here to our destination, we'll have to stop, and he will take his eyes off me, even if it's for a second. A second is all I'm going to need. I'll be away before he even realizes what's happened. Better start making plans.

"Where's the clubhouse, *Cade*?" I emphasize his name, testing it out. I don't know anyone called Cade—I don't think I've ever had to say it before. He huffs out a laugh, changing gear.

"New Mexico. Should take us about thirteen hours to get there if you don't talk the whole way."

New Mexico? My body sinks back into the seat, heavy as a lead weight. That's way further than I anticipated. I thought maybe we'd be traveling for a couple of hours and then we'd arrive, but no. We're headed across three states. That's a good thing and a bad thing. If we were only going to be trapped inside this monstrosity for a little while, that's less opportunity for me to run. But now, the further Cade drives me away from Washington is further that I have to make it back home without them coming after and finding me.

You don't need to make it home, I remind myself. It's like I just told Cade. I'd only need to make it to a police station. Or anywhere I could report what's happened. Then I'd be safe. A surge of adrenalin fires through my veins, electricity around a circuit board, powering me up. I need to be ready, and for that I need energy. I start on the chocolate muffin but then give up halfway through, the food making me feel queasy.

"You mind if I put the radio on?" Cade asks.

I frown, looking at him properly for the first time since we got in the car. "You're *asking* me? I'm your captive. I'm pretty sure you can do whatever the hell you like and I wouldn't have a say in it." It's strange that he would even give me the option.

Cade grunts, dark eyes on the road. "You're not a captive. That's not what this is."

"If I'm not a captive, then let me go." I already know he won't, though. If they were going to help me or do me any favors, they would have done so as soon as we cleared Julio's den out in the desert.

"I already told you. Rebel needs you for something. Once that's done, you can go."

"Bullshit. You're holding me against my will. You may not like the sound of it but that makes me a captive. And it makes you my kidnapper. If you expect me to do something for Rebel, then you're dreaming. I'm not performing sexual acts for anyone. Not willingly. If you make me, then you guys won't just be my kidnappers. You'll be my rapists, too."

Cade's head turns so he's looking at me, mouth slightly open. There's a look of disbelief on his face. "Man, no wonder Hector got rid of you. You've got a tongue on you, you know that?"

I just shrug my shoulders. No way would I have spoken to Hector or even Raphael like that. I would have been too scared. Being in the car with Cade is different, though. "Why did you help me back in that alleyway? Why did you even bother if *this* is what you wanted to do afterwards?"

"*This* isn't anywhere near as bad as you think it is. I helped you because we don't like women being abused. The club has morals. And believe it or not, so does Rebel."

"I doubt that."

"Doubt it all you want. You'll see for yourself soon enough."

"Who is he, Rebel? Who is he to you? The way you say his name's like he's freaking god or something."

Cade smirks. He must press his foot to the floor, because the

Humvee picks up the pace until we're speeding into the early dawn. "He's the president of the Widow Makers," he says. "He's one of the good guys. He's also my best friend."

181. That was the number advertised on Hector's members-only website. I called back to the clubhouse and had Danny, our resident computer hack, check the records, but that's all there was on her. No real name. No background information. Just 181.

She's fucking beautiful, of course. That fact isn't acknowledged or discussed as Carnie and I mull over what to do with her; it doesn't need to be discussed. It just sits there between us, her beauty an obvious truth that's making me seriously fucking antsy. Things would have been a lot more straightforward if she was ugly. I wouldn't feel bad for her, for starters. That makes me a shitty guy, I know, but I'm honest. No point in trying to sugarcoat it. The fact that she looks like a younger, hotter, curvier Penelope Cruz is making it hard for me to think of her as a means to an end. It's making me think of her as someone to be pursued, and that is a bad fucking deal. I don't have time to deal with that. I can't afford to be thinking of a girl when there are important plans to be made. Vengeance to be plotted out. Information to be gathered.

"If you leave her at the clubhouse, we can probably keep her there, out of sight, for three or four days before anyone notices. If we can keep her quiet," Carnie says.

If. That's a big fucking if. I somehow doubt very much that we're going to be able to keep this girl quiet for any length of time. "She can't stay in the clubhouse, Carnie. For starters, which room would we put her in? Everything's being used. And secondly, Keeler and Brassic are nosey as fuck. We tell 'em they can't go into a certain room and what's the first thing they're gonna do?"

"Go into the damned room. You're right. Fuck."

Carnie swerves a little closer to me so that our intercoms don't crackle quite as much. These aren't the lame, bulky intercoms dentists install inside their helmets while they're touring around on the weekend. For starters, we don't wear helmets unless we can avoid it, which we can most of the time. Our intercoms—sleek, small button radios that fit into our ears—were created by Brassic, the Widow Makers' resident tech genius. He was in the army up until three years ago, when he lost the lower half of his right leg. He's fitter, faster, more capable than well over half the other Widowers, but the US Army decided he wasn't fit for active duty so he gave them the finger and joined our ranks—a different kind of army, but an army all the same.

"You know what you're gonna have to do, don't you?" Carnie asks. I hear him laughing, even with the wind whipping away his voice.

"What?"

"She's gonna have to bunk in with you, brother."

"Nope. No. Not happening. She can't."

"Why not?"

"Because I need my fucking space, Carnie. Shit." I paddle the gears with my left foot, switching up so I can go faster. I leave him behind, though I can still hear the bastard laughing in my ear.

"Just sayin', boss. If you want your little witness protection scheme to work, it'd be smart to keep the witness out of the way. At least for a little while, anyway."

I narrow my eyes, glaring at the road. "My little witness protection scheme only needs to work if my plan for all-out violence fails first. And when has all-out violence failed us before?"

Carnie sounds grim when he says, "Never, boss. Not once."

We arrive in Vegas three hours after we leave Cade and the girl. Should have taken four, but we're heavy on the throttle. The city in the desert is roaring already, despite the fact that it's still early in the morning. We rumble down the strip, dodging piles of puke and Nevada PD cruisers pulled up onto the curb, as the local law enforcement round up the wasted people being ejected from the casinos. Gotta love Vegas, city of the damned. Maybe that's why the cartel we've come to see set up their base of operations here—so many drunk people, addicted to one thing or another, to abuse and manipulate.

This is the first time in four years I've been to visit the leader of the Desolladors—the skinners. The Colombian cartel earned their name and their reputation by actually flaying the skin from their enemies' bodies, usually starting on the chest first. That's where most organizations and gangs wear their colors and ink.

I haven't been back here in so long because Maria Rosa, the brains behind the Desolladors, hates coming to America. She's obsessed with the culture, but she hates the people. Like, *really* hates the people. Quite the contradiction. If she steps foot on US soil, there's a good fucking reason for it.

I know she's here now because I pay one of her guards to give me a heads up when he finds out she's on her way in.

Carnie and I turn down one of the side streets off the strip and park up our rides—Carnie grumbles about abandoning his twenty-thousand-dollar baby next to a dumpster behind the Bellagio, but machines like these aren't exactly inconspicuous. Ideally, Maria Rosa won't know we're rolling up on her until we're knocking on her suite door.

Sweat runs like a goddamn river between my shoulder blades, even though it can only be sixty degrees. It takes fucking forever for us to walk up to the MGM Grand. When we reach the entrance to the hotel and casino, Carnie's making noises about getting a beer.

"You really wanna face Maria Rosa after a beer?" I ask, trying not to laugh. Carnie's a lightweight of epic proportions, and Maria Rosa is a deadly viper. She draws on people's weaknesses. I'm pretty sure she sucks out their souls; I just can't prove it. To spend time with her even faintly mentally compromised is asking for trouble. Carnie's never met her before, but he's heard the stories. He lifts one eyebrow, one side of his mouth lifting into half a smile—*good point.*

The MGM is buzzing. People checking in. People checking out. Groups gathered around the casino tables still in their clothes from last night, gin and tonics still being placed into their open hands. The place smells like Vegas glamour and sweat, tinged with just the faintest hint of desperation.

"So, she's on the thirty-fifth?" Carnie asks, already stabbing at the button on the elevator call panel. I grunt, pushing my hair back out of my eyes.

"She's a creature of habit. I can't imagine she's changed."

"Excuse me, gentlemen. Are you visiting a guest this morning?" I turn around and end up facing a wall of muscle, dressed in a suit. The Hispanic guy—a good three inches taller than I am, shaved head, tattoos peeking out above his shirt collar—looks mean. Really fucking mean. He doesn't work for the hotel, that's for sure. The MGM are used to people coming and going from the hotel rooms, no questions asked. Their security detail would never bother people trying to access the guest floors—not even super shady-looking bastards like me and my boy. No, this guy...this is one of Maria Rosa's men. Has to be.

"We're not here to cause trouble. We just want to talk to her," I say.

The guy scowls at me, two deep lines forming between his eyebrows. "I'm afraid I don't know what you're talking about."

"*Nuestra madre nos dijo que siempre estábamos bienvenidos. ¿Quiere que le digamos que nos diste la vuelta?*" *Mother said we were always welcome. You want us to tell her you turned us away?*

Of course, Maria Rosa isn't my mother, nor is she Carnie's mother, but she insists that those she keeps close call her that. By using that name, I've demonstrated who I am to this blank-eyed bodyguard. I'm someone his employer trusts, and I won't have any qualms in telling her he denied us access if he causes any shit.

He stares me down, back rigid and straight, testing me out some more. When I don't back down, he gives me a single nod. "What's your name?"

I tell him. A flicker of recognition flashes across his face. He turns his back to us and begins speaking into the discreet radio he has stowed in the breast pocket of his tailored black suit.

"So much for a surprise visit," Carnie grumbles.

"Yeah, well. I guess it's better she knows we're coming than getting shot in the belly by one of these punks."

"Oh, so that's an option, is it? Fantastic."

"You two can go up. But I'll need to accompany you." Maria Rosa's man has stopped murmuring into his radio. He stares at both of us as he reaches forward and hits the button for thirty-five. We wait in silence. A group of tourists come stand behind us, talking loudly and giggling—four overweight adults and three overweight kids. When the doors to the elevator open, Carnie, the guard, and I get on. The holidaymakers are about to follow suit but then they see our faces. The casual bulge of the gun on Maria Rosa's henchman's hip. The tattoos that cover the majority of our visible skin.

They make the smart choice and don't get on.

The doors close and we begin our ascent. "Give me your guns," the guard says. "You won't be admitted into her presence without surrendering all weapons."

We already know this is how Maria Rosa operates. Smart, really. She commands the most lucrative gambling and drugs ring in the country. There are people who would kill her for that reason alone, to take her business, regardless of the fact that she's faintly psychotic and slices off people's skin for fun.

"We left our guns at home," I tell him. He gives me a look—he clearly doesn't believe that. "You can have our knives, though. That make you happy?" I grin at him, which doesn't seem to ingratiate me to him any further. Holding out his hand, his cold eyes travel over us, as though searching for the telltale bulge of a gun that we're claiming we don't have. I start pulling out my knives—one from the waistband of my jeans, one strapped to my side, one strapped to my ankle. Carnie has more; the guy overcompensates when Margo's not on his hip. All told, the guard has nine knives in his hand by the time we're done giving them up.

He draws his lips into a tight line—not impressed.

The doors to the elevator open then, and a housekeeping maid— a skinny woman with a neat ponytail and sensible shoes—is waiting on the other side. She nearly jumps out of her skin when she catches sight of the sharp blades clutched in the guard's hands. "Sorry, I'll...I'll just..." She doesn't enter the elevator. She spins on the balls of her feet and hurries off down the corridor, glancing over her shoulder at us as she flees. The guard gestures to us that we should follow him.

"She gonna cause problems?" Carnie asks as we follow the hallway around, passing room doors on either side of us.

"She might tell her superior," the guard grunts. "But he's one of ours. They're all ours. It won't go any further."

"Sweet." Carnie pulls a face at his back. Fucking child. I give him a warning look, wondering why the hell I brought him and not Cade. That wasn't really an option, though. There are times when Carnie just can't behave himself, or hold his tongue, for that matter, but in this instance he was the sensible choice. Cade and Maria Rosa... Cade and Maria Rosa have history. She swore a long time ago that she'd have his balls if she ever laid eyes on him again. And Maria Rosa is a very literal woman.

I smack Carnie on the arm, sending him an expression that I hope conveys how much shit he will be in if he fucks this up.

The guard leads us to the end of the hallway, to the very last room on the right. He knocks twice, quietly, and then steps back, presumably so whoever is inside the room can see who's at the door. A rattling, scraping sound follows—the chain being undone— and then the door opens and a huge guy in sweat pants and a muscle tee is standing in front of us, face drawn into a dramatic scowl. Rico Mendez. Rico has been Maria Rosa's personal guard for the past twelve years, by all accounts. He's her personal trainer. He drives her anywhere she needs to go. She fucks him when the mood takes her, although I'm pretty sure she prefers American men. The first time I met him was in Colombia, when he was trying to kill me. He didn't succeed, of course. I kicked his ass and gave him the gnarly scar that still twists the flesh down the left-hand side of his face.

"*Rebel*," he says, as though my very name is a statement in itself.

"Rico."

The man looming in the doorway breaks into a broad grin, booming laughter filling the hallway. "It's fucking good to see you, man. It's been a long time." He holds out his hand. I take it, letting him pump my arm up and down. Slapping me on the shoulder, he pulls me into the suite, still laughing. He points to Carnie, giving me a questioning look. "Who's this? I haven't met this one."

Rico thinks it's hilarious that I took him down. He decided that we would be best friends after Maria Rosa declared she wasn't going to have me skinned alive for breaking into her house. Ever since then, whenever I've had occasion to meet with his boss, Rico's treated me like a long-lost brother. I'm no fool, though. As with all gangs and cartels, camaraderie and hospitality are part of a very tenuous front that will vanish in a heartbeat if you do anything to piss them off. If Maria Rosa decides she no longer likes me, Rico will rip my throat out as soon as look at me. And I wouldn't have a hope in hell of fending him off. Not again. He's not the sort of guy anyone would ever beat twice.

"This is Carnie," I tell him, clapping him on the back when he draws me in close for some semblance of a hug.

"Carnie? You guys are all crazy. None of you have proper names." Rico turns to Carnie, not offering out his hand for him to shake—Carnie hasn't earned that privilege yet—and asks, "What do you call yourself that for? You like meat?"

"Car*nie*, not carn*e*," my boy says, emphasizing the difference between his nickname and the Spanish word for meat. "I'm fucking vegan."

"You don't eat meat?"

"No, I don't. I don't eat anything that used to have *eyes*. That's fucking wrong, man."

Rico runs his tongue over his teeth, narrowing his eyes at Carnie. He makes a low humming sound in the back of his throat—I don't think he's impressed by my prospect. "Men were bred to hunt and kill, my friend. They learned to do that to survive. To feed their families. To assert their dominance over weaker, less intelligent men. That's the natural way of things, huh?"

Oh boy. I've heard people have this conversation with Carnie before. It never ends well. He folds his arms across his chest, flexing his muscles. "Actually prehistoric man survived mostly off things he foraged from the land. Meat was an infrequent substitute to his diet. He survived where other species failed and suffered extinction because he was smart. Because he had a bigger fucking brain than any of the other animals. And look at me, man. You think I have any problems asserting my dominance over weaker, less intelligent men? Do you?" Pulling up to his full height, Carnie leans back, giving Rico a less-than-friendly smile.

The click of heels on tiles breaks the silence. "Are you boys done measuring dicks?" Maria Rosa appears behind Rico, as beautiful and deadly as ever. I always wonder whether it's possible to catch the woman without a full face of makeup and her hair done. I've dated enough girls, really girly girls, to know that even they have their down time. Days when they don't feel like sucking in their bellies and getting dressed up to the nines. Days when all they wanna do is lounge around on the couch in a T-shirt and tracksuit pants, eating Ben and Jerry's from the tub.

Maria Rosa is always perfect, though. Always. And she doesn't look Colombian, either. Bleached blonde hair, green eyes, light olive skin—she looks like Penny from *The Big Bang Theory*. That's no mistake. She's obsessed with the show, addicted, or she used to be.

It doesn't look like much has changed since the last time we met.

"Rebel," she says, holding out her hand. "What a pleasant surprise." I take her hand and kiss the back of it, knowing that she's lying. My visit is about as pleasant as a rough enema.

"Beautiful as always, Mother. So good to see you, too." I lay it on thick, giving her no reason to suspect there are about a million other places I'd rather be than right here, right now, with her. "How long are you staying in the country for?"

She pouts, resting her weight over one hip. If I didn't know her already, the extraordinarily tight red dress she's wearing would have me thinking she is just on her way out to a nightclub. She's not, though. It's just how she dresses, even at ten in the morning. "Oh, I don't know. I'm just checking on a few new business enterprises I've invested in. After that...I could stay a week. I could stay a month. Depends on whether I have any reason to hang around." She strokes a taloned finger down my cheek, tracing her nail along my jawbone and down underneath my chin. She's a notorious flirt. I know better than to even consider going there, though. Cade did and it nearly cost him his life.

I smirk at her, playing the game. Letting my eyes rest on her cleavage a little longer than I should because I know she likes to be appreciated. "Are you going to spend a few days with me here, baby?" she asks, stepping closer to me so that her chest is pushed up against mine. Her tits are almost spilling out of her dress, skin soft and golden and smooth, and it's really fucking easy to see how men get caught up by her. She's sexy, she's powerful and she has stones. I don't know a guy who hasn't been given a boner by the Bitch of Colombia. I'm hardly innocent, myself. I *am* sensible, though.

I take hold of her wrist and kiss her lightly again, on the wrist this time. "I wish I could. We have to be heading back to New Mexico right away, though. I've come here strictly on business."

"Is that why you've brought this one with you instead of that coward Cade Preston?" She actually sounds pissed that Cade isn't here.

I laugh, but it takes serious effort. I can't put a foot wrong here. I can't say the wrong damn thing. If I do, my balls will be forfeit and Carnie will probably end up dead.

"Forgive me for saying so, Mother, but I didn't think you were all that fond of my vice president these days?"

She flicks her wrist at me, making a derisive sound at the back of her throat. "Don't be so ridiculous. I love him. Mateo, everything is fine. You can head back downstairs."

I didn't even realize that the guard—Mateo—was still behind us, loitering in the doorway. He gives her a short bow. "Yes, Mother. I'll be available if you need anything."

I don't like the way he says that, like he thinks she might want us brutally murdered in about half an hour or so, and he'll be ready to oblige her. Mateo leaves, pulling the door closed behind him, leaving the four of us behind in the entrance of Maria Rosa's suite. To say things are a little tense would be an understatement. Rico and Carnie are still utterly unimpressed by one another, and Maria Rosa remains irritated that Cade's nowhere to be seen. She pivots on her skyscraper heels and struts back into the main area of the suite, grumbling under her breath.

"Fucking men. Wouldn't know what to do with...too much to handle. It's his fucking loss, anyway. I wouldn't..." She carries on muttering, the sound of her voice carrying as she vanishes. Rico gestures for us to follow after her, and we do. Inside the suite, a wall of glass stretches from the floor to the ceiling, displaying a panoramic view of the strip, the major artery that supplies the beating heart of the city. It's an ugly, beautiful thing, all at once.

Maria Rosa clucks her tongue, lowering herself gracefully to seat herself at a large glass desk, covered in papers. "So tell me. Why have you come here this morning? I have to say, I'm accustomed to people waiting until they're supplied with an invitation to call upon me." She glances down at her papers, sifting through them, apparently looking for something, and I see it now: she's pissed. I knew she would be. She's just hidden it well until now.

"We've come to discuss a matter of mutual interest with you," I say. Her hand stills on her papers, but she doesn't look at me. She's like a wild animal, aware of our presence, frozen solid, ready to bolt at any moment. Except in this instance, her bolting means her losing her temper and ordering one or both of our deaths. Not only do I have to pick my words carefully here, but I have to say them the right way, too. She needs to be handled with such caution. I've seen guys get their fucking tongues cut out for muttering a sentence she hasn't liked. Thank god Carnie knows to keep his goddamn mouth shut altogether, otherwise I'd be leaving here with a mute prospect.

"What could you possibly have to discuss with me that could be to our mutual benefit, Rebel? You run a small-time club for boys on their bicycles. I run an international business."

"I know, of course. Your organization is in a completely different league to mine, but still, we share common grievances every once in a while. I'm sure you know what I'm talking about."

She does know what I'm talking about. It's well documented that Los Oscuros have been a thorn in my side for years. However, the Mexican cartel has been an equally big thorn in Maria Rosa's side for just as long. Longer. It would be easier for her to ship her drugs up through Mexico and across the border into the states than to fly them direct from Colombia. US border patrol have a keen eye to the sky at all times. It's hard to bribe an air traffic controller at a small airfield, because there are more people to witness a single prop coming in to land. If she were to send her drugs by road, bribing a single border control officer would be a piece of cake. Only problem is, Hector's got all the border control officers on his payroll. And his men protect their investments fiercely against trafficking from outside sources.

He would rather have all-out war in the streets of Mexico than allow one of Maria Rosa's trucks to pass through his turf. In fact, it's come down to that on more than one occasion.

Maria Rosa slips her feet from her heels and holds them out in front of her. Rico reacts instantly, taking a seat so he can lift her feet into his lap. He begins massaging them, mumbling softly to her in Spanish as he works his thumbs into the arches of her soles. "I assume you're talking about the Ramirez dog? Take a seat, please." She jerks her head toward the plush couch a couple of feet away from the table where she's sitting. Carnie and I do as we're invited to and sit down. Carnie lifts an eyebrow in response to the scene playing out in front of us.

He gives me a look I can read all too well—*what the hell is this all about?*

Rico's getting more and more aggressive as he massages Maria Rosa's feet. She lets her head to fall back, one hand rising to touch the skin at the base of her throat. Her eyes slowly close, full lips parting. The whole thing is sexual. Really fucking sexual. I'm used to this kind of bullshit around Maria Rosa, but I didn't exactly give Carnie a heads up.

"So," she whispers. "I heard about your open declaration of war against Los Oscuros. I have to say, I'm very intrigued as to why you would do such a thing. Hector has more men than you. More weapons. And you have, what? A death wish?"

"I have men and guns enough, Mother. Don't you worry about me. As to the why, Hector had someone murdered. Someone I care deeply about. I won't allow that to go unanswered."

Maria Rosa's head lolls, rolling so that she's finally looking at me. Her eyes are burning, filled with the promise of sex. "A woman? Did he snuff out one of your pretty women, Rebel? How cruel."

"Someone of consequence," I say. I refuse to tell her who I wish to avenge. Since he was my uncle, she'll be able to figure out who I am if she discovers Ryan's name, and I can't have that. That information has been well guarded, protected, since the day I founded the Widow Makers, and I don't want that changing any time soon.

Maria Rosa groans, eyes shuttering as Rico reaches what must clearly be a very sensitive spot on her feet. Her back arches off her chair, giving her body an inviting curve to it—the kind of curve that begs a man to touch. Carnie clears his throat, throwing his left ankle up to rest on his right knee. He's clearly trying to hide something, probably the fact that his dick is getting hard, knowing him. I'm immune to this crap now.

"So Ramirez murders someone of consequence and you declare war. And then you show up on my doorstep, looking so good, bringing me some eye candy to enjoy, and I'm not supposed be suspicious, Rebel? Come on." Rico raises her foot up even higher from his lap and licks at her toes, making her gasp. "You think...you think I don't know what you want from...me? *Ahh!*"

"Fuck. Me," Carnie groans.

"You're a smart woman, Mother. I have no doubt you know why I'm here. And because you're smart, I know you'll also see the wisdom in providing support to the Widow Makers. We take down Hector, you get his business. You can ship through Mexico. You strengthen ties to the Widowers, who can then provide extra protection to you while you're in this country."

"And..." Rico traces his tongue across the bridge of Maria Rosa's foot, making her breath catch in her throat. Her whole body shivers. "And you'll contract to run my products for me when I need you to."

This isn't a question. This is a statement that I don't really know I should be agreeing to. Providing protection is one thing. Running drugs is another entirely. The Widowers aren't strangers to transporting the odd key of weed or blow from one spot to another, but what Maria Rosa's talking about is something else entirely. She's talking huge quantities, across long distances. "Our outfit's too small to take on distribution of your operation, Mother. You just said so yourself—we're a small concern compared to the empire you've built for yourself. But I'd be happy to organize local shipments. Share my contacts with you in the east. Set up an expanded network of trusted people who would be happy to work with you."

"I already know people in the east. I don't need more people in the east. I need *you*." Rico's working on her calves now, rotating his thumbs into her flesh, making her squirm in her chair.

Unfortunately, I know what's coming next. I doubt it's avoidable at this stage, no matter what I say. I've lost count of the times when I've been witness to Maria Rosa getting fucked. It's all just part of her madness. Should be a treat for Carnie, though.

"I can help you where I can, Mother. That goes without saying, of course."

Her mouth pulls back into a lazy smile, as Rico's hands climb higher and higher up her legs. "You're a sneaky bastard, Rebel. Don't take me for a fool. I need something from you and you're dancing around it, like you always do."

I just smile. There's nothing else I can do, bar agree to something that will mean I am her employee and no longer her equal. She grins back, just as Rico reaches the apex of her thighs. His hand disappears underneath the skirt of her dress. Her whole body tenses for a moment, then she stretches languorously, like a cat. I wouldn't be surprised to hear her fucking purring.

"All right, Rebel," she says, her voice tight under the pressure of what's happening between her legs. "I'll help you. But you'll need to sweeten the deal a little first, since you won't give me what I truly want."

This is how it is with her. Always something she needs in payment, regardless of whatever she may already be gaining. "What do you want, Mother?" I prepare for her to ask for my first-born son. Good job I don't plan on having any kids.

"Hector Ramirez isn't the only problem I've been encountering recently. A few of my shipments have been seized out at Baker. The DEA have been ramping up their interest in my business transactions the past couple of months. It's very—ahh!—inconvenient."

I keep my eyes up, front and center, careful not to let myself get sidetracked. "And you want the Widowers to lean on a couple of people? Get the DEA to turn their attention elsewhere?"

She shivers again. Rico's hand is quickening under her dress, working faster. He grins at me, though with his lower lip fastened between his teeth, the action looks more like a grimace. Maria Rosa groans, rocking her hips upward. Carnie curls his hands into fists, looking at me out of the corner of his eye. *"Jesus fucking Christ,"* he hisses.

I ignore him. "So you want us to lean on someone for you?"

"I don't...I don't want you to lean on anyone," Maria Rosa gasps. "I want you to bring me the agent's fucking head in a...fucking bag."

So it's murder, then. There's no love lost between the Widowers and the DEA, that's for sure, but murder? That will draw all the wrong kinds of attention.

"Well?" Maria Rosa demands.

"I'll need to assess the situation first," I tell her.

"Ha!" She grinds her hips up into Rico's hands, her eyes closing completely now. "You're such a fucking pussy, Rebel. Don't go shy on me now."

The irony of that statement isn't lost on me. I'm hardly shy. I'm sitting here, conducting a conversation with her about murdering a member of a federal agency while she gets finger fucked by her bodyguard. "I'll give you one day to think on it," she says. "And if your answer's no then you can either...agree to ship,"—she's growing breathless now—"my fucking drugs, or you can handle your problems on your own. Okay?"

"Okay."

"In the meantime, there's one more...thing that I want from you."

"Which is?"

She opens her eyes, lazily glancing from me to Carnie. "Him. I want him to come assist Rico over here."

Carnie's cheeks flush. Of all the Widow Makers, he's the most highly sexed, most fucking reckless when it comes to women. He has a different woman stumbling out of his room every single goddamn morning, and yet right now it looks like Maria Rosa has caught him off guard. "You want me to...you want me to fuck you?" he asks.

"I want you to stick you dick inside my mouth while Rico fucks me," she informs him. *"Now."*

Carnie looks to me, as though I'll be able to clarify whether this is some kind of trick or not. I simply shrug. "Better give the woman what she wants." I hold back from pointing out there's a strong chance she'll bite his cock off. Carnie's a reasonably intelligent guy. He should be able to figure out the odds of something really fucking bad happening all by himself. He shrugs back at me, breaking into grin. "This is one royally fucked-up situation," he says under his breath, but that doesn't stop him from getting to his feet.

The next fifteen minutes are interesting, to say the least. Carnie pulls his dick out—already hard, no surprises there—and Maria Rosa bends over, hitching up her tight red dress. Rico slides himself inside her, pulling the top of her dress down so he can palm her tits. She's practically naked, her long, toned body on show apart from the small section of her stomach that's obscured by her bunched-up dress. Just like she said she would, she blows Carnie while she lets Rico screw her.

Most people would find this situation very graphic. Confronting even. But I know this woman. Her head is perhaps the most twisted place on the face of the entire planet. Because while she's bent over, letting two people penetrate her body, letting them screw her, she's screwing with *me.* She didn't ask to suck *my* dick. She wants me to watch. The whole time she's getting reamed she's staring at me— she doesn't look away once.

So I just sit there and watch. This is my life.

Fucked-up shit like this happens to me all the time.

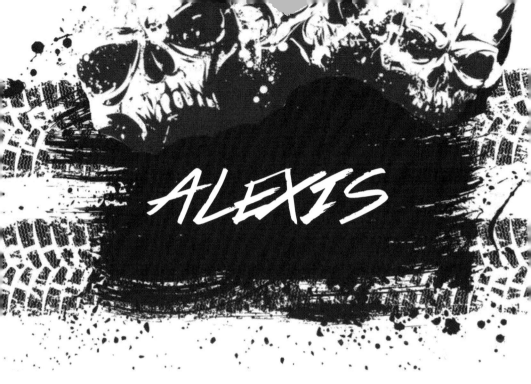

ALEXIS

I end up sleeping most of the day. Maybe it's because I feel kind of safe with Cade, but I let my guard down. I can't help it. It's been so long since I've rested. Even when I have dozed, it hasn't been proper sleep. It's been like dipping my big toe into a vast and deep lake, too afraid to submerge myself for fear of drowning. Or in my case, being raped. So I pass out in the car and I sleep the sleep of the dead, barely waking properly to eat or stumble zombie-like to the bathroom when we stop.

All thoughts of escape fly out of the window.

Through the mugginess clouding my head, I glimpse at the clock on the dash at some point in the afternoon to find that it's coming up on four p.m. I think that's when I realize something's not quite right. Or it might be later, when I wake to darkness out of the passenger window, and country music playing low on the radio.

I manage four words before I slip into unconsciousness again. "Drugged me, you fucker." The words bleed into one another, barely audible.

I hear Cade laughing just fine, though. "Sorry, sweetheart. Easier this way all round, I'm afraid."

I come to briefly when I'm being carried somewhere, carried in the dark. The sound of a motorcycle roaring to life, and voices, talking voices filter in and out as I sway with the motion of someone's gait. And then nothing.

My head feels like it's splitting apart when I wake next. Morning. It must be morning. Bright light blares through a set of thin voile curtains above...above the bed I'm sprawled out across. "What the...?" I'm not wearing the hideous, torn dress anymore. I'm wearing an oversized black T-shirt that says *It Isn't Going To Suck Itself* with an arrow pointing downward. Clearly not something meant to be worn by a woman. So clichéd.

I'm already buzzing with anger as I throw my legs over the side of the bed. That anger swiftly makes way for panic as I realize I'm going to throw up. "Oh, no. Oh, no. *No, no, no, no.*" I get to my feet, the room pitching violently like a ship on rough seas. I don't know where the hell I am. I don't know where the damn bathroom is. I don't have time to look for it, either. I scramble frantically, searching until I find something appropriate, and then I collapse onto my knees, puking up my guts.

The moment is brief but unpleasant. My body is trembling by the time I'm done. I look down at what I'm clutching in my hands, and my stomach drops all over again. A motorcycle helmet. I just threw up in a full-face motorcycle helmet. Great. Why the hell couldn't it have been a trashcan?

I get up, holding the damn thing in both hands, cringing when I pluck up the courage to check out how bad it is. Because it's bad. *Really* bad. The drugged food that Cade plied me with yesterday has mostly been digested, but what remained in my stomach is now seeping into the foam cushioning of what looks like a really expensive piece of equipment.

"*Fuck.*" I look around, properly taking in my surroundings for the first time. The place isn't that big: a timber-built cabin made up of two rooms, the first and largest being a bedroom/living area. The second is a modern bathroom, complete with wet area and an overhead shower, tiled in slate. Very manly. I dump the helmet into the sink and turn on the tap, wincing as the water starts to fill inside it. Back in the main area, I try to figure out where the hell I am.

The huge bed I just slept in resides in the corner. A considerably large leather sofa, soft and cracked with age, divides the space into two. On the far side of the room, a monstrous flat screen television has been bolted to the wall. Bookcases, shelves, a desk with a stool shoved underneath it—the place is full of books and pictures and stacks of magazines. Odd bits and pieces dot the cabin. A snow globe—*Welcome to Chicago!*—sits next to a jumbled sheaf of papers, the skyline of the city in miniature inside, the roofs of the buildings already painted white. A photograph of a slim, beautiful woman with crystal clear blue eyes and a mass of almost-black hair butts up against a coffee maker on the narrow desk underneath the window. The woman in the picture is smiling, flashing teeth as she looks over her shoulder at whoever was taking the image. You can tell she's laughing from the way her mouth is slightly open, her head tilted back. She looks familiar, for some reason. I touch my fingers lightly to the glass of the frame, feeling a bizarre sense of déjà vu.

When I look out of the window, there's nothing but scrubby plant life, orange dirt and shale-like rocks for as far as the eye can see. In the distance, the ridgeline of a mountain range spears up out of the flat plains, made hazy and blue by the miles between us. The landscape is like nothing I've seen before in the flesh—not a place I've ever visited before. Not that I can remember. I'm about to try the handle on the door to the left of the window, ready to see if I am well and truly trapped here or not, when I hear the sound of splashing water.

"*Shit!*" I rush back to the bathroom; the helmet's rolled onto its side and the flow of the tap is splashing off its surface, going everywhere. All over the mirror above the sink, all over the tiled floor. I turn off the tap and grab a towel from one of the racks by the toilet, throwing it on the ground and mopping madly with my foot. I've always been a little accident prone, but this is ridiculous. I'm trashing the place. Not that I should care—I've been bundled up and stolen, drugged and taken here against my will—but I'm not an idiot. I don't want to make the situation worse for myself by breaking or throwing up on everything I touch.

"Hello?"

I stop scrubbing at the floor with my foot, every part of me going still.

"Hello? I brought you some breakfast." My heart's hammering in my chest. Someone's in the other room. I hear the door close, and then heavy boots scuffing on the wooden floorboards. I peek cautiously around the bathroom door, hoping to see who it is without being seen myself. No such luck, though. Cade's staring straight at me, a plate stacked high with pancakes in his right hand. He has some sort of dust in his hair. He doesn't bother with pleasantries. "Rebel's going to be back in an hour or so. Thought you might like to get some breakfast into you and some clothes on before he steamrolls in here, wanting to talk to you."

I slide my body through the barely open bathroom doorway and pull it closed behind me. "This is his place?" I ask.

Cade nods, setting the plate of food down on the narrow desk next to the coffee machine. "Yeah. Built it himself. He's not like the other guys. He prefers the peace and quiet."

"What other guys?" I need to figure out what my situation is right now. How many people are here, wherever we are? Who are they? How far to the next town? What are my chances of breaking out of this cabin and making it to civilization on foot? Cade just smiles at me, wiping his hands down the front of his already grease-stained jeans. He's a good looking guy—dark brown hair, cropped close, warm brown eyes, always with a half-entertained look on his face—but I don't see any of that. I just see a brick wall of stacked muscle standing between me and my freedom.

"No one you need worry yourself about, sweetheart," he says. "You won't be bothered over here."

"When can I go home?" I've somehow managed to keep my cool

since waking up, but it feels like the walls are closing in now. I *have* to get out of here. I *have* to get back to Seattle.

"I told you, as soon as you've done what Rebel needs you to do, you'll be able to go."

"And when will that be? How long with that take? Hours? Days? Weeks?" My chest feels tight, gripped by the concept that I might be trapped here for so long. And even then, Cade could be lying. They could have no intention of letting me go, ever.

Cade purses his lips, shoving his right hand into his pocket. "Look. Wait for Rebel to get back. He'll answer all your questions."

"He said I should direct all my questions to you in his absence."

Cade laughs, glancing back out of the door. "Yeah, that sounds about right." Turning back to look at me, he smiles. "You know why he said that?"

"No."

"Because it entertains him to screw with people every once in a while. I don't have any answers. Only he knows when all this will be over. For you. For me. For him."

"Sounds like a great guy." I lean back against the bathroom door, my head thumping dully against the wood. I want to cry. I really want to breakdown and sob my heart out, but I'm proud. Before I ran into Raphael in the street, it had been years and years since I'd allowed myself to look weak like that. I cried in front of Ramona, too. I do *not* want to cry in front of Cade.

"He may be a total asshole sometimes and he does like to fuck with people, but he's not who you think he is, sweetheart. You'll realize that soon enough. Now, you gonna tell me your name or what?"

"No." I won't do it. Giving them a name to call me by, any name, real or false, seems like I'm giving them power over me.

Cade blows out a deep breath, giving me a look my father used to give me when I was being stubborn as a kid. "Have it your way, then. I'll make sure I come back when Rebel gets here."

I just stare at the ground, feeling hollow inside. I don't know if I want Cade to come back or not. He hasn't exactly been helpful. Not really. The advice he gave me back in that alleyway in Seattle did save me from Raphael's unwelcome attentions, but they also landed me in the situation I find myself in now. Only time will tell if this is better or worse.

I don't look up as Cade leaves. I slowly slide down the bathroom door, covering my face with my hands, and I dare myself not to cry. I manage it, even as I hear the door to the cabin lock behind him.

A bizarre sensation washes over me—a true *how is this real?* moment. I want Matt. I want to curl up in his arms and feel like everything is okay again. I look around this unfamiliar room, nothing making sense, and I'm sure I must be imagining it all. Things like this don't happen. This is the stuff of nightmares and movies, and horror stories young women are told by their elders to keep them safe. It was sure as hell never supposed to happen to me.

REBEL

five years ago

"**A**re you fucking crazy? Get that thing outta here,**"** Cade hollers. The boys have found a vat of oil from somewhere, and the lid is off. I spin on them, not sure I can trust what I'm seeing with my own two eyes. We're smack bang in the middle of fucking Kabul, perched on the roof of a barely standing building, and my men are screwing around with flammable liquids.

"What the hell do you think you're doing with that, assholes?"

Thompson stops laughing, the smile freezing on his face when he sees the look on mine. Both he and Ramon quit attempting to drag the huge, rusted barrel toward the edge of the roof; they stand up straight, Ramon wiping the sweat out of his eyes.

"Well. We was thinking that, instead of wasting ammo on these fuckheads, we could get medieval on their asses. They used to do this in England, y'know? Back when people holed up in castles and shit. They'd pour fuel over the sides of the castles and set it on fire. Very effective."

"Is that so?"

"Yes, Staff Sergeant."

"So you're telling me you want to wait for the enemy to pass by underneath us? And then you want to take this barrel here," I kick the barrel, "and you want to pour it contents over the side on top of the enemy. And you want it to be on fire at the time?"

Ramon and Thompson look at each other warily, obviously unsure what the correct answer is. "Yeeees?" Thompson says.

"And you don't think that's slightly fucked up. That you want to burn people alive, Thompson?"

"It's no worse than they'd do to us, Duke."

"But that's the whole fucking point, isn't it? That's the whole reason why we're here. These people do shit we would never do. Because we're marines, not fucking medieval English castle owners, you fucking moron."

The rest of the squad—Baggs, Paulie, Saunders and Cade—all burst into laughter. I throw my arms over Thompson and Ramon's shoulders, pulling them in close. "Get rid of that fucking thing now, before we set *you* on fire and throw *you* over the side of the roof, huh?" I'm grinning as I say this, but I know how dangerous this place is. I know all too well what it can do to a man's morals. What it could do to *my* morals if I'm not careful.

When I turn around, Cade is watching me with a small smile on his face. He nods at me, scrubbing his hand across his jaw. I'm seriously fucking lucky to have my best friend at my back through this, just as he's been at my back through everything else.

If he weren't here, reminding me of who I am, who I *want* to be, then god knows. Maybe I'd have been throwing that barrel over the edge of the roof after all.

Maybe I'd have been lighting the match.

REBEL

now

My body has that delicious burning ache to it as I climb off my motorcycle. It's taken me far too fucking long to ride from Vegas to New Mexico, but I wasn't exactly rushing. I had a lot to think about. I have approximately ten hours until I need to give Maria Rosa her answer. Either yes, I will kill this DEA agent who has pissed her off so much, or alternatively me and my boys are gonna become her runners, operating on her behalf for, well, forever. When you start working for Maria Rosa, there's only one way you ever end up stopping. And I don't particularly want to die just yet. I have a number of things I plan on doing yet, and I'll be fucked if I let her mess that up for me.

There is one other option: go this thing alone. But Hector's amassed an army over the past few years, ramping up his personal protection. Increasing the volume of his business, which means more hired guns. More people on his payroll. Ergo, less chance of us sweeping in and smashing his operation to bits. Three or four years ago, maybe, but not now. Now, we have to approach things differently. We need backup, and Maria Rosa is the most sensible option. She has as much to gain from Hector Ramirez's downfall as the Widow Makers do.

"You still need me, Prez?" Carnie's still got a shit-eating grin on his face, twelve hours after the end of our meeting with Maria Rosa. The guy has no shame. Usually the dynamic between two guys shifts a little after one of them watches the other get his cock sucked, but things are exactly the same with Carnie. He's a total extrovert. And that wasn't the first time I've seen his dick, either. The guy barely wears any clothes at the best of times.

"No, man, we're good," I tell him. He jogs off across the compound, laughing to himself, shaking his head—my money's on him heading straight to Fee to tell her what happened. She's gonna punch him in his stupid, grinning face.

I think about heading over to the clubhouse, the low-lying, squat building at the far end of the compound, to see if there's anything left over from last meal, but that would mean facing everyone. Dealing with the chatter and having at least three shots of Jack poured down my throat. I don't feel like that right now. I feel like taking a moment. Clearing my head. Breathing, just for a second.

I head in the opposite direction, instead, toward my place. The cabin's outside of the compound proper, over the small ridge that curves naturally around the Widow Makers' HQ. That ridge was part of the reason why I set up out here in the first place. A good natural defense in case anyone tries to fuck with us.

It's winter but I'm still sweating by the time I summit the top of the ridge. The sun's setting to my right, casting angry, long red shadows across the plane in front of me. It's gonna be cold, tonight.

Behind me, the four buildings that make up the compound—the clubhouse, the workshop, the storehouse and the barn—are all lit up. I can hear Carnie somewhere down there, shouting something loud and obnoxious. Laughter follows. Cheering and shouting. I smile to myself as I make my way down the other side of the slope toward the cabin. It doesn't register as odd that the lights are on inside my place. It doesn't seem strange that the door is locked and I have to use my key to get in. The first thing I do when I see the girl sitting on my couch, watching my television, is pull my gun. Force of habit. She scrambles away from me, backing into the corner of the couch. Her eyes are so big I can practically see myself reflected in her irises. She looks terrified.

I catch myself, then—a gun shoved in her face is the last thing this girl needs. But she shouldn't be here. I tell her as much. "You shouldn't be in here. Who put you in here?" Carnie joked about this on the way to Vegas—her needing to bunk in with me. I never gave it serious thought, though. This is *so* not happening. I lower my gun, tucking it back into my waistband. The girl visibly sags, though it's obvious she's still afraid.

"Cade. Cade put me in here when I was passed out," she says. "After he *drugged* me, that is." It doesn't sound like she's too impressed about that. I know people who'd pay good money for the high she received, but it looks like she's not one of them.

"Yeah, sorry about that. We've found in the past that being a little sleepy often keeps the people we're transporting calm. And calm is something we value around these parts."

"How old are you?" she asks. The question catches me off guard.

"Why do you ask?"

She shrugs. "I don't know."

"When you've figured out why you wanna know, tell me and I'll decide whether your reasoning's valid enough for me to share that information with you. In the meantime, I need to talk to my V.P." I kick the door closed behind me, scowling as I bring up Cade's number on my cell. He answers quickly, on the second ring.

"Hey, man, what's up. Are you almost back?"

"I'm already back. And I'm standing in my cabin. Is there something you want to tell me?"

"Ahhh shit. I thought for sure I'd be back before you. Don't blow a gasket, all right? There was nowhere else to put her."

"What about the barn? That's where we usually keep people, isn't it?"

"Yeah, when we plan on keeping them cuffed to the water tank and beating the shit out of them twenty-four-seven. You really think this situation warrants that?" When he puts it like that, I suppose he's right. That does seem a little excessive.

"What about the room at the far end of the clubhouse? The one I used to use?"

Cade huffs—I think I'm pissing him off. Well, tough shit. He knows this place is strictly off limits. "You said you didn't want anyone to know she was here, dude. If I'd dragged her through the clubhouse and up the stairs, someone would have spotted her. And they sure as hell would have wanted to know who she was and why we won't let her out of the room."

He kind of has a point there. "And so this was it? This was the only solution you could think of?" I pinch the bridge of my nose between my index finger and my thumb, feeling a headache coming on.

"She could hardly bunk above the shop with me, man. People are in an out of my place all day long. She'd have been seen in five seconds flat. If you can think of another option, I'll head back to the compound right now and move her myself."

I scowl at the floorboards, the floorboards I laid myself, hammering each and every nail by hand, hating that he's fucking right. "All right. All right. I guess you did the right thing." I exhale, my head working overtime. "Wait, if you're not at the compound, where are you?"

"At the shop. I needed to pick up the gear for tonight. We had late appointments, too, and Chloe couldn't work. I'm finishing off a back piece. Won't take me more than an hour, though." The shop, the Dead Man's Ink Bar, the Bar for short, isn't located within the compound. A twenty-minute ride down a dirt track brings you to Freemantle, the closest town to our location, though to call it a town is a stretch. There are five or six streets with actual stores on them, and then perhaps three or four as many residential streets, and that's it. There was public outcry when the Widowers bought up High Street real estate and unveiled a full-blown, state-of-the-art tattoo parlor. The townsfolk probably wanted another florist or something. Instead they got burly bikers with a penchant for ink and very loud motorcycles. They complained at first, but that soon stopped when they realized the Bar was actually bringing a lot of out-of-towners into Freemantle. People from the surrounding small towns, who otherwise would have no reason to even pass through. More people means more money for the other local stores and diners; the folk who come to get inked at the Bar have to eat, after all. They buy groceries. They replace their old work wear at the army disposal store. Ironically, the business front we use to launder our ill-gotten gains has been really good for the local community.

"Okay, well just get your ass back here as soon as you can. I need to tell you about what happened at the MGM Grand." I don't mention names. The girl sitting on my couch is staring quietly at a seam in the leather armrest, pretending not to be listening, but of course she is. She'd be fucking mad not to.

"Got it." Cade hangs up and I walk around my couch, staring at the girl. This is weird. If I fuck a girl, I do it at the clubhouse. I've never had anyone in here before. I'm not sure I like how normal it feels. It should feel like the place is on fucking fire and I have to get the hell out of dodge.

I sit down on top of my coffee table, still staring at her.

She blinks at me, digging her fingernails into the skin on her right leg. "What?"

"It's time for you to tell me your name." She arches an eyebrow at me. I can just imagine her getting them waxed in some fancy fucking boutique beauty parlor in Seattle, run by Asian hipsters with shaved undercuts and thick glasses. She seems like the type. "Why do you want to know?" she asks, cockiness filling her voice—she's asked me something personal and that's what I said to her. Now she's throwing it back at me. It's fucking adorable.

"I'm asking because I need something to call you. And if you don't tell me your name, I'm going to be forced to call you One Eighty-One. And I'm guessing you won't like being called one eighty-one."

"Why would you call me that?"

"Because that's the reference Hector Ramirez gave you when he uploaded your picture onto his skin site. Hector tags his girls chronologically. The first girl he sold was number one. The fifty-third girl he sold was tagged fifty-three. Using that logic, guess how many girls he sold before he tagged you one eighty-one?"

"So one hundred and eighty other women came before me?" She looks like she's going to throw up.

"Exactly. And he hasn't been caught. The police haven't raided his place out there in the desert. No one has reported his website. No one came to rescue the one hundred and eighty other girls who came before you, and no one is coming for you, either. So if you want reminding of that every single time I call you one eight—"

"Sophia!" She screws her eyes shut, clenching her jaw. "My name is fucking Sophia, motherfucker." She spits out the words like they're poison. When she looks at me again, I can see the fury burning in the depths of her dark brown eyes. She comes alive when she's angry. A thrill of adrenalin stabs through me, sending mixed signals to my cock; provoking such a violent reaction from her is provoking an entirely different reaction from me. For the first time, I see her. *Fucking Sophia.* I don't see her as a means to an end—a potential way to take down the bastard who killed my uncle. I see *her*. I see her as a woman, and she is beautiful.

"All right, Sophia. It's a pleasure to meet you."

"I wish I could say the same." She's flushed, her irritation making itself known on her cheeks as well as in her eyes. Her body language is speaking volumes, too. She's locked up tight, shoulders angled away from me. Her hands are balled together now, interlocking fingers white at each joint, showing how hard she's squeezing.

My father was a fucking asshole—hated me from the moment I was born. He judged me as he saw fit, and I've made sure to prove him wrong at every available fucking turn. But he was right about one thing. He always said I had a stone-cold, manipulative side to me when I wanted to. And I do. That part of me, usually kept under lock and key for civility's sake, pipes up, now, as I look at her. How hard would it be to make her change her mind about me? How hard would it be to alter that body language? It would be a mildly interesting game to play.

Her head snaps up—she stares at me as though she can hear my thoughts and she's daring me to even try it. I can't help the smile that spreads across my face, slow as sin. "Cade says you need me to do something for you," she snaps. "He says you're gonna let me go if I do it."

"And do you believe him?"

She fixes her gaze on mine, staring me right in the eye. There are few people who have the balls to do that. My coloring's always been a little confronting to some people. Unsettling, even. My eyes are a piercing ice blue. They're not the kind of eyes you'd forget in a hurry. It's not vain of me to admit that. I just know how other people work, how they think, and I also know how I affect them. Sophia doesn't look away. She's nowhere near as fragile as I assumed she would be. My interest is now well and truly piqued. "I don't know. I believe Cade believes you'll let me go. But you? I haven't worked *you* out yet."

I almost burst into laughter. *Well, isn't this interesting? I was just thinking the* exact *same thing about you.* "Oh, I'm not a complicated man, Sophia. I do the things I say I'm going to do. I keep the promises I make. If I say something, you can take it to the bank." But I'm lying to her. I *am* a complicated man. I make it my business to be as fucking complicated as I possibly can. If I were simple, I would be easy to pre-empt, and that's not how you survive in the world that I live in. I can't tell from looking at her whether Sophia believes me, but I'm enjoying the way she's sliding her legs up and down against the other. In this case I'm sure it's signifying discomfort, but it can mean other things, too. Sexual excitement for one. I suddenly realize that I want that—to sexually excite her.

"So what do you want me to do?" she asks. The question could not have come at a more appropriate time. A number of things are flooding through my head as I answer her. I manage to keep them to myself, though.

"I need you to testify what you witnessed in that alleyway in Seattle for me, Sophia. I need you to take the stand in a courtroom and tell a judge and jury how you saw a man murdered in cold blood."

Her face goes pale, the angry flush that was still present a moment ago vanishing entirely. "You want me to go up against those men that took me? You want me to go testify against *Raphael*?"

"I do."

She shakes her head, each shake becoming more and more violent. "No. No, I can't do that."

I didn't think she was going to be happy about it, but in the same vein I didn't think she was going to be this aggressively against the idea. Hector's men did kidnap her, after all. "The guy they murdered was a judge. He was a good man. And you won't do this, because?"

She takes a stuttering breath, pushing back into the chair, as though the more space she puts between me and her distances herself from the very *idea* of testifying. "Because I can't. I...I have a family to protect. Raphael threatened them. He said he was going to kill them all. I can't allow that to happen. I'm sorry for the guy that died, but that's it. He's already dead, now. Taking the stand won't help him any. If I do what you're asking of me, they'll find my family. They'll kill my parents. They'll kill my sister, too, but they'll *rape* her first." She shakes her head again, fear written all over her face. "I'm sorry. I *can't*. I won't do it."

REBEL

"Well it's obvious. You can't do either."
I drop my head into my hands, groaning. There was no persuading Sophia that she needs to speak out against Los Oscuros. She wouldn't even listen. She locked herself in the bathroom, and I took the opportunity to leave the cabin, locking the door behind me, too pissed off to try any further. The clubhouse is packed full of Widowers, just like it is every night, but tonight's different. Tonight they know not to approach the quiet table in the corner of the bar that Cade and I occupy when shit is hitting the fan. If they could see the black bag sitting on the bench in between my second and me they might have tried, though.

"You can't involve yourself with the DEA, man. And there's no way the club will pass running Maria Rosa's blow and dope all over the country for her. She tried to strong arm us into that the last time we got caught up in her shit, remember?"

"I do remember. But it was almost worth the risk back then. We had no other leverage. I thought this time she'd agree just for the sake of fucking with Hector."

Cade stares grimly down into the bottom of his rocks glass. I know he's not seeing the burned amber of the whiskey in the bottom, though. He's thinking about Laura. Laura, my best friend. Laura, Cade's sister. Laura, who went missing from my father's estate years ago, never to be seen again. That's what started this whole fucking thing—the MC, the gun running, the small time weed operation the Widowers sometimes dabble in.

I couldn't accept Laura was gone. I left home, set up out here, started up the club. Cade came out later. We decided we would try and find her. Made enough mob contacts that we could submerse ourselves into the seedy underworld of skin trading without being suspected as cops. There were rumors about American girls being sold down in Central America. Mexico. Colombia. We tried Mexico first. A skeevy motherfucker in a bar, selling his own sister out of the back of his van, told us he'd seen Laura, yes, but she wasn't in the country anymore. She'd been purchased by the Desolladors and they'd taken her back to Colombia.

So naturally, that was our next stop. I rolled up on Rico and cut his face open. Cade and I were detained by a very intrigued Maria Rosa for nearly two weeks, during which time she managed to show us that she didn't have anything to do with Laura's disappearance, and also convince herself that she was in love with Cade.

When she said we were free to leave, Cade declined Maria Rosa's invitation to stay behind and be her sex toy, which did not go down well.

Our exodus from Colombia was a rushed one, complete with threats on our lives and absolutely no sign of Laura.

She was in the wind. There were no more leads regarding her whereabouts, no matter which country we asked in or who we asked. Just like that, Laura was gone.

Now, neither of us like talking about her much.

I grind my teeth together, growing more and more restless by the moment. "So what, then? We go after Ramirez on our own?"

"Yeah, sure. If you want to commit suicide and get the rest of us killed, why not? How many Widow Makers are there? Twenty-one?

Hectors got forty people around him at all times. And then there are the hundreds of people he has working on the streets. We go against him without support and we're all dead."

"Then we do nothing. We forget all about him killing Ryan. I let him get away with it?"

Cade slugs back his whiskey and slams his glass down on the table. "Plan B, man. Use the girl. Get her to stand up."

I take my own drink in my hands, rolling the glass between my palms. Sometimes alcohol makes me think clearly, can give me a better perspective when I'm trying to solve a problem. Not right now, though. It's making my head muzzy. "Not an option. Dela Vega told Sophia he's going after her family. He told her he was gonna rape her fucking sister. She says there's no way for him to find them if she doesn't testify."

"That doesn't make any sense."

"It does if she's lying about her name, and she'd be stupid not to. I'm sure Raphael doesn't know her real name, either."

"Is Danny working on finding out who she really is, then?"

I nod, catching sight of our hacker in the corner, laughing with some brunette I've seen him with a couple of times before. He's the best. If anyone's going to figure out who this woman is, it's Danny.

"Okay, well in the meantime you just need to tell her we'll put a detail on her family," Cade says. "Promise her that we won't let anything happen to them."

I grunt, drinking my whiskey after all. I fucking need it. I doubt my brain cells are gonna come up with anything useful tonight. Might as well kill a few of them off. "She's stubborn, man," I say. "Really fucking stubborn. How do you propose I convince her without threatening physical violence?"

Cade slaps me hard on the arm. When I look up at him, there's a broad grin spreading across his face. "You're a fool, you know that? I'm pretty sure you could convince any woman in the world to do *whatever* you wanted. You have a seriously annoying talent for that."

I glare at him, tapping my finger against the rim of my glass. "What the hell does that mean?"

Cade sighs, leaning closer across the table. "I can't believe after all these years you're gonna make me say it. Women find you attractive, asshole. You're a handsome son of a bitch." He's about to finish off his whiskey when he pauses, the glass halfway to his mouth, and says, "Not that *I* think you're attractive, though. *I* think you're fucking hideous."

"Right back at ya, fucker." We raise our glasses, draining what was left in them, and then we sit in silence, listening to the chatter of the club members around us. Carnie's still trying to crack onto Shay. Pathetic. I lean back in my chair, scrubbing my hands over my face. "So you're saying I should flirt with her to get her to do what I want? Am I understanding you right here?"

Cade nods gravely. "A means to an end, my friend. And, come on, she's hardly ugly. I have faith in your ability to mac on some beautiful woman in order to get what you want. You've done it a million times before. I've witnessed it myself."

"Fuck you."

"You deny it?"

I can't really do that. He's right. I have used the way I look in the past to get a girl into bed, and I'm not sorry for it. But this is different. This is Sophia's *life*, the lives of her family. Can I be a total douche bag and potentially put her whole family in danger to get justice for Ryan?

I pose myself the question because it's the right thing to do. But I've already let that devious, calculating part of me out of its cage today; turns out I haven't managed to cram him back into his box. I *can* do it. And using Sophia is a hell of a lot better for a hell of a lot more people than any of the other options open to me. So be it. I'll win her over and convince her she needs to help us, and I'll do it fast. That way I can honor what I've said to her and get her home quickly. *Et voila.* Everybody's fucking happy. Cade refills his glass and holds out the bottle of Laphroaig to me, offering me more. I hold up my glass, resigning myself to my fate. Tomorrow, *Operation: Woo Sophia* will be in full effect. Cade was right—she's all kinds of hot—so it won't exactly be taxing on my part. Might not be as easy as Cade thinks it will be, though. There's only one reason Ramirez would have sold her at such a high price, and that's because she must be a virgin. Virgins aren't exactly the types to jump into bed with a guy just because he pays them a bit of attention. I push that thought from my mind, not wanting to think about claiming this girl's virginity. A hard-on would be seriously fucking inappropriate, as well as the last thing I need to deal with in the clubhouse. "So tell me, Cade. Which part of me do you think's my best feature?" I try not to laugh.

"You're a fucking asshole," he says, shaking his head. "And it's getting late. Shall we get things rolling then?" I place my hand on top of the black bag sitting in between Cade and me. My best friend smirks, tipping his glass in my direction.

"I'll leave this one up to you," he says.

"Why, thank you." I may sound sarcastic, but it's been a while since I've had the pleasure of making a call like this. The Widowers need this, and so do I. The bar's full, club members drinking at tables and leaning against walls. There are over twenty members to the club, and they're permitted to bring people into the bar once they've been vetted by Danny to make sure they're not cops. The place can get pretty rowdy. The arrangement isn't perfect. Fights break out. Members, both male and female, end up sleeping with the wrong person. Shit gets broken. But for the most part we make it work.

I draw some curious looks from the guys closest to me when I get up, Cade's bag of tricks in my hand. Fatty, the Widowers' resident bartender and sometimes chef sees me approaching the bar, sees what I have in my hand, and has an unopened bottle of Texas Trader's Bourbon out on the counter before I can even ask for it. Trader's is the cheapest, nastiest, shittiest bourbon ever made. I can still remember the bottle I had to finish when I first started this thing. My gut twists, also remembering the vast majority of that cheap, nasty, shitty bourbon coming back up again. Violently.

"I thought this might be coming soon," Fatty says, breaking into a grin. "You sure he's ready?"

I knock my fist against the counter, grinning back at him. "Fuck yeah. If the guy can make it through an encounter with Maria Rosa unscathed, he's earned his ink."

Fatty laughs, reaching for a pack of smokes and lighting one. "He's gonna be unbearable after this."

"Oh, I know. If his head gets too big, you can just kick his ass. Cool?"

"Cool."

I turn around, finding that the oldest Widow Makers—Keeler, Brassic, Danny, Foxer and Josephine—have already stood up and are waiting with knowing smiles on their faces. Foxer, the guy responsible for managing the grow we have underway beneath the worn floorboards of the barn, is also in charge of new recruits. I've already spoken to him about what's about to take place and he's green lit the guy. He gives me a sharp nod when our eyes make contact, reaffirming his approval. I may be the head honcho around here, but I don't have time to personally assess every new recruit we get. I value Foxer's opinion as much as I do Cade's, though. He knows what it takes to be a Widower. If he'd said *not now, not ready,* this wouldn't be happening.

"Carnie, you ugly motherfucker!" I shout over the top of the chatter in the bar. Carnie, sitting across the other side of the room, immediately looks up, surprise on his face. He pushes his glasses up onto his head and stands. Everyone else is silent. "What's up, Boss?" he asks.

I collect the bottle of Trader's off the counter and I crack it open in front of him. I wince as I take the tiniest of sips. Everyone in the clubhouse roars, the sounds of their hollering and cheering set to raise the rafters on the place. Carnie, god bless him, looks around, completely confused. I hand off the bottle to Cade, who also takes a really fucking small sip.

"It's time," I tell him. "You're in."

More shouting and hollering breaks out, coupled with the thunder of people drumming their hands and feet against the tables, the floor, the bar. Carnie lifts both eyebrows, smiling cautiously. "For real? You're serious?"

Cade holds up the bottle of bourbon, toasting it at Carnie. "We don't break out this stuff unless we're for real, man."

Nearly everyone in the clubhouse aside from Carnie knows the pain that bottle is going to bring him. There are countless groans as Cade holds it out for Keeler to take. I don't even need to watch to know he won't be taking a big mouthful; every single member of the Widowers will drink out of that bottle before it gets passed to Carnie, and no one will want more than a taste of the vile liquid on their tongues.

"What is that?" Carnie asks.

"That, my friend, is a rite of passage. Once everyone's taken a sip, the rest is for you. And you gotta finish every last drop before I'll ink you." I unzip the black bag in my hand and bring out the ink gun that Cade brought home with him from the Dead Man's ink Bar. It's been about two years since I've tattooed anyone, but that doesn't matter. This particular tattoo is something I can draw without a stencil. I could probably do it with my eyes closed if I wanted to. Carnie whoops, ripping his *Widow Makers MC Prospect* T-shirt over his head.

"Bring it on!"

The bar fills with more laughter and shouting as the other club members all gather around Carnie to slap him on the back and welcome him into the fold. Cade leans against the bar beside me, laughing an evil laugh. "Poor bastard's not gonna be so happy in about an hour," he says.

And he's right. Barely an eighth of the Trader's is gone when it's handed to Carnie. The guy finally understands what he's let himself in for when he takes his first big slug from the bottle. His eyes water, his face reddening to a dark crimson. "Holy fuck! This stuff's worse than lighter fluid."

By halfway down the bottle, he's looking more than a little worse for wear. By the time he's draining the last few drops of bourbon into his mouth, he's already thrown up twice in the spillage bucket Fatty keeps behind the bar.

When I'm presented with a semi unconscious Carnie, carried between Keeler and Brassic and dumped unceremoniously onto the long wooden table that runs down the center of the room, I'm a little buzzed myself. They lay Carnie out on his front, his back bare and just begging for some fresh ink.

The Widowers surrounding me, each and every one of them wearing their cuts with pride, all stand around and watch as I fire up the tattoo gun and begin my work. Carnie sleeps like a baby through the entire fucking thing. Probably for the best. Three and a half hours later, I'm well and truly fucked on *good* whiskey and Carnie has a perfectly straight, perfectly perfect *Widow Makers New Mexico* patch inked into his skin.

"It's a fucking masterpiece," Keeler laughs, slapping me on the back. "You're the only motherfucker I know who can tattoo someone when they're falling off their fucking chair, Boss."

"Fuck you, Keeler," I laugh. "All right. Someone get this sorry bastard out of here. Shay, maybe you can make sure he's taken care of when he wakes up, huh?"

Shay, the girl Carnie's been trying to impress since the day we brought him back here as a prospect, shoots daggers at me. "I'm not his goddamn old lady, Rebel. I thought the Widowers didn't *do* old ladies?"

Her tone is shitty to say the least. I lift an eyebrow at her, too drunk to be fucked with warning her to watch her mouth, but sober enough to tell her what I think of her attitude with one look. "I didn't ask you to wipe his ass for him. I asked you to look out for him. We clear?"

She looks away, pouting, staring at the floor. "Sure. Of course."

"Good."

Cade's at my side, then, throwing his arm over my shoulder. "Time we shut this mother down," he sighs.

"Yeah."

"You gonna be hung over in the morning?"

I punch him lightly in his ribs. "When have I ever been hung over?" It's true. I can drink until I pass out—not that I do that very often—and still be fighting fit when I wake up. It's a god given talent.

"Whatever, man. You need to get your ass to bed. Don't forget. You have a girl to charm tomorrow."

I grunt, trying to tell myself that I almost forgot about the beautiful woman I have locked in my cabin over the ridge. That's pretty fucking laughable, though. Throughout getting Carnie so fucked his eyes began to work independently, and through every minute I was pouring liquor down my throat, marking someone's skin for life, marking him as one of my own, I hadn't forgotten about her.

She was *all* I was thinking about.

It's three am, when I'm headed in the direction of the cabin, the girl *still* on my mind, that I get the text from Leah McPherson. I can just about make out the words:

Your father's term is ending. He needs you to come home and keep up appearances. It's just for one night, big brother. Will you come?

SOPHIA

I lay on the bed, wondering if he's actually going to return or not. Sleep doesn't come easily. On my back, staring up at the ceiling, I jump at every sound or creak in the cabin. I want to be alone, but then again I almost find myself wishing Cade or Rebel would come back, simply so I would have someone to be angry at. Being angry at them from afar is just as easy as it is in person, but face to face has its benefits. I'm hoping, despite how futile that hope might be, that one of them will finally realize how evil this is and let me go. Of the two men, my money is not on Rebel. He was so frustrated when I refused to do what he wanted me to. I get the feeling he doesn't get told no a lot.

I fall asleep eventually. I dream that I'm at Dad's work, at St. Peter's, and both Dad and Sloane are working over me, trying to save my life. I have a gaping hole in my chest, and blood is pouring everywhere. Sloane keeps leaving instruments inside my chest cavity. She's crying and so is Dad, but my sister is inconsolable. She's sobbing so hard she can barely speak as Dad tells her what to do. I want to remind her to take out the scalpels and retractors and swabs she's leaving inside me, but my body won't respond. I have no voice.

Dad straightens up and wipes the back of his hand across his forehead, smearing blood everywhere. His mouth pulls into a tight line—a look of disappointment I've seen many times before. "That's it. She's a lost cause," he says. "Nothing more we can do." He turns to Sloane and throws his arm around her shoulder, pressing a kiss against her temple. "Never mind, pumpkin. I suppose I still have you." He turns around and begins removing his gloves and gown, but Sloane bends down and whispers in my ear.

"All the king's horses and all the king's men…"

"Stop that, Romera. I told you. She's gone." I can't figure out why Dad's calling Sloane by her last name. He pulls her away, but she fights him. She grows more and more hysterical and he wrestles with her, dragging her off down a long, white corridor.

"All the king's horses! All the king's men! *All the king's horses!*"

I'm not listening to her, though. I'm sitting up on the gurney, reaching into my chest, searching for the instruments that were left behind. My fingers don't touch upon anything for a moment, and then I find what I'm looking for. I remove both hands, covered in blood and gore, but I'm not holding scalpels and swabs. In one hand, I'm holding my fake ID, smeared with blood—Sophia Letitia Marne, smiling out of the photo. In the other hand, I'm holding a gun.

I jerk myself awake, my heart slamming in my chest. For a brief, terrifying moment I think my chest is still open. I clutch both hands to my body, feeling solid ribs and breast and sternum, all rising up and down, up and down way too fast.

"Bad dream?"

I barely bite back the scream that's building in my throat. Rebel's standing at the foot of the bed, watching me with his arms folded. With no shirt on. His tattoos aren't limited to his arms and shoulders. They fan out across his pecs, too, down each side of his body in swirling lines of black and red and green and blue. He looks like he's posing for Men's Fitness. Admittedly, with a physique like that, he could legitimately earn good money modeling for those guys. I push myself back in the bed, horrified when I realize I've worn that god-awful oversized T-shirt to bed again. "What the hell are you doing?" I ask.

"Getting ready to go to my father's place. I'm taking you with me. Sound good?"

"Only if your father's place is actually a police station."

He pouts at me, barely hiding a smile. He looks good when he smiles; I hate myself for acknowledging that, but my brain is still reeling from my nightmare. I'm not equipped to be fending off visions of his near-nakedness right now. "My father's the governor for the state of Alabama. He's the chief of police's boss. Does that count?" he says.

"You're not from Alabama."

He smirks now, taking a step closer to the bed. "Why am I not from Alabama?"

"Because you don't have an accent."

"Oh, that's definitive evidence right there. You must be on the money if I don't drawl, huh?"

I shake my head, trying to pull myself together. "If your father's the governor for Alabama, why would you take me to see him?"

"Because he's a righteous asshole and I hate going back there on my own." Rebel turns away, opening up a closet and pulling out T-shirts and full, button-down shirts. He starts making a pile on the end of the bed.

"No, why would you take me, the girl you're holding against her will? You have to know I'll tell him what you've done as soon as we walk through the door."

Rebel reaches up high into the closet and pulls down a North Face duffel bag; he proceeds to place the piles of clothes inside. "You could do that. Or," he says, looking up at me, "you can come with me and keep your mouth shut. You could let me tell you a little more about the guy you saw stabbed to death in that alleyway. You could listen to everything I have to say, and then, when our trip's over, you could make your decision—whether you'll help me or you won't—based on everything you've learned. And then, either way, I'll let you go."

"I told you. I've already made my decision."

"Based on no information whatsoever," he says.

"I'm sorry. Like I said, I have family to protect."

He carries on placing clothes into the bag at the foot of the bed. I watch for a moment, distracted by the shift of his muscles and the powerful lines of his shoulder blades. He's quiet, not looking at me as he works, but then he says, "Okay. Fine. I'm gonna be gone five days. You can stay here and stare at the television. And when I get back, we'll fit you out in a room in the clubhouse. You should be relatively safe in there. Though, there's a lot less to do, of course.

And no TV. Just four walls and a bed."

"You just said you'd let me go either way!"

"Only if you come with me to my father's place and suffer though his annual charity gala with me."

I just stare at him. I can't figure out what the hell is going on with this guy. He's rude, abrasive and pushy, and now he wants me to go on a road trip with him? "All right, fine. I'll come with you. But this is a complete waste of time. I'm not going to change my mind. You may not like your family very much, but I love mine. I won't do anything to jeopardize their safety."

I can't believe I'm agreeing to this. I must be crazy. Scrambling out of the bed, I tug the T-shirt down in an attempt to cover my thighs. Rebel stops what he's doing and watches me, a smile clearly itching at the corners of his mouth.

"If I come with you to Alabama, you have to swear you're not going to rape me."

He almost chokes on his laughter. "I swear, I'm not planning on raping you."

"And you have to promise you're not going to sell me or loan me out to any of your friends so they can rape me."

Rebel holds up three fingers—scout's honor. I doubt this man was ever a scout, and even if he was, the bastard never had any honor. "There will be no raping of any kind, performed by anyone while you are under my protection. Louis' old Princeton pals get a bit frisky when they're on the sauce, but I swear I will defend you to the hilt."

I fold my arms across my chest, shooting daggers at him. "Well, all right then."

"And Sophia?"

"You'd better swear the same. From your choice of T-shirt slogan, I'm a little worried."

"What? What do you mean?" I look down at the shirt. *It Ain't Gonna Suck Itself.*

"One of my boys went to Thailand last year. Said half the chicks there had dicks. Are you—"

"No! God! This is *your* shirt."

He runs his hand through his thick dark hair, sending it sticking up in eight different directions. It still somehow looks like it was styled that way by a hairdresser. "Nope. That is *not* mine," he tells me. "I would hate to hazard a guess as to who it *does* belong to."

"Urgh!" I'm about to reach for the hem and tear the thing off over my head when I realize I'm not wearing anything underneath. Rebel has the look of a positively evil school kid when I glance up at him. He probably thought he was going to get a free show. I shove past him, into the bathroom, locking the door behind me. This room has fast become my safe place. How am I going to cope without a separate space to shut myself away when I need to? How am I—

"Hey, Soph?" Rebel's muffled voice comes through the door. He sounds close, as though he's leaning into the wood, speaking softly. There must only be a couple of inches between our bodies. I take a step back.

"What?"

"Y'all should know, ah'm definitely from 'Bama, baby. Any tahm y'all wan' proof, alls y'all gotta do is holler." He laughs as he moves away from the door, and I rip the T-shirt off over my head, growling under my breath.

The man is a nightmare.

REBEL

I started out murdering people from a very early age, killing my mother as I made my way out of her body. I took a twenty-two-year sabbatical after that. Since then, I've put a good many people in the ground. I like to console myself sometimes, when I'm feeling shitty about things, by reminding myself who those people were. They were violent, evil men. Men who made a living from the abuse of others much smaller or weaker than they were. Afghanistan left me with a zero tolerance for that kind of thing. It's just not in me to let it slide.

As Sophia's showering, I'm wondering whether I should start by telling her how many people I've shot or stabbed, y'know, just to get it out of the way. Shay comes by the cabin with the clothes I asked her to go buy first thing this morning; she's weighted down by all the bags she's holding in her arms, and she's mighty pissed off. But then, that's her usual expression: resting bitch face.

She doesn't step foot inside the cabin. She just dumps everything at her feet, blowing her bright pink hair back out of her face. I can barely keep track of what color her hair is from week to week normally, but the fluoro pink seems to be sticking. Propping a hand on one hip, she casts a disgusted look at all of the bags at her feet and sighs. "You realize, this is probably very, very unhealthy, boss."

"What is?'

"You, hoarding women's clothing. I knew you were kinky, but I never knew you were balls-out weird."

"They're not for me, Shay."

She lifts her eyebrows, nodding slowly. "Uh-huh. That's what my Uncle Donald used to say. He likes to be called Princess now. He's married to some guy down in the Florida Keys. Left his wife and kids. The works."

"Shay?"

"Yeah?"

"Leave."

She eyes the bags one more time. "None of that shit's my style, y'know. If it ain't right, you can't blame me." She saunters off the cabin porch and starts to climb the ridge back over to the compound, hips swinging as she goes. I'm pretty sure she knows I have a girl in here. She just doesn't want confirmation. We had a thing once. A thing where I fucked her and she decided she wanted to be my old lady. That's not how Widowers work out, though. I don't need an old lady. I need an equal who will still shoot someone in the face for me if I need them to.

Shay was feisty from the moment I inked her into the club to the moment I sunk my dick into her on top of the pool table, but the moment she fell asleep on me I knew I'd made a horrible fucking mistake. She changed in a heartbeat. The fire I'd seen in her went out. She wanted to spoon and shit. She wanted to be subservient in all things, and while I do like that in the bedroom, I don't wanna have an empty fucking vessel following me around, day in, day out, waiting for me to tell them what to fucking do.

I gather up the bags Shay left behind and carry them inside the cabin, tipping out the contents one by one. Winter in Alabama isn't that cold. I told Shay to pick up thin sweaters and jeans. T-shirts and dressy tops. Some boots and some lighter shoes. I leave the last bag zipped up—a garment bag, presumably containing the eveningwear I told Shay to get. I shove everything into the duffel bag I've already packed with my stuff, folding the garment bag neatly on top, and then I wait for Sophia to come out of the bathroom.

I'm getting seriously fucking impatient by the time she eventually creeps out, wrapped in a towel. She stares at me, defiance written all over her face, and says, "I don't have anything else to—" She sees the underwear, pair of jeans, light shirt and Chuck Taylors I've left out for her on the bed and shuts up. I pick up the duffel and sling it over my shoulder.

"I'll be outside." I'm feeling pretty damn smug as I sit on the steps outside the cabin, waiting for her. I don't know why I'm taking such perverse, intense pleasure in one-upping her, but I am. It might have something to do with the fact that no one ever questions me. No one ever challenges me, and it feels fucking awesome.

I feel less awesome when my cell phone starts ringing and I find Maria Rosa's name on the caller display, though. "*Fuck!*" I should have called her already to tell her which of her options we were going with. I definitely should not have left it so long that she is now calling *me*.

"Maria Rosa," I say. "Sorry to have kept you waiting."

"I assume you know how much I like waiting, uh?" She sounds bored, but she must be fuming. She's about to get even madder. "What have you decided, my love? What are you offering in return for my help?"

I take a deep breath. "Nothing."

The line goes utterly silent. I hold my tongue, waiting for her to say something. To acknowledge that she's even still there, let alone that she heard what I said.

Eventually, I hear a sharp scraping sound on the other end of the line—sounds like fingernails down a chalkboard. "So you expect me to help you for free? Is that what you mean to say?"

"No, Mother. I'm saying we can't afford to start fucking around with a federal agency. And we won't hand over the Widowers for your personal use, either. That's what you want from us, and it's not possible. So we'll go without your help if we have to."

"You're an arrogant motherfucker, Rebel. You think I couldn't smash your little club into the dirt if I wanted to? You're pathetic."

This is not going well. "Oh, Mother. Of course you could, but I'm hoping you won't. If you do that, we won't be friends anymore. I'd have to retaliate, and you'd do the same. It would be the start of a vicious cycle. And let me tell you, you may think my club is small, but it can be *really* fucking vicious."

"Pssshh. You're threatening me?"

"No. I'm just politely retracting my request for assistance."

"You couldn't be polite if your life depended on it, motherfucker." The tone of her voice changes, then, softening. "But I understand. You don't need my help, anymore? Fine. I'll let you handle Hector on your own. But I'm a business woman, my love. When you're up to your balls in hot water and you can't fucking see a way out—that's when you'll call me again. And my prices will be a hell of a lot higher than they are now, I swear that to you."

I smile, even though I have absolutely no reason to. "I won't call, Mother. I never do. It's kind of my thing." I don't know if she hangs up first or I do. All I know is my phone is in my hands and I'm staring down at the blank screen, wondering what just happened. Maria Rosa is a complete psycho. She could either take severe offence at what's just gone down or she could have forgotten about it by next week. A person can never tell with her. This whole situation is one gigantic motherfucking head fuck.

The sound of the door clicking shut behind me has me reaching for my damn gun again. Sophia backs into the closed door when she sees the look on my face. "I'm sorry. You said you'd be waiting, so I came out."

I stand, cracking my knuckles one at a time. I've been doing that since I was a teenager—a coping mechanism, a ritual I complete when I'm on the verge of flying off the handle. Saved me from kicking Dad's ass about twenty or thirty times, that's for sure. "Come on, let's go." I snatch up the bag and heft it onto my shoulder, setting off to the right, toward the flat, graveled area where we park cars and motorcycles that won't fit into the compound. I don't check to see if she's following. She better fucking had be, though. I've just given Maria Rosa the flick, so now Sophia's our only option. I will pick her up and toss her the fuck over my shoulder if I have to. My boots skid down the loose shale slope that drops away in front of the cabin. I'm almost at the bottom when I hear the cautious, sliding steps of someone coming down after me.

Good. She's doing as she's told. I wait for her, no more than ten seconds, and then I'm walking again, around the buttress of a tessellated rock formation that shields the parking area from view. The Humvee's right where Cade left it when he got back from our little road trip. Alongside the gleaming black beast, a not-so-shit-hot Dodge Charger—blue, rusting wheel arches, a total bomb—has been up on blocks for the past eight weeks. Carnie keeps saying he's going to fix her up, but so far all he's done is sit in the driver's seat and smoke pot for hours on end. If the fucking thing isn't either souped-up and ready to roll or completely gone by the time we get back, I'm towing it out into the desert and firebombing the fucking thing. I throw the bag into the back of the Hummer, growling under my breath.

"Am I allowed to sit back there?" Sophia asks. Her arms are folded across her body, but she's not defensive. She's unsure. I don't have time to be arguing over stupid shit with her right now, so I just shrug.

"Whatever you need, Miss Daisy." She goes to sit on the driver's side in the back and I grab her by the shoulders and forcibly redirect her to the passenger's side. "I know you're a pretty smart girl, so stop planning stupid shit." She's seen too many action movies. I'm willing to put good money on the fact that she thinks she can try and subdue me from behind while we're driving or something, and that isn't gonna happen. Not without one or both of us dying horribly when I flip the damn car. Her look of irritation only proves my suspicions.

I bundle her in the car and hop into the driver's seat, starting the engine.   She stares out of the car window, the muscles in her throat working overtime as she clearly tries to come up with another scheme to get herself out of this situation. I hit the lock button, and all four doors to the vehicle respond instantly, thunking closed. They won't open until I hit that button again. Sophia gives me a tired roll of her eyes—I see it in the rearview as I speed away from the compound and the rest of the Widow Makers. We're silent for a long time. Surprisingly, she breaks the silence first.

"How long does it take to get to Alabama?"

"'Bout nineteen hours." I look in the rearview again and catch the stricken look on her face.

"I am so sick of being trapped in cars. Why do you insist on driving everywhere? It'd probably take a couple of hours on a plane, max."

She'd fucking love that—me trying to herd her through TSA. Her screaming about my holding her captive. Me getting my ass thrown into jail. I reach behind me, shifting so I can grab my gun from my waistband. "I don't know of any airlines that will let me take *this* as carry on," I tell her, holding up the Glock I stole from my father when I was twenty-four. The night Laura went missing.

Sophia tries not to react, but I see her eyes go wide in the mirror. I'm used to being around guns now. Something feels off if I don't feel the weight of the Glock at the base of my spine at all times. For Sophia, a weapon like that is something to be afraid of. For me, it's a necessary accessory that enables me to get through my day without ending up dead.

"You should be careful with that," Sophia tells me, angling her body so her back's half turned to me. Looks uncomfortable. I laugh, returning the Glock to my waistband.

"You think I don't know how to handle a gun?"

"My dad's an anesthesiologist. He's sat in on so many surgeries where guys have been shot in the feet. In the thighs. *In the junk*." She seems especially pleased with that one. "All because the assholes tuck their piece into their pants like a G. So fucking stupid."

I've heard her curse before, but this time it actually registers—the Widowers have plenty of groupies, women who aren't exactly what you'd call ladies. The language on some of them could rival any of the club members. It's not that I think chicks shouldn't swear, but there's something about Sophia. It's just seriously entertaining when she does it.

"What the hell are you grinning about up there?" she snaps. I forget that since I can see her, she can see me in the mirror, too.

"Absolutely nothing. Just enjoying the scenery." Ironic, since we're staring at scrub and dirt and not much else for miles.

"You're just like them, y'know? The men my dad used to come home talking about. Reckless. Selfish. People like you don't give a shit about anybody else."

"I might be those things, Soph, but just to set your mind at ease...I'm not stupid enough to blow my own balls off just because I shove my gun down my pants."

"Oh, I feel so much better knowing that."

"I'm glad."

"You'll excuse me if I choose not to believe you, though. You don't strike me as the intelligent type."

"I don't?"

"You probably didn't even finish high school."

The irony of this statement almost has me wheezing. "Oh, sweetheart..."

"I'm not your sweetheart. And don't call me Soph, either. I don't like it."

I hold my hands up. "All right. Whatever you want, One Eighty-One." She kicks the back of my chair, lashing out hard enough that I actually feel the dig in my back.

"You're a son a bitch," she growls. "I've never met *anyone* as infuriating as you."

Cade told me to flirt with the girl to get her on side, but at this rate I'll be lucky if she doesn't claw my eyes out instead. I just can't help but bait her, though. The opportunity is just too good to pass up. There was a time when the old me would have knocked the new me out stone-cold for even talking to a woman the way I talk to her. But life's a roll of the dice, and people need to evolve to survive. That guy doesn't even exist anymore. I buried him under the dirt floor of a barn somewhere between San Antonio and Floresville, Texas.

"Just thank your lucky stars you're not riding with Raphael Dela Vega right now." I tilt the rearview so I can't see her anymore. We can't carry on like this. The whole point of this trip is to win her over to our side, not to alienate her even further. I'm gonna have to implement the age old practice of thinking before I speak. Trouble is, I've never been very good at that.

Yeah, the guy's a douche bag, but he's right: I am glad I'm riding with him and not Raphael. And the more time I spend with him, the more I can read him. Rebel's not the type of guy I'd ever hang out with voluntarily back home, but despite the way he looks—the tattoos, the hard set to his jaw, the ice in his eyes—I get the feeling that he's not a violent man by nature. And it makes no sense that I believe he'll release me once we're done in Alabama, but I do believe it. More fool me. I could be setting myself up for a devastating disappointment, but what was I supposed to do? Hang around their clubhouse and potentially get gang raped by a bunch of bikers? Not happening. I'd rather take my chances with Rebel. At least there's only one of him.

Two hours pass, and neither of us says a word. I think about my family, about Mom, and Dad, and Sloane, and how they're definitely going out of their minds by now. I feel terrible. My heart is still aching with the pain of it all when Rebel pulls off the highway and kills the car engine.

We're in the middle of nowhere, no buildings in sight as far as I can see. I can think of no good reason why he'd pull over here, and yet he has. Panic flares through me. "What are we doing?"

Rebel twists in his seat, throwing his arm over the back of the passenger chair so he can look at me properly. He runs his hand through his hair, brushing it back, the action an absentminded one. I find my stomach twisting in a most unnatural way—a reaction I do not appreciate.

So.

Time to get this over with.

The guy is hot.

I've done everything I can think of to not think that way, but it's hopeless. He can be an ass and he can be rude, and I can want to punch him in his face, but that won't change the fact that he's smoking hot. He has a small dimple in his left cheek, lower than it should probably be to make him cute. It deepens into a small line when he smiles, a little crooked imperfection that breaks the symmetry of his face and draws my eyes to his mouth. I can't stop looking at his mouth. I even turned away from him entirely when we first got into the car, but that lasted all of five seconds, and now here I am staring right at his lips again.

"We're having a bathroom break is what we're doing. You wanna go first or should I?"

I can just tell he's waiting for me to kick up a fuss about dropping my brand-new jeans and peeing out in the open. He has no idea how many church camps I've been on, though. "I'll go first. Are you sure you aren't gonna come with me? Stand guard in case I make a run for it mid-stream?"

He just laughs. "I'm gonna go out on a limb here and trust you." A *chunk*ing sound echoes around the car—he's unlocked the doors. I unfasten my seatbelt and climb out of the car, headed straight for the back of the Humvee. The massive vehicle is plenty big enough for me to squat down behind without him seeing a thing. It doesn't take me long to finish up. I take a moment to stretch out my legs, though. I'm not used to all of this sitting down. Back in Seattle, I run track. I go rock climbing with Matt.

Oh my god, Matt.

My insides knot when I realize how badly he must be freaking out right now. Mom and Dad, too. It's only been three or four days—with the head injury I suffered, it's hard to be sure—but that will feel like an eternity to my parents. Sloane will be going out of her mind. She's always been so overprotective of me, always thought of me as her responsibility.

I look up, pulling a deep breath into my lungs—the sky's so damn blue. Feels wrong somehow. The driver's side door opens to the Humvee, and Rebel climbs out of the car, sliding on a pair of shades. "Come here for a moment," he says.

"Where?"

"Here." He jerks his head toward the other end of the car. Stepping on top of the tire, he climbs up onto the hood of the Humvee and holds his hand out to me, offering to help me up.

"Why are we climbing on top of the car?"

He shrugs. "Why not? I need a moment. I'm sure you do, too."

I look at his hand, suddenly exhausted by all of this. By thoughts of my poor, worrying parents. By thoughts of how to keep them safe. How to get away. How to cope. It all seems so...insurmountable. I take his hand, allowing him to pull me up onto the hood of the car. I can feel the heat of the engine through the soles of my new Chucks.

Rebel lowers himself so that he's sitting on the roof of the truck, legs kicked out in front of him, crossed at the ankle. Seems like an odd pose for him; he's always so rigid, back straight, chest proud.

Right now, he looks pretty much how I feel—like he's on the brink of saying fuck it and giving himself over to the powers that be, because what's the point in fighting anymore? He nods at the spot next to him, raising an eyebrow.

"You gonna sit down or what?"

I sit down. Arguing with him would be futile. We sit there, side by side, staring off down the arrow-straight road, and for a moment I don't hate him. He pulls a cell phone out of his pocket and taps something into it, and then he turns to face me, frowning slightly. "You believe in vengeance?"

"You mean like revenge?"

He shakes his head. "Revenge is a selfish act. Retaliation for something. Vengeance is a different thing altogether. It's about obtaining justice, usually for someone who can't claim it for themselves."

This is an odd line of questioning but I decide I'll bite. Maybe I wouldn't if he were being a jerk like he was a couple of hours ago, but that's not what's happening. He's pensive, the live wire that apparently runs through him dulled for the moment. "I don't know," I say. "Probably, in that case."

"What if I simplified the question? What if I say, do you believe in justice?

"Then, yes, I do believe."

"Okay." Rebel fiddles with his cell phone again, and then he's showing me a picture on the screen—a picture of the silver-haired man I watched die back in Seattle. He has a huge grin on his face, wearing a really bad Christmas sweater with reindeer on it, and a small kid is sitting on his knee. A baby, really. A little girl. She's smiling so wide her little fat cheeks are round like apples. Can't be any more than two years old.

"That's Maddie," Rebel says. "She's older now, but not by much. She's my cousin, but she might as well be my little sister. Ryan," he points at the man in the picture, "Ryan got married late. His wife

Estelle was in her forties when she had Maddie—surprise kid. They found out she had breast cancer at the same time, and she refused treatment so she could keep the kid. She hung on for three weeks after, got to hold her daughter in her arms, be a mom a little before she went. I guess that's some consolation."

I look at the picture, knowing what he's doing. He wants me to testify so badly that he's willing to pull the old *poor-kid's-mother-died-when-she-was-born-and-now-her-dad's-dead-too* card. It's shitty and it's underhanded. And it's kind of working. "Who's taking care of her now?"

"The state of Washington Child Services. She'll be placed into a care home soon. At worst, some fucking drunk with a penchant for touching small kids will get her. She'll grow up thinking it's normal for Daddy Steve to touch her in her special fucking places. At best, she'll be given to some down-and-out family who don't give a shit about her so long as the government keeps on sending through the checks."

"And how will me standing up in court and testifying against Raphael and Hector change that? If you're so worried about her upbringing, Rebel, why the hell aren't you petitioning for custody of her? She's your blood relative right? You just said she's your cousin." Which makes the man in the photo, Ryan, his uncle. Rebel's refusal to let this drop suddenly makes a whole lot more sense. *His uncle.* God, this gets more and more fucked up by the day.

"I can't have her with me," he says flatly.

"Why not? You afraid looking after a kid's gonna cramp your style? That's pretty fucking selfish."

He clenches his jaw, clearing the picture from his cell phone screen and sliding it back into his pocket. I can tell I've made him angry just by the way he's pressing his knuckles into the roof of the car. "I have a criminal record, Sophia. I live on a compound out in the middle of nowhere with a group of people who all have rap sheets as long as your arms. I'm not fucking evil. If I could take her, I would."

I've accused him of being an asshole from the moment I met him. Turns out I'm an asshole, too. "I'm sorry, okay. I just—"

"A guy in my position, looking like I do, involved in the shit I'm running...you made an assumption about me. An assumption anyone else would make, too. Don't sweat it. But know, the reason why I'm doing this...the reason why I'm *going* to convince you to do what I'm asking, isn't because of me. Not because the man who helped raise me was murdered and I'm pissed about it. Which I am. But because I want justice. Justice for Ryan, because he didn't get to watch his little girl grow up. And justice for Maddie, because of the shitty hand she's just been dealt." He slides off the roof of the car, jumping to the ground. I can hear him pissing against the side of the car. For the moment, I just stay where I am, eyes fixed on some vague, not-there point in the distance.

I don't know what I'm supposed to do. I don't know how he expects me to choose between helping him and keeping my family safe. This is the first time that I've even found myself considering it, and the prospect is terrifying. If I testify, they find out my real name. They can track down my family and Raphael can make good on his promise, regardless of whether he's behind bars or not. He's the type of man who will find a way.

Rebel taps the hood of the Humvee—I can almost see the dark cloud hanging over him. "Come on, we gotta go."

"What would *you* do?"

He looks up at me, eyes sharp. Pained. "What do you mean?"

"If you were in my position, what would you do? If it were Ryan and Maddie who were in danger, would you risk their lives just because it was the right thing to do?"

"Our situations are a little different, sweetheart."

"How so?"

"I would kill anyone that threatened my family with my bare fucking hands. It would never be an issue." He opens the driver's side door and leans against it. "If you do what I'm asking, Sophia, I will do the same thing for you. I swear to God and all things holy, before you right here and now, I will spill the blood of every single member of Los Oscuros before I allow a single one of your family members to come to harm."

REBEL

When she climbs back in the car, she gets in the front.
That's how I know I've made some sort of progress with
her. Is it her finally agreeing to help? No. But maybe, just
maybe, she's not as adamant anymore. Maybe she's thinking about
it. Which is a better situation than we were in before.

She sleeps. For five hours, she lays so motionless, stretched out
as best as she can in her seat, and I drive, glancing at her
occasionally out of the corner of my eye, wondering if she's still
fucking breathing. I can't tell, and she doesn't shift an inch.

We arrive in Dallas just as the day's darkening, the lights of the
city like lightning bugs blinking on and off on the horizon. My eyes
are killing me. My body is used to this, though, traveling long
distances. The Hummer actually provides more comfort than I'm
used to. Sitting on a motorcycle, through wind and rain and
everything other fucking thing Mother Nature throws at us, can be
unpleasant to say the least.

You get used to it. You get used to all of it. The pain in your back.
The wet leather that just doesn't dry out. The guns. The sneaking
around in the dark. The shootings and the stabbings and the dying.

The funerals.

"Mmmm. Where are we?" Sophia stretches out like a cat, just about managing to straighten her legs before the soles of her shoes hit the engine block in the foot well. She blinks at me—she looks like a child as she rubs at her eyes, ridding herself of her sleep. She looks...she looks so freaking sweet in that very, very brief moment that it almost makes my teeth hurt. Catches me by surprise.

"Dallas," I tell her. "Halfway, or close enough. We'll stop for the night."

"I can drive. I just slept for...wow. I slept for a *really* long time." She stares at the clock on the dash like she doesn't believe it's telling her the truth.

"Yeah, I don't think so." I give her the old *you think you're gonna pull that shit with me?* look. "We're stopping. I need to get actual rest, and I won't be able to sleep properly if I have to keep my eye on you the whole time."

She doesn't react to my rejection of her offer—it was clearly expected. Instead, she asks something out of the blue. "Why did you kill off your accent?"

"I didn't kill it off. My father did. He didn't believe a regional dialect was gonna help me through life. Had it trained out of me when I was a kid."

"That's...practical?"

"An obsession of his. He tried to make my mother 'speak properly' too, but it never stuck."

"So she still speaks with a Southern accent?"

"Nope. She's dead." I wait for the awkward silence, but it never comes. Sophia makes a soft humming sound.

"Oh."

"You not gonna tell me you're sorry for my loss?"

"Do you want me to?"

"Not particularly."

"Then I won't tell you I'm sorry."

I grip my hands around the steering wheel, cracking my neck. I shouldn't have mentioned my mother. My whole body feels tight as fuck now. I like that she didn't dive right in with the placations, though. I fucking hate when people say shit like that. It's such a fucking lie. At least Sophia was true to herself. She's in a shitty position and I'm the reason why. I could have let her go back home by now a thousand times but I haven't. I've kept her locked up and refused her requests to leave. She could probably give a shit if my whole family died right in front of us right now.

"Where are we staying?" she asks.

"At a friend's place."

"Another MC clubhouse?" I can hear the worry in her voice. She must have heard about the shit that goes down in places like the Widow Makers' clubhouse. The drinking. The drug taking. The fucking and fighting. She doesn't want to get caught up in any of that.

"No, somewhere else. A motel."

"And...we'll be sharing a room?" She says it carefully, slowly, testing the words on her tongue.

"Yes, we'll be sharing a room. You got a problem with that?"

"You really expect me to say no here? Of course I have a problem with that."

"Well it's tough fucking luck, sugar. Unless you want us both to sleep in the car instead, this is happening. Don't worry—I fully intend on keeping my hands to myself."

I'm getting to know her reactions. I know she's looking at me, pulling that face she pulls when she's pissed. I don't bother turning to check; I just keep on driving into the night. Our sleeping arrangements are non-negotiable. She can't change that by acting like a princess.

"Okay. Fine," she says.

"Okay, fine?"

"Yeah. We get a room with two beds, you stay in yours and I stay in mine and all is right with the world."

If only she knew how many women had begged me to climb up

into their beds with them. *Begged.* Sophia's lack of interest in me only makes me want her even more, which is fucked.

We make it to the Motel 6 around seven. Not just any Motel 6; this is a specific motel run by a specific person. The place looks like any other cheap dive establishment might look, but it's not. It's a kind of safe house for people like me. Alex Draper, a regular guy well into his late fifties, owed pretty much every bookie in America money. I helped him clear a few of those debts with my fists, and I helped him clear the rest of them with a few careful words whispered into the right ears. Ever since then, Alex has been in my pocket. A Widower ever needs a place to keep his head down for a couple of days, he gets sent out to Texas on an enforced vacation.

There's an ancient-looking '78 Honda CX500 leaning on a stand by the entranceway to the lobby. When I see it, my heart gives a kick in my chest. Its royal blue tank has been touched up, I see. In fact, the whole bike looks like it's had minor improvements made here and there. The old girl's been getting some love. I pull up beside it and park the truck, staring out of the window at a motorcycle I'd recognize anywhere, regardless of how many parts got replaced or fixed up.

"What's the matter?" Sophia asks. "You know the person who owns that bike?"

"I do. I knew the guy it belonged to before him better, though. That's my grandfather's old motorcycle."

"Your *grandfather*? Your father, the governor for Alabama, was raised by a guy who rode motorcycles? A guy like *you*?"

Her tone is very suggestive. I hate the way she says that: a guy like *you*. She's right—I'm a criminal and an all-round fuck-up these days—but, still, the more time I spend with this girl, the more I don't want her to think of me that way. "He was my grandfather on my mother's side. And no, he wasn't like me. He was just a guy who loved motorcycles. Building them. Racing them. He taught me to ride as soon I was old enough."

"Does he still live in Alabama, too?"

"Nope. Also dead." I climb out of the Hummer, slamming the door behind me. The ghosts of the past seem intent on screwing with me today. I don't have fucking time for it. Or the energy, for that matter. I lock the truck behind me before Sophia can follow me. I head inside the motel, and Alex is sitting behind the counter, eating beans on toast from a chipped plate in front of him. *Jeopardy!* is playing on a small, decrepit-looking TV that's mounted to the wall. Alex Trebek flashes his pearly whites at the contestants, and Alex Draper catches sight of me and nearly chokes on his dinner.

"Rebel. Wasn't expectin' ya, son." He hammers his fist against his chest, face turning a strained shade of red.

"Yeah, flying visit. Was hoping you might be able to spot me a double room for the night."

Alex gives me that look he always used to give me when I was a kid and he was gambling away my grandfather's money—for a brief time they ran a business together, competing in races all over the country, and my pops trusted him with his winnings. He knew Alex was losing his money, but he didn't really care. Alex was his best friend—hence how he ended up with the Honda CX500 when my grandfather croaked—and it was never about the money for him anyway. All he cared about were the bikes.

"Uh, well, yeah, son. I got the same room you normally use. I keep it free for ya. Just in case." We skip the whole credit card deposit, paperwork bullshit regular guest have to go through, and Alex tosses me the keys. When I head back outside, he follows me to the doorway, squinting out into the darkness. "That a girl you got with you?" he asks. Nosey fucker never did know when to *not* ask questions. I refrain from telling him to mind his own damn business, though. Against all odds, I have a soft spot for the old bastard, just like my grandfather did.

"Last time I checked," I inform him.

He nods, rubbing his calloused fingers over his two-day-old scruff. "That's good, son. Harry would be pleased. About time you found someone nice to settle down with." He squints a little harder, trying to get a better look at Sophia. "She's a beaut, too. Dark-haired. That's good. I never could picture you with a blonde."

"She's just keeping me company. She's not *with* me."

Alex's twisted old mouth pulls up to one side, displaying his crooked, slightly blackened front teeth. "Then you're a mad man, son. She's made for you, I reckon. Better get on that before anyone else does."

I fight off the urge to laugh. If only he knew.

The room's warm, which is welcome. Sophia heads straight to the bathroom and the sound of running water whispers behind the wooden door. I sit on the edge of the bed closest to the door and get ready to make some phone calls. Cade is first on my list.

"S'up, man. You breaking for the night?"

"Yeah. I'll be arriving at Louis' place around three tomorrow. Can you call Leah and let her know we're on our way in?" Leah McPherson works for my father, the one single favor the bastard's ever done for me. She needed to get the hell out of New Mexico, permanently, and I needed to find someone who would take her on, fast. At the time, my dad was the only person I could think of to ask. He goes through housemaids quickly, too abrasive and plain fucking rude for anyone to stomach him for too long, but a sharp-tongued Southern bastard was nothing after what Leah had already been through. I figured she would cope, and she did. Has been coping for the past two years. Ever since, she's been a convenient go-between, passing on messages from my father to me and vice versa. Makes communicating with the old man a hell of a lot more pleasant.

Leah is also very good at passing on information that my father probably doesn't want me to know.

"I'll call her right away," Cade says. And then, "Shay came in here asking who she was buying all those clothes for this morning. She was pissed, man."

"Yeah, well, Shay can be pissed all she wants."

"It's bad juju to have a woman slamming around the clubhouse."

"What do you want me to do about it? Marry the fucking girl?"

Cade snorts. I can hear him shuffling papers or something—must be in my office. He takes care of the paperwork for the Ink Bar and the general running of the compound while I'm gone. "The day you marry anyone is the day hell freezes over. But maybe you could just talk to her. Have a quiet word in her ear or something. Fuck, man, just tell her it wasn't meant to be or something. I don't know."

If he were anyone else, I'd tell him to go fuck himself good and hard. "I'll think about it."

"Great. Now, the Mexicans want more—" Cade cuts off. I think it's just because he was about to say guns, and you can't say the Mexicans want more *guns* on the fucking telephone. Especially with the attention our little community out in the desert attracts. But Cade makes a guttural growling sound that tells me this is something else. Something bad.

"What? Tell me."

"You in front of a TV, man?" he says. "You'd better turn it on."

Oh, boy. When Cade sounds worried like that, it can only mean trouble. I hit the power button on the TV in the room, waiting for the old piece of shit to blink into life. The same *Jeopardy!* show Alex was watching materializes slowly, pixel by pixel, onto the screen. "Which channel?" I ask.

"Any. Just look for a news station. You won't have any problems finding this."

Fuck. If something's happened that's made it to all news stations across America, it must be big. I stab at the programming buttons on the bottom of the TV, searching, until I come across a stricken-looking woman in a pale green suit, staring straight out of the screen at me. She clears her throat, taking a deep breath, as though pulling herself together. "Again, eighteen people have died and seven further people are injured in what is perhaps the most violent gang shooting in Los Angeles for years. Eyewitnesses reported that at three pm this afternoon, a group of men dressed in leather jackets and black jeans entered Trader Joe's on Sunset Boulevard and began indiscriminately shooting at shoppers. It's unclear how many gunmen there were at this time, as security cameras within the store were shot out as soon as the men entered.

"Our sources have confirmed that the reason for the attack is most likely drug related. It is believed an undercover police officer working for the DEA was meant to meet with a handler at the grocery store. Police are yet to confirm if this is the case, or whether a DEA agent was in fact shot and killed, but the tightening of security around the crime scene and the LAPD's notable silence on the matter would lead us to believe this is correct.

"Once the shooting was at an end, the men involved in this senseless, violent attack sped off on motorcycles. Footage here shows three of the men celebrating as they prepare to flee the scene."

The image turns fuzzy as camera footage replaces the news studio, showing a clear image of the supermarket from outside. From the angle of the footage, this camera was covering a small food court outside the entrance, but you can clearly see three men emerging from the left, heads bowed, long hair ratty and hanging in their faces. One of them spins around, must hear something, and then there it is: The Widow Makers' emblem. Our patch. Right in the middle of the motherfucker's back. I can't hear what's being said between them, but they're not fucking celebrating. Their wild arm movements, the way they're shoving at each other as they hurry off screen—they're *arguing.*

"Police are yet to release an appeal for information. Should a member of the public recognize any of these men, we at News 541 want to help. If anyone has any information about these individuals, call in on..." The newsreader rattles of a telephone hotline, the screen frozen on a shot of the three men, bodies all pointed in different angles as they survey the area, faces nothing more than charcoal smudges. The only thing I can make out clearly is that goddamn patch.

"Oh my god."

I jump, hitting the mute button on the television. Sophia's standing right behind me, her body wrapped in a towel, breasts crushed together by the way she's fiercely holding the material tight around herself. Her bare shoulders are speckled with water drops, her hair almost black now that it's wet. Once more, it hits me like a kick in the gut: the woman is fucking beautiful. And she's staring at me like I'm some kind of monster. "What—what have you *done*? That's your club, isn't it? The Widow Makers? Why would you have all those people killed?"

SOPHIA

Rebel just sits there, a tiny wrinkle in between his brows the form of an expression on his face. His eyes somehow look even colder than they normally do, which is saying something. "This wasn't us," he tells me. He stares grimly at the television for a long moment, the muscles in his jaw and throat working, and then gives a small shake of his head. "This was a fucking punishment." He lifts his phone to his ear—I didn't even realize he had it in his hand—and then starts speaking into it. "You still there, man?"

I sink slowly to sit on the edge of the bed next to him, not sure if I should pretend not to be listening. If I should be sitting so close to him. If I should put some clothes on. I don't know what I should be doing. All I know is the news has this story on repeat and for all the world it looks like Rebel and his boys have been out murdering people for fun in Hollywood.

"Yeah. I know," Rebel says. I can almost hear his teeth grinding. "She obviously didn't take our refusal as well as I'd hoped. Now she's gone after her DEA agent and had him killed. And she's pinning it on us publicly, just to fucking spite us."

There's talk on the other end of the phone, but all I hear is my heart beating in my ears. The television's quiet now, but they keep cycling through the same three or four images: a woman running out of the supermarket, dropping a plastic bag on the ground as she staggers away from the madness ensuing inside. A cashier holding up his hands, walking backward. Three men, pushing each other outside, arguing. And then a close-up of one of their leather jackets, complete with grinning skull and double drawn pistols, Widow Makers at the top, New Mexico underneath.

"She'll be expecting that," Rebel says, getting to his feet. "We can't afford to retaliate right now. We need to account for every single member of the club for the past—no, I *know* none of us did this. Fuck's sake, Cade. But the cops, they're gonna be all over this. They're gonna wanna know where everyone was." He starts to pace, pinching the bridge of his nose with his fingers. I was struck by a wave of horror when I first saw what he was watching as I came out of the shower, but now, watching *him*, I know his club is innocent. I just have no clue what the hell's going on.

Rebel makes eye contact with me as he paces, and I don't know what to do. I should maybe look away, give him a little privacy or something, but I'm too confused to do that. So I just look back at him, my heart in my throat, waiting for him to say something that I actually might understand. He stops in front of me, facing me, eyes still boring into my skin, and I feel a little lightheaded. "Burn everything we have on the Desolladors. Bury the guns. Burn the weed. Make our house safe," he says into the phone. "The cops are on their way."

The cops are on their way to the compound. I'm suddenly torn between laughing and crying. The cops, showing up at the compound? If I'd been a little more stubborn, they would have found me there, locked away in a room inside their clubhouse, still plotting a way to escape. I could have been home free.

Rebel slides his cell phone into his pocket and crouches down in front of me, the flashing images behind him on the television casting a blue light around his head, throwing his features into relief. He exhales and places his hands on my bare knees. "Soph?"

This feels like the first time, the first time I've ever been looked at properly in my entire life. Those pale, icy eyes of his almost burn my skin as he studies me.

"Yeah?"

"I need a stiff drink," he says. "I can only have one if you swear you're not gonna try and do something fucking stupid."

He's asking for my word that I won't try to escape if he has a drink? He doesn't need to do that. He could handcuff me to the bed or something and get as drunk as he liked without having to worry about me, but...he's asking me if he can trust me instead. Absolutely crazy. I nod, trying to keep myself from appearing a little too over-enthusiastic. If he doubts me, he will cuff me. And after being restrained so frequently of late, I really don't feel like trying to sleep with my wrists pinned up over my head. "It's fine. I'll behave," I tell him.

"Thank you." He stands, heading for the discolored, yellowing Bakelite phone that sits on the bedside table in between our two beds. He picks it up and stabs one button—must be 0 for reception. "Hey, Alex. Need some whiskey. What you got?" He frowns, but then says, "That'll do. Bring it over?"

He puts the phone down. He doesn't move for a moment, his back to me, his shoulders barely hitching up and down with his breath. Then he tips forward, taking hold of the phone cable, and rips it out of the wall.

Turns out he doesn't trust me enough to leave it plugged in. Definitely smart on his part, but crappy luck for me. He picks up the entire phone and carries it to the door just as someone starts to knock on it. I don't even see who it is. No words are spoken. Rebel shoves the phone through the gap in the door and then takes hold of a bottle of liquor, pulling his arm back through the gap, and then the door is closed again. Whoever was on the other side must be used to this kind of behavior; he leaves without a single comment.

"Are you going to tell me what's going on?" I ask.

Rebel's head snaps up, like he'd forgotten I was even here. "Was that part of our deal? Am I supposed to apprise you of everything that happens in my club now?"

"From the look on your face, this didn't happen inside your club, asshole. Why do you have to be so fucking rude, anyway? I'm scared. You want to keep me calm. The smartest thing you can do is explain what I just saw on the TV, why you're tearing into that bottle like it's your last goddamn lifeline." He really is tearing at it. He can't seem to keep still long enough to focus and open the plastic seal properly. I can tell he's growing more and more tense by the second just from looking at him. I hold out my hand, taking the bottle from him as he passes me. He doesn't stop me. He's too busy staring at the floor as he paces back and forth, opening and closing his hands into fists.

I catch my nail under the plastic seal on the bottle, opening it easily, and I twist the screw cap, wincing at the burning smell that immediately hits my nose. Rebel picks up the television remote and throws it as hard as he can against the wall.

"Fuuuck!"

My heart starts slamming underneath my ribcage. I thought it earlier, that despite how he looks, I didn't think Rebel was really a violent man. Now I can see it, though. I can see how he would be absolutely crazy if the situation required it of him. He blows hard, his breath rushing in and out of his lungs so forcefully I can hear him panting. He storms toward the door and then changes his mind, heading back toward the bathroom. Flexing his hands again, it's as though he's itching for something else to throw.

"Rebel?" He doesn't seem to hear me. "*Rebel.*"

He stops pacing. Stares at me. "What?" he growls.

"You're starting to scare me." I don't know what I hope to accomplish by telling him that, but it's as though I've just struck him across the face. The man who was throwing things and ripping phones out of walls , on the brink of a nuclear explosion, is suddenly gone. He lets out one final, rage-filled exhalation, and by the time he's run out of breath, he's calm. He leans back against the wall, pressing the heels of his hands into his eyes. "Fuck. Sorry, Soph." He takes a moment, fingers digging into his hair, and then he slides down the wall until he's sitting on the floor. "There's a woman. A crazy fucking head case of a woman, who is sorely pissed at me, and this is her way of getting back at me." He jerks his thumb at the TV, shaking his head. "She wanted me to kill this DEA guy. I told her I didn't want the club involved in anything remotely to do with the DEA, so she's gone and killed the fucker and made it look like it was us anyway. To teach me a lesson."

I bridge my knees, still clutching hold of the bottle of...of *Lagavulin?* It stinks like nothing else. Rebel watches me tuck the towel up underneath me so that I'm not flashing him, a wan smile lifting up one corner of his mouth. He looks like he's at a loss. "What does it mean, then? Will the cops come arrest you for this?" I ask.

"Yes," he says.

"And you'll go to jail?" I thought I'd rejoice a little more at that prospect, but the past few hours...I don't know. Maybe I'm changing my mind about him. God, I'm not turning into one of those Stockholm bitches. I refuse. Seriously unhealthy stuff right there. But, from what he's told me, I can see that Rebel's reasoning behind trying to get me to help him is honorable. He's just *really* not gone about it the right way.

"I don't know. I mean, I've been with you the whole time that shooting was taking place. You could always tell the cops we were holed up in here all day."

"And why would the police believe I was hiding out in a motel room with the head of a motorcycle gang, when I've clearly been reported as a missing person back in Seattle by now?"

Rebel leans forward, forearms resting on his knees, his eyes flashing with less worry now and more...something else. Something that makes my skin feel strange, like it's glowing. "Young women run away and lock themselves in motel rooms with hot bikers all the time, sugar. I'd be happy to show you what activities they might engage in to pass the time. And we're not a motorcycle *gang*. We're a *club*."

My cheeks are on fire. I know exactly what he's referring to, of course. He's suggesting we have sex, and that is *not* going to happen. "You swore you wouldn't rape me," I say, using the hand I'm holding the whiskey in to point at him accusingly. He takes the bottle from me and raises it to his lips, eyes locked on me the whole time. He drinks, swallows, inhales sharply, and then grins.

"I didn't say anything about anyone being forced into anything, sugar. I'm talking about consensual participation."

"And why the hell would I consent to participate with you in anything like that? I have a boyfriend, y'know."

"I did *not* know that," he says, shifting forward a little. Closer. Within reaching distance now. He takes another drink from the bottle, pressing his full lips to the beveled rim of the bottle, still watching me. Still making me feel very strange, indeed. He holds up the bottle to me, offering me a drink. "What's your boyfriend's name?"

"Matt." I take the bottle from Rebel, not sure I want to drink from it. I do though; I need something to take the edge of the unexpected tension from this situation. The alcohol that chases over my tongue and down my throat is liquid napalm, setting small fires one after the other as it roars through my body. I gasp, barely able to catch my breath.

Over the past few days, I've been thinking about Matt a lot. What the hell would he make of this situation right now? Would he be wondering why the hell I haven't put any clothes on yet? A bolt of hot embarrassment washes through me, putting out the whiskey fire. Handing the bottle back, I get to my feet. "I should get dressed."

"Why bother? We'll be going to bed soon, anyway, right?" The way he says that—going to be bed soon—is full of innuendo. I hear his meaning clear as day: we'll be going to bed *together* soon, anyway.

"What are you doing, Rebel? A second ago you were freaking out about a shooting that your motorcycle *club* is being framed for, and now all you seem to care about is flirting with me." I tighten the towel around me, suddenly aware that there's very little material between my naked body and his hands. "Shouldn't you be thinking of a way to exonerate yourself and your club?"

Rebel shrugs. He gently takes the whiskey from me with one hand. With the other hand, he slowly traces his fingertips across the bridge of my foot, making me jump. I'd take a step back, but the bed is right behind me, blocking my way. Rebel softly runs up hand up over my foot and loops his fingers around my ankle. His thumb moves in small, careful circles over the swell of bone there, a soft, barely there contact that sends shivers of burning heat sparking upward, firing all over my body. "I think better when I'm distracted," he says, his voice a low rumble in his chest.

I stagger sideways, almost losing my footing. "I'm not gonna be some cheap distraction for you, asshole. I'm not just some hole you can stick your dick into 'cause I'm here and it's convenient."

"And what if I told you I wanted to have sex with you because I like you? Would that make a difference?"

"You don't like me."

"Of course I do."

I turn my back on him, heat welling everywhere all over my body. "Did you bring something else for me to wear, or should I just put my jeans and T-shirt back on again?"

Rebel slowly gets to his feet, his chest brushing against my bare shoulder blades as he steps in between the two beds and unzips the bag he brought with him. I have to hold my breath. He rustles around in the bag and then throws something over my shoulder: another oversized T-shirt. I hold it up, and this time it doesn't say, *It Ain't Gonna Suck Itself.* It says, *Widow Makers MC, New Mexico* and underneath, *Club President.* I spin around, holding it up in the air. "I can't wear this."

Rebel smirks, pulling his own plain black shirt over his head. He starts speaking somewhere between fully clothed and half-naked, his face hidden by his shirt, but I know he's laughing. I can hear it in his voice. "And why not?"

"Because...because I don't want anything to do with your club. I sure as hell don't want your damn logo plastered all over me while I'm sleeping. I won't willingly give you the free advertising."

Rebel looks around, holding up his hands. "Who you advertising to, sugar? Ain't no one here but you and me. Besides, that's not how we roll, anyway. You see anyone outside our compound walls wearing that patch, you tell me straight up. That's against club policy."

"Cade."

"What?"

"Cade was wearing a hoody with this on the back of it the day I met him. In that alleyway in Seattle."

Rebel starts pulling the drawers open on the nightstand, searching for something. "That was different," he says. "That was an exceptional situation."

"Why?"

"Because he was acting on my behalf. He was there looking for my uncle. And he knew what he was gonna have to do if he found Ryan dead. He was going to have to declare war. Gotta be wearing official colors to do that." He lifts out a large notepad in the bottom drawer, apparently having found what he was looking for. He points it at me, lifting one eyebrow. "Now put on the damn shirt."

"Urgh, fine!" I wrestle the shirt over my head, doing my best not to drop the towel as I do so. It feels like he's won, somehow, which is pathetic. We haven't bet anything. He and I are not at war, not really. But wearing his club shirt makes me feel like I'm his property, and that doesn't feel good. The material comes down to my mid-thigh, plenty long enough to preserve my modesty, but I still feel vulnerable all the same.

Rebel's looking mighty pleased with himself when I turn around. "Do not look at me like that," I tell him.

"Like what?"

"Like you want to fucking eat me."

"And what if I do?"

"Just...*stop!*" I throw my wet towel at him, aiming for his smug, smug face. He catches it out of the air and tosses it onto the ground by the door.

"You're not helping matters," he says, his head tilted to one side. "You're really sexy when you're angry."

I lift up my right hand and flip him off. "There. You think *that's* sexy?"

"Yeah. I do actually." He smiles even wider. I think he's going to come for me, then. I imagine how it would play out: him prowling forward, sharp eyes pinning me to the spot. Him reaching up underneath the T-shirt he's given me to wear. His fingers searching for the most sensitive of places between my legs. My hands pushing him away, but my body craving more. This is fucked.

This. Is. Fucked.

Rebel rubs his hand over his jaw, lifting one eyebrow at me. It appears my imagination is misguided; he doesn't come for me after all. He turns around and starts tacking pieces of paper that he tears from the notepad onto the wall. God knows where he found the tacks. And god knows why I'm feeling slightly disappointed.

"What are you doing?"

"Something to occupy my mind while I problem solve. You're welcome to help." He pulls a sharpie out of his back pocket and begins to write. I stand there, mouth open, watching him as he scrawls what essentially equates to hieroglyphs on the papers he's pinned to the wall.

$$\psi(x) \geq \sum_{x^{1-\epsilon} \leq p \leq x} \log p \geq \sum_{x^{1-\epsilon} \leq p \leq x} (1-\epsilon)\log x = (1-\epsilon)(\pi(x) + O(x^{1-\epsilon}))\log x.$$

I angle my head, hoping that a different perspective will give what he's written some meaning. It's pointless, though. The mathematic equation—I'm smart enough to know that's what it is, at least—makes absolutely no sense. "What is that?" I ask.

"This," Rebel says, tapping his pen on the paper, "is a proof sketch for the prime number theorem, using big O notation. I'm gonna use this to try and solve Legendre's Conjecture."

"How long will that take?"

Rebel, shirtless, absolutely covered in tattoos...Rebel, the leader of a motorcycle club, the man who refuses to let me go home to my family, shrugs. "I don't know. Been working on it since I left college. I could prove the conjecture tomorrow. I might never prove it."

"You've been working on this for *years*?"

He gives me a broad, reckless kind of smile. The kind of smile that makes women's insides twist. "Only eight. My old professor's been working on it for over fifty." Turning around again, he starts scribbling at the paper, leaving a wake of marks and symbols behind him that are liable to give me a headache just looking at them. I'm beginning to feel really rather foolish. He's obviously way smarter than I gave him credit for. Way smarter than me, and I accused him of never even finishing high school.

Oh god. He definitely *did* finish high school because he was just talking about finishing *college* eight years ago. I feel rather triumphant when I realize this gives me insight into a little tidbit about himself that he wouldn't share with me earlier. I sit down on the edge of the bed, his bed, clutching one of his pillows to my chest like a shield. "Twenty-nine."

Rebel glances over his shoulder at me, a bemused expression on his face. "Twenty-nine is *not* the correct answer." He carries on scribbling, the muscles in his forearm, his tricep and bicep, across his shoulder blades and down his back all shifting beautifully underneath his skin. "It's not forty-two, either. Might have worked in *Hitchhikers* but this is slightly more complicated."

"Your *age*," I say. "You're twenty-nine. You finished college eight years ago, which means you're twenty-nine."

He doesn't seem even remotely fazed that I've worked this out.

"Am I?"

"Yes."

"And what if I went on a gap year to Europe with an ex-girlfriend in between high school and college? What if I couldn't figure out what I wanted to major in and switched out courses halfway through?"

"Did you do either of those things?"

"Nope." I can hear him grinning, even though he doesn't turn to look at me. He doesn't take his eyes off the paper in front of him and the ever-increasing spider web of mathematical figures. "Hand me that whiskey?" he asks, holding out his hand behind him. I pass him the bottle, wondering how alcohol is possibly the answer right now.

"Seems to me coffee would be more appropriate. I don't think you're gonna solve a super old math problem if you're wasted."

"Solving this problem isn't the point. Solving my DEA/Maria Rosa problem is the point. I just have get my brain working. And since you won't have sex with me, this is the next best thing."

I can't help but laugh. "You think you use your brain when you're having sex?"

Rebel's pen freezes on the paper. He turns, then, towering over me, my face level with his belt buckle. It's as though I can literally feel the heat rolling off his body. He's intimidating and over-whelming, his presence a powerful force to be reckoned with. "Oh, Sophia. I use my brain. Every time I sleep with a woman, I'm using my head to figure out what she likes. How she likes it. What I can do to have her screaming my name until her throat's raw." He takes a step closer, his perfect fucking abs pretty much filling my eye line. He knows how he looks. He knows how perfect *all* of him is. "I'm also thinking up ways for my partner in crime to make *me* happy, too. How she can defer to me, hand herself over to me, let me use her body for my own pleasure." Gently brushing a wet strand of my hair from my face, Rebel makes a low humming sound. It sends shivers through me, making me feel shame for the first time in my life. I shouldn't be reacting this way to him. I just told myself I wasn't stupid enough to fall for my captor, and yet right now...

It's so fitting that he just referred to his sexual conquests as his partners in crime; I get the feeling sex with Rebel really would be criminal. "If the guys you've been sleeping with haven't been using every single part of their bodies when they're fucking you, Sophia, including their heads, then they haven't been doing it right." He takes a drink from the whiskey bottle, and then he offers it to me. "Is Matthew the boyfriend not a very good lover, Soph?"

"That is *seriously* none of your business."

"What you mean to say is, you're a virgin."

I feel like my face is on fire. "I am *not* a virgin!"

Rebel's expression hardens a little, almost imperceptibly, but I catch it. "Didn't Hector check you?"

"Yes, he did. And he wanted me gone, so he told Raphael I was a virgin. He said he couldn't afford the attention I'd bring with me." I shiver at the memory of Hector's fingers inside me. That disgusting look on his face. Suddenly, I feel very sick. I snatch the bottle from him and drink. I drink deep, lighting up from the inside out as the explosive alcohol tears through me. Surprisingly, the burn dulls down after the first few mouthfuls. Rebel folds his arms across his chest, watching me swallow once, twice, three more times. I let my eyes drift a little, catching brief flashes of the ink that marks his skin. A skull sits over his ribcage, crowned in thorns, flocked by birds. A banner runs through the design, and on it, the text: *Forgive Me Father, For I Have Sinned.* Two full sleeves, bursting with color, scroll down his arms. The designs are filled with dragons and water lilies, Japanese designs mostly. The lines of them are harsh and dark, but they're beautiful. On his chest, more birds—two swallows perching on top of the handles of two crossed guns, their barrels pointed downward. In the center of the design, a heart, bright red and bleeding. *Live For Something* runs along the top of the ink. *Or Die For Nothing* is written in cursive underneath. As he lifts his left arm, leaning against the wall, I see something else that catches my attention: Arabic script tracing up the inside of his bicep, leading toward his heart.

"You getting a good look there, sugar?" Rebel asks. Amusement colors his tone, to the point where I feel like kicking myself for being busted checking him out. And I was checking him out. I've seen Matt naked a thousand times, but I've never felt this intrigued by his body. Not even the first time we had sex. Our bodies just came together without any fireworks, whereas right now I feel like it's the fourth of July inside my head and I haven't even touched this guy. I resent that he can produce such a reaction from me. It makes me feel weak.

"Just looking for the prison tattoos," I snap.

"Haven't been to prison. Sorry to disappoint. Been arrested enough times, but they've never been able to pin anything bad enough on me to warrant jail time."

"Until now."

"Yeah, well. Maybe so." He doesn't seem to like me pointing that out. His shoulders are tense when he returns his attention back to his unsolvable mathematical squiggles. I drink more whiskey, trying not to feel anything. Not panic or terror or hope. Or the faint glimmer of interest I seem to be showing in this man, who I should fear with every bone in my body.

Now that I have the opportunity to look properly without him mocking me, I check out the ink on his back. I anticipate it to be the Widow Makers' patch, but yet again I'm surprised. The ink Rebel has tattooed into his back has absolutely nothing to do with the Widow Makers, as far as I can tell. It's a depiction of the Virgin Mary, hands clasped in prayer, head bowed low. She's not what I would have expected from a man like Rebel. She's beautiful.

And she's weeping.

REBEL

Unsurprisingly, I don't solve Legendre's Conjecture. I make zero headway on it, in fact, just like I always do. It serves its purpose, though. It's around two in the morning by the time the solution to my Maria Rosa problem reveals itself to me. Sophia sat and watched television for a couple of hours, drinking the whiskey I offered to her every once in a while, half pretending to watch the TV, half hiding the fact that she was actually watching *me*. Eventually she passed out at eleven thirty on my bed—a lesser man would have considered that an invitation and crawled up there with her—but I kept on working, feeling like I was on the brink of some conclusion and that at any moment it would come to me. And then it did.

I need to kill Maria Rosa.

Of all the crazy, half-baked conclusions ever dreamed up by a guy with a head full of whiskey, this is potentially the very worst of them all. But even once we've cleared this mess up with the DEA, the crazy bitch is still gonna be pissed at me. The only permanent solution I can think of that will keep the club safe and prevent any more civilian deaths is that Maria Rosa must die.

When I wake up in the morning, it's the first thing I'm thinking: *Maria Rosa must die.* Couple that with the fact that I have a raging case of morning glory and a fuzzy head, and things are not shaping up well.

"Oh my god. What the hell?" Sophia's shocked voice really just finishes the whole thing off. I grab the sheet around my waist, making sure she's not exclaiming at my raging hard on. She's not. She's sitting up on the other bed, hair crazy and sticking up at all angles, staring at the wall. When I ran out of space on the paper last night, I just started writing directly onto the wall. Seemed like a good idea at the time.

"I hope you didn't leave a credit card at the front desk," she says, rubbing her head with her hand.

"Alex owes me more than a wall," I inform her. *Bastard owes me his life.* I climb out of bed and hit the bathroom, cupping my seriously painful erection in my hand, not caring if she sees now. Pissing is pretty much impossible. I give up after about four minutes and find her waiting on the other side of the bathroom door, like she's been standing out there, listening.

She looks guilty, but only for a moment. Even with her hair standing up like she shoved her fingers in a power outlet and her skin smelling of stale whiskey, the girl is fucking hot. Can't be denied. She pouts at me, placing her hands on her hips. "I could have run," she says.

"Excuse me?"

"I could have run. You left me alone in here with the door unlocked, and I could have run."

"How d'you know the door isn't locked?"

"Because I just opened it," she tells me.

"Huh." She didn't run. I don't really know what to make of that. I haven't exactly been the best kidnapper in the history of kidnappers; it would totally have served my ass right if she'd done a runner. "Should I be thanking you right now?"

"No. I'm just too hung over to even try it. You need to move the hell out of the way." She shoves past me, elbowing her way into the small bathroom. From there, she pushes me out and locks the door behind her. My ears are greeted by the familiar sounds of someone who's drunk too much the night before, throwing up as though their lives depended on it.

Neither of us are feeling particularly chatty on the remaining leg of the journey to Ebony Briars, the estate where I grew up. We stop for food once and a few more bathroom breaks so Sophia can rid herself of the remaining Lagavulin in her system. Aside from that, my foot is glued to the gas pedal, and the pedal's glued to the motherfucking floor.

Five miles outside Grove Hill, Clark County, I pull over the Hummer and jump out of the driver's seat into the dirt, my skin already itching with the need to fucking leave. Soph watches with curiosity as I pull the bag from the backseat, throw it on the hood and start undressing on the side of the road. "What the hell are you doing?" She leans through the open driver's door, frowning at me. I'm down to my boxers by this point, standing on the side of the road, feet bare, boots thrown into the foot well. I scowl, yanking out a white button-down shirt from the bag, shaking it out. "I'm maintaining the illusion that my father's only son isn't a complete fucking reprobate."

Sophia watches as I slide the shirt on, covering my tattoos, covering who I am, and all for the sake of peace. It's always been this way. Ever since I was born. I may not have had ink all over my body back then, and I may not have worn clothes my father would consider *common*, but I've always adjusted the person I am on the inside. Truth be told, that's far more complicated than throwing on a suit and covering the way I look. I've never been able to truly master the skill of not being me. Not being a disappointment. Hence all the arguing and the shouting, and the years of silence in between.

I catch Soph staring at me, her face half drawn into shadow as the light fades. "What?"

"Nothing," she says, shrugging. "I just...I don't know. I guess you seem too strong willed to be the guy getting changed on the side of the road is all."

I give her a grim smile, flashing my teeth. "If my father thought for a second that I was involved in any form of criminal activity, he'd be the one to hand my ass over to the police. His precious career is far more important to him than his son's freedom. Believe me, it's in my interests, *the club's* interests, for him to think I'm an blue-collar businessman."

"So that's what I should say? If he asks me anything?"

Poor Soph. She really has no clue how this is gonna work. There's an excellent reason why I haven't spent the past two days coaching her about how she's to tell people we met. Who we are to one another. Why I've brought her along in the first place. "I wouldn't worry about that, sugar. He's not gonna ask you any questions."

She looks confused, her eyebrows arching upwards. "Won't he want you to introduce him to me or something?"

I pull on my suit pants, laughing bitterly. "No. No, he won't give a fuck who you are, I'm afraid."

The monstrous old colonial building looms out of the dusk like a ghost ship. My grandfather told me once my mother loved the place because it looked exactly the way it did when it was built in eighteen fifty-three, a constant of Clark Country history that would never change. It's a beautiful old house. Shame I can't look at the place and see anything other than the brutal childhood I spent here.

Sophia sits forward in her seat as we make our way down the long, lit driveway. Lightning bugs flicker everywhere, small darts of glowing orange rising drunkenly from the gardens on either side of us as we approach.

"Well, this is pretty much the last thing I was expecting," she breathes, her gaze drinking in the grand columns and the prestigious, eight-foot-high entranceway. "You grew up here?"

"I grew up here," I confirm. The words grind out between my clenched teeth.

"Incredible."

In the distance, I can make out Cade's family home, lit up like a bonfire against the darkening horizon. Nowhere near as ostentatious as Ebony Briar, the Preston's property is still vast and completely over the top. I'm pretty fucking certain the only reason I never tried to murder my old man as a teenager was because I could escape there whenever his back was turned.

The front door is already opening as I park the car outside the house. Carl, who must be in his late fifties now, is my father's longest-serving employee. Twenty-one years. The guy deserves a medal just for surviving this long. He sidles out of the house, barely opening the door, and jogs down the steps to meet us.

The first thing he does when I'm out of the car is pull me into a bear hug. "You've arrived in the middle of dinner, you crazy son of a bitch," he says, smiling. Holding me at arm's length, he shakes his head, as though I'm different somehow. As though he's trying to marry up some mental image of a past, younger me with this older, more life-worn me. It may have only been four years, and I may not look all that different in my polished Italian leather shoes and my sickeningly expensive tailored suit, but Carl is the kind of guy to see people. Really see them. I wonder, when he looks into my eyes, if he can see the souls of all the people I've killed since we last met.

"So good to see you, Jay. So very good to see you." He grips hold of my shoulders, squeezing tightly. The light's still on inside the car; Carl sees Sophia still sitting in the passenger seat, looking really fucking uncomfortable, and his whole face lights up. "Who is this?" He hurries to open her door—good job, since I haven't had the chance to unlock it from the inside yet. He holds his hand out to her and helps her out of the car, shooting disapproving daggers at me as he does so. "Seems your manners have abandoned you since you left Alabama, boy."

My manners aren't the only things that have abandoned me since I left the south. I left my moral compass on the side of the road somewhere along the way, too. "I know," I tell him. "I'm just the worst."

Carl rubs Soph's hand in between his, the old bugger clearly rejoicing in the fact that I've finally brought a woman home with me. "What's your name, darlin'? I wait for young master Jamie to introduce me and I'll die of old age, seems."

Soph's eyes flicker to mine—the name's obviously stumped her. This will be the first time she's heard anyone call me Jamie. The first time I've heard anyone call me that name in a long time. Only Cade is privy to that information, and he knows better than to call me that. Ever.

She also looks smug, as though she knew someone was going to want to know her name at some point during this visit. "I'm Sophia," she says. "Sophia Letitia Marne." She doesn't realize how weird it is to give someone her full name like that. She's still trying to reinforce it in her head, so it must seem smart. For me, the guy who knows she's *still* lying about who she is, it's a pretty obvious tell.

"I'm Carl. A pleasure to meet you, sweet girl." He kisses the back of her hand, still giving me disapproving glances. "You come on inside now. I'll come back out and gather your bags in a moment, once you're settled."

I give Carl a hearty slap on the back. I've missed him badly. He grins at me, leading Soph up the stairs and into the house. I wait a beat, taking a second to gather myself. I never thought I'd be back here. Never thought I'd be climbing these steps again. And the fact that Soph's here? Yeah, the fact that I'm heading inside with a girl I technically bought as my sex slave at auction isn't helping how surreal the whole situation is, either.

The inside of the house... Scratch that. The inside of the *mansion* is just as grand and austere as the outside. Carl leads me by the hand inside the marble floored foyer, and my breath catches in my throat. Two huge, imposing staircases sweep around, rising up to the second floor, just like out of a Jane Austen book. Likewise, the cut crystal chandelier hanging from the ceiling is beautiful. It spills warm, honeyed light over everything. The heavy gilt-framed paintings on the walls. The plush maroon-colored rugs that dot the polished floor. The Grecian vases, filled with wild flowers, which sit on top of every available surface. Every single item of furniture, from the wing-backed chairs to the perfectly placed buffet dressers, looks old. Old, but beautifully taken care of.

Rebel's behind me, his hand in the small of my back. "Perhaps we could save the penny tour 'til later? We're both kind of tired right now, Carl."

"Of course. It's a really long drive from New York. You both must be dead on your feet," Carl says.

I squirrel away yet another scrap of information that I might need later. Rebel's father and his employees think he calls New York home. They probably think he's some big city hot shot, living it up in some high-rise penthouse apartment or something, when the ironic truth is that he lives in a secluded cabin in the middle of the desert. About as far from New York as you can get, really.

I still can't get over the name. Jamie. He didn't look surprised when Carl called him that—like he was expecting it to happen and couldn't care less. I think I know him better than that now, though. He's secretive. Every small fragment of information I know about him is hard won. And he still never told me how old he was. I have to be close with my guess of twenty-nine, though. He certainly doesn't look much older than that.

Carl squeezes my hand again, smiling warmly. "Well, all right then. I'll go and move that beast of a car before your daddy sees it, Jay. Your room is still where it's always been, son." He slips back outside, pulling the door closed behind him, leaving *Jay* and me behind. I curve an eyebrow at him, waiting for him to speak.

"Louis James Aubertin the third," he says, his mouth pulling down at the corners. "My grandfather refused to call me Louis, though—hated my father—so he called me Jamie. Or Jay." He reaches out absently, touching his fingertips to the petals of a bunch of flowers sitting on a small pedestal at the base of the stairs. "It kind of stuck," he says. "My father refused to call me Louis anyway. Said I wasn't strong enough to carry the name."

I give him a small smile, not sure how I'm supposed to react. "Louis James Aubertin the third. Doesn't exactly roll off the tongue, does it? I prefer Jamie." I don't know why I say this. It's not my job to make him feel better. I owe him nothing, but...I don't know. It's so hard to explain. Every single hour I spend with him leads me away from hating him, and feeling...what? God, it's too complicated to even try and put a name on it.

"Thank you," he says, his eyes resting on me. They seem less hard. Less fierce, somehow. "I prefer Rebel, though."

"Why Rebel?"

A small crease forms in between his brows. He stares at the flowers, stroking his fingers over their delicate petals, being so, so gentle. "Jamie was before. Jamie was an honorable man. Rebel..." He looks at me, wearing a small, almost sad smile. "Rebel does what he has to. Come on. We need to make ourselves scarce."

"Why?"

"Because the very worst thing you can do to my father, besides be *me*, is interrupt him during dinner. Better we see him tomorrow than disturb him while he's shoving food into his fucking face." Rebel holds out his hand. Such a strange thing to do. It's as though being here, around Carl and his impeccable manners, has changed him slightly. I take his hand, feeling conflicted. This situation is bizarre, to say the least. I don't remember the last time I felt this confused. A part of me wants to go back on my word and tell anyone who will listen that I'm here against my will. But another part of me is beginning to...is beginning to *trust* the man now guiding me up the wide staircase, toward god knows what.

He hasn't hurt me.

He hasn't lied to me as far as I can tell.

He hasn't abused me in any way, aside from being incomprehensibly annoying when the mood takes him.

For the time being, and for the sake of my sanity, I'm choosing to believe that he's still an honorable man. That after all of this is over and we've driven back to New Mexico, he *will* let me go.

Rebel doesn't let go of my hand when we reach the top of the stairs. He walks briskly down a long, well-lit hallway that branches off to the left, hurrying, as though he doesn't want to linger. I realize why when I look at the walls.

Photos of him. Everywhere.

Photos of him in a football uniform. Much younger. Unsmiling. Photos of him in a graduation gown, cap perfectly straight on his head. Still unsmiling. Another picture, with another diploma in his hand—I see the name of the institute printed on the mounting of the picture, and my head starts spinning. "Massachusetts Institute of

Technology? *You went to MIT?*"

"I did," he says. He doesn't stop walking. The muscles in his jaw are jumping like crazy.

"Wow." We pass more and more photos. Images of Rebel, sans his tattoos, shirtless and holding trophies, swimming trophies, still unsmiling. As we near the end of the hallway, the photos on the wall change dramatically. They're not of Rebel the over-achiever. Rebel the sporting hero. They're of Rebel the *soldier*. I try to slow, to look properly, but he tightens his grip, walking faster. "Will you—will you just *stop!*" I rip my hand free, backing up a few paces so I can look at the walls properly.

For some reason, my heart is hammering in my chest as I take it all in. The first picture of him is in a dress uniform, buttons shining brightly, hat placed firmly on his head. Unlike in his other pictures, there's a quiet sense of pride lurking in those cool blue eyes of his. He looks so young. Just a baby. "How old are you here?" I whisper.

Rebel sighs, rubbing the back of his neck with one hand. His expression is tired as he joins me in front of the photograph, his chest so close to my back I can feel the heat of him radiating into me. "Fifteen," he says. "I went to a military school."

"And how was that?"

He laughs a hard laugh. "Like winning a five-year-long trip to motherfucking Disneyland. The fun just never ended. They called me Duke. Seems, when your name ends in 'the third', you can't really avoid that shit." His voice is full of sarcasm, but I can hear something else in there, too. Hatred. He hated it there. So why, then, does he look so proud in his uniform? I want to ask, but we're not there yet. He probably wouldn't tell me.

I walk along, looking at the rest of the pictures. In each shot, he gets older, bigger, taller, stronger. That hardness develops in his eyes—not cruelty, but strength. A challenge to the outside world. The photos show images of him with a bunch of other men, always surrounded by other guys in uniform. Even frozen this way, trapped in some millisecond of the past, it's clear they respected him.

Gravitated toward him. There's always an arm thrown over his shoulder. Someone grinning or laughing, pleased to be the guy standing next to him. I see Cade in nearly every single shot, no matter what the landscape in the background—from what must be training grounds at his school to actual army bases. And then...then to the desert.

"You didn't just go to military school," I say. "You signed up afterwards. You were deployed." I turn to look at him. He doesn't return my gaze—just stands there, staring at the history of his life, framed and hung on the walls of his father's home. "Where did they send you?" I whisper.

"Afghanistan." The word comes out flat. Devoid of any and all emotion. Rebel blinks, a visible shiver running through his body.

"And?" I need to know more. I never would have guessed he was in the army, but it makes sense. His club might as well be a military organization, after all. A military organization at war.

"And what? There is nothing else. I did two tours. I left and I didn't look back. The end." He takes hold of my hand again, this time not pulling me quite so determinedly, but drawing me away all the same.

"There is no *the end* on something like that, Rebel. The story's never over. It becomes a part of you. There's just what comes after."

He narrows his eyes at me, opening the final door in the corridor—a room all on its own, separated from the others. "You seem to know a lot about ex-servicemen, Miss Sophia Letitia Marne. Did a couple of tours yourself, did you?"

"No. I was studying psychology before all of...*this*. We studied the way people's perspectives on the world change when they were thrown into tense, dangerous situations and expected to fight. To put the welfare of others in front of their own."

"Are you about to start spouting PTSD shit at me right now? Because if you are, you can fucking forget it." He storms into the room beyond, leaving me standing out in the hallway. Seems I touched a raw nerve. I follow after him, taking in the huge room—

clearly his old bedroom—one detail at a time. The place is flooded with the bloody red light of the sunset, pouring in through two walls worth of massive windows. In the center of the room, a huge bed, already made up, dominates the space. There's not much else in here. A small bookshelf, filled with books. A walk-in closet at the far end of the room. A couple of shelves—

My eyes freeze on the shelves. Three of them, one on top of the other, a foot in between, and evenly spaced on them sit about fifteen snow globes. They're just like the one I found on the desk back in Rebel's cabin. I walk straight to them, my eyes skating over each one—Detroit, New York, London, Paris, Vancouver, Calgary, Switzerland, Wyoming. Niagara. Places mostly within the states, but from cities all over the world, too.

"What's this?" I ask.

"My mother collected them from all the places she went to. I should have boxed them up years ago." Rebel turns his back on the shelves, crossing the room to look out of the window. Huge, ancient trees choked with Kudzu fill the view beyond.

"Chicago. You have one from Chicago back at your cabin. Was that one of hers as well?"

Rebel remains facing out of the window, but I see his shoulders tense. "Yes." Doesn't seem like he's planning on divulging the significance of that particular snow globe—why Chicago was important enough to take with him, while the others remained behind. I don't ask, either. His mood is spiraling. First me prying into the army stuff, and now this... If I get too nosy, he's liable to shut down altogether. My motives for learning as much about him as possible have morphed over the past few days. Originally, I wanted to know so I could tell the police when I eventually manage to report all of this to them. But now, I'm just interested. There's a drive inside me to break the code that is this complicated, hard-headed, kind-of-annoying man. After the photos on the wall and the obvious love Carl has for him, I'm beginning to see beyond his tattoos and the razor blade-sharp look he carries in his eyes. Could he actually be a good guy?

I need to change the subject. "Did you manage to figure out what you're going to do about the shooting?" I ask. Probably not the best topic of conversation to put him in a better mood, but I'm curious. I woke up a couple of times after I passed out last night, already feeling shitty from the whiskey, and he was still scribbling away, trying to find a resolution to his problem. After that, I had nightmares that I was trapped inside that Trader Joe's, scurrying from aisle to aisle, while men wearing Widow Makers cuts stalked me, calling out my name.

"No," Rebel says, sighing. "Not a good solution, anyway. Not an *easy* one."

Nothing about any of this seems easy to me. I hold my tongue, though. "So what are we doing right now? We're just going to wait here until your father summons us?"

"Yep."

"Perfect. Because we just love being cooped up in small, enclosed spaces with each other." I press my fingers into my forehead, sighing heavily.

"I actually don't mind being cooped up with you, sugar."

I think he's being sarcastic again, but when I look up at him, he's not pulling faces. He looks...he looks like he means it. "You've got to be kidding me. I do nothing but complain. How the hell can you find that enjoyable to be around?"

"You're feisty. I like that. And you give me shit. Not many people feel like they can do that."

"Probably because they're tied to a chair, scared for their lives, right?"

He gives that hard laugh again, though this time he actually smiles. Walking away from the window, he sits on the edge of his bed, tipping his head back, sighing. I watch the muscles in his throat work as he speaks. "Guess that all depends on the circumstances of the situation, doesn't it?"

"So...you have hurt people?"

169

"Many people, sugar. Many, *many* people." He looks at me, his eyes zeroing in on me, unblinking. It's like he's daring me to react. Daring me to look away. Daring me to do or say *something*.

"Was there a good reason for everything you've done?"

"*I* think there was a good reason. But would a judge? Or God? Or *you?*" He closes his eyes, and I feel it then, stronger than before. I want to do something crazy. I want to comfort him. I want to help him. I want to be closer to him. How is this possible? I feel like crying at my own stupidity. "I don't know," he whispers. "Maybe."

I turn away from him, picking up a snow globe with shaky fingers. I suddenly don't feel safe anymore, and it isn't because of Rebel. It's because of *me*. Because there must be something seriously wrong with me.

"Are you afraid of heights?" I didn't hear him standing up. He's right behind me, so close his breath brushes against the skin of my neck as he speaks. I break out in goosebumps, unable to control the reaction—half fear, half something far more worrying.

Matt. You're in love with Matt. This man is a self-professed dangerous criminal. You are not *attracted to him. You're just* not. "I'm all right with heights. Why do you ask?" Just like my hands, my voice shakes.

"Do you trust me enough to climb out of this window with me?"

I spin around, giving him a look I hope expresses how mad I think he is for even asking that. "Why are we climbing out of the window?"

He's standing so close, looming over me. I'm not used to being around someone so tall. The Romera women are tall themselves, it's in our genes; I've frequently found myself standing a clear few inches above most men. This is an unusual feeling. Anxious, but weirdly—and this is the strangest part—*safe*.

"We're climbing out of the window because I want to show you something. What do you think?" Rebel's eyes are crystal clear, so sharp and assertive. He stares at me, studying each aspect of my face individually—forehead, nose, cheekbones, jaw, mouth—before he looks up into *my* eyes. "You trust me not to let you fall to your death?" he asks, that odd, deep line forming in his cheek as he fights a smile.

"I suppose I'm no use to you if I'm dead," I reply.

"Exactly." He seems pleased that I've risen to this challenge. Returning to the window he was standing at a moment ago, he unlatches it and opens out the two panes, sticking his head out and looking up. Smirking, he glances back at me and nods. "All right, you have to follow me up. I'll grab you and lift you." With that, he pulls himself out of the window using the lintel to hold his body weight and then he's gone.

"Oh, boy." I stand by the window, flinching when I see how far the drop to the ground is.

"Just climb up onto the ledge. I'll pull you up the rest of the way."

I look up and Rebel's already on the roof, half his body visible as he leans out into space, reaching down for me. "Is this going to be worth it?" I ask, wondering if I can back the hell out now without looking weak.

Rebel waggles his eyebrows at me, laughing. "I can *make* it worth your while."

"Shut up." I clamber up onto the windowsill, the soles of my Chucks not feeling all that grippy all of a sudden. I look for the handhold he must have used to pull himself up and I see it, a small length of iron piping protruding out of the house. Probably designed to drain excess water if it rains. I lean up, my heart in my throat, reaching for it. Adrenalin spears through me as I grab hold of it, and then my body is twisting, moving, leaning out into space.

I'd wanted to do it myself, to pull myself up without his help, but that's not what happens. Instead, I'm left dangling out in the void, one hand holding onto the length of iron pipe, the other scrambling, reaching, grabbing upward for...nothing. There's nothing there.

"Jesus Christ, Soph! What the fuck are you doing?" There's grunting above me, and then hands, big and strong, locking around the wrist above my head. My shoulder sings out in pain as I'm wrenched up, knees, hips, ribcage scraping against the edge of the roof as I'm pulled over it. And then I'm safe. The whole thing takes place in the space of five or six seconds, but it feels as though it took a hell of a lot longer. I lie on my back, chest rising and falling at speed, barely able to think coherently through the roaring sound of my own blood in my ears.

"Well, that was fucking stupid." Rebel slumps back next to me, lying on his back, too. Both our feet are hanging over the edge of the roof, our chests hitching up and down like crazy. "When I say I'm gonna lift you up, you're supposed to fucking let me," he pants.

"I'm sorry. I just…"

"Don't trust me."

I let my head loll to the side so I'm looking at his profile. His lips are parted. There's an angry crease to his forehead, his eyes narrowed up at the sky. "I'm sorry," I say. And I mean it. He wouldn't have let me fall, and I was being my usual stubborn self. I could have fallen and died. Rebel sits up, the back of his suit jacket wrinkled now. He lets out a deep breath, shaking his head.

"This…this is all fucking ridiculous, isn't it?"

"What do you mean?"

"I mean you. My uncle getting murdered. My entire club moments away from being fucking arrested for a crime they actually didn't commit. Now *that's* fucking irony, right there." He gets to his feet, carefully standing on the slightly pitched roof, and then he turns to me and holds out his hand.

"I'm sorry, too, Soph. I should never have put you in this position." I somehow don't think he's referring to the fact that we're now trapped up on a rooftop and I have no clue how I'm going to get down. I take his hand, allowing him to help me to my feet. "My uncle would wanna kick my fucking ass right now," he says. "This would not impress him at all." He points between us, scowling. "Come on. Be careful where you're putting your feet. I was eighteen the last time I came up here, and I weighed a hell of a lot less."

I gingerly follow after him, watching where he steps so I can place my feet exactly where he places his. The roof is pitched on either side as we climb upward, but once we reach the ridge, the apex where the two sides meet, I see that there's a flattened section to the right, a cutout of the roof panel. About twelve feet long and eight feet deep, the platform has been leveled for no apparent reason that I can tell. No air conditioning unit. No access back in through the roof. It's just *there*. Rebel drops down onto the platform, reaching up and turning to face me. By the look on his face, it hits him at the same time as it hits me that what he's doing—lifting me down beside him, like a lover would—is weird.

I tuck my hair behind my ears, clearing my throat. "What is this place? What is it for?"

Rebel places his hands on my shoulders and physically pivots me, pointing me in the direction of the sunset. I feel like I can't breathe; the sight is the most formidable, beautiful thing I've ever seen. It looks like the sky is on fire. "I'm guessing it's for this," he says, removing his hands from my shoulders. He sinks down, sitting Indian style on the platform. I do the same, not daring to take my eyes off the horizon, not wanting to miss a single second of it.

"But how did people get out here? They can't have been climbing out of windows. I think we've just proven that that's not safe."

Rebel snorts, clearly not over the fact that I didn't just do as I was told and let him lift me. "There used to be a small doorway." He jerks his head back, motioning behind him.

"But not anymore?" The wall behind us is smooth brick and render, no sign of a door in sight.

"Louis had it bricked up the day I was born. My mother apparently liked to come up here."

"Oh."

"Yeah. *Oh.*"

We sit in silence for a while, until there's nothing left of the sun, sunken beyond the distant fields, leaving behind nothing but the tiniest glimmer of light. "You can go. In the morning, I'll drive you back to town," Rebel says abruptly.

"What? You're just gonna let me go?"

"Yeah. Why not? Everything else is fucked. Hector and Raphael would somehow find a way out of being arrested, anyway. They'd bribe the fucking judge. Or just kill him, too. Your testimony would be pointless. And after all those people in that grocery store..." Rebel leans back on his elbows, crossing his feet at his ankles. "After all of those random people being killed because of me, I don't particularly want your family's blood on my hands, too. You should just catch the Greyhound back to Seattle."

I can't believe what I'm hearing. Somehow, it feels like this might be a trick. But then again, Rebel looks absolutely devastated. Why would he bother putting on such a convincing act, if he's only just going to tell me he was joking in the morning? That doesn't strike me as his style. Doesn't strike me as the sort of head game he would play. "Do you mean it?"

"Sure. At least I'll have a vaguely clear conscience where you're concerned, if the five-o do come calling."

I hug my knees up to my chin, tears stinging at my eyes. I can't look at him. If I do, I'm gonna start sobbing and I won't be able to stop. He's letting me go. Tomorrow, I get to go home to my family. "Thank you, Jamie."

He bristles at that, doesn't like it, I can tell, but I'm thinking of what he said in the hallway before. *Jamie was an honorable man.* And him dropping this whole thing, setting me free like he said he would, is an honorable thing to do. Far more Jamie than Rebel.

We sit in silence for a long time, until we start to see stars peeking through the deepening blue of the night sky. "I used to bring all of my dates up here to see the stars," he eventually says, pointing up at them. "Never brought anyone to see the sunset, though. That was always something I did alone."

I can imagine him as a young teenager, scrambling up here, sitting and watching for hours. I can imagine him bringing girls up here, too. Making out with them under the blanket of stars. Doing much worse, no doubt. "I'm sure they were all incredibly beautiful.

And incredibly grateful," I say, allowing a hint of sarcasm to pepper my tone.

"*So* grateful," he answers. "Can't blame them, really. Being invited up here was like winning a golden ticket to the chocolate factory." His face is deadpan, though I can tell he's joking. "As far as them all being beautiful, you're probably right there. But you, sugar...just so you know, you'd win the title for Most Beautiful Woman Louis James Aubertin Ever Snuck Up Onto The Roof hands down."

I can feel two hot patches flaming on my cheeks—embarrassment. I hug my knees tighter to me, not sure if I want to look at him or not. "Why do you do that?"

"Do what?"

"Flirt with me. Say stuff like that. Proposition me."

Rebel laughs, unashamed and, unlike me, unembarrassed. "Because I told you, sugar. I like you. I'd definitely try and fuck you if we'd have met under any other circumstances."

"You do that a lot? Try and fuck a lot of girls?"

"No. Never. Just the ones I think might make pliable bedmates."

"What's that supposed to mean? You think I'd be pliable?"

"I think, despite how resilient you are when you need to be, you'd let the right person have control over you if the situation presented itself."

"You mean that I'd let someone dominate me?"

"And you'd fucking love it."

"And you assume that you're the right person?"

"Oh, sugar. I'm the *only* person who could dominate you."

I want to laugh. I want to laugh right in his face, but the arrogance that's normally present when he says something sexual isn't there right now. He's being totally and utterly serious.

"I don't understand you," I whisper.

"Are you supposed to?" he whispers back.

"It's how my brain works. I'm studying psychology so I can understand everyone I ever meet. I like knowing how people work. What makes them tick. But you..."

Rebel smiles. It's a kick-you-in-the-guts kind of smile that I can imagine a boy from Alabama wearing. Slowly, he reaches over and pulls at the lace on my shoe. "Don't bother trying to get inside my head, sugar. It's a dark and fucking scary place. Even I don't want to be here most of the time. You change your mind about the sex, though, and we can talk."

REBEL

I climb my way back down through my bedroom window, and this time Soph trusts me. She lowers her legs down and I catch her around the waist, pulling her back in through the window. I can feel her heart slamming against my chest as I hold her a second too long against me. God, I'm a glutton for the worst kind of punishment. She's not for me. She's for some fuckhead back in Seattle called Matt, apparently.

I intend on keeping my word; I'll drive her to the Greyhound stop in the morning, and she and I will go our separate ways. It'll be for the best. The more I thought about it, the shittier I felt about forcing her to do something she didn't want to do. I've never been that person. Losing Ryan has been seriously fucking shitty, but I can't darken my soul even more by stooping to these new lows.

It's gonna be dark enough after I've finished with Maria Rosa.

I let Soph sleep in the bed, and I fall asleep in the reading chair beside the window, listening to the cicadas' song. When I wake up, the day is barely breaking, and my father is standing over me in his dressing gown.

"So," he says.

"So?"

"You're not even man enough to sleep in the same bed as the woman you're fuckin'? All the girls paradin' around this place in their underwear when you were a teenager, I thought you were at least about to get your dick hard, boy."

And so it begins.

"Good to see you, too, Sir."

"Don't you fucking *Sir* me." My father's always loved his food, but he's a skinny, slight man. I think it makes him self-conscious—that's why he's always eating and eating and eating, never sated. He'd be the fattest man in Alabama if he had his way. Instead, he looks like a half-starved chicken that's had it neck wrung. His wattle wobbles from side to side as he looms over me, shaking. "You've got no respect," he tells me, as though I may not have already known this fact. "You say Sir the same way other people say *dysentery.*"

That one makes me laugh. Comparing himself to shit? Nothing could be more appropriate. Louis doesn't take kindly to my amusement. "Who is she then? Some fucking waitress you picked up? Don't tell me you've got her fucking pregnant, you little shit. If you think bringing her here, showing off your new prize pony will mean I'm gonna give you any money, you are sadly mistaken."

I rocket to my feet, blowing hard down my nose. "You told me to come here, Louis. And what makes you think I need your money? I have *never* asked you for money."

"Well, I just assumed that since you've clearly been spending your meager wage on whores..." He gestures to Soph. I see that she's awake now, propped up on one elbow in the bed, eyes wide. "You probably aren't flush with cash."

I swing for him. In all the years I've been verbally, mentally and physically abused by my father, I've taken everything he's given to me. The dynamic has always been pretty straightforward between us: I killed my mother. My father hates me for it. I deserve anything he throws at me.

But not this time. Not this. Not Sophia.

My fist connects with his jaw. A bright pain lances up my arm, a pain so familiar and welcome that I almost laugh. My father staggers back, clutching his hand to his face. He doesn't fall down—I haven't hit him that hard. Just hard enough to teach him some fucking manners.

A cold rage boils behind his eyes when he looks up at me. "Finally," he says. "Some fucking backbone. After all these years. Good to see the army at least taught you how to hit right."

"No, Sir. It wasn't the army that taught me that. It was *you*." I'm panting, ready to launch at him again, but Sophia sits up in the bed properly now, gathering the sheets around her. Louis casts a very brief glance over her, disgust written all over his face. "It won't last," he says. He's not addressing Soph, though. He's addressing me. "She's a leeching opportunist at best. At worst, a whore with no morals. Mark my words. She'll represent nothing more than an empty bank account and semen-stained sheets by the end of the month. I know a gold-digging cunt when I see one."

That word sounds so much worse when my father says it—he spits it out like a bullet, aiming to hurt, maim, kill. I let my expression fall completely flat. "You need to leave. *Right now*."

"Get your ass down to breakfast. You expect to show up here and not join your family in a civilized manner?" He looks at Sophia again, a sneer of contempt twisting his face. "And if you insist on bringing *her* down, make sure she dresses appropriately. This isn't a fucking cat house."

He turns, striding out of the bedroom, his dressing gown flaring out behind him like a goddamn cape. A sharp, bitter fury rises up in me. It hits me with the force of a freight train. I lunge forward, ready to go after the fucker, but then Sophia's in front of me, her hands pressed up against my chest.

"Don't. Don't do it. He's expecting it."

I let out a small laugh, running both hands back through my hair and pulling. "No, he's not. He has his precious fucking campaign fundraiser tonight. The last thing he wants is a fucking busted-up face while he's asking his fucking Ivy League fucking pig friends for a backhander." I grind out each word, knowing it's true. My father did not expect me to lash out at him. Never in a million years. I saw the look of shock on his face, right before my fist connected with his jaw. I guess he's gotten used to my tolerance of his abuse, but his attitude toward Soph? He can give me shit all day long, but he can*not* call her a whore.

"Well, he's already going to have a split lip and a bruised jaw. That's enough, isn't it?"

I grit my teeth together, trying to bring my heart rate down. "No. It's not."

"Look at me." Soph's hands are on me again, this time on my face. She forces me to look down at her. She's touching me. She's trying to calm me down. That in itself is confusing. My father just insulted her and she doesn't seem fazed. She didn't protest. She didn't tell him she had no choice but to come here—that the very last thing she cares about is his goddamn money.

"Don't give him the satisfaction," she says softly. "If you lose it, he'll know he still has power over you."

I look down at her, adrenalin still firing through my veins, and I do something stupid. It's not even a case of me making a conscious decision to act; it just happens. I fold my arms around her, and I kiss her. She goes still in my arms, hands still flush against my face, as I press my lips against hers. She tastes sweet, just like sugar. Just like the name I've been using to try and irritate her the past few days. I couldn't have known how appropriate it was until now. She's holding her breath as I persuade her mouth open, and then dip my tongue inside. Instead of lowering my heart rate, my pulse is now jackhammering, my blood roaring around my body.

I've wanted to do this since the moment I saw her in the fucked-up prom dress outside Julio's place. I've wanted to run my hands over her body, claim her as my own. I can feel her warring in her head—torn between letting me kiss her, kissing me back, or pushing me away. In the end, she does all three.

She remains still a moment more, but then she begins to sink into me, her back curving, bringing her body closer, her chest pressing up against mine. I bury my hands in her hair, my breath and hers combining, quickening, as she responds to me. Her tongue slips into my mouth, tasting *me* now. Her hands move from my face, sliding back around my neck, until she's wrapping her arms around me, pulling me tighter.

A fire seems to spark within her. She's doesn't even pretend to hold back. She's panting, every inch of her pressed up against me as she kisses me back, like her life depends on it. I was hard the second my lips hit hers, but my cock is straining in my pants now, throbbing painfully, demanding I go further. There's no way she doesn't know how badly I want her; my rock hard erection's pressing up against her, between her legs, making demands all on its own.

I run my hands down her body, until I reach the warm, smooth, bare flesh of her thighs. She shivers against me, making a small, strangled sound at the back of her throat. She wants this. She wants *me*. I slowly move my right hand upward, skimming the material of the large, plain T-shirt she wore to bed, until I reach the curve of her breast. I pause there, waiting for her to move away. To tell me to stop. But she doesn't. I palm her in my hand, groaning when I feel the weight and fullness of her. I can feel her nipple through the thin material of the shirt, stiffening, responding to me.

I want to lick at that nipple. I want to bite and tease and suck at it. I'm lifting the shirt when Sophia finally reacts. She tears her mouth away from mine, a wild look in her eye. Her hand whips out and slaps me across the face. A loud buzzing sound rings in my ear, deafeningly loud for a second before fading away. I touch my fingers to my jaw, stretching it out.

Sophia just stands there, her nipples still peaked and showing through the T-shirt, her lips pouting and bruised from our kiss. "Don't you...don't you fucking dare do that again," she whispers. Her whole body is shaking.

"Why? Because you're so in love with Matthew?" I ask. I can still feel my pulse in every part of my body—some places more painfully than others. Her gaze flickers down to my very obvious hard-on, her eyes shining a little too brightly. I don't even try and hide it.

"You have no right to...I'm not your *possession*, Rebel."

"I know that."

"Then why the hell did you just treat me like I was? Something that belonged to you that you could just take?"

I lean back against the wall, my breathing slowly returning to normal. I don't respond right away. I let it sink in—what just happened. I let her replay it a couple of times in her head, so she can see how ridiculous she's being. "I didn't take anything from you, sugar. I offered it to you. *And you picked up what I was putting down.*"

"I did not!"

I laugh, undoing the top button of the shirt I'm still wearing from yesterday. "Don't they teach you anything about body language in your psychology class, sugar? I know quite a bit about body language." I push off from the wall, standing directly in front of her. Touching my fingers to the delicate, beautifully soft skin around her eyes, I say, "For instance, when someone's attracted to you, their pupils dilate." I can barely see her iris for the deep well of black in her eyes right now. I trace my fingers up the side of her ribcage, fighting back a wicked smile. "Their breathing becomes erratic. Plus, women's nipples tend to tighten. That's an obvious one, given I can see your perfect nipples through the shirt you're wearing."

"Screw you," Soph whispers, stepping away from me. She turns her back, hiding herself from me.

"I'm betting you'd be ready for that, too," I tell her. I move myself behind her, pressing my body up against her back. She goes utterly still again, seemingly at war with herself. Slowly, I reach up, brushing her hair away from her neck, and then I stoop down to graze my lips ever so slightly against her soft, sweet-smelling skin. "I'm betting if I were to slide my hand down the front of your panties..." I slide my hand around her, starting from her hip, heading in that direction. "I'm betting if I were to do that, I'd find that you were more than ready for me to screw you." My fingertips are almost doing it, almost sliding down the front of her lacy white underwear when she slaps my hand away.

"Stop. Please, Rebel. Just stop. I can't...I don't know what the hell is happening right now."

I tuck my hands into my pockets, smiling softly at her. "I can tell you what's happening right now, what's been happening for days, but you won't want to hear it."

"You don't know me, Rebel." She says the words harshly, and I can hear the fear in her voice. She's afraid, because she already knows what I'm about to say, and she knows that it's true.

"You're attracted to me, despite everything, and I'm attracted to you. We want each other, Sophia. It's the reason why you're so terrified right now. And it's part of the reason why I'm letting you go."

I leave the room, my head too messed up to even be in the same room with her right now. She doesn't say anything as I go. She doesn't deny that what I'm saying is true.

When I come across Leah, she's in the foyer refreshing the flowers, dressed from head to toe in the ridiculous maid's uniform Louis insists all his female employees wear. She looks up, sees me charging down the stairs, and grins.

"Well if it ain't the devil himself," she says. She throws her arms around my neck and hugs me. *Thank fuck my hard-on's vanished* is all I'm thinking as I hug her back.

"Looking good, little Leah." She does look good. When I first brought her here, her bruises had healed and she was clean of the heroin she'd been addicted to, but she was still thin. Still quiet and withdrawn. Still broken on the inside. Now, with her hair a natural blonde and tied back in a neat ponytail, the dark purple circles under her eyes gone without a trace, she looks healthy. More importantly, she's smiling. "Feelin' good, big brother," she replies, elbowing me in the ribs. I'm not her brother, of course. It's just what she's called me ever since Cade and I dragged her out of that dingy brothel in Seattle.

"You staying long?"

"Not if I can fucking help it."

She pouts, hitting me lightly on the arm with the dying flowers she's holding. "Carl says you got a girl here. Is that true?"

"For the moment. She's not staying, though. I'll be driving her back into town as soon as I've suffered through breakfast."

"You pissed her off already?"

"Of course I have," I say, laughing. I start walking, heading in the direction of the dining room, and Leah walks along with me. I throw an arm over her shoulder, making her chuckle.

"Why don't you go up there and apologize. Maybe she'll stay."

"I doubt that very much."

"Fucker."

"Bitch."

My father's eyes nearly bulge straight out of his head when he sees me walking in with my arm around one of his employees. "What the hell are you doing now? For fuck's sake, James." He tosses his napkin on the table, releasing an exasperated breath, and I see that Soph was right; he does have a split lip. I let Leah go, giving her an apologetic smile. She returns it, and then hurries out of the room. I'll need to talk business with her later, when the old man has his back turned.

"You realize I should fire her for that," Louis says. "She has to know her place around here. I must have been out of my mind the day I agreed to hire her."

"Must have been," I agree, slumping down in the chair at the opposite end of the table, the furthest from him that I can possibly sit. "I doubt it could have been a moment of compassion."

"Why should I show compassion to someone who can't administrate their lives effectively? It's not my fault the girl involved herself with an abusive partner." This is the story I told him—that she was hiding from an ex who liked to raise his fists to her. The reality of her situation—that she was kidnapped, hooked on drugs and used for sex by countless men against her will? That would have made good ol' Louis squeamish. In his eyes, that, too, would somehow have been Leah's fault. "I take it you won't be staying long?" he says.

"I'll leave in the morning, once your little soiree is over. I think that's just about my limit as far as maintaining this charade goes."

Louis grunts, forking some scrambled egg into his mouth. "In all honesty, I'm surprised you even came. Having not heard from you in four years, I'd assumed my invitation would go unanswered. It's not as though you've felt the need to uphold any of your other familial responsibilities."

I don't bite. He wants to bait me into an argument, but I won't give him the satisfaction. He narrows his eyes, looking first at me and then out of the window. "You know, I'm not as clueless to the life you lead as you might think, son. I know you're not living in New York."

"So you've been checking up on me. How fatherly."

"I need to know what you've been involving yourself in, James. With this re-election on the horizon, the last thing I need are skeletons being dragged out of the closet. No surprises." He points his knife at me, his expression severe. "Tell me right now and I can bury all of your dirty secrets in time, before my competitors have the chance to discover them."

"All right, Pop. Let's see. Where shall we start? Oh, yeah. Okay, since we're talking about burying things, you should know I have a plot of land out in the desert where I've been hiding the bodies of all the people my friends and I have been murdering. Rapists. Drug dealers. Child abusers. You name it, we got it. There are even some crooked government officials out there, actually. Men after your own heart." I lift the glass of orange juice in front of me, toasting him before taking a sip. He just stares at me, his knife and fork gripped in his hands like he's about ready to launch them across the table at me.

"Oh, and then there's the fact that I grow copious amounts of marijuana. I don't deal in the hard stuff, but a bit of pot here and there never started any wars. And I'm sure you'd like to know about the guns? The Glocks and the Berettas and the semi-automatics that I supply to gangs all over America?"

Louis throws down his cutlery, his face turning redder and redder by the second. "You're a spoiled little shit, James. You think of no one but yourself. If you can't respect me enough to tell me the fucking truth, then you should get the hell out of my sight. Now."

I smile so wide my face hurts. Patting my mouth with a napkin, I stand and give him a small bow. "My pleasure, Sir. Honest to god, sincerely, it would be my pleasure."

SOPHIA

I don't know who I am anymore. I never thought I'd become this person.

In August 1973, two armed gunmen forced their way inside a bank in Stockholm and proceeded to take hostages—three women and a man. They held them for five whole days inside that bank, one hundred and thirty-one hours, and during that time, something happened to the hostages. The gunmen got inside their heads. They altered their perspectives so dramatically that when the police finally stormed the building and set them free, the hostages thought their captors were there to protect them *from* the police. One of the women ended up becoming engaged to one of the bank robbers. One of the other women set up a charity canvassing for donations to cover the robbers' legal fees. And so Stockholm's Syndrome was given a name.

When people are kidnapped, they develop defense mechanisms in order to survive. Weirdly, falling in love with a captor, forming an emotional bond with them, improves your chances of remaining alive. The cops even encourage people to do it in certain circumstances. Better your heart keeps beating in your chest, oxygen keeps filling your lungs, and you end up with an unhealthy, undeniable connection to your abuser, than simply being dead, right?

A sick realization dawns on me: that *could* have happened to me if I'd ended up stuck with Raphael as my master.

But that's not what's happened here. I know how the syndrome works. I've studied it. Written a paper on it. The human mind develops these mechanisms when it fears extinction. Only if the stakes are so dramatically high that the psyche will do *anything* to survive. And I haven't felt like that with Rebel. All along, he's been promising me he's going to let me go. And he's never made an advance on me until now. And even then, he didn't exactly force himself on me. I wasn't pinned down and raped.

God, am I just making excuses for him? I don't even know anymore.

All I do know is that when he kissed me, I was shocked and momentarily overwhelmed, but I didn't want to stop him. I only pushed him away at the end because things were moving very quickly and I knew...I knew if I let it go any further, I would have been the one pushing it even further. I sit on the edge of the bed I just slept in, staring down at my hands, not seeing them properly. Wishing I could call my dad and ask him what the hell I should do.

I *know* what I should do, though. Rebel said he was going to let me go this morning, and that's exactly what I should do. I should go, run for the hills and not stop running until I'm safe in my father's arms.

A knock at the door startles me from my panic. Rebel wouldn't knock—this is his room—so it can't be him. That leaves a number of possibilities, none of them particularly good. Carl? Rebel's dad? I don't answer. Whoever it is, I don't want to see them.

I don't get much choice, though. The door cracks open and a short blonde woman, maybe late twenties, stands in the doorway, a broad smile on her face. "Oh, Carl was right. You are beautiful."

I suddenly feel like I'm back at Hector's odd little house and

Ramona's come to prep me all over again. I swallow down the urge to scream at her to leave. She takes two small steps into the room, wringing her hands in front of her, a nervous look on her face. "I'm sorry to bother you. I just...Rebel told me you'd had a slight *misunderstanding*."

"You could call it that." I laugh coldly, not sure how to take this woman. She seems anxious.

"I'm Leah," she says. "Forgive me if this is wildly inappropriate, but...are you like me? Has he brought you here to hide you?"

"Hide me?"

"Y'know. Is someone looking for you? Did they..." She struggles with her words, wrestling each one out like it causes her physical pain. "Were you *taken*?"

My eyes go wide. So, this woman was kidnapped too? My heart lurches, my stomach rolling, like I'm about to be violently ill. After all that crap I was just telling myself about him, Rebel *is* a monster. I'm not the first. He's taken women before. How utterly, terribly stupid of me to have fallen for his bullshit. "You didn't come here of your own volition?" I ask, my voice breaking a little. She doesn't look like she's been abused but that doesn't mean anything. Sick men who like to hurt women find innovative ways of not getting caught. They also don't like being faced with the ugliness of their sins. Keep their women's faces pretty, while underneath their clothes, they're black and blue.

The woman, Leah, jerks back, confusion on her face. "What? No. I was glad when he brought me here. Grateful. He kept me safe. Hector's men fed me a cocktail of drugs each morning, kept me compliant. They did...they did terrible things." Her face turns white, losing the healthy pink glow she had in her cheeks a moment a go. "Rebel came to the house where they were keeping me. He was looking for someone, a girl called Laura. I was the only girl in the house at the time and I fit her description so he demanded to see me. I could hear them arguing downstairs—they didn't want to let him come up, but in the end they did.

"He saw me, saw that I wasn't his friend, but he paid them twenty thousand dollars to take me, anyway. He gave it to them in cash right then and there, picked me up, naked and covered in my own vomit, and he carried me out of that place. He took me back to his place. Not in New York. The *other* place. Said I could stay and work for him, as a cook or I could train to do tattoos, but Hector found out where I was and came for me. He was pissed that his men had let Rebel buy me, and he wanted me back. Cade and Shay hid me 'til he was gone, but by then it was pretty clear I couldn't stay after all. So he brought me down here. I have a boyfriend now, Sam. He's sweet to me. I don't drink. I don't smoke. I make enough money working here to pay my bills and put food in my fridge. I have a good life. I'd never have had that if he hadn't done what he did."

"So...Rebel didn't take you?"

"No, of course not. He saved me. He brought a few others through here after I was settled in. Found them work in the surrounding towns. Figured out new identities for them. Not anymore, though. He sends the girls he buys all over the country—Texas, Florida, Chicago. Doesn't want his father working anything out, I guess. Where is he sending you?" she asks.

"Home," I whisper.

Leah's eyes begin to fill with tears. "Then you're one of the lucky ones," she says. "Go easy on him, okay? I know he's a jerk and you just wanna wring his neck sometimes, but his heart is in the right place. He does shitty things sometimes, but he does his best, okay?"

Leah gives me a watery smile, and then she turns around and walks out the door, tucking her hands into the small pockets of her servant's uniform. I sit there in silence, unsure how I'm supposed to react to what just happened. Completely at a loss as to how I'm meant to process the fact that Rebel is some kind of fucking hero to the woman who just walked out of here.

A cold, hard awareness dawns on me as I think this. Technically, since Rebel did buy me and whisk me away from Raphael's evil attentions, he did the same thing for *me* as he did for *her*.

Should that make him my hero, too?

Fuck.

I shower in Rebel's en suite and get changed into a clean pair of jeans and a thin maroon sweater, and all the while I'm thinking about what Leah told me. Hunger motivates me to go adventuring, but it takes me a solid hour to pluck up the courage to step foot outside of Rebel's room. I'm hoping to find Carl—he was incredibly friendly last night when we arrived—but the first person I run into is Louis James Aubertin the second, pacing down the hallway with a gold capped cane in his hand. From his steady gait, he carries it for aesthetic purposes and not because he needs it. His salt-and-pepper hair has been slicked back, displaying his high forehead and prominent cheekbones. The cheekbones are the only thing he's passed onto his son. I can see nothing else of Rebel in him. His eyes are almost black, unlike Rebel's piercing blue coloring.

"I see you *do* close your thighs long enough to climb out of bed, then?" he says when he sees me. I want to grab that cane off him and smack him around the head with it. His eyes follow mine, glancing down at the cane in his hand. He smiles. "Oh, child, I wouldn't even bother planning on stealing this. It's not real gold, you see. All of my household's valuables are locked away until my event this evening. I shall know who has taken any of my property should it go missing."

"What makes you think I'm planning on stealing anything that belongs to you, Louis?"

His eyes flicker, his mouth pulling down at the corners. He looks away from me, over the handrail of the banister that sweeps down the staircase below us. "Most guests address me as Governor Aubertin when they're residing in my household."

"Oh! Pardon me." I press my hand over my chest, feigning embarrassment. "You've accused me of being a whore and a thief more times than I can count this morning. I didn't think I was a *guest*."

Sharp, narrowed eyes fix on me. Louis pulls back his shoulders, standing with his chest proud. "You are a rude young lady."

"And you're a rude, obnoxious, likely impotent old man," I reply. "I like this game. Wanna keep playing?"

He doesn't appreciate me answering back to him. He doesn't appreciate it one bit. If this were a cartoon, there'd be steam coming out of his ears right now. He steps forward and lifts his cane, pressing the capped end of it directly in between my breasts, right up against my sternum. "If James thinks he's bringing you to my gathering this evening, he has another thing coming. I may need him to play happy families for the sake of appearances, but I do not need you propositioning my peers."

"Oh, believe me, I won't be attending," I snap. "You couldn't pay me to stick around here."

A smug, unbearable smile spreads across Louis' face. "I knew it. I told him as much this morning."

"Told who what?" I growl.

"I told my son not to expect you to stick around much longer than a week. I thought maybe I'd underestimated your staying power, that maybe you'd make it to *two* weeks, but it seems I was wrong. You aren't even going to last a day. How delicious." He taps his cane against the top of my arm—*condescending motherfucker*—and then he saunters down the stairs, leaving me with my mouth hanging open. I have to stop myself from running after him and pushing his ass down the remaining steps.

I've never felt so angry in all my life. It's all-consuming, the rage pumping around my body with each solid thump of my heart. I hate it. I hate how it makes me feel so unlike myself. Jogging down the stairs, swearing profusely under my breath, I manage to find the kitchen. And I also find Rebel. He's sitting at a kitchen island, apparently washed and changed already, and he's eating a sandwich.

He tenses when he sees me, placing his food down on his plate and leaning back on his stool. "I was wondering how long it would take for you to come find me."

"I haven't come to find you. I've come to find food."

He pushes his plate toward me across the marble kitchen island, his expression flat. "Help yourself, sugar."

He probably thinks I won't eat the other half of his sandwich, but the guy is mistaken. I accept the food, taking a decent bite out of it— cheese and pickle—before convincing myself to look him in the eye. "So I met Leah."

"Oh, you did, did you?"

"Did you tell her to come talk to me?"

"Why would I do that?"

"To convince me you're a good guy."

A dangerous smile spreads across his face. "But I'm *not* a good guy."

"Then why would you go around buying up women who've been kidnapped? Finding them safe houses? Creating new lives for them?" I have to know. My mind won't rest until I can figure out how this side of him fits in with the rest. Rebel scowls, angling his shoulders away from me so he's facing the large bay window—it overlooks what seems to be an extensive herb garden.

"Someone really has been talking, huh?" he says. "I helped those girls because human beings aren't meant to be bought and sold as property. I was looking for someone. A friend. I've had to go to these places—the darkest fucking places on earth—trying to find her. And I've been in a position to help the girls that I've found in the process. *Sue me.*"

"Why didn't you tell me?"

He cocks his head to one side, looking at me out of the corner of his eye. "Because you wouldn't have believed me."

"I might have."

He doesn't say anything. I keep eating the other half of his sandwich, thinking really hard. Wondering if what I'm considering is actually madness on my part. It probably is, but after him telling me he's going to let me go, my conversation with Leah and the subsequent encounter I had with his father, I'm beginning to...oh god, I'm beginning to trust him.

"Are you going to take me to the bus station now?" I ask.

He pulls in a deep breath, bracing himself against the cool marble. "I guess so."

And so he does. Carl brings the Humvee around, and Rebel drives me back into the closest town of Grove Hill. He's silent as he drives. Outside a café called The Sweet Spot, he pulls over and kills the engine. My heart skips a beat when he reaches into his pocket and pulls out a roll of money.

"This will get you back to Seattle. You'll be able to grab some more clothes and...shampoo or whatever. They sell tickets inside the café. If you hurry, you'll be able to make the midday bus."

I look at him, at the money he's holding out in his hand. I close my eyes, allowing my head to fall back against the headrest. "Take me back," I whisper.

"What?"

"Take me back."

Rebel, always so self-assured and cocky, now looks confused. My heart beats faster, suddenly scared. What the hell am I doing? My parents flash into my head—how sick with worry they must be. Sloane, too. This isn't just madness. It's *cruel*. If I stay here and I don't contact them, even just to let them know I'm alive, then what kind of person does that make me? Rebel leans over and presses the money into my hand. "You need to go," he says. His eyes flash, as though he can read what's going on inside my head. I close my hand around the money.

"It's okay. I'll stay. I'm not happy about it but I'll do it. I'll testify."

Rebel pulls his lower lip into his mouth. If I'm not mistaken, he does it to hide the fact that he's trying not to smile. I can see it in his eyes, though. "This is because you wanna sleep with me, isn't it?"

"No!"

"Admit it. You're only lying to yourself." He's not even trying to hide his smirk now. I thump him as hard as I can on the top of his arm.

"I'm doing it because you were right back at your cabin. You said you were going to show me you weren't the man I thought you were, and you have. But mostly, I decided to stay because your father said he didn't want me at his party tonight. And you may have noticed, but your father is a massive asshole. Displeasing him will make me one incredibly happy woman."

Rebel tips his head back and laughs. I've never heard it before, his laughter. It sends electricity snapping through my torso, my arms, my legs, my head; it's the most amazing sound. "The Widow Makers say I'm stone-cold, Soph. They say I'm made of ice. When the rest of the club meets you, I'm pretty sure they're gonna say you're made of fire."

My chest tightens at the thought of meeting the other Widow Makers. God knows how I'm going to handle that. Not well, probably. Rebel twists in his seat, staring at me. His hand lifts from the steering wheel, reaching slowly toward me. My breath catches in my throat as he grazes his fingertips along the line of my jaw, his eyes fixed firmly on the point where his skin meets mine. "I swear nothing will happen to you, sugar. I'll keep you safe, no matter what. Your family, too. From here on out, from now until you decide you need to leave, you're under the Widow Makers' protection, and so are they."

REBEL

Soph stares anxiously at the payphone, chewing on her lip. She shouldn't be worried, but she is. "Just do it. Pick up the phone and make the call," I tell her.

Panic flashes in her eyes. "I'm going to break down. I won't be able to stop myself," she whispers.

"It'll be okay. They'll know you're alive and well. They'll stop worrying that you might be dead, and that's the most important thing, right?"

"Yeah, I...I guess you're right." She moves mechanically as she picks up the handset and dials slowly, her finger hovering over each key before she presses it. The dial tone changes, turning into a ringing that I can hear standing two feet away. I watch her face as she waits for someone to pick up.

She grimaces when the ringing ceases and a male voice says, "*Dr. Alan Romera.*" Her whole body locks up. I turn around, gritting my teeth together. I'm a selfish son of a bitch and I know it. Sophia lets out a strangled sob, gripping hold of the side of the payphone. Her eyes look wild when she turns to me.

"Hello?" the guy says on the other end of the phone. A fat tear rolls down Soph's cheek. She swallows hard and then shakes her head, slamming down the receiver.

"Was that your dad?

She nods.

"Why?" I ask. "Why didn't you speak to him?"

"I can't. I just can't," she whispers. Her voice sounds thick with emotion. "If I do, if I speak to him, then I won't be able to stop. I'll ask him to come get me. I won't be strong enough to stay."

She starts crying even harder, and no matter how badly I might want her to think I'm a completely heartless jackass, I can't do it anymore. I move quickly, before I can change my mind, shifting to stand behind her. I wrap my arms around her body, her back to my chest, and I hold her as she cries. She doesn't push me away.

I can feel her heart *bang, bang, bang*ing, its tempo fast and furious around her body. My hands are over her stomach, one resting on her hip, but I can feel her pulse beating there even, through the material of her shirt. She slumps back against me so that I'm the only thing keeping her upright. I'm not sure that it's even a conscious decision to lean on me, but I hold onto her. I hold onto her tight.

Standing on the street in Grove Hill, the place where Cade and I grew up, I'm assaulted by a million different memories as I hold this broken, crying girl in my arms. She turns and buries her face in my chest, and my head is racing. I heard her father say his name on the phone: *Dr. Alan Romera.* I know this about her now, at least. Her last name isn't Marne. It has to be Romera, like her father. A father who's going out of his head, wondering where his daughter is.

"I'm sorry," I whisper. "I'm really so sorry that you've had to do this for me. Can you forgive me?"

Sophia holds her arms in, close to her sides, not wrapping them around me. She's still leaning on me, though, still needing me in some small way. "Maybe." She gasps the word in between breaths. "I don't know. Maybe."

I should ask her again if she's sure she wants to do this, but I don't because I'm a bastard and I need her. I feel like shit. Hollowed-out, evil shit. But still, a brief spark of hope flickers inside me, too. She didn't say no. She said *maybe*, and maybe will have to be good enough for me right now.

It shouldn't matter. I've done some incredibly shitty things in the past to get what I want, and I haven't batted an eyelid. But this, with her...it's different. She's not from the awful, damned world that I call home. She was on her way to being something better than I'll ever be, before my family and my shit messed everything up for her. So now here she is, neck deep in this crap, danger surrounding her at every turn. It's within my power to send her back to safety, but I'm choosing not to. So yeah, it feels like I really *need* her forgiveness. And I'm sure as hell going to make sure I earn it.

SOPHIA

I couldn't bring myself to phone Matt. The hesitation wasn't the same as my reluctance to call my father. I'd just been afraid of falling to pieces as soon as I heard Dad's voice, knowing that still I wasn't going to see him for a while. But with Matt…

I just didn't want to hear his voice, period.

I know Rebel plays a big part in that. As much as I don't want him to, he's somehow worked his way into my head. And, if I'm being honest, into my heart, too. He's secretive and closed off from the world, but he's also in pain. I see it all the time, in the moments when he doesn't think I'm looking. His arrogance fades, leaving him staring off into space with a deep sadness shadowed in his eyes. I have no idea why, but I want to know. I feel the desperate need to find out.

Rebel takes me back to Ebony Briar, the mansion even statelier on approach during daylight hours. He drives the Hummer around the back to a vast garage where he stows the truck, and then he takes my hand, guiding me behind the low-lying building, out toward the trees at the very edge of the property.

I'm grateful. I feel exhausted, and facing Louis Aubertin again before it's absolutely necessary is something that I can do without. I guess Rebel feels the same way. After walking another ten minutes once we've crossed the boundaries of the Aubertin property into the next, Rebel leads me to a twisted live oak, monstrous in size and jacketed in Kudzu. We both sit down. He takes off his suit jacket and rolls up his shirtsleeves, exposing the brightly colored ink on his skin.

"You shouldn't hide who you are from him, y'know," I say. "You should show up to this event tonight in jeans and a T-shirt and fuck whatever he thinks."

Rebel lies back in the grass, his hands underneath his head. "Don't think I don't want to," he says. "But if he's mad at me, he'll punish everyone around him as well as me for it. Leah'll lose her job. And having her here is very, *very* convenient for me."

"Is she...have you—?"

He laughs softly, shaking his head. "She spies on Louis for me. Passes along information. The old man's about as dirty as they come. On the receiving end of so many bribes it's a wonder how he keeps everything straight in his head. Information like that can be really valuable. Who wants what bill to go through. Who's involved in insider trading. Who's addicted to drugs. Who's cheating on their wives. My father has a stream of information coming in at all times, and Leah gathers it all for me."

"And you use that information to get what you want."

"When I can."

"And when you can't?"

Rebel casts a steely look in my direction. "Then I use other means."

I lie back into the long grass, lacing my hands over my chest. "Is this who you thought you'd end up being when you graduated from MIT?"

"No. I thought I was going to be a solider forever. But things don't always work out the way you intend them to, do they?"

"Obviously not."

Neither of us says anything else. The wind blows through the tree branches overhead, rustling leaves and grass and teasing strands of my hair up into the air. I fall asleep. When I wake up, Rebel's sitting with his back against the tree, watching me.

"Getting involved with me is the worst thing you can possibly do," he says.

The words are gripping me by the throat—*I don't want to get involved with you. I'm not going to*—but the intensity of his expression prevents me from lying. Even to myself. "I get the feeling it might somehow be too late now," I say, my voice quiet. "Don't...don't you feel that, too?"

He looks away, clenching his hands tightly into fists. "Yeah. Well. I was kind of hoping you were smarter than me."

"From your math problems and the diploma hanging on your father's wall, I don't think I know anyone smarter than you, Jamie."

I don't know why I call him that. His forehead creases into lines of...worry? "You can't call me that outside of this place, Soph. You need to remember that. It's important."

"I'll remember." I sit up, every part of me focused on him. "I won't do it again. Will that make you happy?"

That small crease in his cheek reappears, completing his rueful expression. "Yes, ma'am." He leans forward, his body close to mine, the smell of him filling my head. Carefully, he plucks a blade of dried grass from my hair. "I kissed you before, sugar. You pushed me away. Next time you want that to happen, you're gonna have to make it happen yourself. You understand?"

I look away, tucking my knees up underneath my chin. Hiding from him. He ducks down, searching for my eyes, but I'm a coward. I close them.

"Sophia?"

"What if I'm too scared? What if I want that now, but I'm too afraid of what comes after?" I feel dizzy as I speak, not sure where I'm drawing the courage from.

"Look at me, Soph."

I don't. I can't.

"*Sophia.*" He shifts his body so that his side is pressed up against mine; his warmth makes my head spin. I feel his fingers underneath my jaw, lifting and turning my head so that I'm facing him. I keep my eyes tightly closed, though, still too paralyzed by the fear that I'm losing myself entirely to acknowledge this. To acknowledge *him*.

I might not be able to see him, but I can sense him drawing even closer. My heart stops altogether when I feel the rough stubble of his cheeks grazing against mine as he presses himself against me and whispers in my ear. "The moment you give yourself to me, it won't be because I've bought you. It won't be because you're afraid of me, or because you want something in return. It'll be because you need me. Because you need me inside you. Because you can't stand this torture a second more. *Then*, you won't be afraid of what comes next. You'll be begging for it."

His heat suddenly vanishes, leaving me breathless. With his close proximity making my head spin a moment ago, now that he's moved away I feel abruptly alone. I open my eyes and Rebel has stood up. His eyes are so filled with hunger that I don't know where to look. Holding out his hand to me, he jerks his head in the direction of the house. "Come on, sugar. We have to go get ready for my father's circle jerk of a party."

The dress probably isn't something I would have picked out for myself, but it's still beautiful. Cream, almost white, with lace around the midsection, it falls gracefully to the floor as I pour the silky material over my head. I feel like a different person entirely in this dress. Someone I would be if I went home and finished my degree. Someone I would be if I had a normal life. Someone I would have been if I'd let him put me on that bus.

With my hair swept to one side, pinned in place and curling down over my shoulder, I feel like I belong in some sort of Grecian legend. I have no jewelry, but I don't need it. The single splash of color I'm wearing—bold, bright red lipstick that I found in amongst the toiletries Rebel brought for me—is embellishment enough.

Rebel, in yet another beautifully tailored black suit, is waiting for me at the bottom of the stairs when I come down to meet him. The smile falls from his face as he watches me approach. I think he approves. The guy he's talking to turns and looks over his shoulder, smiling politely as I stop at Rebel's side. "This is Sophia Marne," Rebel says, introducing me to the older man. "Sophia, this is Drew McKinney. He's my father's campaign manager and our family's oldest friend."

I shake Drew's hand, mirroring the frown that develops on his face when he takes a closer look at me. "Why, how strange," he says, his accent by far the most southern I've heard since arriving last night. "I swear I've seen your face before. Are you...do you work in television?" he asks, breaking out into a grin, elbowing me as though he's caught me out in some grand deception.

"No, no," I laugh. "I've just got one of those faces."

"A beautiful face, I'm sure. Either way, it's a pleasure to make your acquaintance, Miss Marne. I hope this young man is remembering his manners around you?"

I hear Rebel's voice in my head—*it'll be because you need me. Because you need me inside you. Because you can't stand this torture a second more*—and I can't help but smile. "I assure you, he's been the perfect gentleman."

"That's mighty good to hear, my girl. Our Jamie's always been a bit of a rebel. I'm reassured to know he can at least treat a beautiful woman the way she deserves to be treated."

Rebel nearly chokes on the flute of champagne he was drinking from. Obviously the rebel reference just hit a little too close to home. "I think I see my father. We should probably go say hello," he says, clearing his throat. "It was a pleasure to see you again, Drew." Pulling me away through the crowd of people who have already arrived and are milling around the foyer and formal reception rooms, Rebel growls under his breath. "This is my worst fucking nightmare."

His mood doesn't improve. As the night progresses and we're forced to make nice with progressively stuffier, drunker, more passive aggressive people, my escort gets ruder and ruder. His final breaking point comes when his father joins us, as a morbidly obese oiler from Texas is praising Rebel in his service to his country.

"Louis, you must be pretty damn proud of this boy of yours. One tour in Afghanistan is one thing, but two? That's damn patriotism right there, if ever I saw it."

"Yes, my son, the war hero," Louis says. To an outsider, it might look like he's agreeing with the Texan's comment, but Rebel hears the sarcasm just as well as I do. He stiffens, his back ramrod straight.

"I only ever turned out to be the man my father intended me to be," he tells the Texan. "I was sent off to military school on my thirteenth birthday. It was natural that I'd want to enlist properly once my education was complete."

"Yes, that's right. And what did you do when you were in the army, James?"

"I was a Marine." He hardens his jaw, lifting his chin, daring his father to say anything about *that*.

"Hoo-rah," the Texan roars, laughing. He's so drunk he's completely missing the antagonism taking place between the other two men. "Marines are the backbone of the US Armed Forces."

"Yes, of course. Though, coming summa cum laude in his class probably should have meant he was the *brainpower* of the US Armed Forces instead of a glorified grunt."

The governor's tone catches the Texan's attention now. "Oh, come on now. Some people don't like taking an officer's promotion without feeling like they earned it. I respect that."

"You're too kind, Mason. But my son's had an easy upbringing. I'm afraid he's all too used to having things handed to him."

Rebel's eyes flash with hatred and he thrusts his drink into his father's chest. Louis automatically catches hold of it, a look of murder in his own eyes. "*Fuck. You*," Rebel grinds out. "I suppose I became a Marine and put myself in danger every single day I was out there just to spite you, then? Is that it?"

Louis raises his eyebrows, his mouth drawing downward in that sour, unimpressed way of his. "You're not calculating enough for that, son. You're just like your mother was—reckless and...and foolish," he says, taking a deep pause in between words. After all that he's said, after all that he warned, he is the one starting trouble at his own event.

Rebel makes a disgusted sound at the back of his throat. "You're pathetic," he tells his father as he pushes past him. I can feel the Texan gawping at us as I hurry after Rebel, pushing through the crowd of men. Their hungry eyes and wolfish smiles feel like they're burning into my skin, making me feel dirty. I catch sight of Rebel heading through a door at the rear of the formal dining room, vanishing from sight as the door closes behind him. He's waiting for me when I follow after him. His hands are on me the second I step through the door.

"Fuck what I said earlier. Fuck waiting for you to make the first move. I can't do it." His lips crash down on mine, his hands tightening on my waist. My breath feels like it's being pulled from my lungs, making me dizzy as I let him walk me backward, pressing up against the wall behind me. I was expecting him to be angry. I was expecting him to need calming down. I was *not* expecting this.

"Rebel, I don't...I'm not sure this is the best—"

He grabs hold of my hair, winding it around his fist and drawing my head back. "Do you want me to stop, sugar? Do you not want me to sink myself inside you?" I can feel just how badly he wants to do that when he presses his hips up against mine, his solid hard on digging into my stomach. He pulls my hair back further, so that my neck is there for his taking. He lowers his mouth halfway to my skin, his eyes never leaving mine. They spark with fury and lust, combining to create something powerful and overwhelming. "Tell me you don't want me to fuck you 'til you're screaming and I'll let you go right now."

A hot shiver travels through me, making my body feel suddenly weak. God, this can't be happening. Here? Now? It doesn't seem right. I look over his shoulder, seeing that we're in an empty corridor, completely and utterly alone.

"Well?" Rebel growls.

"Fine. I do. I do want you," I gasp. Admitting that is the final breaking point. I've crossed a line, a dangerous one, but right now, here in this moment with his body flush against mine and my skin burning up, I can't seem to make myself care. Rebel growls again, the rumble vibrating through me as he descends on me, licking and biting at my neck. My head's pounding, my blood surging through me, filled with adrenalin and endorphins.

His mouth on me feels amazing. His hands roaming all over my body, his powerful arms bracketing me in place against the wall. The pressure of his cock, demanding and hard against me as he grinds his hips upward. All of it feels incredible and wrong and I don't want it to stop.

"Take off your dress," he commands.

"I...I *can't*. Someone might come."

"They won't," he says. His voice is heavy with need, his hands already pulling at the material of my dress. "This is a servant's walkway. Everyone's out on the floor, doing their jobs. No one will come." I don't get any further say in the matter. Rebel rips the dress up over my head, leaving me standing in front of him in nothing but my underwear. He makes a stifled groaning noise as he leans back and takes me in.

"You're fucking perfect. So fucking perfect." Dipping down, he runs his tongue along the swell of my cleavage, his mouth hot on my body. "Do you want me?" he asks, his breathing coming even quicker than before.

I tell the truth, because it's all I can do. "Yes."

"Do you want me to possess you? To make you mine?"

"Yes. Yes, I do." The very prospect has been the one thing I've been afraid of since he took ownership of me from Julio, but now I'm desperate for it. Begging him, just like he said I would underneath that oak tree.

He's upset. He's pissed off and boiling with anger, but that just seems to add to this undeniable attraction I feel coursing through my veins. "How badly do you want to touch me?" he rumbles.

"Really...*really* badly."

"Then undress me." He steps back, tilting his head back, challenging me yet again, not just to allow this to happen but to participate. To prove to myself that I *do* want this. I slide my hands over his chest, up the front of his white dress shirt, and then underneath his black suit jacket. His mouth twitches, either with the beginnings of a smile or with amusement at the way my hands are shaking. He doesn't tease me, though. If anything, the look in his eyes is keen with curiosity, waiting to see just how far I really will go. I pull his suit jacket over his shoulders, my heart slamming erratically as I feel the hard ridges and planes of his muscular back underneath my fingertips. His physique is hard won. Five years at military school, two tours in Afghanistan and the years he's been running the Widow Makers can't have been easy. I'm definitely reaping the rewards of his labor.

His suit jacket hits the floor. I start working on the buttons of his shirt, aware of his eyes burning into my flesh. Another bolt of adrenalin zigzags through me when he leans into my neck again and whispers, "If you don't hurry up, I'm gonna have to take you fully dressed."

My hands move like lightning, ripping at the remaining buttons, then at the material of his shirt. I've been covertly checking him out for days now, trying not to, trying not to get caught at least, but once his shirt is gone now I can't help myself. I drink him in the same way he's been drinking me in, eyes hungry, barely able to look away.

He is perfection. There isn't a spare inch of fat anywhere on him. I run my hands up and over the bird tattoos on his chest, hesitant but determined at the same time. His breath blows hard across my cleavage, making me break out in goose bumps. "I need to feel your tits up against me, Soph. God, they're fucking amazing." He makes quick work of freeing my breasts from my bra; his fingers barely skate over the clasp before he's ripping the straps down my arms and throwing my underwear to the ground. I'm almost naked; only my panties remain. Rebel grinds his body against mine, pushing me even harder into the wall. He dips down, his mouth moving over the skin of my neck, my collarbone, my chest and then my breasts. I gasp as he takes my left nipple into his mouth.

Fire ignites in the pit of my belly, roaring, sending flames in every direction, burning me up from the inside out. "Oh, fuck. Fuck, Rebel, I need you." My head rocks back, my body feeling boneless. Rebel's hands work their way over me, investigating and exploring every last inch of me. His fingers move down, down, down until they're hovering over the lacy material of my panties.

"Are you ready for me, Soph? Am I gonna find you soaking wet and desperate when I play with your pussy?"

No one's ever referred to it that way before. Only certain men can say pussy and own it without it sounding sleazy or plain weird coming out of their mouths. When Rebel says it, the word sends heat and electricity charging in between my legs. "Yes. I'm wet for you," I whisper. "Please, Rebel. *Please.*"

I can feel him getting harder against me, his cock straining at his pants. Rebel lifts one eyebrow, a ruinous smile teasing at his lips. "If you're lying, sugar, you should know...you will be punished."

I have no idea what form of punishment he has in mind but I'm not sure if it's the bad kind or the good kind. Is there such a thing as a good kind? My head says no, but by the way my body reacts, it might just know something I don't. "I'm ready. I want you, Rebel. Please. I can't..." I can't wait much longer. I've never reacted to anyone like this before.

With Matt it's always felt nice, but in the same vein it has felt rote. Like we're going through the motions, having sex every three days because that's an appropriate amount of time between adventures. With Rebel...fuck, with Rebel, I feel like I'm going out of my mind. I don't think any more of Matt. Alexis was the girl who belonged with him. I haven't wanted to admit it, but Alexis is gone. She might as well have died right alongside Rebel's cousin in the alleyway back in Seattle. Now, I'm Sophia, and there's no way she and Matt would have a future together. She belongs to Rebel, the man standing in front of me, looking at me like he's about to screw me into oblivion.

I start fumbling with his belt, determined to get his pants off him. Rebel slips his hand down the front of my panties, and my hands suddenly still. I can't move, can't react, can't breathe. His fingers find my clit right away—no fumbling around, searching. He makes a guttural, animalistic sound at the back of his throat.

"Oh, sugar. You weren't joking, huh?" Sliding his fingers back, he draws his pointer finger and his middle finger through the slick folds of my pussy, and then he brings his hand up to his mouth. I'm paralyzed as he sucks his fingers into his mouth, humming, the vibration of his vocal chords traveling through his chest into mine. "You taste fucking amazing, Soph. I can't fucking take this anymore."

Unfastening his belt and tearing down his pants, Rebel does what I couldn't do the second his fingers touched me between my legs. His cock springs free, swollen and way bigger that I'd anticipated. I'm no prude. I've not exactly had a vast number of lovers, but I've seen a cock before. And Rebel's is way above average. I feel dizzy just looking at it.

Rebel takes himself into his hand and slowly pumps up and down. He hasn't removed his shoes, so his pants remain around his ankles. That would look ridiculous on someone else, but somehow he pulls it off. I can't take my eyes off his hand working up and down his smooth, slicked flesh. "See something you like?" he asks.

I look up at him, not trusting myself to speak. I can only nod my head.

"Take your panties off, Sophia." Complying, I shimmy the small, barely there material down my legs, kicking them off. While I'm losing my underwear, Rebel's still stroking himself; he pauses for a moment to roll a condom down over his hard-on, completing the movement with practiced ease. His eyes scour my body, taking every inch of it in. "Now press your back against the wall again."

I step back, doing as he tells me, my chest heaving. Rebel comes for me, then. There's no more foreplay, no more talking. He moves up against me and places his hands directly under my thighs, lifting me from the ground. My legs wrap instinctively around his waist, tightening when I feel his cock press up against my pussy. God, I want him. I need him so bad. His hands are everywhere, all over my skin, in my hair. He grinds himself upward, rubbing against my sensitive clit. His lips finds mine, and the two of us breathe our need into each others mouths, panting, tongues skating over each other as we kiss.

He takes hold of my jaw lightly in one hand, holding my head in place so that I'm looking at him. "Look me in the eyes, sugar. I wanna see into you," he says.

I can't take it. The intimacy of staring into his eyes as he slides himself up against me is too much to bear. I can't look away, though. I could close my eyes, but there's something in the way he's staring at me, so intense and focused, as though I'm the only thing he sees or cares about in this moment. I already know, deep down in my bones, that being looked at like that by him will be an addiction I won't be able to shake. "You ready to get fucked?" Rebel growls.

"Oh, god. Holy fucking shi—" I cut off when he pushes into me. My mind goes utterly blank. He feels...he feels huge for that first few seconds. Way too big, I feel like I'm going to burst. Rebel freezes, stilling himself, allowing me to get used to the feeling of him inside me. My nipples burn in the best way, my breasts crushed up against his naked chest. It feels amazing. My whole body feels amazing. I feel my pussy tighten around him, reacting to his presence, and Rebel growls.

"Oh, you shouldn't have done that. You *really* shouldn't have done that." There's a dark, sinister look in his eye as he slides himself out of me and then pushes back in again, harder this time. Gripping hold of me in his arms, he starts up a rhythm, slamming himself into me harder and harder each time.

I can barely breathe. I taste blood in my mouth—I've been biting my lip hard enough to break the skin. Rebel's right hand finds its way into my hair again. He jerks my head back, still inside me, still filling me with himself, and bites at my neck. He's not careful about it. I'm definitely gonna be left with a mark. Right now, I could care less, though. I *want* him to mark me. I want him to make me his. I know with a hollow, terrifying certainty that I'm never going to want to be anyone else's ever again.

Rebel's thrusts grow even faster, his fingers digging into my skin. "You want to come, Soph? You wanna come all over my dick?" he groans.

"Yes! *Yes!*"

"Then get ready. I want you to break apart in my arms, okay? I want to be the only fucking thing holding you together. Let go, Soph. I'm right fucking here. I ain't gonna let you go."

If I'd thought he was driving me crazy before, then what he does next completely blows me out of the water. He slides one hand in between our bodies and he begins to stroke my clit in tight circles, sending wave after wave of pleasure racking though my body. He slows everything down, sliding himself out of me with torturous patience and then carefully pushing back inside.

Pinned up against the wall, my legs still wrapped around his waist, I can do nothing but cling onto him and take it. He has me trembling, on the brink of tumbling over the edge in less than a minute. I tighten my hold on him, staring into his eyes again. He's hidden himself from me since the second we met, barely told me anything that I've wanted to know about him, but while he's inside me, while he's connecting with me like this, I can see who he is perfectly. It's like he just said—he wanted to see *into* me. I can see into him, and I feel like I recognize him. Like he's the piece of me that's been missing all this time and I never even knew it. It's a scary, overwhelming realization. He gives me a scandalous smile, and fire races through my veins.

"That's my girl," he pants. "I can feel you tightening around my dick again. You gonna come for me?"

I nod, my eyes shuttering closed. My body feels taut as a bowstring as I feel the first swell of pleasure rushing up through me, building, building, building until I'm screaming out his name.

Rebel puts his hand over my mouth and pulses inside me, gritting his teeth together as he comes, too. "Holy fuck, sugar," he growls. "You're so fucking tight."

His climax overtakes him then, so that he's leaning his forehead against my shoulder, thrusting hard into my body. I hold him to me, wanting him closer, more a part of me, more fused to me as our bodies ignite.

Eventually, our breathing slows. Rebel lifts his head, that reckless smile plastered all over his face. He's always so cocky, always so sharp-eyed and suspicious, but not now. Now, he folds his arms around me and places me carefully on the ground, looking distinctly pleased with himself.

"I think half my father's guests might have heard that," he says softly.

"Is that why you did it, then? To cause another scene? Get back at your father?" That thought makes me feel less than special. If I'm honest, it makes me feel suddenly very vulnerable, very sick. Rebel grazes his fingertips across my collarbone and down over my breasts, still able to make me react to him. "No, sugar. I did that because I've been desperate to ever since I laid eyes on you. I did it because it's all I've been able to think about for fucking days. It was going to happen eventually. You know that as well as I do."

And he's right. He's telling the truth. Reaching down in between my legs, he traces his fingers lightly over my pussy, growling deep and low in his chest. I know I'm wet from him, slick with my own orgasm. He seems to take great pleasure in rubbing his fingers through my wetness, sliding them up inside me, even sliding them further back, circling his finger around my ass, coating me with myself there, too. No one has ever touched me there before. A spark of embarrassment, coupled with excitement charges through me.

"You're mine, now, Soph. For as long as you want to be, you're mine. And I'm yours," he tells me. "That okay with you?"

I feel paralyzed. I know what I want to say, but I can't bring myself to part with the words. I'm not ready to. I don't know why I feel so strongly for him, and that scares the living crap out of me. If I say it, if I tell him yes, it will feel like I'm walking blindly into something I have absolutely no control over.

He grins at me, watching me intently, and I just *know* that he can tell what I'm thinking. He opens his mouth, is about to say something, but the moment is stolen away by a horrified scream, tearing through the house. For a second I think we've been busted, but the scream doesn't come from the hallway. It comes from somewhere beyond, toward what must be the kitchen.

"*Fuck.*" Rebel snatches up our clothes and grabs me, pulling me to one side, into what turns out to be a closet containing a fuse box and a stack of sealed cardboard boxes. We're barely concealed before the door leading to the party opens and people start to pour into the hallway. A second later and we would have been found for sure. Rebel holds out my dress to me, eyes flashing cold fury. "Hurry. Something's not right."

Another scream echoes through the house—fear and panic combined. I wriggle into the dress, not worrying about my bra or panties. Rebel finishes dressing moments after I do, fastening the top button of his shirt and smoothing back his dark hair.

"Come on." Taking my hand, he leads me out of the closet, ignoring the curious looks of the men and women now loitering in the hallway. The Texan from earlier is standing to one side, a champagne flute still clutched in his meaty hand.

"What's going on?" Rebel asks him.

"A body. Someone found a body in the kitchen. Some hired help or something. Blood everywhere, apparently."

Rebel's expression turns to tempered steel. My arm nearly comes out of the socket as he pulls me after him, pushing and shoving his way through the crowds. He stops in his tracks when he reaches the kitchen. On the floor, just as the Texan said, a body lies in a pool of blood. It's the girl who came to my room, Rebel's friend, Leah. Her eyes are wide, starting to cloud over; her throat lays wide open, slit from ear to ear.

"Oh my god," I whisper. "That's—"

"Yeah." Rebel lets go of my hand, dropping into a crouch, covering his mouth with his hands. Devastation sweeps across his face. He's turned sheet-white.

I go to comfort him. I take a step forward, wanting to place my hand on his back, to say something to let him know I'm there, but something stops me. Or rather some*one*. Across the other side of the room, talking to Louis Aubertin, a man I recognize all too well catches my eye. He has the fucking audacity to smile. I feel like I'm going to throw up.

Hector Ramirez.

Dressed in an expensive-looking suit and holding a cut glass tumbler of what looks like whiskey in his hand, it's obvious he's here for Louis' fundraiser. And from the cold, evil smile he sends my way, it's obvious that he's responsible for the dead girl lying on the floor.

Rebel must see him at the same time I do. Slowly, shakily, he gets to his feet. The man I was naked with, so caught up in only ten minutes ago, is completely gone. It's like he never even existed. "Motherfucker," Rebel snarls. "He should never have come *here*. He should never have known. I am going to fucking destroy him."

Right there, in front of everyone, Hector raises his glass and smiles at Rebel. If the message he's sending with the dead girl on the floor isn't enough, the one in his eyes is crystal clear:

Bring it on, Rebel. Do your fucking worst.

ROGUE

CALLIE HART

ROGUE
Copyright © 2015 Callie Hart

Formatting by Max Henry of Max Effect
     www.formaxeffect.com

LIVE FOR SOMETHING OR DIE FOR NOTHING

For *ALICE*, for being the best bitch in town.

For *RYAN*, for shutting down every bar in Sydney with me.

For *ANDY*, for every single cringe-worthy pun.

For *ASTRID* & *CAMPBELL*. There isn't enough wine and
cheese in the world.

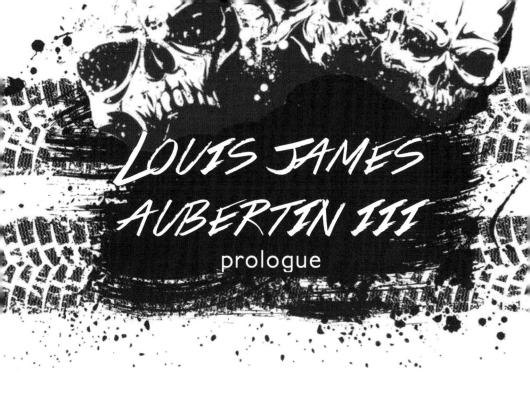

LOUIS JAMES AUBERTIN III

prologue

"You're a fucking embarrassment, you know that don't you? I can't believe you're my goddamn son. If you hadn't been born within the walls of this house, I'd think the wrong child had been brought home from the hospital."

My father throws back the last of his champagne and hands off the empty glass to one of his faceless servants. Faceless to him, but not to me. I know Sarah, know that she just became a grandmother for the first time this morning and no matter how badly my father treats her today, even he won't be able to keep the smile off her face. She gives me a wry shrug, placing the glass carefully on her silver tray, and then she vanishes off into the crowd.

My father is oblivious to the entire exchange. "You had no business inviting people here this evening, James. This is a political event. There are important people here. Serious people. Your little friends aren't suitable company for you to be keeping. You're not a child anymore. Lord knows you might still act like it, but you're not."

I dig my fingernails into my palms, though the action is hidden inside the pockets of the four thousand dollar Ralph Lauren suit I'm wearing. The suit he made me wear. "Cade Preston is a veteran, the same as I am, Dad. He served his country for four years in one of the most dangerous places on earth. And Laura's just been made partner at her father's law firm. How are they not *serious* people?"

My father scoffs. "Cade followed you to the other side of the world because you two boys have always had ridiculous, romanticized notions of war. That's why you both only lasted for two tours. Neither of you accepted the rank owed to you because of your station. You went out there, full of piss and vinegar, thinking it would be easier to start at the bottom rung, where you'd have no responsibility. And then you didn't like it, didn't want to stick it out, so you quit and came home before the job was done."

Louis James Aubertin II loves baiting me like this in public. He knows if he says these things to me in a crowd, there's nothing I can do but grin and take it from him. Makes him feel big. Superior. Thing is, my tolerance for this kind of treatment is wearing really fucking thin. "The U.S Marine Corp is not *the bottom rung.* The Marines are an elite unit. It takes an insane amount of hard work and dedication to even get in. If you think I had no responsibility as a Marine, then you clearly have very little understanding of how the United States Military is run." I don't bother defending the length of time my friend and I spent barely surviving out in the desert. What would be the point? Old Louis has no fucking clue. He'd simply say I was making excuses for myself. He can't possibly comprehend what four long, never-ending years in that environment is like. How the dirt and the sand and the hostile locals and the poverty and the disease and the heat and the IEDs and the amputations and the Taliban and the rape victims and the pain and the suffering all eventually wear you down.

My father's eyes flash with the same unbridled fury I've been provoking in him for years. "I was there in Vietnam, you little shit," he spits. "I was there from the moment the war started until the moment it ended. Don't you tell me I have no idea how the U.S.

military works."

Yes, Old Louis was in Vietnam, and yes he was there from start to finish, but he has nothing to be proud of. He never held a rifle or got his hands dirty a single day of that war. He sat with his other command buddies in a hotel fifty miles away from the jungle, where the only conflict they ever encountered was when the toilet paper was too rough to wipe their pampered, lily white asses on.

I say all of this in my head, but the thoughts don't make it out of my mouth. I press my tongue firmly against the back of my front teeth, just in case a rogue insult should try and escape me. This is how it's been for years now. So many fucking years. Our mutual hatred of one another only magnifies itself as time passes. I hate him because he's a vile, angry, malicious old man. He hates me because I killed my mother.

Fair turnaround.

In truth, I hate myself for killing my mother too, but there wasn't much to be done about it at the time. I had to be born, and fate decided to take the woman who carried me in her womb for nine months, only three seconds after I came kicking and screaming into the world. It was entirely unintentional on my part.

My father swoops down on another of the wait staff, Gavin this time, and snatches up a fresh glass of champagne without uttering a word of thanks. "And what about the girl? Laura Preston is a brash young woman who doesn't know when to hold her tongue. She's only made partner at her father's firm because it's exactly that—*her father's firm*. She wouldn't have accomplished anything if she'd had to fend for herself, James. There's no denying that. And just...just look at what she's wearing, for crying out loud. She looks like a fucking prostitute." He points off across the other side of the room to where Laura, Cade's sister, is laughing with a young guy I don't know, her head tipped back as she lets out a throaty bark of amusement. Her blonde, cropped hair has been pinned up out of her face—a minor miracle, considering it's normal, wild state—and there's the faintest hint of blush reddening her cheeks. She always said she'd never wear make up when we were growing up, and for a long time she didn't. She doesn't need it, and she's sure as hell never been a girly girl, but tonight she looks great with that tiny splash of color brightening her face.

The dress she's wearing is decked out in gold sequins, which reflect the light from the illuminated chandeliers overheard, sending fragments of golden, fiery light dancing and skittering on the walls and on the ceiling. It's not something a respectable Alabama woman would wear in polite company, and that is precisely why she's worn it. I want to high-five her so badly, but that sort of behavior would be frowned upon.

"As soon as the speeches are over, I want the three of you out of here. You understand me? I don't care where you go. Just make sure you're not on the property. God knows what'll happen if the three of you start drinking."

I bare my teeth at my father, arranging my face into a rictus of false civility. "Gladly." Little does my father know, I've already started drinking and I have zero intention of fucking stopping. That would be a really dumb idea at this point in the proceedings. After all, the speeches won't be for another hour. I have to survive this ridiculous circus until then, and I doubt my father would prefer I inhaled a shit load of coke up my nose instead.

I give him a mock salute as he turns and saunters off into the crowd, grinning like we were just having a pleasant father-son catch up and he doesn't have a care in the world. On the far side of the room, the string quartet I saw setting up earlier begins to play, sending the glossy, warm notes of Boccherini's Minuet floating up toward the high ceiling. Such a fucking farce.

Suddenly the tie around my neck feels like it's choking me. Laura looks up from the conversation she's sharing with the young guy I don't know and gives me a small wave, beckoning me over. I don't want to go over there and be introduced to the halfwit son of one of my asshole father's Harvard buddies. I'd rather poke my eyes out with a shitty stick than do the whole run of the mill, *yes, I went to*

MIT. No, I don't know so-and-so. Yes, I served in the military. No, I won't tell you the most fucked up thing I ever saw. No, I won't tell you how many people I killed, you fucking tourist bit. Still, it would seem I have very little choice in the matter. Laura grins at me as I weave my way toward her.

"Jamie!" She throws her arm around my waist, inserting herself into the space at my side so that I naturally put my arm around her shoulders. She looks up at me with those big, brown eyes of hers and winks. "Jamie, this is Edward Lamont. He's the son of one of your father's friends. They..." She frowns, turning back to Edward. "How does your father know the governor again?"

"Oh, they went to college together."

Well, color me motherfucking surprised.

Edward holds his hand out to me, a wall of white, glow-in-the-dark teeth almost blinding me as he sends a smile my way. "Pleased to meet you, Jamie. I've heard a lot about you. Your father is an incredible man."

"Isn't he just?" I pump Over Eager Eddie's hand firmly just the once and turn my full attention on Laura. "Where's your brother, anyway? I haven't seen him yet."

"Oh, he's here somewhere. I think Daddy was showing him off to the head of some private security firm or something. Hey, you're not going, are you?" She has that kicked puppy thing going on as I disentangle myself from her embrace. I know she was trying to use me as a shield between her and Edward, but I really don't have the energy to play nice at the moment.

"Sorry, Lore. I'll be back soon, I promise. Edward, it was a pleasure to make your acquaintance." Laura shoots daggers at me as I duck off into the confusion of people. I'll probably be hearing about it for weeks, but I had to bail. No two ways about it. I can't find Cade in amongst the sea of dusty, gray-haired old fucks and their plastic, bleach blonde wives, so I grab a whiskey from Sarah, ask her how her new grandbaby is, and quietly go about getting drunk alone in a dark corner.

My father moves from one small group of people to the next, continually shoveling canapés into his mouth and pouring champagne down his throat until he's tripping over his own damned size tens. Looks like this year's speech is going to be slurred again. Eventually the quartet stop playing and take a break, and I spy Cade on the other side of the room, talking to Laura and Over Eager Eddie. No way am I going over there now. I've had six whiskeys and I already successfully escaped that clusterfuck once. Cade will come find me when he's had enough of this pretentious bullshit, by which point I will be comfortably numb, anyway.

"Excuse me? Do you...? Hi. Do you know where the bathrooms are? I'm dying over here and I only have a few minutes." In front of me, a petite little brunette with pretty cornflower blue eyes is clasping her hands in front of her stomach, looking like she's about to pee on my father's highly polished parquet. The short black dress she's wearing shows off her tanned, rather delectable legs.

"Do I know where the bathroom is?" I ask.

"Yes. I'm sorry, you probably don't have a clue either," she says, laughing nervously.

"Oh, I know where they are. I grew up here." I sling back the last of the whiskey in my glass and slowly place the tumbler at my feet. I offer her my arm. "Come on. I will escort you there directly."

She looks up at me like a frightened baby deer, her cheeks flushing, but she places her hand into the crook of my arm and follows me all the same. I don't take her to the downstairs bathroom behind the staircase. I don't take her to the one through the servants' walkway, just next to the kitchen. I lead her up to the next floor, straight to the en suite of one of father's overly plain guest bedrooms.

"Thank you. If you go back downstairs and see a really stressed out looking violinist, will you let him know I won't be a second?"

I lean against the wall, pulling roughly at my tie. "You're one of the musicians, then?"

Her cheeks turn crimson. "Yes. I'm...the cellist."

I have a very witty response lined up about her liking a solid piece of wood between her legs, but I keep my mouth shut. She's not the sort of girl you use that kind of innuendo on. She is the kind of girl you tread carefully with. I'm not one for the softly, softly approach, though. There's a fine line between terrifying a woman like this and getting her so wound up that she's trembling at the knees.

"You're very beautiful. Do you know that?"

She swallows. "I—thank you. That's very kind of you."

"Do you think I'm attractive?"

"What?"

"Do you think I'm attractive?"

"Well, that's not a question people normally ask you five seconds after meeting," she says, laughing softly.

"Maybe not. But you're here, working, and I'm here, suffering, and it seems to me that both of us are going to be leaving this place soon. We're probably never going to see each other again. So we don't have much time to waste. If you don't think I'm attractive, I'll happily be a gentleman and go back downstairs. Is that what you want?"

She looks at me like I just told her aliens are invading and the planet is about to be blown to smithereens. Her mouth opens and then closes twice. "I—"

"Don't worry, little cellist. I'll go find your stressed violinist and tell him you'll be down in a second." I make to leave, but she places a hand on my arm, stopping me in my tracks.

"Of course I think you're hot," she says quietly. "You're, like, a young, sexy James Bond in that suit. And your eyes are..." She shakes her head, apparently not sure how to finish that sentence. "Maybe I do want you to be here when I come out of the bathroom. Is that bad?"

Leaning down so that my mouth's mere inches away from hers, I stare at her lips, knowing she wants me to kiss her. Knowing she wants me to do any number of very bad things to her. "Go use the bathroom. When you come out, I'll show you just how bad we can be together."

Her breath catches in her throat, but she doesn't change her mind. She does as she's told and uses the bathroom, and when she comes out I make good on my words.

At the precise moment Laura bursts into the room calling out my name, I have my tongue down the little cellist's throat, her dress pulled down to her waist exposing her breasts, and two of my fingers inside her wet pussy.

Laura screeches to a halt, a horrified look spreading across her face. "*Jesus, Jamie.*"

"Oh my god." The little cellist scrambles back into her clothing, hanging her head as she wriggles away from me. "Oh my god, I am *so* sorry."

"You have nothing to apologize for," I tell her, but she's moving so frantically that she can't hear me. Laura watches her hurry out of the room with her mouth hanging open like a swinging trapdoor. I'm still completely dressed, and thanks to Laura's untimely entrance my hard-on has completely vanished, too. "Perfect, Lore. Just fucking perfect. Have you forgotten how to knock?"

"Are you *kidding* me?" She throws her hands up in the air, staring at me in disbelief. "You're the one up here finger fucking some twenty-one-year old, and you're giving *me* shit?"

It's kind of hilarious to hear Laura say *finger fucking*, but I manage to keep the smile from my face. "What's wrong? You never been caught in flagrante before, Laura Preston? Never been caught with your panties down?"

"No!" She looks like she's lost for a second, and then she's kicking off her monstrous golden skyscraper heels and she's, shit, she's *throwing* them at me.

The first heel misses me by a mile. The second one buzzes my head and hits the huge gilt-framed mirror hanging on the wall behind me, smashing the glass into a million tiny pieces. "*What the fuck, Laura?*"

"You! I can't..." She clasps her hand over her mouth and that's when I notice her eyes are filled with tears. "I can't fucking believe you," she whispers.

Oh, crap. This is not how someone reacts to busting their friend doing something questionable. This is not how they react at all. I cross the room, holding up my hands as I approach her, stooping slightly so I can look her in the eye. "Hey. *Hey*. I'm really fucking confused. Do you want to tell me what's wrong, or should I go get Cade?"

"Don't you dare go and fucking get Cade," she hisses. "You and Cade, joined at the hip, twenty-four fucking seven. You and Cade vanishing off to fucking Afghanistan, leaving me here on my own. I waited here for you for four goddamn years, Jamie. Four years of waking up every single night in a cold sweat, wondering which one of you was going to die first. And then you come home and hardly even...hardly even look at me and..."

Oh.

Fuck.

Seriously?

Her hair, perfectly pinned back when she came charging into the room, has now come loose and is tumbling into her face like it used to when she was a little girl. I reach out, tucking it behind her ear. "Laura—"

"No. Don't! Fuck, Jamie, you just had your fingers inside some girl's vagina."

I consider pointing out that that was my other hand, but then come to the swift conclusion that Laura will probably strangle me to death with my own necktie if I do. I slide my hands inside my pockets, clearing my throat. "Lore," I say carefully. "Is there something you wanna tell me?"

"Fuck you, Jamie. I shouldn't have to tell you. You should already know! Ahhh! Men! Why are you all so fucking oblivious? How can you be that completely blind to what's been staring you in the face since we were kids, Jay. I just...I gotta get out of here."

She's a whirlwind of tense energy and clenched fists as she storms out of the bedroom. I go after her, grabbing hold of her gently by the wrist, trying to stop her, trying to figure this whole thing out in my head fast enough to deal with it right here and now, but Laura has other ideas. She turns on me, hand raised, and her palm makes contact with my face, slapping me hard. I can see from the pain in her eyes that she regrets it immediately.

"*Shit.*" She covers her mouth with her hand. "Shit, I'm so sorry. I just—"

"It's okay."

"I just can't—" Tears roll, round and fat, down her cheeks, dangling like tiny little crystals from her dark eyelashes.

"It's okay," I repeat. "It's fine. We can talk about it tomorrow."

She nods, just once. "Tomorrow," she says. And then she goes, running down the sweeping staircase in her bare feet, tiny sparks of light bouncing everywhere like silent fireworks as the sequins of her dress catch the light.

It's not until the next morning that Cade calls to tell me his sister never made it home.

REBEL

War isn't always a loud, brash thing.

Sometimes, it's a car rolling slowly by the front of your house at night. Sometimes, it's an anonymous call to the police. Sometimes it's the head of a Mexican cartel showing up in small town New Mexico to make your life a living hell. And sometimes, it's three men sneaking through tall grass with guns in their hands, ready to shoot you in the head while you sleep.

I'm bleeding fucking everywhere. One of Hector Ramirez's perimeter guards cut me open with his knife and now the wound is pouring my DNA out all over the grass. I can't be thinking about that right now, though. Honestly, I'm not thinking at all. I'm gripped with the same insanity that's had hold of me since I walked into my father's kitchen and found Leah dead on the floor, her throat slit from ear to ear, and that smug motherfucker toasting me from the other side of the room. There's no room for sanity inside me now. Not after Leah. My uncle was one thing, but add on another innocent woman who I was supposed to be protecting, and there is no more Jamie. Even Rebel doesn't exist anymore. There is only madness and fury, held together with the burning acid of revenge. It's eaten away at everything else until there's nothing left.

I feel a hand on the center of my back, grabbing hold of my t-shirt. It's Cade, trying to tell me to slow the fuck down, but I jerk myself away, hurrying forward. Behind me, I hear him cursing me to hell. Carnie's back there somewhere, too. Just the three of us for this job. As the newest member of the Widow Makers, I shouldn't have brought Carnie along on this particular ride, but the guy's keen as fuck. He totally busted Cade and me as we were leaving the compound. He would have followed us here, regardless. He's had Margo, the gun he named after his mother, locked and loaded ever since he climbed on his Ducati.

The very day after Sophia and I returned from Alabama, Hector showed up with his entourage, walking the streets like he owns the fucking place, drinking coffee outside *my* fucking tattoo shop, sending out a very clear message: *I am here to end this.* And if that's what the guy wants, who am I to argue with him?

I've had enough. I should have sent Sophia away the second I saw that body in my father's kitchen and I realized this thing was never going to make it to trial. Never going to make it past pure, old school, *knife-in-the-chest-while-you're-sleeping* revenge. Soph should be at home with her family, and instead I have her under guard back in my cabin, probably tearing the place apart, raging mad, and all because I've put her in this shitty position. Because where Hector Ramirez goes, so follows Raphael Dela Vega. And after what Sophia told me—that Raphael threatened to kill her whole family and do way worse to her—I'm not letting her out of that cabin until the fucker is dead and in the ground.

"Dude, slow the fuck down. They're gonna see us coming," Cade hisses behind me. Up ahead, the ground floor of the small, innocuous farm house Hector's taken up residence in is lit up against the darkness, pouring yellowed light out onto the wrap around porch that skirts the property. Shadows move inside. I didn't really think for a second I was going to be rolling up on a sleeping house but it's frustrating that there are so many people flitting from room to room. I'm only interested in killing one person: Hector.

After Afghanistan, I have enough blood on my hands to drown myself in. I don't particularly want to add to the body count, but if they stand in my way, if killing them means I get to put an end to Ramirez, then so be it. My soul is already damned to hell. I might as well *really* earn my place there.

The night smells like gasoline and bad weed, the latter of which must be coming from the house. Crouching down low thirty meters from the illuminated building, I scan the darkness, trying to see if there are more watchmen that need putting down. I made a stupid, reckless error before. I wasn't expecting there to be guards so far out on the very perimeters of the farmhouse. When the first guy emerged out of the black night and slashed at me, he took me by surprise. Between me, Cade and Carnie, we managed to put down the four men who rallied to take us on, but it was close. Stupid. I should have been more wary. I'm not just risking my own life here, but Cade and Carnie's too.

"How many?" Cade whispers. My best friend scratches at the beard he's managed to grow in the past few weeks, frowning severely. I can't count how many times we've found ourselves together in this position, crouching in the dark, planning on doing wrong. It's little comfort that the majority of times it was on behalf of the U.S government. We may not be desert rats anymore, but we're still soldiers. We're still fighting a war. Except this is one of our own making, and there's no getting out of it. No backing down. It's *necessary*.

"At least six," I reply.

"I only count five," Carnie chips in. "Three in the living room, one in the kitchen. One in the hallway."

He's right, but his eyes aren't as sharp as mine. I glare up at the farmhouse, holding my breath, slowing my pulse. "And one more. Upstairs. Front left window. He's watching us right now."

Carnie makes a disbelieving sound. "You're fucking crazy. The room's pitch black. You can't see shit."

"Oh, he's there all right. I can see him just fine." In fairness to Carnie, maybe I can't see him in a traditional sense. The room *is* in pure darkness, but I can sense it—Ramirez is there, standing in the murky shadows of the room, waiting patiently for my arrival. I can feel his presence so intensely that the hairs on the back of my neck are standing on end. He's been there all along, just waiting for me to show up. With all the showmanship and blatant peacocking in town, he's been stabbing at my buttons, knowing that with each and every sighting he's coming closer and closer to drawing me out.

I'm a stupid motherfucker.

I'm normally so much smarter than this, but the fury over Ryan and Leah's deaths has had me taking temporary leave of my wits. Cade nudges me with his elbow, grunting softly. "We're here, man. You wanna do this now, we'll do it. But maybe—"

"Yeah, I know." I sigh heavily. Angrily. I want to pound my fists into the dirt in frustration, but where the fuck would that get me.

"You might be wrong," Carnie whispers. "I get bad feelings all the time. Your brain plays some epic tricks on you sometimes."

"He's not wrong, asshole. He's never been wrong." The dull thump of Cade punching Carnie in the arm is quiet, but Carnie's yelp of pain isn't. "Jesus, man. Shut your fucking mouth. You wanna get us killed?"

"I don't think he's seen us," I whisper, ignoring them. "But I can't be sure. Time to leave." Leaving is the very last thing I want to do. I want to storm into that building and shoot some motherfuckers. I want to dig the point of my blade into Hector Ramirez's chest and watch the light go out in his eyes as the steel bites deeper. But Ramirez is a smart guy. He knows I'm coming. There's no way there's only six people in that building. He will have an army of men hidden out of sight, ready to end our lives before we even step foot on the fucking farmhouse porch.

"Come on, man. We'll get the fucker, don't you worry. But this ain't how it goes down," Cade says. I let him pull me back, let his words deaden the boiling adrenalin storming my veins, calling for revenge. I suddenly feel exhausted.

"All right. All right," I take a deep breath, uncurling my hands, not realizing they were clenched into fists. As I retreat from the farmhouse with my boys, ducking low to remain out of sight, I feel sick to my stomach. We're leaving with our lives, but somehow it feels like a defeat. I'm chanting the same words over and over as the farmhouse shrinks and disappears behind us.

This isn't over, motherfucker. It's only just begun.

SOPHIA

I've given up screaming. It didn't get me anywhere for two days so I figured why waste the energy. I haven't seen Rebel in ten days. Ten days couped up in his cabin while he's out there doing god knows what and I've been going bat shit crazy. I thought we were past this. I thought this part was over. I should have known by his silent, brooding mood on the way back from Alabama that things were right back to where we were in the beginning. More fool me for assuming that me agreeing to help him, me turning down the opportunity to flee back to my family, me *fucking him* for fuck's sake, would change things between us. Now, I just feel foolish. For all of it.

There *was* a brief moment where I did get to step outside. Seventy two hours after Rebel put the Humvee in park and bundled me into his house on the hill, locking the door behind me, the prospect, Carnie, showed up and drove me out into the desert, kicking and screaming. He wouldn't tell me why at first, but after an hour of me chewing his ear off, threatening to scream blue murder the whole time we were sitting in his shitty, beaten up Firebird, the guy caved.

"The cops are tearing the compound apart, looking for evidence to link the club to that shooting in Los Angeles."

I'm horrified when it takes me a beat to remember what he's talking about—the shooting at Trader Joes, where all those civilians were killed by men wearing Widow Makers cuts.

"Yeah, one of Rebel's uncle's friends called and gave him a heads up. Told Rebel the police caught the guys who did it in Irvine, still wearing the fake cuts, drunk as all hell. The fat one who was supposed to be the club president confessed that they'd been hired for the job. Gave up Maria Rosa in a heart beat, in exchange for a lesser sentence."

"Is she still going to cause problems then? This Maria Rosa?"

Carnie gets a far away look in his eye that looks almost romantic. "From what I've been told, the Bitch of Columbia causes problems wherever she is in the world. I wouldn't be surprised."

He drove me back to the compound at nightfall and took me straight back to the cabin, ignoring my colorful language and my threats to take him out at the knees.

That was last Wednesday. Now it's Wednesday again. Tomorrow morning I should be getting up at seven and going for a run before heading to my Human Sciences class. Instead, Carnie, with his busted up glasses and his hipster side-parting will bring me my breakfast and refuse to tell me anything, and I'll swear at him or completely blank him depending on my mood. The cycle repeats itself endlessly, over and over.

Tonight, however, Carnie's already dropped off my evening meal. I called him a soulless bastard and threw the plate of meatloaf at his head, but the thing missed him entirely and impacted with the wall. I need to do some serious work on my aim. The meatloaf has sat on the floor since then, getting colder and staler by the second, in amongst the shattered shards of the chinaware.

If Sloane were here she would have figured out how to free herself from this fucked up situation. I can guarantee it. She's resourceful, independent and stubborn, and she wouldn't give up until she found a way to get what she wanted. That makes me even madder as I sit and watch The Hangover for the eighteenth time. The TV in Rebel's cabin has no reception, just a handful of DVDs, all of which are the same kind of stupid, mindless humor I would never normally watch. Now, I've seen every single last one of them. I'm beginning to know them line for line.

Alan is just confessing that he drugged the other guys in the movie when the door to the cabin flies open and Rebel stalks in, larger than life. It's the last thing I'm expecting, given that I've been asking to see him for the past week and a half and he hasn't graced me with his presence. A part of me got to thinking that maybe he was hurt or something. Injured, to the point where he was laid up and incapable of walking. Standing in the doorway now, I can see that he's walking just fine. He glances down at his feet and scowls at the debris from my evening meal on the floorboards.

"What the fuck?" He looks at me like I'm a naughty child, caught misbehaving, and I automatically shrink back into the sofa. I catch myself, almost screaming out loud at how ridiculous my reaction is. I shouldn't be shrinking from him. I'm a fucking prisoner. I'm allowed to revolt if I damn well want to. "Got a problem?" I snap, sitting up straighter.

"Yeah. There's fucking food all over my damn floor. I hand-sanded these floorboards," he growls.

"Then you should have thrown me in the basement or something and had done with it, shouldn't you?"

"Don't fucking tempt me." Rebel steps over the mess and slams the door behind him, locking it before he storms into the room. I try not to flinch as he comes to a stop in front of me. "Stand up, Soph."

I take a deep breath. "*No.*" My skin feels tingly, the same way it used to when I would defy my father. Not that I'm comparing the man standing in front of me with the mild mannered preacher left worrying about me back in Seattle, but this situation feels...it feels very much like I'm about to get punished.

Tilting his head to one side, Rebel drops into a crouch so that our eyes are at the same level. His are ice-blue, cold. Intense. So fierce I can hardly meet them. I'm proud of the fact that I don't look away, though. "What seems to be the problem?" He asks this slowly, as though he's wrestling with his temper.

Had a bad night, buddy? Well guess what? So have I. Leaning forward so my face is closer to his, I breathe deep and even down my nose, trying to tame my own anger. "You're fucking kidding me, right?"

He blinks. He's frozen solid, staring straight at me. He's holding himself back, but from what I'm not entirely sure. Not for a second do I think he's going to hurt me, but there's something about the brooding, stillness of him that's intimidating. "Have you been bored or something?"

"You could say that."

"You know what's not boring?" Calm. He's too fucking calm. It's beginning to put me on edge. He continues speaking softly, but there's a dangerous lilt to his voice. "Being chased down, raped and murdered. That's not boring, right?"

"This place is a fortress, Jamie. I would have been fine out there with everyone else. How many people do you have living at the compound for crying out loud? There must be twenty motorcycles here at any one time!"

He cocks his head again, frowning. He's probably wondering how I know that; you can see nothing but trees and then a distant ridgeline from the cabin windows. With so little to do all day, I've gotten really good at listening, though. I knew nothing about engines before I came here. I don't really know anything about them now, either, apart from the fact that each one sounds different. I've spent hours laying on Rebel's bed with my eyes closed, listening hard. Figuring out which motorcycle was which. Who was coming and going. Not knowing who was riding what, of course, but still.

Rebel's eyes flash, the muscles in his jaw jumping as he grinds his teeth. "Raphael Dela Vega's here. In town."

"Wait. *What?*" My arms and legs suddenly feel very cold, very numb. That...that makes no sense. What would he be doing here?

My anger towards Rebel doesn't matter anymore. Bile rises up in the back of my throat as I try to process this piece of information, but it's as though it just won't settle in my mind. New Mexico is so far removed from Seattle, and so very far removed from Los Angeles. My brain tries to scramble, to come up with some logical reason why Raphael would be here, here of all places. Some reason other than the fact that he must have come for me. I draw a blank.

Rebel shifts for the first time, wincing a little, like he's in pain. "I don't even want him to *see* you here, Sophia. If he does, he'll likely try and find a way into the compound, and then what? Someone's back's turned and you're lying in a pool of your own goddamn blood? No. No way." He says this so quietly, and yet there's such determination behind his words.

"You haven't been by here in ten days," I growl.

He blinks again, staring straight at me. "Would you have wanted to see me?"

"Yes! I sure as hell wouldn't want to be kept in the dark over what's going on in the outside world! You...*we slept together!* And then you're just gone. You lock me up and then you just vanish off the face of the earth."

"So that's it? You just wanted someone to come fuck you? I'm sure any of the boys would have obliged you if only you'd have told them."

I react without thinking. I'm lunging at him, my hand flying out to strike him across the face before I can stop myself. My palm makes contact with his cheek, a loud cracking sound filling the room. "Don't you fucking dare," I grind out. "Don't you dare do that. You fucking buy me like I'm nothing but a lump of meat, like I'm goddamn *property*, and then you make me care about you. You make me think you care about me. You trick me, make me look like an absolute idiot, and then you try and make me out to be some sort of slut, too. Don't you fucking *dare*."

My whole body is vibrating with anger. I've heard the saying 'seeing red' before and I've thought nothing of it, but now I know it's actually a very literal term—it's almost as though I'm seeing him through a red haze.

Rebel runs his tongue over his teeth, slowly lifting his hand to touch his fingers to the red welt on his face where I struck him. He speaks carefully, very slowly. "Sophia, please know, you're just about the only person on the face of the planet who could get away with that right now."

"Yeah? Well, if you don't get the hell away from me, I'm gonna do it again, asshole," I spit.

"I went out with the intention of killing a man tonight. You think I'll have any moral objection to tying up a misbehaving woman?"

I lean forward even further so that our faces are no less than an inch apart. "*Try me.*"

Rebel's calm, overly controlled behavior should have clued me into the fact that he's been on the verge of snapping this whole time. He rockets forward, hands grabbing me by the tops of my arms, pinning me to the sofa. "You really don't want to do this with me, Soph," he breathes.

I do, though. I want to gouge his eyes out. I want to smash my fist into his face so hard that he loses teeth. I want to break his bones and watch him bleed. I think maybe he expected me to back down as soon as he grabbed hold of me, but I don't. I twist underneath him, slamming my knee into his side. He doubles over, huffing out a deep, pained breath. Wrenching my arms out of his grasp, I slip out from underneath him and drive my clenched fist into his side as hard as I possibly can. Rebel grits his teeth, snarling between them, jumping to his feet.

"You're fucking crazy!"

"I guess that's what happens to a person when you lock them away for ten days on their own, and then show up accusing them of being a whore."

"I didn't accuse you of being a whore."

"You may as well have done. You think just because I slept with you, I'd want to sleep with any of your gross, Neanderthal groupies?

I'm not some club hooker to be passed around like a damn party favor!"

He comes at me again, reaching for me, and that's when I notice the blood on his hands. My mind instantly rewinds to what he just said about setting out to kill someone tonight, and I reel back. Oh my god. No, he couldn't have. Did...*did he actually do it?* Rebel sees my anger change to horror and swiftly stops in his tracks.

"What?"

"Your hands, Rebel. What the fuck is all over your hands?"

He looks down at them, a small frown creasing his forehead, eyebrows banking together. The expression he's wearing screams innocent confusion, however the wet blood on his hands screams something else entirely. His face is ashen.

"I don't..."

I scream when he staggers sideways and crashes into the couch, dropping to one knee. "What the hell? Rebel? *Rebel*!" He looks like he's on death door. "Oh, god, please...what's wrong?" I touch his side, the side I rammed with my knee, my hand comes away covered in blood. His t-shirt is drenched with it. I didn't notice before since the material is black, but now that I'm looking closer I can see the dark, wet stain spreading across his stomach.

"Is this...is this *you*?"

Rebel nods, holding one hand to his side. "Go and get Cade."

"What happened?"

"Go and get Cade, Soph."

"Rebel!"

"Jesus, I was stabbed earlier. You just kneed me right on top of the wound. Now, please, fuck...go and get Cade."

I'm not going anywhere. I drop to my knees beside him, tearing at his shirt. "Show me. Show me for god's sake." The bastard deserves to be in pain after everything he's put me through since we returned to New Mexico, but now that he's potentially bleeding out on the floor of his cabin, I'm suddenly not so sure that I want him to die.

He tries to pull shirt back down, but ironically I'm stronger than him right now. A jolt of surprise hits me when I see what's underneath—a seven-inch long gash runs down his ribcage, onto his stomach. And it's seriously deep. *"Are you insane? Why the hell didn't you go straight to the hospital?"* Yelling at him probably isn't the most constructive thing I could be doing, but it's about all I can think of. Rebel grimaces, slumping back so that he's sitting on his ass on the floor.

"It wasn't bleeding that much before you belted me," he says. Unbelievably, he winks at me, like he finds that highly amusing.

"Shit. I'm sorry. I am *so* sorry. God, I need to find a towel." I start pacing, tearing through drawers and cupboards, searching but not finding what I'm looking for.

"It's okay, it's all right. I don't need a towel. Soph. *Sophia!*"

I stop pacing.

"Go and get Cade, okay? He'll be up in the bar, in the biggest building. Go and get him and tell him to bring a suture kit." Rebel reaches up and hands me a key, and it takes me a second to understand what it's for: the door to the cabin. The door to my freedom. I take it from him.

There's an actual pool of blood spreading out around him on the floorboards now, growing bigger by the second. I did that to him. Well, I didn't do it to him, but I sure as hell made it worse. *Fuck.* I run to the door and unlock it, my hands shaking like crazy., and then I'm running some more, running to the left toward a building I've only ever seen from a distance as I've been brought to and from the cabin. Tall, dead grass whips at my bare legs as I barrel head on down the steep hill that leads to the rest of the compound. The night air feels cool in my lungs, pulling at my clothes as I sprint for help.

It occurs to me that I could veer to the right, towards the banks of motorcycles and cars parked off the side. I have no idea how to hot wire a car but I could give it a damn good go. A part of my brain is screaming at me to do it, to let Rebel bleed out on the floor, steal a car and head for the closest police station, but I can't. I just can't make myself do it. Rebel was a major asshole when he came back to the cabin just now, but I saw something in him in Alabama. Something that made me drop my defences and trust him. I can't just let him die.

When I slam though the doors of the main building, I see it must be the Widow Makers' clubhouse. Inside, at least fifteen people stop their conversations, glasses and beer bottles held halfway to their mouths, and they all turn to stare at me. A tall woman, maybe in her late forties cocks her head to one side and blinks like she can't believe what she's seeing. Cade's on the other side of the room, paused mid-hand shake with another, shorter guy with neck tattoos. His eyes nearly pop out of his head when he sees me.

"What in Sam Hell?" Cade drops his friend's hand and storms across the clubhouse bar, murder in his eyes. "You trying to get yourself killed?" he hisses, grabbing hold of my arm. I've had enough of people manhandling me for one day. Ripping my arm free, I step back, ready to knee him somewhere a little more intimate if I have to.

"Rebel needs you. He said for you to bring a suture kit," I tell him. If I were my sister, I could have sewn Rebel up myself. I'm not though, so this is the best I can do. I shove Cade in the chest, trying to transfer some sense of urgency to him. "He's bleeding every-where," I snap. "When he sent me to fetch you, I don't think he had a huge amount of time for you to decide if you were gonna come or not."

Cade scrubs his hand with his face, rolling his eyes. "Jesus, I told him he should go see the doc." He ducks quickly behind the bar, where an overweight guy in an ACDC t-shirt is staring at me with eyes like saucers. It takes me a moment to realize why: I'm half freaking naked. It may be winter, but you wouldn't know it by the temperature in New Mexico. I've been sweltering in Rebel's airless, AC-less cabin. Shorts and tank tops have been my recent staple.

The fact that my shirt is covered in blood really isn't helping matters, either. I try to shrink inside my own skin as Cade grabs a small green case from somewhere underneath the counter, and then he's vaulting over it and leading me out of the bar. I glance over my shoulder just in time to catch the hateful look being sent my way by a beautiful pink haired woman with tattoos. Her eyes narrow at me, and then she's gone as I'm dragged out of the clubhouse and across the compound in the direction of the cabin.

"Is he conscious?" Cade asks.

"Was when I left him," I pant. "There was blood on the floor, though. A lot of blood."

Cade just grunts. He lets me go and takes off without a backward glance to make sure I'm following. Again, I'm presented with the opportunity to escape. Rebel is about to get help. Cade will either stitch him up or take him to get further medical attention. My usefulness in this situation is at an end. I should be ducking into the shadows and vanishing, even if I can't get one of the cars to work and I have to walk to the next town.

I take a deep breath, watching Cade growing smaller and smaller as he runs up the hill to Rebel's place, and then I'm looking over my shoulder, out over the endless, scrubby desert between me and civilization...and I'm shaking my head.

I could die out there. That's not what stops me from running, though. It's the fact that Rebel could die right here, right now and I would never know it.

My head is swimming as I run up the hill behind Cade. I've lost my mind. I must be completely insane to be doing this. My father's face flashes through my head as I summit the hill, running directly back *into* the place I've been desperate to escape from the past ten days. In my head, for some weird reason, my father is smiling.

REBEL

I can't remember the last time I threw up. Certainly not for any reason other than being blind fucking drunk, anyway. I mean, yes, I suppose I do feel really drunk, but that's because I'm losing copious amounts of blood and I can't seem to stem the flow. I'm retching, head spinning, vision blurred when I see a dark shape coming toward me. Coming toward me fast.

"Fuck me, man, what the hell?" It's Cade. His voice reaches me, though it sounds muffled, like I've got cotton wool stuffed inside my ears. "Well, aren't you in a state."

I weakly lift my right hand from the ground and flip him off. Cade laughs. "See why you sent for me now, jackass," he says. "Guy gives you a couple of pints of blood in a foreign country and the next thing you know it's five years later an' he wants the damn stuff back. *Indian giver.*" He laughs under his breath, and my brain works sluggishly, trying to decipher what he's talking about .

Ah, yeah. That's right. Afghanistan. We were in Afghanistan and he was shot. He'd lost a lot of blood. I gave him some of mine. The doctors performed a transfusion because we were the same blood type, and Cade was my brother and I wouldn't just sit by and watch him die while we waited around for the bagged stuff to arrive.

I've been fighting to stay upright, to stay awake, but now that he's here, I feel like I can stop fighting so hard. The bastard won't let me die, I know it. I fall back, my head bouncing off the floor, and then Cade's hands are on my torso, spinning me over slowly so that I'm on my side.

Pain washes through me, like I'm being stabbed all over again. It's weird, though, the ghost of what pain should really feel like. Everything's going numb. That's how it starts…dying. Your nerve endings start playing tricks on you, cutting your brain off from your limbs or making you think you're really cold. At this particular point in time, I feel like I'm half frozen.

"Better…hurry your…ass up," I stutter. It's shock. I know it is. My whole body is starting to shake.

Another voice speaks, catching at my focus for a second. Sophia. My hands involuntarily twitch, my fingers curling inwards, as though reaching for the idea of her. "What…what should I do?" she asks.

I can't see her, but I can sense her close. "Hold this," Cade tells her. I can't see what he hands her. She's standing behind me, breathing quickly, like she's hyperventilating. Pain bites through me, a sudden, sharp reminder of how shitty it is when your nerve endings actually decide to work in situations like this. Carefully, slowly, I look down, struggling to focus my eyes on what's happening to my chest. Cade is quickly, efficiently stitching me back together, my skin tugging and pulling as he forcefully shoves the needle in and out of my skin.

"Any…internal…?" I manage.

"No. No, your insides are just fine, you lucky son of a bitch, now hold still."

I hold still, grinding my teeth together as I'm put back together. I manage to stay awake until the very final stitch is tied off, and then I pass the fuck out.

I could be out for hours, but I get the feeling it's more like fifteen minutes. When I regain consciousness, Cade is standing over me, glaring grimly at me while he wipes his hands on one of my bathroom towels, and Sophia is sitting on the edge of the bed, wearing next to nothing. If I had any blood left in my body, I'm sure it would be headed straight for my dick right now. As it goes, I roll over slowly and throw up over the side of the bed.

"Nice," Cade observes. "Real fucking nice."

"Fuck you, man." It sounds like I've been eating gravel. My head is splitting apart. I fall back onto the pillows, my stomach rolling again, making empty threats. There can't be anything left inside me to bring back up by now. Sophia grimaces at the mess I've made; she gets to her feet and heads for the kitchen bench, rifling under the counters, presumably looking for cleaning products.

"Don't. You don't have to do that," I say, wincing.

Cade lifts an eyebrow, shaking his head. "Sure she does, man. I'm gonna sit here and let you steal half my plasma. I ain't gonna clean up your puke, too."

"Then deal with it," I growl. "She shouldn't have to—"

"I don't mind. I don't want to sit here looking at it, either." Soph drops to her knees and starts mopping up my vomit, which makes me feel about three fucking inches tall. While she's doing that, Cade sets up for the blood transfusion. He must have gone back to the clubhouse and grabbed the tourniquets, lines and needles while I was briefly out for the count.

I lay on my back with my arm thrown up over my eyes while Cade efficiently hooks us up and begins the process. It's such a strange feeling, having blood traveling *into* your body instead of out. I can hear Sophia throwing things into the trash. Can smell the disinfectant she's scrubbing into the floorboards as Cade makes underhanded comments about how fucking stupid I am.

"And by the way," he tells me. "I smoked a bunch of weed as soon as I walked through the door earlier. Don't know if that shit affects your blood, but I sure hope it fucking does. It'll serve you right if you get insanely high and pass out again. You've totally ruined my buzz."

I consider trying to punch him, but just thinking of the effort that would involve exhausts me. I decide on a different tack. "Thanks, man.

"Don't mention it."

I lay there, thinking about the ridiculous shit I said to Soph before she went postal and tried to murder me. I should have kept my mouth shut. I've been completely thrown since we got back here, though. Ten days I stayed away, because me being around her is a bad idea. Actually, no. Before, back when Ramirez didn't know exactly who I was and where my fucking family lived, it was a bad idea. Now he does know and he's shown up on my front door step, it's a fucking *catastrophic* idea. We should never have gotten involved the way we did back in Alabama. I should never have gone after her like that. What a fucking moronic thing to do.

Thirty minutes pass. I spend the entire time mentally kicking my own ass. Eventually, Cade removes the needle from the crook of my arm. "All right. We're done. Here, take this," Cade tells me. I lower my arm, eyeing the four white tablets in the palm of his hand with suspicion.

"What is it?"

"Azithromycin."

"Where did you get it?"

"Carnie had the clap last month. Said it knocked it right on the head." Cade grins as he says this, the motherfucker.

"Fantastic. Now I'm taking medication from Carnie's dick infections."

"I've given you some pretty sweet codeine in there too," Cade informs me. You're gonna feel really good in about twenty minutes."

I take the pills because I don't really feel like heading down to the local doctor's surgery and getting my own prescription of antibiotics. At this stage, I couldn't manage that anyway, even if I really did feel like answering the probing questions that come with a stab wound consultation.

Cade slips out of the cabin, leaving me on my back, staring up the ceiling, wondering what the hell I'm supposed to say to the quiet girl hovering in the corner of the room.

I'm such a complete and utter asshole. I shouldn't have even come storming back up the hill to the cabin when we got back from Ramirez's farmhouse. I should have just kept my cool and stayed on track. Stayed the fuck away. But, oh no, I had to be in a shitty mood. I had to fucking see her.

"Does it hurt?" Sophia's voice is soft, and yet it feels like a slap to the face. One I deserve, and then some. When I open my eyes, she's sitting on the floor a few feet away from the bed, like she's afraid I'm about to jump up and backhand her. Seeing the panic in her eyes makes me feel physically sick all over again.

"Not really," I lie. "Could be worse." *Yeah, I could be fucking dead.*

"You feel a bit better now?" She sounds like she's on the brink of tears. There's a defiant look on her face, but her hands are shaking. I can see the slight tremor as she twists a piece of thread over and over around her fingers. God, she's so damn beautiful. Why couldn't a dude have witnessed Ryan's murder? If she were a dude, I would *not* be having this problem. But then again, if she were a dude, Dela Vega would have murdered her on the spot after seeing what went down. She would have had absolutely no purpose to him. At least as a woman, he knew Ramirez might want to make some quick cash off her.

"I'll be fine tomorrow," I tell her. I won't be fine tomorrow. Truth be told, I'm probably going to be out of commission for days, if not weeks, because of this injury. And being out of commission's something I really can't afford to be right now.

I can't think about that, though. My head is still swimming. Keep my damn eyes open is becoming an almost impossible task, and the bed feels like it's pitching and rolling like a motherfucking sailboat.

"I could have run, y'know," Sophia whispers softly. "I could have just gone, run off into the night and left you here. I'd probably be halfway to the next city by now."

"You mean you'd probably be *vulture bait*," I say, correcting her.

But I know she's right. She could have just left me to die. If she'd made a different decision when I sent her running out of here, there's no doubt about it—I would have been fucking long gone. "Thank you, Soph," I say quietly under my breath. "Thanks for not bailing on me."

Out of the corner of my eye, I can see her expression growing less worried and more irritated. "After what you said to me, I should have. My sister would have probably finished the job if you'd have said that to her. She'd have strangled you to death before you even had *chance* to bleed out."

"Then I'm glad I didn't say it to her. And I'm sorry I said it to you. I shouldn't have. I know you wouldn't screw any of the guys."

"Then why say it? And why leave me here, trapped in this cabin for ten days, after I said I would help you in Alabama? It makes no sense. It's just damn cruel, in fact." She speaks slowly. I can tell she's still furious but she keeps her voice down now. No more shouting and screaming. No more trying to pile drive her knee straight through my ribcage. Given her reaction earlier, I feel like making a show of cowering from her, but it's probably still too early for jokes yet. Besides, I'd probably burst open my stitches if I move, and Cade will not be thrilled if I undo his handiwork. He'll probably stab me all over again.

"If my boys knew you were here, why you were here, or that Raphael is on the look out for you, they'll want to use you somehow," I explain. "They'll want to use you as bait or something to lure Ramirez out, and I'm not taking that kind of chance."

Soph rests her chin on her knees, staring up at me on the bed. "Yeah. Well, I mean, I don't want to be anywhere near Dela Vega or Ramirez again if I don't have to be." She sounds like even the prospect of running into either of those men is enough to give her nightmares. I'd be surprised if that's not actually the case.

"As soon as Raphael lays eyes on you here, Soph, that will be it. I know him. He's a sick motherfucker. He won't ever stop until he gets his hands on you."

Sophia shivers. Shakes her head, like she's trying to shake the very memory of him out of her body. "Why would Ramirez follow you here? Why would he actually search you out? I don't get it."

"We're not playing hide and seek, Soph. Neither side wants to drag this out. The longer we're at each other's throats, the longer Ramirez can't relax or conduct business without watching his back. The longer he can't smuggle his drugs into the country. The longer he can't focus on selling his women."

"And for you? What's this war going to distract you from, Rebel?" she looks dubious.

I smirk, thinking about shrugging my shoulders but then dismissing the idea as entirely not worth the accompanying pain. "The Widow Makers run guns. As an illegal trade, that's how all the syndicates think we make our money. It's how the ATF *think* but can't *prove* we make our money. In reality, the Widowers trade in information more than anything else. Information is far more valuable than gold or silver, drugs or guns. It can build or collapse an empire overnight. The only thing more reliable for bringing a dangerous man to his knees is pussy. And, as you're already aware, we don't sell *that*."

"No," she says, giving me a wry glance. "You only *buy* it."

"If *I* don't, someone else will. Difference being is that I find secure, honest, healthy work for the women we pay for. They leave this compound untouched. If Julio had bought you for himself, guaranteed you'd have already been accosted more times than you could count, and by more men than you could count, too. Would you have preferred that?"

Sophia remains silent. She glares at me like she hates me, but maybe, just *maybe*, like she's also considering that I may have done her a favor. Doesn't look like she'll be admitting that any time soon, though. I pull in a deep breath, testing out how deeply I can fill my lungs without experiencing any sharp, crippling pain.

"Ramirez is here because he's making his first move. He's being reckless. Perhaps I need to be, too."

"I think it's a little late for that, right?" Soph eyes my blood-covered torso with what looks like regret. "I'm really sorry. I had no idea you were hurt. You know that, right? I would never have—"

"Stop. I deserved it. We're all good."

"Still. Launching myself at you like that—

"Is part of the reason why I like you, Sophia. That fiery temper of yours is insanely hot. You looked like some wild Amazon, ready to skin me alive. I was halfway to a boner before you nearly killed me."

Sophia ducks her head, eyes skating over the floorboards, not looking at me. If I didn't know better, I'd say she was embarrassed. "Maybe you *should* use me as bait," she says abruptly. "At least that way, if my presence is somehow a catalyst for drawing Ramirez and Raphael out, then this can all be over. We could all go back to living our lives."

Laughter itches at the back of my throat. Scathing, ironic laughter. I swallow it back down. See, the thing Sophia doesn't quite realize yet is that this *is* my life. When this is all over, if I'm not dead, there will always be someone else to contend with someone else to put down. Someone else who will want to take what is ours.

I can't tell her that, though. She'll run for the hills, and despite my previous pathetic attempt at doing the right thing, I know now that it's just not possible. I have plans for the girl sitting crossed legged on the floor by my bed. Big, awesome, scary plans. I'm going to keep my mouth shut about those, too, though. Right now, there's only one thing I need to tell her.

"I'm not endangering you with those men again, Sophia. No way. Not happening. There are a lot of things I'll risk to end this. I'll risk my own life, and the lives of my club members, if they're stupid enough to volunteer them. I'll risk my freedom and every last cent I own. I'll risk the sun and the moon, and the wind on my face. But not you, Soph. I'll never risk *you*."

SOPHIA

I don't know what to make of this crazy, infuriating, ridiculously hot man. He drives me absolutely insane. One minute he's inside me in a corridor at his father's house, the next I'm being shoved back into his cabin and I'm shut away for 10 days. The man doesn't even speak to me. I don't see his face. I receive no word from him whatsoever. And now, it seems as though he's back in my life again, albeit bloody, bleeding and broken, and I don't know what to make of it.

The sun is pouring through the cabin windows, casting long shadows across the room, highlighting the dust motes swirling through the air overhead as I sleep on the bed beside Rebel. I didn't want to climb into bed with him, but the only other option was the couch and I've been uncomfortable and miserable for long enough now. Why the hell should I have to crash out on the couch? Besides, he's hardly in a position to do anything untoward at this point. The guy was practically dead last night.

It can only be about six in the morning. Already though, I can hear motorcycles arriving and leaving the compound, the brisk snarl of engines startling the birds from the trees surrounding the cabin.

I'm surprised it doesn't wake Rebel up. Mind you, he appears to be sleeping the sleep of the dead. No matter how hard I try, *I* can't seem to accomplish the same feat.

I had unwelcome dreams last night. I know it's messed up, but I haven't thought about Matt since the moment I decided to give myself over to Rebel back in Alabama. I spent the last year dating a guy and I haven't thought about him once. How crazy must I be? Matt was never as thrilling or exciting as Rebel, but he was nice-looking guy, made me laugh. He was *safe*. I feel like I'm doing him a disservice by completely forgetting about him like this. I mean, who does that?

"You look like you're plotting out the world's end." I nearly jump out of my skin when I realize that Rebel *is* awake, and he's actually looking at me, frown lines marking his forehead. Sleep still hangs over him, his gaze slightly fuzzy

"Not exactly," I say. "Just wondering where we go from here?" That seems like the most practical thing to be thinking. It's no longer the sense of limbo that I find frustrating. It's the feeling of complete and utter uselessness. Ever since I saw his uncle Ryan being murdered, I've felt vulnerable and unsafe. I haven't had purpose or place in the world I've found myself in. I've been drifting, cut free from all tasks and activities that might give me some sort of mental stimulus. I've just been afraid and powerless, and that, perhaps, has been the worst part. With nothing to occupy my mind with other than my present situation, I've been driving myself crazy. At least if I know what Rebel's plan of action is, I can maybe help. Maybe I can be a part of the process. I'm kind of stunned by the intensity of his refusal to let me be a part of any plan his club members might come up with. The look on his face last night when he was speaking was so determined; it made my heart swell in my chest in the strangest, scariest way. In that moment he looked like he meant every word, with a depth of passion I couldn't quite fathom. But if he means it, if he really won't allow me to be put in danger again, then maybe there's another way.

Rebel just shakes his head at me. "Don't get any ideas, Sophia. I know this shit is fucked up. I know I should have just let you go when Julio handed you over, but I was too angry to see straight then. I've been even angrier since we left my father's place." He laughs shakily, pressing a hand into his side. "Funny how losing an obscene amount of blood can make a guy cool his heels and start thinking properly again. I'm not normally the guy who runs into a situation guns blazing. I'm the guy who figures out how to disarm everyone without them even realizing." A shadow passes over his face, the light in his eyes dimming. "That tactic's not going to work out this time. This time there will be blood and people will die, and I don't want you anywhere near it. This can't last longer than a couple more days, okay? Once it's all over, I'll personally make sure you're delivered back to Seattle safe and sound without a hair on your head harmed. If that's what you want…"

"*If that's what I want?*" I almost can't breathe around the words. They just seem so ludicrous. "Why *wouldn't* it be what I wanted?"

Rebel just lies there, still covered in blood like something out of a horror show, looking at me. His inhales slowly, then lifts his hand and holds it out to me. "I'm done with the bullshit. If you want me, it won't be pretty. I know I sure as fuck don't deserve you, but I think you're a smart girl. You can feel what's right around the corner for us, right? You can sense how consuming and desperate and explosive it will be if we both just take one step forward. I'm not saying it's not ridiculously dangerous to be with me. To be the partner of someone who lives the kind of life I lead. But *you*…if there's anyone in this world with enough backbone and stubborn-ness to survive it, it's *you*. And you'd more than survive here, Sophia. You'd flourish."

There's a huge, painful lump in my throat by the time he's finished. My cheeks feel like they're on fire. Every encounter I've had with a guy before has been awkward and shy in the beginning. So much beating around the bush. Reading in between the lines. 'Dating,' where no one has a clue where they stand. With the man lying in front of me in this bed, there is no hidden meaning. He's afraid of nothing. He knows what he wants and he speaks plainly. It's terrifying.

"I—"

"You need to think about it. And that's okay. But know this. If you want to be with me, everything will change for you. No more college. No more middle class existence. I'll make you feel like you were sleeping before, like you have no idea how you lived such a placid, quiet existence without me." His voice deepens, sending thrills through me. "I'll fuck you raw, Soph. I'll make you forget what it was like to be with any other man. I'll ride you so hard, you won't remember your own name. I'll be the only thing tethering you to this earth. My sheets will be soaked with your come every single damn night for the rest of your sublime existence. This I promise you."

I feel like I'm seconds away from passing out. *Holy. Fucking. Shit.* No one... *no one* has ever spoken to me like that before in my entire life. And the crazy thing is that I know it's true. I know he means every single word, and more importantly he can deliver. I have absolutely no idea what I'm supposed to say in return to that. Rebel's still holding his hand out to me, waiting for me to do something.

He did the same thing in the hallway at his father's place, asking me to accept him, but I was saved from making any sort of decision by the blood-curdling scream that came from Louis James Aubertin II's kitchen at the time.

There's no one screaming now, though. I take a deep breath, trying to think of something appropriate to say while at the same time assessing what I even *want* anymore. I draw a total blank. "You realize that's impossible, right?" I whisper. "That a girl can't soak sheets with her come."

Rebel lowers his hand. His eyes shine, some sort of mischevious mirth hidden there, just behind the sharpness of his gaze. "You think the female ejaculation is a myth?"

"Isn't it?"

He starts laughing, deep in the back of his throat. It's a wicked, dangerous sound. "Oh, boy. Sounds to me like you've never come properly before, Soph. And that's a crying shame." The laughter dies on his lips, transforming his expression into one of deadly seriousness. "If you let me, I'll be *more* than happy to rectify the situation."

He fixes me with those ice-blue eyes of his, so disturbingly beautiful, and I feel like I'm about to squirm out of my own damn skin. I could barely look into them when we first met, and that hasn't really changed. And now, with him talking about female ejaculation, I'm finding it hard to think straight. "You shouldn't be making bold threats like that, you jerk," I inform him. "You could *not* deliver on that."

He grins. "How little you know me."

Rebel sleeps some more. I find myself watching him, panic coursing through my veins. Three weeks. I can't believe I've only been gone for three weeks. I feel my throat tightening shut when I realize I've missed my mom's birthday. It just slipped me by without notice. Usually Sloane and I will take her out for a girls' day, usually coffee and breakfast in the morning, followed by a spa session, mani-pedis and massages all round. It's been our staple celebrating for the past five years.

The ridiculous thing is that neither my sister or my mother are the kinds of people to enjoy spa days. Sloane was always too focused on her studies and then on her internship, and my mom still thinks every last cent that comes into the house should be squirreled away, banked, invested or donated to the church.

Mom's birthdays are usually awkward affairs.

And this year, instead of getting my toenails trimmed like a prize Pomeranian, I was fucking Rebel in a hallway. Literally. My mom was probably crying hysterically from the moment she woke up to the moment she went to sleep.

"Hey. Hey, what's up?" Rebel reaches up slowly and trails blood-stained fingertips across the line of my jaw. His touch sends violent shivers chasing through my body. I don't even want to mention where the sensation settles, growing and growing with an increasing sense of urgency. I take his hand and place it back on his chest.

"I'm fine. Just still…y'know. *Dealing.*"

"Yeah. Dealing's pretty shitty." He looks down at himself—he's such a mess—and I want to laugh at how insufficient the statement is. I don't think my body remembers how to laugh anymore, though. Screaming or total, terror-filled silence seem to be the only two functions my vocal chords are capable of.

"Your guys all saw me last night," I say, trying to keep my eyes off Rebel's bare chest. I'm morbidly fascinated by the angry red stitches that trail across his stomach and disappear over his side, toward his back. His blood has dried and cracked, turned so dark it's almost black; it creates bizarre patterns all over the tightly packed muscle of his chest and stomach. "I say guys," I continue, "but there were two women there, too. An older, really tall woman, and a younger one with pink hair."

Rebel nods. "Yeah. Fee. Josephine. She's the tall one. She was one of the first club members. And the one with the pink hair…" He shakes his head ruefully. "That one is the bane of my fucking life. The rest of the crew are guys, though. Did any of them look like they were going to lynch you?" he asks.

"They looked stunned actually. Seems like you did a really good job of keeping me a secret."

Rebel purses his lips—god, I want to bite them. I can still remember how amazing they felt all over my body—and then he blinks up at the ceiling, like he's weighing up what he wants to tell me. Eventually, he says, "They're good guys. The Widow Makers isn't like any other club, though, Soph. Everyone has a story here. There isn't a single person here who joined because they think breaking the law is fun. We have a lot of vets here. Like me. Like Cade. After the corps chews you up and spits you out, you kinda feel like...like you've lost your family. Unless they're ex-military too, your blood and bone relatives will never understand what you've been through. The bond you build with the other guys in your unit...they're never *just guys* by the end. Even the guys you hate, the ones who drive you insane, the ones you wanna kill half the time—they're your brothers too." He laughs. "I mean, most brothers want to strangle each other half the time anyway, right? But if someone fucks with them..." Shaking his head, Rebel sighs. "Someone tries to fuck with them and it's game on. Brothers will defend each other 'til the death.

"And these guys who somehow found their way to me, they're even more gung-ho about that stuff than the army. Ramirez has been screwing with me and my family for years now, screwing with our business. These men aren't going to take that lying down. They're going to skin the motherfucker alive, given half the chance. They'll do it by any means necessary. They won't let a girl they don't know get in their way. And some of them haven't exactly had the most stable female role models in their lives, either. A few of them...a few of them don't see a reason for there to be women around the club at all, other than for the occasional receptacle to sink their dicks into.

"I didn't want them getting confused about your purpose here, Soph. So, yeah. You were pretty much the most heavily guarded secret I had. That's seriously saying something. And, no, I'm *not* sorry for it."

REBEL

The next five days are seriously fucking shitty.

Moving is a uphill struggle—even getting up to take a piss is a monumental effort—and when I do feel well enough to sit up in bed, I'm not even allowed to hold a goddamn book. Cade told Sophia not to let me lift anything and, boy, did the girl take him literally. She reads to me. She fucking *reads* to me, and it's amazing. I don't tell her that, though. I sit with my eyes closed, pretending I don't notice *her* eyes are on *me* more often than they are on the pages of Catch 22.

Unlike the first night I was hurt, she doesn't sleep with me in the bed anymore. She sleeps on the couch, arms and legs contorted in the most amusing positions, hair wild and crazy all over the cushions.

I can't believe she's never come properly. That in itself is a travesty. I mean, yes, she came with me in that hallway, but that was rushed, a spur of the moment thing. Definitely not my best work. I can make her come so much harder than that. I can make her feel like her whole body is being ripped apart at the seams if I want to. And I do. I want to open her eyes. I wanna be the guy to show her what sex can feel like if it's done properly, by a real man and not by some pissy, soft college kid. I'm gonna turn her whole world on it's head, and it is going to be so goddamn perfect.

In between what's going down with Ramirez, Dela Vega, and the gigantic fucking hole in my side, I'm sure thinking about a girl is the most insane thing I could be doing right now, but as I lie in bed, staring at the ceiling, Sophia is the only thing occupying my mind.

She may think she's being smart by sleeping on the other side of the room, but she's not as clever as she thinks she is. I've seen the way she looks at me. She's the most transparent person on the face of the planet—every thought she has is usually displayed right there on her face for everyone to see. It's actually quite dangerous, really. Tonight I witnessed her thinking very bad things about me at least three times before she said she was tired and decided to bundle herself up to sleep, and it took every last scrap of will power I possessed to not physically pin her to the mattress and fuck her stupid. If I weren't in so much pain, I would have done it, too.

I think about that instead of the exposed wooden beams over my bed. I think about getting her on all fours so I can lick her pussy from behind. That quickly progresses into me sliding my fingers inside her as I lick and suck. Despite the burning pain lighting up my side, my cock begins to harden as I get a little more adventurous. By the time I've got her sitting on my face, my dick is rock solid and demanding I do something about the throbbing ache. I can't believe I'm horny. I can't believe I'm even still awake, considering the two healthy doses of morphine Cade shot me up with earlier. I've always burned off drugs really fast, though. And my cock's never seemed to know when the hell it should be behaving itself.

I try to ignore the growing desire pulsing around my body. I try to sleep. Across the other side of the room, Sophia turns over, the oversized shirt hitching up to expose bare flesh across her stomach. And her panties.

Fuck.

For a Seattle girl, she's rocking a killer tan. And a killer body to match it.

Go to sleep, Jamie. I try to talk myself into shutting her out, into letting unconsciousness slip over me, but the more I let go of the grip I'm holding on my thoughts, the more they wander to the half naked woman on the other side of the room.

"Jesus," I whisper softly under my breath. "This is going to end badly." I last another minute before I've had enough. I need to act, need to do something about this. I have to.

Getting up is really not fun. I have to tense my abs to hold everything in tight, which naturally hurts when you've just had minor surgery. I feel like if I cough, my intestines are going to burst right out of me all over the floor.

Once I'm sitting upright, I carefully get to my feet. The room seesaws and I have to reach out to brace against the wall before I fall over. Yeah, this is a really bad idea indeed. I'm probably going to pass out well before I make it to Soph.

Still. Loss of consciousness in the pursuit of epic sex is definitely worth it.

With all the speed of a ninety-five year geriatric, I slowly, gradually make my way across the cabin. My head actually clears a little from the movement, which is good and bad in turns. Means I can feel even more, but I can piece my fractured ideas and thoughts together a little better too. Fair trade.

I stare down at Sophia, wondering what she's dreaming about. She's so beautiful. When I was a kid, my mother had a print of Gustav Klimt's 'The Kiss' on her bedroom wall. I used to stand and stare at the fine detailing of that painting, admiring the obvious, captured emotion between the two subjects, and admiring how ethereal the woman looked. That's how Sophia looks now— ethereal. Not of this world. Magical, somehow. She takes my breath away.

I should feel a little guiltier about what I'm about to do, but I don't. She's not going to object. She's going to enjoy every last second of it, even if it kills me. And if I'm wrong and she doesn't want it, I'll stop and she can kick my ass again. Slowly I sink down to my knees and carefully hook my fingers under the waistband of her black cotton panties. The backs of my hands make contact with her sides and her skin is scalding, hot to the touch. She stirs, moaning lightly. I freeze, but then kick myself. The goal isn't to *not* get caught here. I want her awake and writhing against me, damn it. I want her panting my name as I make her come.

I bite back a smile as I let go of her panties, changing tack, and slowly sliding my thumb down, in between her legs. She inhales sharply, back arching up a little from the sofa, but she remains asleep. Her body responds to me, even though she's out cold, which is a beautiful thing. She opens her legs, sliding them apart, sending blood rushing to my head.

She is so amazing. Her body is incredible. My dick presses persistently against my boxers, but I don't touch myself. This will be so, so much better if I wait for her to lay hands on me. I start slowly, rubbing her clit with my thumb in small circles. This is such delicious torture. I want to pull her underwear to the side and taste her, but it's too soon. I want her to be awake for that. I want her to *want* me to. I apply a little more pressure with my thumb, a slow smile spreading across my face as Sophia gradually presses her hips up, grinding herself against me. Mind blowing.

As I lightly press my mouth against the inside of her thigh, I look up the length of her stunning body to see that her eyelids are fluttering open. I guess this is the decisive moment. I ready myself, bracing for the full force of her outrage. Her lips part, the tip of her pink tongue slowly sliding out to wet her lips. She gazes at me blearily. I witness the moment where she fully comprehends what's happening as her eyes clear of sleep, growing wider.

"What—?"

I hold up my free hand, halting her before she can go any further. "Don't kick me. If you kick me, you'll open up my stitches."

"Will I open up your stitches if I kick you in the head?" she whispers.

I nod. "Probably. And let's face it. You might mess up my face. You like my face. You don't want to mess it up."

"You really are something else," she says. She doesn't bat my hand away, though. She doesn't tell me to stop. I press down a little hard, quickening the motion as I continue to tease her clit, and she holds her breath.

"I can stop if you want me to, Soph. I can drag my ass back to my bed, no problem. I get the feeling you don't want me to, though."

"You're an arrogant son of a bitch. What makes you think—"

"Because I can feel how wet you are through your panties, Sophia. And you're really, really damn wet."

"Urgh!" She presses her legs together, trapping my hand between them, scowling at me where I'm kneeling on the floor beside her.

"What now?" I ask, grinning at her. "Is this where you pretend to get all upset and make me remove my hand? Huh?" I have just enough room to continue stroking my fingers over her pussy. She tenses, the muscles in her legs locking up. I can see the need in her eyes, which is almost enough to make me forget rational thought. "*Or* is this when you open up for me and let me slide my index finger and my middle finger deep inside you while I use my mouth on you at the same time."

"You are *not* going down on me," she hisses.

"Why not?"

"Because. I haven't showered since this morning." Her scowl deepens, but I can see her true feelings quite plainly in her eyes again. The idea of my tongue lapping at her clit is turning her on. In case I needed any further evidence, I can feel her panties growing even wetter. They're soaked now. The need to taste her is almost overwhelming, but I manage to restrain myself. I have to wait for her to unclamp her legs from around my arm before I can do anything anyway.

"Sophia," I whisper. "There's no one else here. This is just you and me. Are you afraid of me?"

"I should be."

"Maybe. But *are* and *should be* are two different things. Are you attracted to me?"

She swallows. It looks like it takes great effort. "Yes," she says breathlessly.

"Good. And do you think I'm going to hurt you?"

Answering this question takes a little longer. She stares me dead in the eye, not blinking or breathing while she makes up her mind. Eventually she says, "No."

"Good. Do you think I'm going to try and make you do something you don't want to?"

She slowly shakes her head.

I quicken my movements, rubbing her a little more firmly. Her eyes practically roll back in her head. "Say it," I command. "Tell me you know I won't force you to do anything you don't want to."

"I know you won't force me," she says, sighing. "Oh god..." She closes her eyes altogether.

"Open your legs for me, sugar."

"No, I—" I begin to pull my hand away, ready to back the hell off, but she locks her legs together even tighter. "How about...a *trade*?" she asks.

"I'm not very good at compromising."

"So I've gathered."

"So what do you want to trade?"

"I'll open my legs...if you let me out of here. I want free roam of the compound. Whenever I want."

"No. Not happening." There's just no fucking way. I tug my hand back, trying to free myself, but she's got a pretty damn good hold on me.

"You said it yourself, Rebel. I'm safe here. What could be the harm?"

"You're even more safe in this cabin, sugar."

She gives me a look that I'm sure caused her daddy to melt like butter whenever she wanted something she knew she wasn't allowed. She has that look nailed, damn it. Regardless that I'm aware she's manipulating me, I find myself caving. If she were just in the compound when I knew it was safe, that would surely be okay. A month ago, there's no way I would even be considering this, but now...now she's had plenty of time to work her way under my skin, and I'm in some serious trouble. I really can*not* believe I'm about to agree to this. "All right. Fine. But only when I'm here. Or Cade." I don't know who's more surprised—me, or her. She blinks at me, owlish, and then smiles.

"Thank you."

"Show me how grateful you are. Open your legs for me, sugar."

She doesn't do it for a second, but then she gradually releases the tension in her legs, freeing my arm. In doing so, she's given my free rein to proceed at my own pace. Pulling her panties to one side, I carefully dip my fingers into the slick, wet heat of her pussy. Her face blossoms into an expression of horror when I raise my fingers to my mouth and suck on them.

"Shit no! Don't. Don't *do* that!"

I smirk mercilessly. "Why not?"

"I already told you! I haven't showered since this morning. I'm gross. I'm—I'm *dirty*."

"Oh, sweetheart, you are *not* dirty. You are fucking perfect. You pussy looks, smells and tastes incredible. I'm literally fighting with myself here. I wanna bury my face in there and make you come all over my tongue. It's driving me insane."

Sophia's face loses all color. "You just...can't, okay? It's too embarrassing."

I laugh. "I promise you, sugar, one day very soon you're gonna be begging me to light you up with my tongue. You're gonna crave it more than air. In the meantime, fine. I'll just use my fingers instead."

She looks like she wants to argue with that too, but I slide my fingers inside her before she can get another word out, and the look of sheer pleasure on her face has me fist pumping on the inside. She's so responsive. She reacts to my every tiny movement. She doesn't know it yet, but she's the perfect sexual partner for me. I love to know how the girl I'm fucking is feeling; making a woman moan is the most basic but greatest pleasure in my life. I wouldn't trade it for anything.

Sophia moans for me even as I'm thinking this. Her breath catches in her throat, telling me that I've hit the right spot.

I wonder what she'd do if I did try and make her come properly right now. She'd be freaked out, no doubt. It's not a normal sensation for a woman. She'll feel like she's about to pee everywhere and that will shut her down instantly. No. We'll have to wait on that one. If I get my way, which I definitely intend on doing, then there will be plenty of other times to adventure into unknown orgasm territory.

Sophia's muscles spasm as she tries to fight against the sensations rolling over her body. It's the most amazing thing, watching her wage this kind of war with herself. It's a war she won't win, because no matter how angry it makes her, and how badly it makes her feel like she's losing something somehow, she *wants* me. She wants my fingers inside her, and she wants my tongue working over her clit.

It's not long before my own wants start to make themselves known. I want to fuck her. I shouldn't even be thinking about that— I'm in no position to be undertaking that sort of physical exertion— but sometimes the human body can shock and amaze. Or rather, be annoyingly stubborn and persistent until it gets what it wants. I could make Sophia come now if I wanted to. It wouldn't take much. She's ready to tumble over the edge, and all it would take from me is a little extra pressure, and a little more speed. I hold off, though. She makes a stifled groaning sound when I stop altogether.

"You want something significantly bigger than my fingers inside you, sugar?" I ask, keeping my voice low. Her pussy tightens around my fingers, and I know the idea excites her.

"You're not...sticking anything weird inside me," she says, her voice hoarse.

I can't help it; I chuckle under my breath. "Now why would I want to do that when I have a perfectly good, perfectly hard cock ready and waiting?"

Sophia glances at me down the length of her body. Her hair is mussed and gathered about her face, and her lips are plump and swollen...so fucking sexy. She lifts one eyebrow, arching it for me. "You really do have a death wish, don't you?"

"If I *do* die, make sure Cade gets my bike."

"Why don't you just...not..." She can't finish her sentence, though, because I've started circling my fingers inside her again, and it apparently feels really good. She's gonna feel a million times better when I fuck her.

I can't hold off any longer. My blood is roaring in my ears as I stand up and take hold of her thighs, pulling her roughly down the couch toward me. I still haven't taken her panties off, but there's something really hot about having them pushed to the side, exposing her pussy, so I leave them on. Sophia watches with wide eyes as I push my boxers down over my hips, and then kick them off.

I take my cock in my hand, slowly pumping my fist up and down the hard muscle, shivering slightly at the pressure. It really isn't normal that I'm feeling this way, but if I don't get myself inside her so I can feel that perfect little pussy of hers tightening around me then my balls are going to explode. She probably doesn't even realize she's doing it, but Sophia's digging her fingernails into her thighs, causing the flesh under her nails to turn from blushed pink to white. She wants me. She wants me bad. She doesn't look at my cock, though. It's like she's afraid of it or something. Give her a few weeks and she'll be intimately acquainted with it. This coyness will be long gone. I'm willing to put money on it.

Sliding myself forward, she sucks in a sharp breath when the head of my dick is pressing against her pussy. She seems a little hesitant, so I use it to rub up and down over her clit, over the opening of her pussy. She locks up when I move back a little, toward her ass, so I change direction and focus on the areas she seems okay with. When she starts angling her hips up every time I slide myself over her pussy, I know she's ready.

I take no prisoners. I'm not rough enough to hurt her, to cause her any kind of pain whatsoever, but her eyelids snap open when I thrust myself inside her, all the way, balls deep. "Oh...*shit*," she hisses.

"You have such a dirty mouth." I fold myself over her, not paying any attention to the stabbing pain that sings through me, and take hold of her breasts through the t-shirt she's wearing. No bra underneath. Perfect. Her tits are soft and full, pliable under my hands. She may not do it willingly but her back curves away from the couch, lifting her chest, offering herself to me. I don't need telling twice. I grab the hem of the t-shirt and yank it upwards, revealing her incredible body. Her nipples are tight already, turned a dark pink, flushed with blood. She moans breathlessly when I take her right breast in my hand, palming it roughly. At the same time, I take her other nipple into my mouth and I carefully squeeze it between my teeth.

I've remained very still inside her, enjoying the intense reactions she has every time I shift ever so slightly, but now I start to move again, drawing myself all the way out of her before driving myself back in, slowly but firmly.

"Oh...*ohmygod*." Avoiding my half healed side, she hooks her left leg around me, pulling me closer to her as I thrust, and the extra force is enough to drive me fucking crazy.

I can't stop now. Even if I did split my stitches, I would have to make her come before I could stop this. I need to feel her body seizing up tight. I need to hear the sound of her breath quickening. I need to watch her expression change as the tidal wave of pleasure slams into her.

I'm desperate for all of that to happen, but I'm also a major fucking tease, too. I bring her so close to climax, having to stave off coming myself at least three times before I can't take it anymore.

It sounds like her screams are being ripped out of her throat by force as I slam myself into her over and over again, rolling her clit with my thumb at the same time as I fuck her. I rarely come at the same time as a woman—I'm always far too intent on watching the whole thing play out—but this time I don't have a choice. She opens her eyes at the last second, dark chocolate irises locked right on me, and she whispers my name, my *real* name, and I'm screwed.

I come with her, our bodies both tense and gripped in ecstasy for what feels like minutes but can only really be seconds, and then we're melting together. I rest my forehead against her collarbone, panting, trying to clear my vision of the small starburst of color exploding like fireworks.

"So…is Cade going to be claiming ownership of your bike by morning?" Sophia says softly. She strokes her hand up and down over the skin of my back, oblivious to the fact that she's practically making my eyes roll back in my head.

"The fucker isn't getting that bike for a long time yet," I tell her. "Not until we get to do that at least three or four more times."

She laughs quietly, and it's a fucking remarkable sound.

SOPHIA

My body aches. Burns, in fact. I want to lie still, to sleep forever, or at least another few hours anyway, but I can't. An incessant pounding on the cabin door wakes me before dawn, though the loud hammering doesn't wake Rebel. Seems he can sleep though just about anything. Unsurprising, given how late he stayed up last night, how much morphine he had in his system and how energetic he'd been when he'd pinned me to the couch and fucked me. I'd had to spot him as he weaved his way back across the other side of the cabin, and then he'd pulled me into his bed, refusing to let me go back to sleep on my own. I feel hung over as I disentangle myself from his arms and get up, pulling my t-shirt down to cover my bare legs.

"Rebel? Rebel, man, open up!" a gruff voice hisses. I can tell by the sharp tone of the male voice on the other side of the door that it's Cade, and that he's also super pissed. "*Rebel, open the fucking door.*"

"All right, already," I hiss back. Despite the low light coming from a lamp on the other side of the room, I still manage to stub my toe as I hurry across the room to get the door. My foot is throbbing and my heart is beating out of my chest when I open up, glaring at the two dark figures lurking on the porch. Not just Cade, then—Carnie, too.

"Is he okay?" Cade asks briskly.

"Yeah. Yeah, I think so," I reply. "He's out cold." Carnie gives me a none too subtle once over, his eyes raking over my bare legs, and it's with a considerable horror that I realize I'm not even wearing any underwear. He can't see anything, but I still suddenly feel very naked. Cade gives Carnie a pointed look, clearing his throat, at which point the other man looks away, eyes to the sky.

"We need to come in," Cade tells me. "It's important."

"I gathered, since you were trying to knock the damn door down." I pluck at the t-shirt, trying to pull it down some more as I move aside to let them in. I close the door behind them and Cade beelines straight for the bed where Rebel is still passed out on his back, a very thin sheet barely covering his naked form. Cade clears his throat, scratching at his jaw. He seems to think about how to proceed before grabbing hold of his friend and shaking him hard enough to make his head bounce off the pillow.

Rebel is instantly awake, eyes wide, fist pulling back as he readies to punch Cade. "What the fuck?" he snaps.

"No time for pleasantries," Cade says. "Can you walk?"

Rebel inhales, pulling a deep breath into his lungs. He glances between the three of us, and then nods, resting his hand over his injured side. "I might be able to if you quit shaking the shit out of me, man. What's going on?"

"We got a problem," Carnie says softly. "A big one. You need to see."

Cade grunts. "You need help getting dressed?"

Rebel shakes his head. "Give me a beat. I'll be out in a second."

Cade and Carnie leave without saying another word, both of them wearing grim, frightening expressions on their faces. I've never seen either of them look so angry. Cade's always polite with me, well mostly, anyway, and yet it's like he doesn't even see me as he exits the cabin. I don't know why, but a sense of intense foreboding settles over me. Something really awful has happened. Something beyond comprehension. Something I probably don't want to know about. A wave of panic sings through my veins—panic not for myself, but for Rebel. He's nowhere near fully recovered, and knowing his luck he's probably about to be shoved head-first into a really dangerous situation again.

Slowly, he heaves himself into a sitting position, pressing his hand into his side, wincing in pain. His beautiful body is in bad shape, black and blue, his bruises visible even against the complex, dark background of his extensive tattoos.

"Are you sure you should be moving about?" I ask. "Shouldn't you be resting for a couple more days at least before you head off on some wild goose chase in the early hours of the morning?"

"If Cade comes in here looking like he just did, it means something important requires my attention. He wouldn't ask me to come if it wasn't entirely necessary. So yeah, I have to go."

"Couldn't he just tell you what the hell has happened?"

"In case you haven't noticed, Sophia, Cade is not that wordy. He's more of a show than a tell guy." He winks, groaning as he carefully gets to his feet. I want to give him more morphine, but I get he still has a huge supply of the drug coursing through his circulatory system. More at this point could kill him. Dad used to tell me about that all the time—people who overdose on painkillers, both unintentionally and intentionally, and slip away without even so much as a by-your-leave. It happens so easily. They're dangerous things, painkillers. And highly addictive to boot.

"You feel like passing me a pair of jeans?" Rebel jerks his head toward his closet, brow furrowed in pain. "I think you'll get there quicker than me."

I open up the door to his closet to find the most immaculately organized walk-in I've ever seen. T-shirts, shirts, belts, shoes—everything is placed and folded just so. Puts my room back on campus to shame. I like to think of my room as organized chaos, but the truth is it's actually just chaos. I grab a pair of jeans, boxers and a t-shirt for him, and then I watch as he fights his way into his clothes. I'm about to ask him if he needs me to help him at one point but he holds his hand up as soon as I take a step toward him. The look he shoots me could freeze over hell. Eventually, after a good ten minutes of swearing under his breath, he's fully dressed. I can tell the effort has cost him a lot, though. His face is pale, his forehead lightly speckled with sweat, and he doesn't seem that steady on his feet.

"Are you coming?" Cade calls through the closed door.

"Jesus wept, man! I have a fucking hole in my side," Rebel yells back. He starts to cross the room and I quickly snatch up my own jeans, kicking them on in record time.

Rebel gives me a curious look, arching an eyebrow at me. "Where do you think you're going?"

"With you."

"No, you're staying here."

"Funny, because I was sure you told me a couple of hours ago I could have free roam of the place if I wanted. Did I imagine that?" It takes me a second to realize my hands are on my hips, my own eyebrows raised in challenge. He'd better not take that back. He promised me I wouldn't be cooped up in here any longer. If he reneges on our deal, it won't matter what awful problem Cade and Carnie want to show him right now. He'll have a much bigger problem on his hands: *me*.

Rebel narrows his eyes. "I'm not saying you should stay here for the fun of it, Soph. It's for your own good."

"I'm an adult. How about you let me make my own decisions for once, huh?"

He stares at me a second longer before rolling his eyes. "Okay, fine. But remember, whatever happens, this was your call."

I drop my hands from my hips, trying to hide my surprise. "Great. Thank you."

Outside, Cade takes one look at me and shakes his head. "You won't want her seeing this, man."

Rebel casts a look at me over his shoulder, a guarded look in his pale blue eyes. "She's an adult, Cade. She can make her own decisions, apparently."

A hundred meters from the compound gate, a lone tree stands by the side of the dirt road, silhouetted against the rising sun. From the moment we leave the gate, making slow progress as Rebel hobbles after Cade and Carnie, I can see that something's not right. It's not until we're much, *much* closer that I catch sight of the reason why Cade seems to be so agitated though.

A body.

A body hangs from the tree, upside down, suspended by one foot. The other leg hangs at an awkward angle. The foot which should be at the end of that leg is missing. The hands which should be at the ends of the arms hanging freely below are also missing. And the head... the head is gone, too. Blood mottles the naked flesh, covering the torso, the buttocks, the legs...

The rope, looped around the thick bough of the tree, creaks as the body spins, facing us, revealing that it's the body of a woman. There's what looks like a scrap of blood stained paper stuck to her body, black writing typed across it, but I don't see what it says. I drop to my knees instead, and vomit into the red dirt beneath me.

"Jesus. *A gift, from Los Oscuros?* What the fuck is wrong with this guy?" Rebel hisses. From where I'm bent over double on the ground, I can see that his hands are shaking. I lock onto that sight, willing myself not to look up at the poor woman hanging from the tree, at the awful things that have happened to her. Rebel's hands shake and shake and shake. And the woman's hands are...are just *gone.*

Cade grunts. "And what the fuck is up with their choice of font, too?"

"Yeah." Carnie spits on the ground. "Really says a lot about your intentions. I mean, how are you meant to take someone seriously when the message they send you is printed in motherfucking comic sans?"

"You cut their body into small pieces. That's how you take them seriously. Hector's fucking with us," Rebel says softly. They continue to talk, but my ears are ringing. I can't focus on the subdued conversation that takes place over me, but I can feel the tension pouring off the three men. I can literally taste their rage. I throw up again, screwing my eyes shut, unable to breathe.

Oh my god. I can't... I can't... I can't...

"Bron," Cade says. "Her name's Bron. She's Keeler's girl. I recognize the tattoo." I make the mistake of looking up, then. I see the small tattoo of a rose on the inside of her right forearm, just above her wrist. The bloody stump where her arm terminates is still dripping blood. I heave again, though nothing comes up this time.

"Fuck." Rebel sinks to his knees beside me, his face now completely ashen, devoid of all color. He reaches for me, pulling me to him, though he doesn't really look at me. He's staring at the piece of mutilated flesh hanging from the tree like a slaughtered cow. Slowly, he strokes a hand absently over my hair, the cool blue of his eyes hardening, darkening somehow, turning steely and cold. "Sick motherfucker," he whispers. "That sick, evil motherfucker picked her off because she wasn't inside the compound."

Cade laces his fingers behind the back of his head, turning away from the woman. He squints into the distance, out into the desert, his mouth pulling down at both sides in a grimace. "Yeah. Yeah, looks that way."

"Does Keeler know?"

Carnie kicks at the dirt, shaking his head. "No. No one else knows. I found her this morning when I came back from town. I went straight to Cade."

"Good. You did the right thing. I—*fuck*. God knows how we're gonna break this to everyone." Rebel sounds composed but his voice is utterly empty. I cry in his arms while he strokes my hair, wishing I hadn't been so damned stubborn. If I'd just let him have his way, I wouldn't have the image of Keeler's dead girlfriend burned into my memory. This isn't something that will ever go away. This isn't something I'll ever forget about. This is something that will give me nightmares for the rest of my life.

"They're gonna want blood," Cade says.

Rebel's chin rests on the crown of my head, and for some reason the intimacy of the action calms me a little. "I know," he says. "And they'll get it. We just have to make sure we go about this the right way. He's trying to bait us. Trying to provoke us. If we're angry when we go after him, we won't be thinking straight. We get sloppy, we make mistakes. This *has* to be contained."

"I hear you. But this woman had a foot, both her hands and her fucking head chopped off, Rebel. I'd like to see how you're gonna contain *that.*"

REBEL

Turns out Keeler spent the night away from the compound, visiting his sister in Cedar Crest. At the moment he's
one of our primary tattoo artists at Dead Man's Ink, though.
Today is his day to cover the shop, so Cade and I ride into town and
to wait for him. We cut Bron's body down and drive her back to the
compound first, of course, hiding her out of sight, where the other
guys won't find her before we have chance to tell Keeler. Cade and I
sit in the shop in silence, me bleeding through my stitches, staring at
the walls, neither of us knowing what to say to one another. This
isn't the first time we've seen fucked up shit. Afghanistan was a
savage place. The things we saw there... That was the first time I
really understood, really *knew* the evil man was capable of commit-
ting against his fellow man. Nothing will ever be more brutal than
the atrocities we saw there. But this is different. This is here, on our
fucking doorstep, and this isn't fucking Kabul. This is regular small
town Americana, and this was one of our own.

Keeler's first appointment is at ten thirty, so Cade and I sit and
stew for a good hour and a half before the low rumble of Keeler's
motorcycle rattles the glass in the shop's window frames.

"How you gonna handle this?" Cade asks.

"I don't know. I guess we're about to find out."

Keeler looks surprised when he opens the shop door and finds Cade and me sitting at the counter. Concern flashes across his face. He's young, mid-twenties. Good guy. Not ex-army like most of the Widow Makers. He was beaten by his father from the moment he could walk til the moment he ran away from home—spent some time pin-balling between different drug gangs before he wound up on the wrong side of the law and serving three years for possession with intent to supply. He got his shit dialled in prison. He'd been out for a month when he walked through the doors of Dead Man's Ink for the first time, looking for work. Cade gave him a job on the spot. Took him a clean year to convince me to let him prospect for the club, though. Now I'm feeling really fucking guilty that I caved and swore him in.

"Hey, guys. What's up? Did I leave the door open or something?" He eyes us cautiously, like we're about to ream him out.

"No, dude. Come in. We gotta talk to you about something." I pull out a chair by the counter, gesturing for him to sit down. He looks like he's about to shit his pants.

"Uhhh… should I be freaking out right now? 'Cause I'm freaking out." He slowly walks into the shop and lowers himself into the seat.

"You haven't done anything wrong," Cade tells him. "It's—it's about Bron."

I watch the nervous smile fall from Keeler's face. "What about her?" he says slowly.

I take over. I'm the president of this club. I'm responsible for the people who have joined, and I should also be responsible for their loved ones. I should have known this was going to happen. I tell Keeler what's happened, doing my best to provide as few details as possible. It's impossible to keep the truth from him for long, though. The guy stares at me, as though I'm making it all up.

"Come on, man, stop fucking around. That shit ain't funny."

"I'm sorry. I swear to god, I am so sorry, and we are going to make this right, Key."

"She's dead? She's *dead*?"

"Yes."

"They...they cut off her *head*?"

I scrub my hands over my face, blowing all the air out of my lungs. "I'm sorry. Yes."

"Where is it?"

"What?"

"*Where is her fucking head, man?*" Keeler's voice is nothing more than a whisper, yet his eyes are screaming with rage. He's about to flip his shit.

"We don't know. We'll find out, though. We'll make this right." God, I really hope I'm not lying to this kid.

As predicted, Keeler explodes. Cade and I sit back and watch as he trashes the shop, punching a fist through the door to the back room, throwing the sterilizing equipment, destroying anything and everything he can get his hands on. We let him rage.

By the time he collapses into a heap on the floor, sobbing silently, shoulders jerking up and down as he weeps, there's barely a stick of furniture in the place that remains unbroken.

"Take him back to the compound," I tell Cade. Keep him away from everyone until I get back. No one leaves today, though. Tell the rest of the club they're on lockdown. Tell anyone with friends or family living here in town to make sure they pull everyone in. I'm not having his happen again."

Cade says he'll get it done and then leaves. As soon as he's managed to half carry, half drag Keeler out of the shop, I double over and clutch my side, breathing through the white hot, burning pain that's tearing through me. "Fuck." Breathing is hard again. I don't know if that's from the pain or from Keeler's complete devastation. He deserved better. He deserved for his girlfriend to be safe while he was out of town. I should have fucking known this was going to happen. Hector Ramirez is a sociopath. He's clinically insane. The life of an innocent bystander means nothing to him.

He'd murder the entire town if he thought it would make his point. So I should have known.

"Well, that was quite the display."

My head snaps up at the sound of the voice, already knowing who it is. Already assessing how I'm going to proceed. Hector Ramirez stands in the open doorway of the shop, one hand braced against the frame, the other hand casually in the pocket of his suit pants. He looks mildly amused, like the scene of destruction before him is entertaining. His gaze settles on my side, my hand still pressing against my wound, and his eyebrows slowly rise. Taking *his* hand out of his pants, he places something small into his mouth and bites down on it, crunching.

"You know," he says. "It really is a shame you snuck up on my guards the other night. They're very jumpy men. They tend to react without thinking sometimes. If you'd simply have made your presence known to them and told them you wished to see me, I'm sure they would have treated you in a far more...*civilized* manner."

I grind my teeth together, mentally scanning the shop for a concealed weapon, something to do some serious damage to the evil piece of shit that is strolling into my property like he owns the damn place. Problem is, we don't keep guns or knives here. The shop's raided by the cops on a fairly frequent basis, and precautions have been necessary in the past.

With a slight grunt of distaste, Hector steps over the smashed coffee table between he and I, his leather shoes crunching as he treads on shards of glass. "I imagine you found my little gift this morning?" he says. "I worried that you might not see her. Raphi suggested we leave our present to you right on your doorstep where you wouldn't miss it, however that seemed a little too obvious. I didn't want the police arresting you for murder because there was a mutilated corpse propped up against your boundary wall. Where would the fun have been in that?" He puts something into his mouth again and chews—candied almonds. The bastard always has a pocket full of them. Makes him smell like an old woman.

I curl my fingers to make a fist, hate charging through my veins, seeping into my pores, infecting every last part of me with a rage that won't go unanswered. *Can't* go unanswered. I tried to do this the legal way, I really did. I wanted Ramirez and his men in jail for what they did to my uncle. I wanted them to suffer every horrifying, dark, awful violation possible while they served their time, knowing they were going to die as incarcerated men, never to walk free again. The time for that has past now, though. Now, I just want them all dead. Preferably in the most painful manner possible.

"You shouldn't have killed Leah. You should never have stepped foot on my father's property in Alabama. You should never have followed us back here, and you really shouldn't have harmed a hair on Bron's head, Hector. You think there won't be consequences?"

Hector Ramirez shrugs, pulling a fat cigar from the breast pocket of his suit jacket, apparently done with his almonds. He bites the end off the cigar and spits it onto the ground, then proceeds to light it with an engraved silver lighter. "From where I'm standing, the Widow Makers aren't the formidable force I assumed them to be when I undertook this little adventure to New Mexico, *Jamie*. When Raphi dealt with your uncle back in Seattle and your second in command made grand gestures, inciting war between our people, I thought to myself, '*well, okay now. This might be interesting. Something to distract you from the tedium of every day life, Hector. Thank the lord.*' But no. I arrive here to this dust bowl you call home, and I find a rag-tag group of misfits living out in the desert, sticking their dicks into the locals, *tattooing people for money*." He gestures at the trashed shop, disgust warping his features. "I have to admit, I'm more than a little disappointed."

He makes it to the counter where I'm still bent double, trying to remain calm. Trying not to give away the fact that my right hand is resting on the one weapon we *do* keep in the shop—a prime maple Louisville slugger. I'm in a shit load of pain and my head is spinning, so I have to wait for the perfect moment. If I launch myself at him too early, I'm going down hard and I won't be getting back up again. That means I need him close. Closer than he is now, anyway. And that means I have to keep him talking.

"You made a huge mistake in coming here, Hector."

"Ahh, you think so?" He pouts, pulling on his cigar, holding the smoke in his mouth before he blows it out in a thick cloud. The smell reminds me of my father—he always smokes after dinner, ever the traditional southern gentleman. It takes me a mere second to connect the dots when I see the familiar Havana Red paper seal of my father's favorite brand wrapped around the rolled tobacco leaves in Hector's hand. He is *literally* smoking one of my father's cigars. This is an action designed to piss me off, to drive me crazy, but all he's succeeding in doing is distilling my anger into clarity. I don't see red. I don't react. My recklessness the other night, the recklessness that got me stabbed, isn't normally how I operate. Push me to the edge and I get smart. Poke and prod at my buttons and I come up with new and interesting ways to return the fucking favor. I've got my shit handled now, but then Hector Ramirez doesn't know that about me. He knows nothing about me whatsoever. He's massively underestimated both me and my club if he thinks he's going to succeed in baiting me into stupidity twice.

He comes closer, standing on the other side of the counter. "You know...I believe I recognized the woman with you at your father's home, Jamie. Can it be that you arranged for Julio Perez to purchase my little One Eighty-One on your behalf?"

One Eighty-One, the number he assigned to Sophia in order to sell her. Motherfucker. I glare at him, willing him dead. It's the only way I can maintain my relative calm. If he says her name...if he so much as mentions her again...

"That was very underhanded, you know. I can't say that I like you tricking me out of her like that. Bad business. My good friend Raphael has aired his concerns about her association with the Widow Makers. He's...*worried* about her safety. Normally, I'm careful to ignore Raphi's council, however in this particular instance

I think he may have a point. *I want her back, Jamie.*"

My vision blurs in my peripherals, my heart rate doubling. No way. No fucking way is he having her. "You're certifiable if you think I'm handing her over to you, asshole."

Hector shakes his head, as though he expected more from me. He looks away, out of the shop window, biting down on the fat cigar in his mouth. "I'm sorry to hear that. But I suppose these things can't be helped. If you are not willing to return the girl to me, I will simply take her from you. You won't be able to stop me. And this way, when she is back within the confines of my household, performing for my pleasure, I will not treat her well, my friend. I will treat her like the whore she is. I will ruin her. I will make her obey me in everything. She will be degraded and tortured, and when I have had my fill of her, I will kill her. And this time I will make sure to send you her head and her hands instead of the rest of her body. No. I will keep the rest of her body. A pussy is still a pussy, after all, no?"

I don't feel the pain in my side anymore. My head is no longer fuzzy, my vision no longer blurred. Everything is crystal fucking clear, and my body is vibrating with fury. Only a second ago, I was clinging to the fact that his provocations wouldn't work on me, and I honestly believed that to be true. But now, with this? I *cannot* stay calm. I *cannot* keep a cool head. Sophia is a game changer. I swore I would protect her, and now Ramirez is threatening to violate her dead body?

No.

Just. Fucking. No.

He doesn't see the baseball bat coming. I whip it out from under the counter so fast that he has zero time to react before I'm swinging. Back in Alabama when I was a teenager, my father used to force me to stun his livestock with a sledgehammer before their throats were slit—'*one fierce blow to the temple, boy. What's the matter? Are you a fucking pussy or an Aubertin? God, you disgust me.'*

There were other, far more humane ways to end the animals' lives, but my father derived some kind of sick pleasure in watching me cry as I swung that sledgehammer at his cattle. He had me do it over and over again, hundreds of times. I hated every second of it, disorienting those cows so they could be slaughtered, but the experience taught me a lot. I've had plenty of experience. So when I slam the baseball bat into the side of Ramirez's head, it's with a precise and brutal force.

Ramirez's head rips around, the cigar flying out of his mouth. He drops down to one knee, making a low, gurgling sound at the back of his throat. Blood. There's blood all over the baseball bat, and Ramirez's head is pouring more of the bright red liquid down his face, soaking the crisp white collar of his shirt. I vault over the counter, already lifting the bat in my hands, ready to bring it down on his head again. I'm prepared to keep on lifting it and bringing it down until the man in front of me never gets up again. I can't have him hurting Sophia. I won't fucking allow it.

I'm two seconds away from landing another, terrible blow when Ramirez starts laughing. That was the gurgling sound he was making—laughter, while choking on the blood gathering in the back of his throat. "You...you really caught me with that one," he says, grinning. His teeth are covered in blood—bright white obscured by crimson. "Oooh, Jamie. You should see yourself," he growls, looking up at me, dark eyes burrowing into me. "You look fearsome. You look like the kind of man who's unafraid to kill another to protect what is his. Perhaps you're not such an unworthy adversary, after all. Your father was wrong. You do have a backbone."

"My father can go fuck himself. And so can you, motherfucker." I swing, and this time the bat connects with Ramirez's shoulder, sending him crashing to the floor. The crazy bastard curls up on his side amongst the shattered glass and laughs long and hard. He's insane. Has to be. He must know he's about to die, and yet his only response is this complete and utter hysteria. "Like I said," I growl. "You should never have come here, Hector." I raise the bat over my head, gripping it in both hands, and I'm ready. It's been a long, long time since I've killed a man, but this right now is well deserved.

Hector killed Ryan. He killed Leah, and Bron. And now he's a threat to Sophia? I won't even feel bad about ending him. My conscience will be clear. There's nothing on earth that can stop me from finishing this, here and now.

It's at this exact moment that I'm thrown off my feet. It feels like I've been hit by a Mack truck. My back smashes against the counter, and my body wants to sink to the floor but I can't because my muscles have locked and my jaw is clenched so tightly that my teeth feel like they're going to shatter. Pain claims every nerve ending I own from my head to my toes. I can't make a sound, but if I could I'd be yelling out in agony. Barely able to even move my eyeballs, I look down at the source of my pain and realize that there actually *is* something on this earth that could stop me. Two things, actually. The first, a fifty thousand volt Taser gun, the prongs of which are embedded into my chest. The second, the female police officer standing in the shop doorway.

"You wanna run that by me one more time, asshole?"

Detective Lowell, DEA, does not seem entertained by my response to her questioning. In fact, she looks severely pissed off. She likes things tidy. I can tell that just from looking at her—her immaculate gray pant suit, and her immaculately styled hair, and her immaculately understated make-up speak volumes. And questioning me in my messy, smashed up shop while two paramedics make sure I don't have any lasting injuries from where she shot me with her Taser is making her less than congenial. Funny, really, since I'm feeling so bright and shiny. If bright and shiny could also be described as fucking broken and in serious amounts of pain.

"I told you. I was just showing a prospective client some of our sporting memorabilia."

"I assume you're talking about the baseball bat?"

"Yes, ma'am."

"And you were showing it to him? By pile driving it repeatedly into his face?"

I glance up at her, wincing as one of the EMTs uses an alcohol swab to clean a cut above my right eye. "You saw me hitting that guy with my bat?" My tone of voice is borderline shocked. "That doesn't sound like something I would do at all."

Lowell exhales sharply, hands on her hips. "You had the thing held high over your head. Your *potential client* was prone on the ground, laughing. It sure as hell looked like you were about to use the thing to shut him up."

"Why would he have been laughing if I was beating him, Detective? That sounds crazy."

Lowell looks like she's about ready to pick up the bat and smash *me* over the head with it. She jerks her head toward the offending article lying on the ground where I dropped it. "Doesn't look like sporting memorabilia to me. Looks brand new."

"Not true. It's signed. Super valuable."

"I can't see a signature anywhere on that thing."

"It's there. It's just hidden underneath all the blood. See...*there*." I point. "David Ortiz."

David Ortiz hasn't signed the bat. But *I* did when we hid it under the counter. It's a fairly decent forgery. Lowell gives me a cold, dead-inside kind of look. "You think you're funny? You think this is a joke? This is jail time right here, buddy. Serious jail time."

"Detective, please. He's telling the truth." On the other side of the room, Ramirez is being aided by another EMT; his left eye has almost swollen shut and his arm is in a sling from where I dislocated his shoulder. "He was just showing me the bat," he says. "I fell and hit my head. I assure you, there was nothing untoward taking place when you shot at Mr Aubertin."

Lowell glances between the two of us, her brows drawn together, scowling furiously. "You're both horrendous liars. You think I don't know who you *both* are? You think I'm stupid? You think it's a coincidence that *I* am here, in the middle of bum-fuck-nowhere Hicksville, New Mexico, sitting here with the both of you? Because rest assured, it is *not*."

I shrug, giving her my best *I-don't-know-what-to-tell-you* face. "I'm no one special, Detective. I run a tattoo shop. And this gentleman—" I choke on the word. "—Just came in asking about getting some work done."

Lowell laughs a hard, stony laugh. "All right, just stop. Don't fucking bother. I'm sure I'll get the truth out of you back at the station. You're both under arrest." She reads me my Miranda rights first, and then repeats the process with Ramirez. As soon as the EMTs are done assessing me, I'm cuffed and bodily dragged out of the shop by two deputies. Ramirez isn't far behind. As I'm shoved into the back of a police cruiser, I catch Ramirez grinning at me out of the corner of my eye.

I know him. I know he won't change his story at the station, and neither will I. Lowell is about to be frustrated at every turn and I suspect I'm likely to spend the next twenty four hours in a holding cell, but I couldn't care fucking less. It'll give me time to think this thing through. It'll give me time to make plans.

I'm sure Hector Ramirez will do the same.

SOPHIA

I can't get the image of that headless woman out of my mind. It's there, every time I close my eyes for the rest of the day. Horrifying. The most awful thing I've ever seen. Rebel, Cade and Carnie kept their cool, but I could tell the sight had disturbed them, too. Rebel's hands were shaking as he walked with me back to the compound. Still shaking when he pulled me to him and lay with me on his bed for half an hour in silence as I cried.

He left me shortly after to go find the woman's boyfriend in town, and I've sat in his cabin ever since, staring at a wall, wondering how this can really be my life. I find myself thinking about Matt again. I made a choice to stay with Rebel back in Alabama. I've thought myself crazy many times since then. I could have gone back to my old life and to safe, boring Matt. I'd never have been exposed to mangled, headless corpses if I'd stayed with him. I'd have had a Costco account and checked out books from public libraries. I'd have visited wineries on the weekends and eventually had some kids and rescued a dog from the pound. I would have had a mundane, safe life I'm sure. Everything would have been fine.

But *Rebel*.

It's inexplicable. It's the worst decision I've ever made, and yet all the same, headless corpses or no, here I am, still sticking to it. What does that say about my mental state? It's dark by the time Rebel returns. He never told me what time to expect him back, so I haven't been worried, though when I catch sight of him that changes. He looks way, *way* worse than before if that's possible. He looks like he's literally nearly dead on his feet. Cade helps him through the cabin door and dumps him on the end of the bed, and I can do nothing but stare at him with my mouth hanging open.

"What...what the hell happened?" Rebel lies back on the bed, exposing the lower half of his stomach, which is red with fresh blood. It's then that I notice the two small holes in his black t-shirt. "And what the hell happened to your clothes?"

"He got hit with a Taser," Cade says dryly. "And then arrested by the DEA. I don't know, man. I leave you alone for five fucking minutes and look at the state of you."

Rebel groans. "I appreciate your concern."

"*What?*" My ears must be playing tricks on me. Rebel is so damned nonchalant, like being arrested and Tased is an every day occurrence. As soon as the thought hits me, I realize that perhaps it really *isn't* so uncommon for him, though. "You feel like explaining what happened?" I say.

"Love to. I kind of need a second, though," Rebel replies, pressing his knuckles into his sternum—he's in a lot of pain, though I know him well enough to know that he'll never say so.

"You should get into bed, man," Cade tells him.

"Not yet. We need to go to the clubhouse. The others will be raging if we don't explain all the cloak and dagger bullshit before the end of the day. They deserve to know."

Cade shakes his head, throwing his hands in the air. "Why the fuck did I just drag your ass up the damn hill, then?"

Rebel slowly turns his head to look at me. "Because we had to come get Sophia. It's time the rest of the club met her properly. I'm sure they're all asking questions."

Cade laughs. "That's one way of putting it. They were about ready to lay siege to this place this morning in order to find out who the hell she was."

Rebel's face takes on serious expression. "I hope you informed them how unwise that would be?"

"I did. And they didn't like it."

"They don't have to like it. They just have to do as they're told."

I haven't seen this version of Rebel before. He's angry, that much is obvious, but he seems focused, too. Determined. He's been intimidating since the first moment I met him, but right now he's downright scary. He looks at me again, taking a deep breath. "This is what you wanted, right? Free rein of the place. Freedom to see and talk to whomever you like? Well, this is it. Do you want to come with us to the clubhouse?"

I bite my lip, images of Costco and the fiction section of a Seattle public library flashing before my eyes. I slowly shake my head, feeling slightly hysterical. It's the challenge in his eyes. The look he gives me that tells me I need to be strong in order to immerse myself in this life.

I fold my arms across my chest, tilting my chin up in acceptance of his challenge. "Sure. Okay. I'll come."

Rebel's eyes flash cold steel. "Fuckin' A."

My memories of the clubhouse the other night are pretty hazy. I was too concerned with getting Cade to follow me back to Rebel in order to assess my surroundings, but now things are different. Now I have plenty of opportunity.

The place is cavernous—an old remodelled barn with high rafters and recast concrete floor. Long wooden tables and benches line the room, and smaller tables dot the edge of the space. A bar runs the length of the back wall, stocked with a multitude of different bottles of scotch as well as everything else you might expect to see in any normal bar.

There is a sea of people gathered inside, seated at the benches and hovering by the bar. Most are men, huge guys with arms full of tattoos, larger than life, scary as all hell. There are a few women and kids, too, all of whom look generally terrified and out of place. Everyone stops talking when they catch sight of Rebel. And me.

A woman at the back of the hall gets to her feet straight away. I recognize her—she was the woman who gave me the dirty look as I raced out of here behind Cade. She's different to the other women packed into the clubhouse. She's inked up, her nose pierced, pink hair pinned back in a messy topknot. She's wearing a torn Sepultura t-shirt and a snarl on her face that already spells trouble. Beside me, Rebel hangs his head, apparently sensing the same thing.

"What the fuck is going on, man?" she snaps. "We've been sitting here with our thumbs up our asses all day. Keeler's missing, and Cade hasn't told us shit. And who the fuck is *she*?" The woman stabs her finger at me like I'm an invading alien and she's ready to go Independence Day on my ass.

"Sit down, Shay. And shut your damn mouth. This isn't how we're doing things," Rebel says. His voice is monotone, controlled, but even I can tell he's irritated by her outburst.

The woman—Shay—shakes her head. "That's bullshit, Rebel, and you know it. You can't keep us in the dark, and you can't bring random women—"

"I SAID SIT THE FUCK DOWN AND SHUT YOUR GODDAMN MOUTH, SHAY!"

I nearly jump out of my skin as Rebel explodes. His face, completely colorless for the past five days, is suddenly bright red. His body is shaking, shoulders tensed, hands clenched into fists. "Today has been a seriously shitty day. Do *not* make it worse," he hisses.

Shay blanches, the hostility falling away from her. She looks very much like a frightened little girl, which I'm betting is a rare event. I'm also betting it's not very often that Rebel loses his cool; nearly every single person in the clubhouse looks stunned. Shay slowly sits down, and everyone else keeps their lips tightly sealed, clearly waiting for Rebel to speak.

Eventually he does. "This morning, Hector Ramirez sent us a very clear message. Carnie discovered the body of a woman hanging from a tree on the dirt road into town. It was Bron, Keeler's girlfriend. She'd been decapitated, her hands and one of her feet removed. Her body had been hung upside down from the tree."

The room explodes into sound. Forty people start shouting at once, the sound of their anger deafening. The obvious club members, the men with Widow Maker tattoos and leather cuts, are the angriest. In the corner of the room, a tall, skinny guy with long blond hair jumps out of his seat and rushes forward, limping ever so slightly. "Where the fuck is Keeler? And where the fuck is Ramirez? We have to kill the bastard. He's gotta fucking pay, Rebel."

Rebel blows out a deep breath. "Keeler's just taking a beat, Brassic. And Ramirez is holed up in a farmhouse on the other side of town. He was arrested this afternoon, as was I."

He goes on to explain that Ramirez showed up at their tattoo shop after Cade left and made some poorly veiled threats, at which point he'd laid into him with a baseball bat. I stand beside him, listening in horror as he goes through the motions of describing how he was then shot with a Taser and taken down to the local sheriff's department. Cue one very angry DEA agent, ten hours of very aggressive questioning, and then he was allowed to call Cade who came and got him. The tension in the room is at boiling point by the time Rebel finishes his story.

Brassic, the tall, blond guy who asked about Keeler, slams his palm down onto the table in front of him, sending an empty glass shattering on the floor. "When are we going after him, Rebel? We can't let this stand."

"And we won't. I know you're all angry. I'm angry, too. But we need to be smart. If you can come up with a solid plan of attack that doesn't end up in most of us dying and the rest of us in prison, I'd love to hear it. If not, then we need to take some time to figure this thing out. That DEA agent was intent on getting answers out of me. I'm sure she was the same with Ramirez. She told me plainly that she was in town with a crew, and that they weren't leaving until they get what they came for. That includes Hector Ramirez on charges for drug trafficking and murder, and the Widow Makers locked up for the LA shooting at Trader Joe's."

"We were cleared of that, man! The cops arrested the guys the Desolladors hired to frame us. They admitted everything!"

"I know that. You know that. Lowell knows that. She's pissed, though. Anything she can pin on us is a win for her. We're living under a microscope right now, guys. If we put one foot wrong, we're all fucked."

Rebel's words don't seem to have any effect. Or certainly not the one he's clearly hoping for, anyway. From the snatched words I overhear from people's conversations, it sounds like no one cares if they get caught, sent to prison, shot or killed. They just want revenge.

"You still haven't told us who *she* is," Shay repeats. She moderates her tone this time, but it's clear she's furious over my presence. Rebel fixes her in an artic stare.

"She was witness to my uncle's murder in Seattle. Hector and Dela Vega kidnapped her and we had Julio arrange purchase of her. She's my guest here, Shay. That's all you need to know."

"So Hector and Raphael found out you had her and came here looking for her, right?" A rumble of dissent goes up amongst the crowd. Shay can hardly keep the hatred from her face as she locks eyes on me. Rebel does something that surprises me next. He steps in front of me, blocking me from her view. "You look at her again like that, Shay, and you and me are gonna have problems. In fact, best not to look at her at all, you read me?"

"She's put us all in danger, Rebel. And you brought her here without telling any of us," she spits. "Don't you think we had a right to know about this? Don't you think it would have been smart to tell us if you were bringing danger to our doorsteps?"

"It sounds very much like you're questioning my judgement." Rebel's voice is all gravel and hard edges. He sounds like he's about to go off at the deep end. Cade places a hand on his shoulder but Rebel shakes it off. He looks around the room—I can't see the expression on his face, but I'm betting it's terrifying. "This is not a democracy," he says slowly. "This is not a fucking day spa. You don't get to question me or go against my wishes. I've always done my best by you guys. I've always done my best to keep you safe. As of this moment, if any of you are unhappy with my leadership or think the threat Ramirez and his men poses is too great to your safety, I invite you to leave. No repercussions. No hard feelings. However, if any one of you so much as thinks of stepping out of line and putting this club in further danger, I'll strip the motherfucking ink out of your backs right here and now." I can see the hairs on the back of his neck slowly rising. The silent pause that follows is uncomfortable to say the least. Half the Widow Makers are looking at their feet when Rebel continues. "And should any one of you so much as think about making life here difficult for Sophia, you're going to have to deal with me personally. Old or young. Man or woman. You've trusted me for the past five years, followed me through hell and back, so trust me now when I say this: you have *never* seen me pushed to my limit. Do *not* fucking test me. It will *not* end well."

When we get back to the cabin, Rebel puts me in his bed and tells me he'll be back, and then I watch him through the half open bathroom door as he strips down to his boxers and methodically washes the blood from his body. He's constructed beautifully, the planes of his muscles twisting and shifting in unison as he moves carefully around the bathroom. I can tell his side is still bothering him. And now he has two angry looking purple bruises planted in the middle of his chest where the prongs of the Taser made contact as well. There's a lot of grunting and wincing as he cleans himself up. Sloane would tell him to sit his ass down so she could help him, but Rebel...he probably wouldn't comply. He's fiercely proud. He's used to this—I can tell. If I try and interfere, he'll probably shut down and instead of making progress we'll be backtracking. I leave him to clean his wound and replace his bandages himself. He throws back what I'm assuming are more pain killers and antibiotics, and then he braces against the counter and stares at himself in the mirror for what feels like a very long time. He doesn't seem to like what he sees.

When he comes to bed, I'm still intimidated by his performance back at the clubhouse. Intimidated enough that I pretend to be asleep. He sees through the ruse, though, pulling me to him without fear of waking me. He doesn't say anything. He just strokes his hand over my hair, breathing deeply in the darkness, and I listen to his heart charging underneath his ribcage. He's running a fever, his skin burning against my cheek as we lay there. I wonder if he'll be a little better by the morning. Probably not. I mean, it's going to take longer than a few days to recover from a serious injury like that, especially if he keeps moving around, attacking people with baseball bats and getting shot by DEA agents. I get the impression that tomorrow will be more of the same, somehow.

It doesn't take long before Rebel's breathing evens out. I'm chasing sleep myself, but before it can claim me a thought strikes me. An unpleasant one. It takes me a moment to pluck up the courage to speak. When I do, my voice is nothing more than a whisper in the dark. "Rebel?"

"Mmm?"

"That DEA agent? You think she'll come here? You think...you think she'll recognize me?"

He inhales, then rests his chin against the top of my head, the same way he did this morning when he comforted me. It all feels too familiar. Too safe. Too right. "Yeah," he whispers back. "She'll come here. She'll probably recognize you."

"And then what? What do I tell her?"

He's quiet. Too quiet. I already know I'm not going to like his response. "You tell her one of two things, Sophia. You tell her I kidnapped you and you've been held against your will for the past few weeks."

"Or?"

"Or you tell her you left Seattle of your own free will. That this is where you want to be. That this is your home now. Here with us."

It feels late when I wake up. Sunlight pours in through the window above the bed, warming my skin, though I'm cold. I've been used to half-surfacing from sleep throughout the night and feeling Rebel's body kicking out enough heat to warm me in the dead of winter, but now I can tell I'm alone. I don't open my eyes. I lie very still, listening. Sure enough, the sound of someone moving around at the other end of the room reaches me, confirming that Rebel's up and about. Slowly, carefully, I turn over and crack my eyelids, searching him out.

He's still in his boxers, standing in the open doorway of the cabin, with what looks like a notepad and paper in his hands. There's a small snow globe at his feet—a snow globe of Chicago's skyline. Back at his father's house in Alabama there were at least twenty more of them, from different cities all around the world, collected by his mother. The snow globe from Chicago is the only one he has here with him, though. Not for the first time, I wonder what makes that one in particular so special.

"Sleep okay?" Rebel asks. He hasn't turned around but he's figured out that I'm awake. I pull the covers up around my body a little closer, fighting the urge to hide completely.

"Yeah, I guess."

"Good." He pivots and freezes with the sunlight casting him into silhouette as he faces me, pen in one hand, paper in the other. He's so damn beautiful. Not jock pretty like Matt was. No, Rebel's body bears a striking similarity to a vase my mother keeps on her side table at home. Sloane and I were playing when we were kids, soccer inside the house, and we'd knocked the vase off the table. It had shattered into a thousand tiny pieces. Mom was devastated. It took Dad a solid three weeks to figure out where each tiny sliver of porcelain belonged and to glue it back into place. I think Mom loved the vase even more once Dad had finished the job. So much painstaking effort had gone into repairing it that it didn't matter to her if it was riddled with a spider web of fine chips and fractures. I have no idea who has spent so long over fixing all the injuries to Rebel's body—many people, I'm sure—but his body somehow seems more beautiful for all the scars and imperfections. Matt would whine like a little bitch if he rolled an ankle during football practice. I'm yet to hear Rebel complain once about the fact that his belly was half-ripped open, or that he was shot up with thousands of volts of electricity.

I can just about make his features out as he gives me a grin that would take me out at the knees if I were standing. "You done, or should I come closer and give you a better look?" he asks softly. "You keep peering out of those covers at me and I might just come back to bed."

"That sounds like a threat."

"It is. And more. I'll make good on the promise I made you the other day, if you like?"

It takes me a second to remember what he's referring to. When I do, my cheeks feel like they're on fire. He's referring to making me come. Properly. Showing me that the female orgasm isn't just a myth. Holy shit...

Rebel stalks into the room like a panther, like now he's had to chance to think about making me scream and he's decided it's a really great idea. I have no idea if he's just trying to scare me or if this is something more. And I have no idea if I want it to be more. It makes me feel safe to pretend I don't want him, but it's exhausting and I've never been good at lying. Even to myself.

Truth is, I'm addicted to the man.

I should hate him. I should be scared of him. I shouldn't want him anywhere near me, and yet...

"You can do what you want," I whisper. "You normally do."

He gives me a smirk. "Well, well. I do believe that wasn't a no." He walks back into the cabin, holding his torso rigid—I can see he's already freshly dressed his wounds again this morning—as though he's trying not to pull his stitches. I never thought I'd be the kind of person to look at a man like this. Like I'm hungry for him. It's embarrassing, but it's also freeing in some weird way, too. Sex has never been a big deal for me. It's never played a huge role in my life. Ever since Matt and I got together, I assumed I just had a low sex drive and that was okay because he was always pretty vanilla about things and would finish up quickly anyway. But now... now I know my sex drive isn't low. It's just been dormant, laying in wait for the right person to come and awaken it. As I lay in Rebel's bed, rubbing my feet together, trying not to think about the building pressure between my legs or the wicked look that's spreading across his face, I'm pretty sure I've found that person. Or rather he found me.

"I'm just saying. Would it matter even if I did say no? You seem to get your own way most of the time, regardless of what anyone else has planned."

He stops dead in his tracks. "Not all the time, Soph. Not with this. You think I'd force you to fuck me?" He's lost that playful air to him. It's vanished in a puff of smoke. Instead, he looks...hurt?

"No. No, that's not what I meant. I...I just—"

"Think that I would coerce you in some way?" He frowns deeply, those blue eyes of his clouding over. It takes less than the space of a heartbeat to realize that I've said the wrong thing. I regret opening my mouth instantly. I should have thought.

"No. I don't think you would ever coerce me. I really don't. I shouldn't have said that. You just...you make me feel like I'm...out of control."

"You are *always* in control, Soph. *Always*. If you haven't figured it out yet, I'm at your disposal, day or night. My club members step out of line and they'll know about it, but you can pretty much get away with murder. I'm not a fan of games, Sophia. I've kept my mouth shut since Alabama because you looked terrified at the time, but I told you back in that hallway that you were mine for as long as you wanted to be. *And I was yours.* You didn't take my hand. You were scared by the idea of it, I know. But it's still true. That hasn't changed. As long as you're here, with me, you have nothing to be afraid of. And that includes me."

I can't think of the right thing to say. When he looks at me the way he's looking at me right now, I can't think straight at the best of times. But coupled with the intensity in his voice and the way my body has just responded to his words, I don't have a hope in hell of forming a coherent sentence.

He sighs, throwing the notepad and pen down on the end of the bed. "I'm going to figure out how to shower with all of these bandages. You can get some more sleep if you like." He turns and heads for the bathroom door.

"Rebel, wait!"

He does. Glancing over his shoulder at me, he waits for me to speak. Me being me, I'm hoping that he'll let me off, cut me some slack, not make me say it, but of course he's him and that's not how this thing works. I'm learning that slowly. Frustration courses through my veins. Why can't he be a gentleman about this and just come get into bed with me? Rebel shakes his head, a small, barely-there smile twitching at the corners of his mouth.

"Be brave, sugar. I know you are. You just gotta prove it," he says softly.

In a million other situations, I'd get stubborn on his ass. I'd slump down in the bed, hiding under the covers, and I'd let him go take his shower, refusing to step up to the plate. This is different, though. If I did that right now, I wouldn't be winning. I'd be losing, big time. I let out a shaky breath, pulling myself up a little in the bed. "All right, fine. I don't want you to go for a shower. I want you to stay here. With me."

"Oh? And why would that be?"

I could kick him in the shins for being so quietly smug, but it's actually a very sexy look on him. He pulls it off well enough for me to be squirming in the bed as he slowly faces me again. "You know why," I tell him.

"You have to tell me."

"Because..."

"Because?" He takes another step closer to the bed.

"Because...I want you."

A bright fire burns in Rebel's eyes. "How?"

"I want to feel you on top of me, pushing my legs apart, pushing your way inside me. I want to get lost in you."

"You want me to fuck you hard or slow, Soph?" He seems fascinated by the words I'm forcing out of my mouth. He seems to be savoring every last one. He stares at my mouth as he stalks purposefully toward the bed.

"Slow," I whisper. "I want you to fuck me slow. I want to feel every last movement. Every last second that you're inside me. I want to feel your arms tight around me, so I can barely breathe. I want to forget."

He gives me a sharp look. "Forget about what? Bron? Dela Vega?"

Slowly, so slowly, I shake my head. Why is this so damn hard to say? I've come this far now—the rest of it should be easy. It isn't, though. Opening my mouth, telling him what I want, is the hardest thing in the world. I've climbed mountains and overcome so many ridiculous obstacles recently, and yet *this* is where I flounder—here, trying to tell him the truth. He makes me feel small. Vulnerable. *Afraid.* "No," I say. "Not about them. I want to forget where you begin and I end. I want to forget what it feels like to exist without you. I don't want to dance around this anymore. I was scared back in Alabama, you're right. But now the only thing that scares me? The only thing that scares me is *not* being with you."

As he rushes the last few steps to the bed, Rebel doesn't seem to care about his injuries anymore. I think he's going to jump on me, rip the covers from my body and devour me, but he doesn't. He kneels on the bed, sitting back on his heels and bracing his hands on his thighs, staring at me, his chest rising and falling quickly. "You have no idea..." he growls. "You have no idea what I want to do to you, Sophia. But you're about to find out. Are you ready? Do I have your consent?"

Panic grips me, but I force myself to let go of it. In the past I'd have grabbed hold of this fear with two hands and refused to let go, giving myself an excuse to back out of whatever situation I found intimidating. I can't afford to be that way, though. Not if I want to find out where all of this leads. Despite every single warning bell going off in my head, that's exactly what I want. I nod, slowly drawing in a deep breath. "Yes. Yes, you have my consent."

Rebel eyes glitter. I can see his intention in them, and it's both thrilling and frightening at the same time. I know he's going to come for me now, but knowing it and seeing it happen are two very different things. When he bends slowly, placing both hands on the bed in front of him, and begins making his way closer, I feel like I'm about to pass out.

"You want me to come inside you, Sophia?" he says, his voice a low, dangerous rumble in the back of his throat.

"Yes."

"Good girl." He moves so he can peel back the comforter that's still covering me, and then he takes a second to inspect the length of my naked legs. The t-shirt I'm wearing seems really damn short all of a sudden. As if that bothers Rebel, though. He gently makes contact with my skin, running his hands lightly up the outsides of my thighs. I break out in goose bumps at his touch, sending violent shivers chasing through me. When his hands hit the hem of the t-shirt I'm wearing, he fingers the material, following the stitching along the hem until his hands meet in the middle. I know things are about to get crazy when his eyes meet mine and I can see the lust burning in them. "You know you should be naked right now?" he says. I'm going to respond, going to tell him that I want to be, but I'm not given the opportunity. Rebel grips the bottom of the t-shirt in both hands and pulls, splitting the material right up the middle.

The action is violent and makes me jump, but he doesn't hurt me. The t-shirt's in ruins, though. Completely unsalvageable. It's kind of ridiculous that I've been wearing a shirt that says, *It's Not Going To*

Suck Itself anyway. Rebel removes the rest of the shirt from my body with persuasive hands, but he doesn't touch my naked breasts. Doesn't even glance at the rest of my bare flesh. His eyes remain locked onto mine, his breathing growing faster and faster. His skin is still boiling hot. He's still feverish, though he doesn't seem likely to let that hinder him in his current activity. Once I'm naked and lying on the bed in front of him, Rebel carefully positions himself in between my legs, kneeling over me.

"You're a problem, Sophia," he tells me. "You're like the most complex, infuriating math problem I've ever attempted."

I curve an eyebrow at him, trying not to look at his increasingly noticeable hard-on. I smile a little, determined not to hide my body from him, even though the effort is killing me. "More complicated than Legendre's Conjecture?" I ask.

Rebel laughs. I could be wrong, but I get the impression he's a little impressed. "You remember what it's called, huh?"

"What it's called, yes. If you asked me to draw it out, that might be a problem, though."

"Oh, well, we can solve that." He leans back and grabs the pen he was using before, pulling the cap off with his teeth. How such an action can be sexy, I have no idea, but he manages it. It's hot as hell, in fact. He spits out the cap and then holds up the pen—a blue sharpie—giving me a questioning look. "You ready for me to get mathematical on you, sugar?"

"You want to scribble messy equations all over my body?"

When he opens his mouth, he's switched on the Alabama charm. "Why, I'm a tattoo artist. I ain't never made a mess on nobody's skin. And I sure as hell ain't ever *scribbled* on anyone, either. Now, please be so kind as to oblige me while I create a work of art on your already perfect body, darlin'."

The southern accent has always made me cringe, but when Rebel speaks slow and deep the way he just did, I find myself reacting very differently. Very differently indeed. I want to press my knees together again, to stem the building need I'm experiencing, but I can't because he's still kneeling in between my legs.

I am frozen marble as he takes the tip of the sharpie and begins to slowly draw on my hipbone. From there, he travels upward toward my belly button in an arcing beautiful cursive that incorporates long, sweeping blue lines and curlicues that dip down low onto my stomach. He doesn't rush. He takes his time. I feel every hot breath he takes as he works over me, frowning in concentration.

I have no idea what true values the numbers or shapes represent as he marks them onto me, but he was right; this isn't a scribble, and it's sure as hell not messy. It's remarkable. He works for another fifteen minutes, his movements becoming slower, more considered, as the seconds tick by. My nerve endings jump every time tip of the pen makes contact. My heart races a little faster every time he exhales over the expanse of my bare skin. Eventually, I realize he's noticed my involuntary reactions and he's taking his time with me on purpose, drawing this out, making it last longer.

His pen travels down, down, down, and I clear my throat. When he looks up, his face is already lit with a savage grin that I haven't been able to see until now. "Little uncomfortable?" he asks.

"Just wondering if you're going to color me in entirely is all."

He laughs again. "I think you'd look great as a smurf. I've only just discovered how hot it is to watch you jump and squirm when I do this. It's made my cock rock solid, Soph. All I can think about is how beautiful you'd look if I were tattooing you for real and this was a gun in my hand. I think watching you writhe around while you were getting inked would have me coming in a heart beat."

A cold, strange shudder runs through my body—half dread, half excitement. There were lots of girls at school who had tattoos all over their bodies, some of which were real works of art. I never looked at them and thought, 'yeah, that's me,' though. I never planned out what I would look like if I were to have some serious ink going on. It never even crossed my mind, mainly because I knew what my father would say if I came home with a tattoo. He'd lose his freaking mind.

"I'm not letting you tattoo me," I tell him. "No way in hell."

"Why?" Rebel puts the cap back on the pen and tosses it over his shoulder, looking devious. "Afraid?"

"Is this the part where you tell me I'm a chicken and it wouldn't hurt?"

"Oh, no. It can hurt like a bitch, sugar." Slowly, he ducks down and licks the skin just above my belly button, never taking his eyes off me. "It's just that some pleasures are worth the pain. You wouldn't know about that, I'm sure. I'll show you if you like?"

I've never wanted anything as much as I want him now. I think he can see that in my eyes, because he smiles. "Are you wet yet, Sophia?" he whispers. "If you're not ready for me, I can always color you in some more."

I nod, struggling to keep my hands still beside me. It's as though they have a mind of their own. I want to touch him. I want to bury my hands in his hair. I want to trace my fingers over the deep purple bruises on his chest, and then I want to gently kiss both of them. I imagine what his skin would taste like if I licked him the same way he just licked me, and my hands curl into fists. "No more coloring," I whisper.

"As you wish." Rebel kisses my body, sending wave after wave of pleasure soaring through me as he moves from the very start of the equation he's just drawn on my hip, up, up, up my ribcage, until he reaches my left breast. It's far from cold in the cabin, but my nipples have tightened to almost painful proportions already. It's cruel, cruel torture when he takes my nipple into his mouth and gently sucks, trailing his tongue over my sensitive flesh, flicking it with the tip of his tongue.

"Oh...*oh my god.*"

He sucks harder, and my back arches off the bed, curving into his body. I can feel how badly he wants me now. I've already seen how big he's gotten but to feel his erection digging into my belly makes this whole situation seem more...I don't know. Surreal in some ways? Because this isn't me. I'm not the girl who grinds her hips up against a guy I barely know as he teases my nipples with his fingers and his mouth.

Rebel palms my right breast with his free hand, kneading lightly, breathing hard down his nose. Every single muscle in his body is tight and tense as he slowly starts to rock against me, pressing his cock against my pussy, creating the most amazing friction. I forget I'm meant to be a timid mouse in this situation.

I wrap my arms around his neck, pulling him closer to me. Rebel groans as he continues to grind his body against mine, and the sound of his pleasure sends a sharp, demanding shockwave of need through me. I want to hear him make that sound again. I want him to be inside me when he does. My hands are working quickly, then, pulling at the waistband of his boxers.

Rebel takes hold of my left hand first and then the other, pinning them above my head. "I thought you wanted this slow."

"I do."

"Then don't tempt me."

He slides down my body, and then he's pulling my legs apart even further, making a pleased humming sound at the back of his throat as he stares at my pussy. If I weren't so turned on, I'd probably be cringing. Instead I'm biting on my bottom lip like a character out of some trashy romance novel, feeling electrified by the way his eyes travel so slowly over me.

"You want my tongue, sugar?" he growls.

"Yes. Yes, I want it," I pant. "*Please.*"

He chuckles under his breath, running his hands down the insides of my thighs. "You're incredible," he tells me. "Just...fuck-ing...incredible." When he dips and teases his tongue over my clit, my head starts spinning. I have no idea how guys learn how to give head, but Matt could have done with some lessons from the school Rebel attended. He knows exactly what to do to set off those fireworks in my brain. It occurs to me that he's probably so good at it because he's had years and years of practice with god knows how many women, but the thought is fleeting. Neither my body nor my mind will allow me to think about things like that right now. Not when I could be floating on this cloud, feeling like the tether holding me to this earth could snap any second and I could drown in nothingness. It's what I want. No, it's what I *need*.

Rebel has me on the brink of coming and he must know it. Just as it feels like I'm climbing, lifting, rising to the top of some giant roller-coaster, he slides his index finger and his middle finger inside me and every last synapse in my brain starts firing.

"Jesus, you really do taste like sugar," he groans. "I can't get enough of you." He only has to pump his fingers into three or four more times before he pushes me over the edge and I plummet, heart hammering, hands clinging to the sheets, vision narrowing and my ears ringing.

It takes me a moment to realize my thighs are locked tight around Rebel's head and his tongue is still working over my clitoris, stretching out the end of my orgasm, making the muscles in my stomach and the backs of my legs twitch and flex.

"Oh, shit. Stop, stop. *Please*! Stop!" I'm laughing uncontrollably, but it's manic, pleading. He's driving me crazy. I'm way too sensitive for him to carry on. He stops, rocking back on his heels, a very smug smile spreading across his face.

"You taste like candy," he says, as he gets up off the bed and finally removes his boxer shorts. I've been waiting for this for a long time. Sure, we had sex in the hallway at his dad's place, and, yes, we did it again the other night, but I've never *seen* him. Never had the chance to check out what he's got going on down there. Rebel seems to know that I want to see him properly. He doesn't rush back onto the bed. He stands, shoulders back, covered in bruises, favoring his good side, but he doesn't hide his cock. If anything, he's pretty damn proud of it as he remains frozen to the spot, allowing me to get a good look. And he has every right to be proud. Matt was pretty straight laced, but he did like to watch porn with me every once in a while. Rebel easily rivals any of the guys we saw in those 'movies.' His cock is perfection. It's actually *beautiful*. That seems like a strange thought to have about a penis, but it's true. It makes me want to do weird things...like take a plaster cast of it and make myself a personalized Rebel dildo that I can tease myself with it when he's not around.

"I take it you like what you see?" he asks. "You've got this look on your face. Somewhere between complete carnal lust and over-whelming relief."

I laugh. "Overwhelming relief?"

He nods, climbing back up onto the bed, back up onto me. "Yes. Like you thought I somehow tricked you before and I was going to have a micro-dick."

More laughter, though it's strained now. I can feel him between my legs, pressing against the entrance to my pussy. If he so much as takes a deep breath, he'll be inside me. And god, I want that. "I'm not...sizeist," I tell him.

"Doesn't matter." Rebel pushes forward just the tiniest little bit, but the feeling of him entering me makes me dizzy in the best possible way. "Even if I had a two inch cocktail sausage for a dick, I could still make you come with it. I could still make you scream my fucking name. I know what I'm doing, sugar, and it makes me seriously fucking hard to bring you pleasure. Now, are you ready for me to make you come?"

His gaze penetrates me deep. The heat from his body on top of me is making my head spin. "I'm ready," I tell him. And he pushes into me, slowly, with purpose, staring me in the eye, his arms braced either side of my head as he sinks deeper and deeper. He feels...he feels *amazing*. Before, things have always felt amazing, but this is something else entirely. He doesn't pull back straight away; he holds himself in place, holding me in his gaze, and it feels like something clicks. That sounds ridiculous, but it's true. It feels like the last tiny shred of resistance I may have habored concerning this man is gone, banished, destroyed, and now I'm screwed. I won't be able to hold myself back anymore.

I'm surprised by the look in Rebel's eyes when he finally pulls back, drawing out of me so he can repeat the motion. He looks surprised. A little shocked even? He shakes his head, grinning a little, and then he really takes my breath away. He supports himself with one hand, and then cups my face with the other, bringing his lips down on mine. Kissing him isn't something I've daydreamed about. I haven't allowed the thought to cross my mind. We kissed back at his father's place, but we were both desperate then, fighting to control ourselves. We were ripping and tearing at each other like wild animals. Those kisses were intense and powerful, but our mouths were crashing together, devouring one another. Now, the way he kisses me is purposeful and direct. His mouth is soft on mine, but he's in control. Lowering his full weight on top of me, he leans on his elbows, which frees up his other hand to brush the hair back out of my face, trace his fingers across the line of my cheekbone, my jaw, my temple. He moves slow just like I asked him to, but he makes sure he's deep inside me each time before he draws away. I move with him, feeling trapped and safe beneath him at the same time, both scared and whole.

This is nothing like the encounters we've shared before. This feels honest. Like a promise somehow. He holds onto me so tight as he fucks me. It's not long before both of us are shaking with the effort of keeping ourselves together. I lock my legs around his waist and we come at the same time, Rebel growling into my neck, crushing me to him as he climaxes.

We lay together, panting, unable to move as the early morning sunshine shines down on our bodies, and I realize that he gave me what I asked of him. He made me forget. He made me forget where he began and I ended.

And it feels perfect.

REBEL

Burying a body's never fun. When you're only burying part of it, it's even less fun. Back in Afghanistan, my boy and I buried fucking dismembered arms and legs all the time. The Marine Corps were pretty diligent about making sure the pieces of people they were sending back to the States all belonged to the same body, but I'm guessing often times DNA got a little fused together. Not a pleasant thought. Really fucked up, in fact. I made sure the army knew I didn't want to be flown back to Alabama if I was K.I.A. Told them I wanted to be cremated and scattered to the four winds from a rooftop in Kabul. Last thing I ever wanted to do was give my asshole father the pleasure of interring me in the Aubertin family mausoleum instead of burying me with my brothers in a military cemetery. He didn't respect the time I spent overseas. He would have stuck me in the cheapest pine box he could find, left me on the bottom shelf underneath my mother's dusty coffin, blinked a couple of times at what remained of his only son, then casually locked the door. He wouldn't have returned until it was time for his own empty husk to be shelved and forgotten about, too.

Motherfucker.

Burying Bron is a different affair entirely. I'm sick to my stomach and in pain, but I figure if I have enough energy to make Sophia come then it's only right that I have the energy to go out into the desert and dig a grave with Brassic.

As I thrust the shovel into the sun-baked dirt three miles south of the Widow Makers' compound, sweat running in rivers down my back, running into my eyes, salt in my mouth, my head spinning just enough to let me know this is a really bad idea, I'm trying not to think about Sophia. I'm trying not to think about how edge-of-a-knife this whole thing is. I'm ready to burn the whole fucking world down for this girl. I wonder if she knows that? I wonder if she knows how many people I'd tear limb from limb myself in order to keep her safe.

I'm not like her, though. I don't wear every single thought I have on my face, or in my body language. I keep things close to my chest. It's the only way I've survived this world for so long.

Other members of the club have survived by alternative means. Cade's stone cold like me, but his temper is legendary. People don't fuck with him, because they know the consequences will be dire to say the fucking least. Shay uses her body to protect herself. She'll make you think you're about to get the ride of our life, when in actual fact you're about to get a stiletto blade slipped through your eardrum and into your gray matter without a by your leave. She really is a true widow maker. The guy I'm digging this grave with, Brassic, is our resident bomb maker. He won't hurt you with his fists. He'll hurt you with a pound of C4 and a remote detonator while he's a mile away slamming back a shot of whiskey.

He doesn't talk while we dig. Neither of us do. He's angry that I wouldn't let him go after the guy who killed his best friend's girl last night when his rage was peaking, but he won't show it openly. Good thing for him, too. I'm not in the mood to be questioned. My side is killing me, and all I can think about as our shovels make dry, *shink, shink, shink* sounds in the dirt is that I somehow have to fix this fucking Ramirez mess under the noses of the DEA. Highly fucking inconvenient.

"We're digging this hole for the wrong person, you realize," Brassic says. It's the first thing he's said since we started working, and it's so true it makes my head pound.

"I do know."

Brassic grunts. He's slick with sweat like I am, except the vast expanse of his back bears the Widow Makers' club badge instead of the Virgin Mary that I have inked into my skin. She was my first tattoo, my holy lady. The space had already been taken by the time I started the Widow Makers, and besides, it's better for me not to have any club markings. There are times when I need to go places, see and do things that I wouldn't be able to if people suspected I had affiliations to a biker gang. In those instances, if they knew I was the *president* of a biker gang, I'd be murdered on the spot.

"So when, then?" Brassic asks. He sounds tired; I know for a fact he was up all night with Keeler, drinking and smashing the shit out of the workshop in one of the outhouses, so his head must be killing him.

"Soon. Really soon, man," I tell him.

"And you'll give me free rein?"

I mop my brow, eyes still stinging, my head swimming, and I say, "Buddy, when this thing goes down, you don't need to worry. You can turn the bastard into red mist and I will thank you for it."

In the distance, thick plumes of dust billow up into pale, washed out blue of the sky overhead. Cars. Three of them. I can't see what kind they are or who is driving them, but they're traveling fast.

We walked out here to clear our heads. We fucking walked. Brassic turns giving me a concerned look. "We need to get back?" he asks.

I have a sick, anxious feeling in the pit of my stomach as I watch those cars speeding toward the distant compound. "Yeah. Yeah, man. We need to get back. *Now.*"

SOPHIA

I've never noticed that Cade has a slight limp before. I notice it well enough when he's charging across the compound toward me like a crazy person, though. He favors his left side, skipping his right foot behind him ever so slightly as he charges in my direction with a stony expression on his face. I can feel the worry pouring off him when he pitches up in front of me.

"You should get back up to the cabin, Soph."

"Why?" No way am I going back to the cabin. I have no specific reason for being in the courtyard outside the clubhouse but I'll be damned if I'm being sent away again already. I am sick of being cooped up. Sick of feeling a prisoner. Cade must see me bristle; he blows out an exasperated breath, holding his hands up in the air.

"We got visitors, okay. And not the nice kind. Better you aren't here for it," he says.

I feel like being stubborn some more, but the look on his face tells me that might not be wise. "Who is it?" I ask.

"Don't know. Not DEA, but still... no one good. C'mon. Get back up the hill. *Please*. Jamie will kill me if I let anything happen to you."

He looks genuinely concerned. Out of the corner of my eye, the woman with pink hair from last night, Shay, emerges from the clubhouse, pulling on a dirty white t-shirt over her florescent pink bra. Classy. She shoots me the foulest look ever, and then frowns as she squints into the distance beyond the compound gates. When I follow her gaze, I see what she sees: tall columns of dust, red and brown, growing closer and closer. Too close, it would seem. The hood of a black car is visible, only meters away from the gates, but there are more behind, following.

"Shit," Cade hisses. The first black car screeches to a halt, kicking up more dust and debris as it almost crashes into the gates. The sound of hot metal ticking reaches us, and then the loud *crack!* of a gun being fired. Sounds like it came from inside the car. I can just make out the shape of a figure slumping forward in the driver's seat, and then the car's horn starts screaming, blaring out obnoxious sound into the quiet.

"Ah, sweet Jesus." Cade steps to the right, blocking me from view of the car. He sends Shay a sharp look that she returns, arms folded across her chest. "Make sure this one doesn't come to any harm," he tells her.

She scowls and then spits on the ground at her feet. "Rebel said not to threaten her. Didn't say nothing about *protecting* her."

Cade pivots on the balls of his feet and begins marching toward her. He looks like he's about to tear her head from her shoulders. She holds up her hands, taking a step back, eyes wide. "All right, all right! Fuck, man, it was a joke."

Cade's not in the mood for jokes, though. "Just do as you're fucking told, Shay."

A high pitched screaming joins in the sound of the car horn, and suddenly there are people climbing out of the first car while a second and a third pull up alongside the first, blocking the gate to the compound entirely. I couldn't see it before, but all three vehicles are completely riddled with bullet holes.

A tall, leggy blonde in a tight black dress and red stilettos emerges from the first car. She looks like a wild animal, dark eyes round and filled with madness. As soon as she's on her feet, she turns and unceremoniously drags the lifeless body of a huge man out of the car behind her. He looks like he's half dead; given the amount of blood spattering the woman's arms and legs, he could actually be all-the-way dead.

Shay's mouth hangs open, surprise taking over her features. "Is that...?"

"Maria Rosa?" Cade finishes. "Yeah. Yeah, it is."

It takes me a second to remember who this woman is. I've met so many new people and been introduced to so many new threats recently that this recalling where Maria Rosa fits in takes a beat. I get there fairly quickly, though. Maria Rosa. What was it Carnie called her the day the police came to search the compound? That's right...the Bitch of Columbia. The head of the Desolladors Cartel—the woman who tried to frame Rebel by sending men in Widow Makers cuts into a grocery store in Hollywood and mowing down women and children.

"What the fuck is she doing here?" I whisper this under my breath, unable to give force to my words. I'm too disbelieving, too stunned, too completely horrified to grasp what I'm seeing in front of me.

"I don't know," Cade replies. "But it looks as though, as per usual, the psycho bitch has brought trouble with her."

"Help me! *SOMEBODY HELP ME!*" Maria Rosa topples to the ground, tripping on her own heels as she tries to drag the extremely heavy looking body toward the gates. She spins around, fury and panic lighting up her face. She sees the man standing next to me and the panic vanishes, completely replaced by anger. "What the fuck is wrong with you? Get over here, Cade. Get over here and fucking help me."

More people pour out of the cars—all men in black suits and white shirts with guns in their hands—but Cade remains utterly still. His eyes look cold. Dead, almost. "You really are insane if you think for one second you're getting through those gates, darlin'."

Maria Rosa lets go of the man's arm and stalks up to the metal railings of the gate, a wicked snarl twisting her features. I can tell that she's a beautiful woman usually, but at the moment she looks like medusa—her hair is everywhere, her eyeliner smudged down her face, bright red lipstick smeared. She's hysterical, and from what I can tell about to get much, much worse.

"You let me through these gates, Cade," she snaps. "Let me through, or I'll make sure this one finds his way inside all by himself. He's been telling me all about how he'd like to fuck the pretty little thing you have hiding in your shadow."

I only put two and two together and realize she's talking about me when she jerks her head at one of her men and Raphael Dela Vega appears. He strains against the taller, broader man holding onto him, desperately trying to get free. I spot the crude spider tattoo on his face and it all comes rushing back to me—him telling me how he was going to rape and kill my mother and sister right in front of me. I feel dizzy, like I'm about to pass out. He's haunted my dreams, but this is the first time I've laid eyes on him since the night Rebel bought me. I've tried to pretend he doesn't exist, tried to pretend he's dead somehow, that Hector tired of him and got rid of him, but no. Here he is in all his savage glory, only twenty feet away from where I'm standing now. And Maria Rosa's threatening to set him free on our doorstep. Irrational as it may be, I'm terrified. Since the gunshots, car horn and Maria Rosa's screaming took place, twenty Widow Makers have materialized out of the compound buildings, all holding guns, all ready to put a bullet in this woman's head for fucking with their club name. I *know* they aren't going to let Raphael anywhere near me, but still… I can feel his eyes crawling all over my skin, can sense the dark things he wants to do to me, and it makes my heart squeeze in my chest.

"Shoot them all," Shay says. "We don't need any of them alive. Just fucking kill them all."

For the first time since I've met the woman, I finally find myself agreeing with something that's come out of her mouth. Less than a second after I think this, the weight of that hits me in the gut like a battering ram. Kill them all. I want them all dead. There are perhaps eleven people on the other side of the gate including Maria Rosa and Raphael, and I just agreed that I wanted them all dead.

Who am I becoming?

They're drug dealers, murders, human traffickers and rapists. If my father were here, he would forgive them of their sins and invite them inside so he could help their wounded. I want to double chain the gate, douse the bastards in petrol and strike a match.

I would watch them burn.

Maria Rosa snatches a gun from the guy standing closest to her and holds it up, aiming though the bars of the gate at Cade. "If you kill us," she hisses, "I won't be able to tell you what Ramirez has planned for you, will I?"

I'm still all for killing her, but Cade falters. Shay cocks a mean looking gun, holding it up with both hands as she moves closer to Cade. "She's bluffing. She doesn't know anything about Ramirez. Let me put a fucking bullet between her eyes, man."

"You think Rebel would do that?" he asks.

Shay's determination flickers, only for a second. Only for the briefest of pauses. It's enough for Cade, though. "Exactly. He'd want to know what she knows first. And *then* he'd kill her."

I don't like his tone of voice at all. It sounds for all the world like he's about to do as she asks. "You are *not* going to let her in here, right?" It seems like sheer madness that he would even consider such a thing, and yet he gives me a tight-lipped smile and starts walking toward the gate.

"You, Rico, *him*,"—he points at the guy holding onto Raphael— "and Hector's guy. That's it. Everyone else needs to get gone. Then you can come in."

"You're crazy!" Maria Rosa laughs scornfully. "I'm not walking into the lion's den with only one able-bodied guard. You must think I'm stupid."

"No, I think you're desperate otherwise you wouldn't have come here. The choice is yours, Mother."

Mother? My head is spinning. Why the hell would he call her that? It makes no sense. No one else seems to find it strange, though. The Widow Makers surrounding me are all wearing severe expressions, hands resting on their guns, some blatantly holding them out like Shay. I'm the only one who looks lost, I'm sure. Cade shrugs, smiling in a dramatic, all of a sudden way that is totally out of place.

"When you make up your mind, you let me know, okay?

Meantime, I'll be in the clubhouse drinking a cold one." He begins to turn around, turning his back on the crazed woman on the other side of the gate, but she starts screaming again.

"*¡Te odio! usted es un enfermo, el mal hijo de puta!*"

Cade faces her again, grinning. "Oh, don't worry, Mother. I hate you, too."

There's pure murder in her eyes when she lowers her gun. "Fine. Just the four of us. But trust me...if you value your life and the lives of your precious Widow Makers, you won't lay a finger on me or mine."

Cade draws an ex over his chest. "Cross my heart and hope to die."

"I've hoped you would die many times over already, *cabron.*"

"Likewise." Cade stares at her until she loses patience and starts barking at her men in Spanish, presumably telling them to leave. They look unsure at first, and then afraid as she gets angrier and angrier. Eventually seven other men climb into two of the cars, start the engines and leave.

"There. Are you happy now? Rico is *dying*, motherfucker. Let us inside."

I have no idea who this Rico guy is, but he sure as hell seems important to Maria Rosa. Cade grunts, still grinning, though the humor has vanished from his face. He looks like he's grimacing as he slowly strolls to the compound gate and punches a code into the keypad to the left. The metal screeches as the gates swing open and then Maria Rosa is charging into the compound, holding up her gun. She marches straight up to Cade and presses the gleaming metal directly against his heart.

"You'd better fix him," she spits. "You'd better fix him, or there will be consequences, asshole."

I'd be curious to see what these consequences are, now that twenty angry Widow Makers surround her. Cade says something, but I don't really hear it, though. The two of them talk, anger and antagonism lacing their voices, and I stare at Raphael, feeling panic rising in the back of my throat. He's still being restrained, though the evil motherfucker isn't struggling anymore. He's staring right back at me, unblinking, apparently unfazed by the situation he finds himself in. He seems only intent on one thing: *me*. And the look in his eyes is enough to make the blood run cold in my veins.

"Well? Sophia? Can you do it?"

"Huh?" I tear my gaze from Raphael, shaking, to find that Cade has moved again and he's standing beside me. His eyebrows are raised in question. "What?" I ask.

"Can you take a look at the guy? You're studying medicine, right?"

I just look at him blankly. He can't...he can't actually be serious. Can he? "What? *No!* I study *psychology*."

Cade laughs like this is the funniest thing ever. He turns around, throwing his hands up in the air. "Well, there you have it. No doctors here, Mother. Sorry." He doesn't sound sorry. Not even a little. "I mean," he continues. "I can pull a slug out of him, but I can't guarantee I won't do more damage than good. He looks like he's on the way out, darlin'."

Maria Rosa sends him an icy stare. And then she turns it on me. "You're lying," she informs me. "You *are* a doctor."

"I'm not." I'm really damn glad none of these people know my father or my sister are actually doctors. They would probably assume I know what I'm doing by association or something. Turns out Maria Rosa doesn't need such information to make calls like that, though. "Bullshit. You can save him." She sounds like she's determined to make this the truth by sheer force of will. She's mad. I'm convinced of that fact when she turns her gun on me and removes the safety. "Get over here," she commands. "Get the bullet out of him and sew him up. You can do it."

"I—" I shake my head, not quite sure what to do. "I have no surgical experience. I'll kill him."

"Oh, no, princess. You kill him, and I kill you. I don't think you want that. You want to die?"

"Of course not."

"Then get over here and fix him!"

I can see that the man on the ground by the gate, Rico, is beyond saving. His lips and eyelids are blue, which I'm educated enough to know means he stopped breathing some time ago. I'm betting that if I walk over there and place my fingertips against his neck, I'm not going to find a pulse. I'm also betting Maria Rosa does not want to hear that, though. She seems like she's on the brink of a complete meltdown.

"I don't have any equipment. I'd need a sterile room, and surgical tools. I—I don't even have a needle and thread, let alone forceps. You do know what a psychologist is, right?"

Maria Rosa doesn't answer. She moves in a flash of tight Versace and highly impractical Manolos, and suddenly she has me by the hair. Both Cade and Shay move at the same time, trying to put themselves in between me and the woman, but Maria Rosa has a firm grip on me; my hair feels like it's about to be torn out at the roots.

"For fuck's sake," Cade groans under his breath. "If you really wanna piss Rebel off, you're doing a stellar job."

"Do I look like I give a fuck about Rebel?" Maria Rosa spits. "I only care about Rico." She proceeds to drag me toward Rico's body, jabbing me every few paces with what I'm assuming it the barrel of her gun. Raphael starts laughing in that rattling, weird, unnerving way of his. His cackling bounces around the compound courtyard like a mocking bird call. He stops laughing as I pass him to say, "I hope you're ready, slut. I'll be skull fucking you before the end of the night."

Anger rolls through me. I want to punch this woman in the ribcage for handling me like I'm shit, for bring that man in such close proximity of me, but I know she won't hesitate to shoot if I piss her off.

The Widow Makers all move in unison, crowding in around, all just as angry as I am. They may not know me or like me, but they love Rebel. As far as they are concerned, I am his property and Maria Rosa should not be interfering with me in any way.

Cade is beginning to look seriously worried. Maria Rosa shoves me forward roughly, and I fall to my knees beside Rico. My heart is charging so hard, I can hear my blood pumping in my own ears. The sound becomes a deafening roar when I feel the muzzle of the gun pressing into the back of my head.

This is not good. This is not good at all. I have no way of saving this man. I have no clue what I'm doing. Now that I'm closer I can see the bullet hole in his stomach, though, can see that someone has ineffectually tried to stem the flow of blood by ramming a black silk scarf into the wound. Right into it, like that was the best option available to them. Even I know that was a bad idea. That scarf has got all kinds of bacteria all over it, and now that bacteria is happily breeding away inside the torn up vital organs of a dying man.

"Begin," Maria Rosa commands.

"I told you, I don't have any instruments."

She crouches down beside me, craning her face into mine, baring her teeth so that she's showing gum. *"Use. Your. Fingers."*

"I am not sticking my fingers inside his body. No way!"

Pain comes, then—a sharp, piercing pain at the back of my head. My vision dances, pinpricks of light bursting everywhere, but I don't lose consciousness. I do fall forward, though—my hands land right on Rico's torso. The man's eyes flicker open, and he gasps soundlessly for oxygen once, twice, and then his eyes roll back in his head. He starts to convulse, pink foam pouring out of his mouth.

"Ahhhh, Mother, the bitch killed him," Raphael laughs. "She's trouble. I told you, no?"

Maria Rosa lets out an anguished squeal. I look up, and see that she's hitting herself in the side of the head with her gun, pulling on her own hair. Tears tremble on the ends of her eyelashes, ready to fall any second. "He's not dead. You check him. Check his pulse," she growls.

I do check his pulse. It's thready and weak, but I can feel the irregular twitch of his heart beneath the pads of my fingers. Thank fuck for that. "He's not dead," I say. I hate how my voice shakes. I hate that I'm afraid right now, but it can't be helped. I keep finding myself in these situations. If I don't get shot in the back of the head in a couple of minutes and my brains aren't splattered all over Rico and the dirt and everywhere else in between, maybe I'll be less frightened the next time this happens. *Maybe.*

Maria Rosa grinds her teeth together, repositioning her gun in her hands again. "Okay. Now you get that bullet out of him, bitch, or I'm going put three in you. Do you hear me?" she screams.

I look from her to Cade and back again. Cade has his gun in his hands pointing it at Maria Rosa, but he looks torn. "I could shoot her if you want, Soph. I can't guarantee she won't shoot you first, though. It's your call. What do you want me to do?"

"God, don't shoot her."

"All right. Well, you'd better get your hands inside Rico then, before the bastard dies." He doesn't look at me while he talks. He stares intently at Maria Rosa, unwavering, hands steady. I think about changing my mind, about telling him to shoot her, but would he be able to do it before she killed me? Probably not.

So there's nothing left for it. My hands are covered in blood and dirt from when I toppled forward a minute ago. I scrub them against my jeans, doing what I can to get them clean, and then I lean over the ghostly white body in front of me and I do something neither my father nor Sloane have probably ever done: I stick my bare, filthy dirty fingers inside an open stomach wound. It feels innately wrong, and, worryingly, it feels cool. Should he really be this cold? The human body should sit at an average 98.6 degrees Fahrenheit, but the inside of Rico's stomach feels a lot cooler. This could be normal, though. I'm not a doctor. I know shit about trauma and what happens when someone goes into shock.

"Can you feel it?" Maria Rosa asks.

"No." All I can feel is intestines and a whole lot of blood that I'm assuming is not meant to be there. I twist my fingers around inside the wound, attempting to locate anything metallic, hard or sharp, but my fingers feel like they're tearing through wet paper. It definitely doesn't feel right. I think I'm killing him even quicker. My suspicions are confirmed when Rico starts convulsing even harder.

"What are you doing? What did you do?" Maria Rosa screams.

I pull my hand out of Rico, choking on panic, readying myself for the sound of the gunshot that will end my life. Do bullets travel faster than the speed of sound? I think they do. At least I won't have to hear the herald of my own demise. I guess that's something.

My heart nearly explodes out of my chest when I do hear the gunshot, though. I feel instantly numb. My breath fires in and out of my lungs in impossibly short blasts, and I flinch, waiting for the pain to kick in.

It doesn't happen.

Through the high-pitched buzzing in my ears, I can hear someone roaring in anger, and someone else screaming at the top of their lungs. That's what I should sound like. I should sound like I'm in agony, like the person screaming, and yet I feel nothing.

Hands are on me next, pulling at me, patting me down.

Rebel. Rebel's scooping me up in his arms, lifting me to my feet. Hold me to him, swearing over and over again in my ear.

"Fuck, Soph. Fuck. Fucking hell. Are you okay?"

I look down, and Maria Rosa is on her side, clawing at Rico's very dead body. She's bleeding from her shoulder, blood everywhere, all over my white tennis shoes. Her black mascara has bled all down her face too, now. She's the one who's screaming, the one who got shot. Not me. I'm okay. I'm okay. I'm okay.

"Soph! Tell me you're not hurt!" Rebel shakes me, trying to get a response.

"Yes! Yeah, I'm fine. I'm not hurt."

Rebel lets me go then. I think I might fall, but I somehow manage to keep myself upright. I watch him as he stalks around the compound, glaring into the faces of the Widow Makers who are still standing around us with their guns in their hands.

"*I* had to do that?" he hollers. "You're all standing here with your dicks in your hands? I had to get here and do that, and none of you acted?" He stops in front of Cade, his face less than an inch away from his vice president's, his chest rising and falling so fast. He looks crazy. He looks like he's about to straight up murder Cade. "What the fuck were you thinking?" he grinds out.

"I was thinking that the crazy bitch had a gun pressed against the base of Sophia's skull and I wouldn't be able to take her out without something really terrible happening. What would you have done if I'd taken the shot and Soph had been killed, you fucking asshole?" Cade shoves him. I've never seen anyone do something so risky. If anyone's going to get away with it, it's Cade, but Rebel doesn't look very happy right now. He looks like he's about to go supernova. I hold my breath, waiting for him to do something crazy, for him to smash his fist into his best friends face or pull his gun on him, but he doesn't. He glares at Cade for another few seconds, and then turns away from him, facing me again.

Maria Rosa writhes on the ground, swearing angrily in Spanish. She's bleeding pretty heavily, her blood mixing into the dirt with Rico's. Rebel ignores her, stepping over her body like she's a mild inconvenience, unworthy of his attention. He stands in front of me, his shoulders hitching up and down, a frantic energy still pouring off him in waves. "Come with me," he says.

He holds out his hand and I'm too stunned by the events of the past few minutes to object or refuse him. I take it, my legs feeling unstable as he guides me across the compound toward the clubhouse. As we pass Cade, Rebel growls under his breath. "Get a prospect to clear that shit up, man. And get her and Dela Vega out of sight, will you? Make sure they're...*comfortable*."

A shiver runs up my spine at the tone in his voice. When he says comfortable, I know he means something else entirely. He opens the door to the clubhouse, muttering under his breath when he surveys the place and finds it void of all life. We weave between tables and abandoned chairs, making our way toward the bar at the back of the room. Once there, Rebel opens another door into a back room. The small, dusty space is filled with torn-open boxes containing bottled beer, empty milk crates and cleaning equipment. The shelves on the right hand wall are a jumbled mess of spirits and...and *guns*. Guns, just sitting there like casual objects that don't hurt, maim, kill. Rebel lets go of my hand and picks up a small, silver handgun, sliding it into the waistband of his jeans at the base of his spine. "Come here," he tells me, gesturing me close. I move to his side, not sure what he could possibly want to show me in here aside from the weaponry and liquor. "Look," he says. "Pay attention. There's a small catch up here, right in the corner." His hand moves to the very top corner of the wall by the shelves. Sure enough, I see what he's referring to—a small, black switch in the shadows. I would never have noticed it if he hadn't pointed it out.

"See if you can reach it," he tells me.

He's much taller than me, but I'm still tall. I have to stand on my tiptoes but I can just about graze the smooth metal with my fingertips.

"Press it," he says.

When I was kid, my favorite thing to do on a rainy Sunday afternoon once we got home from church was to watch Indiana Jones with my father. I have awful images of some terrible booby trap springing into action if I do what I'm told and hit this switch, but I know that's ridiculous. Rebel wouldn't be telling me to do it if it would be bad for me. My nerve endings still crackle when I press my fingers against the catch, though. A loud clicking noise cuts through the tense silence, making me jump. I jump even more when the wall—what I thought was the wall—swings back to reveal yet another door. This one is made of steel, looks reinforced, and has no visible handle or keyhole. To the left, a narrow keypad sits on the wall, glowing softly in the darkness.

"Watch," Rebel tells me. "The code is One Seven Six Three." He punches the code into the keypad as I observe, my arms wrapped around my body. I'm starting to feel really shaky. Maria Rosa's arrival and Raphael's presence is catching up with me. I feel like the world is crashing down on my head and I have no means of stopping it, of holding back the tide.

The keypad is silent as Rebel presses the keys. He hits the green enter button and the door chunks and releases. Rebel doesn't allow it to open properly, though. He closes it and holds his hand palm-up to the keypad, giving me a tight-lipped smile that holds absolutely no humor. "Now you," he says. "Show me you remember the code. I need to know you can open this door."

He's incredibly intense. He's clearly so stressed he's not really functioning, and yet at the same time there's an eerie calm resting over him. It's way more frightening than if he were simply raging mad. I slowly punch in the access code to the door and hit the green button afterward, just as he did, and the door swings open.

"Okay. Good. Follow me." Rebel moves through the door into the pitch-black darkness beyond. I hesitate a second, but then follow behind him, unwilling to push him even a little while he's in this state. The heavy steel door closes behind us, and suddenly I feel like I'm trapped in a tomb. A dark, impenetrable tomb that I have no way out of. My chest tightens ever so slightly, the first strains of panic setting in, my heartbeat noticeably quickening.

"Rebel?"

His arms are immediately around me, his chest up against mine, his lips pressing against my forehead. He holds me in the dark and breathes. I can feel the impossible speed of his own heart beating against mine, and I know he's having trouble holding himself together. So strange. He always seems so unflappable, like a bomb could go off right next to his head and he'd still be able to think straight.

"Fuck, Soph," he whispers. "Just...I can't..."

My cheeks burn, my head swimming as he draws me even tighter and crushes me against his body. Is...is he this freaked out because of *me*? Surely not. Despite Maria Rosa, Raphael, Hector, dead Bron and dead Rico, I'm selfish enough to enjoy this fleeting moment in the dark. My fear has completely vanished. With his arms around me, it feels as though nothing bad could ever reach me here. Such a bizarre feeling.

"If something like this happens again, Sophia, this is where you come. You hear me? You come straight here. Promise me."

"But where—"

"Promise me!"

"Okay, yes. I swear it. I promise."

Rebel draws back, pulling in a deep breath. He lets me go then, and the fear returns with the force of a freight train. It's amazing to me that I can be this terrified as soon as his presence is gone, and yet no more than a second ago I felt so safe.

Rebel moves around in the dark, not fumbling, apparently sure of his surroundings, and then the blackness vanishes as a strip light flickers on over head, casting a stark white light over everything inside...inside the huge office we're now standing in. It's immediately obvious whose office this is. On all four walls, white board material has been scribbled over from the floor to the ceiling; nearly ninety percent of the scribble is mathematical in nature, and absolutely none of it makes sense. Well, not to me, anyway.

Two large desks, one at either end of the room, are piled with papers, and some seriously expensive looking computers sit among the madness, apparently gathering dust. In between them on the far wall, a huge server stands like a tall, dormant monolith, all dark metal and LEDs that remain unlit.

Rebel watches me as I walk around, taking in the weirdness of the place. He leans against the tidier of the desks—I assume it's his—observing me like I'm some sort of endangered zoo exhibit. "What is this place?" I ask him.

"This place is bomb proof. This place can withstand all hell breaking out around it, and no one will be able to get in. This is where you're safest if something bad goes down."

"And the computers? The server?"

"Information. It's all just information. Bank accounts. Blackmailing. Satellite images. P.I. reports. *Burial locations.*"

"So this...this is what you have on people. All of the dirt you've gathered over the years. This is all leverage?"

"Yes."

In the distant recesses of my mind, I recall Julio discussing some files Rebel was holding over him, which was why the guy drove across the state in the night to pick me up from Hector's place: Rebel was bribing him.

I quit my investigating, leaning against the other desk, facing him. "Very valuable, I'm sure."

"Yes."

"And you showed me how to get in here. You'd trust me in here all by myself?"

He nods. "You think you're a flight risk, Sophia, but you're not. You're as invested in me as I am in you."

"I don't think so." I don't know how invested in me he thinks he is, but regardless...I don't want it to be true. Caring about this man will only get me killed; that much is obvious.

Rebel looks away, focusing on the wild, red text marking the wall by his head. He folds his arms across his chest. "You know why you resist me so much, Soph?" he whispers.

I narrow my eyes at him, trying not to let him see what I'm thinking. "Because you're rude and arrogant, and you left me alone in a cabin for ten days?"

He smiles softly, allowing his gaze to fall to his feet. "Nope."

"Oh no? Well, please enlighten me, then. Why do I resist you so much?"

"Because you're in love with me, and you're afraid."

"*What?*" I consider picking up the large rock that's being used as a paperweight on the desk next to me and chucking it right at his head. He is such an asshole. "You are dreaming, my friend," I inform him.

"We're not friends. We're much, much more than that and you know it."

"Jesus, you...you just have no shame, do you? Where do you get off saying stuff like this?"

"I find shame is usually a wasteful emotion. It occurs after an event or certain actions have taken place. There's no sense in beating yourself up over something you can't change or effect, right? I think you're actually uncomfortable because I say what I think. I don't sugar coat anything. And I've never been afraid to admit what I want, Sophia." He rubs his fingers over the stubble on his jaw, piercing me with those blue eyes of his. "You, on the other hand... you're afraid of admitting anything to anyone, ever. Must be exhausting."

I don't answer him. I don't really know what to say. I want to be stubborn and hard with him, tell him he couldn't be more wrong and he should keep his half-baked theories to himself, but I am so done. I don't have the energy to fight or bicker with him. And besides, it's becoming harder and harder to deny that what he's saying isn't actually the truth. Fuck him. Fuck him and his ability to see right through me. Rebel starts to laugh. "You don't need to say a word, sugar. You know it's true, and so do I. I can wait, though. If you ever feel like being honest with me, I'm ready to hear it."

His voice softens out at the end of this statement, the laughter slipping away. He sounds muted, soft, almost pensive. I want him to put his arms around me so he can hold me and make the whole world go away again, but won't that just be proving him right? Instead, I turn away from him.

My eyes land on a file sitting on the overflowing desk. Scrawled across the front of it in black, blocky capitals is one word: MAYFAIR.

"What's Mayfair? Is that, like, a code for something? A place?"

Rebel sighs heavily. I can hear his boots grinding against the bare concrete underfoot as he paces the length of the room; he takes the file from me and places it back on the pile of disorganized binders and papers. "It's a name. A guy back in Seattle. Cade's been looking into him."

"Is he connected with Hector and Raphael?"

"No. He's not someone we need to worry about right now, Soph. We have other things to take care of. Namely Maria fucking Rosa."

I learned how to waterboard somebody without killing them back in Afghanistan. There's a trick to it. If you pour the water too fast, shove the rag down their throat too far, you'll drown them straight away. If you go too easy on them, they can hold their breath and they'll never break. As I fill up a four-gallon canister with water from the outside tap close to the clubhouse, I spend a moment reflecting on how little Maria Rosa is going to like this. That's probably the understatement of the century. She's going to fucking *hate* it.

The roles are usually reversed in situations such as these. She tortured the ever-loving shit out of me when she found me and Rebel snooping around her place in Columbia. I spent three days strapped to a chair while she tried to ascertain if I was there to try and kill her or not. The experience was a frustrating one for her. Being in the Marines, you learn how to withstand torture. You learn how to keep your damn mouth shut and give nothing more than your name and rank, and Maria Rosa wanted me to be screaming. I was a disappointment to her in the beginning, but then later she confessed my silent stoicism turned her on. Wasn't long before she was straddling me, grinding herself up against my cock, torturing me in a different way. That seems like a long time ago now.

She was unconscious when I carried her into the barn and down into the hidden basement, making sure to bolt the hatchway behind me when I came back up for the water. I trussed her up pretty tight when I tied her to the single, lone wooden chair down there, but she's a wily one. No, not just wily; she's a goddamn contortionist. I've had first hand experience of that. I'm yet to fuck another woman who can fold herself up into a pretzel the same way Mother can.

I try not to think about all the things Maria Rosa can do that other women can't as I carry the canister of water back to the barn and unbolt the hatch. Down the stairs I carry the carton, along the badly lit corridor, water sloshing out onto the dusty concrete, onto my boots, not thinking about the things Maria Rosa can do with her tongue.

Jesus.

When I enter the very last room on the right, the woman in question is slumped forward in the chair, chin resting on her chest, a thick river of blood drying down her arm and her leg. She looks like she's out cold, but if there's one lesson I've learned in this life, it's do not trust Maria Rosa. She's a master manipulator. I'm sure Rebel would have a couple more very choice names for her, too.

She fucked with the club.

She fucked with my sister.

And now she's fucked with Sophia.

It takes a lot to get Jamie to the point where he'll bury you as soon as look at you, but we're past that point now. I kind of feel sorry for the woman. He's not going to go easy on her. Not even a little bit.

I pull the rag I found behind the bar in the clubhouse from the back pocket of my jeans and lean against the wall with the huge container of water at my feet, tearing the rag into long strips. This is where the boss finds me.

He's not looking too shit hot.

"You tried to wake her up yet?" he asks.

I shake my head.

"All right. Let's get this over with. I shouldn't have reamed you out. I know you were only looking out for Sophia. I lost it. I'm sorry."

I shrug.

"Don't give me that shit, man. You'd have lost it, too. You'd have blown a fucking gasket if that had been Laura."

I lock up at the sound of my sister's name. We'll go weeks, sometimes months, without speaking of her. Both of us just knows that she's the reason we're here though, neck deep in stinking shit that makes us both sick, drives us both crazy. We'll never be able to get out until we find out what happened to her, one way or another. And then make whomever is responsible for her disappearance pay. Dearly. That day will be the day Jamie and I lose our souls for good.

I shoot him a shitty look. "So you're comparing Sophia to her now, is it? You really must love her or something."

Rebel's eyes narrow so dramatically, they almost disappear entirely. "Maybe. Maybe not."

I throw one of the balled up pieces of rag at him, and it hits him in the face. "You're so full of shit, man. I saw the way you looked at her the second she climbed on the back of your ride in that fucking disgusting yellow dress and I knew we were all doomed."

The ghost of a smile flickers across his face. Bending to pick up the piece of rag I threw, he grunts. "Like I said. Maybe. Maybe not."

Maria Rosa groans. It's not the kind of groan she'd fake. She'd want to sound sexy, even through her pain. No, this is the kind of groan someone makes when they're in agony and their head's not working right. Rebel turns his attention to her, and I catch a glimpse of how much trouble she's in…

If the look on my brother's face were to be categorized by a single act of violence in recent history, it would be codenamed Hiroshima. He's going to kill her. I can read that fact in every line of his body. He's wound so tight, I'd be surprised if he even waits for her to wake up before he starts on her.

"Are you okay, man? I can do this on my own if you need me to?"

"And you won't end up fucking her brains out instead of teaching her a lesson?" He lifts both eyebrows at me, clearly convinced that this is what will happen if I'm left alone in a room with her.

"I can get it done." And I can. Ever since Laura went missing, the closest we ever came to finding her was at Maria Rosa's place. Too many people told the same story. Too many people said she had her. Rebel and I turned her place upside down once Mother let us have free rein, but there were those three days. Those three days where she was deciding if she hated or loved us. She could easily have had any girls she was hiding in her villa relocated, never to be seen again. Buried, thrown into a ditch somewhere for wild animals to pick their bones clean.

Yeah, I can get this done.

I know he won't agree to leaving me here with her, though. Even if he did think I was capable of making her talk all by myself, his conscience wouldn't let him. He'd never ask me to do something he wasn't prepared to do himself. That's how we've ended up in this situation so many times. *Together.*

Maria Rosa stirs again. She makes a delirious, gurgling kind of sound at the back of her throat, and then her head lolls back, eyes finally shuttering open. Rebel clenches his jaw, readying himself. This is not going to be fun for anyone involved, but he's angry enough right now that it won't trouble him as much as usual.

"Good sleep, Mother?" he growls. Slowly, he begins to pace around her in a circle, wrapping the torn piece of rag around his fingers over and over again. "You're planning on gracing us with your presence, I see."

Maria Rosa's pupils dilate, desperately trying to focus on her surroundings. She's very clearly having problems, though. She's lost a lot of blood. And she was hysterical before that anyway. God knows where they were before they came burning out of the desert, but something serious obviously went down. Serious enough to end Rico, anyway. Rebel told me about the last time he saw Maria Rosa in Vegas—that she and Rico put on quite a show for Carnie. She fucked Rico right in front of them. Even back in Colombia, it was fairly plain that Rico was in love with her. It was only a matter of time. The woman can never resist a man who fawns over her, no matter if she's attracted to him or not. She'll fuck a guy just to make him purr. From the show she put on as Rico was dying, however, I wouldn't be surprised if she actually had some form of feelings for the guy. Not real feelings, of course. She's not capable. But some sort of...*tolerance* for him. More than she ever felt for me, that's for sure. She repeatedly said she was in love with me, but you don't attempt to stab someone you're in love with to death. At least not in my limited experience.

She blinks drunkenly up at Rebel, and everything seems to hit her all at once—Rico dying, threatening Sophia...she probably remembers Trader Joe's and the heat we pulled from the DEA last, because an ashen, gray color sweeps across her face, turning her into a ghost.

"Oh, my, my," she whispers. Her words are slurred but still audible. "I suppose this is quite ironic, no?"

"Not really," Rebel replies. "I'd say it was more...*karmic retribution*. Do you believe in karma, Mother?"

"Only the bad kind." She leans forward and spits on the floor—blood and saliva mixed together. "I'm guessing you're very angry with me, my love."

Rebel laughs. He tips his head back and howls so loud I'm sure people in town can hear him. "You could say that. Yes, I'm just a *little* bit mad with you. Can you blame me, though? I mean, you sent men in to a grocery store wearing Widow Makers' cuts and you had them kill a whole bunch of innocent people. That wasn't very nice, was it?"

Maria Rosa rolls her eyes. "It was a warning. Nothing more. The cops were never going to charge you. That's why I had that fat one wear the president's cut. The police would do a little digging and pull up the club's details, see your handsome face and know it was the wrong guy, and they would figure it out. That's why I chose Los Angeles not New Mexico, you spoiled little shit."

"*I'm* the spoiled little shit?" Rebel grinds his teeth. I just stand there, leaning against the wall, waiting. At some point one of them is going to drag me into this, but until then I'm quite content sitting it out on the sidelines. Rebel shakes his head, scowling at Maria Rosa.

"You're petulant, and you have the stones to call *me* spoiled? I came to you for help in good faith, and now look at where we are."

"We are here because you have no fucking sense of humor, Rebel. We're here because I messed up your pretty girlfriend's hair. Kind of pathetic, don't you think? She's still pretty. She still has all of her hair. Even though she killed Rico."

It was plain to see that Rico was on borrowed time when they pulled up in those cars, but trust Maria Rosa to see it that way—Sophia didn't save him, therefore she killed him. "There will be...consequences for that," she wheezes.

"Oh? Consequences? You really think you're getting out of here alive?"

"I do. I don't think you're a cold-blooded killer, Rebel. More's the pity. I would respect you more if you were, I think."

There's only so much of this baiting Rebel will take before he eventually does snap. I've only seen it once before, and it was messy and brutal, and it took three weeks to get him to calm down afterward. If we can avoid that outcome, that would be great, but Mother loves to wind a guy up. She teased and tormented me for hours and hours at a time. Difference is, I handled it. Rebel will wrench her head off before he puts up with this much longer.

He slides his hands into the pockets of his jeans, looking around the room like he's never been in here before and all of this is new to him. Like we haven't had these kinds of conversations plenty of times before, with plenty of different people. This is the first time we've had a 'chat' with a woman, but then again Maria Rosa hardly counts. She loves to skin people, for fuck's sake. She's wielded the blade herself more times than any of us can count.

Rebel walks over to the container filled with water and plunges the rag he's holding into it, so that his hand comes up running water everywhere. There's no showmanship, no bravado. No drawn out production over it. He knows it's pointless trying to scare Maria Rosa, just like I do. This won't be about terrifying her into telling us everything she knows about Hector. This will be us bending her to our will, and then when bending doesn't work, breaking her. And *then* she'll tell us.

That undoubtedly makes us evil people, but this is a very unique situation. Maria Rosa really fucked up with that stunt she pulled. She should have gone back to Colombia and continued trafficking her blow. Threatening Rebel and then framing the club? Yeah, that was never going to end well.

"Open wide," he tells her.

"I'm not normally so eager to please, but...whatever you say, my love." Maria Rosa opens up, unflinching, unwilling to show that she's even slightly afraid. Sophia reminds me of her a little, in a way. While Soph is admittedly a little more intimidated by our fucked up world, she wears this look of defiance wherever she goes, like she's ready to throw down should the need arise. I respect that about her.

Rebel jams the rag into Maria Rosa's mouth. He then gestures for another one from me. I wet it in the container and hand it over. That goes into her mouth, too. And then another. And another. He's hitting her with this hardcore. She really won't be able to breathe in between rounds of water being poured into her mouth, but it doesn't look like Rebel cares. He kicks out Maria Rosa's feet from underneath the chair and grabs her by the ankles, pulling her down so that her head is tipped back. The position looks sexual, especially with Rebel standing with one leg either side of hers, but it's not. He stands like that in order to lift up the heavy water container without tearing open his stitches anymore. Maria gives Rebel a dead-eyed smile around all of the material he's forcing into her mouth.

He smiles back, holding her face in both of his hands. "What happened to you, Mother?" he asks. He genuinely looks like he wants to know, though there's a touch of madness to him. "Something fucking *terrible* must have happened to you." She looks up at him, not even attempting to speak, not even attempting to answer his question.

He tilts the water canister, and we begin our adventure.

No matter who you are, no matter how strong your will, if someone pours a gallon of water into your mouth when it's stuffed full of rags, you're going to choke. You're going to splutter. You're going to half drown. Maria Rosa does all of these things as Rebel pours and breaks, pours and breaks with a grim efficiency.

Predictably, she doesn't tell him a fucking thing. Eventually she loses consciousness. Rebel straightens, glaring down at her limp, soaked body, and shrugs his shoulders. "Well. I guess that was a pointless exercise."

He sounds way too calm. Frankly, it's a miracle that he's functioning on any rational level at all. "You're not gonna wake her up?"

Rebel grunts, tips his head back, closes his eyes, and then draws in a deep breath. "No. No point. If I carry on with this shit, I won't be able to stop until she's fucking dead."

At least he knows this. That in itself means he's keeping his shit together. Kind of. "Can you stay with her?" he asks. "When you leave, have Carnie come sit down here and watch both rooms. Make sure Mother and Dela Vega are behaving themselves. In the meantime, do what you have to. Find out what she's doing in New Mexico, and why the hell she thought it was a good idea to come here."

"Has to have something to do with Ramirez, right?"

Rebel slowly shakes his head. "Maybe not. Remember that DEA agent she wanted me to sort out for her?"

"Yeah."

"Well, it took me a while to put the pieces together, but the DEA agent that picked me up yesterday...?"

"Lowell? She's the same agent? *No way.*"

"Way."

"What are the chances?"

"Pretty high, actually." Rebel rolls his neck, opening his eyes. He looks at me, the cold blue of his irises almost the color of ice. "She's in town because of Ramirez. He and Maria Rosa are the two biggest drug importers into the United States. It's normal that the same unit would be investigating them both. She must be the big, swinging dick, this Lowell. She's a viper for sure. Find out what you can about her from Maria Rosa when she wakes up. In the meantime, perhaps you could dig the bullet out of her, please? I don't feel like finding her dead tomorrow." He cocks his head to one side, surprise chasing across his face. "Weird. I actually mean that."

SOPHIA

I don't go to Bron's funeral.
I didn't know her, and besides...if I were to look at her oddly shaped figure, wrapped up in layer upon layer of white sheets, I'd know it looked odd because the poor woman is without her head, hands and one of her feet. I'm doing my best not to recall the image of her hanging by her one remaining foot as it is. And the club still doesn't know or trust me. A funeral is a deeply personal event. I don't want to intrude.

I spend my time reading in the cabin instead. Pretending to read. Really, I'm trying not to be hyper aware of the fact that Raphael is so close. It does not feel safe with him no more than a hundred feet away. Rebel assured me he was tied to a freaking chair, that there's no way for him to get to me, but the hairs on the back of my neck keep standing on end every time I hear the cabin settle.

Later, when Rebel returns from mourning with his club, he tells me to grab a coat and follow him. For the first time since he came and collected me from Julio's compound, he tells me to climb on the back of his Ducati and hold onto him tight.

When I was a kid, maybe about seven or eight, Dad took me to see Santa Claus at Christmas. He took me to an expensive department store, the kind that hire genuine white-haired old men with real beards—men who didn't feature on any sex registers. My father sat me on Genuine Santa's knee, and he told me to tell the old man everything.

Santa had gentle brown eyes, the eyes of a Labrador or a Golden Retriever. When he asked me what I wanted more than anything in the world, I told him I wanted to be just like my big sister. My parents loved her more. She got all the best presents. She was really smart, so she understood what our father was talking about half the time. I wanted to be just like Sloane.

I felt that way for a long time. I was about sixteen before I realized that the eternal quest to Be Like Sloane was a futile one, and it was just as well being Alexis as it was being anyone else. Better, in fact, because being myself required very little effort, and being Sloane took so much concentration that I couldn't concentrate on anything else.

I think about what Sloane would or wouldn't do a lot, though. I'm think about what she would do now, as Rebel places his hands over my mine, wrapping his fingers around the trigger of the gun I'm holding. The gun he told me to take hold of back in the storage room in the bar.

In the distance, somewhere out toward the highway and civilization beyond, all that remains of the daylight is a hazy pink band, burned orange where it meets the horizon. The sky overhead is darkening with every passing minute, revealing a deep, rich blue, scattered with the pinprick of stars.

"Hold it like this. Make sure you keep your finger straight along the length of the gun up here. Don't curve it around the trigger just yet," Rebel tells me.

"This what they teach you in Motorcycle Gang 101?" I'm full of snark, since he dragged me out of his cabin in the dusky night air and refused to tell me where we were going or why. I shouldn't have been surprised that he would lead me out into the middle of nowhere and want to teach me how to shoot a gun.

Little does he know I can already fire a gun perfectly well. Dad taught me when I was a teenager, the same way he taught Sloane. I keep this information to myself. Having Rebel's chest pressed up against my back, feeling his warm breathing in my ear, is too nice to pass up. It feels wonderful, actually. I lean back into him, feeling him tense and then ease at the contact.

"No," he tells me. "Not motorcycle gang 101. Military School. Very different organization, I assure you, sweetheart."

It slips my mind from time to time that Rebel even went to Military School. And then I remember the dozens and dozens of pictures on his father's wall, and it seems entirely normal that the man standing at my back fought for his country and defended his people. Being a protector is second nature to him.

"Now, when you fire," he tells me. "Don't pull at the trigger. Don't jerk it. Squeeze it softly. Don't hold your breath. Just inhale..." He removes his left hand from over mine and places it over my sternum, above my belly, making a satisfied sound at the back of his throat when he feels my ribcage rise. "Good. Now, nice and steady. When you breathe out—"

The report of the gun fire shatters the silence in the desert. Fifty feet away, the rusted Budweiser can Rebel balanced on top of a round fence post jumps into the air—a direct hit. No more than two seconds later, the echo from the shot comes back to us, weakened by the distance it's traveled but still bracingly loud. Rebel grunts. He sounds more than a little bemused. Using the index finger on the hand resting over my chest, he digs me in the ribs, burying his face into my neck.

"Cheat," he growls.

"I didn't cheat. I did what you told me to."

"But you've already done it before, haven't you? And you had me thinking you were completely ignorant to the workings of a gun."

"I did no such thing. You just never asked."

"Hmmm." He stabs me with his index finger one more time,

making me squirm. "Come on, then. Show me. Show me what you're made of."

He must trust me implicitly. Without a backward glance, he sets off toward the fence line, collecting beer cans from the ground as he goes. The loaded gun in my hand could easily be used to put an end to him, but he knows me. He knows how I feel about him, irrespective of whether I'm ready to admit to it or not.

I watch as he stoops and collects two more cans. I'm not prepared for the wall of emotion that hits me sometimes, for absolutely no reason. He can be doing the most inane thing—scratching at the stubble on his chin. Talking to Cade. Spinning a pen absently in his hand. Picking up beer cans for me to shoot—and I'll be hit with this sensation that just feels so damn...*huge*. Like it's taking me over, ferocious and unstoppable. Like it would be impossible to run from, no matter how hard I tried or how badly my lungs burned, or how painfully my legs ached.

When he straightens, Rebel finally glances over his shoulder at me and he smirks. "You okay?"

"Yeah, I'm totally fine. Why? Why wouldn't I be okay?"

More smirking. "Because you've got that look on your face."

"What look?"

"The look you get when I've just made you come really hard and your ears are still ringing."

Blood rushes to my cheeks. Man, this guy. He has some nerve. "I don't get a look when you make me come."

"Sure you do. It's like this." He tips his head back slightly, mouth open just a fraction, his hair falling back out of his face, his chest heaving. He looks incredible. And he does look like he's just had the best sex of his life. I'm struggling to keep myself in check. A very large, turned on part of me wants to command him to remove his clothes at gunpoint. *Slowly.*

Rebel's grinning when he lowers his head to look at me. "Sweetheart, you think I'd ever quit fucking you unless I knew you were satisfied? That face is how I know I've done my job properly.

It's the most beautiful, sexual thing in the world. I've memorized that lust-filled, sex-doped expression in great detail, which is why I recognized it two seconds ago when I caught you staring at my ass."

"Oh my god, I was not staring at your ass!"

He just laughs, turning his back on me again so he can carefully start balancing the beer cans on the tops of the fence posts again. "Why not? I have a great ass."

I can't deny that—he most definitely does have a great ass. It's just frustrating that he *knows* it is all. "Just get the cans up there, jerk."

"Yes, ma'am. If you hit all of these without missing, I'll treat you to something very special. Would you like that?"

"An Audi R8?"

He shoots a raised eyebrow over his shoulder at me. "You really don't know the meaning of inconspicuous, do you? A car like that would draw some serious attention around here. Either way, no. No Audi R8 for you. You'd get a far better ride out of what I'm offering, anyway." He looks positively evil as he says this. There's no doubting what he's referring to. I'd have to be stupid to miss the innuendo. He oozes sex when he's like this—intense, fixated and just a little wild. He's much calmer than he was earlier. His nervous tension pours off him just as strongly as his lust, though. He's not in a good place. Flirting with me might be a great way to distract himself, but I get the feeling he wouldn't follow through on any of his promises. He's just trying to rile me.

I decide to put the theory to the test. Purely out of curiosity, of course. Not because holding a gun in my hands always makes me feel heady with power, and his rather obvious comments have me tingling all over my body. "Okay," I say. "If I hit all...*five, six,* seven cans, you'll give me the ride of my life, huh?"

Rebel places the final, seventh can on top of one of the fence posts, straightening up. From the way he sets his shoulders, pushing them back, the cheeky glint in his eye turning very, very serious, it's clear he didn't expect me to take up his challenge. "Yes, ma'am. You can't miss a shot, though."

"What happens if I miss? No crazy sex for me?"

"Oh, no." He stalks toward me, something dark and dangerous now playing in his eyes. "There'll be sex for you alright. The tables will be turned, though. It'll be your job to please *me*. Your job to blow *my* mind. You'll have to do absolutely anything I tell you to, without question. That's a big responsibility." He pauses, crossing his arms over his chest. "I'm not so sure you can handle it."

I pull a face, shaking my head, trying to laugh off the highly sexual tone in his voice, but I can't. His words, the thought of obeying him, doing as he tells me, working to please him and sacrificing my own pride in order to do so...it's weirdly appealing. I want him to use me. In some perverse way, I want to lose this challenge so I can find out exactly what he would have me do. It would be the most eye-opening experience. I'd sure as hell know an awful lot more about his desires and kinks if I submitted to him like that. And if there's one thing I've ever been sure of in my life, it's that Louis James Aubertin the third has many, *many* desires and kinks he hasn't introduced me to yet.

"I can handle it," I say softly. "I can handle anything you throw at me. You should know that by now."

A smile twitches at the corners of his mouth. "Kidnapping, maybe. Having a gun pointed at your head, sure. But this? *Me*, uncut and uninhibited? Not holding back? I don't think so, sweetheart. *I think you'd be terrified.*"

He neglected to mention Raphael. After Raphael, nothing will ever scare me again. Certainly not Rebel. He told me himself that he would die to protect me. Common sense dictates that he would then be the last person to hurt me. Intentionally, at least. I smile, pouting a little. "I guess we'll see then, won't we?"

Rebel stands at my side like a statue carved out of marble as I line up my first shot. He doesn't look at the tin can waiting to be knocked off it's post; he stares at me instead. The heat of his gaze is palpable. Swallowing, I take aim, adopting the stance he had me shoot in before. Both my hands are on the gun, even though I can probably make it with just my right hand for support.

"Don't miss, sweetheart," Rebel says. "I promise you, I'm holding you to this deal. Whatever the outcome, you'll have to deal with the consequences. Do you agree?"

"Sure. Why not."

"All right, then. Better get to it." He holds out his hand, palm up, an invitation to get my ass in gear and get firing.

I try to be too cocky as I let off the first round. The can makes a high-pitched, metallic *ting*ing noise and leaps into the air. Dad would have given that a ten. The second shot is only an eight. The bullet hits the can slightly off center, but the impact sends it flying all the same. Rebel clears his throat. "Nerves getting to you?"

"Nope. You're just standing way too close, soldier boy. Why don't you back up a little?"

Rebel laughs. "Afraid you might hit me?"

"Perhaps. I mean, I doubt you could take any more injuries at the moment. A gunshot wound to the leg would likely finish you off." I make a show of aim the gun at his right leg, but the bastard doesn't seem concerned. He paces toward me instead of moving out of the way, until he's standing right in front of me. For some reason, following him with the gun seems like a smart thing to do. The muzzle ends up pressing into his chest, and he's not blinking, breathing, moving. He's staring at me and it feels like the whole world has stopped.

"If you're planning on shooting me, you should probably do it now, Sophia."

"Why now?" My hand shakes. It feels as though I have a jack-hammer pushing blood around my body and not a fragile human heart.

"Because today...today has been one of the worst days of my life. If you wanted to put me out of my misery right now, I wouldn't stop you. On the other hand, tomorrow I might wake up full of piss and vinegar and want to go hunt down Hector Ramirez. I might decide to go round two waterboarding the woman we're hiding under the barn. And I might just feel like asking you to marry me. A good night's sleep can really change a man."

"You waterboarded Maria Rosa?"

Rebel lets out a bark of laughter. He looks away, scanning the horizon. A dimly burning sliver of copper, rapidly disappearing below the rocky ridgeline in the distance, is all that remains of the sunset. He squints at it, frowning. "I just implied that I've been considering asking you to marry me, and you object to the fact that I dumped a bucket of water over a woman who threatened to kill you not only seven hours ago."

"Yes, but you were joking about the proposal part. I know you were, asshole." He has to be joking. Has to be. There's just no way he's being serious.

He steps forward just a little so that the gun digs deeper into his chest. There's a weighty look in his eyes. I don't know what to make of it, of his body language, of anything that's happening right now, but I know I'm beginning to feel a little freaked out. He's so close, I can smell him—entirely natural, and yet addicting at the same time. I can't get enough. "Why am I not being serious?" he asks. There's no doubt that he's looking and acting very serious, but my brain just won't comprehend the prospect that he's not fucking around.

"Because! You know. You're a smart guy. There's no way you'd ask a girl to marry you if you'd met under the circumstances we did. Especially only a month after that meeting, too."

"Why not?"

Oh my god. I'm beginning to think he's lost the plot. "Because you're meant to date for a couple of years, see if you like someone before you marry them, Rebel."

He pulls a dismissive face, rolling his eyes. "It takes you *years* to know if you like someone? Sounds like horse shit to me."

"Of course not. That's not what I—" I pause, take a deep breath, then start over. "There are steps you're meant to follow. You're meant to live together first."

"You're already living with me."

"You're meant to meet each others' parents."

"You've met my dad. He's a total ass-swipe but you've *met* him. And anytime you want, I'd be happy to meet your folks. You know, I scrub up well in a good suit." He winks at me.

I ignore him, because this is all far, far too absurd. "You're out of your damn mind. You're being a jerk, pushing this because you know I'll say no and you just want a reaction out of me."

"If thinking that makes you feel better, Sophia, then that is totally okay. Though, I think in the profession you were studying back in Seattle, the way you're acting at this moment might be termed as *avoidance.*"

"Get the fuck out of the way, Rebel. Am I supposed to be shooting these cans or not?" Even as I snap at him, I realize that what he's saying is true, though. I am deep in the grips of avoidance. But, hell, shouldn't I be? I mean, what a crazy, half-baked, insane thing to bring up. We barely know each other. And I'm more than a little intimidated by the man. If and when I get married, it's going to be to someone who didn't pay a considerable amount of money to buy me from a Mexican skin trader. I'm going to know my future husband intimately. I'm going to know his favorite color and what he thinks of Stevie Knicks. I'll have heard stories from his childhood so many times already that I'll know them by heart. We'll have traveled together and explored different countries, seen and done so much together that...*that it will feel like we've already had all of our adventures? That we have nothing left to learn about each other?*

It hits me like a punch to the gut. People place so much emphasis on getting to know your partner before you agree to spend the rest of your life with them. Perhaps...god, I don't even want to think it, but I can't seem to stop myself. Who ever said knowing someone inside out is a good thing? Could that be why so many marriages fail? Because there are no adventures left to be had? No secrets to be uncovered? No mysteries left to untangle?

I shake my head, forcefully shoving the thoughts out of my mind.

What the fuck is wrong with me? My father would have conniptions if he knew what was going on in my mind.

Rebel's wearing a shit eating, I-*know-what-you're-thinking-and-I-like-it* look on his face when I climb back out of my head. "You wanna shoot the cans, that's okay with me. You forget…I get to strip you naked either way, though, Sophia. It's win/win for me."

A shiver crawls up my spine, my skin breaking out in instant goose bumps. This bet is a win/win for him, but does that mean it won't be a win/win for me, too? Would obeying him, doing what he tells me to do without question, be that terrible for me? I somehow don't think it would. "Maybe I'm…maybe I'm curious," I whisper.

"Then why bother with our little shooting lesson? You're clearly a crack shot. Why not just say, *'Jamie, I want you to take me back to the cabin, and I want you to show me what it means for you to be my master.'*"

My hand is trembling on the gun so badly that I'm suddenly worried I might accidentally shoot him. Despite the cool night air of the desert, my palms are slick with sweat, as is the back of my neck. "You told me I shouldn't call you Jamie," I say quietly.

Rebel leans in, filling my head with the smell of him. "Oh, sugar. If you were going to say those words to me, I'd definitely want you to call me Jamie. At least then, when you eventually *do* run away like any sane person would, I can replay the sound of your voice telling me that. And it will be for *me*. Not the guy who's wrestling to keep his people together. Not for the guy who didn't protect his uncle. Not for the guy who's been searching for his best friend's missing sister for what feels like forever. It'll be for the guy who came back from Afghanistan never thinking he'd find a woman strong enough or brave enough to take him on."

I lower the gun, letting it hang down by my side. "I've already told you. I'm not going to run."

"Then it looks like you're the crazy one, not me."

"Looks like it." I can't believe what I'm about to do, but I know it's happening. I'm ramping up to it, a part of me panicked and scared yet unable to talk me out of voicing the words he wants to hear me say. "Jamie, I want you to take me back to the cabin—"

Rebel moves like a whirlwind. He catches me up, wrapping his arms around me, pinning me to him so hard that it feels like our bodies are fused together. He's kissing me, then. Kissing me so intensely that pinpricks of light start exploding like fireworks behind my closed eyelids. His hands are in my hair, roaming all over my body, palming my breasts, moving over my thighs. The moment is so unexpected and fierce that I begin to wonder if I'm imagining it. My imagination has never been this good to me, though. He slides his tongue into my mouth, exploring me, tasting me, and I follow his lead.

The gun I'm holding drops to the ground, and then my hands are in his hair, arms winding around his neck, and he's lifting me up so I can wrap my legs around his waist. His hands cup my ass, holding me up. When he pulls back, he's breathing heavily, his chest heaving, his eyes bright and shining in the near darkness. "We can still have amazing sex without you finishing that sentence, Soph. Don't say something you don't mean. Don't say something you can't take back."

A frisson of fear sparks in the pit of my stomach, but that's all it is—a small nagging sensation. When I look into his eyes and see what's in store there for me, how giving myself over to him will be so, so much more, that fear fizzles out and vanished entirely. "I trust you," I tell him. I lean closer, crushing my breasts up against his chest in order to whisper in his ear. "*And I want it.*"

His reaction has me gasping out loud; he grabs hold of my hair in his right hand and makes a fist, pulling my head back. "Then do it. Say it," he growls.

"Jamie, I—I want you to take me back to the cabin, and I want you to show me what it means for you to be my—my master."

A slow, wonderfully sinister smile spreads across Rebel's face. "Sophia?" he says.

"Mmm?"

"You may not want to talk about it this second, but you *are* going to marry me. You know that, don't you?"

I feel weak and helpless in his arms, but not in a bad way. I also feel safe. Protected. At peace. I know, no matter how many other men I could potentially meet in my lifetime, no matter how special they might be able to make me feel, I will never meet another man like this. I will never feel as special as the way he makes me feel. I bury my face in his neck, hiding from the truth in his eyes and the truth in my heart. I can't face it yet. It's too damn frightening.

Rebel laughs silently, his shoulders moving up and down. He presses his lips against my temple and then stoops to collect the gun I dropped on the ground. I'm still clinging to him, legs wrapped around his waist, arms around his neck, when he shoots out the remaining cans.

"Come on, sugar," he whispers into my hair. "Let's get you home. Time to show you what you've been missing.

REBEL

I take a corner, leaning my Monster into it, and Sophia's thighs tense ever so slightly. My dick is suddenly harder than reinforced concrete. Fuck Maria Rosa. Fuck Agent Lowell. Fuck Hector Ramirez and his evil piece of shit right hand man. All I care about right now is what's gonna happen when I get Sophia through the door and into my damn bed. I doubt very much we'll make it to the bed in all honesty. At this rate, as soon as we pull up outside the compound I'm probably going to be bending her over my motorcycle and fucking the living daylights out of her just to warm her up. She has no idea what she's getting herself into. No clue whatsoever.

Up ahead, the compound is lit up against the darkness like a beacon. We pass the huge tree where Carnie found Bron's body as we head toward home, and I can feel Soph judder against me. No matter how much time passes, that tree is always going to have evil connotations for her. For me, too. I'm not normally one for wantonly destroying living things, but I make a mental note to come out here tomorrow morning to take a chainsaw to the damn thing. I'll use a pickaxe to dig the stump out, and then I'll fill in the hole so it looks the same as the rest of this desolate landscape. Shame, really.

There are plenty of people milling about when we pull through the compound gates. I park my motorcycle up alongside the long line of machines behind the barn. Cade's out the front of the clubhouse smoking a cigarette. He sees us, gives me a curt nod of his head, but he doesn't come over. He'll have things to tell me—if anyone can make Maria Rosa part with information, it's Cade—but he must see the small shake of the head I give him. He'll wait for me to come find him later. After my business with Sophia is at an end.

The girl beside me has her shoulders drawn back, chin tilted proudly. She's set her jaw, and looks extremely defiant as I gesture for her to lead the way up to the cabin. She sets off without batting an eyelid.

"That woman hates me," she says.

"What woman?" I don't really need to ask, though. There's only one possible person she could be referring to. Shay needs to calm the fuck down, or she's gonna get called into my office and we'll be having words. Really unpleasant ones. Sophia jerks her head to the right, where Shay is leaning against one of the storage units, talking to Dex, one of the Widow Makers' longest standing members. She's glaring at Sophia, sending her the foulest look imaginable. She seems completely oblivious to the fact that I'm even here. When she does notice me I shoot daggers at her and she looks the other way, eyes to the ground. When I was a kid, Ryan taught me how to treat a woman. Southern manners are hard to shake off, regardless of where you end up living and regardless of how other people may treat the fairer sex. Shay's something else, though. She's enough to make me forget my manners entirely.

"You guys used to sleep together, right?" Sophia asks.

She's far too astute for her own good. I can see the awkward look on her face out of the corner of my eye; I know telling her the truth is only going to make her feel weird, but in the same vein I'm not going to fucking lie to her. I never will. "Yeah. Couple of times, back when she first showed up here. I put a stop to it very quickly."

"Why? I mean, she's a beautiful woman. You didn't think so?"

I laugh, placing my hand non-too-subtly on Sophia's ass as we climb the hill toward the cabin. "Sugar, a girl can be just about the most stunning thing to ever walk the surface of this planet, but if she's ugly on the inside then it's only a matter of time before she's ugly on the outside, too."

"So she's a bad person?"

I take a beat to think about this. "No, not bad. Just damaged. Seriously, *seriously* damaged. This club is a family, though. You don't kick out the problem child just because they have problems, right? You try and help them."

"And if they just don't want helping?"

"Then you lock them in their rooms until they start behaving themselves." I am really not beyond considering this with Shay if she continues to act like a spoiled little bitch. "The thing about Shay is she hates to lose," I say.

"And she thinks I've won?" Sophia sounds incredibly amused by this idea. I slap her on the ass. *Hard.* She stifles a cry, which has my cock throbbing in my pants. She can try and stifle her cries all she wants, but before the night is out I swear she won't be able to help herself anymore. Her throat will be sore from all her screaming, in the very best way.

As soon as we're through the door of the cabin, I have her in my arms, feet off the floor, and I'm charging across the other side of the room toward the bed. I must take her by surprise, because Sophia goes rigid, stiff as a board.

"Shit," she hisses.

I throw her down on the mattress so hard she bounces. There's a look of poorly disguised fear in her eyes as she blinks up at me, her breasts straining against the thin material of her t-shirt as she breathes in and out in quick time. "Are you afraid of me, Sophia?" I growl.

Her cheeks are stained with a delicate, rather attractive shade of crimson, as are her lips and the base of her throat. She swallows, and then nods. "A...little."

"You can't be. If this is going to work, you can't even be a tiny bit frightened." I crouch down at the foot of the bed, grabbing her by the ankles. Pulling her forward, I only let her go when her legs are either side of me, her feet almost touching the floor. I look her in the eye along the length of her beautiful, perfect body, and grin. "Sit up."

She slowly props herself up on her elbows, and then pushes herself upright so her breasts are at my eyelevel. They are so incredible—I want to tear her shirt right off her back and go to town on them, licking and sucking, but I don't. I need to make sure she understands what's about to happen first. And what will *never* happen. "Look at me, sugar," I whisper. "Look me in the eyes."

Until now she's been looking everywhere *but* at me. It's so important that she knows I'm telling the truth when I say what I have to say now, though. If she doesn't, she's likely to flip the fuck out and panic and I don't want that. I may be about to make some serious demands of her, but I want her to enjoy them all. I want her to come so fucking hard on my dick.

"Soph, tell me what you're afraid of," I say.

She bites down on her bottom lip so hard, the skin turns white. I reach up and press my index finger and middle finger against her mouth, making a disapproving sound. She releases her lip and takes a deep breath. "I'm...I'm afraid I'm not going to like not being in control. I'm afraid I won't like being told what to do. I'm afraid—I—" she stumbles over what she wants to say, but I already know what it is. I give her a moment to finish, but when she doesn't I complete the sentence for her.

"You're afraid you'll feel trapped and unable to escape. You'll be frightened, because you think I'm going to treat you the way Raphael wants to treat you. To hurt you. To take something from you that you don't willingly want to give."

She looks away. Again I reach up, but this time it's to gently turn her face back to me. "I'm not Raphael. I don't like to hurt women. I would never, *never* force you to do something you didn't want to. We're going to push your limits, perhaps, but having those limits is

347

okay. If you honestly don't want to try something, then all you need to do is say so and that's it."

A slow smile gradually forms on her face. "So... we're going to have a safe word?"

I laugh. "Sugar, 'no' is the only word you ever need to say. 'No' should never *not* be enough." It makes the blood boil in my veins to think that she's told someone no before and it *hasn't* been enough. I'm sure she didn't welcome Hector inspecting her to see if she was a virgin. I'm sure she didn't consent to Raphael pawing all over her, breathing down her neck, telling her all the vile things he wanted to do to her. If he'd taken it further...if he'd actually... Fuck, I can't even think about that. My rage would be a brutal, swift, consuming thing.

"Thank you," she says softly. "No's good enough for me."

"Good. Now. Do you want to know what *I'm* afraid of?"

It's very rare that Sophia looks shocked. She does now, though. It's almost comical to be honest, but I can't laugh because I actually am freaking out a little. Today isn't the best day to tell her this; I know that. But the thing about perfect moments is you don't know they're perfect until they've already passed you by.

Fuck it. Here goes.

"I'm scared because I'm in love with you, and I don't know what to do about it." I sound confident as all hell when I tell her this, but my head actually feels like it's about to implode. I only manage to sound that way, because it's true. I *am* in love with her. It's fucking inconvenient, and a genuine surprise to me, but it's true.

Sophia's eyes grow really round. She sits very still, not breathing or moving. Eventually, she says, "You're not joking, are you?"

I shake my head.

"Well, fuck."

"I know. Messed up, right?"

"Ha!" She stares at me, and I think she's not really taking this in. Not believing me, anyway. I can tell by the mildly angry look on her face. "That's really low," she says. She laces her fingers together, gripping tightly, her knuckles blanching. "Why would you do that?

Why would you tell me that?"

"Because…I've never told anyone before. It seemed like the right thing to do."

"You've never told anyone you loved them before?"

"No. Never."

"What about your…" I know she was going to say my father, and I know she then realized how stupid that would be; I watch it all play out on her face. "What about your Uncle, then?" she says. "What about Ryan?"

"Nope. Never. He was a pretty stiff kinda guy. I know he loved me in his way, but he never said it. I think he would have kicked my ass if *I'd* have told *him*."

"And there were never any girls you dated? You…you never fell in love with any of them?" She's beginning to sound incredulous. I don't know if I should be offended, or I should be finding her complete and utter disbelief entertaining.

"No. Never been in love."

"But you're…"

"I'm what?"

"You're insanely hot! I just…I can't…"

"Lay back on the bed, Soph."

"What?"

"But we're not…you just told me that you're in love with me. I can't—" Sophia covers her face in her hands, shaking her head from side to side. She's not coping well at all with this new piece of information. I stand up, crack my neck, and then I push her onto her back, eliciting a strangled scream from her.

"What the fuck? You—"

"I am your master for the night, remember. It's time for you to start doing as you're told."

She goes still again, staring at me—seems that's all she's done the past fifteen minutes, like I'm some strange, alien creature she can't possibly comprehend—and then she lets her hands fall either side of her on the bed. "Okay," she says. "Okay, fine. Show me."

I head for the bureau on the other side of the room, slide open the top left drawer, and take out a pair of scissors. They're old. Really old. They have Winchester Gun Co. engraved on the handle, and they're really fucking sharp. Sophia's face goes blank when she sees them. She doesn't object, though. She doesn't get up and make for the door. She remains where I left her on the bed, watching me cautiously.

"What are you going to do with those?" she asks, her voice flat.

"I'll show you. We're going to go through some rules, though, sugar. Are you going to obey them?"

"Shouldn't I probably know what they are first?"

"No, you shouldn't. That's the whole point." I've only played this game with three other women, and nearly every single one of them hesitated here. It's not in a person's nature to strike bargains or agree to things without prior knowledge of their responsibilities beforehand. However, Sophia shocks me when she doesn't miss a beat.

"Okay, then. I'll obey your rules." Her voice doesn't waver. She means what she says, that much is clear, and the effect that has on my body is insane. I've never been so proud in all my life.

"Good girl. Rule number one: when I tell you to do something, you do it immediately, without question. That one's simple. Number two: don't speak until you're spoken to, or there will be consequences. Number three: you don't come without my permission. Simple, right? You think you can handle that?"

"Yes. I can."

"Okay. From here on out, we're operating under these rules. Shall we begin?"

"Yes." Her response is barely loud enough for me to hear, but I can see it in her eyes: she's intrigued. I'm sure Matt-the-boring-ex never did anything even remotely off the wall; this is probably going to be a real education for my poor little Sophia. I make my way back to the bed, scissors in hand, and I climb up onto the mattress on my knees beside her. She lies still, watching the sharp, silver object in my hand with just the right amount of trepidation to tell me she's concerned about what comes next.

I start at her right ankle, taking hold of the cuff of her jeans and then opening the scissors, sliding the lower blade beneath her clothing. Sophia sucks in a sharp breath but remains still, just like she's meant to. There's understanding on her face now—she knows what I'm about to do, and in truth she looks a little relieved.

The scissors cut through the denim material easily; I could probably just run them upward and slice through from her ankle to her waistband in a few short seconds, but where would be the fun in that. This is a sensory experience, after all. The sound of the scissors cutting through one inch at a time is half the fun. And Sophia feeling the cold, hard metal against her warm skin is another very big part, too. She gasps the first time I lay the flat of the lower blade against her calf. I don't leave it there long. I don't want the metal to heat up, and besides, too much contact will desensitize her. She'll become used to the sensation and it won't be shocking anymore.

When I reach the middle of her thigh, I go even slower. She's breathing fast, not looking at the piece of metal in my hand or what I'm doing to her clothes. She watches me, her mouth slightly open, the tip of her tongue darting out to wet her lips, a slightly doped up look in her eyes, and it's all I can do to stop myself from forsaking the scissors and tearing her damn clothes off with my teeth.

My hard on is digging into my jeans, caught up, beginning to throb like a motherfucker, but this is too delicious to stop. I will wait until the pain reaches unbearable levels before I quit my little game and rearrange so that things are a little more comfortable. Sophia tenses a little when I make the final cut through the right hand side of her jeans, right at the top, through her waistband. Folding the material away from her leg, I see her lacy black underwear for the first time and my blood starts roaring through my body, all chasing through my veins, charging in one direction: to my cock. Before I know it, I've reached that unbearable level of pain and I have to adjust my dick. Sophia watches me do it, looking shy yet hungry at the same time. I can't wait to get through destroying her clothes so I can bury my tongue in her pussy. I can't wait to taste her come all over my tongue, sweet and delicious and all mine. And I really can't wait 'til she's digging her fingernails in my back, desperately trying not to make a sound, to not displease me while I fuck her so hard her whole body shakes.

I lean down and place a feather-light kiss on her exposed hipbone, warring with myself as I fight not to take things further. To kiss her lower. A little to the left. A little further down again. I know she's feeling the same anticipation I am when she angles her hips up a few millimetres; she catches herself and freezes almost straight away, but I sit back on my heels, giving her a warning look.

"Careful, sugar. That nearly counted."

She opens her mouth, wants to say something, but yet again she catches herself. She's good at this game so far, but things haven't even begun to get difficult for her yet. Not too long from now, it's going to take everything she's got to stay silent, and I am going to relish the moment when she breaks one of my rules. It's going to be absolutely fucking perfect.

I cut the other leg of her jeans off her body, watching her struggle to keep still the entire time, and then I take the scissors to the flowy shirt she's wearing. I cut down the arms, and then straight down the middle, biting back a smile every time she twitches when the cold metal makes contact with her belly, her arm, her chest.

"Get up," I tell her. "Stand here, in front of me."

She climbs out of the ruins of her clothes, leaving them behind on the bed, and it's almost like she's leaving behind the scared, frightened part of her. I gather up the material and dump it on the floor at the end of the bed, and then I sit on the edge of the mattress, surveying her in her underwear.

She doesn't cover herself or hide. She simply stands there, waiting for my next command. She's good at this. Perfect, in fact. "Come here," I say, opening my legs so she can stand between them. She takes two steps forward so she's right where I want her. There's only a flicker of doubt in her eyes when I raise the scissors and slowly slide the blade beneath the lacy material of her panties at her left hip. The soft snip of the metal cutting through the lace is the only sound in the room. I cut the material at the other hip, too, and her panties flutter to the floor, nothing to hold them up anymore.

Now she gets antsy. She shifts from one foot to the other, pressing her thighs together, and I tut. "You want me to punish you, don't you, sugar. You're asking for trouble." Again, she wants to speak but she doesn't. She frowns at me instead, her fingers curling into fists by her sides. She's self-conscious. God knows why, she has the most incredibly sexy body, but she is, I can tell. She wants to keep me from seeing the one part of her that no one ever sees. But I have seen her. I've gone down on her often enough to be on very good terms with that part of her body. I'm willing to put good money on the fact that her ex never went down on her. Not properly. He should have made her feel comfortable with her body. She doesn't know that her pussy is beautiful, that I could happily look at it all day long as I made her come, and she would have a fight on her hands if she tried to stop me.

I take the scissors and run the point from a couple of inches below her belly all the way up until I hit the under wiring of her bra. She knows what comes next. Her hands make fists again and this time they don't uncurl. She looks up, away from me, eyes fixed on a point on the wall straight head. Her shoulders lift up and down rapidly, like she's afraid I'm going to cut her. She knows I won't, though. She's hardly a shy woman. She'd be waling on me in a second flat if she thought I was going to do her any harm. I love that about her.

She's still focusing on the wall when I cut through the slender strap between the cups of her bra, freeing her breasts. "Take it off, sugar," I growl. Her eyes meet mine again as she obliges me, sliding the thin straps that I've left intact over her shoulders and down her arms. Completely naked, she stands in front of me like a statue, not moving, not saying anything, doing exactly as I told her to. Her obedience is remarkable, given that I know she wants to cover herself up. I place the scissors on the floor and kick them under the bed so they're out of the way, and then I tell her what I want from her next.

"On your knees, Soph. Be a good girl now."

She gives me a sharp look, eyes narrowed, but she only takes a moment's pause before she's lowering herself to her knees. I'm thinking she must be pretty pleased with the fact that her pussy isn't at my eye level now, but little does she know that's about to change.

"Good. Now, open your legs for me, sugar."

"But—" She clamps her mouth shut as quickly as she's opened it, but it's too late, the damage has already been done.

"Oh dear..." I send her my most fucked up, smug, wicked looking grin. "Looks like someone broke a rule."

"Oh come on, I didn't mean to. I—"

"You did it again. And here I was, thinking you were doing so well." I try my best not to laugh when I catch sight of the mortified expression she's wearing; she must have been counting on the fact that she wasn't going to break my rules, and now it looks like she's done it twice.

She wants to defend herself, to say it wasn't her fault, I provoked her, but she manages to stop herself from speaking this time. Crying shame, because racking up three individual punishments in under a minute would have been a record.

"You know I have to teach you a lesson now, sweetheart. I can't let that slide. I would if I could, but...y'know...rules are rules and all. Spread your legs for me, princess and I'll go easy on you."

Sophia rolls her eyes and sighs, presumably resigning herself to her fate. Without another word, she does as I've told her, opening up for me. She doesn't just open a little ways either. She pushes her legs out as far as she can do in this position, exposing herself to me.

"Good girl. Now lie back on your heels, so they're still underneath you but your back is arching away from the floor." She does as she's told again. In this position, her breasts are close at hand for me to palm as I sink down to the floor and proceed to go down on her.

Some men like to drive fast cars. Some dudes go fishing. But this, right here, giving head to Sophia, is my favorite pastime. I know she loves it, even though she likes to think it's embarrassing. It's fucking hot. She's fucking hot. I'm painfully aware of the fact that I'm fully dressed as I stroke my tongue slowly across Sophia's clit. But this is part of her punishment. I'm not going to get naked with her now. I'm not going to fuck her either, no matter how badly my balls are aching. I'm going to tease Sophia, send wave after wave of pleasure shooting through her body. I'm going to make her sweat and writhe and moan, and when she comes it will be the best orgasm of her life. And after, when she's sated and limbless, sleep rolling over her, I'm going to tell her that next time I'll stop right before she climaxes if she misbehaves herself. And I will leave her like that without a second thought.

So this is what I do. Soph's attempt to stay still and keep quiet is a valiant one, but in my head I guestimate it's a mere four minutes before she completely loses it. She doesn't even seem aware that she's bucking and grinding her hips against my mouth—which incidentally drives me fucking insane. She's so fucking beautiful. I watch the sheer bliss on her face as I continue to use my tongue to bring her closer and closer to coming, and for the first time since I was fourteen years old I nearly end up making a mess of my pants. She's practically tearing the floorboards up with her bare hands when she finally comes.

It's the most spectacular, amazing thing to watch. Her back arches off the floor, chest heaving, thighs clamped firmly around my head, and she screams. She screams loud enough that the guys down in the clubhouse must now either assume I'm murdering her or that we're having ten-out-of-ten, hard core sex.

When her body stops shaking, Sophia looks up at me out of half-closed eyes and scowls. "I'm in serious trouble now, aren't I?" she says breathlessly.

I laugh, and then I slap her thigh, which doesn't seem to amuse her as much as it entertains me. "Oh, fuck yeah, girl. You have absolutely no idea what I get to do to you now. The only thing that will save you now is that tattoo we talked about."

"No way! I am *not* getting tattooed."

"We'll see." I crawl up her body, placing kisses on her hot, sweet-smelling skin. I'm practically planking over her when I reach her mouth.

"I think you should be inside me now," she pants through our kisses.

The way she says it, the way those words sound coming from her full, biteable lips, almost makes me cave. I stay strong, though. "Sorry, sugar. You were a bad girl. Only good girls get what they want."

I leave her there on the floor, naked and still panting.

REBEL

Cade's not in the clubhouse. Normally after taking a girl up to my cabin for a couple of hours and then reappearing looking frustrated as fuck, I'd garner a few catcalls from the other Widow Makers, but tonight the mood is overly drunk and sombre. After Bron's short and simple funeral, no one's in the mood for jokes. They're in the mood to get fucked up and fight.

Three chairs and one table have been smashed by the time I manage to make it across the clubhouse bar and up the back stairs to the handful of bedrooms we have set up there. No one lives here permanently. The Widow Makers have either chosen to live in town with their families, or they have rooms in the many outhouses that make up the compound. That's probably why people think we're some sort of fucking sex cult. Cade has a place above Dead Man's Ink in town, but he won't have gone back there tonight. Not without speaking to me first. He'll be holed up in the one room that's permanently reserved for him on the top floor, waiting to spill whatever bullshit lies Maria Rosa told him when I left the two of them alone.

I lay my fist against the last door on the right, not surprised when

Cade opens it right away. He must have heard my boots coming down the corridor. A gift from the U.S. Marine Corp: the ability to hear a man sneaking up on you from a mile away.

Semper Fi.

My brother in arms looks absolutely exhausted. He steps back so I can enter the room, which is sparse and OCD neat. He claps me on the back, giving me a tired smile. "You look much better than you did before, man. I think you got out of there at the right time."

"Did she say anything else?"

He shakes his head. "Nope. She did try and convince me to fuck her, though."

"What is wrong with that woman? She gets shot and waterboarded, and in the next breath she's trying to get you to stick your dick in her?" Cade gives me a rueful look that tells me it might have been worse than that. "Jesus. I don't think I want to know," I tell him.

"I'm sure you don't. Come on. Let's do this." Cade knows where we have to go next. He knows what has to be *done* next, too. Raphael Dela Vega has polluted Widow Makers ground for too long already. I won't have him here, freaking Sophia out, causing trouble amongst the club members. They know Hector Ramirez's right hand man is in one of the holding cells underneath the barn. It won't be long before someone's suggesting we chop the motherfucker's extremities off and send them back to Ramirez in ziplock baggies.

The guy has got to go. No way are we sending him back to his employer, though. No. No fucking way is that happening. If I'm honest, I'm all for the chopping off extremities and leaving them for Ramirez to find, the same way he did with poor Bronwyn, but we don't have time for that. Gunshots fired? A convoy of strange, unlicensed, shot-to-hell black cars burning out of town, headed straight for us? It's a goddamn miracle that Lowell woman isn't hammering down the gates already. There was nothing to be done about him until dark, though. With a long range scope—paranoid perhaps, but a possibility—it would have been all too easy to spot a couple of guys wrestling with a noncompliant Mexican guy in broad daylight. Now we just have to hope that if Lowell is out there and she's got people watching us, they don't have heat imaging or night vision. If they do, we're gonna be fucked.

There's a goddamn riot unfolding in the bar downstairs as Cade and me sneak out the back. Normally I'd start knocking heads together, but it's better for everyone involved if the guys continue raising hell here instead of following us. Outside, the desert air is cold and the sky is an explosion of stars.

Cade jogs across the courtyard—there's still blood everywhere. I should make Maria Rosa come clean up her fucking mess before I even consider setting her free—and opens the barn door, slipping inside. He holds the door open for me, and then we're shrouded in pitch-blackness. A pale yellow flame is struck into existence, which sends long fingers of narrow shadows stretching up to the barn rafters. Cade looks like some sort of horror movie character as he holds the tarnished zippo he's lit up to his face.

"You want me to turn on the overheads?"

"No. Would only draw attention. Dark is better."

I'm regretting my words two seconds later when Cade is falling over sideways, crashing into me, hissing under his breath. He goes down hard, almost taking me with him. The zippo skitters out of his hand, skidding across the roughcast concrete floor, though the flame remains lit, guttering and then strengthening again.

"What the hell, man?" I grab hold of Cade by the shoulder, trying to pull him up in the half dark. He grunts, and then there's the sound...the sound of a second person moaning? What? No one else should be in here. No one else should even know we have people in the basement. My hand's reaching for the gun in my waistband when Cade swears loudly.

"Fuck, no. Damn it, it's fucking Carnie."

"*Carnie?*"

There's more moaning. Cade gets to his feet, moving his considerable bulk out of the way, and then I can see Carnie too in the meagre light being thrown off by the zippo. Sure enough, he's flat out on his back, a two-inch long gash along his right temple. His eyelids flicker open, but even from here I can see his eyes themselves are not working properly, don't seem to be focusing on the men standing over him.

"What happened?" Cade demands. "What the hell are you doing up here, passed out cold, man?" He shakes Carnie hard, which seems to do the trick.

"Uh...I was...fuck. I was...heading down to take some food to Mother and the other one. I opened the padlock on the hatch and he...he sprang out. He had a broken chair leg in his hands. He must have hit me over the head with it."

When I first walked back into the clubhouse and Cade told me Ryan had been killed, it took me a beat to process what he was saying to me. Took me a minute or two to comprehend what he was telling me. Not so this time. As soon as the words are out of Carnie's mouth, I'm in fight mode, already predicting what will come next. Dreading it with every fibre of my being.

I grab hold of Carnie by the collar of his cut, pulling him off the ground so my face is in his. "How long? How long ago?" I yell.

"I don't...I don't know. What time is it?" Carnie's still struggling to string words together. Means he was probably hit over the head pretty hard. That also means he could have been out for a considerable amount of time, too. I let go of him and he drops to the ground like a sack of flour.

This cannot be happening. It just can't. "*Fuck!*"

Cade draws his gun and sets his jaw. He knows what this means, too. Raphael Dela Vega is an unhinged bastard with no sense of self-preservation. He won't have fled the compound. Not yet. He's been fixated on one thing and one thing only for a long time now, and he won't leave here until he's gotten what he's been dreaming about.

He has been dreaming about Sophia.

SOPHIA

When night falls over the desert, it suddenly feels like the world ceases to exist. Out there, beyond the lights and sounds of the compound, all drunken shouting and the furious roar of motorcycle engines, there's nothing more than a sea of black ink and an endless void that stretches for as far as my mind can imagine in every direction. No, there are no roads or general stores. No dive bars, and no all-night diners. The compound feels so very isolated and alone. It kind of freaks me out.

My body is still humming from Rebel's ministrations when I get up and draw the blinds on all the windows. God knows where he's gone. I didn't really get a chance to ask him before he fled the cabin, looking very pleased with himself. He knew exactly how cruel he was being when he decided not to stay and have sex with me. Can't have been pleasant for him, either, but still… the guy is evil.

I'm grinning like a moron as I think this, though. Grinning so hard my face hurts. He's turned me into some sort of pathetic teenager, which is ironic because I was never like this back then. In high school, I was driven by the need to excel in my schoolwork, and definitely not to pursue the attention of boys. And now here I am, turning my back on my studies in order to be with the most unsuitable person on the face of the planet.

But, in saying that, maybe he's not the most unsuitable person. If just that one thing about him were different, he would be prime take-home-to-meet-the-parents material. He's intelligent. He's a gentleman (for the most part). He was in the army. He went to MIT, for fuck's sake. But then the kicker...he's also the head of a motorcycle gang. What would Mom and Dad say if they knew what I was doing right now? A pang of guilt sideswipes me out of nowhere as I really take on board what they probably believe has happened to me by now.

They have to believe I've been murdered.

There isn't a way in this world they would ever believe I just decided not to come home when given the opportunity. So I mustn't have had that opportunity. They must think I was stabbed or shot, or worse, that I was raped and beaten to death.

God, I am the worst person on the face of the planet to leave them wondering like this. My heart feels like a lead balloon sitting heavy in my chest as I find new, un-shredded clothes to put on.

I should call them. I should just stop being such a fucking coward, and I should tell them I'm okay, even if I end up hurting them by not going back to Seattle. Straight away. Not going back to Seattle *straight away*. I will have to go back at some point. Don't I? I can't hide here forever.

The t-shirt I've stolen from Rebel's closet is clean and soft and smells deliciously of him as I pull it over my head. My moral compass starts spinning, then. Why can't I stay here for a while? At least until everything with Ramirez dies down. I have excellent grades. I could always go back to college next year if I want to. There may even be a college in New Mexico that—

I can't help but smile as I hear the cabin door creak open. He thought he was such a smart ass when he high-tailed it out of here, leaving me on the floor, needing so much more of him. And now look. He's back within ten minutes, no doubt ready to teach me a lesson. I get half way through pulling the t-shirt over my head, but then there are hands on my hands, stilling me. I'm half naked, only my head and shoulders covered by the soft, dark material. Something about that is so kinky. I'm essentially blindfolded for all intents and purposes. He could do anything to me and I would never see it coming.

"So," I say breathlessly. "You changed your mind. Will this be part of my punishment?"

"Mmm-hmm."

His stubble grazes me across my shoulder blades, my skin immediately turning to goose bumps as he places his lips against the curve of my neck. Slowly, his hands travel from mine down my arms until they're hovering just above my breasts. I want him to touch me. I want him to touch me so badly. I arch my back pressing my breasts upward, catching my breath in my throat, waiting for him to gently slide his palms downward, following the swell of my body.

However, when he does move his hands down, it's not gently. He takes hold of my breasts, grabbing with rigid, calloused fingers, and then he squeezes so hard I'm momentarily blinded by the pain.

"Ahhhh! What...*what the fuck?* No! Stop!" For a second, through my confusion, I think that this is the real punishment Rebel was talking about and I am frightened. Very, very frightened. And then it hits me. There's no way Rebel would ever handle my body like that. Like he hates it and he wants to hurt it. I may not have been with him for years and years, I may not know what his favorite color is, or what all of his childhood stories are, but I know he would never do that to me. Never in a million years.

Which means...

Terror is a living, breathing thing, snaking its way through my insides.

Oh, god, no...

Oh, god, no.

My whole body locks up tight when I hear the sound of very familiar, very evil laughter in my ear. "Oh, I knew you would have such a pretty little cunt. I knew you would love me pinching your perfect titties like this."

Raphael.

Raphael is here, with his hands on me, touching me. Hurting me. I try to drag in a breath but it's impossible. My ribcage feels like it's in a vise and I'm never going to wriggle free. My brain eventually connects my difficulty to breathe with the fact that Raphael has wound one of his arms around my chest and is squeezing tightly.

The next three seconds are a blur. I tear the t-shirt away from my head, which leaves me completely naked. Better naked than blind, though. I thrust my elbows backward, slamming them into Raphael's body, contacting with his side and his arm. He doesn't let go, though. If anything, his grip grows even tighter.

"GET THE FUCK OFF ME! LET ME GO!"

"I won't be letting you go, princess. Not this time. This time you're mine. Struggle, bitch. Fight me. Come on...make me believe it." I can't see his face but I can hear the sneer in his voice. He's loving the fight almost as much as he hates me. Because he does. He *despises* me. He's the sort of man who hates all women, purely because of their sex. I know nothing I say is going to get me out of this situation. I'm going to have to fight my way out of it, and I'm going to have to be smart about it, too.

I'm gripped by panic and fear, but somehow my brain is still working. Through everything that's happening, feeling trapped and ultimately terrified, I manage to form one coherent thought: *stop giving him what he wants.*

I fall limp in his arms.

"Que—?"

He's shocked at my response. Me deciding to play possum was the last thing he must have expected. I'm sure he knows that's exactly what I'm doing too, but now he has to do something with me. He has to put me down or spin me around or...or *something.* I know it, and he knows it, too.

"You think you're so smart, huh, *Puta.* So fucking smart. You always think you're one step ahead of me. Well, you're not." I realize he's right when he quickly shifts his hold and wraps one of his arms around my neck, applying pressure. Fuck. He's going to try and choke me out.

"Don't worry, princess. You'll be asleep soon. I'll have so much fun with you while you're sleeping. And when you wake up, you'll be all tied up and begging me to knock you out again. Won't you? Won't you, you little fucking slut." He braces his muscles, tightening everything as he pulls back, applying even more pressure against my windpipe. My head is already spinning. Pinpricks of light dance in my vision, floating around like drunken flies. My arms feel weak; they feel them as I scramble at his arms, trying to prise them free.

That's not going to work. Too weak. Too dizzy. No strength. Can't...

I reach further back, fingernails clawing at the ripped material of his shirt, searching for...searching for god knows what. My heels hammer against the floorboards as Raphael lifts me higher, putting even more pressure on my neck. I have seconds. Mere seconds to get out of this, or it will all be over. I will pass out, and I will never want to wake up again, knowing what he will have done to me while I am out cold. My fingers suddenly hit something fleshy, something soft. His face.

I keep scrambling, scratching, trying to claw at him, but it's not working. It's not working. Raphael starts to laugh again—a maniacal cackle that sounds unhinged. I'm on the verge of losing consciousness, but the madness in that laughter gives me the strength for one last push. One last grapple at his skin.

I feel something wet and moist underneath my fingertip, and I know this is it, my final chance. Raphael tries to swing his head around, to move away from my hand, but I butt my own head backward, cracking my skull against what feels like his nose, and then my index finger is digging into that soft area of flesh I touched a second ago.

Not bone. Not cheek. Not chin. No. My finger is digging right into his eyeball, and Raphael is screaming.

I know I've done some serious damage when he drops me like a hot coal and clutches both hands to his face. The world is suddenly in Technicolor; my head feels like it's splitting apart from the brightness and loudness of it. Blood thumps through my veins, charging full tilt as I try and crawl away from him.

"PERRA DE MIERDA!" Raphael stumbles into the wall next to him and then punches it, leaving a smear of blood on the plasterwork. I can't tell if it's from the action of actually hitting the wall or if it's from his eye. A river of blood runs down his face, and his left eyelid is swollen shut, puffy and oozing fluid. With only one eye open, he sees me on the floor and lets out a howl that chills me to my very core.

I should have moved quicker. I should have been on my feet and running as soon as he let me go. I couldn't breathe, though. I could barely see straight myself.

He falls on me, grabbing hold of my ankle and dragging me across the room toward the bed. "You should not have done that, you fucking psycho," he growls. "Are you a good catholic girl, princess? Are you?" He slaps me hard across the face, landing the blow across my ear. A high pitch whine buzzes through my head. When the sound dies down, Raphael is screaming obscenities at me, shoving his face in mine, spitting everywhere.

"I'm going to make you wish you'd never been born. I'm going fuck you raw. I'm going to make you hurt. You've brought this on yourself." He hits me again, snapping my head around with the force of his blow. With his right hand he presses my head down into the floorboards so hard I can feel the skin above my eyebrow splitting open. It feels like my skull is about to crack open. With his other hand, Raphael begins to fumble with the belt around his waist. It doesn't take much to imagine what's coming next. I screw my eyes shut, trying to think, trying to figure this out. Trying to find a way out of this. It's when I open my eyes, the sound of Raphael's fly unzipping snapping me back to reality, that I see my salvation, though.

I don't have long.

I reach under the bed.

I stretch.

I stretch so hard it feels like my shoulder is about to dislocate.

I close my fingers around cold metal.

And then I'm twisting as best I can with my head being pressed into the floor, and I'm stabbing and I'm stabbing and I'm stabbing.

I only stop when Raphael Dela Vega slumps over me, a heavy, dead weight, pumping long, hot jets of arterial blood all over my naked body.

"Ohmygodohmygodohmygod." I shove him off of me, and then I'm clambering to my feet, backing away, backing up until my shoulders hit the wall and I can go no further. Shit. *Shit!* I clamp both of my hands over my mouth, trying not to see the mess I've made of Raphael. I want to look away, but I can't. My eyes are locked on the shiny pair of scissors—Winchester Gun Company—that are sticking out the side of his fucking...out the side of his fucking neck.

I pitch forward and brace my hands against my knees, and I throw up.

I don't stop until I feel hands around me. I think for a second that it's him. I think it's Raphael, that I didn't do the job properly. I start flailing, arms and legs everywhere, fighting for my life. And then I smell that smell. The one from the soft t-shirt. I smell that smell, and then I know everything will be okay.

Rebel crushes me to him, and the world turns black.

REBEL

Sophia sleeps in one of the bedrooms in the clubhouse most of the next day. When she's awake she showers over and over again, crying continually. I stay with her. I don't really know what to do to make her feel better. This is all my fucking fault. I allowed that motherfucker to remain alive and breathing on Widow Makers' ground. I should have put a bullet right between his eyes the moment I saw him standing there, but I didn't. I allowed him to live, and so in turn I allowed him to attack Sophia. She's hurting and she's in pain, and it's all because of me.

The third time she wakes and lumbers heavily to the shower, I sit on the edge of the double bed, sheets twisted up and practically knotted from where she's been tossing and turning, and I hold my head in my hands. There's nothing I can do to fix this. She wanted her freedom. She didn't want to be watched over twenty-four seven, but I shouldn't have listened. There shouldn't have been a moment of the day that I wasn't by her side, especially with that piece of shit festering away in the basement.

I allow myself a moment of weakness, and I think about Laura. It was the same with her. I turned my back for five minutes, and then she was gone. What the fuck is wrong with me that I keep letting this happen to the people around me. They always seem to get hurt. A part of me wants to shut the club down. These people that have followed me out here into the middle of nowhere, who for some reason trust me to know what I'm doing, have misplaced their faith in me. I keep proving that, time and time again.

And Sophia. She has to go back to Seattle. Like, *yesterday*.

Just the thought of what I have to do makes me want to head directly downstairs, grab a bottle of Jack from the shelf above the bar, get on my bike and then find somewhere quiet where I can drink myself into a stupor. There was a time when I probably would have done that, but I can't now. I have a responsibility to the woman quietly tearing herself apart in the shower.

I walk numbly down the hall, take my flick knife out of my back pocket, and then I twist the lock on the bathroom door open from the outside. The room is so full of steam, I can't see my hand in front of my face.

"Soph? It's me. It's Jamie." I speak loudly, so she knows I'm there. The last thing I want to do is surprise her. "Jesus, have you even got the cold tap turned on, girl? It's like a sauna in here." I know why she's scalding three layers off skin from her body, though. She feels dirty. She can still feel his hands all over her body.

This, sadly, is not the first time I've had to take care of a woman who's been mistreated by a man. It is the first time that I've felt like I'm dying myself, though.

From behind the steamed up glass shower screen, I can make out the small shape of Sophia, curled up in the corner of the tiled shower. "Can you...can you just..."

She wants to ask me to go away. She's trying to ask that of me, but she can't seem to finish the sentence. I should be a gentleman and give her what she wants. Walk right back out the door, lock it again, and give her the space she craves. But I can't. Instead, I open the shower door and I climb right in there with her, fully clothed. T-shirt, hoody, jeans, sneakers. I leave it all on. Me stripping off my clothes would be a shitty idea, even though I have zero intention of trying anything on with her.

I'm soaked the instant the stream of boiling water hits me. Sophia looks up at me, arms wrapped tightly around her body, knees drawn up to her chest, and I can tell there are tears running down her face in amongst the beads of water from the shower head. "What are you doing?" she mumbles.

I smile sadly down at her. My throat feels like it's swelling fucking closed. She looks so small. So vulnerable. She stabbed Raphael eleven times before she drove those scissors into his neck, but to look at her now you wouldn't think she was capable. I'm really fucking glad she was.

"Just checking in," I say softly. She doesn't reply. She leans her forehead against her braced arms, her body shuddering. Fuck. I've never felt like this before. I've never felt this...useless. Even when Laura went missing, I still felt like I had a purpose: Find her. Bring her home. Apologize. Sophia's sitting right in front of me, though. I haven't lost her in the same way I lost Laura. Bringing Sophia home is a different task altogether.

I lean against the wall and slowly slide down it, not making any sudden movements, until I'm sitting on the floor next to her. I don't touch her. She must hate me. She must blame me. She has every right to. I told her everything would be okay, and it was anything but.

We sit there in silence for a long time, the water feeling hotter and hotter with every passing moment. The skin across Sophia's shoulder blades turns from a violent scarlet to a bruised looking purple. She doesn't seem to notice when I slowly adjust the temperature of the water from blisteringly hot to something a little more manageable.

We sit some more.

Eventually, I feel the need to break the silence. "I'm going to drive you home tomorrow," I say slowly. "I'll drive you myself." She doesn't look at me, but I can feel her tensing, though; I know she must have heard me. "It's...for the best. I don't want anything else happening to you. Not because of me. I can't—I can't tell you how sorr—"

"You don't want me anymore."

I stop talking, turning my head to fully look at her properly. "*What*?"

"You're sending me away. You don't want me anymore," she says. It's really hard to hear her over the constant battery of the water against the slate tiles, but I can just about make out what she's saying.

"No...no, of course I want you, Sophia. Fuck, I..." My heart feels like it's being stomped on repeatedly every time it beats. How can she think that? How can she honestly think I don't want her anymore?

"I probably disgust you," she says.

Oh, god. Being stabbed at Ramirez's place hurt. Being tasered by Lowell was breathtakingly painful. But *this* pain? This pain makes me feel like I'm dying. I would hurt less right now if someone took a knife, slammed it into my chest, and twisted with all their might. "You're crazy if you think that, sugar. You have no idea. I...*I am so fucking proud of you.*"

Slowly, she raises her head, peering at me sideways, a blank look on her face. Her hair is plastered down her cheeks, her neck, her back in dark, wet streamers. "How? How can you be proud of me? He nearly..."

"Because you defended yourself. You didn't give in. And he didn't get what he wanted from you, Soph. You didn't let him. It takes so much strength to do what you did." I mean every word. Since I started buying these women from the skin traders, I've come across so many girls who were overcome by the dark places they found themselves in. A lot of the time, giving up felt safer than standing their ground. That was how they coped, how they stayed alive. I'm pretty sure giving up wasn't something that even crossed Sophia's mind.

"I'm not strong," she whimpers. "I'm not."

I want to smash my fists into the wall, but that won't help her. More violence is the last thing Sophia needs in her life, and so I wrap my arm around her shoulders instead, pulling her to me. "You are the strongest fucking person I know, okay. Don't you ever fucking doubt that. And you do not disgust me. I fucking love you, okay? I fucking love you."

It's as though she finally gives in and breaks all at once. She's stiff as a board one second, resisting me, and the next she's crumpling, falling slack, and then climbing into my lap, throwing her arms around my neck, clinging onto me as though her very life depends on it.

Since I raced up to the cabin yesterday, my heart trying to climb up and out of my mouth, I haven't been able to touch her properly. She's flinched every time I've gone near her. Seems that her reluctance to have any sort of physical contact with me has passed now, though, and I am so fucking relieved I could cry.

"It's okay, Soph. It's okay." I gently stroke my hand over her hair, my eyes clenched tightly shut, and she cries into my soaking wet clothing, fisting my t-shirt in both her hands. When she stops crying and just breathes against me, I turn off the water and wrap a towel around her body, and then I carry her back to the bedroom.

Sleep takes hold of her.

When she wakes up, it's dark and I tell her I have a job for her. Confusion clouds her face as she looks at the pair of heavy-duty gloves I'm holding out to her.

"Why are you giving me those?" she asks.

"Because digging's hard work. I doubt your hands are already covered in calluses, sugar." She doesn't ask me why she's going to be digging. She gives me what can only be described as a baleful look, but then takes the gloves and gets dressed in the jeans and sweater I brought down from the cabin for her.

Outside in the courtyard, a huge bonfire is blazing, cracking, spitting, sending burning hot red and orange embers spinning upward into the black night. Cade took a chainsaw to the hanging tree. I couldn't do it, so he stepped up and got it done. A small crowd of Widow Makers, Brassic included, stand around the fire with beers in their hands. They watch with silent respect as Sophia and I walk by. When she first came here, the guys were dubious of her. New people, especially pretty young women, are always cause for suspicion around these parts. But now she's not the girl who lead Ramirez back to New Mexico, to our doorstep; she's the girl who killed Raphael Dela Vega. That will forever earn her kudos with my guys. Even Shay nods her head as we pass. There's no anger in her eyes tonight. She just looks weary, and I kind of get it. Being as angry and as confrontational as Shay is twenty-four hours a day, seven days a week, must be exhausting.

Soph and I climb up into the Humvee, and she doesn't mention it but she must know I have Dela Vega's body in the back, out of sight. I drive thirty minutes south, heading in the opposite direction from the spot where we buried Bron yesterday. Lowell hasn't paid us a visit yet but there's every chance she's having the compound watched, so I don't turn on the car's headlights. I just drive in a straight line, my eyes accustomed to the dark, and Sophia stares out of the window, her thoughts clearly weighing heavily on her mind.

When we stop and get out of the car, the night air smells weirdly like eucalyptus and something else. Something sweet that I can't put my finger on. The dark shadow of Sophia's form moves quietly around the car, where she opens the rear passenger door and takes out the two heavy shovels I put there before we set off.

"How many times have you done this?" she asks me. Her eyes shine brightly, full of pain and sadness, but they're dry. I get the feeling I won't see her crying over Raphael Dela Vega again; the firm set of her jaw and her ramrod straight posture speak volumes.

I want to lie to her and tell her I'm new to this. That I haven't been burying people out here in the desert for *years* now. But I can't. What would be the point in deceiving her? She's a smart girl—maybe too smart for her own good—and she must already know the truth. I want her to know me, dark, evil things included, and telling her otherwise would only be misleading her. "Too many times to count, beautiful girl."

"Were they...were they all men like Raphael?"

Nodding, I drive the point of my shovel into the ground. "And worse. Far, *far* worse."

She seems to think about this for a long moment, the sweet smelling breeze lifting tendrils of her dark hair about her face, and then she nods. "Okay."

"Okay?"

"Yes. If they were worse than Raphael, then they deserve to be here. I get it."

I'm not prepared for her acceptance of this knowledge, so I don't have anything to say at first.

The two of us start digging; it's not long before Sophia sheds her sweater, stripping down to the thin t-shirt I gave her to wear, and I'm naked from the waist up. We're both sweating and breathing heavily by the time the hole is deep enough to dispose of Raphael's body.

I purposefully haven't covered him up. He's all blood and horror and loose-limbed madness as I heave him out of the back of the Humvee and drag him under his arms to the grave we've prepared for him. His skin a strange mottled purple color, apart from where he's covered in his own dried blood, which has turned the color of rust and dirt.

"Are...are his eyes meant to look like that?" Sophia asks softly. She's glancing at Raphael's already decaying body out of the corner of her eye, as though, if she only manages to glimpse him in small snapshots, she'll be spared the true horror of what she's done. That won't do her any good, though. That's why I left him uncovered. She *needs* to see him. She *needs* to come to terms with the fact that she killed him.

"Yeah." I drop Raphael on the ground, and then go to stand beside her. Taking her hand, I draw her to my side, trying to stem the body-wide shivering that seems to be taking her over. "That always happens."

Her fingers feel icy and cold in mine. "Do you know why?" she asks.

"It's the potassium breaking down in his red blood cells. Makes the eyes go cloudy."

"He looks...looks like he has cataracts. He doesn't look *real* anymore." Taking a deep breath, she finally looks at him properly. "I get why you're making me do this," she whispers.

"Tell me."

"Because you want me to have closure. You want me to be the one who buries him. You want me to be the one who shovels dirt onto his body and sends him away forever. You want me to understand he's never coming back, and he's never going to hurt me again. That's why."

I don't say anything. I don't need to. She's hit the nail on the head; without this sort of closure, she'll only ever remember him with his hands on her, trying to force himself on her. He would always seem stronger than her in her mind. More dangerous. He would forever haunt her. Now, like this, broken, just a slowly degrading husk, he has no power. Yes, he looks terrifying, covered in all that blood, staring up at the star speckled night sky with his mouth yawning open in surprise, but he also looks small. Weak. Incapable of causing her any more pain.

I nuzzle my face into her hair, breathing her in, trying to transfer some of my strength to her. She's already so damn strong, but that's irrelevant. If I could carry this burden for her, I would. If I could have been the one to kill him, I would have. I *should* have. I don't ever want her to hurt or suffer any more than she has to. "Do you want me to help you?" I whisper.

She squeezes her hand in mine, taking a deep breath. "No. No, it's all right. I can do this."

She gets to work. Even after she's pulled on the gloves I gave to her at the clubhouse, I can tell she doesn't want to touch Raphael.

She has to in order to get his body into the hole, though, so she steels herself and then grabs him under the arms, the same way I did when I dragged him from the car.

Raphael was a big guy, and Soph is nowhere near as strong as me, so it's not as easy for her to maneuver him to the side of the grave. She doesn't give up, though. She positions his body directly beside the gaping hole in the ground and then she straightens, staring down at the man who's plagued her dreams since that night back in Seattle.

"You were a vile piece of shit in life, Raphael. And you're a vile piece of shit now. Fuck you." She trembles as she spits on his body. Trembles as she uses her foot to shove him roughly into his final resting place. He lands face down, which feels highly appropriate. A strange sense of pride washes over me as my girl tosses the first shovel-load of dirt into the hole.

"My father would have a fit if he knew I was doing this," she says.

"Burying the man who assaulted you?"

"Burying him like this, face down, with no blessing and no prayer for his soul."

"Your father's religious?"

She remains quiet for a second. I know it's hard for her—she still hasn't given me her real name, and I haven't pushed for it. I know her last name is Romera, or at least her father's last name is, but even that wasn't information she volunteered. I heard him say it when she called him on that payphone back in Alabama. She still feels conflicted about parting with information that might endanger her family, and I get that... But *she* has to get that I am not a danger to her family. She *must* know that. The main threat to her family is now being covered with the dirt she's letting fall from her shovel.

I don't think she's going to answer me, but then she speaks after all, talking in muted, quiet tones. "Yeah. He's a preacher for all intents and purposes. My family are pretty devout Christians."

I had no idea about this, but it fits. When I first met her, she had that uptight air about her that spoke of a sheltered, strict upbringing. That's gone now, lost to the four winds. Now, she seems like an entirely different person.

I sit on the ground by the graveside and watch as she labors to fill it in. The work is backbreaking but she doesn't complain and she doesn't ask me to do it for her. With every load of dirt she piles on top of Raphael Dela Vega's body, she seems to become more and more confident, her back straightening, her eyes flashing with determination. When it's done, Sophia drops the shovel to the ground, rips off the gloves I gave her, and sinks to the ground beside me. My arm finds its way around her shoulders instinctively, and she folds into me, resting her head on my shoulder.

"About what you said before," she says.

"Which part?"

"The part about you driving me back to Seattle."

I cringe at the words. "Yes." It's going to hurt like a motherfucker taking her back home, but it's the right thing to do. What I should have done weeks ago instead of dragging her further and further into this mess.

"I don't want you to drive me back," Sophia whispers.

Hearing her say that is like a punch to the gut. I understand. I don't like it, but I will respect her wishes. "Okay. Public transport's out of the question, though. I need to know you've walked back through your front door okay. I'm sure Cade won't mind taking you if you pref—"

"No, that's not what I mean." She looks up at me, frowning slightly. "I mean, I don't want to go. I mean I want to stay here. I want...*I want to be with you*."

I've known pretty much from the beginning that she was attracted to me. It was fairly obvious from the way she acted around me and how often I caught her staring. I was hardly shy about the fact that I was into her, too, though. This, however, is a huge surprise. She looks a little stunned herself.

"I thought you'd jump at the chance to get out of here, Soph. Don't you want to go home? See your parents? Your sister?" I stroke my hand over her wild, wavy hair, dreading whatever she's going to say next. I want her to be safe. I want her to be a million miles away from Ramirez and his men, even if Raphael is no longer a concern. But I also want her in my line of sight at all times, close enough that I can touch…

"I'm going to call my dad," she says. "I want them to know that I'm okay. And I want them to know that…that I'm not coming home."

"Perhaps you should think about this before you make any rash decisions."

"I have. It's all I've been thinking about for days. I don't think I can go back to who I was before, Jamie. I'm not…I not the person I used to be."

When she calls me Jamie, I feel like I *could* be the person I used to be, if I tried really hard. That would mean giving up this whole enterprise, though. It would mean admitting that Cade's sister is gone and that we're never going to find her. After so long, I think I've already come to terms with that fact anyway. Admitting it is hard, though. Admitting it to Cade would be fucking impossible. We barely talk about her anymore. He must have come to the same conclusion that I have, but she's his blood. He won't stop looking until he's found out what happened to her one way or another. And I won't abandon him.

"This club is intense, Soph. Being here means you're going to be more and more involved in the way we live our lives. Is that something you can put up with?"

"Yes. I want to. I—" She turns to face me, eyes about as wide as I've ever seen them. She's so fucking beautiful. I want to wrap her in cotton wool and keep her safe. Forever. "I want to be a part of it," she whispers.

"Be a part of the club?" This…this is guaranteed the very last thing I ever expected her to say. I still don't think I've understood her correctly. "You want to be a *part* of the club?"

"Yes. I want to do what Carnie did. I want to prospect."

"*No. Fucking. Way.*" She's gone mad. I shouldn't have made her bury Raphael. It must have caused severe trauma to her brain.

"Why not?"

"Come on. Let's get in the car." I help her to her feet, and then I'm half guiding, half dragging her back to the Humvee. She doesn't make a sound when I open up the passenger door for her and usher her inside. Slamming the door closed, I hope the loud noise will be an end to the crazy conversation, but Sophia's ready and waiting for me.

"Shay's a woman. Fee, too."

"That's correct. They are."

"So why can't I be a Widow Maker? If they can be, then surely I can be, too."

I start the engine but I don't put the Humvee into gear. I swivel in my seat so I'm facing her, desperately trying not to launch myself across the other side of the car so I can shake some sense into her. "You can't join because it's dangerous, sugar. Things with Ramirez are about to get grade A fucked up. I'm trying to make your life safer, not even more dangerous."

"Do you honestly think Ramirez is going to forget all about me now that Raphael's gone? Am I still not the only person who can testify about your uncle's murder?"

"*Raphael* killed Ryan. Raphael's now dead. There's no way to prove in a court of law that Hector ordered him to do it. That ship has well and truly sailed. The cops are never going to fix this. *I'm* going to have to fix it. *The club* is going to have to fix it. It's going to be all out warfare, and that bitch Lowell is going to be along for the ride. God knows how it's all going to end. I don't want it to end with you swinging from the end of a rope, missing your fucking hands and feet, though."

"Why are you reacting like this? I thought you'd be happy that I wanted to stay, Rebel."

Rebel. Huh. No more Jamie. That's probably for the best. I punch the steering wheel, grinding my teeth together, expecting to feel them crack under the pressure. I can't seem to think straight all of a sudden. My entire body feels hot, my senses working overtime to keep up with my rising anger. "Have you forgotten what I said to you the other day? I told you I was fucking in love with you. That means I will let you go. That means I will kiss you goodbye and I will help you pack you shit into the back of this car, and I will let another fucking guy drive you out of here. It means I will never see you again if that's what I have to do, because I love you so goddamn much that I'd rather my whole world come crashing down around my fucking ears than have you killed because of me. Go back to Seattle, Sophia. Become a psychologist. Marry boring Matt and have a ton of children. Go to book club and drink too much Sauvignon Blanc on the weekends. Get a divorce at forty and find yourself all over again. Live the clichéd, middle class life that I can't give you."

I'm blowing hard, my lungs burning when I shut my mouth. I've never really known what it is to feel like this—utterly destroyed. It's come as a complete and very unwelcome shock to me that I am going to be fucked when she goes, but she *needs* to see it's for the best. She *has* to.

It takes me a long while to realize that she's not saying anything. When I look at her, Sophia's staring dead ahead, arms folded across her chest, eyelids unblinking. She's practically vibrating with rage. Her tone is even and flat when she begins to speak; I can tell it's taking everything she's got to remain calm enough to get her words out. "Over the past few weeks, you've been stabbed, nearly bled to death right in front of me, attacked by Ramirez, shot with a Taser and arrested by the DEA. You think I wouldn't worry about you if I went back to Seattle? You don't think I would be sick to my stomach every second of the day, wondering if you're alive or you're dead? Fuck, Rebel...*you don't think I'm in love with you, too?*"

She gets out of the Humvee, slamming the door so hard behind her that I'm surprised the damn window doesn't shatter. I watch her storming off into the desert, the pale blue of her t-shirt fading fast into the darkness as she hurries away from the car. For a moment I can't move. I can't think straight. *She loves me, too?* She loves me too.

I feel like she's just punched me square in the jaw. I mean...*how*?

I finally get my shit together in time to realize that she's been totally swallowed by the near pitch-blackness outside and I should definitely find her before she vanishes for good. I get out of the car and run after her.

She's not too hard to find. Standing with her back to me, she's only made it thirty feet from the car, and she's crying. "I should fucking hate you," she tells me. "I shouldn't give a shit about you, whether you live or die, but I do. That day you took me up on the roof of your dad's place, you said something to me and it's been stuck in my head ever since. You said, 'Don't bother trying to get inside my head. It's a dark and scary place. Even I don't want to be here most of the time.' But I couldn't help it. I wanted to get inside your head, and you..." She turns around, stabbing her index finger into my chest. "You invited me in. You didn't for one second try and stop me from developing feelings for you. So why should you get to care more about me than I care about you? And why the hell am *I* not allowed to take risks to make sure *you're* okay? I have nothing to go back to, Rebel. I have a family and a college degree and I have an apartment sitting empty in Seattle, but if you're not there with me then I have *nothing*."

I can't fucking breathe. I can't...

I grab hold of her and pull her to me, wrapping my arms around her and holding her so tight to me that she probably can't breathe either. She presses her face into my chest, clinging onto me, and we just stand there, not letting go. Not saying anything. Not moving.

This woman has turned me fucking inside out. I reach down and lift her up, my hands underneath her thighs, and she wraps her legs around my waist without question. I just hold her there.

"You want this? You really want this, knowing what it involves?"

She pulls back, her eyes slightly red and puffy. There's real grit there, too, though. So much fire. She swallows, and then says eight words that will change things for us both forever. "I want *you*. And I'm not going anywhere."

This is pure fucking madness, but I can't help grinning. One of us will end up dead soon enough, but in the meantime I'm sure things are about to get really fucking interesting. "You realize you're going to need to learn how to ride a motorcycle now, right?" The thought of her in charge of a bike is instantly hot. Her intensity breaks as a small smile spreads over her face.

"Seriously? That would be kind of badass."

"Oh my god," I groan. "You're gonna be the death of me, woman."

"Huh. And here was me thinking I would try and keep you out of trouble instead," she says softly, biting her lip.

It occurs to me how fucked up this is—the fact that we've just disposed of a body in the desert in the middle of the night, and I'm swiftly developing a hard on. I laugh like a maniac because I can't help myself. "All right, then. Sophia Romera, consider yourself the newest prospect of the Widow Makers Motorcycle Club."

RANSOM

CALLIE HART

RANSOM
Copyright © 2016 Callie Hart

Formatting by Max Henry of Max Effect
     www.formaxeffect.com

LIVE FOR SOMETHING OR DIE FOR NOTHING

For you,

for reading.

THANK YOU.

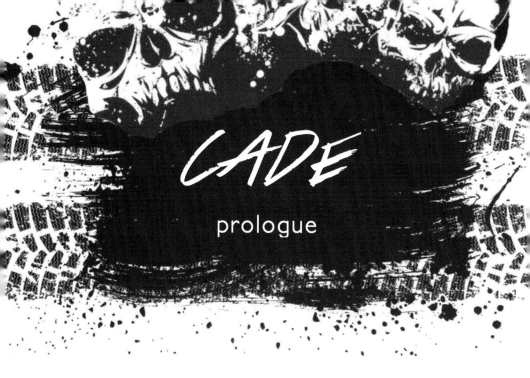

CADE
prologue

"**D**on't even think about it. Don't you dare even think *about it, motherfucker.*"

The weight of my rifle sits heavy in the crook of my shoulder. Both of my hands are on the brink of going numb. My skin feels damp and clammy from lying out in the tall grass for so long, but I can't move. Nope. No way. Hector and his men disappeared five days ago and haven't been seen since. Ever since then, Rebel's had people watching the farmhouse, waiting for them to return, and it just so happens I'm on duty when the black sedans roll down the long, winding driveway toward the two story building. I wasn't on watch when the bastards left, so I have no idea how many people departed or how many will be returning, but my math is pretty good. Three cars just rolled up, tires crunching on the gravel driveway, headlights spearing the darkness, casting long, narrow columns of light over the field I'm currently laid low in, over the two story building in front of me. Over the three-walled barn that crouches low to the right of the building. *Three* sedans. So potentially fifteen people all in. Can't imagine Ramirez cramming three grown ass dudes into the back seats of his vehicles—that would be far too undignified—so realistically we're looking at twelve men, maximum. I'm definitely outnumbered, regardless of how many passengers the cars carry.

I don't worry about being seen. I spent years perfecting the art of camouflage in the military. I can just as easily make myself invisible here in the middle of bum fuck nowhere, New Mexico, as I can in a forest or a city. No, I won't be seen.

Ramirez obviously has ideas about remaining invisible, as one by one the cars switch off their headlights, coasting the last fifty feet down toward the house with silenced engines and a cloak of darkness to conceal what's going on inside the vehicles.

I mutter under my breath again, willing my eyes to adjust to darkness. "Sneaky fucker. You can't hide from me." I close one eye, shifting the rifle across an inch so I can switch from my left to my right while I get used to the shadows. When I open my left eye again, I can see pretty well. Well enough to make out the shapes of bodies moving in front of the house.

Ramirez knows we've been watching him. He has to. That's the only reason he'd be taking such precautions. He hasn't counted on the fact that I have better than average night vision, though. Or the fact that the huge DSLR camera I've brought with me is state of the art and can discern images in the dark without the need for a flash. I place the rifle in the grass next to me and power up the camera, holding it up so I can look through the lens. God, this thing's fucking good. Three men go inside the house. Another figure climbs the stairs up to the porch and then turns, looking back over his shoulder. My itchy trigger finger comes in handy when I make out the man's face. I react quickly, shooting off a picture of Hector Ramirez, and a large part of me is pissed at the fact that I switched over from the rifle to the Canon. It would have been a clean shot. I could have put a bullet between his eyes and no one would have noticed a thing until the bastard's body hit the deck. I would have been long gone.

Ramirez disappears inside. My night's work here is done now.

I've laid hidden for long enough. I've seen the devil himself return back to Freemantle, and now I need to get my ass back to the compound to let Rebel know. Slowly I begin to pack up the camera. I work silently, not making a sound—don't want to attract any attention to myself as I sneak back to the road where I hid my bike. That would be a big mistake. I nearly have everything secured when I hear the commotion up by the farmhouse. It sounds like feet kicking at dirt, scrambling, and the dull sound of someone's shouts being cut off.

"He—HELP!"

I have the camera unpacked in a heartbeat. Another shout echoes across the fields, and a flock of birds explode from the tree line of the forest on the right. Tiny black silhouettes cartwheel across the sky, zigzagging this way and that.

Shut the fuck up, old man, someone hisses up by the house. I hold the camera up and look through the lens—takes me a second to figure out what I'm seeing. There are too many arms and legs in play. It looks like there's a fight taking place, more than two people involved. I see a flash of white hair through the camera lens, and then the terrified face of a guy I don't recognize. He's being restrained in a headlock as three other men attempt to pin his arms to his sides.

God knows what the hell Ramirez's men are doing with this guy, but it doesn't look like the grey-haired man is a willing participant. "Let me down. The police are going—"

Looks like the police aren't going to do anything. Ramirez's flunky, the one who was holding the old man in the headlock, apparently grows tired of trying to choke him out and instead raises the butt of his gun, bringing it crashing down on the top of the guy's head. I take a picture just before the gun magazine makes contact. The old man falls limp in the arms of Ramirez's thugs, and they drag him into the building, up the stairs and across the huge porch way. From inside the building a light is turned on somewhere, sending a warm pool of yellow light spilling out into the inky blackness. I should leave. This situation could blow up very quickly. I could find myself in some serious shit. I don't move, though.

There's something so familiar about the old man. I've seen him before, I swear I have. Ramirez's men drag him backwards up the porch steps and I see his face once more, this time in profile. A memory itches at the back of my mind, teasing me, almost rising to the forefront of my recollection before scattering and vanishing into smoke.

"*¡Apagar la luz!*" an angry voice commands. "What the fuck are you doing out there?" Ramirez himself appears in the doorway, expression twisted with fury. He slams his hand against the light switch on the wall and all is blackness again. I can still hear the man fighting as he's half dragged, half carried inside the building, and I can still hear Ramirez's men swearing as they try to subdue him. The sounds are cut off with the loud slamming of the heavy front door.

My ears buzz as silence falls over the field. A dull thudding noise comes from the house, just once, and then there's nothing.

Who the fuck *was* that? I can't think of a single reason why Ramirez would kidnap an old man and bring him way out here, but then again who knows what's going on in the crazy fucker's mind. The old guy could be a part of his operation somehow. He could have fucked up and done something bad enough to warrant a visit from the Los Oscuros cartel head himself. Seems unlikely—Hector would surely just send someone else to deal with such trivial things?—but it's possible. Anything is possible when you're dealing with a megalomaniac like Ramirez.

Rebel's going to want to know about this immediately. I pack up the camera and the rifle, and I hunch down low, skirting the perimeter of the field as I head in the direction of my motorcycle. It takes five long minutes to negotiate the terrain back toward the road. The narrow dirt track bends back on itself about a hundred meters from the farm house, the remaining mile long stretch of unpaved driveway obscured from view by a tall bank of trees. I hop

386

out from the undergrowth and jog quickly along the track, still keeping low, my mind racing. If Jamie thinks this guy is somehow an innocent party, he won't rest until he's made sure the guy is safe. If he even suspects for a second that the man being forcefully taken inside the farmhouse was an official like his uncle Ryan was, he'll tear the place apart brick by brick looking for him. He still feels responsible for his uncle's death. The past six months have done nothing to ease the burden of his guilt; it still troubles him every time someone mentions the name Hector Ramirez. Or Raphael Dela Vega for that matter, though Raphael won't be causing us problems anymore. Not unless he digs himself up from the shallow grave he earned himself and starts telling tales, which is highly unlikely.

My bike is only a few hundred meters up ahead. In the distance, across the sweeping, open swathes of land that stretch between here and Freemantle, tiny lights flicker like lightning bugs, orange and white. I nearly jump out of my skin when a pair of lights much brighter and much closer suddenly flare up in the dark, directly in front of me.

"Fuck!" I duck down, swearing again under my breath, taking cover in the head high brush and bushes next to the road. My heart is hammering, racing away at an unstoppable pace. What the fuck? Another car? The headlights in the road were close—too close not to have noticed me headed toward them. The metallic clunking of a car door opening and then quickly closing reaches me where I'm hunkered down in the ditch beside the road. Footsteps on the dirt. The sound of a lighter being struck.

"Come out, come out, Mr. Preston. We'd like to have a chat with you," a male voice says. *Mr. Preston.* So they know exactly who I am. *Fuck.* How many of them are there? I can't see anything from my vantage point, so it's impossible to assess how bad this situation really is. I'm guessing it's really fucking bad. The footsteps grow closer, and I smell the faint burn of cigarette smoke on the air. "We just want to talk to you," the voice says again; it's thick with a Spanish accent, though the English is next to perfect. I'm guessing whoever this guy is, he was born in the states, but Spanish is his first language. "If you make us come looking for you, we might change our minds," he says.

I'm hardly likely to hand myself over to them. That would be suicide; I'd put money on it. I stay very still in the brush, holding my breath, trying to calculate if I have time to rip the rifle from its bag and assemble it in time to shoot this motherfucker in the face.

"You're being very foolish," the voice advises me. "Mr. Ramirez is a reasonable man. Sitting down and having a conversation with him might actually be beneficial to you and your friends. You surely can see the wisdom in this?"

But I can't. Ramirez is a psycho with zero morals. If I let this guy take me back to the farmhouse to 'talk', I can guarantee there won't be any talking. There will only be torturing. Torturing and bleeding.

The sound of footsteps draws even closer. Jesus Christ. No, I definitely don't have time to assemble the rifle. I'm such an idiot. I should never have taken it apart—or at least not until I was well clear of Ramirez's land. I'm going to have to use my bare hands to get myself out of this. Good job I've been trained extensively in how to murder an opponent that way.

"All right. Have it your way," Ramirez's man says. "Don't say I didn't give you an alternative."

The brush next to me explodes as a loud cracking sound fills the night air. He must have shot into the ditch by the side of the road, hoping to hit me. Anger bubbles in my veins—that's such a shitty way to kill someone. Such a cowardly way to take care of business. There's no honor in blindly shooting into the dark, hoping you hit your mark. You're supposed to look a man in the eye when you kill him. You're supposed to be present, so you can face him, own what you're doing. Take responsibility for it. Take pleasure in it sometimes.

Another gunshot rings out, and a shower of dirt rains down on me. That one was much closer, maybe less than twelve inches from my head. He's getting warmer and there's nothing I can do about it.

If I start moving now, I'll be giving my position away. If I don't, he's going to have to come down here and find me personally. The fucker had better pray he doesn't have to do that, 'cause I'm going to fuck his shit up good and proper if I lay hands on him.

"Sure you don't want to change your mind, Mr. Preston? Hector will be far more lenient if he knows you chose to come and see him voluntarily. Maybe he'll leave you most of your fingers." He's goading me now, trying to get me to respond so he can figure out my position. I'm not falling for it. My heart rate has leveled out, slowing to a normal rate. I'm in control. I'm not some unseasoned kid who's gonna start begging and pleading for his life the moment things start to look a little sticky. I can lay here and hold my breath forever. Unless he comes and finds me, he's going to have to get real lucky with that handgun of his. Even then, he's going to have to shoot me in the heart or the head, because taking a gunshot wound to any of my extremities, my shoulders, or my stomach isn't going to kill me, and I'll still be more than able to kick his ass, no matter how much blood I'm losing.

Silence returns for a long while, drawn out and tense. I have plenty of time to work myself up, allow myself to get angrier and angrier. This stupid fuck has no idea what he's getting himself into. If he knows my name, then that kind of indicates that he knows *me*. And if he knows me, he knows that I don't go down in a fight. For *anybody*, no matter how big, small, tattooed, or pierced. He could be a professional UFC fighter and it wouldn't matter. He'd have to knock my head clean off my body in order to stop me from coming for him.

A short burst of gunfire rattles out, and bullets strafe the vegetation to my left, closer toward the car. He's getting further away now—much further away. Relief is a sweet, sweet thing. Looks like I'm going to get my mini hand-to-hand battle soon, after all. I risk ducking up for a split second, checking to see where the guy's standing now, but it's hard to see anything with the night so heavily upon us. Out here there's no light pollution. The moon's barely a slip of silver in the sky, a very tiny crescent. I can just about make out the shadowy outline of someone moving around up ahead, but I can't judge distance. Not like this.

I have to move quickly or not at all. I have less than a second to make up my mind—do I stay hidden, or do I take this motherfucker out, risking whatever repercussions there may be from whoever else is sitting in that car?

I barely think about it. I've never been the type to sit on the sidelines and wait to see what happens. I'm an all or nothing guy. Leaving the camera and the rifle behind in the grass, I creep up the bank in front of me as quickly and as quietly as I can, and then I launch myself out onto the road, hands up, ready to pile drive my fists through this asshole's head. I only need to stride about three paces before he's right there in front of me, about my height and about my weight. He looks momentarily stunned as he whips around to face me.

I don't give him time to lift the shining metallic object in his hand. I'm too close to punch him, so I grab hold of him by the collar and jerk him forward, bringing my head down at the same time so I can head butt him.

A head butt is like a bomb going off inside your skull. If you know how to do it right, you can cause some serious damage to a person with minimal effect to yourself. I've had a lot of fucking practice. The guy's nose explodes when I hit him, blood spraying everywhere. He yelps in pain, dropping his gun, trying to stagger away from me, to hold his hands to his face, but I'm right there, moving with him, catching him square on the jaw with a powerful right hook.

"That one's for you, shithead," I tell him. "And this one? This one's for your boss." I hit him with everything I've got. My fist lands directly to the side of his head, just below his temple, which may or may not be a good thing. A temple shot like that can easily kill a man. He goes down, sinking to one knee, holding a hand up, as if that will be enough to ward me off. I'm more of a boxer than a UFC guy. Mauy Thai and kickboxing aren't my wheelhouse sports, but I still use my knees when the mood takes me. I grab the back of the guy's head, planting the back of my hand against his skull, and I lift my bent knee quickly, slamming it straight into his face. Something makes a sickening cracking sound, but I can't tell what. He's already a pulpy mess of swollen flesh, so I haven't got a clue what's actually broken and what's just covered in his blood.

My opponent topples forward onto the dirt track, falling face first to the ground, groaning quietly. I have to say, I did think that was going to be slightly more difficult. He was full of talk; I figured he'd at least land a few decent punches before I rung his bell. He didn't even get his hands up. Fucking pathetic. I grab his gun and make my way over to the car, where the driver's side door is yawning open.

This is where things could get really bad for me. This is where someone I can't see could shoot me in the face. The car's high beams are on, blinding me, preventing me from making out anything inside the vehicle. Adrenalin is surging through my veins as I carefully head around the side of the car, hunched over, ready to stop and drop if I need to. Turns out I don't. Ramirez's guy was bluffing. He was alone all along? That was a ballsy fucking move. I get closer and check the back seat.

Nobody.

"Well, that was a crap shoot, huh?" I say. Ramirez's guy doesn't hear me, though, because he's out cold on the ground right where I left him. I go back to him and sigh, standing over him, wondering what the fuck I should do now. If I leave him here, at some point someone will find him. The cutthroat, savage part of me thinks I should probably just kill him. Shoot him in the head with his own gun and drive his sedan out into the desert, have myself a little bonfire. But then again, I'm not the man I used to be. Killing doesn't thrill or excite me these days. This guy's out cold, defenseless, and yeah, my own thoughts from a moment ago replay in my head, chastising me: there really is no honor in killing a man without looking him in the eye.

Fuck.

So what, then? I bundle him up and take him back to the club compound with me? Where the fuck would we put him? The basement underneath the barn is dangerously crowded these days. Our permanent resident takes up a lot of fucking space. And Rebel's head would probably explode if I showed up in one of Ramirez's cars with a body in the trunk. No. That's not going to work.

Crouching down, I grab hold of the guy by his hair and yank his head back so I can get a proper look at him. His face really is a mess. He's going to look like shit tomorrow, that's for sure. The guy blearily cracks an eye, consciousness fighting to return. "Morning, sailor." I grin and wave with my free hand. "Little sleepy, are we?"

"Fuck. You," he wheezes. I think some of his teeth might be broken.

"Oh, I think *you're* the one that just got fucked, sunshine." My Spanish is better than okay, but I can't make out what he says in response to this, either because the language is too colorful, or his jaw is shattered. "Okay," I tell him, nodding. "I'm gonna pretend like I caught that and move on. Since we're here, y'know, *chatting*, I have a question for you."

The guy starts laughing, though it looks like it really hurts. He spits blood out of his mouth. "I ain't...answering no questions for you, *cabron*."

I tighten the grip I have on his hair, yanking his head back a little farther. Leaning down, I shove my face into his. "You will if you ever wanna see out of your right eye again."

Both his left and right eyes swivel to look at me, so wide I can see the whites. "What you gonna do?" he snaps, bravado in his voice. "You ain't gonna do nothing."

I give him the same sour smile I used to give my grandmother when she made me eat her famous rabbit stew—the woman was a saint, but she couldn't fucking cook to save her life. "Shall we find out?" I glance around, trying to find a rock the right size and shape for my purpose, but then I see something even better, far more suited to the task at hand. On the ground a few feet away lies a smouldering cigarette—the very same cigarette the guy lit when he got out of his car, I assume. How ironic. I reach over and pick it up, holding it in the air for my new friend to see.

"Do you think this would hurt?" I ask. Hovering it close to his face so he can feel the heat, I give him a closer look at what I'm going to be stubbing out into his eyeball if he doesn't play along. "*I* think it would. But that's just me."

"Don't you fucking dare," the guy spits. "Ramirez won't stand for it. He'll wipe out your whole club if you even touch—"

I do more than touch him with it. I roll the brightly burning cherry of the cigarette onto his skin, right on his cheekbone, leaving it there long enough to make him whimper in pain. A stream of Spanish comes pouring out of his mouth, but once again I have no idea what the hell he's saying. His eyes are watering, rivers of tears running down his face. "Yep. That really looked like it hurt," I say. Putting the other end of the smoke into my mouth, I pull on it, dragging the fumes down into my lungs. "So, yeah. I think I'll aim a little higher next time."

"Fuck you. I don't even know anything. I'm just a fucking driver, man!"

I tut, giving him my disappointed face. "You knew who I was just fine. I'm confident you'll be able to answer this question for me."

The guy glares up at me hatefully. "Ask your fucking question then, and let me fucking go."

I almost laugh at his indignant tone. "All right, all right. Your boss has been gone for five days. He just came back from...*where*?"

My captive scowls. "Who knows? I don't have a fucking clue."

"That's a shame. And there you were, telling me your were a driver a moment ago. Drivers usually know where they're driving *to*." I roll the cigarette on his face again, grimacing—you forget after a while what human flesh smells like when it's cooking. This reminder is unpleasant to say the least. Ramirez's guy howls as I leave the burning ember on his skin for longer this time.

"Fine, fine! Fuck! He was in Seattle. He was in Seattle."

I take the cigarette and put it back in my mouth. Seattle? That's a little too coincidental. Too much has gone down in Seattle in the last six months for that to be a fluke. Ryan was killed there, after all. That was where Ramirez was due to be tried for murder. And it was in Seattle that I first laid eyes on Sophia. "What was he doing there?" I ask.

"He was looking for someone. Some old guy."

"And he obviously found him. I just saw him being hauled inside the farmhouse back there." I draw on the cigarette and blow a smoke ring, thinking. "Who is he? And what does Ramirez want with him?"

"*I* don't fucking know what he wants with him!" the guy hisses. "I don't get to question every single fucking thing Ramirez does. He says point and shoot, and I point I shoot. I don't know why, man. All I know is that he's some doctor. Some dude who makes sure people are put to sleep when they're operated on or some shit."

"An anaesthesiologist?"

"Yeah! Yeah, one of those."

The cigarette is burning down to the butt. I only have another minute before it's spent and I have to find something equally as effective to play with. "And his name?" I say. "I'm sure you know his name."

"Alan. Alan Romera," he says, spitting the information out quickly. "The guy's name is Doctor Alan Romera. There! Are you happy now? Fuck you, man. Let me fucking go."

SOPHIA

I used to dream about white picket fences. I refused to admit it, though. I swore I'd never spill my secret. Never in a million years. My sister, Sloane, wouldn't have understood. Since we were tiny, all she ever wanted to do was follow in Dad's footsteps and become a doctor. She was so driven and focused on her career that the idea of a husband and a family just never occurred to her. I asked her once whether she was going to get married and take time off to have babies after she graduated from medical school, and she just looked at me like I was a perplexing puzzle she couldn't quite figure out. Mom and Dad would have been thrilled to know I wanted to build a home and a family for myself, but I could never voice my dreams to them for some reason. They made me feel uncomfortable in a way that I didn't know how to handle. Embarrassed, almost. Nearly every woman I knew wanted to achieve greatness, to strive for some seemingly unobtainable goal, to grow and better themselves. It seemed like wanting a family was such a small dream. Pointless in the grand scheme of things, as though being a mother or a wife was always meant to be a secondary role I was meant to play, and my main purpose in life was something far greater.

It's laughable to think back on all the hours I spent slogging away over test studies and group assignments in college now, though. I never planned on witnessing a murder, getting kidnapped, being spirited away across two states, and falling in love with the president of a motorcycle gang. It never crossed my mind that I might end up running away from everything I ever held dear to me. That I would be laying in bed with a man who stole my heart so thoroughly that I feel like I can barely breathe without him by my side.

It's been six months. Six months since Jamie found me. The best and the worst six months of my entire life. I'm used to waking up next to him now. I'm used to the roar of motorcycle engines rumbling in the dark as members of the Widow Makers MC return to the compound—I don't even notice the sound anymore. I sleep like a baby, my head resting on Louis James Aubertin III's chest, his arms wrapped around me, and it seems utterly normal that twenty armed men are sleeping in a bunk house only a hundred feet away from us. It's strange how time and exposure to violence can dull its impact on you. It's strange how one decision can change your life forever.

"You still sleeping, Prospect?" Jamie whispers into my hair. Sunlight lances through the gap between the heavy curtains, casting long fingers of gold and white across our bodies and up the opposite wall. Dust motes hover in the still air, refracting the light. I've been watching them spin for the past twenty minutes, enjoying the way Jamie's naked body feels tangled up in mine, while I've listened to his heartbeat beneath my ear. It's always the same: slow and steady, never erratic or unpredictable. It calms me. No matter what's going on in our lives, no matter how much shit seems to be raining down on us, he's always there, steady like his heart beat, always watching over me.

"Mmm. You'll never get tired of that, will you?" I whisper.

He strokes a hand lightly over my hair. "What?"

He knows exactly what I'm talking about, but I humor him all the same. "Calling me Prospect," I say, prodding him in the side. Ever since that night in the desert after we buried Raphael together, the night he agreed that I could prospect for the Widow Makers, he's taken great delight in calling me that name. He finds it amusing that his girlfriend has to bend over backwards twenty-four seven in an attempt to be accepted into his motorcycle club.

"I guess not," he says softly, stroking his hand up and down my bare side, making me shiver a little. "It's good to know you have to behave yourself and do as your told. What can I say? This power I hold over you has gone to my head."

He's so fucking ridiculous. He knows I rarely do as I'm told, and he knows I rarely behave myself. He's clearly asking for trouble. I can hear the smile in his voice, taunting me. I tilt my head so I can graze his chest with my teeth, biting down a little. "You're dreaming, buddy."

"Such a pleasant dream, though." He moves quickly, shifting out from underneath me, throwing one leg over mine and pinning me to the mattress. Taking hold of both my hands, he secures my wrists high above my head. Not for the first time, the pale icy blue of his eyes shocks me. They're beautiful. Haunting. He's so incredible I can hardly bear it. His torso, packed with muscle, is covered in tattoos— some in Farsi, some in English. Two colorful birds rest on either side of his pecs, and an intricate skull complete with thorns and roses covers his side. Beneath, the words: *Forgive Me Father, For I Have Sinned.*

The last tattoo is fairly ironic, given that Jamie could care less about his father. Or these days he doesn't, anyway. Louis James Aubertin II is a megalomaniac. One of the most vile, spiteful people I've ever come across. How Jamie didn't end up the same way is a mystery. He leans down, rubbing the tip of his nose against mine. "Were you planning on riding your Ducati today?" he asks.

I shake my head. "I don't think so."

"Good." He sucks my bottom lip into his mouth and bites down hard. "I'm about to fuck you senseless, sugar. By the time I'm done with you, you're not gonna be able to sit down properly for a week."

Heat flowers all over my body. God, I don't know how he still does this to me. I have a very limited frame of reference—my ex, Matt, was hardly the most sexual person on the face of the planet— but I'm pretty sure most people grow comfortable with each other. The intensity of first love burns off, to be replaced by something calmer and deeper if you're lucky. But with him, with Jamie, that hasn't happened. The fire that existed between us from the very beginning still remains, burning strong, coupled with such a fathomless love that only seems to strengthen as the seconds pass. I never knew a person could feel like this and stay sane. The power of such a love constantly feels like it's about to overwhelm me, rob me of my senses, take what little control I have left within me and dash it into pieces. And it feels incredible.

Jamie shakes his head as he looks down at me. He has this way of staring into me that makes my head spin. I don't feel like I'm *me* when he looks at me like this. From the expression on his face, it seems as though he's seeing something magnificent and beautiful for the very first time and it's bringing him to his knees. There's no way he can be seeing *me*, the girl he calls sugar. I've seen myself in the mirror, after all. I know I'm not an entirely unattractive girl, but Jamie's reaction to me always takes me by surprise. Dipping down, he presses his mouth against mine and hums. I love kissing this man. Our bodies were made for each other, and so were our mouths. When he kisses me, it feels like I'm coming alive. I melt into the bed, allowing my body to fall limp as he increases the pressure of his lips against mine. His bare chest brushes against mine, making my nipples tighten and grow hyper sensitive, and Jamie breathes out hard—I can see the way the contact affects him, his skin breaks out in goose bumps.

He's so warm. Groaning softly, he lowers himself down onto me and I feel like I'm suddenly on fire, prickling all over from the heat he's kicking out of his body. Using one knee, Jamie pushes my legs apart and adjusts his position so that he's in between them. His cock is hard already, trapped between our bodies, placed in a position that sends waves of excitement through me. He angles his hips up and presses forward, and it feels like my whole body is surging with electricity. My clit is already swollen, my pussy already wet—Jamie feels just how wet I am and swears under his breath.

"Jesus Christ, Soph. You have no idea what that does to me. Fuck. You're always so ready for me. Always so turned on. You're so fucking sexy. I can smell it on you."

A long time ago, I would have blushed at this. I would have tried to hide my face in embarrassment, buried myself under the covers and tried not to break down from mortification. Now, I know better. I know that he really does mean it. When I'm turned on, he's turned on. It works both ways. And he's right—he can smell how turned on I am, because I can smell it on him, too. He smells like sex in the very best way. His body puts out the most intense, amazing scent when he's about to fuck me, and my own body responds in kind. It drives me absolutely crazy.

"D'you wanna get punished now, Soph?" Jamie licks at my lips, tracing the tip of his tongue over my mouth, and I can't help myself. I arch my back up off the bed, crushing my breasts against his body, moaning.

"That depends. How are you going to punish me?"

"You're not cleared for that information, I'm afraid." He nips at my top lip, pinching my flesh between his teeth just hard enough to make me cry out. "But I can show you if you'd like. Sound good?"

I nod, breathless, and Jamie grins wickedly. "Good girl. Why don't you start off by showing me how well behaved you're going to be?" He may know that I never really do as I'm told as a prospect for the club, but in this situation Jamie is king and I am his humble servant. It thrills me to give him what he wants. It excites me to the point of insanity to obey him in every way. Jamie knows this all too well. "Suck," he says, opening his mouth. He darts his tongue past my lips and I do as I'm told, sucking his tongue, licking at his mouth, trying not to get too ahead of myself just yet.

My arms are starting to ache in the most delicious fucking way. He's still holding them high over my head, pinning them to the pillow above us, and my wrists are burning. He won't let go unless I ask him to, and I'm not about to do that. I love feeling vulnerable with him. I love feeling like he has absolute control. He's so much bigger than me, stronger, more commanding. He could really hurt me if he wanted to, and something about that knowledge tips me over the edge every time. I know with every molecule of my body that he never *would* hurt me. He makes threats and sometimes even promises, but it's all bullshit. Under no circumstances would he ever do anything I didn't want him to do, especially if it might cause me harm.

Jamie groans as I suck a little harder on his tongue. He pulls back and ducks down, nuzzling into the crook of my neck so he can bite and kiss me there. My neck is my biggest weakness. My whole body hums with excitement, goose bumps everywhere, as he uses his teeth and his tongue on me, sucking, making me pant as he grinds himself against me between my legs.

Letting my hands go, he leans back, palming his cock. "Roll onto your stomach," he tells me.

Oh god. This is going to be so intense. I turn over, planning on sliding my legs in between his so that he's straddling me, but Jamie has other plans. He grabs me by the ankles and spreads my legs again, jerking me toward him as he pulls me down the bed. I'm exposed, open to him, my pussy laid bare as he continues to stroke his hand up and down his erection. "Fuck, Soph. You are in some serious trouble right now, girl. I'd apologize ahead of time, but I get the feeling you're going to like this."

I should probably protest. As the Widow Makers' prospect, it's my job to prepare breakfast for everyone in the mornings. Just one of the shitty tasks I have to complete without bitching. If I bitch, I add time onto my term as a non-member of the club. Letting Jamie have his way with me right now will make me late, and being late to put food in front of twenty hungry bikers is a very bad idea. But still…I can't do it. I can't say no. This is going to be too delicious.

"You could still apologize," I tell him. "At least pretend you're sorry that you're about to get me into trouble."

Behind me, Jamie growls. "No way, Sugar. I don't hand out apologies unless they're one hundred percent necessary. You can get your ass up and go start scrambling eggs if you like. I'd prefer not to, but I can finish off this job by myself if you have someplace to be." He slaps my right ass cheek, making me hiss.

The pain is both shocking and amazing at the same time. "Sounds about right," I say though gritted teeth, smiling, waiting for the burning pins and needles to subside. "I'm sure you'd be just as satisfied if you jerked off and had a Kleenex moment, wouldn't you? I'm basically surplus to requirement."

"Not true. Sinking my cock into your pussy is definitely way more fun than taking care of business myself. But, y'know. I'm a guy. I've had a lot of fucking practice. I'm pretty good at making myself come."

"You're pretty good at making *me* come, too."

"Damn straight." Jamie takes hold of me by the hips, pulling at me so that my ass is sticking up in the air. "I plan on having a lot more practice at that, too."

I flush with embarrassment, and then with heat as I feel his fingers skate over my ass cheeks and then in between them, touching first my pussy and then bringing his hand back, tracing the tips of his fingers up, over my asshole. We haven't really done this before. Not often, anyway. Jamie knows it's taboo for me, knows how turned on I have to be for him to even approach that area of my body. My palms are already sweating as he applies a slight pressure, rubbing the pad of his thumb against me, teasing but not pushing inside.

"You're wet for me, Soph," he says under his breath. "I can fucking *see* how wet you are for me, and it's fucking beautiful. Can you feel it?"

I shudder, trying to calm my breathing. "Yes. Yes, I can feel it."

"Do you want me to taste it?"

I'm convinced that no one on the face of the planet has ever been turned on as badly as I am right now. It's as though I can feel the need flowing through my veins with every elevated, frantic beat of my heart. He's going to destroy me one of these days. "Yes. Fuck, yes. Do it."

"*Mmm.*" Jamie makes a savage snarling sound at the back of his throat as he scoots back so he can gain access to me with his mouth. His tongue is hot and persuasive as he licks at my clit. "Goddamnit, Soph. I'll never get over this. I never will. You taste so fucking good. I wanna eat your pussy all day long."

I'm inclined to let him. He's so fucking good at it. My body sings with anticipation as he rubs at the entrance of my pussy; I know he's going to slide his fingers inside me soon, and I know how amazing it's going to feel. My breath stutters out of me when he does it; he finds my g-spot immediately, curving his fingers down and forward at the same time so that I can feel the unique, intense pressure that always starts to build when he massages that spot inside me.

When we first started sleeping together, Jamie told me I hadn't come properly, and he was right. Ever since then, he's shown me time and time again that my climaxes can only get better and better. He's had me howling and begging all over the compound, desperate for release while he administers the sweetest, most intense sexual torture to my body. Right now is no different.

"Shit, Jamie. Oh my god."

"That's right, baby. That's right. Let go for me. I wanna feel you letting go." I only grow tenser as he carries on laving and sucking at my clit, though. He pumps his fingers inside me, swearing quietly when he feels my pussy contract around him. "You getting close?" he asks.

If I wanted to, I could probably quit trying to hold onto my sanity with such determination and allow myself to succumb to the orgasm I can feel building. I don't want to yet, though. I'm not ready for this to be over. I want him inside me when I come. I want to feel weakened and at his mercy as I slip beneath the waves of my pleasure. I shake my head. "Not yet. Please, not yet."

Behind me, he laughs. It's the most sensual, thrilling sound—it sends chills racing all over my skin. "You're a glutton for punishment, sweetheart. How hard do you want me to make you come?"

"Really fucking hard."

"So hard you can't stand?"

"Yes."

"So hard you can't remember your own name."

"Yes."

"So hard I have to change theses sheets when we're done?"

I close my eyes, pressing my face into the very sheets he's talking about. I have them balled up in both my clenched fists. "God, yes," I hiss.

"Okay, baby. You asked for it." Jamie licks me again, but this time he's not licking at my clit. He licks my ass, and I buck against his mouth, surprised by the sudden heat and the intimacy of the gesture.

"*Fuck*! Fuck, Jamie. I can't—"

"Yes, you can. Stay very still for me, sugar, there's a good girl. I'm gonna take care of you. I'm gonna give you what you want." His fingers are still inside me, thrusting into my pussy. He slowly slides them out of me, and then pushes them back inside much more forcefully. I gasp every time, my voice hoarse, my throat stinging as Jamie fucks me with his index and middle finger. It feels so fucking good.

I had no idea I'd like what he's doing with his mouth, but every time Jamie licks my ass, the pressure from his tongue growing and growing as he works, I find myself falling apart piece by piece. This is incredible.

Seriously. Fucking. Incredible.

Jamie pauses, sinking his teeth none-too-gently into my right ass cheek. "You want my finger in there, beautiful?"

I don't normally go in for this kind of thing, but he's got me so worked up and crazy that I find myself nodding. More than that—I physically ask for it. "I want you to, yes. I want to feel you in my ass, Jamie. Please…I can't take it anymore."

"*Fuck.*" Jamie sighs out further colorful expletives as he gently, carefully pushes his finger inside me. I break out in an instantaneous sweat, my legs trembling as he moves little by little. It's such an overwhelming sensation. The combination of pleasure and pain is dizzying. "You want my cock inside you, too, Sophia?" Jamie whispers. "You want me to fuck you in your pussy while I fuck your ass, too?"

My cheeks are the color of a freshly painted fire truck. I know this because it feels like they're on fire themselves. For a second I don't really know what to say. I don't know if I can handle that. I don't know if my body can take that much attention.

"*Sophia.*" Jamie slides his thumb inside my pussy at the same time, gently pumping both fingers in and out of my body. I gasp, clutching the bed sheets tighter. "Don't overthink it. It'll feel good, I promise."

Jamie doesn't make promises lightly. He'd never say something like that in order to get his own way. And he'd sure as hell never promise me pleasure and then not deliver. It's a point of pride for him.

"Okay. Okay, yes." My voice is quiet but I sound like I mean it. Like I want it. Jamie grunts, repositioning himself between my legs. His breathing is fast and labored like mine. His cock presses against me as he grinds his hips against my ass.

"I want to feel you come all over me, okay, sugar? I want to feel you getting tighter and tighter as you come all over my dick and my fingers. Can you do that for me?"

I can't speak. I can only nod. Jamie leans back and pushes himself slowly inside me. "Damn it, Soph," he hisses. "You feel fucking good."

I feel so full as he works both his cock and his fingers inside me, thrusting both into me at the same time, carefully, slowly, deeply, making me shake and shiver. It's like nothing I've experienced before. Nothing I've ever come close to feeling, and it's amazing.

"I can feel myself inside you," Jamie says. "I can feel my cock getting harder."

I nod, clenching my jaw. "So can I. It feels incredible." And it does. Jamie rubs his free hand lightly up and down my back. I want to feel his hands all over me, stroking me, caressing me, but he's kind of busy, and I'm kind of enjoying what he's doing too much to stop him.

"Holy fuck." Jamie digs his fingers into my back, slamming himself into me harder now. I can tell he wants to fuck the sense right out of me, but he's holding back. He doesn't want to be too rough when he's fingering my ass at the same time. I almost want him to, though. I want to feel like I'm being owned. I want to feel like my body is not my own for just five minutes. It's a strange, dangerous thought. I push back against him, forcing him deeper as he fucks me. Jamie slaps my ass with his free hand, growling.

"Is that how it is, sugar? Is that what you want?"

"Yes. Fuck, Jamie, please. Fuck me harder." I'm sure I sound like a clichéd porn star, begging to get pounded on by some gigantor-dicked playboy, but my pleas are genuine. I want him. Need him. Must have him.

Jamie obliges me.

My eyes roll back into my head as he speeds up, thrusting into me over and over again, and I can't keep myself together anymore. I feel like I'm sinking into the mattress, my ass still sticking up in the air as Jamie fucks me, and it's as though I'm rising up out of my body. I feel weightless, feather-light, seconds away from hitting the ceiling. Jamie groans as he slides his finger in and out of my ass.

"You ready now, sugar?" he asks me. "You ready to come for me?"

"Yes. I can't hold out much longer."

"Then don't. Let it happen. Come for me, baby. Come on." The very last of his will power apparently burns off; he doesn't hold back anymore. I feel like I'm being lit up from the inside as Jamie slams himself into me. I feel drunk, high, lost and found all at once. When the first rushes of my orgasm hit me, they hit with brute force strength, undeniable and unstoppable. Jamie must feel it, must feel the difference in me, because he starts swearing again.

"Oh my god, Jamie. I can't—I can't—" I lose the ability to speak altogether. I can only pant and moan and cry out as I'm swept away in the riptide. Jamie roars as he comes with me. He removes his finger and takes hold of me by the hips with both hands, and he fucks me hard and deep. We writhe against each other as the pleasure wanes, sensitive and stupid from the endorphins flooding our systems, and Jamie strokes my body, peppering me with light kisses all over my back.

Eventually he pulls out and lies down next to me. He smiles, brushing my hair out of my face. "You're very flushed," he announces. "Seems to me someone just had the servicing of her life."

I stick my tongue out at him, lifting my heavy arm so I can playfully pinch his nipple. "Nope. I got the servicing of my life last week from a guy named Rebel."

Jamie pretends to scowl. "I hear that guy's an asshole."

"He is. But I love him."

Now he frowns. "I thought you loved *me*?"

"I do. I love you both. More than I should, I'm sure."

He grins, waggling his eyebrows. "Good thing I'm not a jealous guy." He wraps his arms around me and pulls me to him so that my head is resting on his chest once more. The sun is still bullying its way through the gap in the curtains, laying in thick gold bars across our bodies. Jamie runs his fingers up and down the leg I've thrown over his body, tangled up in his own legs. His fingers don't deviate outside of the thick band of sunlight that marks my skin.

We lay like that for a long time, him stroking my hair and my body, humming quietly, until Carnie comes and hollers that he wants his damn breakfast through the cabin door. I tame my hair, throw some clothes on and leave, kissing Jamie on the forehead before I go. I know that when I kiss him later on down in the compound, whenever he drags his lazy out of his bed, I won't be kissing the same person anymore. I'll be kissing Rebel, the president of the Widow Makers Motorcycle Club, but it will still be as perfect. It will still be as magical.

CADE

Used to be that the hatch to the basement underneath the barn would get rusty. Anytime anyone wanted to go down there, they'd need to take a hammer and chisel to the handle and prise it open with brute force. Not the case these days.

Now the damn thing's opened so often the hinge doesn't even squeak anymore. Breakfast, lunch and dinnertime, someone has to go down into the basement to feed our current guest, and usually that someone is me. I don't carry out the task because it's something I enjoy. I draw the short straw every fucking day because the job is so unpleasant that no one else will do it, and besides, the other Widow Makers' arguments *are* kind of valid: our guest *does* insist that I'm the one to feed her and clothe her, as well as take her out every evening so she can stretch her legs.

Today, Soph doesn't seem to want to get her ass out of bed and make breakfast, so I've had to concoct something on my own. I told Rebel what I saw—an older guy, who appeared to be Alan Romera, being dragged into Ramirez's place. He was understandably furious, but he's kept the information from his girlfriend thus far. Said it would be for the best, until we can confirm it really is her father. I have to tell him later that it *is* Dr. Romera, one hundred percent, no doubt about it, which isn't a conversation that I'm looking forward to. So yeah, I'll let the prospect stay in bed and I'll cook myself if it means I can avoid spreading that delightful news.

The scrambled eggs, toast and sliced up fruit I've cobbled together aren't going to be up to standard for our picky, precocious guest, but guess what? I don't give a fuck. I lower myself down the rungs of the ladder that descends into the basement, using one hand to climb and the other to hold the plastic tray of food I'm carrying. Back when we realized we'd have to detain our guest for longer than we'd originally anticipated, Jamie had a proper AC and ventilation system installed down here, so thankfully it's cool and doesn't smell of shit and dried blood anymore. I head to the door at the end of the corridor and open it, readying myself for the abuse I'm about to receive. I've come to accept it now. The verbal and physical abuse (pathetic though it may be) I endure every few hours has become a regular part of my day. In fact, I find it kind of cute, now.

Inside the room, Maria Rosa, former head of the Desolladors Cartel, is sitting on a beaten up sofa, reading a battered copy of Lady Chatterley's Lover. When Rebel shot her six months ago and we locked her down here, Maria Rosa's English was pretty clipped. She could get by just fine, but she sure as hell couldn't read in anything other than Spanish. Now she seems to be demanding a new book every time I come down here.

She knows I've entered the room, but she doesn't look up from her page. Sometimes it's like this—she'll pretend I don't even exist as I leave her food and clear away the remains of her previous meal. She'll lay down on her bed and close her eyes, pretending to be asleep as I collect her dirty laundry and dump it outside for Sophia to pick up later. But then there are other days, when she's like a deranged hellcat, jumping out from behind the heavy steel door, trying to claw my eyes out of my head as she tries, for the one hundred millionth time, to escape.

This morning doesn't seem like an escape attempt kind of morning. Maria Rosa slowly puts down her book and stands, stretching, arms high up over her head. She looks like a cat when she does this, limbs long, fingers spread wide, head back, spine arched. She makes a quiet sighing sound as she turns around and bends over, reaching for the ground. The tight sweatpants she's wearing—they read *Juicy* across the ass—don't leave much to the imagination.

Her attempts to seduce me have ranged from subtleties such as this to blatant insanity, where I've opened the door to find her naked on her bed, her legs spread wide, while she teases her pussy and begs me to come fuck her. She stopped doing that a while back. Still, every once in a while she'll try something like this, something designed to pique my interest. She should know by know that crazy bitches don't get my dick hard.

"When is he coming to see me?" she purrs. "I need to talk to him."

I put down her breakfast on the small chest of drawers we had brought down here for her, kicking the door closed behind me. "What do you need to talk him about?" This line is as old as the hills. She *always* needs to talk to Rebel, and Rebel *never* wants to talk to her. Funny, that.

"I need more space," she says. Her voice is light. Breezy, almost. "I can't work out down here like this. The place is too cramped. How am I supposed to stay in shape when I can't run? Or do yoga?"

I can't bite back the laughter that itches at the back of my throat. "I don't think Rebel cares about you staying shape, darlin'. I think he cares about you keeping quiet and not trying to stab people in the neck with a plastic knife whenever they come in here. Or throwing your own shit. I think he cares about you not doing that."

"I only did that once." She pouts. Even without make-up, she's a very beautiful woman. There are certain concessions Jamie's made for her, certain demands he's met in return for her vague cooperation, but make up hasn't been one of them. "And I only did that to demonstrate how undignified this whole arrangement is, baby. I shit in the corner of the same room that I eat, sleep and bathe in. That's fucking insulting, no?"

I smirk, grabbing her wash bag. "He's already knocked through three of the rooms to give you more space. He's not gonna give you any more."

"But I need a treadmill," she whines.

"You're dreaming. It's not gonna happen."

"*You* could make it happen," she says quietly. "If you really wanted to."

"But here's the crazy thing, Maria Rosa. I *don't* want to."

"Why not?" She seems genuinely confused.

"Hmm. Could have something to do with the fact that you tortured me for three days in Columbia? Could also have something to do with the fact that you were severely unhelpful when Rebel and I were searching for my sister? And for Jamie, I'm gonna say it's because you fucking framed our club for the murder of eleven innocent people who were just trying to do their weekly grocery shop in Los Angeles."

Maria Rosa laughs, head back, her voice tinkling like a silver bell. She's fucking insane. "Oh, yes. *That.*"

"Yeah. *That.*"

"It's been three years. I thought he would have forgotten about that by now."

I shake my head. I'm almost tempted to roll my eyes. "It's been six months, you lunatic. And even if it had been three years, you know Rebel. You had a bunch of civilians killed for no goddamn reason, and then you tried to pin it on us. A lifetime could go by and he's never gonna forgive you for that shit."

She pulls an ugly, disgusted face. "So fucking sensitive. Worse than a woman. He offended me. Of course I was going to retaliate."

Rebel refused to be her whipping boy. There was no way he was ever going to agree to run drugs for her, be her hired help whenever the fuck she felt like it. It was ridiculous that she even thought he'd go for that deal. I don't argue with her, though. It'd be a pointless venture. The woman is completely unreasonable. She really does believe that her actions were justifiable. "Eat your breakfast, Maria."

"Wait." She crosses the room, skipping a little to get to me before I can let myself out. "I'm so fucking bored in here, baby. Can't you stay a little while? Entertain me?" She already knows by the face I'm pulling what my answer will be. "*Or...*" she says, grabbing hold of my arm. "I could entertain you instead? I seem to remember that you liked it when I used to entertain you."

I didn't really have much choice when she chose to 'entertain' me before. I was strapped to a chair, naked, a zip tie cutting into my wrists, blood trickling down my finger tips, and she did everything in her power to figure out what would get me hard. She had girls come and blow me. She had people come and fuck in front of me. She let her bodyguard fuck *her* in front of me. Nothing worked. It drove her crazy. In the end, it was her frustration, her desperate, inexplicable need to sexually excite me that made it happen. And it was a conscious decision. She tried to force it, but that's not me. She could tease and play with my dick from sun up to sun down and she wouldn't have gotten anywhere until I decided to let it happen.

Maria Rosa's full, swollen lips part as her tongue darts out between them. Her hand slides down my body, traveling from my arm to my cock. She squeezes. Hard. "We used to have fun, baby. I know I'm in Rebel's bad books, but that doesn't mean I have to be in *your* bad books, surely?"

"You're the *only* person in my bad books, woman. Now get your hand off my dick before I break your goddamn fingers."

She grins up at me, not believing me for a second. "Come on, Cade. When was the last time you had a woman's mouth around you? A real woman's mouth. A *passionate* woman, not some silly little American girl."

"Back when I met you, you always wanted to be one of those silly little American girls, didn't you?" Her hand is still exactly where she left it, and she's squeezing harder. She leans into me, crushing her breasts up against my chest.

"That was before I got locked away in your motherfucking basement. Now I know how stupid that was. I've had a lot of time to think. I'm proud to be a sensual, sexual Columbian woman. You can keep your stupid, blonde airhead bitches."

"Either way. It's not happening. So move your hand. If you want someone to play with, I'll send Carnie down here. I'm sure he'd be happy to oblige you."

She lets go, her repulsion at the thought very clear on her face. "Oh please. That little boy? He's a child."

"He's thirty. And you didn't say that when you made Rebel watch you suck *his* cock in Vegas, now, did you?"

"That was different. That was for Rebel, not for me. And it definitely wasn't for that stupid boy."

I lean down close so I can whisper into her ear. "I'm gonna let you into a little secret, Mother. Rebel isn't attracted to you. He never has been, and he never will be. So you can suck as many dicks in front of him as you like. You can let an entire football team take turns at fucking you. It won't make the slightest bit of difference. He thinks you're a crazy, manipulative, evil piece of shit. He wouldn't piss on you if you were on fire. Do you understand?"

Maria Rosa steps back, the smile slipping from her face. A cold glint forms in her eyes; dark though they may be, right now they're frostier than Rebel's pale blue irises. She's gone from horny and devious to malicious and spiteful in a heartbeat, and I know that my time down here with her should most certainly be coming to an end. "He can think whatever he likes of me," she says slowly. "He can pretend that he's going to punish me down here in this fucking box forever. He can treat me like an animal, deprive me of my basic rights as a human being, but trust me when I tell you this, Cade Preston. I *will* get out, and when I do there will be hell to pay for this. There will be blood spilled, and people will die, and I will stand over his grave and I'll piss on *that*. And I will piss on yours after his. Only *then* will my rage be tempered." Her hand whips out unexpectedly, and she slaps my face, hard enough that the enclosed space echoes with the sound of her palm making contact with my cheek.

Slowly, I run my tongue over my bottom lip, tasting blood. "There she is," I say. "Be careful, Mother. One of these days...I'm going to slap you back."

She spits, thankfully smart enough to do it at my feet instead of in my face. "Bullshit. You're not man enough to raise a hand to me, *bastard*." Even as she swears at me, curses me, I can see the fire sparking inside her. I can feel it burning off of her. She thrives on this kind of conflict. I know as soon as I step out of the door behind me, she'll be tearing off her clothes and making herself come. She won't be able to stop herself.

"Eat your fucking breakfast," I whisper. "Or don't. I don't give a shit." I turn and leave, quickly inserting the key into the lock on the door, opening it and slipping through before she can try to dash through after me like she normally does.

I stand there, fuming, blood racing like wildfire through my veins as I stare at the steel door that once more separates us. I can't stand this shit anymore. Someone else is going to have to be her fucking delivery boy. She can fling her own shit and throw as many tantrums as she damn well likes. I'm fucking done.

But still...

My heart is tripping over itself right now. My skin feels hot, prickly, uncomfortable against my clothes. Fuck that fucking bitch. Damn it. I slump back against the concrete wall behind me, Maria Rosa's wash bag at my feet, and I stare up at the low ceiling, my retinas burning from the harsh glare of the strip lighting.

Her touch didn't turn me on. It was her anger. Her pure, unadulterated fury. She's fire and brimstone, the epitome of a woman scorned, and I do believe her when she says she'd do anything in her power to destroy both Rebel and me if given half the chance. But I know she'd want to fuck me senseless before she killed me. I can see the war of emotions in her all too clearly, and loathe as I am to admit it, I want to fuck her just as badly as I want to kill her, too.

My hand automatically moves to my dick. I managed to control myself back in there, but I'm having less luck out here. I'm growing harder by the second, my body overheating, feeling like I'm about to boil over. I don't even think about it; I unbuckle my belt and unzip my fly, my head kicked back, still leaning against the wall. I let my jeans fall down over my hips and I pull down my boxers a little, allowing my erection to spring free. It would feel so much better if Maria Rosa *was* on her knees in front of me right now, swirling her tongue expertly around the head of my cock, moaning as she tasted me, moaning as I grew harder than granite deep in her throat. But I couldn't trust her not to bite the fucking thing off. I couldn't trust myself not to lose control and grab hold of her so I could hate fuck the living shit out of her until she was screaming out my name.

I run my hand up and down the length of my dick, breath catching in my throat. She's dangerous. Wanting her in any way, shape or form is probably the stupidest thing I could ever do, and yet right now it's taken every scrap of will power I possess to stop myself from opening that door back up and destroying her pussy.

I work my dick, holding myself tighter and tighter as I edge closer and closer to coming. Soon I'm frantic. My legs are shaking, my head spinning when I explode, a jet of semen spilling all over my hand, onto the floor, almost hitting the opposite wall. I grind my teeth together, holding in the need to groan as my body convulses and trembles.

God.

Holy fuck.

What the hell is wrong with me? I feel numb and boneless as I pick up Maria Rosa's wash bag and open it up. Her black panties are the first thing I pull out, which is kind of fitting. I can see that they're used. I'm not a complete pervert, though. If I were, I might consider holding them to my nose and inhaling deeply. Even the thought of doing something like that makes me angry—a sensation at odds with the equally prominent desire to give in and just do it. I wipe myself with the black cotton, cleaning myself up, and then I use the panties to mop up the mess I made on the floor, too. The scrap of material is sticky and saturated by the time I'm done.

I throw them back into the wash bag, knowing that I'll be cleaning the entire contents myself this morning instead of leaving it out for Sophia to do. It might be a shitty prospect job, but there's no way I want my boss's girlfriend handling my fucking come.

I'm bemused as I climb the ladder out of the basement. I lied to Maria Rosa. I told her that crazy bitches didn't make my dick hard, but it seems as though that was an out and out lie. Crazy bitches *do* make my dick hard. They make it very hard indeed.

SOPHIA

"**Get that fucking bitch out of here.** *Now*." **Shay glares at** Carnie with the intensity of a thousand violently burning suns. The two of them have been sleeping together for months now, but for some reason Carnie turned up to the clubhouse this morning with a skinny blonde on his arm, and red lipstick smudged all over his smug face. I sigh as I fix up three more plates of bacon and eggs and shove them down the bar. It's kind of pathetic that these two can't get their shit together. Carnie collects one of the plates I slid down the highly buffed wooden bar top, and then he picks up another. He holds out the second one to the skinny blonde, who I'm sure has never eaten a strip of bacon in her entire fucking life.

"You're not the only one who can have a slip up, Shay," Carnie says. "We're all human here. Right, guys?"

The other members of the club weren't born yesterday, though. They know backing Carnie up right now is essentially picking a side, and picking a side is basically the same as signing your own death warrant when it comes to Shay. She's completely psychotic most of the time. Angry and volatile. Not a one of these men or women would willingly bring her wrath down on their heads without good reason, and this is definitely not a good reason. She can fight her own battles with Carnie. Better to let the two of them go three or four rounds and then forgive each other than find yourself trapped in the middle of a life long vendetta that will only end in tears.

None of the Widow Makers look up from their plates. Carnie pulls a face at Cade, who's sitting alone at the table reserved for him and Jamie. "Pussies," he says under his breath. And then, louder, he says, "I don't see what the problem is, Shay. Your other boyfriend gets to eat breakfast with us. Why shouldn't the girls I fuck share the same privilege?"

Sounds like Shay's bruised Carnie's ego a little. She stands up from the table where she was eating and folds her arms across her chest. She's wearing that look on her face that can only mean trouble. "If you're referring to *Cade*," she says, glancing over her shoulder at the dark-haired guy sitting alone, "then he's hardly my *other* boyfriend, in the same way that you aren't my boyfriend either. Cade and I fucked. Get over it. He gets to eat in here because he's the motherfucking *vice president* of the club, you moron."

The clubhouse falls quiet. All conversation ceases. Cade stops eating, putting down his knife and fork on either side of his plate. He doesn't look up at the fracas taking place. Instead, he grinds his teeth together, making his jaw muscles flex as he studies the mess of egg yolk and blackened bacon in front of him.

Carnie makes a disparaging sound at the back of his throat. "Great. Just fucking great, Shay. Tell everyone, why don't you."

"Sure I will. No one fucking cares, Carnie! You're the only one who has a problem with this. Why don't you take your peroxide hooker down to Denny's, okay? The food's better there, anyway."

"Hey!" I slam down my serving spoon. "If you don't wanna eat the food I make, Shay, then drag your own ass into town and have done with it." Shay and I have gone toe to toe a couple of times ourselves. I knew from day one that there was never going to be any love lost between us, and that if I wanted to become a member of this club I was going to have to stand up to her, irrespective of whether it mattered to me or not. Her head rocks back, eyes narrowing as she fixes me in her sights.

"Calm your shit, Sophia. Not everything's about you. Your food will do just fine," she snaps.

"What a compliment." I roll my eyes. "Carnie, why don't you and your friend eat outside in the sunshine? It's too small in here for bickering right now. The walls are closing in."

"Y'know…" Carnie shakes his head, his mouth pulling up into a bemused smile. "For a prospect, you sure do get away with telling us all what to do an awful lot. I wonder why that could be." We all know why I get away with blue murder: I'm the president's old lady. Carnie won't ever air that fact out loud, though. Rebel will string him up from the rafters and use his torso as a punching bag if he does. I'm about to come back at him with a retort about children being easily led, but a loud, metallic scraping sound cuts through the humid, stifling air inside the clubhouse and everyone stops talking again. Cade towers over everyone, hands planted on the table in front of him on either side of his silverware—he casts a dark, weary look at Carnie.

"You'd better watch your mouth, man," he says quietly. "It would be a pretty shitty start to my day if I had to kick your ass for being rude to Soph."

"See! This is what I mean," Carnie says, throwing his hands in the air. "She gets preferential treatment because she's blowing the boss."

"No one said this was an equal opportunities organization. If you don't like it then you can always leave, Carnie. Just remember to leave your ink at the door."

Leaving the Widow Makers is just like leaving any organized crime outfit. It's never as easy as it might seem. Even if Carnie hadn't had access to highly sensitive, high dangerous information that could really hurt the majority of the club's members, which he *has*, then he'd still have to get the huge tattoo marked into his back removed. And that is a particularly unpleasant and painful procedure that involves whiskey, knives, blood, fire, burning and bleeding. Carnie begins to turn a sickly shade of green.

"I was just pointing out that—"

"People that point tend to lose their fingers," Cade growls.

"Yeah. Well…"

"And I'm not sleeping with fucking Shay, you idiot. I don't shit where I eat."

Carnie looks at Shay, confusion all over his face. He looks so turned around that I almost feel sorry for him. I've got no idea what the hell lead to Shay telling this lie, but there's no way I would have believed it for a second. I'm surprised that Carnie did either. Shay looks unapologetic as she swipes her plate up from the table and scrapes the remaining food from its surface into the trashcan at the end of the bar.

"Why did you tell me you'd fucked him?" Carnie demands.

"I have. Just not recently," she says.

"Not in the last *five years*," Cade corrects. Shay turns purple, but she nods her head.

"You wanted to know. You *asked*. You were being a little pissy bitch about guys I'd slept with before that you might know. When I told you about Cade, you didn't stick around long enough to hear that it wasn't a current thing. You made assumptions, because you're a hard-headed jerk, and now here we are, with you sticking your dick into a walking Hepatitis factory."

The blonde, who's stood quiet for the most part up until now, sets down the food Carnie passed her. "I think I'll just get going," she fake whispers. She looks like her temper is rising but thankfully she's managing to keep a hold of her tongue; Shay will rip it out her overly-botoxed mouth if she doesn't.

"I didn't fuck her properly, baby," Carnie says. "I swear I didn't. I put my cock in her ass last night, but it didn't feel right. I stopped. Tell her, Denise. Tell her I didn't—" But Denise is walking out of the clubhouse, swaying a little on top of her six inch hooker heels, and she doesn't look like she's going to be stopping and turning around any time soon. God knows how she thinks she's going to get back into town from here. Late last year, not too long after I arrived here with Jamie, we found one of the club member's girlfriends strung up from a tree on the road leading from town to the compound. Her hands and one of her feet had been cut off. Along with her head. Ever since then, we don't allow people to walk alone out there, especially women. Carnie was the one who found Bron, so it's surprising he's letting her wander off now.

His eyebrows are drawn together, pulled upward in a look of puppy dog hurt. The lenses of his thick-rimmed black glasses are huffed a little at the bottom, suggesting his temperature is up. It's hotter than hell in the New Mexico desert in summer as it is; arguments and bickering only makes the weather more unbearable.

"You should have explained," he says to Shay.

"And you should have dropped the machismo bullshit for just a goddamn second and let me actually finish my sentence." She has a good point. She doesn't seem too fazed by the fact that Carnie's been out fooling around with another woman. In fact, she seems frighteningly calm. If Rebel had done that to me, there would be hell to pay. I'd have his testicles in a heartbeat. The relationship I share with the head of the Widowers is different to most relationships inside the club, though. Monogamy isn't high on most people's list of desirable moral traits in a partner. That goes for the male members and the female members alike. No one seems to want to be pinned down—not when you could be having fun with a whole bunch of different people at the same time. Sloane would have something choice to say about the arrangements that take place here under this roof once night falls. Probably something about the risk factors of highly communicable venereal diseases, and how syphilis is a really bad look on people these days.

Carnie grabs his cut from the counter and shrugs it on. "We're not done talking about this," he says.

"Whatever you say, baby. You're the boss." Shay smiles at Carnie, but it's not a real smile. It's a grimace, teeth bared, and the message is clear for Carnie to read. He's *not* the boss, and if he even *tries* bringing this shit up again, Shay's going to castrate him with a rusty butter knife.

Carnie shakes his head. "Fuck," he mutters under his breath. Leaving his breakfast behind, he exits the clubhouse, presumably to go and grab the blonde he allowed to leave a moment ago and take her home, wherever that might be.

Shay sits herself back down, not saying a word. Everyone feels the burn of Cade's gaze directed at her head, though. He looks pissed. Eventually Shay acknowledges him, rolling her eyes. "What?"

"Don't ever drag me into your shit again, woman. It won't end well. You feel me?" His dark eyes look almost black as he stares at her. Shay grumbles something under her breath. Cade rarely gets mad, but right now he doesn't appear to be all that happy. "I'm sorry. I didn't quite hear that," he growls.

"I only told him the truth," she snaps. "I didn't lie. We did sleep together Cade, no matter how badly you might want to forget about it."

"You're right. It would be lovely if I could forget about it, but you seem to keep bringing it up for some fucking reason, and I can't seem to put my finger on the why of that. If we have problems, Shay, just let me know and I'll happily resolve them with you."

I'm waiting for Shay's caustic response to that, but the door to the clubhouse swings open and Rebel walks in, scanning the room from side to side as he makes his way toward the bar. From the tense look on his face, he's heard raised voices and he's seriously not in the mood to be dealing with them. "What's the problem?" He slams his gun down on the woodwork, blowing a long breath out down his nose.

"Nothing. Shay was just about to head into town to check on the shop. Right, Shay?" Cade doesn't really seem to be giving her a choice. Shay is suddenly expressionless, her face utterly blank. She gets up and gathers her things, slinging her patch covered cut over her shoulder.

"Yes, sir," she says, her voice clipped, devoid of any inflection or emotion. The change in her is miraculous, and yet I've seen it a thousand times before. She blows hot and cold, fire and ice, her tongue sharp enough to flay the skin from a man's back most of the time, but the moment she's faced with the man I love, she's suddenly docile and compliant.

"Come back here after lunch. I'll send someone else out to relieve you," Rebel says.

Shay gives him a quick nod and then she silently leaves the clubhouse, leaving a handful of bemused Widow Makers behind her. Ever since Hector Ramirez showed up in Freemantle and decided to terrorize the Widow Makers any way they could, it's been necessary to have someone armed and ready to respond at the club's tattoo shop. I'd kind of thought Ramirez might have grown bored and left New Mexico by now, gone back home to his cartel in Mexico to oversee his drug operations, but it seems as though he has far more patience than anyone gave him credit for.

He was furious after his right hand man, Raphael Dela Vega, went missing. He vowed not to leave until Raphael was found, and so I guess that means he'll never leave because Raphael is gone for good. I should know—I killed him and buried him out in the desert. Rebel shoots me a brief smile as he sits down with Cade. I try not to listen to their conversation as I clean up after breakfast, but it's hard not to. I've felt an uneasiness in the compound over the last few days. An uneasiness I can't put my finger on, but that I know is there all the same.

I hear two words that send shivers all over my body: *Los Oscuros*. And then I hear another two words that cause a bolt of panic to rise up my throat and relay around the inside of my head, so powerful and strong that I can feel my pulse beating in every part of my body.

Alan Romera.

That name should never be slipping out of Rebel's mouth. It should never be a name spoken inside the walls of the Widow

Makers' clubhouse. It shouldn't be uttered in any motorcycle clubhouse period. When I was initially captured by Raphael, he found my fake ID in my purse and assumed that Sophia Letitia Marne was my real name. I wasn't exactly in a rush to correct him, given that he kept on threatening to rape and murder my family as soon as he could find them. I'm not sure why I haven't told Rebel the truth, that Sophia isn't my true identity, but... I suppose it felt safer. Better if I kept my family and my old life as far away from this new one as humanly possible.

So now that Rebel is whispering *that* name, the name of my *father*, out loud, it feels as though my lies are catching up with me.

He says the name again as he talks in low, hushed tones with his second in command. Suddenly I don't feel all that well. My stomach is churning and my head feels light, like there's nothing inside it. My hands are prickly, numb, rubbery all at once.

I look down at the wet, soapy plate I'm holding slips from my hands, and I watch as it seems to fall to the floor in slow motion. I know it will smash. I know it will explode into thousands of pieces when it hits the floor, and I can do nothing but observe as it does exactly that. The clubhouse falls silent. Eight people all turn and look at me, frowning, surprised, irritated. My eyes lock with Rebels and an entire conversation takes place in the brief heartbeats that follow. He knows. He knows *exactly* who I am.

And something is very, *very* wrong.

REBEL

I didn't push. I never did. It seemed like a bad idea back when Soph first came to the compound. She was livid, seven which ways from crazy, and calling her out on her secret seemed like the dumbest fucking move I could make. I always knew though, knew who she *really* was. I've been waiting for the past six months to see if she would ever come clean, to trust me, but the day never arrived, and now it seems as though I don't have the luxury of giving her space anymore. I don't have the luxury of giving her time. We've run out of both, because something terrible has happened, and I have no idea how we're going to find our way out of this one. I've held my tongue and waited the past three days, hoping that I'm wrong, hoping the information Cade dug up is wrong, but it appears all the hoping was for nothing. Hector Ramirez, the motherfucker that had my uncle murdered in cold blood, has kidnapped Sophia's father and brought him here to New Mexico.

It makes no sense. When we were back in Ebony Briar for my father's charity ball, I heard Soph's father say his own name when he answered her phone call. She hadn't said a word, had hung up almost immediately, but I'd heard him say his name. I never told anyone else. When we got back to the compound, my curiosity was undeniable; I wanted to know everything there was to know about this strange, fiery woman I'd fallen in love with, so I did my due diligence. I did my digging. I looked up Alan, and then I moved on to his wife and his two daughters, Sloane and Alexis. I found pictures online. I read Alexis's school reports. I looked up her Facebook profile and then wanted to kill some fucking moronic guy called Matt that kept posting on her wall, calling her every name under the sun because she'd left him and wouldn't respond to his texts.

I got to know the other side of Sophia that she kept hidden, and I felt fucking weird about it. I knew I should wait until she offered up the information voluntarily, but shit. I'm a curious fucking guy, okay? I'm not perfect. I have my faults just like everyone else, and I needed to know if there was anything important about her that might cause problems for the club further on down the line. Some dark secret that might show up and bite us on the ass.

I found nothing, but during my momentary foray into P.I. work I did see many, many photographs of her father. That's why I recognized him when Cade brought me observation shots of a dark-haired male in his late fifties being dragged up the porch stairs of the farmhouse Hector bought, hands zip tied behind his back, a rag stuffed into his mouth. I thought for a moment that maybe I was being paranoid, but no.

"Are you sure? Any chance he was lying?" I ask.

Cade fidgets in his seat. He hates this almost as much as I do. Over the past six months he's grown close with Soph. He watches over her like a big brother, always keeping one eye on her whenever we're here in the compound, and both eyes on her when we're not. He nods, sighing. "No. No. He had no reason to. The guy spat out the name along with three of his teeth after I gave him a couple of right hooks. They definitely have Alan."

"Fuck."

"Yeah. You could say that."

"Did Hector's guy say what they're planning on doing with him?"

Cade looks troubled. "After he spilled the name, he said Hector wants the girl. That he's planning on offering her a trade, that she hands herself over to him in return for the old man's freedom, otherwise he's gonna dig him a shallow grave out in the desert and put a bullet in his head. Not before he's cut off a few fingers and toes here and there, I'm guessing."

"Right. So how do we get this guy outta there without Sophia finding out?"

Cade taps a finger on the blank screen of his cell phone, frowning. I've been through hell and back with this man. I've seen him wear this expression so many times before that it seems almost commonplace now. It shouldn't have to be, though. He shouldn't have to be this pissed off and stressed out ninety percent of the time. When we got out of the military, that should have been the end of this kind of worry for the both of us, but instead he lost his sister, was accosted by a mad woman in Columbia, got locked up in Chino for a spell, and now he's dealing with this bullshit. There has to be an end at some point for the poor bastard.

"I don't know yet," he says. "But we'll figure it out right. We always do."

I grunt. "Yeah. Because if Hector Ramirez is known for anything, it's making good on his threats. Alan Romera isn't the kind of man who can withstand torture for very long, Cade. He isn't that kind of man at all."

The sound of something smashing over my shoulder had Cade and up on his feet in an instant. I twist around, my pulse slamming, my body ready to fight, and I see Sophia standing on the other side of the bar, her face white as a sheet. She looks like she's about to burst into tears.

"She fucking heard us," Cade says softly. "So much for keeping her out of this, man. Jesus Christ." He leans back in his seat, groaning, but I can't take my eyes off Sophia. She's locked onto me, bottom lip trembling, accusation in her eyes, as though I'm the one who's been keeping secrets from her this whole time. I mean, yes, I

427

wasn't going to tell her about this particular problem until we had a solution to it, but still. That's excusable. That would have been for her own good.

"Rebel?" she whispers.

I can hear her perfectly, which makes it all the more reasonable that she could hear the lulled words I was sharing with Cade. Damn it. So fucking stupid. "Come on, Soph. Come sit down. We need to talk."

She slowly shakes her head. "I don't want to. I—I can't."

"You need to, sugar."

Her head shaking grows more violent. "I need some fresh air." She charges out of the clubhouse, palms crashing into the wood of the door, making a loud slapping noise as she bolts out into the blistering sunlight. I'm up and out of my seat before Cade can even suggest it; the very last thing Sophia needs right now is to freak the fuck out and go speeding off on her motorcycle, trying to find her father. This is exactly what I find her trying to do when I head outside into the courtyard. She's throwing one leg over the seat of the slick Ducati I bought her with the Irish green gas tank, and her hand is in her pocket, presumably searching for her key.

"What the fuck do you think you're doing?" I stand in front of her, placing one leg on either side of the front wheel, my hands on the handlebars of the Ducati. If she wants to go burning out of her, all hot under the collar, then she's literally going to have to run me over, junk first. I'm hoping she likes my junk far too much to do that.

"Move," she snaps. The fire in her eyes is wild, almost out of control. The blaze has already caught inside her, and is burning hotter and hotter by the second. I have little hope of putting it out.

"Sophia, what do you think you're going to accomplish by racing over there? You're gonna give Hector exactly what he wants. He'll cuff you in the basement and let each and every single one of his boys fuck you, and he won't let your father go. He'll end up dead, and you'll end up broken and bleeding. And then *I'll* end up dead, too."

"No, you won't." Her dark eyes glint with steel, like she's seeing some other outcome to this course of action.

"Of course I will. Do you think I'll let you leave here without me? Fuck, Sophia, do you think I wouldn't die trying to break into that place to get you out? Jesus Christ. Did you think I was just gonna sit here on my ass while you went off half cocked to confront one of the most dangerous men in the goddamn country?"

She doesn't look impressed by my anger. "You can do whatever you like, Jamie. If my father is in trouble,"—pain flashes in her eyes now—"in trouble because of *me*, because I didn't go home when I should have, then it's up to me to rectify the situation." She pulls her keys out of her back pocket finally and fumbles them, trying to get them into the motorcycle's ignition. I watch her for a second, wrestling with myself. How the fuck am I supposed to talk her down right now? If I were in her position, I'd be feeling exactly the same. Nothing would stop me from going after Hector. Nothing at all. Except, maybe…

"Sophia? Sophia, look at me." I place my hand over hers, stilling it as she struggles to stop shaking long enough to slide the key home. She looks up at me, furious and scared, and my heart aches.

"Sophia. I'm not going to let Hector do anything to hurt your father. Do you trust me?"

She blinks. "How can you stop him? What if he's already hurt him? What then?"

I shake my head. "*Do you trust me, sugar?*"

I know her, and because I do, I know she's desperately fighting the urge to say that she *did* trust me, but then she found out I was keeping this from her and now she doesn't know what to think. She knows me, too, though. She knows I wouldn't have kept information from her unless it was because I wanted to be sure, because I didn't want to panic her unnecessarily. That knowledge makes her hold her tongue.

She says this instead: "What am I supposed to do, then, Jamie? Sit around on my ass and keep my mouth shut until you've figured out what our next step should be? Anything could be happening over there in that farmhouse. My father's not a tough guy, okay? He's gentle. Soft. He's a Christian. He's not cut out for this kind of thing."

Her words mirror my thoughts. Alan Romera really isn't cut out for kidnapping and physical abuse. He's not the kind of man who will be able to withstand extreme violence. Alan's the kind of man to give his interrogators everything they desire immediately, without question, which is tough because he actually doesn't possess information or property that Hector wants. His only valuable commodity is his life, and he won't be in possession of that for very long if we don't play ball. The weird thing is that Hector hasn't asked for anything yet. The details of Alan's kidnapping had to be beaten out of one of Hector's lackeys, where usually I'd expect him to play his cards right out of the gate. Hector's hardly patient. He's hardly the sort of man who sits on an ace when he can lay it out and watch the chaos ensue afterwards, rubbing his hands together in delight as everyone around him falls apart.

I sigh, knowing what's going to come out of my mouth next and not looking forward to it. Sophia isn't going to like it either, but she's just going to have to deal with it. "I'll go over there. Cade and I will go. We'll talk to him, figure out the lay of the land. It's our only option."

Sophia shakes her head, no, even before I've finished speaking. "I won't be left behind. I'll lose my mind, wondering what the hell is happening to both my father and then you two on top of everything else. I'll have a goddamn nervous breakdown. I am coming with you, Jamie, whether you like it or not."

I can see from the look on her face that she means business. She won't back down. Highly inconvenient, given what that means for us now. She's going to hate me. "Okay. Fine. You can come." I rub at the back of my neck, trying not to swear and failing miserably. "Come back inside, though, sugar. We need to talk about it. Figure out what our plan of attack will be."

My beautiful girl narrows her eyes, swallowing. "Don't even think about trying to put me off in there, Jamie. I've made my mind up."

"I can see that."

She stares at me a moment longer and then slowly climbs off the motorcycle. "All right. Let's do that then. Let's figure this out, and then let's get moving. The longer my father's trapped over there with Ramirez, the worse it's going to be for him."

I had so much doubt in my mind when Soph said she wanted to become a Widow Maker. I had no idea if she was going to be strong or fierce enough to handle all the shit we put ourselves though. Ever since she became a prospect, she's been proving herself braver and more ferocious than many of the oldest club members, though. She's deter-mined at all times to get her own way, to be involved, to change things somehow.

We go back inside and Sophia sits down heavily at the table with Cade, as if her bones are made of solid steel. Cade gives me a knowing look as I go to fetch us all coffee. Neither of them see me fetch the Zolpidem from the drawer underneath the bar—the same sleeping pills Cade used to knock Sophia out on the journey from Julio's place to New Mexico. Neither of them notice me crushing up three pills and tipping the ground up powder into one of the mugs I've filled with dark black liquid. I'm careful to make sure Sophia gets the doctored coffee when I set them down on the table.

"So what do we do? Tell me there's a way to fix this," she says, lifting the mug to her mouth and drinking. Cade sends me a look that tells me he knows exactly what I've done, and exactly how much trouble I'm going to be in because of it. I scowl at him. Over the next fifteen minutes we talk about ways in which we might be able to rescue Alan, and Sophia starts to go a little cross-eyed. The Zolpidem is potent to say the least.

Eventually Soph begins to realize something's up. She looks at me, eyes glazed, and I see the moment when she understands what's happening to her. She glances dopily down at the coffee I gave to her, and the betrayal in her eyes is impossible to miss. "You… motherrr …fuckkker," she slurs.

Cade manages to catch her just as her eyes roll back into her head. I'm gonna be in so much shit when she wakes up.

REBEL

Cade swings the Humvee around a sharp bend, hugging the turn so that I need to brace myself against the dash. I'm used to his hectic driving. Two tours together in Afghanistan and I'm really fucking grateful he drives like a Nascar boss. He's saved our asses more than once by putting his foot down when we were drawing heat. The drive into town is only twenty minutes today, less with Cade at the wheel, but I have enough time to send Danny, the Widow Maker's resident hacker, a text:

> **Me: Find me a number for Ramirez? Or one of Ramirez's men. ASAP?**

I get a response twelve minutes later:

> **Danny: 505-328-9887. Hope there's a shot of Jack headed my way for that, man.**

There'll be more than a shot of Jack in it for him if this number puts me in touch with Hector. I copy and paste the number into contacts and hit the green call icon, and then I wait. Cade watches me with one eye as I hold the phone to my ear and I wait. Buildings begin to appear, dotted out in the desert on either side of the road. As the phone continues to ring and ring, more houses and a gas station spring up in front of us, signaling that we're approaching the town limits.

"No one picking up?" Cade asks.

"No," I tell him, canceling the call. "Fucking frustrating. Danny never normally gives out bad information."

"Danny *never* gives out bad information. *Period*. Maybe try again?"

"Yeah." I about to hit redial when the phone lights up in my hand, flashing **UNKNOWN NUMBER** on the screen in time with the shrill tone that fills the car. I look at Cade. "Coincidence?"

He looks doubtful. "No such thing, right?"

"Mmm." I answer the call, not saying anything, holding the sleek black metal up against my ear as I wait for the person on the other end of the line to say something. At first, it's so quiet I think maybe the connection didn't take, but then a loud cracking distorts the line, followed by a series of smaller cracks and crunches, and I know someone is there. Someone who just so happens to be eating something by the sound of things.

"I was wondering how long…" a voice says quietly. It's Hector, of course. Hector, with his thick accent, eating his godforsaken sugared almonds, sounding as cool and collected as ever. I fucking *despise* the man.

I play along. "How long *what*?"

"How long it would take you to call. Or show up. Or do *something*, anyway. Alfonso told me he had a run in with one of your boys. Sounded like your delightful vice president. And in light of the information Mr. Preston obtained, I assumed you'd be in touch sooner rather than later."

Hector's a well-educated man. My guess is he was schooled in America. Probably went to an expensive, exclusive college, where he studied economics or business. No doubt his parents, whoever they might be, wanted him to relocate permanently stateside and make a new life for himself. Become something. Accomplish all that they couldn't in Mexico. Of course, I could be wrong. He could have simply watched a lot of television and learned English that way, or maybe his parents were criminals too and they taught him everything he knows, but listening to him speak now I get the distinct impression that I could easily have studied alongside him at MIT. There's something really intimate about talking on the phone with him. Like he's actually here, sitting with me, whispering into my ear, and it's creeping me the fuck out. My skin is literally crawling.

"Let's meet," I say. "Somewhere public. Let's just hash this shit out once and for all, shall we?"

"Hmm, well..." Ramirez ponders this silently. "I have a full schedule today, Jamie. I'd be happy to host you at my rustic, charming farmhouse, though. If you have the time."

"Oh, come on now, Hector. I'm not that stupid. If I walk through your front door, I won't be walking out again. You and I both know that." We've had someone watching his place night and day ever since he showed up here in New Mexico, and there are never any less than twenty armed men moving and rotating through his property. If I went on over there, gave a polite knock on the front door and asked to come on in, I'd be dead within a minute.

Hector laughs. "Worth the offer, right?" He laughs some more. Crunches some more. "So where would you propose we have this very public meeting of ours, Jamie? And who will you be bringing along with you?"

"Just me and Cade. Outside the public library off Main. Come now. We'll be waiting." I hang up before he can object. There's no real reason why Hector Ramirez should come and meet with us given that he's the one with the leverage in this situation, but he has to make his demands after all. And I know the guy. He'd never pass up an opportunity to rile me in person. There was a time when I'd do the occasional shift at Dead Man's Ink, purely for the enjoyment of tattooing and meeting new people, but not anymore. Hector and his boys make a point of walking down Main Street every morning and every night just before dusk. They come to see if I'm around; they come to show their faces, to show they're not going anywhere anytime soon, and I have a pretty fucking short fuse these days. I want to hurt him. I want to do unspeakable things to him, so I stay away, keep my wits about me, and I bide my time, waiting for the day *I* go rolling up on *his* place of business.

"Why there?" Cade stabs a finger at the buttons on the Humvee's radio until static crackles out of the speakers. For a second I'm transported back to the desert, and I'm straining to hear snatches of distorted sound from my hip radio as bullets whip and sing overhead. Cade frowns. "Why the library?"

I block out the chatter of the radio, staring straight ahead out of the windshield in front of me. "Because *she's* back. Because she's brought a team, and it looks like she's staying."

Cade knows precisely who *she* is. Denise Lowell, agent for the DEA. Lowell was pursuing Ramirez last year, and arrested both him and myself after we had a bust up at Dead Man's Ink. She tried to lay the pressure on me back then to talk, to say something that might incriminate Ramirez (and potentially myself) in illegal activity. I got the feeling, as I sat there in that interview room being interrogated by her and her little DEA friends, that she wouldn't have really cared where I slipped up or what I inadvertently confessed to. She would have taken a misdemeanor crime and somehow twisted and turned it, moulding it like clay, until it was suddenly murder one. She's the type of woman who can perform magic tricks like that.

"Is she here for him?" Cade holds onto the steering wheel tight, glaring at the straight road ahead of him. Any moment now he'll have to turn right, pull off into the sleepy, lazy town of Freemantle, but until then he looks intent on gunning the engine as hard as he possibly can.

"I don't know. I fucking hope so, man. I *really* fucking hope so."

CADE

Rebel's looking twitchy as we get out of the Humvee and walk across the street. There are some kids playing on the patch of grass outside the library; they have some kind of electric skateboard and three of them are watching as the tallest, gangliest pre-teen zips up and down the sidewalk, wobbling, looking like he's about to fall off and crack his head open any second. To be honest, I'm surprised that there even *are* four kids in Freemantle. I can't say that I've ever noticed any before. I don't even think there's a school here.

Rebel puts his hand in his pocket and pulls out a roll of twenty-dollar bills. "Hey." He beckons to the kid on the skateboard. "Wanna make some money?"

The tall kid cocks his head to one side, coming to a stop. "How much?"

"Forty bucks. But you gotta split it between you. Ten each."

"Pssshh. Ten bucks is nothing. What do you want us to do?" Four sets of owlish eyes blink up at my friend like he's a god.

"Are you any good at math?" he says. All four of them shake their heads. "Okay, well how about I make it simple for you. Who's got a pen and some paper?"

The smallest kid takes off his backpack and produces both articles. Rebel scribbles something down on the paper and hands it over to the tiny kid. He can't be any more than six or seven. The kid squints at the scrawl on the paper, frowning, and then spins it upside down, trying to make sense of it that way. Rebel turns it back.

"Take that into the library and find the answer for me. It'll be in a mathematics book, I promise."

"Which one?" Tall kid's looking suspicious.

"I don't know. But I'll bet you a hundred bucks you'll find the answer in there. You just have to look for it."

Unlike Freemantle, there were a lot of kids in Afghanistan. Hundreds of them, teeming, running up and down narrow alleyways, vanishing and emerging from the shadows when you least expected it. It wasn't a place for a kid to be. *Ever.* Jamie used to pull this shit with them over there, too. He'd pull out a bunch of money and bribe them into completing some time consuming, pointless task for him that would take them far away from the dangerous situation we'd shown up to deal with. Afghani kids wouldn't have been complaining about ten bucks each. They'd have been climbing over themselves to take the deal and disappear. Half the time they wouldn't even complete the task he'd set them. They'd just run off with the cash, as far as they could get for fear that they'd fail and he'd ask for the money back. Didn't matter, though. Jamie would have accomplished what he set out to do, and the kids would be gone.

The motley crew in front of us discuss his proposal in loud whispers before Tall Kid turns around and holds out his hand. "Deal. And if we figure out the answer to the equation, we get a hundred bucks?"

Jamie nods.

"On top of the original ten each?"

"Correct."

"Cool. Let's shake on it."

Jamie tries not to smile as Tall Kid accepts the deal on behalf of his compatriots. "And don't cheat. If you're out here in the next fifteen minutes, I'll know you googled it. You need to look it up in a book."

A chorus of groans goes up from the small crowd. Tall Kid rolls his eyes. "Fine." He takes the money from Jamie and the four of them begin making their way toward the library, pushing and shoving each other.

"Pity you can't do that with Soph," I say, elbowing him in the ribs.

"I'd be fucking broke if I had to bribe her every time I wanted her to do something." Jamie climbs up and sits on the lone park bench, ass on the back, feet on the seat. "I'd rather have money in my back pocket and a spirited girlfriend any day of the week." He winks, and I can only imagine what kind of shit those two get up to in the bedroom. Jamie's not one to kiss and tell, but I heard them well enough when I was waiting for Soph to come cook breakfast. It sounded like he was murdering her or something, and she was strangely fucking happy about it.

"Where's Lowell set up shop?" I ask, doing my best to shove Jamie and Sophia's weird sex life out of my head. Jay points over my shoulder, up toward the second story of the tiny women's clothing store on the other side of the street. There are three sets of windows up there, each shut tight, which is weird for such a swelteringly hot day. Net curtains block the view inside, but I can imagine Lowell has already noticed us and has camera lenses pointed our way.

"Why d'you wanna do this in plain sight?"

"Because if I know Lowell's here, Hector knows Lowell's here, too. And he's not gonna pull any weird shit if he knows he's got half a federal agency jammed up his ass. Or at least I'm assuming he won't."

"Probably." I turn my back on the windows again. "Think she can monitor the conversation?"

Jamie looks at me. Shrugs. Looks away down the street. He turns a cocktail stick over and over between his teeth. Neither one of us have worn our MC cuts into town; we're both in jeans and t-shirts, baseball caps turned backward on our head, sneakers on our feet. We're just two guys in our late twenties. Or we would be if we weren't covered in so many tattoos. Military tattoos. Club tattoos. Things that your average civilian might not recognize, but a cop definitely would.

We wait for a while. We don't speak. We've been friends for so long now that we don't need to open our mouths to communicate. I know what he's thinking from the way his forehead creases, or the way his eyes seem to flash occasionally, transmitting information and his mood in a way that few people can pick up on. He says the same of me. He knows if I'm pissed or happy by the nervous energy that pours off me. According to him, the air around me might as well be sparking with electricity when I'm about to go nuclear on someone. Regardless of the fact that I might seem perfectly calm to anyone else, Jamie always knows when to grab me by the collar and drag me away from a fight before it can start.

After about fifteen minutes, a black sedan with tinted windows slowly rolls down the high street, only the driver visible as the vehicle approaches. Jamie slides off the bench and gets to his feet. "Here we go," he says under his breath.

"Here we go," I agree. I think I see a bright glance of light flash off one of the upstairs windows across the street, but when I look up they're all still closed up, the curtains still at the glass. Jamie's gaze flickers up there at the same time as mine, however, so I know I'm not imagining things. The sedan comes to a stop alongside us, and rear door closest to us.

Hector Ramirez climbs out.

He's wearing a dark navy shirt, almost black, shot through with purple pin stripes, and his pants are long, heavy looking things that make me want to sweat just from looking at them. Hector isn't sweating, though. He looks cool and refreshed, like summer isn't kicking his ass the same way it is everyone else.

"*Gentlemen.*" He dips his chin, lowering his head in a curt nod. "So wonderful to see you, as always."

Beside me, Jamie's hackles are up already. I can tell by the way the muscles in his jaw are jumping, flexing, as he locks Ramirez in his gaze. "*Hector.*" He offers out his hand, and I can imagine how much the gesture costs him. Jamie's a good guy. He's a good guy until you do something to piss him off, or fuck him over in any way. When that happens, you quickly realize he can be decidedly *bad* when he wants to be. Ramirez knows that all too well. Maybe that's why he wears a painfully smug smile as he accepts Jamie's hand and shakes.

"I can only imagine why you would have chosen such a place to meet," Ramirez says, smiling, flashing his teeth. "But I can assure you, you would have been perfectly welcome and perfectly…" He pauses, eyes skirting down and to the left, as though he's trying to assess if we're being watched. Or listened to as the case may well be. "*Safe,*" he finishes. He turns that shit eating grin on me next and I have to fight down the overwhelming urge to plant my fucking fist in his face. "Mr. Preston, you look a little upset. Would you like a tea? Coffee? I'm about to send Alfonso across the street to grab me something. I'm sure he wouldn't mind collecting something for you, too."

As he says this, a broad, barrel chested guy climbs out of the sedan's front passenger seat, his face mottled purple and blue, his left eye swollen shut, burn blisters under his eye. I recognize him instantly—easily done, since I beat the living shit out of him not too long ago. He gives me a look that could sour milk. "I think I'll be okay without," I say. I smile, grin in fact, as Alfonso backs away, staring at me with hate in his eyes as he goes to grab his master's coffee.

I know without a doubt that he'd be dead if he were working under Maria Rosa's employ. She wouldn't tolerate any of her men giving away her secrets, no matter how hard they were punched repeatedly in the face. Ramirez doesn't strike me as the kind of cartel boss who would let something like that slide, but chances are he's waiting to serve Alfonso's punishment to him when he least expects it. The shitty part is Alfonso probably knows his boss is going to put a bullet in the back of his head one night soon, and there's nothing he can do about it.

"Now. What would you like to speak about, Jamie? I'm sure it must be pressing to drag me out here in the middle of the day on a Tuesday." Ramirez leans back against the sedan, his hand reaching into the pocket of his heavy suit pants. I instinctively assume he's going for a gun, but I don't move to act on my assumption. Not yet, anyway. If Lowell sees me pull a gun, I'm going away for a very long time. Besides, I can judge a man's intent in his eyes. Ramirez definitely looks like he would happily skin us alive right here and now if he thought he might get away with it, but he knows he won't. He doesn't pull out a gun from his pocket. Instead he pulls out a handful of almonds, some sugared some plain, and he offers them first to Jamie and then to me. "Sweet tooth. I have the worst sweet tooth. I can't seem to stop eating these things. I suppose there are worse addictions to have, though, no?"

Jamie doesn't take any of his almonds, and neither do I. We both simply look at him like he's crazy, which he is. Patently. Jamie clears his throat. "I heard you have a friend in town. A *mutual* friend."

Ramirez pops an almond into his mouth and bites down on it, smiling. "Alan? My good friend *Alan*? I had no idea you two knew each other."

"We do. Very well. I'd like him to come stay with me if that's amenable to you." Jamie lifts one shoulder in a poor attempt at a shrug. "We do have more room for guests after all."

Ramirez wags a finger at Jay, like he's just made a joke. His eyes crease at the corners, showing how blatantly amused he is at the prospect of merely handing Alan over without a by your leave. "You sure do have a lot of room over there, you're right. I don't know, though. Alan's pretty happy with me right now. He knows his daughter is going to come pay him a visit soon. He seems very invested in seeing her." His eyes turn cold all of a sudden, hardening, the creases created by his smile morphing into something sour and angry. "I believe she'll be by any day now."

Jamie steps forward, growling under his breath. "She won't be going anywhere near you or your farmhouse, Hector. She's not your property."

"Of course not. People can't belong to other people. This is America, Jamie. What an absurd thing to say." Ironic that he chooses to say this, when he makes hundred of thousands of dollars a year, perhaps millions, selling people as sex slaves. There's a chance he makes more money selling people than he does selling heroin and cocaine. A junkie will pay twenty bucks for a baggie. A rich gentleman with certain proclivities and the means to keep them secret will pay considerably more to satiate *his* addiction. Jamie's seething, but he's also doing a pretty damned good job at remaining calm.

"If we drop our conflict," he says, "will you let him go?" It's wild that he's dropping our pretence so quickly, but what's even wilder is the suggestion he's making. Drop the conflict with Los Oscuros? I can barely believe what I'm hearing. We went to war with the cartel because Ramirez had Jamie's uncle murdered. It was the straw that broke the camel's back, and it broke Jamie's heart at the same fucking time. Now he's just willing to forget that, forget about getting justice for Ryan and walk away?

Ramirez looks bemused by the thought. "I don't see that there's ever going to be a way out of this conflict for you or for me. Not without blood spilled. Life lost. You've been quiet for the past little while, and I've sat in that cramped farmhouse waiting for you to snap. Waiting for you to make your move. And you've done nothing. I have to say at this point, I want a more...*physical* ending to this game of ours if only so I won't feel like I've been wasting my time in this godforsaken place, day in, day out for what frankly feels like an eternity."

"So you refuse?" Jamie doesn't move an inch. I don't want to take my eyes off of Ramirez in case the guy truly is certifiable and he does make a move here, but I can tell something is very wrong with the man standing next to me. He's about to lose his fucking mind.

Alfonso appears from the café next to the women's clothing store on the other side of the street, coffee cup in hand, still shooting me stink eye. He hands the coffee to Ramirez and then hovers, standing there. "Get back in the car," Ramirez snaps. Alfonso glowers at all three of us, and then does as he's told, reluctantly folding himself back into the passenger seat.

"Yes, I refuse," Ramirez says. "Of course I fucking refuse. Tell me something, Jamie. Where is Raphael?"

Raphael. Raphael Dela Vega. I'd like to say I haven't even thought about him in forever, but that couldn't be further from the truth. Jamie never gave me details, but I know the fucker is buried somewhere out in the desert, and that Sophia had something to do with it. I can't imagine her taking someone's life, but then again Dela Vega was a special guy. I'm pretty sure nearly everyone he met wanted to drive a knife into his heart, and with good reason.

"How the fuck should I know where he is?" Jamie's voice is level and even, but it holds a hard edge to it. It's hardly an admission that he had something to do with the guy's disappearance, but it's hardly a denial either. Not a *real* one, even if he does claim so with his words.

Ramirez stares Jamie down, not breathing, not blinking, not shifting an inch. The two of them stand their ground until Ramirez turns away, fishing more almonds out of his pocket. "That's a pity. He's my favorite employee, you know. I'd be really fucking upset if I found out something had happened to him. God only knows what I would do." He tosses an almond into his mouth and then washes it down with some coffee.

His threat isn't even a veiled one. He knows perfectly well that Raphael is dead and that the Widow Makers are responsible. And now he's going to punish us by taking it out on Alan, demanding we hand over Sophia, otherwise there'll be hell to pay. It's what we expected at the end of the day. I step forward, placing myself between Jamie and Ramirez—it's only a matter of time before Jamie's temper gets the better of him and he goes for Hector. There's only one reason he would ever do something so reckless, and that's if Sophia is in danger. Right now, Ramirez's attentions towards Jamie's girlfriend certainly constitute danger. Jamie will tear his throat out on the street in front of countless witnesses and risk going to prison if it means keeping her safe.

Ramirez smirks, bowing his head. "We men are alike, you know?" he says softly.

"And how the fuck did you come to that conclusion?" I crane my neck, staring down at him. I've never considered myself overly tall—I'm 5'11", pretty average for a guy—but I tower over Ramirez. The guy is pretty short; maybe that's why he decided he needed to get into the organized crime business—to obtain the power that his physique couldn't command through fear. If that's the case, then he's doing a pretty damn good job of it. Lesser men would be cowed by him. They'd think twice about fucking with his business or his employees. Rebel and I are probably the only men to have stood up to him in a really long time, which from the look on his face is very entertaining to him. His smile grows even broader.

"We are focused individuals," he says. "And we're unfamiliar with not getting our own way. It gives us a certain determination that other men lack."

Behind me, Jamie makes a really unhappy sound. "You're right," he says. "We're not used to being told no. We're also really fucking patient. We've been waiting for the past six months, Ramirez. That doesn't mean that we'll wait forever now, though. Don't be fooled. If you think we're just going to sit by and let you torture an old man to get what you want, you'd be mistaken."

Ramirez raises one eyebrow. "Torture? I don't have a fucking clue what you're talking about, Jamie. I don't torture people. Like you, I'm a simple businessman. I moved to New Mexico as a tax break. Nothing more. And Alan...why would I even want to harm a man like Alan? He's a good, god-fearing man. In fact, I think his presence in my household has been very grounding so far. I'd hate to see him go."

This is all an act, purely for Lowell's benefit. It's unlikely Hector would openly admit to kidnapping Sophia's father, but fuck. This whole sugar-wouldn't-melt bit is sickening. We need to get out of here before Jamie goes postal and tries to knock the guy's head clean off.

I give Ramirez one last dark, warning look and then I turn around to face my friend. He looks like his blood is boiling in his veins. "Come on, man. Time we got out of here. Doesn't look like we're going to accomplish anything."

His eyes look like chips of ice—cold and pale. They're filled with violence. "There's no reasoning with the unreasonable," he says quietly, almost under his breath. He's not talking to me, or even to Hector. He's retreated inside his own head, and he's making plans. Dangerous, awful, bloody and undoubtedly illegal plans. My favorite kind.

It's about fucking time. The confrontation I can see brewing in Jamie's mind is long past overdue. It should have happened the moment Hector showed up in town and rented that fucking farmhouse. I jerk my head in the direction of the Humvee, and Jamie walks away, his eyes still vacant, his hands clenched into fists by his sides.

Turning our backs on a man who wants us both dead is a very bad idea, but he needs to know we won't be intimidated. We *will* spill his blood. For Ryan, Jamie's uncle. For Leah, the woman Ramirez had killed back in Ebony Briar. And now for Sophia's father. There's no two ways about it: the man is going to die, and he's going to do it horrifically. Because when Jamie gets that look in his eyes, there is no alternative. There's only pain and horror. There's only begging and pleading. There's only death.

"I'll see you soon, gentlemen," Hector calls after us. "I'm sure of it.

In fact, tell that little whore of yours that she has one week. One week to pack up her things and show up on my doorstep. Any longer than that, and I fear Alan might need to go."

Jamie twitches. That's all he allows himself as we head back to the car. He twitches, and Hector Ramirez laughs.

SOPHIA

I dream that I'm fucking Jamie, that he's deep inside me, hard and rigid, making me feel tight and full, and when I wake up I'm so angry I throw a glass at the kitchen wall in his cabin. I shouldn't be having sex dreams about the bastard when he betrayed my trust like that. I shouldn't be waking up, my head still thick with lust, my clit still aching, my pussy still wet, when the grade-A motherfucker doped me up and shut me away in his private little sanctuary all over again.

I half expect the door to be locked when I storm over to the cabin's only point of entrance or exit, and yet when I yank on the handle and pull toward me, it opens wide. Probably because Jamie knew by the time I woke up, it would be far too late for me to rush out and do anything to interfere with his plans, whatever they may be.

"You are *so* going to regret this," I tell him, growling the words even though he's not around to hear them. He'll get the picture later on, though. I'll make sure of it. The courtyard down by the compound is empty. Night is creeping across the desert floor toward us, a visible line between light and dark, and the air is heavy with the scent of chili and something more organic, floral and completely out of place in this dry, lifeless dustbowl. The smell teases me, bringing memories half floating to the surface of my mind before they sink out of view, unseen and unremembered, and I'm left feeling strangely hollow and unsatisfied.

God, I'm going to fucking murder Jamie. If Ramirez hasn't already completed the job, of course. My boots are thick with dust by the time I reach the clubhouse. I stamp my feet outside the entrance, knowing that I'm going to be responsible for cleaning up any mess I make in the morning. This whole prospecting thing is far less glamorous than I'd assumed it would be, but everyone here has paid their dues at some point. Every single member of the Widow Makers Motorcycle club has cleaned dishes, cooked meals, and swept floors. It's the natural order of things. I'm fired up and pissed off right now, though, and knowing that I'll have to clean the clubhouse from top to bottom tomorrow, as I have to clean it every Wednesday, is making my black mood even blacker. I can't wait to get my hands on that fucking asshole. He really shouldn't have done that. I mean, how am I supposed to trust him when he drugs me, simply because I have my own mind and I refuse to do as I'm told every time he opens his mouth?

Inside the clubhouse, there are only a few people sitting at the tables, drinking bottled beer and talking, laughing, watching a fight on the small, crappy television that's been mounted on the wall by the door. Carnie and Danny are playing pool on the other side of the room, and Fatty is in his regular spot behind the bar, leaning on the beer taps, scratching at his rotund belly. He blinks suspiciously when he sees me headed toward him. No one else even acknowledges my existence.

"Sophia," he says, straightening up. "You want somethin', honey?"

You're absolutely fucking right I want something. I want a set of rusty scissors to castrate my boyfriend with, but I don't tell *him* that. "I need to get back there," I say, pointing behind him.

Last year, when Maria Rosa was locked in the basement below

the barn and shit was flying at us from all angles, Jamie had shown me where his 'office' was—through a heavy, reinforced steel door in the back, behind the bar. Fatty gives me a worried look. He seems surprised that I'd even know the office was there.

"I don't think that's a good idea, Sophia. Jamie doesn't like people back there without him."

In fairness, that is true. He really doesn't like the other Widow Makers knowing that there's valuable information in the vault. He does his best to only disappear there late at night, when he figures it will be much quieter and no one will ask questions.

"I'm going back there, Fats. You can let me by, or I can fight my way past you. You'll have a hell of a job explaining to Rebel why his girlfriend is covered in bruises and is bleeding."

"Shit, girl. That's just plain evil."

"Sorry." I'm not really, though. I'm too mad to even come close to sorry right now.

"You know you're putting me in a crappy position. He's gonna be pissed with me either way."

"I can guarantee you he'll be more pissed if I have a black eye and I'm limping."

"Jesus." Fatty looks around, presumably to see if anyone's watching our exchange. He scowls at me, and then lifts the bar hatch, allowing me to skirt around him and into the back. It's dark and dingy in the stock room, the tight space crammed full of liquor bottles and snack food, as well as the dry store ingredients used to make breakfast, lunch and dinner each day for whomever happens to be kicking around. To the far right, in the shadows, the large steel door Jamie showed me stands, sealed shut, impenetrable. Except he gave me the code to get in if there was ever an emergency, so it doesn't pose a problem for long. I punch in the numbers he told me months ago. He made me repeat them back to him so I would remember—one seven six three. The heavy door swings back, yawning open, allowing me inside. I don't know why I've come. I just know that I want to piss Jamie off, and this is one sure fire way of accomplishing that.

Last time I was here, the desk to the left was stacked high with papers and all kinds of files, some of which were so full they were bulging open, splitting apart at the seams. The desk on the right was flanked by two huge computer screens, and a bank of tall servers sat behind it, humming quietly, lights flashing on and off at random intervals. The servers are still there, as are the computers, but now the desk on the left is tidy, a small stack of papers neatly lined up close to the edge of the polished wood. In the very center of the desk, a single file sits, the dark blue cover flipped open, and inside a picture of a tall, frightening looking guy in dark clothes sits on top of a few pieces of paper. He's not looking at the camera. It's clear this black and white image was shot from a distance without the man's knowledge. He looks like he's angry, about to climb into a car parked outside a huge warehouse—I think it's a Camaro. I flip the image over and there's another photograph underneath it, this time a close up of the guy's face.

People always say that Jamie's eyes are startling because of their stark color. This guy's eyes are disturbing too, but they're so dark they're almost black. They're full of rage and violence, as if he's quietly simmering, fury flooding his veins, and any second he's about to explode. There's no doubt about it; this man, whoever he is, is a dark, dangerous individual, and I'd be happy if I lived a long, healthy life and never had cause to run into him.

The third picture underneath the close up is a mug shot. The guy's holding up a black board with a string of numbers on it, and underneath it says, **MAYFAIR, ZETH**. The name rings a bell, but I can't think where I've heard it before. The way he stares down the lens of the camera in this picture, his expression flat and lifeless, is even more worrying than the image previous. He looks like he's hollow, dead inside. I find myself wondering what he did to end up with his mug shot being taken. Probably murdered someone, cut their head off and wore it like a goddamn hat or something.

I don't know why I carry on flicking through the file, but I can't seem to stop myself. I'm intrigued by the kind of information Jamie gathers about people, and to what end? What does he want with this guy? Admittedly there isn't much to the file. Just a few printed out sheets of paper with very few details on them—the name *Charlie Holsan*. A Seattle address that makes my head thump. I know exactly where the address is, on the other side of the city from the hospital. An up and coming area where an apartment in a decent building will set you back a couple of million dollars. Is that where this guy lives? It doesn't seem like his style.

More photographs at the back of the file. One of him talking to a tall, handsome black guy in a sleek, obviously expensive suit. Another of him sitting behind the wheel of the black Camaro again. The third and final picture makes my throat constrict. It's a picture of the same guy, this Zeth Mayfair, and he's dressed in bright orange overalls—the kind you're issued in prison, which is clearly where he is given the chain link fence and the scary looking tattooed people in the background of the picture. He's not alone. My throat has tightened, making it difficult to breathe, because he's talking to someone in the picture, someone I recognize, and I'm finding it hard to believe what I'm seeing right now. It's Cade.

He's talking to Cade.

"What the...?" Cade was in prison? He's wearing the same orange overalls, after all. He looks skinnier, less muscle, and his head is shaved, but it's definitely him. I've spent the past six months living at close quarters with the guy; I'd know him anywhere. The two men appear to be deep in conversation in the picture. Not a tense, heated conversation. It's as if they're just chatting. Cade is actually smiling, and this Zeth guy looks a little less intense than he does in all of the other shots. He may not be smiling, but I get the feeling that the clear looseness in his body and the ease with which he's leaning against the brick wall beside him means a lot. I don't think his body language would be the same if he didn't feel like he was talking to a friend. A good friend.

I gather all of the photographs and the papers back together and slide them inside the file, flipping it shut. I feel like I just invaded Cade's privacy somehow. This is a part of his past, and I went snooping. Unintentionally, but still. I don't know why I should really care. Cade's loyalty has always been and always will be to his friend. If Jamie asked him to shoot his own mother in the face, I'm pretty sure he'd damn well do it. They're closer than brothers. But he and I are friends now, too, I'd say. We've been left alone together too much, spent hours in cars and days holed up inside the same buildings to not know each other and to not care. At least that's how I feel. He might feel very differently.

Either way, I try to place the file back in the spot where I found it, hoping he'll never know that I saw it. It's just easier that way.

It's not really a surprise that Cade's been locked away. As the months have passed by, I've been allowed to see more and more of the illegal activity the club is involved in. The Widowers don't sell drugs, but they do move them from time to time. Weed, mostly. Large quantities of it that get picked up in one location, usually a couple of days' drive away, and then dropped off somewhere else, far, far away from Freemantle and the permanent location of the club.

There are guns, too. The gun runs are a little more intense. They're closer to home and happen quickly, and I can usually tell one's about to happen by the nervous energy that lingers in the compound. Assault rifles. Hand guns. Large and small, all kinds of weaponry is trafficked not only by Cade, Carnie and the others, but by Jamie, too.

I feel sick to my stomach when I think about *him* getting busted and locked away for gun running. Cade must have been sentenced for a lesser crime. I don't know everything there is to know about the judicial system, but I sure as hell know enough to realize that Cade would definitely still be serving time if he'd been caught with assault rifles. The ATF usually tend to frown upon the possession of unregistered, unlicensed weapons like that.

I spend another few seconds waiting around in the secret room behind the bar, waiting defiantly for Jamie to come back and find me here, but then I change my mind. I want to tear him a new one for what he did, but I also want to know he's okay, and I want to know what he's discovered about my father. Is he safe now? Is he okay? Is he even alive? Anything could have happened while I was sleeping. Jamie could have gotten himself shot. He could have gone to Ramirez's place and discovered my father dead. Alternatively, my father could well be free now and he's so angry with me over what I've done that he simply refuses to come and see me. I wouldn't blame him for that. There isn't a day that goes by that I don't regret not telling my family I am safe. But as each of those days flew by, slipping through my fingers like grains of sand, the concept of reaching out to them and telling them I was alive became harder and harder, until it almost seemed impossible.

I'm sure most people would think I'm a terrible human being, but turning back never seemed like an option. I'd love to say I wanted to stay because I wanted to help bring Hector to justice, but the truth of the matter is that I was scared. I was scared because Raphael was still lurking in the shadows, and I know without a doubt he would have followed through on his promise. He would have discovered who I was eventually, the same way Hector has now, except he wouldn't have kidnapped my dad, or my mom, or my sister. He would have killed them where they stood. He would have raped Sloane, and probably Mom too, and it would have been on me.

After Raphael died and he was no longer a threat, it was too late. I was already in too deep. I'd killed a man. And besides, I may have pretended for a while, but there was no way I could fool myself. I was in love. I couldn't have left Jamie if I'd tried. No one has ever made me feel so safe. So protected. It's ironic. I'm in the most perilous, dangerous situation of my life here in New Mexico, and yet I've never felt safer. That's because of him.

And even though he fucked up today (which he will pay for in spades), it's because he refuses to let me get hurt. It's infuriating, and it's frustrating, especially since I'm meant to be prospecting for the club, but at the end of the day, his actions are because he loves me just as fiercely as I love him.

I leave his office. Pulling the weighty door closed behind me, I make my way back out into the bar and I know something is up as soon as I see the look on Fatty's face. His expression is a wary one, his eyebrows half way to his hairline, his lips pressed together to form a tight line. His eyes flicker to his left, and I see the cause of his discomfort: Jamie and Cade sitting at the bar, each with a shot of whiskey in their hands. Jamie doesn't say a word.

"Did you find him? Did you find my dad?" My heart is thrumming in my chest like a small, trapped bird.

Jamie and Cade exchange a tense look. Jamie says, "Yes, he *is* with Hector. We didn't see him, though," and the blood drains from my face.

"Do you think he's okay?" Seems like such a stupid thing to ask, but I have to. I need to know. I need to look them both in the eye and see whether they think my father is alive and well, or if they think maybe it's possible that he might already be beyond saving.

"Hector hasn't done anything to him," Cade says. His voice doesn't waiver. I see no doubt in him. "He would have inferred that he had otherwise. He wouldn't have been able to help himself."

I look to Jamie—I need to hear him say the same thing, or my mind will be racing. He gives me a curt nod, pulling in a deep breath. "It's true. He's a smug motherfucker. He wouldn't have been able to keep that to himself. As far as we know, Alan's unharmed."

As far as we know. That's hardly a reassuring statement, but it will have to do.

"I see you were checking out the office," Jamie says. His eyes lock onto me as he raises his rocks glass to his mouth and takes a large swig. He remains fixed on me as he swallows.

"Don't look at me like that," I snap. "You have absolutely no right."

He pouts a little. "I didn't say a word."

"You didn't need to." Cade manfully tries to hide the smile I can see hovering at the corners of his mouth, but he fails miserably. I press my palms down on the countertop, leaning toward them both. "And *you* can quit that, too. I know you played a part in what he did."

Cade holds up his hands. "I fucking didn't. That's all on him."

Jamie's mouth drops open. "*Traitor.*"

"You knew he was going to do it, so you were complicit. That's exactly the same as participating, so you're both in the dog house."

"Very unfair. I would have let you come with us," Cade says. Jamie makes a face, demonstrating exactly what he thinks of that statement.

"You're so full of fucking shit. Would you have let Laura come? *No. Fucking. Way.*"

As always when someone mentions Cade's sister, the atmosphere instantly shifts. Jamie tenses, knowing he's brought up a touchy subject, and Cade attempts to appear unaffected. He is affected, though. For all the money the club has, for all the time and all of the resources they've invested looking, they haven't even come close to finding Laura. It's been years now. So much time has passed that I doubt either one of these men believes they're going to find her again, and yet they refuse to stop looking.

My stomach twists at the thought. Just like Laura, *I* am someone's sister. Is Sloane looking for me, the same way Cade is looking for Laura? Does she shut down every time someone mentions my name? God. I feel like my insides are being ripped out. I don't want to think about this now. I can't. I have to deal with my Jamie situation. I duck underneath the bar hatch so I can walk up behind my boyfriend and whisper in his ear. Jamie bows his head as he listens. I try not to let the smell of him distract me from what I want to say—a really difficult feat to accomplish, since he smells divine.

"If you ever drug me again, if you ever lock me away again...if you ever try and prevent me from doing something I want or need to do by force..."

"You'll cut my balls off?" he whispers.

"No. I won't cut your balls off, Jamie. I'll *leave*. You'll wake up one morning, and my things will be here. My toothbrush will be sitting next to yours. My clothes will still be in the closet. My pillow will still smell of me. There will be a thousand things here to remind you of me, but *I* will be gone. And I *won't* be coming back. Do you believe me?"

Jamie turns his head to look at me. Our noses are almost touching. I am so in love with this this man that it kills me to say that I'll leave him, because it would be the hardest thing I've ever had to do. I mean it, though. I can't live this way. There are some things I can tolerate if I absolutely must. I can handle feeling restricted and trapped here in the compound a lot of the time. I can deal with Shay and her stinking attitude. Even knowing that we have a homicidal Colombian woman still living in the basement under the barn is something I can live with, so long as I know she's not getting out any time soon. But this? Feeling like I have no free will? Feeling like I can't trust him? That just won't fly.

Jamie's eyes are shining brightly. His facial muscles are relaxed, but I can tell just by looking into his eyes that he doesn't like the words that are coming out of my mouth. He huffs down his nose, his tongue poking out ever so slightly so he can rub it along his bottom lip, wetting it. "Okay," he says softly. "Yes. I believe you."

"So you won't do it again? I need to hear you tell me that you won't."

He doesn't say anything for a long time. Cade's no longer sitting beside him, I notice. He must have slowly gotten up and crept away during the last few minutes, leaving us to our muted conversation. Eventually, Jamie blinks, his eyes narrowing a little. "I won't say it. I can't, Sophia."

I stand upright, reeling away from him. I wasn't expecting him to say that. I was expecting him to be contrite. To swear that he'll respect my wishes and take them—*me*—seriously. Instead, he's...he's *refusing*? It makes no sense. "Should I just pack my bags and go now, then? Maybe that would be easier for the both of us." I sound angry. Hurt creeps in at the edge of my voice—an annoying tell that I could burst into tears at any moment if I don't wrangle my emotions into check and fast.

Jamie closes his eyes. "I'm not saying that because I don't give a shit if you come or go, sugar. I'm saying it because I love you. If I have to lose you to keep you safe, then I won't think twice. I'll risk having to let you go if it means that you don't end up raped and dead in a ditch with your limbs chopped off. I'd be miserable, and my heart would feel like it was never going to beat again for as long as I lived if you were gone, but I'd be happy at the same time, because I'd know you were far, far away from here and you were alive. Wouldn't you do the same if it was me?"

I have a lump in my throat the size of Texas. If I breathe, if I even think about blinking or moving, even a millimeter, I don't know what's going to happen. I'm conflicted, being dragged in so many different directions all at once by my emotions that I can't decipher what I'm thinking or feeling right now. The pain in his voice upsets me. The fact that he won't see things my way angers me. And the beauty of his sentiment makes my heart feel swollen and bruised. Almost guilty somehow. How can I be mad at him, or hold his actions against him, when he goes and says something like that?

He means every single word. There are no closed doors with him. Those crystal clear blue eyes of his allow me to see directly into his soul, and I know he's telling the truth.

"You can be mad at me all you like. And yes, you can go whenever you like, Sophia. I won't ever try and stop you from leaving here if that's what you truly want. But I want you to listen to me, and I want you to really listen to what I'm about to say, okay? Can you do that?"

I feel like being stubborn and denying him his request, but when I look at him I can see how earnestly he's asking. He's not trying to be a dick; he's not trying to make me angry. It's hard to say no to the man when he's looking at you the way he's looking at me right now.

"Fine. Say what you want to say. I'll listen. Properly, I swear."

Jamie nods. Spinning his scotch glass around and around on the bar in front of him, he stares at the liquid inside, apparently trying to construct what he wants to tell me in his head before he allows himself to say it out loud. After a long, drawn out minute, his gaze returns to me.

"There was an English guy in Afghanistan. He was a member of the Royal Marines but the British government loaned him to us as an informant. He'd been taken prisoner by a group of rebels after his unit's transport hit and IED and killed everyone but him. For nearly two years the rebels kept him hostage in a cave system, giving him just enough food and water so that he could survive. They would torture him every day. They wanted to know everything he knew. They would pull his fingers and his toenails out one by one. They would pull his teeth out too, whenever he wouldn't give them information they wanted. This guy, Andrew, he held out for months. He took the pain and the torment, and he let them take his fingernails and his teeth, until the people who were holding him captive realized they weren't going to get anything out of him.

"Now, that was a really bad position to be in for Andrew. The only reason they were keeping him alive was because he was worth something. If he wasn't valuable to them alive in any way, he sure as hell would be valuable to them dead. See they don't just kill people in the shadows. They want the world to see. They gather their friends. They gather the world's media. They make us watch on television as they force their prisoners to tell lies about their countries, and then they make us watch as they cut off their heads and burn their bodies in cages.

"Andrew nearly died that way. They sat him down in front of a camera and they told him what they wanted him to say, otherwise they were going to have their friends in England track down his wife and two small kids, and they were gonna have them murdered in their beds. You always think you won't cave, that nothing they can do or say to you will make you give in and repeat the hatred they want to spread, but when they threaten your loved ones..." Jamie looks pained. He flinches a little, small creases forming between his eyebrows. "So Andrew sat down and said what they wanted him to say, and they filmed it. The bastards restrained him while they tried to slit his throat from behind, so the camera could see. They almost finished the job. Andrew had a scar that ran from his left ear too his Adam's apple, but that's where it stopped. Miraculously one of our units launched an assault on the caves. We had no idea they were holding anyone captive there. We'd had intel that they were using the location as a munitions cache and we wanted to take it out.

"So they stormed the place and Andrew only got his throat half cut. He came and worked with Cade and me for a long time. He told us in graphic detail about the shit those guys did to him. The kinds of torture they were capable of. And he told us that it paled in comparison to the atrocities he saw committed by the cartels in Mexico. He cried like a baby when he told us about *that*. He'd gone in as part of a task force to rescue a British government official who had been taken right off the street in Juarez. They'd found this guy and his wife in an open grave under a bridge in the middle of the city. The bodies had been mutilated beyond recognition. When the marines attempted to recover the bodies, they'd realized that both the official and his wife were still alive. They were fucked up and bleeding, missing skin, missing fingers, both of them missing their tongues and their eyes. Their ears. Her breasts had been cut off. His dick. They were just raw pieces of meat, and they'd tossed their bodies into a hole while they were still bleeding.

"The *cartels* did that to them. Not even a hardened marine who'd been held captive in the desert and almost died at the hands of some of the most immoral men on this planet could talk about the shit he saw in Mexico without his hands shaking. And *these* are the people we're dealing with right now, Sophia. This is the type of madness we're involving ourselves in. Cade and I were deployed. A lot of the other Widow Makers are ex military, too. We've all had training. We've all been in combat situations. We've been to the dark places of this world and we've already puked our guts up. We've already seen enough to make it difficult to sleep at night."

He stops talking for a second. Gives me a second to digest. I already know what he's going to say next, and the gravity of his words really hit home. I grip hold of the counter, leaning into it, tired and terrified as Jamie continues.

"And you want to go racing after these guys half cocked, Sophia. What about your upbringing in Seattle as a preacher's daughter, living with everything you could possibly need, never having to make hard decisions or real sacrifices, qualifies you to face off with these guys when grown ass marines cry like babies at the mere thought of it?"

My ex, Matt, used to tell me I was sheltered. He used to tease me about the fact that I wasn't street smart at all, and it used to drive me crazy. If he had said everything Jamie just said to me back then, I'd have lost my fucking mind. He would have been making fun of me, trying to be hurtful by making me feel silly, but that's not the case with Jamie. I know he's not trying to call me spoiled. He's not trying to mock me, or criticize me for the way I grew up. He's merely pointing out facts. I *am* the daughter of a preacher from Seattle. I didn't grow up on the streets. I was taken care of. I was loved. I *didn't* have to make hard decisions or make any real sacrifices. I was privileged, and I never wanted for anything. I have no military training. I've never really fired a gun properly. Not really, under pressure, when it matters. I feel, all of a sudden, very foolish.

Jamie's eyes are grief-filled, his entire body tense with worry. "Tell me you'll consider that, Sophia. Because I'm fucking worried out of my mind over you, over this whole fucking situation, and I feel like everything is about to spiral out of control."

His dark hair, normally buzzed close to his head, is a little long at the moment. Jamie runs a hand through it, pulling on it as he leans one elbow against the bar. He really does look like he's worried out of his mind.

I take a second to really think about what I would do in his place, and it dawns on me that I wouldn't react in any other way. I've been so overtaken by my own vim and vinegar, pissed off about my civil rights being infringed upon, that I haven't seen what this is doing to him. It's absolutely killing him.

I step into him, wrapping my arms around his neck, and I hold onto him as tightly as I can. "I'm sorry," I whisper. "I shouldn't be, but I am. Things would be so much easier for you if you'd never met me. You'd have dealt with Hector a long time ago. He probably wouldn't have come to New Mexico at all. If I weren't in your life, everything would be easier."

Jamie's arms find their way around my waist, and his lips find their way to the sensitive skin of my neck. He kisses me, and then sighs, leaning his head against mine. "If you weren't in my life, sugar, I'd only be half a man. I wouldn't trade knowing you, caring for you, loving you, for anything in the world."

REBEL

Afghanistan

I can smell smoke. I can smell something else on the night's breeze as well, something heavy and acrid, organic almost, and a knot forms in the pit of my stomach. There are no alarms going off to signal something significant is happening, but I'm gripped with foreboding. Something is fucking going down, I know it is. I prop myself up on one elbow, squinting into the darkness, and Cade is already sitting up in his bed on the other side of the room, a mirror image of me, concern etched deeply into his face.

"You smell that?" he whispers.

"Yeah. Yeah, I do."

"You know what it is?"

I shake my head, no, though I have a worrying suspicion that I actually *do* know and I just don't want to admit it to myself. "Better check it out," I say.

Cade flings his legs out of his cot, shoving his socked feet straight into his polished boots that are sitting next to his bed. I do the same. We're both already dressed, t-shirts tucked into our pants, ready to rock and roll. In the army you learn pretty fucking quickly that you have to go to sleep fully geared up. Too many times we've been called out in the middle of the night and needed to move quickly. Takes too long to wrestle into your clothes when there are people screaming at you and sirens wailing in your goddamn ears.

I don't wake the rest of the unit yet. Since we haven't officially been called to duty, it would be a mistake to drag everyone out of their cots when we might not be needed. Cade and I are hardly quiet as we exit the tent we've called home for the past eighteen months, but the other ten men we bunk with don't even stir as we head outside into the darkness.

Immediately, we see the source of the burning smell. On the far side of the base, a tall column of smoke is rising in a great billowing cloud up toward the sky. The base's fire trucks are already positioned by the high chain link fence that borders the encampment, and their hoses are jetting arcs of water over the fence onto the small tents and shanti buildings on the other side.

Normally we would have been told to move along the Afghan locals who chose to set up camp right next to the base. Too dangerous to have potential insurgents sleeping on our doorstep, maybe building bombs in their shelters, strapping themselves up with C4, ready to make martyrs of themselves, but these people were all old women and children. Put out of their homes by bombings, they had no one to protect them and nowhere else to go. The Colonel decided it was permissible for them to stay alongside the base for a week until troops could be spared to relocate them somewhere safer, away from the open gunfire and the burning cars in the streets. Right now, it doesn't look like anyone is going to require relocating, though.

"Holy shit," Cade says under his breath. "What the fuck?"

What the fuck is right. There were maybe two hundred people here when we went to sleep, at least seventy tents and make shift shelters pitched up twenty feet away from the fence. Now every single one of those tents and shelters are on fire, and there are women dashing around, jaws hanging open, low wailing coming from their mouths as they try to find their friends and loved ones.

"*Fuck.* You think those assholes came down here and set fire to their own people's tents? Why the fuck would they do that?" Cade covers his mouth with his hand, frowning at the scene unfolding before his eyes.

A woman stumbles out from a tent close by, howling in pain. She's on fire, the long material of her clothing engulfed in flames that lick at her body, rising upward as she runs in the direction of the fire trucks. The guys douse her with water, putting the flames out, but she doesn't stop howling. It's the most ungodly, terrible thing I've ever heard. I won't be able to free myself of the sights, sounds, and smells of this night for a very, very long time.

The radio I carry on my hip emits a burst of static, which I barely notice. Cade has to take it off my belt and place it in my hand before I realize that Richter, our platoon leader, is barking out orders to me and I haven't answered him yet.

"—can see your ass from where I'm standing, Squad Leader. Answer your damn radio!"

I hold the radio up to my mouth, still blinking at the fire. At the tents that are on fire. At the *people* that are on fire. "Yes, sir. Sorry, I hear you. Just a little shocked that the base isn't in full meltdown right now."

"That's what they want. They're up on the hillside. Patrol saw three or four men up on the ridgeline watching through sniper scopes. They want chaos, and we don't aim on giving it to them. Go wake up your men."

"Yes, sir."

"I want those fuckers' heads on sticks, Duke. Go get 'em for me."

"Sir, yes, sir. They'll never see us coming."

"That's what I like to hear."

The radio falls silent, and Cade and I run back to our tent, less dazed now that we have a purpose. I'm whooping and hollering by the time I tug the flap back and duck inside our billet. "All right, assholes, on your feet! On your feet! On your feet! We got work to do." Ten bleary-eyed men are suddenly sitting upright in their bunks, moving automatically as they reach for their boots and their gear. They don't gripe or complain. They're all so used to this that their bodies function instantaneously, performing rote mechanical movements that were drilled into them back in basic training.

By the time everyone has their kit on and the straps of their M4s slung over their necks, my men are wide away and ready to fuck shit up. They live for this stuff. More often than not, they're sitting around, trying not to cook in the Afghan heat. Being called out on a mission is the most exciting thing that can happen any day of the week. Being called out on a mission in the middle of the night is even better.

Normally we'd load up into transports and burn rubber out of base, speeding toward the location of our targets, but this time we're on foot. The hillside that flanks the base was considered a major security risk by the higher ups when they were considering where to plant our three-thousand-strong camp, but in the end their concerns were overruled by General Lockwood, who felt the location—close to four hotspots in the near by vicinity, along with the fact that it is only a ninety minute drive to Camp Leatherneck—out weighed the risk that it would be on lower ground and subject to an increased chance of attack.

The knife-edge sharp ridgeline to the west rises up into the night. It's clear, no cloud cover, and neither the light coming from the base behind us or the fire beyond can dampen the blanket of stars suspended over our heads, shining bright. Cade's a reasonably tall guy, is only a couple inches shorter than me, and he's a broad motherfucker, yet as we navigate our way around the back of the ridge, ducked low to the ground, trying to stay out of sight, the guy doesn't make a goddamn sound. None of my men do. For a brief, twisted moment I'm proud that they're such well trained killing machines.

The slog up the four hundred meter slope shouldn't take us as long as it does, but our cover will be blown if we don't tread carefully at this point. When we come close to topping the hill, I send the newest, youngest recruit, Atherton, up ahead to scope out the situation. The rest of us crouch in the dark, breathing quietly, the warmed metal of our guns pressed against our chests, listening to the sound of our hearts slamming in our chests as we wait for him to return and tell us what he's seen.

Three minutes pass by. Below us, a loud splintering, cracking sound rips through the night, and a ball of fire boils up toward the sky, casting long shadows behind us as it flares. "The *fuck* was that?" Cade hisses.

I stare down at the camp, narrowing my eyes, trying to figure that out for myself. The swell of flames from the initial explosion dies back, and it's clear to see it originated on the other side of the camp's fencing, where the Afghani women and children were camped out. Not our fuel supplies then. But whoever sparked that thing must have had access to a huge quantity of accelerant. How the fuck did they manage to get that through the checkpoint? And was it meant to blow inside the refugee camp, or inside *our* camp?

Cade shakes his head, chewing on something between his front teeth. "This is absolute bullshit. Those people came to us for help. They were camped right next to us, for fuck's sake. How could this happen?"

I keep my mouth shut. I'm about to tell him to do the same but Atherton emerges out of the darkness, face as white as a sheet, and my focus turns to him. "Well? Who's up there?"

Atherton shakes his head. "No one. Well, four men, but they're all dead. Their hands..." He shivers. "Their hands have been glued to their rifles. Their eyelids are glued open too. They've all been shot in the head. They're...they're *ours*."

"Ours?" My stomach dips, like I'm on a rollercoaster and I've just been rocketed down a steep drop. "US soldiers?"

Atherton nods. He looks like he's about to pass the fuck out. "I don't recognize them. I haven't been here long, though. Could be they're from our platoon. Could be they're from another camp."

"We have to get up there," Cade snaps. A rumble of agreement goes around the other men.

"We can't."

Cade looks horrified. "What do you mean, *we can't*? They're our men. Our *brothers*. We can't just leave them there."

"Why would they leave them up on the ridgeline with their hands glued to their weapons and their eyes glued open, Cade? There's only one reason: they left them there for us to find. They know we patrol this hillside religiously. Daily. *Hourly* sometimes. I have no idea why they want us up there at the top of the hill, but they're trying to draw us there."

"If it were a trap, why wouldn't they have killed me when I just went up there to recon the area?" Atherton asks.

Cade answers on my behalf. He looks like he's seen the truth in my logic now. "Because you're one guy. If they pick you off, then the rest of us head back down and report what's happened. If you come back here, tell us what you've seen, rile us all up and we go charging up there to get our men, they can pull the trigger and kill twelve of us. They're playing it smart."

This reasoning isn't enough to stop my men from wanting to barrel up there to get our guys back, even though they know it's the truth. Most of them develop hard, stony-faced expressions as I order them to march back down to camp. Halfway there, I radio back to Richter and tell him what we found. I can hear the rage coloring his voice. He tells me fifty-three of the Afghani women are dead, along with thirteen of the kids. As we approach the camp, we can see their lifeless bodies lined up in rows along the fence line. Worse, we can *smell* their bodies.

In the morning, the sun, white and cold somehow, peeks over distant mountains much steeper and foreboding than our little hill. A team of marines from Leatherneck report four of their men are missing, and at oh eight hundred hours, an IED blows the top of the ridgeline, creating a crater sixty meters across, sending rocks and boulders raining down on the camp and into the valley.

They obviously grew tired of waiting for us to go up there.

REBEL

I wake up in the night, sweating. Sophia is already awake, staring at the ceiling, worrying her bottom lip between her teeth. I'm hardly surprised. She's so wound up right now that I'd be shocked if she's slept at all. I don't know if she's realized I'm conscious yet. She just lies there, staring up at the ceiling, not fidgeting or moving an inch. I blow out a deep breath, shifting over onto my side.

"You were having a bad dream," she whispers.

"Yeah," I whisper back.

She says nothing more about the fact that I must have been tossing and turning, which I love her for. I don't really feel like talking about Afghanistan. I especially don't want to talk about that night, when it seemed like the whole world was enveloped in death.

"Cade was in prison," she says.

I'm mildly shocked by this statement. "He was. For nine months."

"Nine months isn't very long. What did he do?"

"*Nothing.*" The word is heavy on my tongue, weighty and painful, and also true. Cade didn't do anything to land himself in Chino, but he took the time and did it without complaining. I will always owe him a debt for that. "This isn't the first time the club's been watched by a federal agency. The ATF were interested in us once before, a couple of years back, but they couldn't pin anything on us so they picked up Cade for possession of an unlicensed weapon. It was stupid. *I* was the one carrying the gun. We were in a car, and they pulled us over. Cade grabbed the thing from me before I could stop him. We were on our way to meet an informant who claimed they had information about Laura, and Cade told me I had to go. I had to make the meeting, otherwise the guy would be in the wind and we'd never find out if his information was legit. So they arrested him, took him in, and I couldn't do a fucking thing about it. Took my uncle nine months to get him out of that place. The wardens were trying to make him talk on the inside. They locked away in the SHU for months on end. Refused to let him have visitors or talk to his lawyers. Eventually they couldn't keep hold of him, though. They let him go, and Cade came home."

Those were hard months. Knowing that he was shut away because of me was fucking shitty, but knowing that the information had lead to a dead end and he was serving time for no reason was a bitter pill to swallow. Next to me, Sophia cups her hands over something on her stomach, something round and shiny—one of my snow globes. I don't need to ask which one it is; I already know it's the one from Chicago. Has to be. I reach out, skimming my fingers over the cool surface of the glass globe. Sophia's never asked me about my snow globes—this one in particular—though I know it plays on her mind. She's too smart; she knows there's a story there, given the fact that I keep it separate on its own on my desk. I'm not ready to offer that story up voluntarily yet, however, so I take the plastic and glass from her and set it down on the bedside table next to her. Tiny flakes of white swirl inside the globe, falling silently on the Willis Tower, 900 North Michigan and the Lake Point Tower, barely visible in the thick darkness of the room.

After a while, she asks, "Who's Zeth Mayfair?"

In all honesty, I haven't thought about that name in a long time.

Cade's mentioned him a number of times since he got out of jail, but he's been a peripheral player, someone who hasn't affected our daily lives here in New Mexico. "He's a friend of Cade's. Kind of. He works for a guy in Seattle, a guy we suspect has started to trade in women."

"You think he might know something about Laura? The guy he works for?"

"No. Charlie Holsan's only just starting to dip his toes into that shit. Cade thinks it might be a good idea to talk to his friend, though, see if we can convince him to question his boss about any girls he might have heard about going missing a few years back."

"And you don't think it's a good idea?"

I shake my head. "My cousin works for this guy, too. It's messy. We went to see Michael a while back and stormed over there to Charlie's place but he managed to talk us down. We didn't end up seeing him. Since then I've had time to look into Holsan. He's fucking crazy, a real nasty piece of work. It would be a mistake to confront him about selling girls. And this Zeth guy doesn't seem to have anything to do with that side of Holsan's business, so it's unlikely he can get information from him anyway. Better to just watch and wait, see what happens."

Sophia makes a soft, *mmhhh*ing sound. "Cade obviously feels differently. That's why he has a whole dossier on the guy in your office?"

"Yeah. Maybe." I could explain to her that Cade's just going through the motions now, but it's too painful to admit out loud, even to myself. Laura's been gone for so long that the possibility of ever finding her and bringing her home seems remote. I'm nearly positive that Cade thinks his sister is dead. It's easier for him to believe that. If she's dead, she's not being raped repeatedly, over and over again. She's not being abused and tortured. She's not in pain and suffering because we can't fucking find her anywhere on the surface of this godforsaken planet.

Sophia rolls onto her side, facing me. "I've been lying here for the past few hours, trying to decide if I should call the cops," she says quietly. "If the police got involved, if they knew Ramirez has my father, they could storm the farmhouse and get him out of there before they could do anything to harm him."

"*God*, Sophia—"

"But then I realized that there's no way to get the authorities involved without implicating you in my kidnapping. They'd dig and discover something about the Widow Makers that would land you or Cade in trouble, not to mention the other guys. So I just lay here in the dark, trying to think of a way out of this situation, trying not to resent you because of it, and I've been so angry, Jamie. So fucking angry, I could taste it, and I didn't like how it made me feel."

She has every right to be angry. It would be a fucking miracle if she wasn't. I asked her to stay here to help put Ramirez away; I asked her to testify, but Hector turning up on our doorstep, moving himself and his whole goddamn crew into town, less than four miles away, really threw a spanner in the works. He made it fucking personal. He threatened her, and the time for legal justice came and went. Instead, I've been holding my breath, waiting for Ramirez to make the first move, and that hasn't done anyone any favors. "And what about now?" I whisper. "Are you still angry?"

She nods, tears welling in her eyes. "Yes. But I don't want to be. I just want it to go away. I want my dad to be safe and sound back in Seattle. I want somehow for this all to be okay. Can you tell me that it will? Can you ease my mind? Because right now I'm teetering on the edge of a nervous breakdown, and I'm pretty sure I'm about to lose my balance."

Slowly, I brush the loose strands of hair out of her face that have escaped her messy ponytail. She closes her eyes, her eyelashes nothing more than the suggestion of black smudges against her cheeks in the darkness. "I can't promise you anything, sugar. I wish I could, but I can't. It would be unfair to lie. What I can tell you is that I'm going to do absolutely everything I can to make sure this doesn't end in disaster. I'll sacrifice everything I have to make sure your father gets back to Seattle, and I'll bury anyone who tries to prevent that from happening. All I can promise you is my best. And in case you haven't noticed—" I place a feather-light kiss on the end of her nose, "—I'm kind of a badass. So don't fret yourself, beautiful girl." I let the Louisiana creep into my voice as I speak, and a tiny smile plays over Sophia's lips.

"You *are* kind of a badass. But you're also a jerk," she informs me.

I slide my hand underneath her head so I can wrap my arm around her, pulling her to me. "Do you love me?" I whisper.

She speaks so softly. So quietly. Like she's almost afraid I might hear her. "Yes. I love you so much."

I kiss her temple. "Good."

"Do *you* love *me*?"

"So much it scares the shit out of me sometimes," I whisper. And that's the god's honest truth. I care about this woman so much. Too much, I think. If I didn't care about her one way or the other, I'd be free to do whatever the hell I pleased around here. I could have launched a Hail Mary, attacking Ramirez in his farmhouse and ending this bullshit months ago. I could have torched the place with everyone inside. I would have had to fight off the memories of all those women and children screaming out in the desert, but I could have done it. With with Sophia here, I have to remember who I am, though. Who I *want* to be. She told me once that I was still a good man, and over the past few months I've found myself craving to be that for her more and more. To be someone good and honest and kind. I thought those days were long gone for me. I've done too much, seen too much, hurt too many people to believe that I could ever go back to being wholesome again. But something about Soph makes me want to fucking try, and it's so goddamn inconvenient that I could weep.

"I don't think you've ever been scared a day in your life," Soph says into the dark. I try to stifle my laughter, but it escapes me, coming out in hard, clipped bitter sounds.

"Oh, I've been afraid. More times than I can count. Any man

who's found himself on the other side of the world, watching his friends get blown up, shooting thirteen-year-old boys because they're about to firebomb a hospital, running around inside sandstone houses, screaming at the top of his lungs, trying to survive, to save other people, to make things right...anyone who claims to have done that and remained unafraid is a fucking liar. *Believe me.*"

Sophia doesn't say anything. I don't think she *knows* what to say. I run my hand up and down her naked back, letting my fingers trace over the soft silkiness of her skin, and I feel her body slowly, unwittingly responding to me. She probably doesn't even realize she's doing it, but her back arches, pressing her breasts up against my chest as she shivers a little.

"Can you do something for me, sugar?" I say.

"Yes. What?"

"Come up here." I turn suddenly, taking her with me, lifting her on top of me as I lay flat on my back. I can feel her everywhere, our bodies flush against one another, hot and slightly sweaty—with summer in full force, that's almost impossible to avoid. I love tasting perspiration on her skin, though. It's sweet and salty at the same time, and the gentle sheen of it on her skin gives her a sexy, flustered look.

Sophia's bottom lip is only inches away from my mouth, plump and deep red, swollen a little, it would seem, from where she's been worrying at it with her teeth.

"I don't want to think about it anymore," she whispers. "It's so exhausting. I just want to feel...I just want to be free of it all. Just for a moment."

"I can do that for you, sugar."

She gives me a wry smile. "You seem pretty sure of yourself."

"I am. I have a proven track record, after all. Would you like me to demonstrate my capabilities?"

She nods silently. I want to bite at the smooth, soft, delicate skin of her neck for some inexplicable reason, hard enough that I leave a mark, but I feel like that kind of foreplay might not be appropriate in these quiet, heavy hours of the morning. I cup her ass in both my hands instead, squeezing slightly, testing my boundaries. Her ass is phenomenal—her curves are perfection in so many ways; she has a butt most Hollywood celebrities would pay good money for. My hands are just big enough to grasp the swell of her toned cheeks. She breathes in sharply when I spread them apart a little, running a finger over her exposed flesh, down, down, toward her pussy.

She's not soaking wet yet, but she will be soon. For now, I stroke my fingers over the soft skin of her pussy lips, enjoying how smooth and responsive she is. I love teasing her from behind like this. Coming from a different angle means our bodies are still crushed together, hers on top of mine, and I can still feel her heart beating against my ribcage, feel her chest rise and fall against me. It's fucking perfect.

My dick is growing harder by the second. Sophia must be able to feel it digging into her as it increases in size, pressing into her belly, demanding attention. I want to push my way inside her so badly. It would be easy enough; I could grab her by her thighs and yank them apart, pull her up a little so we were in the perfect position for me to slam myself home. Where would the fun in that be, though?

No, I need her to be ready for me when I finally sink myself inside her. I need her to want me more than she's ever wanted anything in her whole entire life. Only then will I know I've fucked her right. I kiss her, winding her hair around my free hand, holding on tight so I can control her head. I work my tongue over hers, stroking the inside of her mouth with the tip, tasting her, licking her, making her breath quicken as she writhes on top of me. *Fuck yes.* Gradually, she begins to grind her hips against mine, causing the most intense friction between our bodies, making my dick throb.

My balls are aching like they're about to burn up and ignite from the inside out—they need her hands on them, her wet, hot, perfect mouth—but I can wait. I'm on a mission, and Sophia has no idea what I'll do to accomplish it. "Kneel," I say to her. I pant the word into her open mouth as she moans. "Get up on your knees, Sophia."

She looks at me like she doesn't understand for a second, and then realization dawns on her. "Okay." She straddles me, her beautiful tits bouncing a little as she repositions herself. I can't stop myself from cupping them in my hands, rolling her nipples, my balls aching even more when the delicate pink skin of her areolas tighten, puckering into sensitive buds, just begging me to twist and pinch them. Sophia's back arches when I do this, her chest heaving as she grinds her pussy against my dick. She's definitely much wetter now. My cock is slick with her as she rocks back and forth, and it's almost impossible not to lift her for a second so I can grab hold of my shaft and pull her down on it.

"Fuck, sugar. You're so fucking sexy. I can't take it. Come here." I take hold of her by the hips and I do lift her up a little, but not so I can fuck her. I guide her up my body, pulling her so she has to crawl on her hands and knees up my body. At the same time I slide myself down the bed, and within a second she's kneeling over my face, her pussy slick and glistening, no more than an inch away from my tongue.

"God, Jamie. Fuck, I don't know if I can—"

I know all too well that she *can*. She's been self conscious about me going down on her before, so hovering over my head like this is bound to make her uncomfortable. I want it though. I need it badly. "Sit on my face, Sophia. Be a good prospect and ride my mouth like it's my goddamn dick. Do it now."

She hesitates.

I growl, deep and low in the back of my throat. "If I don't have your clit on my tongue in the next three seconds, I'm going to punish you." So much for avoiding inappropriate foreplay in the silent, heavy hours of the morning. I can't help it, though. I can see every single last pink, delicate, perfect fold, can smell her sweetness, can almost, *almost* taste the saccharine, silkiness of her and I'm about to lose my fucking shit.

"Jamie, I—"

I dig my fingers into her thighs, warning her. I mean it. I really will punish her, and while she'll have an orgasm so powerful she'll probably be bed-ridden for the next twenty-four hours, the things I'll do to her will make her feel far more vulnerable than this. "*One*," I say.

"Please, Jamie. Please, I need you to fuck me," she whimpers.

"*Two*."

"Oh my god, don't," she cries. "Please, please, please. I can't take it!"

"*Three*."

"*Jamie!*"

It's too late now. I gave her a chance to take the easy road. She didn't take it. Now she has to accept the consequences of her misbehavior. I take hold of her by the waist and move her off of me so that she's not kneeling over my face anymore. I'm sad about the change of scenery, but I'll get my own way in a moment. Sophia scrambles, trying to get away, but I snake my arm around her waist and I pin her to the bed. She starts laughing, her fingers trying to prise my arm from around her, but she knows she's got no chance. It's so strange to hear her laughter. Only a few moments ago, it seemed like she was never going to laugh again, and now it's as though the tables have been turned. I'm glad they have. She needs this, if only for a little while. A brief moment where everything is on hold and she can clear her head.

"If you don't let me go right now," she says, "I'm never blowing you again." She can barely keep a straight face as she says this. That's how I know she's lying through her back fucking teeth.

"You wouldn't be able to stop yourself, you love my cock in your mouth."

She shakes her head from side to side, squirming. "Nope. It's the worst. Arggghh, it's the worst!" She dissolves into throaty, gurgling laughter as I tickle her with my left hand, still keeping hold of her with my right. I can't help but laugh too; she thrashes on the bed, her legs kicking frantically as I tease her sides and her belly with my fingertips. Her laughter will transform into something very different in a few short moments. She's going to be begging me to lick her. She's going to be screaming out my name, and I won't oblige her until I know she's going to behave herself in future.

"I'm going to let you go now, Sophia," I tell her. "And I'm going to get something. I'm telling you now, if you move from this bed there will be hell to pay."

She nods, unable to speak, unable to catch her breath properly. "O...okay. I won't. I won't move, I...swear."

I don't trust the little minx, but I have to do it in order to grab the items I've decided I'm going to use on her, so I don't have a choice. I release her and she flops backward onto the mattress, grinning at me. "I didn't think you'd make me smile," she whispers, biting the knuckle on her index finger. "I didn't think I'd be smiling for a very long time. Thank you."

"You might not be thanking me in a minute." I prowl toward the closet and open it up, fetching the coil of rope I've left there on the floor. Sophia's eyes glint, full of fire when she sees what I have in my hand.

"What are you going to do with that?" she asks. I don't answer her. I head into the bathroom, and I come back a second later with my other hand behind my back, hiding the white plastic object I just retrieved so she can't see what it is.

"Jamie?" She says my name as if it's a warning. "Jamie, don't even think about using eyebrow tweezers on my sensitive areas." She blushes a little. "I should have just let you eat me, shouldn't I?"

I give her a slow, sadistic nod. "Yes, ma'am. Yes, you really should." I climb up onto the bed, still hiding the contents of my left hand. "On your stomach," I command. "Better do it right away, or you're gonna make things even worse."

"What if I don't want to?"

"Then we go back to sleep."

"That doesn't sound like it would be too dire a consequence."

"Maybe not. But I won't fuck you for a month. That will be even worse than what I have planned for you now. I'll tease the living shit out of you, I'll get you so close to coming every single day for thirty-one days, and as soon as you're about to tumble over the edge...I'll suddenly remember I have somewhere else I need to be."

Sophia's mouth falls open. She looks horrified. "You wouldn't. That's just cruel."

"*On. Your. Front.*"

"Fine. Have it your way," she says, pouting. "But just so you know, I'm not going to enjoy this on principle."

She will. She really will. She won't be able to deny herself. She rolls onto her front, falling limp like a ragdoll, sulking in the most comical way. I'm smirking on the inside, but on the outside I imagine my expression is pretty severe. This is going to be an experience she won't be forgetting any time soon.

"Spread your legs," I tell her.

She does as I ask, opening her legs wide, and I'm tempted to duck down and bury my tongue in her pussy anyway. That would be cheating, though. I take hold of her ankles and pull them together instead, grabbing the end of the rope and quickly tying a honda knot with one hand, then threading the loop over both of her feet. Jerking it tight, I take her closest hand and guide it behind her back, until she's almost able to touch her own ankles. Perfect.

"Are you about to hog tie me?" Sophia asks.

"Perhaps."

She tenses a little. "I don't know how I feel about that."

I sit back on my haunches, stopping what I'm doing. "Take a moment to decide then." I want her to be thrilled right now. I want her to be filled with adrenalin. I want her heart to be racing. But I sure as hell don't want her to be fucking frightened in any way, shape or form. I would never do anything against her will. If she tells me no, she'll be too freaked out to do this, then I'll untie her and let her go immediately, no two ways about it. I'm not that kind of guy.

A moment passes where Sophia considers her options. After a

full minute of silence, she reaches behind her with her other hand, offering it to me, so they're both resting in the small of her back. "Do it," she whispers. "I want to know what it's like. Show me."

I tie her quickly and efficiently, until her wrists and her ankles are bound together, finishing the job in a matter of seconds. Sophia strains at the ropes, testing them, trying to see if she can escape them. *I* tied the knots, though. No way they're coming loose until I *un*tie them again.

"You're going to beg," I tell her. "You're going to scream. I'm only going to stop what I'm doing if you say *Kansas*, though, Sophia. Got it?"

"Yes."

"Say it. Say it, so you'll remember."

Sophia twists on the bed, making soft whimpering sounds. "Kansas," she says breathlessly.

"Good girl." I dive right in. I don't give her time to overthink anything or worry about what I'm going to do to her. I pick her up— she weighs next to nothing after all—and I spin her over, holding her up by her waist. She gasps, her body bucking as she tries fruitlessly to maintain her balance, but she's not going to be able to do that. She's going to have to rely on me to keep her stable, and I'm only going to do that if she lets me have my way with her. I lay down on my back and I lower her on top of me, her feet and hands tied behind her back; her knees are the only part of her body that make contact with the mattress. She's almost back in the same kneeling position she was in before, hovering over me. I hold onto her by the ankles, providing a stable platform for her to rest her weight.

"Fuck, Jamie. Fuck you," Sophia pants. "You're going to do it anyway, aren't you?"

"Fuck yeah I am. I told you, sugar. I want you riding my face like it's my goddamn cock." I shift down in between her open legs, and she can't buck or wriggle away. She has to stay very still or risk toppling sideways off the bed.

"Look at me," I tell her. She looks down the length of her body, her chest heaving, her tits rising and falling as she hyperventilates, and my cock starts throbbing again. It feels like I'm about to blow my load everywhere, and she hasn't even touched me. Fuck, *I* haven't even touched myself yet. Sophia makes eye contact with me as I slide my tongue out of my mouth and gently flick her clit with it.

"Shit," she hisses. "Oh my god." She blinks, her eyelids fluttering, but she doesn't close her eyes. She watches me as I've asked her to. Slowly, I work the tip of my tongue back and forth, applying just the right amount of pressure to kick things off. Sophia gasps for air like she's a woman drowning.

She tastes fucking incredible. There's something about eating pussy. It's always been one of my favorite parts of sex, but eating Sophia's pussy is a whole different ball game. She doesn't have one of those barely-there pussies, everything neatly tucked away. She has pussy lips, and I fucking love sucking on them. Teasing them. Teasing her everywhere—over her clit, over the slick, wet entrance to her pussy, down, over her asshole. Everywhere.

Sophia's soon shaking, trembling, her whole body vibrating as I work my magic. She makes frantic, desperate sounds as I suck gently on her clitoris, laving my tongue up and down quickly with the very tip of my tongue again.

"Fuck. Holy shit, Jamie. This is...this is..."

Driving her fucking wild. I can tell by how wet she is. It's turning me on like crazy every time the sweet, glossiness of her pussy hits my tongue. She shied away from it when I asked her just now, but it's not long before she's rocking as best she can against my mouth, grinding her hips, riding me just like I wanted her to. She loses herself, completely withdrawn as she ascends toward her climax. I hold onto her tight, sucking, licking, swirling my tongue, as she grows more and more frenzied. Her tits bounce like crazy as she rocks, and it's a miracle I'm not coming all over myself as she suddenly screams, head tipped back, chest proud, and she comes hard in my mouth.

"Oh my god! Oh my god!" She repeats this over and over as she comes, her body still shaking. I hold onto her tight, making sure she doesn't go anywhere as I continue to flick my tongue against her overly sensitive clit. "Shit, Jamie. Shit. Stop, please! *Kansas, Kansas, Kansas!*"

I probably wouldn't stop if not for the safe word; it's far too much fun watching her flip her shit. I need her to trust me, though. I need her to feel safe, so I stop.

Quickly I place her down on her stomach and untie her hands and feet. She's boneless, unable to move as I spin her over onto her front and retie just her hands this time.

The item I collected from the bathroom has tumbled to the floor. I pick it up and hold it so she can finally see it. Her eyes, dazed and glazed over one second, are suddenly round and alert the next. "You are *not* using an electric toothbrush on me, Jamie."

"Oh, but I am." I turn it on, and Sophia pales a little at the high-pitched whir.

"I can't take it. My clit will literally fall of my body."

"I bet it won't. I bet you'll enjoy it an awful lot. Open your legs, Sophia. Open them for me and I won't have to go find another toy to tease you with after this one."

She swears under her breath. "Remember. *Kansas*," she says, and then she opens her legs. She's soaking wet. If she weren't I might have rethought the toothbrush, but it won't make her sore if she's like this. It'll send her into fucking outer space, and I will have the pleasure of watching that happen.

Carefully, I apply the vibrating end of the toothbrush against her clit, and Sophia's hips rise as her eyes roll back into her head. She's amazing. She's so fucking beautiful. I watch for the next three minutes as she falls apart, and I take hold of my dick when she comes, finally stroking it, squeezing hard as she screams and pants. Her orgasms are impressive, consuming things.

I let her catch her breath before I allow myself to fuck her. Her eyes snap open, her lips slightly parted when she feels me slide inside. "God, Jamie," she whispers.

"Wanna call Kansas?" I ask.

"No. No way." She loops her bound hands over my head and hugs me to her. I fuck her with the force of a derailed freight train. After so much teasing, my dick is so sensitive, so hard, so ready to fuck that I have to fight off my own orgasm twice before I give in. Sophia's thighs tighten around me, holding me deep inside her, my balls covered in her come, and I explode.

When it's over, when we're both spent and exhausted, our bodies tangled up in each others, our lips numb from the thousands of kisses we rain down on each other's skin, we sleep like the dead. And I don't think either of us minds.

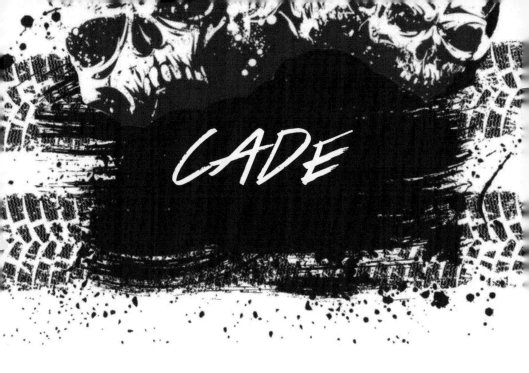

CADE

I've never really wanted to hit a woman before I met Agent Denise Lowell. A part of me still cringes away from the idea, the southern gentleman in me skirting away from the concept of planting a right hook squarely into the jaw of a five-foot-five blonde, but when I see her getting out of a black sedan on the other side of the compound fence, I find my fingers curling in on themselves, forming fists.

She's wearing aviators and a pale grey pant suit that screams power, her tailored white shirt tucked in at the waist. A tall, cookie-cutter generic dude gets out of the passenger seat, also wearing sunglasses, also suited, but nothing about *him* screams power. There's no time to let Jamie know we have guests. I send Carnie a warning glance, carefully suggesting with my eyes that he should run up to the cabin immediately and let our boss know what's going down. I, on the other hand, walk slowly toward the gate with my hands shoved into my pockets, all evidence of my terrible mood hidden from sight while I feign indifference over the fact that the DEA are on our fucking doorstep.

Lowell's already got her badge out and is holding it up for me to see, sunlight glinting off the polished metal. "Hello, Mr. Preston. Glad we finally get to meet properly."

I think she wants me to be impressed that she knows who I am. Like maybe I should be intimidated or something. I was stationed in Kabul and Helmand Province though, so this bitch had better try harder. "Dee Dee. I wish I could say the feeling was mutual. It isn't, though. What can I do for you?"

"I need to speak with Rebel. Is he here?" She's pressed her mouth into a pinched line, the edges of her lips turning white. I don't think she liked the whole Dee Dee thing.

"I don't know where he is. We don't keep a tracking collar on him. I'm sure *you'd* like to, though, right?"

Lowell flips her aviators up, resting them on top of her head. Squinting, she looks off over her shoulder into the flat, dry, dustiness of the desert, her face in profile as she muses over my words. She'd be a pretty attractive woman if only she wasn't such a raging bitch. "I'm fully aware that your club isn't happy about my presence here in Freemantle, Cade. I'm also aware that you and your friend Jamie have some serious problems with authority. The Widow Makers run guns. You guys run drugs, too. You're the least of my concerns, though. I'm more worried about the outside influences you've attracted into town, and what it is they might be up to here. I need Hector Ramirez in jail or back in fucking Mexico. Either way, I can't accomplish this without evidence, and with no one willing to give up information they have on him, that's making my job really hard."

"Mmm. I don't really know many people that would want to make your job easy for you, Dee Dee. You don't exactly ingratiate yourself with folks. Not as far as I can tell anyways."

She sends a withering look my way. I'm sure she's had dudes' balls retracting inside their bodies with that look. "I'm not in the business of making friends. I'm in the business of ensuring that the streets of this country are safe. If I have to rub a few undesirables up the wrong way in order to achieve that, then I say all the better."

"Jamie's not going to help you. He doesn't have anything that can put Ramirez away. If he did, he would have brought it to you a long time ago." This is the absolute God's honest truth. I snagged the camera footage of Sophia being dragged into the side street by Raphael last year, but that's literally all it shows. She's on the street one minute, Ryan appears the next, and then Raphael is having both of them dragged kicking and screaming into the alleyway after that. Maybe that's enough to arrest Hector with, but he's a smart motherfucker. He wasn't actually there when Ryan was murdered.

The only real evidence Jamie has against Ramirez is a person—Sophia—and there's no way he's willing to put her at risk. Not now. He was all for it back when we bought her from Julio, but now that they're an item it's pretty much impossible. He knows how unsafe it would be for her and her family.

There are plenty of files sitting in Jamie's office that contain incriminating information about the Mexican cartel boss, but there's nothing damaging enough to put him away. Ramirez always has other people to do his dirty work for him. Lowell shrugs her shoulders, pouting a little. "Well, I'd like to hear that from his mouth."

"And like I said, I don't know where he is."

Lowell arranges her face into an ugly smile. She points over my shoulder, behind me. "Funny that. I believe I can see him heading this way even as we speak."

I turn and see that she's right. Jamie's heading down the hill from his cabin, bee-lining for us at a frightening speed. He looks seriously pissed off. Carnie's hot on his heels, following after him.

I grin back at Lowell. "Good luck, lady." I take three large steps back to make room for Rebel as he pitches up in front of the compound gate, breathing heavily. "I didn't think the DEA paid social visits," he says.

"Oh, we do. Only when we're feeling magnanimous, though. Only for people we take a *special* interest in."

"And how do we remove ourselves from your special interest list,

Denise? We don't really like people showing up here unannounced. It makes our club members...twitchy."

"Oh, I'm sure you have nothing to be twitchy about. Right?"

I hang back, waiting to see how Jamie plans on handling this situation. He's way more diplomatic than I am normally, but can tell by the way he charged down the hill toward us that he isn't in the mood to be cordial today. "Cut the shit," he snaps. "What do you want?"

Lowell glances at her partner, who appears to be just about as vacant and useless as a human being can be and still qualify for the title. She sighs heavily, shoving her thumbs into the waistband of her dress pants. "I just want to do the right thing. I just want Hector Ramirez to be handled in the correct way. Now, I hear from multiple sources that you're a good guy. That you like to do the right thing too. You were deployed out in Afghanistan for two tours, weren't you? How does a guy go from serving his country to breaking her laws in such a short space of time?"

"If putting Ramirez away is your primary focus, Denise, maybe you should spend more time pursing that goal instead of Googling my ass. I'm sure that would be far more productive use of tax payers' resources and effort."

Lowell scowls. "I have minions who do my Googling for me. It's really no skin off my nose. And besides, I get the feeling that leaning on you will get me Ramirez in the end. Call it intuition."

"You can call it whatever the fuck you want. Are we done here?"

"That depends on whether you want to talk to me about your uncle," Lowell says. Jamie's hands twitch, but aside from that he shows no sign of annoyance or recognition.

"I don't have any uncles."

"But you did, didn't you? Your uncle Ryan was murdered last year. He was found down a back alley in Seattle. Didn't take much digging to discover he was presiding over a murder trial that Hector Ramirez was being prosecuted for. Ryan ended up dead, and the case was dropped. I found that highly coincidental."

Jamie folds his arms across his chest, staring Lowell down through the wrought iron bars of the compound fence. "I hadn't spoken to Ryan in years. I had no idea he was involved with Ramirez. Now if you'll excuse me, I have some business to take care of."

"Tattoo shop business? Or gun running business?" Lowell smiles a sickly sweet, innocent smile that makes my fucking teeth itch. I'm sure it has an even more unpleasant effect on Jamie, since he's standing that much closer and she's aiming the smile at him. He takes three deliberate, slow steps toward the gate and stops right in front of her.

"*Fuck. You. Denise.*" With that he turns around and walks away from her, heading in the direction of the workshop and barn. Lowell watches him go, eyes slightly narrowed, thumbs still tucked into her waistband. She only turns away when Jamie's disappeared into the building beyond and she can't drill holes into the back of his head anymore.

"We'll be back," she says lightly; I'm assuming she's talking to me, but who the fuck knows? Who the fuck *cares*? She can come back here as many times as she likes. She'll never find guns here. She'll never find drugs. It would take her twenty years to get inside Jamie's office, and even when she did, she'd only find a few burnt out servers and three destroyed hard drives.

There's only one thing Agent Denise Lowell might come across that could cause us problems, and that's Sophia. Hopefully, that will never come to fruition. Hopefully Lowell never lays eyes on the girl again, otherwise our shit will seriously be fucked up, and my best friend will likely be arrested and sentenced to life imprisonment.

Better hope and pray it doesn't come to that. "You should get a pet, y'know," I tell Lowell. "It'd be calming. Give you a reason to actually go home at night."

She angles her head, glaring at me. "Thanks for the concern, Preston, but I have enough on my hands as it is. I don't need a dog under foot, pissing and shitting all over the place when I have *you*."

SOPHIA

"Pack a bag."

I nearly jump out of my skin when I hear Jamie's voice behind me. I didn't notice him entering the clubhouse. Ever since Carnie burst into the cabin and told us about our DEA guests, I've been holding my breath, worrying about what's going to happen if Lowell decides she wants to come on in and make trouble. A part of me has been ready to duck out of the back exit and jump on my bike, burn off down the dirt road that leads back toward civilization, head away from the compound and from my friends here simply so that my presence doesn't cause issues. Carnie told me to *'stay the fuck here'* though, and despite how badly I wanted to run, I managed to do as I was told, keeping out of sight until the DEA cars sped off down the long dirt track back in the direction of town. Now, down in the compound, Jamie looks like he's about to go on a killing spree. My stomach is doing backflips as he storms across the clubhouse toward me. "What?"

"Pack a bag. We need to get out of here."

I can't be hearing him right. Surely he can't actually be suggesting we leave Freemantle? "I can't go anywhere, Jamie. I'm not leaving my dad here."

He makes a frustrated growling sound; when he reaches me he takes hold of me by the wrist, pulling me toward the exit. "We have six days, sugar. Six days before anything bad happens to your father. That gives us six days to go figure this shit and get our asses back here."

"You're trusting Ramirez to stick to his word? Are you *mad*?" He has to be if he's being even remotely serious right now.

Steel and ice flashes in his eyes. The cold blue of his irises seems even colder as he sighs, guiding me outside. "Sophia. I don't trust him, no, but he's not going to do anything, believe me. He wants to be holding the pliers when it comes down to it, and he wants an audience. Ramirez loves to fuck with people. He's not going to break the rules to his own game. Not when it's so much more satisfying to have us scrambling, trying to figure this out."

A sinking feeling low in my gut tells me this logic is madness. I want to yank my arm free and confront him in the middle of the court yard, ask him if he's really being this naïve, but Shay and Keeler are standing in front of the workshop, watching us, and the last thing I want or need is Shay cat calling at us as we fight in front of them. I'm liable to try and claw her eyeballs out of her head.

"Where the hell do you think we're going to go?" I hiss. "You told me when we first met that Maria Rosa's the only person crazy enough to go up against Hector, and in case you haven't noticed we've had her locked in a fucking basement for the past six months."

In the distance, plumes of orange dust rise up from the horizon— Lowell and her DEA friends still high tailing it back to their base. Jamie heads in the direction of the cabin, anger pouring off of him in palpable waves. "She was our best bet, sure. She wasn't our *only* bet, though. There's someone else."

I don't like the sound of this someone else. Anyone powerful enough to take on the Los Oscuros cartel has to be seriously dangerous themselves, and undoubtedly into some really fucked up, illegal activity. "Who, Jamie? Who the hell are you talking about?

And why am I really worried right now?"

He slows, his urgency abating ever so slightly. Letting go of my arm, he scrubs his hands over his face, groaning. "Perez," he says. "Julio Perez."

My head starts spinning in the most disconcerting way. *"Julio Perez*? The man you had collect me from Ramirez? The man who sells women? The man you despise?" I can't comprehend what's going on in Jamie's head right now. He has to be desperate to even consider this move. He hasn't told me much about the tense nature of the relationship he shares with Perez, but I do know he has something on him. Something bad. Information on one of those hard drives that could put Perez away for a really long time. The last time they met, when Jamie came and took me from him in the middle of the night, Julio swore he was going to find a way to free himself from Jamie, and at the time I got the distinct impression shooting him in the back of the head wasn't something Perez had ruled out.

"He's not likely to be too happy about doing me a favor," Jamie says through gritted teeth. "He hates me, but he hates Hector more. Los Oscuros poses direct competition to both his skin trade and his drug trafficking. If he can get Ramirez out of the picture, his income goes through the roof, especially since he has connections in Mexico."

"But he's not going to do anything that gives you more leverage over him. That's just madness, Jamie. He's gonna tell you to go fuck yourself."

"We have a twelve hour ride ahead of us. I'll have figured out that part by the time we get there."

"Oh god." This whole thing sounds like a horrible idea.

"Don't freak out. It's going to be fine," Jamie says. But I can tell from the tightness in his voice that he's not a hundred percent sure it will be.

Twelve hours is a seriously long time to sit on a motorcycle. It's better now that I'm actually riding my own bike and I'm not perched on the back of Jamie's, but still. Sore shoulders. Sore back. Sore hips. Sore ass. Every part of my body is humming with pain. We stop to stretch our legs and get gas, but it's not enough; the dull ache returns within ten minutes of being back on my Ducati, and all I can think about is blasting my skin with a hot shower and falling asleep in a soft bed.

The only thing that keeps me from complaining is the thought of Dad, asleep on a cold, damp floor, no hot showers or soft beds for him. He's probably wondering what the hell happened to land him in this predicament. Has Ramirez spilled the beans about me? Has he told my father I'm shacked up with an outlaw, the leader of a motorcycle club that has one boot firmly planted in highly illegal activities, the other shoved up the Los Oscuros cartel's ass?

I really fucking hope not—no matter how much I've let my family down, I don't want them thinking badly of me, ironic though that may be. It seems as though Hector delights in causing hurt wherever he goes, though. He's probably taken great pleasure in showing my dad what a miscreant his daughter has become.

It's dark when we cross the border into California. There are no streetlights or cars on the roads. The sky overhead is cloudless and vast, a myriad of stars bowed from horizon to horizon, clustered so thick and shining so bright that it takes my breath away as I follow the constant red glow of Jamie's tail light up ahead. We ride for another hour through the night before he pulls off the highway at a dingy looking motel and parks up out front. I pull in beside him, killing the engine on the Ducati, trying not to groan as I sit up straight, stretching out my back.

"Are we stopping here?" I ask.

492

Jamie nods. "We'll head on over to Julio's place first thing. If we come charging out of the desert at this time of night, his men will shoot us on the spot. Better they can't use the dark as an excuse for any accidents they might try to instigate."

Fucking perfect. So there's a chance we might end up dead. I guess I knew that when we set off. Julio's a piece of shit, and from the high fences and the razor wire I saw circling his home when I was there last, it's pretty clear he doesn't take too kindly to uninvited guests. Jamie climbs off his bike and heads into the motel; the building itself has been painted a rather gaudy color of pink, and there appears to be a Star of David painted above each and every single one of the entrances to the rooms. A flickering sign above the reception reads: *Queen Of Hearts Motel*, though it seems that half of the letters only work half of the time.

Jamie's gone for five minutes. When he returns, he has a key in his hand and a sour look on his face.

"That was like pulling teeth," he says. "The old guy in there is ancient. He had a fucking sawn off shot gun leaning against the wall behind his desk."

I try and figure out if this makes me feel safer or even more concerned for our wellbeing, but I can't decide. We both take our small backpacks up to the room on the second floor the ancient guy allocated us, which overlooks a drained swimming pool full of trash and rotting leaves, and Jamie pretends not to notice the craters in the building's plasterwork that can only have been created by gunshots. Shotgun blasts by the looks of things. I know he sees them, though.

Inside our room, Jamie tosses his bag down on one of the beds and starts typing something into his phone. After a second he frowns, then holds his cell up for me to see the screen

'Three teenagers attacked in rural Queen Of Hearts Motel. Girl's mother shot dead in pool by elderly desk clerk.' There's a black and white picture of a pool underneath the tagline, the same pool that sits in the yard outside our room, except in the photograph it's full

of water, and there's a woman floating face down in the middle of it. The article shows a date two years ago.

"Seems we can't escape trouble." Jamie lets out a deep breath. He takes me in his arms and immediately works his way underneath the light jacket and the t-shirt I wore to ride in. "I need to ask you something," he says. "And this is the worst fucking time for me to ask this, but I'm sick and tired of waiting."

I angle my head, tilting it to one side, narrowing my eyes at him, trying to figure out what he's talking about. "Waiting for what?"

"For this." Jamie reaches into the back pocket of his jeans and takes out something small and round and shiny. I don't give myself time to look at it properly. I'm instantly panicked. Terrified. I screw my eyes shut, trying to back away from him.

"Oh, no, you fucking don't." He winds an arm around my waist, holding onto me tight, stopping me in my tracks. "What the hell d'you think you're doing, missy?"

"God, Jamie. Not now. I don't—I can't even—" I can't even *think* straight right now, but Jamie won't let me finish my sentence. He places a finger over my lips, cutting me off.

"Open your eyes, silly girl."

"I don't want to." I've just ridden a motorcycle across three states. My whole life is in turmoil, upside down and inside out, and I feel like I'm about to really lose it. I can't open my eyes. If I do, I'll see what he's holding in his hand, and I won't be able to take it. It'll be too much, too overwhelming, too scary, and I'll end up doing something stupid.

Jamie presses his lips against my forehead, his mouth hot and pliable as he kisses me gently. "Yes, you can. You've done much harder things. You survived being kidnapped. You made it through three days at my father's house. You've lived with a biker gang for the past six months. You defended yourself against a man who wanted to do you harm, and you helped me bury him. All of those things were harder than this."

I shake my head, still trying to wriggle free of his grasp. "Jamie, this—I can't do this now. It's not the right time."

"That's my point. There won't *ever* be a good time." He sighs heavily. His grip loosens, releasing me ever so slightly, but I can tell he doesn't want to. "Please, Soph. Don't run away from this. You can see what I have in my hand and you can listen to what I have to say, and you can shoot me down if you like. Or you can do the opposite. But don't just fucking run away from it. I know you better than that. You're going to feel shitty if you don't deal with this."

He's right. I will feel shitty, I know I will, but that doesn't stop my heart from pounding away like a jackhammer inside my chest. My head feels like it's too full, so much pressure building inside it, and I don't know what to do. It's as though it could explode at any moment. Slowly, cautiously, I open my eyes. I make sure to look up at him—that feels safe enough, though it really isn't. When I see him and the open, hopeful look on his face, I know I won't be able to escape this.

"I'm not going to get down on one knee, sugar, and I was born in Louisiana. I was taught there was a proper way to do this kind of thing, so you should know how much it pains me to shirk tradition. But I know it's not what you want.

"So this is just me telling you that I want you to be my wife. Asking you if you would do me the greatest of honors. I want to be your husband. I've never wanted anything so much in my life." He blows out a deep breath, both his eyebrows rising up his forehead. "You know, I thought when I got out of the army, the hell I'd been living through was over. Shitty thing was, it had only just begun. The moment Laura went missing, everything got so fucked up. I never for a second thought something like this would happen."

"Something like this?"

"Something huge. Something special. Something important. I didn't want to love you, Soph. Fuck, I did everything I could to try and prevent that from happening, but this thing between us was out of control before I even saw it coming. I didn't stand a chance. And neither did you. You can't fucking deny it."

I can't deny it. I'd like to. It would be so convenient to tell him he's wrong, and while I do love him, I don't think we're in that place yet. The trouble is, I know we *are* in that place. I could marry him tomorrow and it would feel so right. The mere thought of him calling me his wife makes my insides feel like they're on fire, my veins racing with adrenalin. But the way things are right now...I don't know. It would be dangerous to commit to a promise like this.

"Tell me what you're thinking?" He rests his forehead against mine, his eyes only a few inches away, his lips so close I can almost feel them on me. "I can't tell you how all of your concerns are pointless and invalid if you won't tell me what they are."

"I only have one," I whisper.

"Say it."

"Getting married is something I've dreamed of since I was a little girl. I know you probably think that's stupid, but I couldn't help it. And in all of my daydreams about falling in love and getting married, my father has always walked me down the aisle. My mother has always done my hair for me. She's always been there, crying in the pews. And my sister has always been my maid of honor. We fight like cat and dog, and we rarely see eye to eye, but I love her. I've always known I'd ask her to be there for me when the time came. And now, my father's being held hostage and my mom and sister think I'm dead. I can't get married without them, Jamie, I just can't."

He cups my face in his hands. "Okay, then. We won't get married unless your family can be there. I can agree to that." He kisses me lightly, his mouth finding mine, his tongue skating between his lips to graze against me, and a deep, penetrating wave of fear rises inside me. I've never been a *what-if* person, but there are so many of the cursed things hounding me right now. What if we can't get Julio to help us? What if Hector kills my father? What if I have to hand myself over to the cartel in order to save him? But worse still, what if we *do* manage to free my father but he wants nothing to do with me anymore? What if he never wants to lay eyes on me again, let alone give me away to the man who technically kidnapped me and refused to set me free?

Jamie brushes his fingers along my jawbone, humming softly at the back of his throat. "I know what you're thinking, sugar, and there's no sense in worrying about that at the moment. I *know* it's going to work out. I *know* I'm going to hear you say 'I do.' I know it deep down in my bones. So please…let me put this ring on your finger? Let me hear you say the words. I'm going to lose my fucking mind if you don't."

I hold my breath, wishing I was as certain as he is. I trust him, though. The past six months has been a cat and mouse game where I try to pretend I *don't* trust him and *I* know better, but the truth is I'd happily place my own life in his hands if he said he knew I'd be safe. God, I must be certifiable. I release the breath I'm holding, trying not to shake. "Okay. Okay, Louis James Aubertin the third. I'll wear your ring. I'll marry you."

Jamie smiles, and it's the kind of smile you don't see very often. It's like sunlight breaking through clouds. His eyes are shining brightly as he holds up the ring he's been hiding while we speak, and I can't seem to form words. It's lovely. A princess cut diamond, not too big and not too small. Simply set on a white gold band. It's not an ostentatious, gaudy thing. It's pretty and feminine. I love it as soon as I lay eyes on it.

"*Jamie*…" I whisper.

"You like it?"

I nod, trying not to get teary, though that seems pretty much impossible as he slides the ring onto my finger. "It's so beautiful. It's perfect."

Jamie smiles down at my hand, sadness creeping into his expression. "It was my mother's. I knew it would fit you."

For some reason, the knowledge that he's giving me his mother's ring makes my throat feel like it's swelling shut. It's a monumental act on his part. He has so little left from his mother. Being given her engagement ring feels like an honor I don't deserve somehow.

"Are you sure? Are you sure you want me to wear this?"

He dips down and kisses the ring on my finger, grinning at me. "Are you kidding me? I never want you to take it off." He picks me up and carries me to one of the queen beds, raining kisses down onto my face, my neck and my collarbone as he does so. "Close your eyes," he tells me. "I don't want this to be the place where we have sex for the first time as an engaged couple."

"What the hell are you talking about?" I laugh, clinging onto him tightly, while he nips at my bottom lip.

"Close your eyes. You'll see."

"Fine." I squeal as he throws me down onto the bed, landing on top of me. The weight of him feels good, heavy but also reassuring in a way. He brackets my head with his arms, supporting himself over me as he brushes his fingertips over my face, skating them over my forehead, my temples, over my cheekbones and down the bridge of my nose. He rubs the pad of one of his fingers against my lips until I part them for him, and then he slides it inside my mouth, wetting it against my tongue, pressing it against my teeth, his breathing growing quicker as he trails it over my lips, wetting them too.

"You're so fucking beautiful," he whispers into my mouth, his breath hot, sending shivers all over my body. My skin breaks out into goose bumps, so sensitive as he shifts on top of me. I can feel the ache building between my legs already, and I know that soon it will be undeniable—a demanding pressure that will have to be sated otherwise I'll go mad. Jamie teases my lower lip with his finger again; he licks at it, then licks over my bottom teeth, tracing the ridge of them with the tip of his tongue, applying enough force to make himself groan. "You mouth is so perfect. Are you going to let me fuck it, Sophia? I love feeling your lips wrapping around my hard cock. It's the most incredible thing..."

"Yes," I say softly. "You can fuck my mouth."

"Are you going to tease your tongue around my shaft? Are you going to lick and suck on my balls like a good girl?"

"Fuck. Yes."

"Good. And when I'm done with your mouth?"

"You can take whatever you want," I pant. "I'm yours. I'll do whatever you ask me to."

"That's right, sugar. Such a good girl. Now I want you to do something for me."

"Anything."

"I want you to imagine we're back at your place in Seattle. I want you to imagine you're getting ready for bed. You're alone, you've just gotten out of the shower and your body is still soaking wet. Can you do that for me?"

This is new; we've never played this game before. I wonder where he's going with this, I want to ask him, but that would spoil the surprise I suppose. He loves when I follow his lead without question. It turns him on so much, and that, in turn, drives me wild. "Yes. I can do that," I say breathlessly. I keep my eyes closed, trying to place myself in my old room back in Seattle just as he's asked me to. I try to imagine the feeling of the beads of water rolling down my skin, between my shoulder blades, over my buttocks, over my breasts. It's surprising how easy it is to picture it. And it's surprising how hot it's making me.

Jamie licks at my lips, gently running his thumb over my chin, downward, over the column of my neck into the base of my throat. "You're drying yourself, slowly, and you rub your towel between your legs. It doesn't take long for you to realize how good that feels—the warm, soft material causing friction against your pussy. It's turning you on."

"*Yes.*" I can imagine it when he says it all too well. My hips press up a little, grinding against his, but Jamie leans back, moving so that our bodies are no longer connected there. I feel the loss painfully.

"Tut, tut," he growls. "You're on your own, Sophia. You know what that means, don't you?"

I shake my head slowly from side to side, sucking my lip into my mouth. "No."

"Oh, you do. You've felt like this when you've been on your own plenty of times. And you know exactly what you need to do about it. So do it."

I haven't masturbated in front of him before, so the prospect is making me feel a little embarrassed. Still, the idea of unbuttoning my jeans and sliding my hand down my panties is kind of a turn on at the same time. I move slowly, my eyes still closed, knowing Jamie's watching me intently as I reach for my pants and I undo them. My breath catches in my throat.

"That's it. Good girl." His voice is thick with lust. I can hear rustling sounds next to me, and I know instinctively that he's unfastening his own pants. He's stroked his own cock many times when we've been fooling around and he's been getting ready to fuck me, but this is different somehow. It feels kinky. Knowing that he's going to jerk off while he watches me finger my pussy has me blushing red all over my body. I can tell by the hot flush that burns at the base of my throat and over my cheeks.

"Take everything off," he whispers into my ear. "I want to see *everything*. Keep your eyes closed though."

I do what he asks, keeping my eyes firmly shut as I remove my shirt first and then my bra. My nipples are erect, hard and tight at the prospect of what might happen next. I squeeze them between my fingers briefly before I reach down, pushing my jeans and panties down over my hips and kicking them off as smoothly as I can. I lie back down, my back arching slightly off the bed, trying to picture what Jamie's expression is like right now as he takes in every inch of my body, greedily studying and devouring my nakedness. I can hear his breath quickening next to me, and even though he's not touching me my heart begins to pound.

Hesitantly, I slide my right hand down my body, over my stomach until my fingertips are resting in between my legs, my index finger and my middle finger working their way through my slick flesh until I find my clitoris. I'm already so fucking wet. I knew I would be, but I'm a little shocked at *how* wet. How turned on I am. Jamie makes a low, frustrated sound next to me, and I can tell he's enjoying this.

"Open yourself up," he says softly. "Show me." I use my other hand to do as he asks, spreading my pussy open so he can see every last milimeter of me, and he groans. He moves on the bed, kneeling I think, probably so he can get a better view. "Now touch yourself, Soph. You're lying on your bed, and your legs are spread wide open. You're touching yourself with your fingers, gently, cautiously, and you're enjoying how good it feels to make your body react like this."

Holy fucking shit. Just listening to him say this to me is driving me insane. It feels a little wrong to be rubbing my clit while he watches me, moving in small circles over and over the swollen bundle of nerve endings, trying not to moan as the pleasure begins to build inside me. My fingers are slick and wet, making my job easier; I slowly slide my fingers down a little, so I can tease myself around my pussy, and Jamie swears under his breath. I want to open my eyes, to see what he's doing, to see how *he's* touching himself, but I also don't want to spoil the game. Instead I push my index finger inside myself, gasping a little at the sensation.

"Does that feel good?" he asks.

I'm so swept away in this that I can't speak. I just nod, pushing my finger deeper, my back bowing off the bed, fireworks going off inside my head. I won't have to do this for long. I'm going to come so quickly. Something about being watched has me feeling completely outside of myself. Jamie shifts on the bed again. The mattress dips and then I feel his hands hooking under my thighs, dragging me toward the edge of the bed. Still I manage to keep my eyes closed, though I whimper when he roughly pushes my legs further apart and positions himself between them. I can feel his breath on my pussy, so I know he's not going to fuck me. Not yet, anyway. No, he's moved both himself and me because he wanted a better vantage point, and now he's watching me touch myself up close.

"Jesus Christ, Sophia. You're incredible."

I'm not even thinking anymore. I palm my own breast, rolling my nipple, gasping as I squeeze it tight. It feels so fucking good. My brain has completely shut down, ceasing all coherent thought. All that matters is Jamie's eyes on me, feasting, enjoying the show I'm putting on for him.

"Now imagine that you know you're not alone, Sophia," he says. "Imagine that someone's entered the room, and you know they're there with you, watching you. How does it make you feel?"

"Wet," I pant. "So fucking turned on. I can't help it."

"You want to look, but you know you're not allowed. So you keep on touching yourself, knowing you have an audience, getting wetter and wetter. Do you want to feel *him* touching you, Sophia? Do you want *his* hands on your body?"

"Yes. Yes. Fuck, yes!"

"Do you want his tongue on your pussy, sugar?"

I can't even answer this question. The thought of Jamie going down on me right now is almost too much to bear. I writhe on the bed, increasing the pressure I'm applying to my clit, rubbing in faster, smaller circles as I'm overtaken by my need for him to touch me.

"I'm afraid if you want something, you're going to have to say it," Jamie says, his voice low.

"Fuck, yes. Yes, I want it. I want his tongue on my pussy. I want *your* tongue."

Somewhere far away, I can hear him laughing a wicked laugh. His hand is suddenly on mine, ripping it away from my body as he licks and laves between my legs. The sensation is intense and soul shaking, and I can barely keep myself together. When he grazes my clit with his teeth, I can't do it anymore.

"Fuck, Jamie. Please. *Please*, I need you. God, this is insane."

"You *need* to lay still," he tells me. "You *need* to let me taste you. You *need* to let me make you come with my mouth."

I fist the over starched sheets underneath me, incapable of speech and incapable of laying still. If he wants that from me at this point, he's going to have to strap me down and gag me or something. That might not necessarily be such a bad idea. It'll take

502

time, though, and I couldn't bear him to stop what he's doing. I'd be hysterical.

"God, sugar. You taste so fucking good. I could do this all day," Jamie groans.

I buck my hips against his mouth, my back bowed so far that only the base of my skull and my butt are in contact with the mattress. I squeeze my breasts, my nipples, pinching them until they send darts of pain racing through me, and still it doesn't seem enough. My body is electric, my soul is fire, and every single sensation I feel, powerful and devastating, is connected to another more intense sensation that threatens to disconnect me from consciousness and reason.

Jamie doesn't get to continue for very long. I'm primed, ready to go off. I try to squirm away from him as my orgasm rips through me, my vision whiting out as a million pin pricks of pleasure explode all over my skin, but he grabs hold of me by the thighs, refusing to let me go. He forces my legs open as he carries on teasing me with his tongue, his hold tight and unescapable, and my climax deepens, creating almost painful waves of ecstasy that sink down into my bones.

"Shit. Shit, Jamie. I can't—I can't—God, *stop*!"

He does stop then, an evil laugh reaching my cottonwool-filled ears. I can only just hear him above the muted ringing sound that's humming inside my head. My lips are twitching like crazy, along with the rest of my body. Jamie nearly has me rolling off the bed when he places one last, quick kiss on my pussy, sucking the slick heat from me. I nearly knee him in the head as my body spasms.

He pulls back, giving me a moment to regroup. "You're amazing when you come," he says. "Fucking amazing. I love watching you lose your shit. It's my favorite pastime."

He says that a lot. I'm beginning to believe his ass. "Can't. See. Straight." I pant. "Can't. Move."

Jamie's laugh grows louder. "We'll have to see about that, sugar. I'm gonna fuck your mouth, remember?"

I do remember. I think I'm going to need another minute, but my clit has other ideas. I'm still so sensitive, so over the edge, but I'm aching between my legs at the thought of Jamie's hard cock inside my mouth. "I know. I want you to. I want to feel deep in my throat."

"You're about to," he whispers. "But first, open your eyes."

My eyelids feel like they're glued shut at first, refusing to obey me, but eventually I manage to crack them open. Jamie's naked—god only knows when he slipped out of his clothes—and he's standing between my legs at the end of the bed, still stroking his dick, cupping his balls in his other hand. The hand he's using to stroke his cock is slick and wet, and the tip of his cock is shining, too, covered in pre-cum. That only ever happens when he's incredibly turned on—so turned on that he can barely restrain himself as he fucks me. I've always had trouble walking afterward when he's turned on like that. I love that feeling—the soreness that comes from a hard fucking. It reminds me for days how he claimed me, how he worked my body until it was pliable. Until it was *his.*

"You look like you're about to do some damage with that thing," I say, my voice hushed, laced with desire.

Jamie presses his lips together, looking up at me from underneath drawn brows. It's such a fierce, dangerous look on him that I begin to shake with anticipation.

"You couldn't be more right," he tells me. "Just you wait and see. Get up off the bed, Sophia. Come and kneel in front of me."

I love kneeling for him. Having him towering over me is so sexual; I feel vulnerable, so small, completely at his mercy, which makes my head spin. I get up and coerce my limbs into doing as they're told so I can sink to my knees in front of him. My lips already feel swollen and pouty from where he's kissed me, bruised almost, and I know they're about to be even more so. Jamie steps forward, brushing the tip of his cock over my lips. "Are you ready?" he asks.

I nod, looking up at him, eyes wide and unblinking, knowing how that makes him feel. He shakes his head, muttering something softly, and then he rubs his fingers over my mouth, parting my lips open, sliding his index finger inside.

I suck. I flick my tongue over the end of his finger, and Jamie's head rocks back, exposing the strong column of muscles in his neck. His Adam's apple bobs as he swallows. "Jesus, Soph. Goddamn it."

I allow myself a small smile. I love having this kind of effect on him. It's so gratifying, to know that I can bring him to *his* knees if I really want to. He's still cupping his balls in his other hand, squeezing and gently massaging; I take over, ducking down a little so I can use my tongue on him there. Jamie sucks in a sharp breath, the muscles in his thighs tightening up, locking, keeping him in place as I run the tip of my tongue over him, wetting him, sucking him into my mouth.

"You have no idea how fucking good that feels," he pants.

I'm sure I have a fairly solid idea. He did just send me spiraling into oblivion with his mouth a few minutes ago after all. He uses both hands to take hold of my hair, and I tentatively move upward, taking the tip of his hard, rigid length into my mouth. He curses, his hands tightening their grip on my hair. He wants to push all the way into my mouth, his hips thrusting forward a little, but I tease him, pulling back, only allowing another inch of him inside me.

"Oh, it's like that, is it?" he groans.

"Mmmhhh." It's hard to respond with my mouth full of his dick. Jamie pulls on my hair slightly, angling my head back so I have to look up at him once more. "I'm going to come so hard in your mouth, Sophia. My cock is gonna be so far down your throat, you're not going to be able to breathe. You want that?"

Back when we started embarking on sexual escapades together, I would have been intimidated by this statement, but not now. I've been here before. He's done exactly what he's saying he's going to do now, and not only did I enjoy it, but I wanted more. Maybe that makes me a slut. Maybe that makes me dirty. So be it. I don't care, either way.

I nod, telling him how badly I want that with my eyes. Jamie's chest rises and falls quickly as he grows more and more excited. "Good girl." Still holding onto my hair, he tips my head back even farther and begins to push himself into my mouth. There's no teasing him now. I can see the look of intent in his eyes, and he wants more than that. He wants *everything*.

He's so fucking hard in my mouth. I can taste the pre-come all over his cock, and it drives me crazy. He so goddamn beautiful, so powerful and strong. The deeper he pushes into my mouth, the harder he becomes, until he's rock solid and throbbing against my tongue, the roof of my mouth, the back of my throat.

"Fuck," he hisses. "Oh my god."

I massage him as I suck, taking hold of the base of his shaft as I slowly slide my mouth back up his cock. I'm so fucking pleased with myself when his eyes literally roll back into his head. I watch his stomach muscles flex and contract as I lick and suck at him. He seems to oscillate between trembling uncontrollably and then becoming completely paralyzed as I work my mouth up and down, making sure to take him as deep as I possibly can every time. Jamie makes a frustrated, rumbling sound that has me shivering down to my toes.

I don't think it's possible for him to get any harder, but somehow he manages it. I know when he begins to thrust into my mouth that he's getting close. I squeeze the base of his cock hard as his movements grow faster, more labored. I know all too well what that will do to him; he swears again, growling through his gritted teeth, and then he's roaring as he comes, his legs shaking as he tries to remain upright.

I never knew what it was like to almost reach orgasm simply because you made someone else come. Not until I met Jamie. I swallow every last drop as he pours himself into my mouth, and I feel myself glowing. I eventually let him go, and Jamie drops to his knees in front of me, scrubbing his face with his hands.

"I swear you're going to kill me one of these days," he tells me.

"I hope not."

Jamie blows out a deep breath and grins at me. He plants a kiss on my forehead, and then takes me in his arms, pulling me over so that I fall on top of him as he sags to the floor. We end up in a pile of tangled limbs, my head resting on his chest, and we lay there for a moment, both breathing hard, Jamie's heart hammering beneath my ear. For a split second, everything is perfect. There is no Hector Ramirez. My father isn't being held hostage. Agent Denise Lowell has crawled back under whichever rock she came from.

There's nothing.

There's nothing but me and Jamie, and the beautiful ring he just put on my finger, and everything is perfect. I know it can't be this way forever, but for now it's more than enough.

REBEL

Honestly, I didn't think she would say yes. I mean, why the fuck would she? Doesn't make any sense. Things would be so much easier for Sophia if she packed up her shit and went back to Seattle. Well, maybe not Seattle given Ramirez's interest in her, but somewhere else. Somewhere I couldn't find her. She surprised me when she agreed to my proposal, but then again Sophia regularly surprises me, almost on a daily basis. I didn't expect her to want to prospect for the Widow Makers, and I sure as shit didn't expect her to stick with it once I gave her the green light. Being a prospect is basically bullshit. She's had to babysit drunk bikers, clean up their puke, stand watch outside while deals are going down, cook breakfast every morning, clean the clubhouse, and put up with every sexist remark under the sun while she's been wearing that prospect cut, and yet she hasn't complained. Not once.

Maybe the guys have gone easy on her since I made it clear they were to show her respect, but still. Being a prospect is fucking terrible. I definitely wouldn't want to do it.

I find myself grinning like a fucking tool as Soph pulls up next to me outside Julio's compound. She yanks her gloves off her hands, and Mom's engagement ring flashes in the sunlight, sending fractured rainbows dancing in all directions. She catches me looking at it there on her left hand and slaps me on the arm.

"Focus. We're about to walk into the lion's den. You can't be smirking like the Cheshire cat."

She's right. Julio will probably see it as a sign of weakness or possible insanity if I go in there looking like this. It takes me all of ten seconds to master my expression into one appropriate for the situation. All I need to do is remember why we're here, after all, and my smile suddenly feels like it's land sliding off my face to be replaced with a stern, downturned grimace.

"That's more like it." Soph swings her leg over her bike, climbing off, and I do the same. Julio's men are slowly approaching the gate to the compound, assault rifles butted up against their shoulders, dark eyes fierce and pissed off. Sophia tenses at the sight of the weapons, but her reaction is barely noticeable. I only note the way her shoulders rise a little because I know her so well. To an outsider or a stranger, she would appear to be completely at ease. Her poker face is phenomenal.

"What the fuck you doing here?" a tall, skinny guy yells over to us. "This is private property."

He's obviously new. The three other men that are with him, guns also raised, snicker at his expense. One of them whispers, "That's *Rebel*, man. The Widow Maker." The tall guy in the middle squints at me, as if he was expecting someone more impressive.

"You can't be here, man," he shouts. "You weren't invited."

"I have an open invite, *ese*. Might want to check that with your employer." Beyond the four men, on the inside of the compound in front of Julio's Spanish style villa, numerous cars are parked in rows. Mercedes Benz. Maserati. Bugatti. Lamborghini. There must be at least eight million dollars lined up in front of the house, shiny and colorful in the early morning sunlight. The tall guy makes a *tsk*ing sound with his tongue, waving the muzzle of his assault rifle in front of us.

"Ain't nobody getting in here today that ain't on the list. Julio said so. No exceptions."

I lean against the gate, propping myself up with one elbow. The smile on my face is disingenuous to say the least. "Why don't you go see if I'm an exception, asshole? I'll wait right here."

"You're gonna be waiting a long time, motherfucker. Maybe I should just shoot you right now before Mr. Perez comes out here and does it himself."

"Julio hasn't shot anyone in nearly ten years," I say. "And even if he tried, the fat fuck would probably miss. Now be a good little boy and run along, tell him he has visitors. Visitors that don't appreciate being left hanging on the doorstep."

The tall guy lowers his rifle, looking at me and then at Sophia like we have three heads apiece. "Did you not hear me, shit eater?" he snaps. "Get the fuck out of here right now, or these guys will shoot you."

Next to him, his three friends all look at each other, shaking their heads. "We ain't shooting Rebel, man. No fucking way. He's protected."

This is news to me. I'm protected? Man, Julio really doesn't want those files I have sitting on a hard drive back in Freemantle falling into the wrong hands. He knows the club voted for me to release the information we discovered about his operation to the cops. He knows, without me around to talk some sense into the club, the details I have stored on him in my office would become public knowledge very quickly.

"Alright. One of you go and get the boss, then. *Fuck*!"

The three other guys look at each other like they don't know what they're supposed to do. Tall Guy jabs the closest of them with the muzzle of his gun and hisses at him, baring his teeth. "*¡Ir a buscar al jefe, idiota!*"

The other guard hurries off with a murderous expression on his face, his hands gripped tightly around his weapon. Sophia inches a little closer to me, hands by her sides, though I can tell by the way her fingers twitch that she wants to take my hand. She won't, though. She knows better. Doing so will make us both look weak. She straightens her back instead, her gaze traveling from one man to the next, unfazed by the lecherous, openly lewd looks they give her while they wait for their comrade to return with Julio. I'm so fucking proud of her. There was a time when she would have shrunk away from men like this. They would have reminded her of Raphael, and the memories of him trying to assault her would have had her cowering on the ground. These days, she's strong. Stronger than I sometimes give her credit for.

The guard returns less than two minutes later, sporting a split lip, fury in his eyes. He speaks in hushed tones to the other men, stabbing a finger in our direction, and then he spits on the floor at the tall guy's feet. The tall guy threatens to hit him, but then he turns and faces us instead. "Julio says you're okay, man, but you gotta sit by the pool and wait for him to finish his business. We'll shoot your ass if you wander anywhere else in the house."

"Fine by me. I could use some time to work on my tan." I grin at the dude, flashing my teeth. Waiting for Julio by the pool is no problem, but I am curious as to what kind of business he's conducting here at the moment. There are clearly a lot of rich people here judging by the cars. I doubt they're all here to buy and sell drugs. Drug dealers drive beaten up Fords when they're carrying. At least the smart ones do. And no way Julio would conduct that kind of business out of his home, either. That shit goes down out in the middle of the desert, at night, when you can see a car coming for fifty miles in any direction.

The gates roll back wide enough for Soph and I to slide on through, and then the tall guy closes them behind us again, as if he's afraid there are other interlopers loitering on the other side, waiting for their chance to sneak on through.

God knows how many people are here right now, but as we're walked into the villa and out into the courtyard through the entranceway, a sea of chatter bubbles up around us. At least eight men sit at glass-topped tables dotted around the kidney shaped pool, mostly gathered around the far end, where a small waterfall feature cascades down into the deep end. At first I only see the men, but then something about the way Sophia stiffens next to me has me doing a double take. At the feet of the each of the well-dressed guys, a woman is kneeling or on her hands and knees, mostly naked. Some of them are sitting, heads bowed, eyes on the ground, hands tucked under their asses. Some of them are blowing the guys on the chairs. Some of them are bent over, while one or two of the men slide fingers into their pussies or their asses.

Sophia looks away, turning her back on the scene, her face a little grey. The guard who has escorted us through Julio's villa smirks, displaying a set of yellowing, rotten teeth. "Bad day to bring a bitch out into the desert, huh, *ese*?"

I take a step toward him, snarling, but the asshole steps away, laughing a high-pitched hyena laugh. "Better keep an eye on that one, *cabron*. Julio's other guests have big appetites. Your whore looks like she might be their type."

It's pretty pathetic that I react to him, but my blood is boiling in my veins. I'm ready to uppercut this fucker and toss him head first into the shallow end of the pool, but Sophia places a hand on my shoulder, stopping me.

"Don't. It's not worth it," she whispers. "Let's just sit down and wait for Julio."

She's right—fighting with Julio's men, low life scum though they may be, really isn't worth it. It definitely won't ingratiate us to our host, that's for sure.

Soph sits with her back to the bizarre scene on the other side of the courtyard, leaving me with a full on view from the other side of our small glass table. There are two small red spots of color staining Sophia's cheeks, and I immediately know they're not there from embarrassment. Certainly not from excitement. She's *angry*. So angry that her hands are shaking as she stacks them one on top of the other in her lap.

"You don't seem too shocked by that," she says.

I clench my jaw, looking down at my hands. "I'm not. I've seen a lot worse."

"*Nice.* Good to know." She looks disgusted.

"Not because I wanted to, Sophia. Because Cade and I were looking for his sister. That was the kind of place Laura would have ended up. Those are the kinds of things she would have been forced to do. I don't take pleasure in fucking unwilling women, sugar. I don't take pleasure in watching them get fucked, either."

Sophia hangs her head, biting down on her bottom lip. "I know. I'm sorry, that was a stupid thing to say."

"From the looks of things, none of those women are unwilling participants, though. They all look like they're enjoying themselves."

Sophia blinks up at me like I'm simple. "You can't be serious?"

I shrug. "Julio's women are paid here, Soph. Most of them, anyway. He doesn't keep stolen women here. He's too smart. If anyone comes through his place that doesn't want to be here, he's quick to sell them on right away. He knows the cops would be investigating him in a heartbeat if they suspected he had missing girls here. And he knows I'd be putting a bullet in his head if *I* suspected it, too.

"But you *know* he does it."

I sigh, running the pad of my index finger up and down the handle of the flick knife I'm carrying in my pocket. We didn't bring guns, thinking Julio's men would search us. Seems as though they didn't really care if we were carrying, though. "I can't prove it. Like I said, he's smart."

We sit in silence for a few minutes, the quiet interrupted only by the sound of flesh on flesh and women moaning. Sophia shifts uncomfortably in her chair every time someone gasps or calls out, and I try not to shoot daggers at any of the men who cast their eyes over my fully dressed girlfriend as if they're trying to imagine what she looks like naked.

Julio finally appears after what feels like forever, waddling toward us, tucking a huge, tent-like short-sleeved linen shirt into his enormous pants. He does not look like a happy man.

"I didn't think I'd be seeing you again so soon, my friend." He says *my friend* like it's an insult, which it undoubtedly is designed to be. "Something tells me you wouldn't be here unless you absolutely had to be." He's been fixed on me, scowling deeply, but his expression shifts when he sees Sophia. Astonishment flashes across his face, his eyes growing wide. "Well, this is unusual. I thought you'd be dead in a ditch somewhere by now, girl." He offers Sophia his hand but she looks away, refusing to meet his gaze. Her hands remain stacked in her lap.

"You'll have to forgive Sophia. I don't think she approves of your party," I say.

"Maybe you both ought to join in. I'm sure she'd enjoy it then."

"I think there's more chance of your balls miraculously becoming separated from your body to be honest." I smile, tilting my head back, looking up at him. "I'd hate to invite you to sit down in your own home, Julio, but it'd make this whole thing a little easier if we were all seated around the same table. I imagine standing up for extended periods of time isn't all that fun for you, anyway."

Julio mumbles something unintelligible, his jowls swinging from side to side. "You're a son of a bitch, Rebel. What the fuck you think you're doing, showing up here like this? You fucking crazy?"

Over his shoulder, a woman throws her leg over a guy's head, grinding her pussy against his face, which makes it hard to take Julio seriously as *his* face grows redder and redder.

"I didn't think calling ahead would be smart," I answer. "I'd have shown up and no one would have been here."

"True. I'd have made sure we were all down in Tijuana, drinking cerveza and fucking big-titted Latina beauties."

I spread my hands in front of me—*see what I mean?* "We need to talk about Hector Ramirez," I say.

Julio sits himself down heavily in the last remaining chair at our table; it creaks, groaning under the considerable weight of the man.

"I don't see what we have to talk about, my friend. Hector Ramirez is your problem, not mine."

"Is that so?"

He shrugs, spreading his hands in front of him. "I 'm aware that he has been camping out on your front lawn, stinking up the neighborhood, ruining your little slice of Americana. While his gaze is turned toward you, it's not focused on Mexico or the border. Or the goods that I choose to ship back and forth for that matter. And with Maria Rosa still missing, it's very convenient for me to have Ramirez playing Cowboys and Indians with you. Mexico is mine for the taking."

Fuck. I haven't even considered what might be happening with Ramirez's business while he's stateside, occupied with the Widow Makers. Of course he's not paying attention to what's going on back in Juarez. I'm sure he's left men behind to manage his operation, there's no doubt about that, but the kind of men you leave behind are the kind of men who are easily bribed. They're probably pocketing a couple of hundred dollars every time Perez wants to import or export a shipment, and then looking the other way.

I catch a frown on Sophia's face. She looks like she's kicking herself for not considering this outcome, too, though I have no idea why. She doesn't know how the politics of this world works. Not really.

Julio waves over one of his armed guards and tells him to bring him three beers. Once the guard is gone, Julio says, "Tell me what you want to discuss. We'll see how our conversation proceeds from there. But trust me when I say this, my friend. The return on whatever you want from me had better be fucking impressive."

"I want Ramirez dead. That's what I want to discuss with you. And the return on that is obvious. Right now, Mexico *isn't* yours for the taking. Mexico is on loan. As soon as Ramirez is done in the states, what do you think's going to happen? He's going to head straight back to Juarez and he's going to butcher the guys who've been turning a blind eye to you and yours. He's going to seek retribution because you encroached on his territory, and he's going to murder half of your men. I wouldn't be surprised if he takes control of your California business just to prove a point. And then what? You've had your ass spanked and you're broke. Doesn't sound too great to me. If you help us get rid of the fucker once and for all, Mexico really *will* be yours."

Julio narrows his eyes, staring at me. He laces his fingers together, resting his interlocked hands over the paunch of his belly. "And after, when Ramirez is gone, the Widow Makers will just stand by and allow me to conduct my business freely? Is that so?" He laughs, the sound scathing. "I don't think so. I know you too well, my friend. You cut the head off a hydra and you expect that to be the end of it. You expect it to die quietly forever, never to be heard from or seen again. That is not what will happen. I am a man who loves money. I love women and drugs and power. I'll simply take Ramirez's place, and that won't sit well with you. You'll turn your eye to killing me, too."

"I don't give a shit what you do after Ramirez is dead, Julio." It almost kills me to say this, but it's all I've been able to think of. I told Sophia last night that I would have figured out what leverage we could use in return for Julio's help, and this is it. This is all I could come up with. Allowing Perez to deal his drugs and sell his women goes against everything I stand for. If I'd had to strike a deal with the bastard six months ago, this would never have been on the table, but so much has changed now. Now, there is Sophia. Now, I don't have a fucking choice.

Julio looks at me for a very long time. Eventually, he says, "Are you a man of your word, Rebel? People say this about you, but I need to look you in the eye and hear *you* say it."

"I am."

"And you know what happens if you go back on your word in our world, no? It doesn't end well for me or for you."

"I know what happens." He'll come after the club. He won't have any other option. Even if he knows he'll lose his life, he'll have to.

His honor won't allow him to take any other course of action, and if he does come after the Widowers who knows what will happen. We'll probably slaughter his men if it comes down to a numbers game, but it would be a miracle if we came through the other side unscathed. Loss of life would be a certainty, and I don't think I could handle knowing it was avoidable somehow.

Julio glances at Sophia out of the corner of his eye. "I would make it a personal point of interest to ensure that some very unpleasant things happened to your friend here if you reneged on any agreement we came to. That is something you should understand, my friend."

Well, shit. Julio has no idea how close a *friend* Sophia is. If he did, he sure as hell wouldn't be tossing around threats like that. He'd be doing his absolute best not to make eye contact with her, or even look in her general direction for that matter. I grind my teeth together, pressing my palms against the tops of my thighs to prevent myself from making fists and knocking the shit out of him. I plan on warning him, giving him advanced notice that he can expect to be digesting food through a stomach tube for the rest of his life if he even *thinks* dark thoughts about Soph again, but I don't get a chance.

Soph gets to her feet and takes a step toward Julio, so she's standing right next to him. She bends down and smiles. "I'm not the same frightened girl you bundled into the back of your car six months ago, Mr. Perez. I'm someone entirely different altogether, and I'd appreciate it if you wouldn't talk about me as if I wasn't sat two fucking feet away from you. Otherwise there might be consequences for *you*."

Julio blinks up at her in a very owlish manner, confusion written all over him. I have no idea what my girlfriend thinks she's doing right now, but holy fuck if it isn't hot. Julio Perez doesn't let grown ass men with a history of violent murder talk to him this way. The slender brunette with the bad temper seems to have him on the back foot, though. He looks at me, his mouth slightly open, and jerks his head back. My hand is itching, ready to reach for the knife in my pocket—I'll slit the bastard's throat if he harms a hair on her head— but Julio's serious expression melts into one of disbelieving amusement. He laughs, the sound of his mirth echoing around the enclosed courtyard loud enough that one of the women servicing the men on the other side of the pool yelps and falls off her patron's lap.

"This one...you'd better get rid of this one, Rebel," Julio says, wiping his eyes. "She's too much for you to handle. Hell, I think she'd be too much for any of us to handle."

I avoid looking at Sophia. I don't want Julio to see it in my eyes— how much this girl means to me. If he suspects for a second that I'm in love with her, it'll plant a seed. He'll always know that he can use her against me if he needs to. in hindsight, it's better I kept quiet and didn't say anything about his threat just now. "She knows when and when not to open her mouth," I say.

"Women in my home usually only open their mouths so someone can shove a dick down their throat."

I don't smile. "All Widow Makers are equal. We don't persecute members based on their sex, and we don't let people threaten them, no matter who they are. You won't need to harm a single one of us, because we won't renege on our deal." I meet Sophia's eye and silently tell her to sit her ass down. She obliges me, though I can tell she doesn't really want to spend another moment sitting at a table with this pig. Especially with things ramping up on the other side of the pool now. One of Julio's wealthy guests is openly fucking a bleached blonde woman with a rose tattoo on her thigh, and the sounds of their skin slapping together is resounding around the courtyard the same way Julio's sour laughter did a second ago.

"So how do you propose we get rid of Ramirez, then?" Julio takes a sip from the drink in front of him, his eyes never leaving me. "He's always protected. He goes nowhere alone. We'd need to do something pretty crazy to get to him."

"We can do crazy. It's just how far you're willing to go..."

Julio pouts, shrugging his shoulders. "For the Mexican border, I'd be willing to go very far, my friend."

"Good. Then call Ramirez and tell him you want to arrange a meeting. Tell him you have a business proposition for him."

"Pssshhhh. Ramirez knows I would never discuss my business with him. We haven't spoken in over seven years. He'll be suspicious."

"Let him be. Let him think you're trying to out smart him somehow. If he's focused on you and your men, wondering what game you're playing, then he's going to be temporarily blindsided. He might just forget about the Widow Makers for three seconds. You'll be at his farmhouse. You'll propose that you combine forces for one huge run from the south. Make him an offer he can't refuse. Keep him and his men distracted for as long as possible."

"And in the meantime, you'll be moving into position, getting ready to sever the fucker's head from his body, yes?"

"Exactly."

"And how do you plan on doing that without getting all of us killed?" Julio asks. He takes another long drink from his beer, his eyes glinting over the glass.

"Don't you worry about that," I tell him. "The Widow Makers will have that covered."

CADE

Jamie and Sophia are gone for three days. They return just after dark on the third day, the throbbing engines of their motorcycles making the beer glasses on the shelves of the clubhouse rattle and chime against one another. Shay's first to the door to see for herself who's just pulled up at the compound gates, despite the fact that we can all probably identify the individual rumble of not only Rebel's bike but Sophia's Ducati now, too.

Shay swears under her breath when she rips the door open. "There's a car with them. A Humvee, like ours."

I get up to see for myself. Jamie didn't say to expect company when he returned from the Californian desert. Seems like he brought some home with him all the same. It's impossible to tell who jumps out of the Humvee, but from my vantage point out the front of the clubhouse, I can plainly see my best friend climbing off his motorcycle, as well as Sophia, standing next to him, removing her helmet, shaking out her hair.

"What the fuck is he doing?" Shay hisses. "Things were never like this before. We were just fine, flying under the radar. Now we've got the DEA and a fucking cartel on our doorstep. And now *this*."

"And what's *this*, Shay?"

She folds her arms across her chest, frowning into the darkness, clearly pissed off beyond words. "I don't know yet, but I can guarantee you it's nothing good."

Carnie throws an arm over her shoulder, hugging her to his side. "Rebel knows what he's doing, babe. We all trust him. Right?"

Shay doesn't answer as quickly as she should. Finally she clears her throat and says, "Sure. Of course we do. It's not him I'm worried about. It's *her* I don't trust." She spins on her heel and heads back inside the clubhouse, collecting a bottle of scotch from the bar as she walks by. Her hurried footsteps are thunderous as she runs up the flight of stairs to the second floor, where she and Carnie have taken to sleeping.

"Think I should go after her?" Carnie asks.

"Who the fuck knows. Shay's your Rubik's Cube to figure out, not mine. I gave up on that one pretty much the moment I met her."

Carnie grunts. I don't think he likes to be reminded that the girl he's hooking up with is difficult to say the least. Impossible would probably be a better word. He steps back inside, leaving me alone in front of the clubhouse, listening to the soft susurrus of crickets whispering in the distance while I wait for Jamie to come find me.

I'm strangely calm. If there were a problem, Jamie wouldn't be standing around, talking to the strangers he's brought back here under the cover of night. He'd be kicking the crap out of them and I'd be over there with him, doing the same. I hear Spanish passing back and forth—must be some of Julio's men. I'll wait for Jamie to call me over before I intrude. These things can be tricky. Political. Perez's men have no love for me, the same way they have no love for Jamie. Better they deal with just the one of us for the moment. I rest my shoulder against the doorjamb, biding my time.

Across the courtyard on the other side of the compound, the barn looms, a grey-black shadow, shot through with white where the woodwork has been painted around the yawning entrance and the window frames on the upper level. Underneath there, through that rusted hatch, Maria Rosa is probably prowling like an animal, pacing back and forth, plotting and scheming like she usually does.

I haven't seen her since I jerked off in the hallway. Carnie's been begrudgingly taking her the meals that are prepared for her, and when I asked him, he said she hasn't hit on him once. He seemed almost disappointed by the fact. After what Rebel said took place in Vegas, poor bastard likely thought she'd be into him or something. She said it herself, though: she thinks Carnie's a little boy. She used him to put on a show for Rebel and the guy never realized it.

I wonder what she'd do for me—what kind of messed up, fucked up, kinky bullshit she'd instigate if she knew I'd be willing to sit and watch it. The thing about Maria Rosa is that she's intriguing. I want to know how she works. I want to know what drives her. When you know what drives a man, or in this case a woman, you discovered their undoing. It's easy to defeat your enemies if you know what they desire more than anything else in the world. You simply take that from them—the ability to ever obtain their desires—and you remove their reason for living. I want to know her deepest, darkest fantasy, and in turn I want to use it against her, to destroy her. It only seems fair for the abuse I suffered at her hand in Columbia, and it only seems fair for the men, women and two kids that lost their lives that day in the grocery store in LA.

"'Cade? Cade, meet Andreas Medina. Andreas is Julio Perez's second in command."

I look away from the barn, back to where Rebel and his guests were a moment ago, only they're not there anymore. They're standing right in front of me, as is Sophia. Five of them in total. Two Widow Makers, and three of Julio's men. Sophia looks exhausted, like she's dead on her feet. I'm betting that was her longest ride yet. Must have wiped her out. Standing beside Jamie, a skinny Mexican with a haunted looking face and deeply sunken eyeballs grimaces at me. No smile.

"You're the one who declared war," he says, looking me up and down. He obviously doesn't think it was a good idea. "Ballsy," he says. "I got no idea how you thought you were gonna win, but still..."

"Oh, we're gonna win. You wouldn't fucking be here if your boss didn't think so too."

Andreas bares his teeth. "My boss and I have differing opinions sometimes. I'm sure you and Rebel don't always see eye to eye."

Sophia places a hand on my shoulder, giving me a tired smile. "You'd be surprised," she says, as she walks past me into the clubhouse. Jamie seems to be happy and content, but I can sense the tension on him. I know he's got a lot to tell me, but he can't exactly spill everything now. It'll have to wait until later.

"What's the plan?" I ask. "Are Andreas and his friends staying in the compound?"

"Yeah. I'm gonna set them up in the clubhouse. Julio's going to be arriving in the morning. Maybe our other guest should watch a movie instead of taking a walk this evening?"

He's talking about Maria Rosa, of course. Now's around about the time that I'd have to restrain her and walk her around the back of the compound, let her climb up the hill towards Rebel's place three or four times before taking her back down into the basement, but then again I haven't had the pleasure of that duty recently.

Jamie ushers the men into the building behind me, following Perez's men inside last. As he passes me, he whispers in a low voice, "They can't know about her, man. They can't even suspect. Keep everyone away from the barn while they're here, yeah?"

"Sure thing."

"And their Humvee? There are some in the trunk. Can you take them down into the armory? Be fucking careful, Cade. *Seriously.*" He looks worried for some reason. Jamie's never worried. Whatever is in those boxes must be dangerous shit.

"Should I come up to the cabin when I'm done?" I ask.

Jamie nods. "We have a lot to talk about."

The boxes are full of fucking C4 explosives. No wonder Jamie said to be careful. On deployment people would lose limbs all the time fucking around with this shit. I carry the boxes one at a time, gingerly balancing as best I can with my load in my hands, pressed against my chest as I descend down into the basement, where we keep the rest of the club's munitions. Takes me four trips to complete my task. I have no idea why the fuck Jamie brought so much back with him—there are enough explosives stacked up next to our semi automatics and live rounds to take out half of New Mexico—but I guess he'll explain that when I head up to the cabin. I'm about to lock up behind myself and head topside when I hear screaming down the hallway.

"*Fucking pigs! You're fucking late. Let me out of here!*" a loud, hollow, metallic sound vibrates down the corridor as Maria Rosa slams her palm against the steel door to her quarters. She's none too happy to be missing her evening stroll, it would seem. "*Fucking asshole! Carnie, I can hear you out there, you shit!*"

I stop in my tracks. I shouldn't. I should leave her to her screaming and her cursing, head straight back up the ladder and ignore her, but for some reason I find myself hovering.

"*Get Rebel down here,*" she spits. Her words are muffled, but I can hear the vitriol in them just fine. "*Get him down here. I've had enough. I've fucking had enough, you bastard.*"

Back in Columbia, Mother's empire has undoubtedly been dismantled, warred over, torn apart and claimed by a hundred two-bit cocaine dealers. No new cartel head rose to power and took over the Desolladors after Maria Rosa went missing. Jamie's had Danny monitor local news and our informants since the day we locked her down here, so we'd know about it if they had. No one has come to save her. Her people didn't rally to rescue her like she insisted they would during those early days. She's been down here alone, and every day for the past six months she's been angry. Furious at the way she's been treated. Listening to her pound and shout through the door now, though, she sounds different. She sounds as though she really has had enough. She sounds like she's given up.

I don't know how I get there, but I find myself standing in front of her door. Maria Rosa falls quiet, as if she can sense my presence. I can hear her sniffing on the other side of the inch-thick steel.

"Carnie's up in the clubhouse," I say. "We have guests. You're gonna be stuck down here for the next few days."

"Cade?"

I bite my tongue.

"Cade? Please, open the door. I fucking can't stand this anymore."

"Perhaps you should have considered that before you took on a guy who isn't typically known for his forgiving nature."

"Fucking shit," she spits. "I tortured you for three days. I lost my temper and tried to pin something shitty on you. You've locked me away for *months*. I haven't seen daylight in...in..."

She clearly has no idea how long it's been. "You had people *killed*, Mother. Innocent people. You know how he feels about that."

She's silent for a moment. "We're people who kill people, Cade. That's who we are. You know this. When I die, the lord will judge me for my sins. He'll weigh the acts of my life and I will have to settle the balance. Until then, I can only be who I am. Who I was *made* to be."

Everything goes silent. She doesn't say another word. I stand there in front of her door for a moment, her words ringing in my ears. I can still hear them repeating over and over again as I finally walk away.

SOPHIA

I wake up in the morning, and a light, fluttering sensation is dancing in my stomach—the same kind of feeling I used to get every year when I woke up on Christmas morning and I could hear Mom and Dad moving about downstairs, organizing our presents and making breakfast. It should be a good feeling, an *excited* feeling, but today it's not. I'm scared out of my mind. Today, we're attempting to rescue my father from Ramirez's farmhouse, and I have no idea if we're going to be successful. He might end up getting killed in the process. Hell, all of us might end up getting killed in the process. I fucking hate that we're having to use Julio Perez to distract Hector, and I especially hate the fact that his right hand guy, Andreas, came back with us yesterday.

The man is disgusting—an evil pig almost as abhorrent and revolting as Raphael Dela Vega was. They were cut from the same cloth at birth; I have no doubt in my mind that Andreas is a nasty piece of work, and that we can't trust him as far as we can throw him.

I turn to wake Jamie up, but I find the other half of the bed empty when I roll over. I didn't hear him get up; god knows how long he's been gone for, or how long I've slept in for, but for some reason I feel like I've been alone here for a long time. Hours, at least. I was exhausted yesterday when we got back to the compound. Every single muscle in my body ached. When we got home and tumbled into bed, Jamie offered me a massage, winking, promising me much more than that, but I'd been too tired and sore to even take him up on the offer.

I climb out of bed and do a quick recon of the cabin, looking to make sure Jamie's not in the bathroom or passed out on the couch for some reason, but he's not. The clock on the wall reads nine thirty-eight am. Jeez... We went to bed late, well after midnight, but I think this is the first time I've come close to getting eight hours sleep in month. Jamie must have had someone else pick up the prospect's chores this morning. I'm sure a riot nearly broke out amongst the other club members—*why the hell should Sophia get preferential treatment, just because she's your girlfriend?*—but I can also imagine the look Jamie will have had on his face should anyone have dared say this, and how quickly they will then have shut their mouths.

I shower and head down to the clubhouse, my skin prickling when I see there are more cars lined up alongside the Humvee Andreas drove in last night. That means Julio is here, no doubt. The guy insisted on breaking up the drive from Cali to New Mexico on account of his considerable size and how uncomfortable it would be to sit for so long without moving around. It actually bought us some breathing space, though. Inviting a cartel boss into your home is sometimes a good way to do business. Sometimes, it's death wish.

Loud chatter and raucous laughter spills out of the clubhouse when the door swings open and Shay comes barreling out of the building, just before my hand reaches the handle. She almost careens into me, her expression thunderous and angry, her lips compressed into a straight white line.

"Oh look, it's Sleeping Beauty," she snaps. "What time do you call—" She stops short of whatever she was about to say, her eyes wide, staring down at something on the ground. "What the *fuck*?" she whispers. I look for whatever is freaking her out so much, but Shay grabs hold of me by the wrist and raises my arm, a deep frown etched into her face. "What the fuck is *this*?" she says.

I finally realize what she's seen, and heat floods my cheeks: the ring. Jamie's mom's ring is still sitting on my left hand, shining in the morning light, and Shay is staring at it like it's the most offensive thing she's ever seen.

"Shay—"

She digs her fingernails into my skin. "Is this what I think it is?"

"Yes." I'm not going to lie to the woman. My relationship with Jamie is none of her fucking business. And the fact that I'm now engaged to him really isn't either. I should tell her to mind her own damn business, but there's no point. She's not stupid, and she would never leave me alone until I told her the truth. Her eyes look like they're welling up with tears. She opens her mouth to say something to me, but then her gaze grows distant over my shoulder and her jaw snaps shut. I nearly topple over as she barges by me, muttering under her breath.

"Christ, Shay, what the hell is wrong with you?" I spin around, angry enough to chase after her and confront her, but then I see Jamie walking toward me, alone, and I realize why Shay bolted. She's hardly going to be rude to me if he's there. He won't tolerate her being shitty to me, even though I can handle Shay along with anyone else just fine these days. He's wearing his *don't-fuck-with-me*, face as he arrives next to me.

"What was that about?"

"She saw the ring," I tell him.

"Fuck. The last thing we need today is for her to start causing problems. You okay?" He folds his arms around me, hugging me gently, and he smells of soap and clean clothes. I breathe in, pulling him into my lungs, trying to hold onto this moment a few seconds longer before we have to deal with anything else.

"I'm fine. I just forgot it was there to be honest."

"Gee. *Great.*"

I bite down lightly on his pec through his t-shirt. "That's not what I meant. It's just...it's strange that we made this huge decision three days ago and no one else has known about it until now. It kind of felt like it was a secret. Like we shouldn't be talking about it or something."

He leans back, looking down at me. "Do you want it to be a secret?"

"No. No, I don't."

"Good. After this shit today is over, we'll celebrate properly. I have a bottle of scotch in the back with your name written all over it."

I smile, thankful that he seems so sure we'll still have something to celebrate after our run in with Ramirez is through. So many things could go wrong. There's every chance we'll be coming back here later empty-handed. It doesn't bear thinking about. My father doesn't deserve this. He lost his youngest daughter, has probably thought she's dead for the past little while, and now he's been kidnapped and dragged across three states through no fault of his own.

This is all my fault.

I had a choice back in Ebony Briar, back when Jamie told me I could leave and go home to my family, and I did something very cruel. At the time I thought I was doing the right thing. It seemed noble to remain behind and help the Widow Makers bring Ramirez to justice, but after a while I began to see how that wasn't the case at all. Jamie and the rest of the club are resourceful people. They would have found a way to right the wrong that had been done, regardless of whether I was there or not. I chose to stay at that point because I had fallen in love. I chose to stay because leaving seemed impossible, because I would have been leaving my heart behind.

Now I have to fix this. I have to make sure Dad gets home safely to the family he has left, and I have to make sure nothing like this ever happens again. "Is Julio here?" I ask.

Jamie nods. "Yeah. He's leaving after six tonight. Ramirez has had people out all night, setting explosives down the driveway toward the farmhouse. Looks like he plans on blowing a hole in the damn place if Julio pulls any stunts. We're going to have to approach over the fields to the rear of the property, and we're going to have to wait until dark."

"I didn't think Ramirez would be laying charges." This is worrying news, though Jamie doesn't seem all too fazed by it. He runs a hand over my hair, kissing my temple.

"It's all good, sugar. We have plenty of explosives of our own."

The day drags unbearably. I can't help but feel like Ramirez is probably onto us, expecting us to pull a stunt like this with Julio in town. Cade hides Julio's numerous vehicles out in the desert, so none of Ramirez's men can spy them from a distance sitting right there in our compound. Perez and his men lounge around in the club house, complaining about the domestic beer Fatty keeps serving them. They must have had five drinks each before Cade politely suggests that they grow the fuck up and get their heads straight for what's about to go down. Andreas looks like he's on the verge of jumping out of his seat and starting a brawl, but Julio yells at him in Spanish and his right hand man begrudgingly sits back down.

They're halfway to sober by the time six o'clock rolls around and it's time for them to leave. Jamie briefs the rest of the Widow Makers, choosing a team to go with him on the run—Cade, naturally. Keeler. Carnie. And *me*.

There was no way on earth I was staying behind on this one. No way in hell. I was preparing for a heated, violent argument about me coming along, but then Jamie goes and surprises me by calling out my name anyway.

"Are you serious?" I ask. "You want me to come?"

He nods sternly. "You made it pretty clear that drugging you really isn't an option anymore. And I know if I leave you behind here, you're only going to wait until we're gone and then follow us. Better if I have you by my side, where I can see you and keep you safe."

"This is fucking bullshit!" At the back of the clubhouse, Shay rockets to her feet. "I've been a member of this club for nearly six years now. I'm one of the best marksmen the club has, and I can fight just as well as anyone else. Why the fuck haven't I been called up?"

Jamie sighs heavily. "This is going to be like neurosurgery, Shay. You don't do precision work with a hammer. You do it with tweezers and a microscope. If we go charging in there with a huge team of people, our cover will be blown immediately. We can't afford to risk that."

She shoots daggers at him, folding her arms across her chest. "Seems to me we're taking a lot of risks these days. And all for the wrong reasons. What happened to helping the girls, huh? What happened to finding Cade's sister? Seems to me, the club's purpose has had a shift in direction over the past few months, and none of us were told about it."

"What's that supposed to mean?"

"It means the Widow Makers are nothing more than your hired help these days. You only call on us when you want us to protect her," she says, stabbing a finger at me. "And now here we are, working with the Mexicans to go save *her* father. She has nothing to do with this club, Rebel. She's not one of us. Why the hell should we be endangering *our* lives to fix her problems?"

Jamie's furious. I'm furious, too, but nowhere near as outraged as he is. I can practically see the steam blowing from his ears. The thing about Jamie when he's angry is that he doesn't blow up or start screaming and shouting. He gets quiet, his movements more precise, his voice clipped and tight. All three of those things are happening now as he says, "You're not going to be risking anything, Shay, because I didn't call you up. And in case you missed it, Sophia *is* one of us. She's a prospect. When she's outside the walls of this compound, she's wearing the same cut you wore when you prospected for us. We've been here before, haven't we? I'll tell you what I told you six months ago. If you don't like the way things are being run, feel free to leave at any point. And feel free to leave your ink behind at the same goddamn time."

I didn't know what he meant the last time I heard Jamie tell Shay she could leave her ink, but I do now. You can't just walk out on the club. Joining is a commitment and a responsibility. It's something you have to take seriously, which is why the prospecting period is so long, aside from the fact that the other members need time to work out if you're going to be a liability or not. So wanting to leave is a big deal. Shay will need to have the Widow Makers club emblem scoured from her back with fire or acid if she wants to pack up her shit and go. Some people try and cover the huge back piece with something else, but the work is never good enough; if that's the route you want to go down, Jamie and Cade have to inspect the new ink, and nine times out of ten it won't be acceptable. The club's banner will still be all too clear, and they'll take your skin anyway.

On the other side of the clubhouse, leaning against the bar, Julio starts to laugh. "Trouble in paradise, my friend? You can say whatever you like about my operation. My men aren't dumb enough to question *me* like that. It would mean death for them, and they know it. Bad business, letting women play at big boy games. Haven't I told you this before?"

Jamie doesn't respond. He's too busy burning holes in Shay's head. "Do we have a serious problem here, or can we get on with the task at hand?" he demands.

"Whatever." She turns her back on him. "Get on with your precious task at hand. I'll be right here when you get back." Sarcasm drips from her voice. She's not happy, but then when is she ever? Cade shakes his head, rubbing his hands at his temples. The other members of the club are all looking to Jamie, waiting for him to tell them what to do next. Julio, Andreas and the rest of the Mexican crew file out of the clubhouse, all of them still smirking at the discord they just witnessed.

Five minutes later, the people Jamie called up including myself are all climbing on our motorcycles, watching Julio's Humvee burn off into the settling dusk.

The skyline is a deep pink, tinged with burned orange—a smudged blur of color that looks like it was violently splashed across the desert. An ill portended prophecy perhaps. Those pinks and oranges will deepen to crimson before long, a brutal and bloody horizon, and all six of us will find ourselves riding toward it.

Cade and Carnie talk in hushes tones as Jamie stands beside my Ducati, checking and rechecking the clip of the Glock he's holding in his hands. "Don't hesitate. You see anyone you don't recognize and you shoot. Have your gun up and ready at all times. Don't leave my side. If shit goes bad, get the fuck out of the farmhouse and back to the bikes. Make your way back here, no matter what. We'll all be following behind you."

He wants me to turn and run at the first signs of trouble, but he has to know I won't leave him. If shit goes bad, it means we all need to stand our ground and fight. I won't be leaving if Cade or any of the other Widowers are hurt. And if he's hurt? God, if *he's* hurt, I'll die before I get back on my bike and ride off into the darkness. He doesn't need to hear me say this, though. He needs to hear me tell him I'll do as he asks for his own peace of mind, so this is what I do.

"Of course. I will, if that's what you want."

He nods once, a hard, sharp, military nod. I think that's who he needs to be right now: a soldier, and not my fiancé. After he hands me the Glock, he still cups my face in his hands and kisses me deeply, though. "Be *careful*," he whispers. "I'll never forgive you if you get yourself killed."

"I'll be dead so it won't matter," I say, smiling.

"I'll shoot myself in the head and find you on the other side, just so I can kill you all over again, Sophia. Don't even fucking joke about it, okay?" There's worry in his eyes. I don't like that. It's dangerous. If he's worrying about me, then he's not focusing on what he has to do in order to get us through this. I want to say something about it, but in the end I don't need to. Jamie steps back, head down, checking his own weapon, and when he looks back up at me, his eyes are cold, flinty, cool as ice. He's done being Jamie. Rebel stands before me in all his savage glory, and I know without a doubt his head is back in the game.

"Okay," he says, his eyes passing over me like he doesn't really see me. "Let's do this. Let's ride."

SOPHIA

My father sat me down once when I was little and spoke to me about violence. Of course, him being an ex-preacher and a man of God, he quoted passages from the bible.

"The Lord tests the righteous, but his soul hates the wicked and the one who loves violence.'

'For we know him who said, "Vengeance is mine; I will repay." And again, "The Lord will judge his people.'

'Do not envy a man of violence and do not choose any of his ways.'

'You have heard that it was said, 'An eye for an eye and a tooth for a tooth.' But I say to you, do not resist the one who is evil. But if anyone slaps you on the right cheek, turn to him the other also.'

He taught me to be forgiving and just. He taught me to be kind and to allow mercy into my heart. He told me that to pardon those who trespassed against me, just as it says in the Lord's Prayer, was one of the most righteous, Christian things I could ever do in this lifetime. I'm thinking about this as we stalk silently through the back fields toward Ramirez's farmhouse, and I'm wondering what my father would say now if he was asked about vengeance. Would he still stay the hand of justice, choosing to absolve Ramirez for the things he may have done to him, or will he have had a change of heart? Maybe he'd like to pull the trigger himself when Ramirez's head is blown off. Maybe he'd like to be the one holding the dagger that plunges into the cartel leader's throat. I don't know. I just can't picture it.

"Five men upstairs," Cade whispers. "Three downstairs that I can see."

"Two to the rear of the house, too," Rebel whispers back. "There has to be more. No way there are only ten people guarding this place. Carnie, skirt around to the front. Come back with a head count. See if Julio's Humvee is parked up there yet, too." It should be. Julio left a clear thirty minutes before we did, and we've had a tricky approach to the farmhouse, too, traversing at least a mile's worth of uneven terrain in the dark to sneak up on the cartel from the rear. Carnie nods and then takes off into the inky darkness without saying a word. If he's pissed about Shay not coming along on this run, he hasn't said anything about it. He's dressed in black, the same as the rest of us. The only flash of color I can see as he disappears from sight is the small patch of skin on the back of his neck. After a second that vanishes, too, and Carnie is gone. The four of us that remain crouch low to the ground, chins tucked into our chests, weapons primed and loaded in our hands. I feel like a fraud, holding onto the Glock like I know exactly what the hell I'm doing with it, when in actual fact I've only fired a weapon like it a couple of times.

I'll make it work, though. I know enough to remove the safety, aim and fire the thing, and that's really all I need to know right now.

Carnie doesn't come back for a while, and Cade begins to get twitchy. He bounces up and down on the balls of his feet, pulling a face, probably in pain from the circulation cutting off to his lower body as we crouch. Rebel watches him, his right index finger moving slowly up and down as he caresses the slide of his gun. "What d'you think?" Rebel asks. "Too many of them?"

Cade exhales, studying the farmhouse. He shrugs one shoulder, pursing his lips. "Fucked if I know, man. You're the one with the gut feelings about these things."

Rebel looks back to the building, frowning at it slightly. "I don't know this time. There are too many variables." Carnie returns like a ghost, barely visible, parting the tall, wavering stalks of grass as he hurries back to the group. I'm praying for good news, but I can tell right away that he hasn't seen anything to make him feel confident about this plan. In fact, he seems kind of spooked.

"There are so many cars up there," he says, sinking down beside me. His body may very well be shoved up against mine, but it's Rebel he's talking to. "At least seven. Julio's Hummer is there, but it's blocked in. Ramirez obviously had someone barricade him in in case things go south. There are motorcycles up there, too, man. Three of them. Harleys. Expensive ones."

"You recognize them?" Rebel asks.

Carnie shakes his head. "They're not local to here, whoever they are."

Rebel raises an eyebrow at Cade. "What club would align themselves with Ramirez?"

"None that I know of. Hector hates the clubs. He does everything he can to fuck them over."

Rebel's brows bank together; he looks deep in thought. "Well, there's nothing we can do about outside involvement now. Julio's expecting us to break up this little dinner party in less than thirty minutes, so we'd better get moving. We'll stick to the original plan."

"What about their escape route?" Keeler asks. "If their Hummer's blocked in, they won't be able to book it out of there when the first explosions go off."

Cade makes a *tsk*ing sound between his teeth, shaking his head. "That's not our problem. Julio's a grown ass man. He'll figure it out."

"Exactly." Rebel places a hand on Cade's shoulder, fixing those cool blue eyes of his on his friend. "You good to go?"

"Sure am."

"Okay. Go and lay the charges. We'll give you ten minutes. After that we'll head through the back door and lay ours. We'll wait for your signal."

Cade nods. "I'll be right behind you."

"Don't stand on anything stupid," Rebel whispers.

Grinning, Cade pops up from the ground, tightening the straps of the backpack he's wearing. "You know me. I never put a foot wrong." And then he's gone.

Rebel shifts the backpack he's wearing, too—it's identical to the one Cade just vanished with, and its contents are the same: fifteen pounds of C4. I cringe at the idea that he's carrying that amount of explosives on his back, but no one else seems overly concerned. I know next to nothing about materials like that. According to both Rebel, Cade and the internet, C4 is fairly stable until you prime it with an igniter. We won't be doing that until the very last second, after we've gotten rid of Ramirez's guards on the lower floor.

Ten minutes tick by slowly in reverse.

After what feels like forever, a car alarm starts wailing around the front of the building, high-pitched and ear-shatteringly loud. Rebel smirks, pulling back the slide on his gun. "That's it," he says. "That's our cue. Come on."

My heart is in my throat as he gets to his feet, still bent low at the waist, and begins to run toward the farmhouse. Carnie and Keeler are up and following in an instant, and weirdly enough, so am I. I don't think twice. My palms are sweating, my blood pumping in my ears, but I'm not afraid. I definitely should be.

I would be if I was following anyone else into this nightmare, but following Rebel is different. I *trust* him. I *believe* in him. I *love* him. I will follow him until the ends of the earth if needs be.

"Hey! Hey! ¡detener! No te acerques más!" A loud shot rings out into the night, followed by a high, metallic zipping noise. I hunch down lower, still running, as a bullet rips through the air to my right, close to Carnie. Carnie swears under his breath, returning fire, but the report of his weapon is drowned out by a deafening, roaring sound that detonates somewhere around the other side of the building. A wall of light, sound and heat ripples past us, and twisted shards of metal rains down from the sky.

"Fuck." Rebel dodges a piece of warped shrapnel. "Keep going! Keep running!"

Up ahead, the gunman who fired at us a second ago has his back turned on us, facing toward the house, obviously trying to figure out what the hell is going on. His body is lit up in silhouette, framed in black against the orange glow that's spilling through the windows and the open backdoor of the farmhouse. Carnie takes advantage of the opportunity and fires his gun again, and this time he doesn't miss. The guard jolts harshly, his arms rising in the air, and he lets out a strangled shout. He sags to his knees, his gun falling from his hands, and then topples forward into the grass.

We reach him just as Cade barrels around the side of the building. Rebel rounds on him, gun raised, ready to shoot, but then he sees who it is and turns away. He spins around just in time to catch another of Ramirez's guards appearing in the doorway ahead of us.

The world is in chaos. Another explosion rattles the window frames of the building, so I don't hear Rebel's gun go off. I only see his arms kick back and then the guy's head bursting like a watermelon as he tries to lift his own weapon too late. Blood and tiny fragments of bone shower Rebel and I, spattering our faces and our chests.

"*Inside, inside, inside!*" Cade hollers. "Move."

Rebel's already running; he jumps over the body of the man he just killed and sweeps his gun from left to right, scouring the room for further assailants. Keeler is right behind him, followed by Cade and then me, with Carnie bringing up the rear. "Find the door into the basement," Rebel shouts back to us. "Cade, take Soph. Find her father."

"No! I'm staying with—" A strong hand on my shoulder drags me sideways pulling me in the opposite direction Rebel heads off in, and Cade is in front of me, his face an inch away from mine. I want to slap him. My arm is half raised, my hand well on its way to making contact with his face, but Cade grabs hold of me by the wrist.

"You can't go where he's going, Sophia," he says. "He's about to descend into hell. You aren't ready for that."

"Fuck you! I *need* to go with him!"

Cade shakes his head quickly. "Do you want to get him killed? Is that what you want?"

"Of course not!"

"Then do as he says and come with me. We'll do what we have to do, we'll find your dad, and Jamie will do what he has to do, too." His hold on my wrist increases to painful degrees. I'm about to argue further, but then I realize Rebel's gone and a confusion of people are scrambling to get by one another up ahead, which can only spell certain death for me and Cade.

We're in a large, well-stocked kitchen. This is the first time I've taken a beat to look around see where we are. To the left, the door to the pantry is wide open, revealing stacks and stacks of food, tinned goods, cleaning products, as well as two guns sitting abandoned on the edge of a shelf. To the right, a closed door with a heavy-duty padlock bolted to it. Straight ahead of us: chaos. No one seems to have noticed Cade and me hovering in the dark kitchen yet, but that won't be the case for long. Through the melee of limbs and well-tailored suits ahead, I make out Julio Perez's face, contorted into a rictus of rage. His cheeks are purple, his jowls shaking.

A gun goes off, followed by another and then another, and Cade yanks me to the side, to the right, toward the door with the padlock bolted to it. He holds up his gun and fires at the heavy Yale lock, and the thing shatters, falling to the floor. He opens the door, then, and grabs hold of me, pulling me to his side.

"Follow. Follow me," he says. With his gun held up by his head, Cade moves through the door and into complete darkness. I'm right on his heels, my own gun gripped tightly in both hands. Through the door, a set of stairs descends into the pitch black. I stick close to him, my heart fluttering as I try not to panic. Fuck, this is so bad. God knows what's going to be waiting for us down here. Ramirez's men have undoubtedly set up a dungeon where they torture their captives. My father's probably naked, chained to a wall, missing at least three of his fingers, bloody, bruised and broken. I don't know if I can witness that, knowing that it's all my fault.

I feel like crying.

Crying is pointless right now, though. I have to keep my shit together. I have to stay focused. Anything could happen, and I need to be ready for that. When we reach the bottom of the stairs, Cade fumbles, his hand brushing the wall, and light suddenly explodes everywhere, illuminating our surroundings with harsh white florescent light. "What the fuck?" Cade hisses.

"Oh god." I cover my mouth with my hands, the handle of my gun pressed against my lips. "What the hell is this?"

Cade looks around, just as confused as I am. The basement is filled with boxes. Boxes from the floor to the ceiling. Shoe boxes, hundreds of them stacked one on top of the other, except these boxes don't contain shoes. They contain a myriad of dildos, strapons and other weird and wonderful sex toys, each depicted by a large, colorful image on the side of the cardboard.

My father is nowhere to be seen. In fact, it's clear this space is being used for some rather kinky storage purposes and not for torturing people at all. "Is there another room?" I ask, searching for a doorway. "Is there another place he might be down here?"

Cade scans the large space, the muscles in his jaw popping as he thinks. "No. There can't be. This area is the exact footprint of the farmhouse. This is all there is."

"Then where the fuck is my father?"

"Your father's *dead*, bitch."

Cade and I both spin around at the same time. Both of our guns are raised. The man standing behind me, halfway down the steps into the basement, has his gun already trained on us though—on my head specifically—and his finger is on the trigger. "You even think about trying to shoot me and I'll blow her fucking head off her shoulders, Mr. Preston." The guy looks like he's been fighting already, though his bruises look old, faded, more green and yellow than the stark blue and purple you'd associate with fresh injuries. His cheeks are a mess, covered in scabs.

"Figured Ramirez would have dismembered you and fed you to the pigs by now," Cade says, laughing. He sobers, saying, "Your face is *seriously* fucked up, Alfonso. "

Alfonso, whom Cade has apparently met before, glowers; he looks like he's ready to shoot both of us in the face anyway, irrespective of whether we shoot at him first. "I'm like a cat," he says. "I have nine lives. I'll still be here, working for Hector long after you and the rest of your Widow Maker scum are dead. We won't even bury you. We'll drag your bodies out into the desert and let the buzzards have you. The crows will peck out your eyeballs."

"Sounds unpleasant," Cade says airily. "But I made myself a promise a while back. I swore my body would be buried in Louisiana. Definitely not in a fucking desert, be that an American desert or an Afghani desert. So I'm going to have to decline your offer, I'm afraid."

"It was *not* an offer. It was a *promise*." He laughs. "How do you think you're going to get out of this basement, you fool? I'll kill the girl if you take another step."

I see Cade shoot a glance my way, but I keep Alfonso in my sights, training my gun at his head. Cade sighs heavily, as though he's exhausted by the conversation. "I don't give a shit about the girl. Do your worst. I have a bullet in this gun right here and it's got your name on it. No way some piece of club pussy is going to stop me from burying it right between your eyes."

REBEL

Three seconds feels like a lifetime when there are eight guns pointing at your head. The second I step through the doorway and into the front family room of the farmhouse, Keeler and Carnie on either side of me, every single gun in the room swings at us, locked and loaded. Behind me I can hear Cade yelling at Sophia, but I can't think about that right now. He'll take care of her, I know he will. Right now, I have to stay alive.

Ramirez is in the corner of the room, and there are two heavy-set guards standing in front of him, protecting him with their own bodies. Andreas Medina is on the ground, bleeding on the carpet by the looks of things, though he's aiming a gun at one of Hector's bodyguards. He fires, and the guy on Hector's left staggers backward. He holds his hand to his head, which just so happens to be where Andreas shot him, and a look of abject confusion flits across his features. A second later that confusions dissolves as he falls to the ground, dead.

"What the fuck?" Ramirez yells. "Julio, your man just shot mine!"

Julio spits on the ground, pulling out a small silver gun from the inside of his suit blazer. "They're about to shoot the rest of them, too, *pendejo.*" The tiny little pistol goes off in Julio's hand, and then the other guard in front of Hector dies, blood running down the front of his white shirt as his heart, suddenly ripped apart, ceases to work.

Everything happens so quickly. Ramirez is unprotected, but only for a moment. More of his men charge in through the front door, bloodied and burned from the explosion that Cade set. As we'd planned, they all ran out there when Cade set the car alarm off, and they were caught in the blast a few moments later. Sadly some of the fuckers survived, though.

"*¡Abajo! Soltar las armas!*" the guy out in front hollers. He's fucking crazy if he thinks any of us are setting our guns down. He obviously didn't get the memo about Julio's guys being on our side for the time being, because he doesn't even cast a look in their direction. Not even when one of them cocks their gun and shoots him in the side of the head, sending brain matter and gore flying across the room.

"This is fucking *madness!*" Ramirez reaches for his own gun, but Julio gets to him first, barreling into him, pinning him against the wall. He holds him there, fury all over his face, his cheeks wobbling as he curses his enemy in Spanish.

"*Kill. The. Old. Man.*" Ramirez grinds out, clawing at Julio's meaty hands, wrapped around his throat. "*Kill. Him.*" he repeats, louder this time. A badly burned guy in a singed grey suit nods, and then goes racing off to the right, around a corner, sprinting as fast as he possible can.

"*Fuck. Oh, no you fucking don't.*" I go after him, crashing into the wall as I try and make the corner; there's a staircase in front of me, and Ramirez's guy is almost at the top of it. I aim and fire at him but the bullet misses, impacting with the wall at the top of the steps. The guy swerves out of sight on the landing. I charge up the stairs, taking them three at a time. I reach the top step just in time to see him racing down a long, narrow corridor and then turning to the right, vanishing again. A bone jarring shot rings out, echoing down the corridor, coming from the direction Hector's guy just ran toward, and my stomach backflips.

He's killed Sophia's father. He's fucking shot Alan, and now's he's dead. It can't be. It just *can't* be. I storm down the corridor, ready to put at least five or six bullets in the back of this motherfucker, but when I skid around the corner Hector's man is lying on his back on the polished floorboards, and another guy is standing over him, looking down at his gun.

He looks concerned, stricken, like the fact that he just shot the man on the ground was a complete accident. His expression transforms to one of anger. "You're too late," he says. "I already killed him. As soon as the car blew up outside, I slit the old man's throat."

The thing about slitting someone's throat is that it's a messy job, though. Perhaps this guy *has* slit Sophia's father's throat. Perhaps he did it from behind and that's why he's not covered in blood, but I *know* people. I know when they're bluffing. The guy in front of me doesn't look like he's telling the truth. I aim on finding out if I'm right or not. He holds up his gun and fires it at me.

I drop to the ground just in time, laying flat on the hard wood. Almost at the exact same time, I pull the trigger on my own weapon, shooting him in the knee. He falls sideways into the wall, screaming out in pain, and I take the opportunity to take his other knee. No more running for this guy. Probably no more walking, either. I get up and walk over, standing over him. He's dropped his gun, which I collect from the floor and slide it into the back of my waistband. "Any more weapons?" I ask.

He shakes his head. He really is a terrible fucking liar. Placing the heel of my sneaker on top of the ruin of flesh and bone that used to be his right knee, I begin to apply pressure.

"I'm not bending down there to check you, only to get shot in the face," I advise him. He screams, his bloodcurdling cry bouncing off the narrow walls.

"All right, all right. *Here.*" He draws back his suit jacket and there's his back up, strapped to his chest. I pull the engraved, ostentatious firearm out of the holster and tuck that down the back of my pants, too.

"Which room?" I growl.

"I told you. He's *dead.*" I place more of my body weight on his mangled knee. "Fuck, man. Fuck! Stop, stop, stop!"

"Which room?"

"That one. The one on the end. On the left. Fuck!"

I remove my sneaker, shaking my head. "Don't get any ideas," I advise him. But it's too risky. I can't just leave him here, bleeding on the floor. Too easy to get shot or stabbed in the back. "Sorry, man." I shrug as I take a final shot after all, shooting him in the head.

No time to feel bad now. Downstairs, it sounds as if all hell is breaking loose. Hopefully, for my sake along with everyone else's, Sophia is safe. I run to the end of the hallway, booting open the door on the left, and it takes me a second to find what I'm looking for. On the other side of the room, hunkered down in the corner between the bed and the wall, is Alan Romera. His throat is in tact, and he seems otherwise unharmed, which is a minor fucking miracle. "Alan? Dr. Alan Romera?"

The old man blinks at me, eyes cold and contemptuous. "If you're going to shoot me," he says, "get it over with. I'm not afraid to die. My Lord and Creator is waiting for me at the gates of heaven, ready to receive me."

Well, damn. I'm not prepared for that. I smirk as I cross the room, wondering how the hell a guy like he ever fathered a child like Sophia. "Don't worry," I say. "The big guy upstairs is gonna have to wait a little while yet to receive you, buddy. If I don't get you out of here safe and sound, I don't get to marry your daughter. And I fully intend on doing that really fucking soon."

Alan's eyes almost pop out of his head. I don't know if this is because I mentioned Sophia, because of what I said about marrying her, or because of my language. Frankly I don't care. I just need to get the fool out of here before he cops a stray bullet to the back of the head or something. Holding out my hand, I offer to help him up.

Alan stares at me like I'm either the second coming of Christ or the son of the devil himself. Cautiously, he places his hand in mine, allowing me to pull him to his feet. At least five days' worth of stubble marks his face, making him look disheveled and grizzly. From the stains and the rumpled nature of his shirt and pants, I'd say he's still in the same clothes he was wearing when Ramirez had him snatched from the side of the street, but other than that he looks fairly healthy.

"You know my daughter?" he asks.

"I do. She's downstairs, probably getting herself into a world of trouble. Now if you don't mind, I'd like to get back down there to make sure she's safe."

The guy seems really out of it, as if he can't really believe any of this is happening, but I don't have time to hang around and pander to him. I place one of the guns I just liberated into his hands, and I try not to shake the shit out of him when he looks at it like it's a coiled snake.

"You know how to fire that thing?" I ask.

"Of course I do," he says indignantly. He pulls the slide back and checks the chamber, and then removes the safety. "I'm a man of God and I'm a healer, but I'm also not an idiot."

"Good for you, Doc. Now come on." I hurry from the room, wondering how the hell I'm going to get him safely through the shit fight that sounds like it's escalating downstairs. I have very little time to weigh my options. I hear Alan making a strangled choking sound behind me as he steps over the two dead bodies in the hallway. I look back to make sure he's still following and he is, so I keep going. We creep as quietly as we can down the stairs, and as we reach the ground floor I hear Carnie yelling at the top of his lungs.

"Fucking die already! Fucking *die*!"

I duck around the corner, back into the front family room of the farmhouse, and Carnie's wrestling with a guy on the ground, on his back, his arm locked tight around his opponent's neck. They're alone—everyone else is notably missing. Ramirez's man has turned purple, and his tongue is fat, sticking out of his mouth as he claws at Carnie's arm. He's managed to kick both of his shoes off, and I watch as he thrashes at the floor in his socks, floundering, flailing, growing weaker and weaker as he tries free himself. Carnie grunts, tightening his hold, bowing his back as he strains, and the guy in his arms falls slack. When Carnie lets him go, shoving him off him, the dead man's mouth falls open, and the tip of his tongue dangles down onto his chin, half bitten off.

"*Jesus Christ.*" Beside me, Soph's father is white as a sheet. He covers his mouth with one hand, staring down at Carnie who is heaving and panting, laid out on his back with his eyes closed, catching his breath.

"Don't worry, Doc. I doubt anyone's waiting at heaven's gates to receive that guy," I tell him.

Alan trembles. He reaches into his pocket and takes out a handkerchief, mopping at his brow. "You may be right. But still…"

Once upon a time I would have been stunned myself. But serving in the military changes things. It changes everything. Nothing will ever surprise or horrify me again. I grab hold of Carnie by the arm, pulling at him until he sits himself up. "Where are the others?"

"Outside," he pants. "Out the front. Julio's gone fucking crazy."

"You okay? Can you watch the doc?"

Carnie takes a deep breath and hauls himself to his feet. "Yeah, I got this. Go."

Outside, body parts lay strewn in the long grass. The air is choked with copper, making the back of my nose itch, reminding me of memories I'd rather forget. Under foot, something snaps, cracks, crunches every time I take a step. It's almonds. There are sugared `almonds on the ground everywhere. The external wall of the farmhouse is painted in blood, and Julio and his men are standing around in a half circle while someone screams and shouts loud enough to wake the dead.

"Sick. Mother. Fucker!"

I know the sound of flesh striking flesh well enough to know that someone is taking a serious beating. I know the sound of flesh on broken bone, too. Whoever Julio and his men are watching right now is pounding on dead flesh, or close enough to it anyway. I look around, trying to catch sight of Cade and Sophia, but they're not here, or at least not where I can see them right now anyway. I head for Julio, noting that every single one of the four men he brought with him appears to be alive, though perhaps slightly bruised and bloody. I'm about to ask him if he's seen the rest of *my* guys when I stumble onto Keeler repeatedly pile-driving his broken hands into Hector Ramirez's skull.

"She was pregnant," he sobs. "She was fucking pregnant, and you chopped off her fucking head."

I halt in my tracks, my heart climbing up out of my chest and up into my throat. Bron? Bron was pregnant? Oh, god. Keeler carries on openly weeping as he slams his fists into Ramirez's head and chest. The leader of the Los Oscuros cartel doesn't move. He doesn't twitch. He doesn't flinch. As far as I can tell, he's dead.

"I wanted to do it myself," Julio tells me under his breath. "But this one seemed like he had a bigger score to settle."

Shit. I don't know what I'm supposed to do in this situation, but I can't just let Keeler grind Ramirez's head into the dirt. I don't care if he kills him. I couldn't care less if Ramirez checks out of this world in the most undignified, terrible way possible. I do care about Keeler's mental state though. If he smears Hector's brains all over the porch with his bare hands, that's going to affect him. It's going to take a piece of him that he won't be able to get back.

I nearly take an elbow to the face when I wrap my arms around him, pulling him away from Ramirez's body. "Get off me! Get the fuck off me! I'll fucking kill you!" he wails, over and over again. I collapse onto the ground, Keeler braced against my body, and I hold onto him tight.

He shakes and cries, and I continue to hold him. I don't let him go until his hysteria passes, leaving him limp and exhausted.

No one's moved. No one's tried to figure out if Ramirez is still breathing. Carnie and Alan stand in the doorway, watching on, and it feels as if the world is holding its breath, waiting to exhale.

"I'm sorry, man," Keeler whispers. "I'm really fucking sorry. I shouldn't...I shouldn't have lost it like that."

"It's okay. It's okay. Just take a minute. It's all going to be okay, brother."

But it's not. It's not, because *that's* when the world exhales.

That's when we hear the gunshot.

SOPHIA

I can't believe what I'm hearing. Cade's voice sounds so disconnected. So inhumane. It's like he's flipped a switch somewhere and he's not feeling anything. I almost find myself believing the words that are coming out of his mouth. But they can't be true? Can they?

"She's caused nothing but trouble since the day she showed up, man," he says. "She's distracted my friend. Brought Ramirez here. It's her fault that one of my brothers' girlfriends is dead. If she hadn't come back to New Mexico with us, it would be status quo as usual. So no. I really don't give a shit if you shoot her in the head. Have at it, Alfonso. Either way, I'm walking out of this basement, and I'll be climbing over your dead body in order to do it."

"Bullshit," Alfonso snarls. "You're just trying to rile me. She's Rebel's bitch. You wouldn't just let me kill her."

Cade pulls an ugly, disinterested face. "Only one way to find out. Test your theory."

"How about you *don't* test that theory." I adjust my grip on my gun, sweating over every inch of my body. "How about you let us both by and none of us gets hurt. I just want to get my father and go."

"And *I* told *you*, your father is fucking dead, *whore*. We killed him days ago." He glares at Cade, shaking his head violently from side to side. "I'm not letting you walk out of here, asshole. No fucking way. You humiliated me. You *scarred* me. You're going to wish you'd never been born."

"You'd be surprised how many people have said that to me," Cade muses. "None of them ever followed through, though. Some of them tried, of course, but...you know how these things go." Alfonso looks like he's boiling inside. I've never seen anyone look so angry before. Cade takes a step forward, eyes fixed on the man hovering halfway down the stairs, standing between us and freedom. "Once upon a time, I might have felt sorry for a guy like you, Al. I might have gone a little easier on you the other night. It was pretty clear you were a pathetic, weak, useless sack of shit. I might have just broken a rib or two and let you leave with your pride in tact, but I don't know. After years of dealing with spineless, pitiful losers who can't get anything done, I just couldn't take it anymore. I just had to make you feel worthless. See, I *enjoyed* it." Cade takes another step forward, smiling at Alfonso in the most arrogant way.

"Stop right there, motherfucker. Don't you take another fucking step." Alfonso briefly swings his gun around and points it at Cade, but then he swings it back, aiming it at my head. A jolt of adrenalin fires through me, mixed with a considerable stab of relief. I suddenly know what Cade is up to.

He doesn't want Alfonso to shoot me. He wants Alfonso to shoot *him* instead, presumably so I can get a round off and put the bastard down. It's a horrible, horrible plan that will never work, but I'm sure he knows that. He's a smart guy. Why the hell would he even dream of risking his life on a long shot like this?

"Your mother must have been so fucking disappointed in you," he says. "I have no idea how you fooled Ramirez into hiring you, but he must be kicking himself pretty hard too right now. You can't even come down here and do this right."

"You're a fucking dead man." Alfonso trains his gun on Cade, giving him exactly what he wants. He's going to shoot him, no doubt about it. I want to scream. This is really fucking bad. If Cade gets shot and Alfonso kills him, he'll be shooting me three seconds later and Cade's sacrifice will have been for nothing. I can't breathe. What does he want me to do? How can he expect me to get this right? I'm not Jamie. I haven't been to war with him. We haven't saved each other's asses more times than I can count. My father is probably already dead, and the guilt of that will cripple me for the rest of my life. If I have to carry the guilt of Cade's death around with me, too, I don't think I'll survive it.

"Do it," Cade snaps, sneering at Alfonso. "Take your fucking shot. *Take it.* What's the worst that can happen?"

That last comment seems odd. *What's the worst that can happen?* Why would he be talking Alfonso through this? It makes no sense. It dawns on me almost instantaneously, though: Cade isn't talking to the man on the stairs. His, *'take the fucking shot. What's the worst that can happen?'* is aimed at *me*, and he's waiting on me to follow through and squeeze the trigger.

I can think of plenty of terrible things that can happen. I could list them off in my head, but there's no time. There's no fucking time whatsoever. Cade takes yet another step forward, gritting his teeth. "Come on!" he shouts. "Fucking do it! DO IT!"

I fire. For good or for bad, I fire. The recoil of the weapon exploding in my hands sends a shockwave of panic through me, and for a moment I'm too stunned to react. Time catches up quickly, as though someone is leaning on the fast forward button, and I see Cade launching himself toward me. Alfonso has disappeared from my line of sight, but does that mean that I shot him? Is he fucking dead? I don't have a clue. The oxygen leaves my lungs as Cade tackles me to the ground. I make a pained *ufff*ing sound as he lands on top of me, his body covering mine, and I can't breathe, hear, or see anything. My ears are still ringing from the gunshot. Cade rolls off me and spins onto his back, gun raised, pointed at the stairs, but

Alfonso isn't there.

Another shot rings out, loud and violent. A bullet hits the concrete wall next to my head, and Cade starts firing, this time aiming at the ground where we were just stood a second ago.

Alfonso is sprawled out on his side, grimacing, his shirt and his neck drenched in blood. I didn't kill the bastard but I certainly managed to injure him. Cade's gun barks again, and Alfonso's body jerks as the bullet hits him in the stomach, just below his ribcage.

"Fuck." Cade grabs me by my shirt and literally slides me behind the wall next to us. A tower of boxes topples over between Cade and Alfonso, sending rubber sex toys tumbling out over the floor.

"You fucking whore!" Alfonso screams. "This isn't over. This isn't fucking over!"

"Oh, yes it is." Out of nowhere, Rebel is tearing down the basement stairs, Carnie behind him. The two of them are shooting rapidly, over and over again, and Alfonso is bleeding freely. They shoot him countless times, in his torso, his legs, his arms, and finally, when Rebel hits the bottom of the stairs, in his head. The air smells metallic, of gunpowder and blood.

Through a haze of concrete dust, Rebel emerges like some kind of ruthless god. He's covered in blood, his shirt torn, his right hand bleeding, but he looks invincible. He looks terrifying—a nightmare in the flesh—and I have never been happier to see him.

He drops down to his knees and takes me in his arms, his hands frantically roaming all over my body, looking for injuries. "Jesus, Soph. Are you okay? Tell me. Are you fucking okay?"

"Yes, yeah, I'm fine, I'm fine." I really am, which is a goddamn miracle. I should be dead, or at least severely injured, and yet I'm pain free, completely fine. Weird. Not that I'm complaining. Rebel holds my face in his hands, his cool eyes traveling over me, trying to find signs of discomfort, despite my protests. "I'm okay, I promise," I say, leaning my forehead against his. He lets out a deep breath, hugging me to him. "Are *you* okay?" I ask.

"I'm fine. Everyone is fine."

"And..." God, I don't think I can say the words. "My dad? Is...we were too late, weren't we? Is he...is he dead?"

Rebel slowly shakes his head, a tiny smile playing at the corner of his lips. "No, sugar. We weren't too late. Your dad's alive. He's just fine. He's waiting upstairs for you now." He places a deep, slow kiss on my lips, and my head swims. I'm so fucking relieved. I'm ecstatic. My father's alive. He's alive, and he's waiting to see me. I used to resent my father, feel stifled by him most of the time, but right now I've never needed him more.

"I don't know about you, sugar," Rebel says, brushing his thumb along the rise of my bottom lip. "But I'd like to get out of here before the cops show up. What do you say?"

I manage a weak smile as he helps me up from the floor. "I say I couldn't agree more. Let's get the fuck out of here."

REBEL

Ramirez is dead. Keeler is still sitting on the porch with his head in his hands when we go outside. He informs us that Julio told him to remind me of the agreement we came to, and then he left. Keeler stops talking. He rocks silently back and forward, knees drawn up underneath his chin, and we leave him in peace. Grief is a funny thing. You think revenge will fill in the hole that grief causes inside you, but more often than not revenge only makes the hole deeper. Bottomless, in some cases.

Alan Romera stands like a statue when Sophia steps out onto the porch. His face is carved marble, his shoulders rounded in on his body, as if bowed under a great and unbearable burden. Sophia bursts into tears the second she lays eyes on him.

"Daddy?" she whispers.

"Hey, pumpkin." The Doc twists his filthy handkerchief over and over in his hands, looking very unsure of himself. "Are you...are you all right?"

Sophia nods. "I am. I'm *so* sorry. God, Daddy, I'm sorry."

I back the fuck off. Sophia doesn't need me loitering on the peripherals as she tries to explain where she's been for the last six months. He's going to hate me. He's going to fucking *despise* me. Cade saved his daughter in one way, but I was the one who really took her away from him. *I* was the one responsible for guilting her into staying here in New Mexico.

There's so much blame to be thrown around, though. So many fingers to be pointed. I'm too fucking tired and worn into the ground to bother with that right now, so I let Sophia tell her father the truth, and I accept how he's going to feel about me.

At the end of the day, it's how Sophia feels about me that matters, and I'm hopeful that that won't be changing any time soon. As she speaks to her father, I see him shaking his head, her bowing hers. At once point, the doc takes her head and holds it in his, and she collapses against him, sobbing silently. I want to go to her and take her in my arms, to comfort her, but it's not my place. Hard though it may be for me to remember, she was the light of someone else's life before she was the light in mine. Alan hasn't seen her in six months. They both need this time together to heal the hurt between them.

I wait twenty minutes; it feels like an eternity. I'd give them even longer, but Cade points out the red and blue flashing lights approaching down the distant fire road leading to the farmhouse and it really is time for us to go. All six of us run over the back fields, heading toward the bikes we left stashed there. Alan makes noise about staying, talking to the cops, explaining to them what happened. It's only when his daughter tells him how that will pan out for the rest of us that he gives in and runs.

We're about three hundred meters from the bikes when the loud, crashing sound of another explosion tears through the early hours of the morning. We all stop, mouths hanging open as the farmhouse goes up in flames. Wood detonates in every direction, rocketing straight up into the air, and the night sky is alive with fire and smoke.

"You set your charges," Cade says, staring back over his shoulder at the inferno.

I don't say anything. Just nod. It had to be this way. We couldn't allow the cops to match our DNA with blood spilled at the scene. They'd have found evidence of every single one of us inside that house. We'd all have been fucked.

The police lights soon blend in with the warm glow cast off by the burning building, and we move on. The sound of our motorcycle engines rumbling into life is blotted out by the roar and crackle of the fire at our back.

I carry Sophia's father on the back of my bike as we head back to the compound, and no one stops us. We travel across the desert, aching in our bones, tired and exhausted, and as the miles pass us by and the stars wheel overhead, I do something I haven't done in a very long time.

I pray.

I thank the higher powers of the universe, whomever they might be, that we all made it through tonight safely. I show my eternal gratitude for the fact that the woman I love wasn't hurt, and that she didn't lose her father. Beyond that, my mind is empty and my heart is full.

Sophia is safe.

The club is safe.

That's all that really matters.

I know something's up as soon the compound gates peel back and I see Danny sitting on the steps to the clubhouse, waiting for us. He looks just as tired as we do, which is worrying since things here should have been quiet compared to what just went down on the other side of Freemantle. There's blood in the dirt. Blood on the ground by the barn.

Cade sees it, too. He's tensed, his hands gripped into tight fists at his sides as he jumps off his bike and hurries over to Danny. "What's wrong? What happened?" he demands.

Danny cracks his knuckles, shaking his head. "Shay," he says. "Shay went crazy after you left. She said…"

"She said what?" Cade

"She said she was going to show you what a mistake you made tonight. She was so angry. No one could stop her."

Carnie's off his bike and standing in front of Danny now, his arms wrapped tightly around his body. "What did she do, man? What did she do?"

"She shot Fatty in the fucking head, man. She went down into the barn, and she…" Dread passes over Danny's face. "She let her out," he whispers. *"She set Maria Rosa free."*

REBEL

epilogue

We should have killed Maria Rosa a long time ago. Cade told me over and over again how sure she was that she was going to get out of the basement, *so* fucking sure, and I didn't listen. I mean, why the fuck would I? The door to her cell was an inch thick. She was injured for a long time. How *could* she escape? I should have known better. I should have seen Shay's betrayal coming a mile off as well. She's been simmering for months, quietly and sometimes not so quietly mad over Sophia's presence in the compound. There are steps that should have been taken a long time ago, and now a Widow Maker is dead, and a psychotically dangerous woman is on the loose.

Two days have passed since the farmhouse. I thought we'd have some tearful phone calls back to Seattle, where the Doc and Sophia both told their family they were fine, that they were both alive and well, but that hasn't happened. Sophia's mom is away on some church retreat in the wilds of Alaska, so she doesn't even know Alan was missing. As for Soph's sister, Sloane is so entrenched in her studies that it's normal for her to be MIA most of the time anyway. So it goes that after some long, painful discussions, Sophia has come to a difficult decision, and once again she's making sacrifices for the club.

I hug her to me, throwing my arm around her shoulder as we walk down the hill toward the clubhouse. Night is all round us, pressing in from all sides, endless and eternal. There are no clouds, but the stars seem to be strangely absent, too. Everything is blackness—a strange, heavy kind of night.

"Are you sure you want to do this?" I kiss Sophia on top of her crown, holding her to me. She's shivering a little despite the warm breeze, which teases at her hair, lifting strands, sending them whirling up around her head.

She takes a deep breath and then lets it out slowly. "Maybe," she says. "Maybe not. I thought this would be over by now. I just thought..."

"You can pick up the phone, you know. All you have to do is pick up the phone and call them. No one in the club will think badly of you for it. You know that, right?"

She nods, biting her lip. "I do. But this kind of makes sense in a way. I just can't believe my dad agreed to it. He's always played everything by the book. He's a conformist. He's never broken a law in his life. The fact that he's about to lie to the cops...a DEA agent, at that..." She shakes her head, stunned. "I never thought he'd do this. Never in a million years."

I'm more than a little surprised too, but then again I know exactly what Alan's going through. I know there's nothing I wouldn't do for this woman, no matter how drastic or complicated it seemed. The morning after the farmhouse, Lowell came to the compound, and this time she had a warrant. She ripped the place apart. Thanks to Shay, there were no weapons on the property, and no hysterical Columbians locked in the basement. Lowell went away frustrated and furious, promising to figure out exactly what part we played in Hector Ramirez's demise, along with our involvement in the transportation of weed and cocaine. As soon as she walked out of the door, Cade said we needed someone on the inside. Someone who could tell us what she was up to. How close she was getting. And Alan Romera put up his hand.

"I'll tell her Alexis called me, asking for money. I'll tell her I know she's with you and that I think she's being held against her will. If she thinks I'm in communication with my daughter, she'll be in touch with me regularly. I'll feed her information. She'll tell me what she knows, too, surely?"

Soph looks around at Cade first and then back at me. "If she thinks I'm here against my will, she'll come after you."

I smile, trying to reassure her. "And maybe she does. But you just tell her the truth. That you want *to be here. She won't be able to disprove that. We alter a few of the details relating to* how *you came to be here, maybe, but other than that..."*

She nods. She squeezes her father's hand, tears in her eyes. "What are you going to tell Sloane? Mom?" she whispers. Her voice is thick; I can hear the ache in it. I can feel perfectly well how badly she wants her mom and her sister back in her life, and it damn near kills me.

Alan's eyes shine brightly, too. He places a perfunctory kiss on his daughter's head and then squeezes her hand back. "I can't tell them this, pumpkin. I can't lie to them. Not if I can avoid it. So maybe I just don't tell them anything. Maybe that's for the best. I'll be there for them. I'll take care of them and support them. And when the time comes, we can tell them absolutely everything together. It will be better that way."

I can see in her eyes that Sophia doesn't believe this. She knows there's no other way of allowing her father to help, though, which he is determined to do. "Okay. Okay, so I guess that's it, then."

And so the plan was set into motion. Alan called the DEA this morning and told Lowell Sophia had contacted him, asking for money. Lowell took the bait immediately. Alan had to leave right away to get back to Seattle, where he'd arranged to meet up with Denise, which had the added bonus of forcing her out of New Mexico as well. It's temporary, of course. She'll be back with a vengeance.

The goodbye Sophia shared with her father was heartbreaking.

The fact that he knows she's alive and safe, and he can contact her when he wants is of some comfort to her, though. She seems sombre but less panicked than she has been of late.

Raphael is gone. Hector is dead. Justice has been served for my uncle. For Leah. For Bron. For the pain and suffering that Sophia endured. We may be left walking a tightrope with the DEA, but our future is looking a lot less fragile than it did a month ago. Everyone can feel it.

Loud music and laughter spills from the clubhouse doors as Danny reels drunk out into the night. He staggers off toward the barn, mumbling something about fresh air. Sophia and I hover outside the building for a moment, arms around each other, listening to the raucous shouting and revelry taking place inside. I think about the black bag I had Cade hide under the bar earlier—the bag with my tattoo gun neatly packed away inside, and the black ink I plan on marking this beautiful, brave, wonderful woman with in just a few hours. She has no idea what's about to happen, of course. She has no idea that I'm about to make her drink a foul, disgusting bottle of whiskey and make her lie down for me so I can tattoo her, making her a full, official member of the Widow Maker's MC.

I wrestle with the smile that wants to spread across my face as she looks up at me, her eyes wide and clear. "You look like you're up to no good," she tells me, tucking her hands on the inside of my t-shirt. "You've got that look on your face. It's making me nervous."

I kiss the end of her nose, sighing. "Well. Y'know. You can always call Kansas."

She won't, though. I know her inside and out, and she knows me. We were born for each other. Our futures hold pain and suffering, there's no doubt about it, but the joy and the beauty of what we will experience as we share our lives with one another outweighs the hurt. It will all be worth it. I can see it now, and so can she. I can tell by the way she's looking at me.

"Still want to marry me?" I whisper into her ear.

She makes a soft, subtle sighing sound at the back of her throat.

"I still want to marry you, Louis James Aubertin the third. In spite of everything. *Because* of everything, I still want to be your wife."

"Good. Then let's go inside. I have this bottle of scotch I want you to try."

CALLIE'S NEWSLETTER LOTTERY

As a token of her **appreciation** for reading and supporting her work, at the end of every month, Callie and her team will be hosting a **HUGE giveaway** with a mass of goodies up for grabs, including vouchers, e-readers, signed books, signed swag, author event tickets and **exclusive** paperback copies of stories no one else in the world will have access to!

All you need to do to automatically enter each month is be signed up to her newsletter, which you can do right here: **http://eepurl.com/IzhzL**

*The monthly giveaway is international. Prizes will be subject to change each month. First draw will be taking place on Nov 30 2015, and continue at the end of each month thereafter!!!

ABOUT THE AUTHOR

Callie Hart is the international bestselling author of the Blood & Roses and Dead Man's Ink series.

If you are yet to dive into either series, book one, **Deviant, is FREE** right now!

If you want to know the second one of Callie's books goes live, all you need to do is **sign up at http://eepurl.com/IzhzL**.

In the meantime, Callie wants to hear from you!

Visit Callie's website:
http://calliehart.com

Find Callie on her Facebook Page:
www.facebook.com/calliehartauthor

or her Facebook Profile:
www.facebook.com/callie.hart.777

Blog:
http://calliehart.blogspot.com.au

Twitter:
www.twitter.com/_callie_hart

Goodreads:
www.goodreads.com/author/show/7771953.Callie_Hart

Sign up for her newsletter:
http://eepurl.com/IzhzL

TELL ME YOUR FAVORITE BITS!

Don't forget! If you purchased the Dead Man's Ink series and loved it, then please do stop over to your online retailer of choice and let me know which were your favorite parts! Reading reviews is the highlight of any author's day.

I must ask, though...if you do review, please do your best to keep it spoiler free or indicate your spoilers clearly. There's nothing worse than purchasing a book only to ruin the twists and turns by reading something by accident!

66186270R00328

Made in the USA
San Bernardino, CA
09 January 2018